THE MARE BUCKED, HINDQUARTERS GYRATING AS SHE KICKED AT INVISIBLE DEMONS—

One boot slipped free as Doyce slammed back into the saddle, her foot chasing after the missing stirrup. An impossible task—her hard landing in the saddle had set the mare off as if a burning brand had been lashed to her tail. Whipping the air, the reins dangled tantalizingly beyond reach, and the stirrup bounced and banged against her leg. In the midst of this, a gloating voice slithered through her mind. *"You won't like the Sunderlies. Turn back while you still can. Go home now!"*

"A wonderful idea!" she sputtered, clinging as best she could, Khar flattened beneath her and protesting all the way. "But I think I'd rather return on foot." Her shiver of fear as the strange message flashed through her was overwhelmed by panic at the mare's inexplicable behavior. The mare spooked and veered when she least expected it, though once Doyce glimpsed something unfurling, waving from a low branch as the horse charged by.

Both Jenret and Arras peppered her brain with useless advice and misguided warnings. They meant well, feared for her safety, but *they* weren't astride a panicky beast. *"Jenret, keep following,"* she begged, *"you can't miss the trail, believe me!"* At the end of the trail would be a bruised and battered body—hers. . . .

SUNDERLIES SEEKING

BOOK ONE OF GHATTENS' GAMBIT

Gayle Greeno

DAW BOOKS, INC.

DONALD A. WOLLHEIM, FOUNDER

375 Hudson Street, New York, NY 10014

ELIZABETH R. WOLLHEIM
SHEILA E. GILBERT
PUBLISHERS

First Printing, November 1998
3   4   5   6   7   8   9

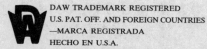

DAW TRADEMARK REGISTERED
U.S. PAT. OFF. AND FOREIGN COUNTRIES
—MARCA REGISTRADA
HECHO EN U.S.A.

PRINTED IN THE U.S.A.

In fond memory of the
eager young women we were,
and in tribute to the wiser women
we've come to be:

Antonia Bignelli Totten
Elise Carlson Burrows
Susan Cunningham Wofford
Sylviane DeCerbo Cresman
Lynda Kaplan

Because I remember, yes, I remember . . .
and wish us love and joy in 1999!

*"We carry within us the wonders we seek without
us:*
There is all Africa and her prodigies in us."
—Sir Thomas Browne,
Religio Medici (i, 15)

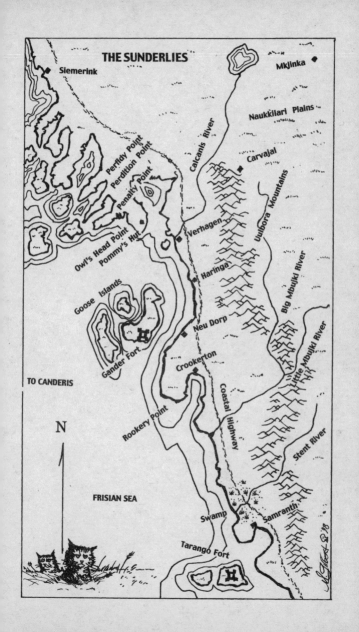

✤

PART
ONE

✤

White streamers of breath gusting in the afternoon air, two youths, a boy and girl, thundered toward the gnarled apple tree, their feet hammering frost-hardened earth and stiffened grass. A small, gloved palm slapped the moisture-darkened bark in triumph, nearly an arm's length ahead of the boy's chapped hand. A glance over her shoulder convinced the girl to dodge, and pop up on the tree's opposite side, excited but wary at her win.

The setting sun, descending so quickly at the height of winter's solstice, cast a wavering beam of pink and gold at the girl, emphasizing the contrast of blue-black hair and white complexion, while adding a ruddy depth to the boy's unruly red-brown thatch. He leaned forward, hands on knees, panting, and the girl ventured round, her heady victory tinged with concern. Closer, closer, a hesitant wool-clad hand on his back.

He spun at her then, slamming her shoulder against the tree trunk and mashing his back against hers, straining for leverage, vertebrae meshing with vertebrae. A retaliatory elbow brisked his ribs and he shoved harder, exploiting the distraction to sneak one foot on a root, raise himself a fraction higher. His other foot edged toward the leaf-strewn mound beside the apple tree, the mound with the carved stone at its head.

"Am too!"

Confident from years of practice, she kicked to snag his ankle, discovered he'd anticipated her and shifted clear. *"Are not!"* Her mouth was set firm, steam trailing from her nostrils. *"And you're cheating again!"* Righteous color flooded her face. *"Standing on Barnaby's grave, aren't you? Unfair, you cheater! Bratty to treat Barnaby like that!"*

The odd thing—or odd it might appear to a stranger—

was that not a single syllable leaked into the raw afternoon air. The only sounds to be heard were the distant caws of crows, breathless exertion, and the thud of competing bodies throughout the exchange.

The boy suddenly moved away, abashed, and the girl nearly stumbled at the loss of support. "Sorry," his voice rang overloud, gruffly concerned as he gripped her arm to steady her.

Slinging her arm over his shoulder, she leaned against him, catching her breath. "Why does it have to mean so *much* to you? I can't help it, you can't help it." He nodded unhappy agreement, refusing to meet her eyes. "You'll keep growing, and I won't. Boys do that—get their growth later than girls."

"I know, I know." As if avoiding her, he sat, chapped hands grabbing wrists, arms pinioning his knees. Sinking beside him, she tucked an arm through his, looked, then silently offered one of her wool gloves. "Didn't lose them," he protested. "Know exactly where I left them."

"Uhuh. The glove graveyard, right?"

"No!" He pulled back as if stung, except for the quirk at one corner of his mouth. "I'm sure that Barnaby's stealing them." Serious now, "I still miss him, Sis."

Barnaby. No words, aloud or in the mindspeech abilities they shared, were necessary to evoke Barnaby's image. Barnaby, the white-and-tan terrier who'd shared their lives practically from their birth until just after their tenth birthday, six years past. That tongue-lolling smile of doggy delight, the barks of glee and, most of all, the all-accepting, warm comfort of his compact, wriggling body. He'd viewed the twins as his gods, and all children deserve to be the center of the universe to some loving creature. His devotion straightforward, uncomplicated; his allegiance had been total despite his odd past. Only the Shepherd-Seeker Harrap and his bond Parm could elicit an equal devotion from the terrier, a tenderness mixed with guilt.

They both shivered, ducking closer together, not so much at the gust of wind that showered dead leaves on them as at the thoughts of their past . . . and of their future. Today marked the anniversary of their naming day, the party tonight. A door opening on adulthood, once they finished their Tierce in the spring.

"Well, I don't want to be a eumedico," the boy addressed his knees, head pulled tight into his collar as if someone might cuff him for the statement.

"Me neither!" She shivered at the thought, her expression pale and pinched. With her free hand she fumbled in her pocket, pulled out a lucifer and held it tight, poised to strike it with a thumbnail.

"Jen!" the boy reproved, plucking it from her and tucking it in the corner of his mouth. "Might catch Davvy's eye if you trained as a eumedico. Give you something in common to talk about," he teased, stopping as he glimpsed the tear trembling in her eye. "Sorry."

A sharp whistle split the air, a red-cheeked face topped by a tousle of dark hair appearing over the split fence like a rising moon. "There you are! Hurry! Come on, Jenneth, Diccon—you can't miss it! It's going to be glorious!"

"Miss what?" collided with "When did you get here, Harry?" as Diccon Wycherley rose, pulling his twin sister Jenneth to her feet.

"Just after lunch." Harry hopped the fence, doing a little dance to entice them to hurry more quickly. "Aunt Mahafny's going to race Mama! Parse finally finished the roller chairs! Hurry! If it gets too dark, they'll postpone it!"

Ungloved hands clasped together, the two ran after their cousin, Harry Muscadeine, worries about adulthood temporarily abandoned.

"Fare ye well!" Claudra Thomas embraced Doyce. "I know what you're planning to do."

Hugging the older woman, Doyce Marbon craned back to study the Resonant omsbudswoman's accepting smile, the stately figure with its crown of braided hair. "Mindsnatcher!" she teased, as only one Resonant might do with another.

Claudra shook her head. "It's written on your face, in your stance. That look of pinched determination you take on when facing an unpleasant duty. Well, you've given enough. Time to let others shoulder the burden, though it's still a heavy one." Again she shook her head, this time in wonderment. "Never did I think someone like me, one of the Gleaner generation, would be responsible for reconciling Normals and Resonants. By rights, that task should have been Faertom's."

"And you've taken up where he left off." Doyce squeezed Claudra's strong hand, wondering how she could remain so strong in mind as well as body. Faertom's death still hurt, brought back unwanted memories, as did Darl Allgood's death—both killed trying to save two children, to salvage a future from a shrouded past that made all Gleaners symbols of fear in Canderis. Gleaners, more properly Resonants—that was the accepted term nowadays—were average, ordinary people gifted with the powers of mindspeech. "We Resonants need you to be our voice, give focus to our concerns."

"I know. I'd not have it any other way—if only for Faerclough and Faerbaen, and all the other young ones, the ones young enough to change, who want to be a part of society." As she adjusted her hair, she chuckled. "And that husband of mine mutters and grumbles about 'the good old days' when we lived sequestered on our island. Mind you, he's selling twice as many boats as he used to—we've hired six workers, three Normals and three Resonants!"

"Are there many who prefer the past? Miss it?" It puzzled her, that there might be those more comfortable with the shadow world of the outcast, the constant fear of discovery.

"Some always view the past with a rosy hue. Though I'd suspect more Normals would agree than Resonants. Still, there's security in knowing your 'place,' even if it's not a very good one." Turning to the desk, Claudra stroked the large cat weighting down the paperwork. "Do what you must, both of you." With that advice, the older woman left.

Pensive, Doyce forced her concentration on the paperwork in front of her as she resettled herself behind her desk, refusing to race through it or surreptitiously count how much still remained—reading the synopses of the last oct's activities, eight days' worth of circuit cases. As Seeker General, she must know what each Seeker Veritas Bond-pair had encountered as they rode the length and breadth of Canderis, hearing both civil and criminal cases.

"But never passing judgment, you might remember that when assessing your worth." The large ghatta with the bold gray-brown bull's-eye swirls against her dark coat yawned once and regarded a pristine white paw, deciding it didn't require washing.

Without raising her eyes from the report, Doyce waved her pen suspiciously wide of the inkwell. *"And have you ever had your beautiful pink nose inked black?"*

Khar'pern, Bondmate of her beloved human, Doyce Marbon, drew back with a moue of disgust. Well, yes, truth be told she *was* vain about her petal-pink nose and her white muzzle, the way it set off her amber eyes and the dark stripings on her forehead. **"Is it indelible ink?"** Despite herself she shivered at the thought.

Doyce ignored her, so Khar pressed on. **"We determine truth and falsehood, but it's not our duty to pass judgment—ever. That's what the Conciliators are for. Why—after sixteen years as Seeker General—are you starting now? And on yourself—your ability to do this job?"** It struck the ghatta how complacent she'd become—not a particularly pleasing thought, but a true one. But Doyce had never had that luxury, not in the complex roles she'd found herself thrust into: Seeker General, late-blooming Resonant, and wife and mother.

After careful consideration, Doyce transferred another page of report to the left-hand corner of her desk, made a check mark on the tally she compiled each oct. Someone else could add this oct's tally to the octant report. How sensible to track cases by the problems they represented, categories for the obvious and the obscure. After all, sometimes the not-so-obvious revealed a subtle patterning of its own, shining light on hidden problems.

"And what have I accomplished here?" She longed to say it aloud, shout it, actually, but worried who remained on call outside her office. While a faint electrical current ran around the room's perimeter to ensure none of the ghatti inadvertently overheard what was discussed within, a shout would carry—the sound at least, if not the precise words. *"What, beloved? Tell me. Oh, I've done my level best to help Resonants adjust to living openly amongst us, to help Normals adjust to the fact. I suppose it's helped—barely."* Despite herself she mimicked aloud, "Some of my best friends are Resonants, but I wouldn't want my sister to marry one!"

"**Well, she did,**" Khar interjected.

"Stop quibbling! You know what I mean. I wanted things to become better, move faster, see substantial change. I thought I could . . ." an uncomfortable shift in her chair. *"But everything frays a little more, never mends quite enough. Jenret and I . . . my relationship with the twins. . . . Lady bless and save me, Khar, they're my children and I barely know them! I've spent too much time here! Too much wasted, worthless effort!"*

"**Never wasted, never worthless,**" the ghatta protested as she shoved her head against Doyce's bowed shoulder. "**You and Jenret *have* been more separate of late, but you can remedy that, especially if you work as diligently as you do at this. Diccon and Jenneth will be fine . . . *are* fine. It's just the flightiness of youth.**"

"But I swear I don't truly know them, haven't ever really known them. If I even understand Jenret anymore—what goes on in his head, his innermost thoughts, his dreams and desires. . . ."

That final statement worried Khar, made her realize her own fears were more rationally grounded than she'd suspected. Doyce's switch from the universal to personal particulars told her more than she'd wanted to hear. No, she'd not considered it proper to pry; when Doyce was ready to share her quandary, she would. Rawn *had* been right, the midnight-hued ghatt glum with worry over Jenret and Doyce.

Silly to hope, silly and stupid if one were one of the ghatti, those giant catlike creatures blessed with not only mindspeech, but also the ability to winnow truth from falsehood. It was just that even ghatti found that truth could be unpalatable at times. Still, she pressed on, hoping to shake Doyce out of her mood, too aware what the last sheet of paper contained. "**And your premier accomplishment as head of the Seekers Veritas involved the installation of porcelain flushers at Headquarters, I suppose?**"

Reluctantly Doyce laughed. "Let it be recorded that I, Doyce Marbon, Seeker General, improved the sanitation of Headquarters—indeed, of Canderis as a whole—with my relentless battle for indoor plumbing!" Hooting, Doyce leaned back in her chair while Khar crouched over the pen, hiding it.

"No good, Khar. I've a whole drawerful. You'll get ink on your white belly—and it is indelible."

With bad grace Khar edged clear. One last chance, something she'd resolved not to do, not and put further pressure on her beloved bondmate. **"But what about me? Don't you care what I think? How I feel?"** Shame, shame, enough to forfeit a spiral of growth and wisdom with the Elders to beg thusly—and willingly forfeit it if she succeeded.

"Oh, beloved, I care so deeply!" Hands, knuckles ink-stained, cupped the ghatta's head, fingers ruffling behind ears, thumbs tickling under the chin until an unwilling purr broke forth. *"It's just that no matter what, we'll be together. That's what counts, being together—not where we're together, not what we're doing together. That's what I want with Jenret, the twins, too."*

Point out that Doyce *was* with Jenret, the twins? That it didn't matter what they did, where they were, as long as they were together? Khar shook her head, gently extricating herself from the loving hands and raising a hind foot to scratch the itch behind her ear that Doyce had incited. No, she understood what Doyce meant, what she felt, and that would have to suffice.

"Ready?" She took a deep breath, reached for the pen. Her signature started off weak, tentative, but concluded with a bold flourish as Doyce Marbon signed her resignation as Seeker General of the Seekers Veritas.

"Honoria! Nori, wait!" Jenret Wycherley hurried after the younger woman crowned with corn-yellow hair. Corn-yellow was what she dismissively called it, but to him it conjured up the sunny yellow at a daisy's heart, its core fringed by pure white, slender petals. He dodged, evading bodies that seemingly materialized out of nowhere to obstruct his path, people with piled armloads of presents, food, drink, extra chairs, the Lady knew what. He certainly didn't know and didn't want to—not until he'd spoken with Nori.

"Ineffectual, incidental—and in my own house, no less!" he grumbled, eluding his sister Jacobia, only to collide with Lindy, the twins' companion for their first ten years before she'd wedded Bard. Her eyes perused him calmly but too searchingly for his own peace of mind.

"Hardly that, Jenret, but you *are* underfoot if you don't plan on doing your share."

"I *know*." Straining over her shoulder, he caught a glimpse of Nori. Damn, she had her cloak, had almost gained the door! "I'll be back, labor to your heart's content—even leash the twins—but I forgot to tell Nori," he tried to slur his pet name into " 'Noria. Honoria. If she's returning to the mercantile, I need to remind her—" he brushed by Lindy, shame surging at his facility in spinning a skein of lies designed to tangle him deeper and deeper.

"Honoria!" A restrained hail, he hoped, not desperate or pleading, but enough to attract her attention, make her single out his voice from amongst the rest. Whether she'd actually heard or simply sensed his need, on reaching the front door she gave a diffident half-turn, her momentary hesitation working to Jenret's advantage. Arras Muscadeine, Marchmont's Defense Lord, burst through the front door, effectively blocking Honoria's exit and giving Jenret the opportunity to catch her.

Flushed with good cheer, Arras Muscadeine pulled Jenret into his massive embrace, leaving Honoria inbetween— hardly unpleasant as far as Jenret was concerned. Extricating himself, he companionably slapped Arras's shoulder and crooked his hand around Honoria's elbow, swinging her clear of his brother-in-law and out the door.

Arras's mindvoice jovially teased his brain, hitting too near the mark. *"No flirting, Wycherley! Nothing wrong with a pipe dream, but married men can't have more than that!"*

Provoked beyond reason, Jenret glowered at the closed door, praying that Nori wouldn't inquire as to the cause of his vexation. "Nori, please. Stay for the party! You've as much reason to join us as anyone else—especially after all your hard work. Don't disappoint the twins by leaving so soon!" Lady above, would he offer up his own offspring to keep her by his side? Truth was, his dependency had grown, and the time fast approached when he'd need to rely on her even more.

She stood as tall as he, their eyes meeting, and that always roused him, the idea of dominance, the challenge of staring one another down. And Honoria wasn't above bolstering his ego if she thought his resolve had weakened. "We'll set sail to the Sunderlies soon, though not soon enough for me. We have to be patient, bide our time." As the import of what he'd said sank in, he shook his head, wondering if Rawn were near enough to have 'read him. "Not that I'm the best one to preach patience!"

Her voice—always so light and fresh, yet capable of stinging sarcasm on occasion—her breath, caressed his cheek as she leaned close, unwilling to broadcast their business to outsiders. "I've waited this long—I certainly know how to bide my time. But I *should* go back to the mercantile, business first." Pensive, she bit her lip, releasing it to bestow a smile on him. "Mayhap I *will* stay for the festivities. I've presents for the twins—not that they'll notice one more or less tonight."

He nodded, eager that she'd be present to hear tonight's announcement, gauge people's reactions to it.

"But promise me, Jenret, give me your word." He kept nodding, knowing he'd promise her anything, faithfully fulfill his obligation if she could straighten out this unholy tangle.

"Tonight belongs to the twins, to you and Doyce. I'll enjoy it from the sidelines where I belong. After all, the fewer who suspect our alliance, the better off we'll be." Hand on his forearm, she teased, "Going back to the house? Ready to do your share?"

Mutely shaking his head, he walked on a bit farther, determined to distance himself from her. He let the rapidly chilling air prick his skin, serve as an antidote, allow him to think rationally. Damnall, it was nearly over! Well, actually it had just begun, preludes concluded, the real action about to commence. And high time for it! As he waved good-bye to Honoria, his mother Damaris, Jacobia, and Rawn bore down on him.

"Given your glum looks, I think I'd rather face a Guardian cavalry charge!" The somber expressions that echoed from one face to another never altered. "I suppose you're all planning on riding roughshod over me, talking me out of something."

"I wish you'd reconsider, Jenret." His sister Jacobia gave a significant glance back at Honoria's retreating figure.

"I *have* considered and reconsidered, Jacobia. Believe it

or not, I consider more things than you can possibly imagine, secure in your little numerical world." Win her over, and he'd be safe—or safe enough. "Don't you remember an adventure into Marchmont? Seems to me I distinctly recollect someone saying 'There'll be another Wycherley accounted a leader amongst the merchanters!' "

"Jenner, you *are* a leader in so many things! It's just that I've had more time to devote . . ." He couldn't bother to listen to the rest, had heard it all before.

"Rawn, am I right in this?" If he required acid proof of the rightness of his resolve, Rawn would tell him straight out.

Tongue flicking to remove a bit of butter-cream frosting from his upper lip, Rawn never lost his dignity. **"You're right, but some of your reasons are wrong. Don't you realize how this will hurt Doyce? Already has—in case you haven't noticed."**

Hardly the answer he'd wanted to hear, but now his mother took her turn, hands clasped, her self-control overriding her urge to wring them. "I still can't believe this has returned to haunt us after so many years. The past should be dead and done. Jadrian may have been overly harsh with Pieter Rutenfranz, but he was totally within his rights."

"And I can't believe you never told us anything about it until Jacobia mentioned our problems!"

A helpless shrug, a movement toward Jacobia for support, and Damaris spoke in a slow, considering voice. "Because it was an isolated incident, over and done with. Your father fired Pieter for embezzlement and severed ties with his family's company. It was right before, right before . . ." And now her elegant hands did begin to twine until Jacobia clasped one and he took the other, held it against his chest.

"I know, I know," he soothed. "Right before Father killed Jared, and Jared swept his mind clean. 'You had more urgent things to worry about—running a mercantile, consoling a little boy who'd lost his big brother, who couldn't grasp why his papa now cried like a baby when he lost at childish games with his surviving son.

"That was why when the Monitor contacted me, I decided to shoulder this burden. You've done enough, and Jacobia wasn't even born then. Mayhap I'm not going about it in quite the manner you'd prefer, but I think we'll see results." A quick bow of homage to his mother, his sister, a half-salute to Rawn, and he ran lightly toward the house. "Now, if you'll excuse me—if I don't keep my word and help out, Lindy will box my ears just as she did with the twins!"

Quick-walk the path away from Headquarters without looking back, smile, nod, toss a comment to a passing Seeker, but don't stop to chat. One brief, almost furtive pause as Doyce caressed the bronzed knee of Matthias Vandersma for luck, Khar stretching her pink nose to the bronze nose of Kharm, first Bondmate of them all. *"This has been one of the finest parts of my life. But it's not my whole life, Matty. Please understand. You couldn't conceive of a life beyond the Seekers because they were your creation. But I can, and I must."*

Hurrying now, Khar and Doyce strode along the flagstone walkways, her ultimate goal the little stone house on the farthest edge of Headquarters property, the house that she and Jenret and the twins called home. Or rather, it had been little once, but had grown just as the twins had, a new kitchen wing added, a two-story addition that had also lifted part of the original roof to match.

So big, too big now, so often empty. Jenret spent most of his time at the Wycherley mercantile, in charge since his mother, Damaris, had retired and married Syndar Saffron soon after her husband Jadrian's death. His passing had been a relief to all concerned since Jadrian's mind had been rendered totally blank some forty years ago upon killing his son Jared, whose untutored, unrestrained Gleaner skills had been viewed as an inexplicable curse upon a proud lineage, recessive Gleaner ability abruptly burgeoning in a seemingly normal family. Almost another era, it seemed. Despite herself she shivered over Jared's fate, Jadrian's as well, all too thankful that Jenret had realized his Resonant abilities far later in life, as had she. Not like the twins, Resonants from the womb.

Given Doyce's busy workload, it had made more sense for Jenneth and Diccon to spend the majority of their time at their father's mercantile just outside the city. And as that gradually became the norm, Doyce had found herself preferring a more spartan suite at Headquarters, the empty, echoing house a reminder of how difficult it was to successfully balance her life.

"No one ever mentions that the scales get tired, too," Khar gibed as she quick-footed it along the path, the flagstones icy damp beneath her paw pads.

Squinting against the setting sun Doyce stopped short, the ghatta's expression obscured in shadow and light. *"What scales, Khar?"*

"The scales you constantly use to weigh your worth, your success. Up, down, down, up, toss a burden on this side, counter it with another task in the opposite pan. Always seesawing." Despite her narrow-eyed disapproval, Khar kept one ear flickering, twisting this way and that to gather the sounds. What? What was it? Yells, cheering, friendly jeers . . . not that far away. No danger that she could judge, but something was definitely up.

Tapping her foot, annoyance plain, Doyce snapped, *"Well, it's not always easy finding equilibrium. But then, as a mere human, a fallible Bondmate, I can never aspire—"*

"Shh!" Both of Khar's ears swiveled as she lifted her head in concentration. Warning alarums going off at the ghatta's demeanor, Doyce listened hard as well, sending her senses soaring, stretching her mindpowers. Too many mental signatures fogged her brain: Diccon and Jenneth, her nephew Harry, her sister Francie, Mahafny, Parse and Sarrett and various of their brood, Harrap, and a host of others.

"What in the name of the Lady's going on—some escapade, I hope?" Angling off the walkway she cut across the winter-singed lawns, drawn by the racket. *"It's not trouble, is it?"* Too much time spent in dealing with Resonant-Normal problems, and still they flared on occasion, just as a brush fire buries itself under ashes, beneath ground cover, smoldering, creeping along, only to abruptly explode into a full-fledged blaze under the right circumstances. And generally far from watchful eyes, determined souls who'd risk all to extinguish such enmity.

Breaking into a sedate trot, the ghatta flung back, **"Not the sort to give you nightmares, but with the twins involved,**

**not to mention Harry and Parse, it's bound to annoy some-
one—like you."**

What was Parse's quicksilver mind toying with now? The
Monitor should have insisted he move his workshop beyond
Gaernett's Ring Wall after the last explosion. Making do
with a grimace rather than a groan, Doyce increased her
pace, only to realize they'd reached the stone wall that
bounded this segment of the grounds. Damn, which gate
was closer? Left or right? The shouts, the banter, grew
more raucous, but she could scarcely see where she
stepped, the wall and shrubbery blocking the setting sun's
final rays. Perched partway up a cherry tree, Khar began
edging along a pliant limb, intent on peering over the wall.
"Which way, Khar?"

With a scramble and a muffled mew, Khar sprang, gaining the top of the wall. **"I think,"** she mustered as much
dignity as she could, **"that I'm getting a bit old for these
short cuts. You, too. But climb straight over if you can.
Otherwise you'll be too late to see."**

Constructed of rough, irregular stone, the wall stood two
meters high, low enough so Doyce could just manage a grip
on the top. Fingers digging in for dear life, she sprang as
high as she could, only to discover she no longer could
press her own weight upward. A faint snicker from Khar.
"I am in the prime of my middle years, a mere fifty-five.
You, however, Khar, are fast approaching antiquity—remember that," and sucked a scraped finger.

She'd anticipated delivering additional comments in a
similar vein but couldn't spare the breath. Reaching up, she
took hold again, blindly dragging her boot along the wall
to locate an outcrop of stone to support her foot. Yes,
there, up a little higher . . . now the other foot . . . her left
hand slipped, and she felt the sting along palm and inner
wrist. Not going to slip down, not and have to start over
again! Shift the left foot now. *"What can you see? What's
happening?"* she begged, unwilling to plead aloud.

**"Well, you're likely to frighten small, susceptible children
when your face pops over the wall."** A momentary side-
groom. **"You should see yourself. Face purple, eyes bulging, hair an unruly rat's nest—as usual."** Finding another
outcropping, Doyce levered herself higher, flung an arm
across the top of the wall, grazing Khar's flank. **"Anyone**

who thoroughly assessed the situation first would have noticed the maple just beyond has a convenient overhanging branch. Now hurry or we'll miss everything."

"Mmph!" Swinging her right leg over, Doyce heard her pantaloons rip—once at the knee and once at the back seam. *"Miss what, dammit? What's going on, what's happening?"* Heart pounding, she sat atop the wall, twisting to take in everything at once. A milling throng, mostly children and youths—though more than a scattering of adults—jostled each other, slowly began splitting in half, thickly lining each side of the narrow street that leveled here after cresting a small hill and a sharp curve. Considering that Parse exhibited the enthusiasms of a twelve-year-old, the crowd's makeup was right.

Two boys half-lost in oversized, hand-me-down wool jackets busily unfurled a cloth strip, bits of bedsheet, and Doyce prayed their mother had been prepared to sacrifice it. "Finish line?" she hazarded. "Finish to what? Is Parse arranging some sort of race?"

Testing the way, Khar stretched, front paws walking down the wall until gravity demanded that her rear quarters follow. **"Parse's finally finished the prototype of his rolling chair—two versions, no less."** Glancing back as Doyce hoisted herself on heels and hand, ready to jump, she interjected, **"No! Hang on to the top, lower yourself, don't jump! I can already hear your ankles and arches protesting."**

Aggravated but still sensible enough to obey a useful suggestion, Doyce did as she'd been bidden. Even so, the ground rose to meet her harder than she'd expected. Dusting her hands she turned, belatedly aware she could see far less now that she stood on the ground. "Is he testing them, then? Now? It's almost dark, it could be dangerous."

"If I were you, I'd ask who's doing the testing." The ghatta wove through the holly shrubbery more fluidly than her Bondmate.

"Two . . . ouch!" Branches snagged her pantaloons, jacket sleeves, and tabard, tore at the purple-and-gold trim denoting her rank as Seeker General. Oh, for the old sheepskin tabard she'd worn riding circuits. "Two versions?" Damn all, why hadn't she worn her sword, sliced through this ridiculous hindrance? It dawned on her then.

"Not the twins? Parse's birthday present to them? Sarrett would never let him. . . ." What Parse lacked in practicality, his mate Sarrett made up for, blessed with abundant common sense, business acumen, and beauty.

"Well, there's still some disagreement up top as to who's steering and who's serving as ballast for each 'chariot,' as Parse calls them. But according to Per'la, I doubt you'll approve of anyone involved."

Wonderful. The alleyway between the two shops was crammed with rubbish awaiting disposal, much of it dragged off the street to clear the way. Backtracking, she tried another route, heard another muffled, exultant cheer explode from a host of lungs at the high end of the street. "I swear, if the twins are involved in this, they get paddled first, then Parse!"

"Why not deport them all to the Sunderlies, heinous varlets that they are?" and Khar earnestly wished she'd bitten her tongue instead. Hadn't she been told in strictest confidence? Oh, Rawn'd be within his rights to give her a tongue-lashing for breaching it. And just when she yearned for the big, black ghatt to lick and groom her, soothe her aches away, the soft caress of burred tongue sleeking matted fur. Casting her mindvoice wide, she asked all the other ghatti who watched for confirmation as to the charioteers. Unbelievable! Parm and Saam were involved as well!

"I wanted to steer, or at least ride," Diccon groused, working against the throng encircling Parcellus Rudyard and his wheeled chairs. "Come on, give way," he shouted. "Best spot now's the finish line!"

"Assuming they make the curve and stay upright," someone pointed out, more than gleeful at the prospect of a crash. "Only thing that might cross the finish line is a stream of blood," added another with a certain morbid satisfaction.

Fidgeting now, frantically jiggling beside Jenneth and Diccon, Harry plucked at hands, sleeves to capture their attention. His hazel eyes widened, apprehensive at overhearing the advice, well-founded and not, offered to the drivers and their human "ballast." "I never thought! She won't get hurt, will she? Papa's gonna skin me alive if she is, if any of them are."

Diccon crooked his arm around his cousin's neck, smothering him close in a brusque hug while he met Jenneth's equally worried eyes, the same hazel as Harry's—and well they should have been since Harry's mother was Francie, Doyce's sister. *"They're way too old for this! Are they crazy?"* he demanded, hoping Jenneth had a reasonable explanation.

Cautious, he kept his mindvoice in the strictly intimate mode that he and Jenneth had shared since the womb; Harry already showed strong Resonant ability but had become increasingly unpredictable as he approached puberty. Sometimes he'd "stumble" into their private conversations like a china shop bull, and other times he'd miss an obvious and direct mindquery. Diccon sympathized; Harry's mindpowers displayed the same unreliability Diccon'd experienced with his speaking voice the past few years—breaking high or low. Jen had been lucky, puberty hadn't affected her except, mayhap, for making her more skittish, wary, uncertain of herself. Other Resonants didn't gain their abilities until adolescence, while those like Harry suffered embarrassing times, old, familiar skills suddenly awkward, uncontrollable. Still, no point in letting Harry "overhear" their worry, easy enough to sense it without that.

Jenneth gnawed at her lower lip. *"Aunt Francie hates being overprotected. Yes, she's crippled, but she says you never know what your limits are till you try."* Almost pugnacious now, her lower lip thrust out. *"She's no more crazy than you or Harry. You were* both *volunteering without a second thought. She's given it that—and more. Now come on!"* Grabbing Harry's hand, she expertly eeled her way along, only to discover the crowd had formed a human barrier between her and the street.

Now they contended with Gaernett's regular citizenry, tired, intent on trudging homeward after a day's hard work. A final tug and she extricated Harry from the crush, Diccon momentarily lagging behind him. No need to tell him to follow, he always would, always did. Just as she followed if he gained the lead. Well, usually he led and she followed—except in races. The recent memory left her warm with delight.

"Well, I planned to let you steer. Wouldn't have raced without you." His gentian blue eyes, so like their father Jenret's, glared around, then glanced off her. For a teen unassuming in build and coloration, such brilliant, long-lashed eyes gave him an awesome advantage when he chose to use them. It was one of the few things she was jealous of when it came to her twin. He leaped as if goosed when several young women in the crowd whispered behind their hands, staring admiringly in his direction.

With Harry sandwiched between them, they ran down the walkway toward the finish line at the end of the street. "Please," Harry implored, legs pumping, " 'Speak Kharpers! Tell her what's going to happen. Mayhap Auntie Doyce can stop Mama!" Kharpers was his "baby" name for Khar; his slip emphasized his building worry. "I'm 'speaking Papa, but I can't find him yet!"

They exchanged a look over Harry's head. "Should we?" Jenneth worried aloud as they both swung Harry up and over a chubby child toiling after his package-laden mother.

"What good will it do?" Grunting, Diccon eased Harry down. "The only way to stop them is with a coil of rope—assuming you can anchor one end to an anvil or three! Mama'd agree—they're all as stubborn as she is!"

"Well, Mama could alert the Guardians, have them step in, halt it." Jenneth had implicit faith in the Guardians, Canderis's compromise between a standing army and a constabulary. They were all *so* handsome in their crested helmets, so good-natured yet serious, willing to do anything needful to keep the peace. If that meant dismissing the cheering crowd, dampening Parse's excesses—like this race—to protect those who might take hurt from it, they'd do it in a flash, she *knew* they would, even if their popularity temporarily suffered.

A rumble from above and behind, the crunching of wheels initially overpowered by rising laughter and cheers. The crunching quickened, louder now, nearer, gravel skittering, spraying a wall.

"Hurrah! They must've taken the curve!" Diccon leaped to see, fist spearing the sky. "Yes! Now run, run if you aim to be at the finish line!"

❖

"Through, please! Excuse me! Coming through!" Damn it, she couldn't see a thing, though the crowd's reactions served as a crude barometer as to what was happening. The crowd wasn't rude, but it lacked any reason to look behind, discover the Seeker General struggling to breach a passage.

"Out of practice," Khar announced. **"Forgetful, too. Any Seeker worth the tabard—senior or retired—carries a staff. They issue them for precisely such occasions."**

"Thank you very much!" she huffed, and her suppressed venom registered, convinced someone to marginally yield, let her wedge herself into the packed crowd, smelling of hot apple cider and peanuts. "Khar, give me a hand here."

Lingering at the fringes, Khar considered, hating the thought of having her beautiful white feet trod upon. Humans were so inconsiderate sometimes. **"It'd be easier if you'd just Resonant them. 'Speak them and they'd let you pass."** A barking dog, keyed to the breaking point, pranced and bounced, seizing forearms, nipping legs. **"I'm not imitating him."**

"Khar, I can't inflict my mindvoice on them, it's precisely that sort of casual arrogance that makes Normals so uncomfortable." "Coming through! That's right, move a bit!" *"That sense of being herded like cattle obeying some subliminal command. Help me stop this silliness before someone's hurt. Khar, please!"*

"Oh, all right," Khar-the-Long-Suffering agreed. If catering to Bondmates' whims counted, each and every ghatt and ghatta should have reached the Eighth Spiral of Enlightenment. Did the Elders *ever* take that into account? No! Even the Elders were less trying at times. With a snarl and a hiss she dove at the dog, and the dog, torn between sheer joy at finding a playmate and stark terror at its nature, gave a shivering howl as it darted into the press.

It wasn't a long, rangy dog, but it was tree-trunk broad and solid beneath its shaggy rust and black coat. A hiss and a swipe, claws carefully retracted, convinced him to retreat faster. Khar daintily followed at its heels, Doyce behind her as the audience found itself shoved willy-nilly, some tumbling over the dog's wide back as it slammed behind their knees. *"Where're the twins?"* Doyce prayed for Khar's reassurance. *"They're not involved in this, you prom-*

ised me they weren't. I swear I'll tan their hides if they are. Yours, too."

With a touch of wounded dignity, the natural accoutrement of a long-suffering ghatta, Khar lifted her head, let her senses roam. **"Since you won't 'speak them yourself, I predict they'll be arriving very shortly."** .

Half-tripping over the dog as it stopped short, Doyce righted herself against a convenient neighbor. *"And if I 'speak them, they'll vanish so quickly I'll never catch up with them."* Genuine discomfort with and reluctance at employing her Resonant powers made parenting a difficult task, especially with offspring who accepted such gifts as being as natural as the air they breathed. Being the parent of children with far superior Resonant skills, she often alerted them to her anger, and her exasperation well before she caught up with them, giving them time to placate, soothe, or feign complete innocence before she could reprimand them.

Almost to the curb now, one final line of bodies to break through and she'd see whatever it was she wasn't supposed to witness. Pass silent censure on Parse's latest idiocy, assuming she could make out the details in the near-dark. As if hearing her thoughts, nimble children began shinnying up posts, were boosted onto adult shoulders as street lamps were hastily lit. The light dazzled, half-blinding her. Something hard banged her thigh, began rocking; a second shove forced her that way again.

Wrapped snug in a red cloak, a little girl of five wobbled above Doyce's head, fully as amazed as Doyce as she craned her head at the sight. Short she might be, but no five-year-old should outstrip her. "What . . . ?" she exclaimed and felt her serviceable gabardine pantaloons snag. She grabbed to free them, only to discover the protruding nail, the vertical slats. Ah, the child perched on a barrel someone had rolled out to give her a ringside view. Except she couldn't see through the child.

At the moment the dog, still overwrought and highly bewildered at the role reversal that had sent a very large cat chasing after him, found himself nose-to-nose with Khar. His moist black nose snuffled the pink one. **"Ugh!"** Khar hissed her annoyance, and with that, it dawned on the dog precisely what his canine obligation was regarding cats, even very large ones. With an exultant "Woof!" he dug in his feet and lunged.

Tired of evading human feet, humiliated at being sniffed by a dog, and piqued that the scene threatened to degenerate into a free-for-all, Khar drew on instinct and Seeker training: she leaped for Doyce's shoulders to get clear. Startled, off-balance, and painfully aware the Seeker General's woolen dress tabard didn't protect against claws the way sheepskin did, Doyce staggered. Counter stepping to help Doyce regain her balance, Khar shifted to Doyce's other shoulder just as the crowd rotated leftward, staring up the street at the strange vehicles thundering along at breakneck speed. Hip-checked, Doyce slammed into the barrel and tumbled, taking it down with her, the child tossed skyward.

A harried glimpse told her the child had been caught in midair with no ill effects as Doyce worked to heave herself off the barrel. Momentum sent it rolling streetward, Doyce on hands and knees atop it, unsure how to get clear. Instead, it continued rolling, Doyce's dismount attempts propelling it faster, Khar still riding on her back.

The boy holding one end of the finish line spun and crashed like a duckpin as they rolled by, and Khar, in the vain hope of halting them, snatched the end of the line in her teeth as it flew by. **"Faster,"** she urged, **"or slower, or we're in trouble."** She, at least, rode high, could see the action, although Doyce had no pressing desire to view what she could already vividly imagine: in mere instants Parse's wheeled chairs would flatten them!

Feeling like a performing circus animal, Doyce cast a desperate look leftward, all too conscious of a sound like a runaway wagon on a downhill slope. "Ware!" she yelled. "Ware!"

"Mama? What are you—" A second well-known, well-loved voice joined the first, "Mama. You should be embarrassed, acting so silly at your age—" With perfect timing Jenneth and Diccon each grabbed a barrel-end, Diccon catching his mother as Doyce went catapulting at the unexpected braking. Khar sailed clear, her nephew yelling "Kharpers, I've got you!" When had Harry arrived? With a grunt Jenneth upended the barrel, and Diccon deposited Doyce on top, the twins flattening themselves beside it.

And with a muttered prayer, Doyce raised her sweat-drenched face to see Mahafny Annendahl and the Shepherd-Seeker Harrap bearing down on her, tightly followed by her sister Francie and Seeker Holly Benedykt in the second chair. A roar, a whizzing rush of air, and they spun by, faces blurred, mouths open in warning shouts that drifted back to her.

"I truly don't want to know." She fixed her children with a frown. "Not right now, at least. But later, definitely. Oh, very definitely. And if you utter one word of this tonight . . ." she left the threat unfinished for increased potency. Abashed, the twins and Harry nodded as one before dashing after the chariots. The glint of their mind-laughter, sharp and diamond-bright with youth and high spirits, tickled her mind.

Three ghatti—Saam, Parm, and P'roul—trotted down the center of the street, a judicious distance behind the cloud of dust now settling. Parm, a calico with markings only a demented, drunken painter could have envisioned, stopped short and sat to scratch his chin. **"Did you see? Round and round, wheels spinning and flashing! Oh, I tell you, ooh!"** The steel-gray ghatt cuffed Parm's head. **"Ah, well, never mind."** He scampered to catch up with the others. **"Like a trained bear on that barrel! If I could convince dear old Harrap . . ."** and his mindvoice drifted off on another tangent.

Thankful her jacket and tabard concealed her split pantaloons, Doyce marshaled her composure as she limped homeward. A mental wince at her tardiness—a fine help she'd been in preparing for the party! Despite her organizational abilities and her attention to detail, party arrangements weren't one of her stellar skills, and the lack elicited a twinge of guilt. A sad case, to say the least—a mother who'd prefer not to involve herself in planning this special festivity for her two, her only children. Not only wasn't she good at it, but she derived no real pleasure from it.

"Parties aren't the only way a mother shows her love." Khar boasted a minor scrape to the left of her forehead where the fur runs sparse between ear and eye. A faint rolling gait indicated her right hip hurt.

Pausing, Doyce scrubbed her jacket sleeve across her face and bent to blot at the ghatta's wound. **"Don't worry, I'll clean it later, or have Rawn or Saam wash it."**

Straightening slowly, both hands pressed against the small of her back, Doyce groaned. "Patching wounds. *That* I do well, those years of training as a eumedico still come in handy."

A shaky laugh as one of the crowd's laggards good-naturedly shouted, "Did ye drain the barrel first, Seeker General?"

"Lady bless us, Khar, we look as if we've been in a drunken brawl." Unshed tears clouded her voice. *"Khar, it's not just missing the party planning, not even enjoying it. . . . I never baked cookies with them, kissed their tears away . . . oh, the thousand-and-one things good mothers do. No! I was too busy, always doing what I had to do! They'd run to Lindy first, or Jenret, before they'd run to me to soothe their hurts. Lindy was a better mother to them than I was, and she was only a child herself."*

Resolutely padding ahead, forcing Doyce to follow and not make a further spectacle of herself here in the middle of the street, Khar listened first to the shamble, then the slow, steady tread of her beloved's feet. **"You loved them and still love them. You were there when it really mattered and thrust the other tasks aside. What they're now discovering is how *much* you loved them, enough to try to make the world right for them and their kind, so that they'd always be safe, secure. Cookies are nice but don't last very long. What you've done is more important in the long run."**

"But all Jenneth and Diccon wanted and needed then was a lap and love, not the whole world!" Then finally, begrudgingly, *"Point taken. How did you ensure P'roul and Khim knew you loved them?"*

The cottage lights now streamed welcome ahead of them, laughter, silhouetted figures passing by the windows, rushing in and out the doors. **"Cuffed them when they deserved it, washed their ears, nipped them, wrestled with them."** Her muzzle screwed up in distaste. **"And gifted them with mice, dead and alive. At least you weren't subjected to that! What we do for love!"**

Doyce rippled with shaky laughter, and Khar prayed her mirth had carried sufficiently. Jenret and his mother, Dam-

aris—so similar in looks, if nothing more—stood arguing at
the eastern corner of the house, Jenret's actions stiff and
jerky with shame and anger, denial. What words she'd
caught hadn't sounded promising—blast Rawn for not
warning her Jenret was in one of his moods—and hoped
Doyce hadn't noticed or overheard them. With a muffled
curse Jenret stalked off toward the back of the house. Hugging her elbows, shoulders hunched—from the cold or the
coldness of Jenret's words? Khar wondered—Damaris remained, stepping forward to greet them.

A brief hug and she eased away, holding Doyce's shoul-
ders, inspecting her up and down. "I didn't think the
Seeker General fought her own battles—or are you shy of
Seekers, not to mention Guardians, at the moment?"

"No, but your grandchildren age me more every day.
Amongst others I could mention." Doyce threw up her
hands as if that explained it all. "How much time before
the festivities begin? Enough for a quick bath?"

Damaris considered, shaking her head in regret. "No,
most everyone's here, and the twins are upstairs changing.
They came pounding in as if fiends were snapping at their
heels—or at least their mother. Who, I gather, has been up
to some interesting activities."

"Please, don't ask!" She shared a look with Khar.
"We're slowing down, old dear. They've beaten us."

Khar sat, looking Damaris in the eye, until the older
woman turned away, masking her discomfort. "A quick
wash and change is the best you can hope for. You ought
talk with Jenret, Doyce. Something's bothering him. You
know how he is when one of his highs or his lows seizes
him, always too profligate with his emotions." With that
Damaris linked arms with Doyce to head toward the door.
"I'll hold the well-wishers at bay while you make for the
stairs. Those pantaloons look beyond salvaging."

"I've a surprise for you tonight, for everyone." Doyce's
hectic gaiety made Khar wince. "Jenret should be thrilled
by it."

Khar ached as she scurried up the stairs, both from the
pain in her hip and from her beloved's words. Blast the
truth! But it was true only as far as it went, and if the
ghatta had a say in it, an older truth would outweigh a
newer one. Still, she'd be reassured if Doyce would actively

participate, stop being uncertain about verities. Humans, even Bondmates, made their lives *so* messy!

Absentmindedly kicking off a sandal, he scratched his shin with his bare toes, sighing. No relief; the sensation remained, the unquelled itch resided in his brain. The suspicion—no, knowledge—that the figures lied, except he couldn't locate where, how. Whoever was responsible showed fiendish cleverness at clouding the numbers, creating plausible line items he'd entered without thinking twice—until recently.

Damn it all! His big, square office was designed to be airy, bright during the mornings, shady and cool later; that was how one survived the Sunderlies climate. But today he'd left all the floor-to-ceiling windows closed, the louvers shut tight as if to conceal his oversight. Made it dark, hot and still as a tomb, no breezes wafting through. Shifting the oil lamp closer to his elbow, Ozer Oordbeck winced at the heat it shed and cleared the abacus beads.

Start again. Start again and think. Don't just think, think crafty, deceptive, fraudulent. Oh, he'd seen scams before, but never one quite so subtle and far-reaching. Had he become complacent, too bogged down by the sheer mass of entries to really "see" them? With a tug at his gauzy white caftan Ozer peeled the fabric from his sticky skin. Then he rested his head in his hands, elbowing the abacus aside. The beads click-clacked, offering their own tsk-tsking reproach.

How had it come to this pass? And what did he plan to do—keep searching out the lying figures or ignore them? Ozer Oordbeck prided himself on serving as factor for the Wycherley-Saffron textile enterprise here in the Sunderlies. A responsible position, prestigious, even, and he'd been thrilled at being chosen for it because of its complexity and scope—and because of the salary it offered. The upkeep on a household with twelve children was daunting, even in the Sunderlies, where at least clothing and shelter were minimal needs. Twelve! He named them over in his mind, six of his own and Zandra's, six nephews and nieces, the children of Zandra's sister, Gelya, now widowed. Why sort them when he loved them equally, his own regardless of paternity.

Hadn't he immediately alerted Jacobia Wycherley when the first minor discrepancies riveted his attention, warning her someone sought to take advantage of them? Errant figures meant errant shipments, errant debits and credits—shrouded mysteries, the kind that bled a company dry if they weren't discovered, stopped. So he'd ferreted deeper into back records, digging for other instances, other entries or numbers that looked subtly wrong. Had hied himself away from Zandra, Gelya, and the children to visit the weaving sites, the warehouses. But there were so *many* to inspect, to instill with his own sense of vigilance!

His resolve had become tinged by practicality. It was just too much for one man—he couldn't be everywhere at once. Spend a day vetting the quality of an incoming delivery of loose-weave cotton, and he fell a day behind in his figures and the rest of the paperwork. He should have asked—no, insisted—that Jacobia let him hire a junior accountant to bear some of the burden.

Revised reports poured from his pen, more and more isolated incidents, but so little hard evidence. And each instance decreased the bottom line, the profitability of Wycherley-Saffron. Oh, not by a great deal, but enough to be worrisome, especially if there were others he'd not yet flagged. Each discrepancy was scrupulously reported back to Canderis and Jacobia Wycherley, with the devout hope that a fresh set of eyes, a different sensibility, might focus on the overall picture that apparently blinded him. Pray that his problems would be viewed as supervision strained thin, not a plot to line his pockets at Wycherley-Saffron's expense. Straightening, he flicked the abacus beads at random, listening to the zing and clink as they shot up and down, but seeing nothing, normally mild blue eyes blank with hurt, surveying something personal, private, that clashed and clanged in his heart.

Of course then the letters had started, just after he'd written Jacobia Wycherley, pleading that she come to the Sunderlies to help him. An admission of failure? Or the sign of a responsible employee who knew when to alert his superiors to problems beyond his power to solve? He didn't care how she interpreted it, not once the letters arrived—

and so far there'd been but two. STOP LOOKING FOR
ANSWERS, read the first, NOT IF YOU VALUE YOUR
TWELVE CHILDREN. The second had been more ex-
plicit: GIVE IT UP, OORDBECK. YOU CAN'T SAFE-
GUARD TWELVE CHILDREN EACH MOMENT OF
EVERY DAY . . . AND NIGHT. WITH TWELVE,
YOU'LL SCARCELY NOTICE IF ONE GOES
MISSING . . . OR BLIND.

Twelve, twelve, and all equally precious in his sight.
Sight! Moaning, he scrubbed the heels of his hands against
his eyes to dash away the dampness. How could he be so
hot when his skin felt clammy to his touch? Resolute, he
picked up his pen, started rereading his report from bottom
to top. Mayhap if he reviewed it dispassionately, discarding
all preconceived notions, a burst of insight might strike,
lightning-bright. Loyalty—to his family? Or to his employer? Which was more important? Or loyalty to himself,
to what he perceived as right and just? An ironic thought,
here in the Sunderlies with its population of recalcitrant,
unrepentant criminals! Well, honor wouldn't save any of
his children from blindness—or worse. Mayhap Jacobia
Wycherley wouldn't come. Then he'd continue on his own,
as best he could.

A knock startled him, his face going paler than the sun-
bleached eyebrows and lashes that made his face look so
naked, vulnerable. "Come in." Good news? Bad news?
Anything and everything appeared an omen these days,
even the simplest, most unambiguous things.

A head popped round the door, the face shiny with
sweat, daubed with smeared ink. His nephew Rudy, ap-
prenticed at seventeen to his uncle, and a wizard with figures, fingers flying, knuckles tapping as he made his
calculations, all without an abacus. "Uncle Oh-Oh, I think
I've snagged one. Not big, but interesting." He swung inside the main office, leaning against the door until it firmly
latched behind him. "We generally pay for transport in the
octant *after* we've received the fabric bolts, yes?"

Nodding agreement, Ozer strove to look encouraging,
wondering what Rudy was driving at? "Yes. We usually
buy and pay for the bolts close to the end of each octant.
But they're delivered to the warehouses at the beginning

of the next octant—takes a few days for them to arrive. You know that. We pay delivery charges then."

A mischievous look flitted across Rudy's face, downright impish. A rub to the bridge of his nose left a new ink track. "Well, have you ever noticed we're paying for more wagons than we had shipments? Oh, just one or two, mayhap three. But it happens time after time." He waited, then rushed ahead. "It matches the bolt shipment for the *same* octant, but only if that figure's higher than the other.

"I mean, we bought enough bolts to fill seven wagons last octant; eight this time. Well, we should be billed for seven wagons *this* octant, eight wagons *next* octant, right? Matches what we bought last time but transported now. We've been billed for eight. It's easy to forget, assume the two figures should match."

Eyes wide, Ozer's mouth formed an "o" of comprehension, sudden understanding. Lady bless the boy for catching his negligence! One more puzzle piece, another debit, another way to cheat Wycherley-Saffron. The overbilling wouldn't amount to much, but would build over time. Obvious—and right in front of his harried nose. "Good work, Rudy!" Only then did he notice how stiffly Rudy held himself, his left shoulder and arm immobile, gesturing with the other. "What's wrong with the arm, lad?"

Rudy shrugged, grimacing as his left shoulder rose, then gestured with his right noncommittally. "Mashed it 'gainst a wall, Uncle Oh-Oh. Some show-off dagga boys, pushing and shoving. What else is new in life?"

"You weren't hurt any worse than that, were you? Did they threaten you, try to hustle you off?" He shuddered at the randomness of life and death—not the neat order of numbers. But they were no longer as neat as he'd assumed. Coincidence? Or the possibility that they—whomever *they* might be—had chosen Rudy to teach his uncle a minor lesson, but a major truth.

Rudy grinned, the grin any self-sufficient young Sunderlian gave at the casual dangers of life. "Didn't stay to find out. Showed them the back of my heels, just as you taught."

Ozer Oordbeck felt almost calm. Dagga boys were a fact of life, especially in Samranth—like packs of wild dogs in the hills. Just as feral, too. They were part of the reason he kept such close track of his twelve, so they wouldn't run with the pack. Still, no need to jump to conclusions just because of the letters. "Feet as fleet as your figuring, Rudy. Good lad."

"Are you ready yet?" Jenret Wycherley tapped his foot, had been tapping it forever, tonight, the only outlet he had for his mounting frustration with the stodgy predictability of his life, its passionate lack of so many things. Well, that would change, soon enough. *"We'll be the last down. Should have been greeting our guests from the beginning."* A tug at his midnight-blue wool jacket to settle its band more easily at his hips. Almost black, looked it in certain lights. A simple band of embroidery down the front of his white shirt, scarlet pyramid shapes, no less—dashing.

The same, always the same, and Doyce the same as well. Consistency meant boredom, the stupor of sameness. Why 'speak her, why share his mind with her and her with him when they both knew how monotonously predictable they'd be? Even her habitual lateness was predictable. When hadn't she been late, when hadn't she put something else, someone else, ahead of him, of the twins? Well, at least *he'd* been available for Diccon and Jen more often than she ever had. At least they could count on him! Which meant he'd turned utterly predictable as well! More mercantiler than Resonant-Seeker. Make him feel old, weighted by life—and here he was, younger than Doyce!

Struggling with an earring Doyce glanced over her shoulder, away from the mirror. "So go down, Jenret. Greet everyone. I'll be along shortly." She spoke the words aloud and that, as much as anything, indicated to him that she again presented some façade, not her inner feelings.

"No, I'll wait." He'd lost this battle, lost it before it had even begun, but he'd not wave the white flag yet.

"Since when did it become a battle? A war you fight against each other?" Rawn, his coal-black ghatt Bondmate, stretched across the foot of the bed, kneading his paws in Khar's haunch until she began switching her tail and narrowed her amber eyes at him.

"It's not a battle." A weak denial, and a relief that both

Resonant talent and Rawn's special mindspeech provided an intimate mode, no one existing to hear except the other.

Rolling onto his shoulder, languidly pulling his paws clear of temptation, Rawn yawned, then lifted his head to glare at Jenret. **"Beware of a flank attack while you and Doyce are clashing weapons, complaining whose tasks are more demanding. Besides, you're always demanding."**

He was about to question Rawn about the flank attack when Doyce spoke. "Jenner, I can't get this earring in. Help me?" Her plea, even for something as silly, as trivial as that, touched him—a tenderness he'd half-forgotten—and he came 'round the bed while she sat at its foot. Earring in hand, he reached for Doyce's chin to tilt her head. Funny, he now harbored no jealousy of the garnet rose she always wore in memory of her lost lover Oriel. Though he *had* been jealous for longer than he cared to acknowledge, had insisted on replacing those special earrings with a pair from him, as if to insure he possessed her, her love. And she'd point-blank refused, calmly stating her love for him but protesting that one didn't cancel the other, that Oriel's memory was equally special.

Enough to make him sulk—and he had. Until Khar had explained that some other token could symbolize his and Doyce's love. The star sapphire on its chain had been his compromise. Damn, wasn't she wearing it tonight? "Jenner, we have to talk." She winced as he jabbed the earring post. "What's wrong, what's bothering you? I feel as if you're withdrawing from me, have been for some time."

As he fumbled, the earring leaped from his fingers, a relief to stoop in search of it, shield his face. "Nothing, love," though his words growled in his throat, guilt turning them rough and mean.

"It has to be something, Jenret. We have to talk, we need to talk, there're things I need so much to tell—"

"There, got it!" he crowed, springing to his feet. "Now, steady, if you please." His graceful fingers regained dexterity, and he fitted the earring through, slipping on its backing.

Doyce grabbed his hand, held it to her cheek, leaving him rigid with surprise. "Jenret, talk to me! Please, I'm so afraid that—"

For some reason her fear, her need, angered him, as if

it were too late for that, and he didn't know whom to blame. "You never take time to listen, really listen to me anymore!"

Staring at his hand as if she truly couldn't identify it, she let it slip free and rose, rummaging atop her bureau. Snatching up the chain with its star sapphire, she let it slither through her fingers to clatter at his feet. "Mayhap that's because you never really tell me anything anymore!"

What halted any further exchange was a chorus of low, warning growls from the bed. **"Enough!"** Khar spat. **"Truce called,"** cautioned Rawn, looking every bit the stern enforcer. **"Finish dressing and go, both of you. Children fight fairer, more openly."**

They both stood, frozen in shock and embarrassment, until Jenret stiffly scooped the chain off the floor. Unclasping it, he held it out, inviting her to enter the circle of his arms. With a look inscrutable enough to make the ghatti proud, Doyce slipped inside, Jenret's familiar touch brushing the back of her neck. "Jenner, I *do* love you," she whispered.

"I know, love, I know," and he kissed the back of her neck, the touch of his lips burning cold. Was it so hard to say he loved her in return? But he couldn't make himself shape the words.

Left hand tight to his waist, right arm fully extended, Diccon snapped his arm inward, turquoise silk flaring, tasseled ends swishing by his nose. Despite his best efforts, the shimmering fabric tangled, folding back on itself before dangling limply floorward. His face scarlet with effort, he shook the end of the sash as if scolding it. *"Jen! Hurry up, please!"* he exploded, *"The blasted sash won't behave!"*

Ankle boot in each hand, Jenneth padded into her brother's bedroom. She wore a cream-colored shirt and chocolate-brown pantaloons topped by a short overvest of chocolate, coral, and turquoise bargello patterning. Beneath it peeked a coral sash with turquoise tassels girding her slim waist. *"And they say women take forever getting dressed,"* she chided.

Snapping the end of his sash at her, he gave a low whistle, freeing a hand to make circling motions. *"Turn around, Jen, let's see."* A blush touched her cheeks, but she spun obediently, lithe and flowing as the ends of her sash. *"Beautiful, Jen, absolutely beautiful,"* Diccon beamed his approval and truly meant it. *"If Davvy doesn't notice you tonight, we'll have proof positive he's blind!"* Jenneth colored more deeply, whether at the compliment or his comment about Davvy, Diccon couldn't judge. He considered, *"Of course, it might be more effective if you* wore *the boots, don't you think?"*

The left one narrowly missed his ear, and he deflected it with an elbow. After all, he'd expected her to throw it— could tell precisely when she'd let fly, just as he knew that she knew as well. Always attuned, always anticipating each other, so very different yet so very much the same. No one knew him as well as Jen, and no one knew her as he did— so it had been since the womb.

With a complicitous grin Jenneth retrieved her boot and tugged them both on. Hands on hips she inspected Diccon's sash, already well on its way to bedragglement. *"How do you do it, Dic? Make such a muddle of things?"* Taking the sash and shaking it, she smoothed it as best she could. *"There's no hope—and no time—to teach you, so let's finish this quick as we can."* Measuring out a length of sash from her brother's waist to his knee, she forced his hand down to gingerly pinch the edge. Backing with the other end until it stretched taut, she raised her eyebrows, motioning him toward her with one hand. *"Slow and even, turn, turn, turn. That's it,"* coaxing him along.

"Worse than dancing!" he groaned as Jen held up a hand to halt him. "Keep me at arm's length, or I'll tramp on your feet!" With quick, efficient motions she tied his sash, deftly teasing the knot to shape it and combing the tassels with her fingers. She found his vest—for a wonder of wonders slung on the back of his desk chair, not crumpled in a corner—and held it for him. It matched hers, although the turquoise predominated within the chocolate-and-coral patterning.

"Diccon, you shaved again!" A melodramatic hiss over the word "shaved."

"I should hope so! Just because I shaved three days ago

doesn't mean I couldn't use another!" Now it was his turn
to look faintly abashed but pleased.

"Well, the stubble might have proved an advantage, however much there was," Jen taunted. "You could have terrified Helwys with it, threatened to scratch her!"

Diccon moaned, resting his forehead on his sister's shoulder. "Save me!" he whimpered and met his sister's dancing
hazel eyes. "Promise me that for tonight, Jen. You know
how my magnetic personality attracts the poor child!" Helwys was the twelve-year-old daughter of Parse and Sarrett,
and until recently had been a perfectly pleasant child to
sport with, they'd both agreed from their vantage point of
four additional years. But womanhood beckoned Helwys,
leaving her captive to puppy love, not to mention a generous padding of baby fat.

"I promise," Jen raised her right hand in pledge. "Just
don't be cruel, she idolizes you."

"I know, I won't." Grabbing a hairbrush, he attempted
to slick back his hair while he polished his boots on the
back of his calves. "It's just that she's always shadowing
me and sighing, looking up at me with those big, adoring
eyes. Reminds me of Barnaby—except he had more sense."
He spun his sister toward the door. "About ready to go
down and celebrate? The happiest of naming days to you,
Sis."

"And to you, Brother. Mama and Papa down yet?" They
started out, arms linked.

"You never take time to listen, really listen to me anymore!" The harsh words echoed down the hallway from
their parents' room.

"Because you never really tell me anything anymore!"

The twins froze, then sped from the sounds. *"Why tonight, of all nights?"* Diccon's face had gone tense, and he
clutched Jen's arm tighter for comfort, his and hers. *"At
least argue in mindspeech, not let the whole world hear!"*

Jenneth's eyes filled, the hazel shading turning green-
blue. *"It's all they seem to do lately."*

Tugging her in his wake, Diccon made for the stairs.
*"Come on, there's nothing we can do. Besides, look who's
at the bottom!"*

Craning to see, Jenneth caught a glimpse of Davvy
McNaught standing with his back to them at the landing

and she hurried. Diccon gave a surreptitious mindcall, and Davvy, a Resonant-eumedico, obediently turned in mock-surprise to stare up at them.

"Jenneth, Diccon!" he called, "Felicitations of the day! And may the coming year bring you joy as new-minted adults!" A pretend stumble, as if in shock, "Jenneth, you look stunning tonight, radiant. Womanhood becomes you!" Aglow with eagerness, Jenneth almost floated toward the inviting hand Davvy held out to her.

But at that moment a pleasant contralto voice called out. "Diccon, Jen, my loves! Happiness today!" and Davvy pivoted in its direction, clearly in the grip of some powerful emotion, his welcoming hand falling limp at his side.

"Lindy, how are you? How're Bard, Byrlyn?" he asked a little too heartily.

Hugging his sister's arm tighter, Diccon pressed his shoulder against hers in solidarity. *"Don't worry, Jen. There'll be time later. You know how he gets when Lindy's around."*

Chin high, lower lip trembling between her teeth, Jenneth continued down unsteadily, each step a blur through a haze of grief. *"When is he going to realize he can't have her? She's Uncle Bard's wife and that's that!"* Her fingers crumpled Diccon's sleeve as she blindly clutched his arm. *"I'm not a child any longer, even he should be able to see that!"* Again a hollow, empty feeling swallowed her heart, insecurities blooming, expanding, and she yearned for the reassurance of a lucifer or two, igniting them, watching them burn to nothing while she composed herself.

Diccon frowned, gave an imperceptible headshake. *"No, Jen. You promised me . . ."*

"I won't, I just . . . when I have . . ." She shrugged, appeasing him, but her mind still circled, wildly relentless. How could Lindy betray Uncle Bard like that? But she hadn't—couldn't! Jenneth knew Lindy would never do such a thing, loved her too much to doubt her. It was just that . . . how did Lindy attract someone so innocently, effortlessly? Someone over whom Jenneth herself pined.

"No, it isn't fair, Jen, but it's life."

❧

"Lindy!" His hand, the glowing warmth of his flesh almost melted her resolve, his warm brown eyes on her, too eager, too obvious. Lips pursed in a frown, she reclaimed her hand, her resolve, relieved his face resumed the pleasant mask he wore in her presence. Despite his years, his accomplishments as a rising Resonant-eumedico, the boy within shone forth: merry eyes half-covered by shaggy brown bangs, braggadocio and shyness combined; more comfortable in those days around adults than other children, legacy of his early years as an only child, the spoiled pet of the Research Hospice in the Tetonords. And protector of the little girl she'd once been, two years his junior.

What she could not, would not show Davvy McNaught, was the depth of her own reciprocal emotion, nor even hint at the chance that they might share these emotions in the future. She'd felt the potentialities ever more strongly of late, those strange foreshadowings of the future she sometimes experienced. Unwanted knowledge of happenings in distant places at the same moment they transpired, or the daylight visions that presaged an event tomorrow, an oct, or octant later . . . or never at all, except in her own mind. Burdened with such uncanny abilities, she wasn't one to daydream lightly.

"Davvy, I've a million things to do," Lindy Marlin Ambwasali whispered a caution, her icy flesh now tingling and warm. "Make yourself useful. Help Bard in the kitchen, check the wine and fruit punch. Please!" When they were inadvertently alone like this, his mere presence unnerved her, made her wary.

Pulling him away around the corner into the hall, out of sight of the twins, she admonished, "Pay a little more attention to Jenneth tonight. Some grave flattery, a touch of flirting. It's her name day, after all." Davvy had the grace to look contrite.

"I know. You distracted me. I can feel her 'come-hithering' in my brain—she doesn't even realize she's projecting it." His eyebrows soared upward, vanishing in his bangs. "It's so hard to contemplate—Jenneth the temptress, the seductress!" Ashamed at her reaction, Lindy choked back a chuckle. "She's practically a niece to me. Hard to entertain romantic thoughts when you've changed someone's diapers!"

At the lofty age of twenty-eight Davvy clearly considered the twelve-year gap between Jenneth and himself an insurmountable barrier. No matter that eighteen years separated her from Bard. It was hard, Lindy acknowledged, to admit their relationship with the twins could evolve from mentor/protector/minder to equals, adults. "Well, a little kindness, a little compassion for unrequited love might let it bloom and fade a bit faster." Lindy shook a finger in his face. "Be kind, let her down gently. She'll come to believe it her idea to drop you, not yours."

"Be kind, let him down gently," he mimicked with savage scorn. "Just as you've done with me all these years?"

She turned toward the kitchen, back stiff with reproach, finally relenting enough to take a few unwilling steps toward him, her expression grave, as always. "And each time I dash your hopes, you raise them again, unsolicited, don't you? I told you from the beginning I'd marry Bard—and I did! I never lied—I told you I love him!"

That was the utter truth, no lie. She *had* loved Bard, *did* love Bard . . . but she loved Davvy more. That was her secret, her purgatory. If Bard were the cool, sustaining water that refreshed her soul, then Davvy was the heady wine that made her spirits sing. What she couldn't say was what her foreseeings presaged: marriage to Bard, then marriage to Davvy. But she must be wrong, *had* to be! For that meant Bard's death, looming somehow, somewhere along the future's path. What she "saw" in many tomorrows was often clouded, never as fully revealed as she might wish for interpreting it. So say nothing, raise no false hopes for either of them, let alone carve Bard's doom upon his brow.

The memory surged over her again: travel, a storm-tossed ship; strange, exotic places; hot, humid, and bursting with sensuous, riotous growth, like a forcing house. Bard, uncharacteristically, quietly happy, almost at peace with himself, and then . . . and then? She didn't know, couldn't see. But travel? Not likely. After years of riding the circuits as a Seeker Veritas, Bard had retired early, unable to continue after his sister's death. Oh, he did his share of training Novies, or substituted on holidays or vacation times, but otherwise her dear Bard only grumblingly ventured beyond Gaernett. Wedded to his cookery, his bakeshop, his catering, devoted to his wife, his little daughter, Byrlyn. And overwhelmingly solicitous of the child, a substitute for Byrta.

Amazing how her mind could race, cover so much uncharted territory in such a fragment of time, because she realized now that Davvy answered her. "No, you never lied, Lindy." Yet that arrested moment had aged him, or at least schooled him in maturity.

A paw swatted her skirt and she reached down, caressing the ghatt's sleek head, tracing his white forehead star. "Yes, I'm coming, M'wa. Tell Bard I'm on my way, gossiping when I should be working."

"And I'm on my way as well. Duty calls." A sudden dimple flashed in Davvy's cheek. "Hard labor—flirting to do. What better present for a girl's sixteenth birthday than genuine admiration? If I do it properly, perhaps I'll make you jealous!"

Panicky, she eyed M'wa, wondering if the ghatt transmitted this conversation to Bard. Stretching front paws to her waist, the ghatt tilted his head, and she gave a rub behind his ears, those ears bereft so long of Seeker earrings, put aside after Byrta's and P'wa's deaths. No, if anything, M'wa understood all too well, was grateful for what she'd elected to give Bard—her love and affection. Not once had she ever known M'wa to pry where he shouldn't, as tender with her feelings as he was with his Bond's.

It steadied her, that shared glance with M'wa, and she couldn't resist tossing a gibe back at Davvy. "Then I'll flirt with Diccon! See how you like that!"

"A contest!" Stroking M'wa's shoulder, old friend and comrade that he was, Davvy saluted and headed back to the celebration.

Paper hats, noisemakers, and the torn remains of silver-foil crackers littered the room; leftover cake and half-drunk cups of punch crowded every surface, inviting spills. Everyone had eaten to excess and some, Doyce noted a bit sourly, had drunk more than enough. Herself included, and she set her punch behind her, well out of reach. The remnants of crushed fruit in the bottom floated like bloated, water-logged corpses.

Khar shoved her muzzle into the cup, lips drawn back as she inhaled. **"Doesn't smell like a corpse, not unless you pickled the body,"** she announced. **"Like the Bannerjees with their specimen jars. Besides, you haven't drunk much—not like some I could mention."** A pointed look in Jenret's direction as the ghatta wrinkled her nose in disapproval. **"Rawn should knock the cup from his hand,"** but the black ghatt across the room refused to rise to her bait. Instead, he stolidly hunched his head tightly to his shoulders, patience already sorely tried.

Stifling a burp, conscious of the leaden sensation in her stomach, Doyce slipped to the fringes of activity, preferring to participate from a distance in the laughter and games. *"Lady help me if Bard hears me burp. He'll suspect his cooking calls for bicarbonate."* Pursing her lips, she forced the rising gas back down. *"It wasn't the food. Nor the drink. Couldn't do justice to either, in fact."*

An easy chair crammed with shabby, floral-print cushions beckoned, a comfortable sanctuary relocated in an out-of-the-way corner to make space for an expanded buffet table. Now the buffet had been pushed back as well, creating a narrow alley to negotiate to reach the chair. Khar took the short route, directly under the buffet, the tablecloth trailing along her tail as she emerged.

"Tell me, Khar. Do you ghatti truly have a third eye? One on the tip of your tail?" Capturing the striped tail, Doyce gave it a little shake.

Twisting to groom, Khar licked ruffled fur into place. **"Of course. That's why we ghatti are superlative at blind-man's bluff. You always forget to tie a handkerchief over my tail."**

Settling into the chair with relief, Doyce watched as the game began. The twins had planned to flout tradition, skip blind-man's bluff this year, unwilling to tamper with their new status as adults by indulging in a silly children's game. But too many pleas from adults as well as children had forced the twins to relent. A mindless game, but fun—especially when played earlier in the evening before the younger children became so boisterous.

"And of course you're not cheating if—because of my oversight—your tail-eye can see."

A rippling purr of agreement as Khar squeezed beside her in the chair, dislodging a pillow. Funny, she had no idea what had brought it to mind, but these pillows had come from the Sunderlies.

Handkerchief over his eyes, Davvy obligingly bumbled around the room, desperately lurching after every stifled laugh, head cocked to track the shuffle of fleeing feet. As Diccon sidled behind his sister, he winked in Doyce's direction and slammed his hip into Jenneth's, propelling her into Davvy's arms. A payback of sorts, Doyce suspected. Moments before little Helwys had donned the blindfold and had unerringly hunted Diccon like a hawk; Jenneth had tossed Harry into her path, a lure for her to strike.

"They're growing too fast, Khar. Can't we stop them?" But the ghatta avoided answering, cushioning her head on Doyce's thigh.

Swinging in a wide circle, her coral sash flying, Jenneth tracked the noises she heard, mouth intent beneath the blindfold. A quick feint in the opposite direction, and Jenneth's arms closed tight around Honoria, passing by to clear the buffet. Laughing, Jenneth ripped off the blindfold and let go in shock, managing a game smile. Although Doyce hadn't expected Honoria to join in, too coolly condescending for such frivolity, Honoria let Jen tie on the blindfold. And quickly—too quickly to soothe Doyce's heart—Jenret stepped obligingly into her path. Whoops and giggles as he kissed her cheek. Somehow the game had lost its savor. A game, only a game. A foolish, childish game—put it firmly out of mind.

Working through the throng, Holly and Theo approached from either side, their Bondmates P'roul and Khim pausing to greet-sniff Khar. Unable to shake old habits, Khar gave both a thorough but brief ear-wash. Such maternal ablutions caused a remarkable similarity of expressions on both childish and ghatten faces, Doyce decided: a long-suffering look and squinted eyes. Catching the drift of her Bond's thoughts, Khar muttered, **"I shouldn't—I know they're too old. Don't you think, though, that till the day she died, Inez wanted to check behind your ears?"**

A tall, broadly-built woman in her early thirties, Holly

let out a satisfied groan as she loosened the sash over her tabard. To hear Holly, a waist was the one gift she truly desired; while her bosom was respectable, the rest of her was tree-trunk wide and straight, a firmly-padded monolith. Hard to believe she and Theo were first cousins, only their height similar. Theo was even taller but almost cadaverously thin; anyone running into him would be bruised on the various knobs and angularities of his joints. Holly gestured at his plate, Theo's fork rising and falling with the staccato rhythm of a famine victim finally encountering food. "Third piece, so help me by the Lady!" she moaned and snatched Theo's plate. Tauntingly, Theo licked the fork. "Enough! Each bite you take travels and relocates around my middle!"

An old, familiar battle between the cousins, and Khim and P'roul chortled as they rubbed against Doyce, backs arched, tails high. **"Wonderful that we ghatti don't have to watch our weight."** Khim prepared to duck as her sib, P'roul, aimed a swat at her, ever vigilant to slurs against her Bond.

Joints popping like haliday crackers, Theo squatted with the grace of a folding skeleton, whispering at Doyce. His breath, frosting-sweet and warm, tickled her ear. "S-so, is it t-true? I m-mean truly t-true?" Laying a hand over his dice-sized knuckles, she heard his stammer with surprise; he generally managed to conquer it among old, familiar friends.

Holly had eased herself protectively on the arm of the chair, dark brown eyes filled with concern. "But why now?" she chimed in, warily glancing to see if any noticed their huddle around Doyce.

"Yes, it's true, and you know it—consider your sources." Doyce studied her lap, picking at the folds of her brown silk pantaloons, fashionably wide and swirling to mimic a long skirt. "I won't ask *their* source, since it isn't official until tomorrow morning." A tug at Khar's tail, and the ghatta twitched with pretend startlement, not to mention false innocence. "As to why now? Well—" she paused, and Holly reached for her other hand, held it. The love and concern radiating from them, from P'roul and Khim, threatened to sweep her away, evoke emotions she wasn't capable of handling tonight. For sixteen years Holly and Theo had held a special place in her heart, only to be expected, given their Bondmates: P'roul the offspring of Khar and Rawn, Khim the offspring of Khar and Saam, yet the same litter.

"Why not? Sometimes you know the time has come. . . ." Her eyes started to tear, self-discipline temporarily deserting her just as a small voice floated up from behind her chair.

"Auntie Doyce? Need you, need a hug." With a gentleness that belied his ungainly-looking hands, Theo reached to retrieve a little girl of seven, folding her into his arms before depositing her in Doyce's lap.

The solace of burrowing child enveloped Doyce as thin arms trapped her, a pale gold face nuzzling her neck. Every muscle felt coiled and tense as a spring as Doyce stroked between her shoulder blades, protruding like tiny wing nubs. "Byrlyn-love, Byrlie-Barl, what's the matter?" A rapid mutter, impossible to catch. Still, she suspected what ailed Bard and Lindy's only offspring.

Chin propped on Byrlyn's head, she caught Theo's eye. "Why don't you two see if Arras plans to serve the celvassy? It's potent enough to jolt the eight Disciples in their orbit, but just a touch does settle the stomach after a big meal."

Holly patted her shoulder to acknowledge the hint. "I could use some myself—overindulged in Bard's cooking, as usual," and she and Theo unobtrusively withdrew, their ghatti following.

"So?" Kissing the child's ear, she let Byrlyn resettle herself to peer at the crowd, careful, nonetheless, not to jam Khar with her knees. One hand sought her mouth, but she fought the urge, planting her thumb beneath her nose, fingers curled near her eye. Such restraint cost the child dear; Byrlyn had sucked her thumb until well after her fifth birthday. "So?" Doyce tried again.

"I am *not* Auntie Byrta!" the child wailed. "I'm *me*. Don't want to be Byrta! I love Papa, but he makes it so *hard*. Think he loves Byrta more'n me!" She gulped, swallowing hard as she rammed her fist to block the tears. "Don't look like Auntie Byrta, do I?"

Doyce struggled to construct an honest answer for the child she'd held on her naming day. What had the past imprinted on the present? No new-minted coin deserved a second stamping.

Byrta, Bard's twin, as like as like could be, despite the difference of gender, and both so lithe and golden-skinned, tight curls the color of maple sugar, eyes like blue-hazed smoke. Bound to each other beyond all accounting, yet always "outsiders," the odd ones out, somber, silent offspring of a Sunderlies native and a Canderisian woman. Their connection had been so complete that no others could contend. A mental communion as well, not precisely Resonant powers, but a shared connection of mind and spirit.

Byrta, dead now, along with her Bondmate P'wa . . . the giant broadsword inexorably arcing at the weaponless Bard, Byrta's mad advance to protect her brother, her sword insignificant as a shaft of wheat against the broadsword's hungry harvest. Her severed head . . . flying through the air . . . Bard catching it . . . pressing his lips against hers. . . . The memories wracked Doyce, a part of her for better or for worse. And if a part of her—what of Bard?

But the here-and-now required an answer, one designed to console a child.

"Sometimes he calls me Byrta, even *thinks* I am! When he does that, I won't answer, I won't!" Byrlyn's words sputtered against Doyce's throat. "And . . . and . . . now . . . we go off sometimes, someplace quiet, and he . . . he sits with his back to me!" Her tears flowed, a silent stream of them. "And he . . . he says, 'Concentrate, think what I'm thinking, tell me what I'm thinking.'" A tiny wail, like a fearful mouse, frantic not to expose itself to further torment or suffering. "I *don't* know what he's thinking! Don't want to know. I just know I'm *me*, not Aunt Byrta!" Her shoulders rose and fell with rhythmic sobs.

"Well, of course you're Byrlyn, you're *you*, no one else is like you. Understand that, child. You're *you*, not Byrta." Rubbing circles against the thin back with one hand, Doyce dug into a pocket to find a handkerchief, half-wishing those little wing nubs would sprout into wings, let the child fly away. "But, my Byrlie-Barl, remember. When you were made, it took your mother and your father to do it. Not to mention a pinch of your grandparents on both sides, aunts and uncles and cousins—they all contributed a bit to the broth that makes you You. Fact is, I'm sure you've got your Grandma Marlin's handsome, stubborn chin." She bit her lip, unsure what more to say, how far to intrude.

"Want me to speak with your mother?"

A gusty sigh ruffled the handkerchief, followed by a healthy nose blow. "Mama tries, yells at Papa when she catches us. But she can't be around all the time. And I don't want to hurt Papa."

"I've known Bard, your papa, a long time. I could remind him who *you* are—his lovely daughter, his one-of-a-kind child?"

"One-of-a-kind child! Just *me*!" A watery giggle before the child turned grave again. "Nooo. Don't think so. His heart hurts when someone reminds him Auntie Byrta's gone." A mature perception for such a small child.

"Well, there's always M'wa. How about that? Khar or I could 'speak him." Something had to be done, and whether Byrlyn approved or not, she'd warn someone of the burdens of the past the child was being forced to carry on her small shoulders.

Long legs, tired of being folded, sought freedom over the arm of the chair; Khar's nose and whiskers tickled bare skin where ruckled pantaloons and drooping hose had parted company. "Nooo. That'd be worse." Pensive now. "M'wa's all Papa has left of the past. Don't want them to argue, fight over me." Now her arms and trunk extended over the chair's opposite arm. "Just needed to make sure I was Me, 'cause I get wondering sometimes. Had to make sure, Auntie Doyce."

"You're always You to me, love."

Shifting in Doyce's lap for a better view of the gathering, Byrlyn tilted her head, rolling her eyes back in an alarming fashion, "Who're *you*, Auntie Doyce, if you're not Seeker General?"

Right now Doyce refused to consider the question—or the answer. "Scoot, child. Emmelot and Arndt need someone to play with them."

As the children began to flag, exhausted but stifling yawns to avoid threats of bed, the celebration slowed, adult con-

cerns took center stage—reminiscences, future plans, josh-
ing and jokes, anecdotes that opportunity and alcohol
coaxed from even the most reluctant and shy. Young and
old displayed flushed cheeks, drowsy eyes, and the easy,
open camaraderie that long friendship engenders. The fire
had burned low, even the lamps and candles casting a
softer, more intimate light against the dark outdoors. Peering out the window someone announced, "Snow flurries!
Send one of the ghatti out, check for tracks! It'll be our
first official blizzard if the tracks show!"

Feeling absurdly expectant with the secret of her resignation as Seeker General, Doyce yearned to deliver her news.
Yet each time she strove to reveal it, her voice refused to
command the crowd, interrupted, balked at every turn: a
renewed drift of laughter, some drollery's aftermath; an intense but affable argument resumed; or Parse and Sarrett's
youngest, Serphin (known to his siblings as Serpent, Snake,
and Worm) sobbing after a fall. And never once, even once,
could she flag Jenret's wandering attention, alert him to the
significance of her announcement.

Instead, Saam caught her eye from across the room, a
match to Mahafny's assessing appraisal from their chair by
the fire. A blanket draped the retired eumedico's lap; her
gnarled fingers, practically useless now, rubbed Saam's
back, the heels of her palms working up and down his steel-
gray length. Come to think of it, she hadn't yet chided
Mahafny or her sister about Parse's ill-considered chariot
race.

Despite her glimpse of him this afternoon, she'd avoided
admitting to herself how greatly Saam had aged, even more
so than Rawn and Khar. Sprawled on Mahafny's lap, his
increasing thinness was all too obvious. He'd endured so
much to honor his pledge to watch over her and Khar.

Eyes slitted with pleasure at the massage, his 'speech
drifted to her lazy as smoke, though it masked a real concern. **"We ghatti can announce it from the rooftops just
after the Bethel chimes midnight. Bound to attract their
attention. It's right, Doyce. Follow your heart, be Doyce
and no one else."**

*"Well, like it or not, I'll always be someone else—mother,
wife, sister, friend, ex-eumedico."* A little shrug, a smaller
smile. Seeing him so frail, so increasingly worn by time,

forcibly reminded her how far she and Saam went back—
to Oriel, his first Bondmate and Doyce's lover, a victim of
her stepson Vesey, maimed in both body and in his Gleaner
soul, and his perilous quest for knowledge and power. She
shook herself, clutching at the present, Saam awaiting her
answer. *"I'd rather you didn't 'speak it from the rooftops,
old friend. The temperature's dropped, and the tiles and
shingles are icy. No broken hips, if you please."*

**"And always remember to land on your head, it'll lessen
the damage,"** Khar chimed in.

**"If I weren't so comfortable, I'd make you regret that,
my pink-nosed beauty."** As he shifted and stretched,
Saam's eyes brightened, time fading, falling away to reveal
what a magnificent ghatt he'd been in his prime. **"I could
ask a certain ghatten of ours to handle the task for me."**
Perched on the arm of Theo's easy chair, Khim perked up,
highly interested, but Saam gave no further command.

**"Khar, don't distract me from Doyce's problem. A ghatti
serenade? No, too much like a flourish of trumpets. The
answer, I think,"** Saam paused, bobbing his chin, **"is simply
to fill your lungs with air and force it out. Pretend you're
playing one of those blasted, blatting long horns that Arras
and his fellow Marchmontians cherish so."**

Obedient, Doyce inhaled as the conversation faltered
into a natural lull and found her voice, launching it. "Ladies
and Gentlemen, Dear Ones all, I've an announcement to—"
The buzz diminished even further, heads craning to gauge
where the interruption came from, so reticent had she been
all evening. Abruptly breaking off his conversation with
Honoria, Jenret interpreted the pause as his cue, even silence submissive to his every whim. More than a little inflamed from too much celvassy, he pushed clear of the
table, lifting his voice and raising his glass.

"I've saved the best for last—a surprise for you all, and
a special naming day gift for the twins." Breathless, he
paused, one stubborn dark lock falling free over his forehead, and he swiped at it. "As you're all aware, my sister
Jacobia and I are joint partners in a recent mercantile venture in the Sunderlies. She journeyed there several times
when she set things up, but I've had projects here at home
to handle."

Cocked eyebrows, murmurs, the room awash with curiosity. Helpless, Doyce realized every eye had wandered from her, no one to interrupt with "Jenret, Doyce was announcing something important, too. . . ." It didn't come, not one reasonable voice—not even Mahafny's—and the strained expressions on Damaris's and Jacobia's faces, the simmering glower on Syndar Saffron's were hardly enough to muzzle Jenret.

"Oh? No, Arras." Jenret tossed his head as if a fly buzzed round it. So Arras Muscadeine *had* come to her rescue, had employed his Resonant skills to privately rebuke Jenret for trampling over her announcement. "Whatever Doyce has to say, I'm sure it can wait." Those blue, blue eyes sought her at last, yet didn't seem to see her, "Can't it, dearheart?"

"Jenret, please," she begged, loath to plead or, worse yet, shame him in public, convince him yet again her position as Seeker General took precedence over anything else. *"I wanted to tell you before, I tried—"*

"And you'll tell us all later, won't you? This is too special to wait." He tossed his hands into the air, his expansive smile encompassing the room, embracing everyone except her.

Khar's flickering tail tip accelerated. **"Push back, don't let him push you. You're so afraid of crossing him, starting an argument, that you don't stand up for yourself. Make him listen! You avoid it because it's less effort."**

A false smile pasted in place, Doyce clamped her hands between her knees to hide their shaking. *"I might hear things I don't want to hear. It's too late, he has the wind in his sails, I can't—"*

Couldn't—or wouldn't? Didn't dare? Which? But Jenret seized the floor as if the brief interruption had further whetted people's appetites for his news. "I think it's high time *I* visit the Sunderlies, spare Jacobia another trip. And since it's winter break, the twins have time before their final Tierce begins. Assuming Diccon and Jenneth want to go with me!"

Capering like a dancing bear around an astonished Jenneth, Diccon finally propelled them both into their father's arms for an exuberant hug. Beaming, Jenret tucked a proprietary arm around each. "Anyone care to join us? After all, the more, the merrier—especially friends!"

A long ocean voyage, an exotic southern land, the promise of warm climes in the depths of winter; a land peopled
by Canderis's most hardened, unrepentant criminals, exiled
there in punishment for their crimes; a land of stalwart
individuals who'd voluntarily emigrated, thirsting for adventure, exploration, and new business. And most of all,
the land Bard's gentle forebears—his grandfather and his
three wives—had left so long ago, with their prime herd of
beef cattle, to create a new life in Canderis. A rare occurrence, such reverse migration.

A hollowness expanded in the pit of her stomach, her
body but a thin shell containing it. Why now? Why—once
she'd made her decision to resign—did they all plan to
desert her?

Khar's tail still flickered, her ears back-tilted with dismay
as Rawn bowed his dark head in abject apology. **"Well,
we've no Seeker obligations now. We could go, too."** A
demanding white paw tapped Doyce's knee, but still no
words surfaced, unable to escape the void. **"Beloved, *tell*
them!"**

But Harry's frantic jig had attracted not only his father's
attention, but everyone else's. "Papa! Let's go, too! Please?
Marchmont trades with the Sunderlies. King Eadwin would
approve a visit—even though you're not commerce minis-
ter!" Struggling to contain his high spirits, act mature and
sensible, Harry managed to stand still, stand tall. "I'm
nearly as old as Jennie and Dic, so I'm practically grown
up. It'd be a good experience for me to have under my
belt!"

"Ask your mother, see if she wants to go," Arras
growled, trapped between his son's ebullience and Francie's
consternation. At least Francie openly revealed what she
felt, secure in her love for Arras; a twinge of envy struck
Doyce.

With difficulty Francie rose, leaning into Harry's careful
charge at her, his outstretched arms pleading. The boy had
learned early to treat his mother like fine china, so fragile,
yet so strong, as if her body's infirmities had tempered her
mind and soul. Harry wrapped an arm around her waist to
serve as her willing crutch. "Mama? Would you? Go to the
Sunderlies, I mean?" His eyes begged her permission.

"I can't imagine anything I'd like less!" Yet her tart rejoinder was undercut by Arras's equally boyish delight at the hint of adventure. "If your father can abandon his precious politics, can believe the kingdom won't topple without him, I see no reason why you two can't go. Provided," she let the pause lengthen, "you bring me suitable—and costly—presents to show your gratitude. Such as your two bodies, safe and sound!"

This time Harry did bowl her over, her weak leg buckling as he caught her, righting her and holding her secure until she found her feet. "Sorry—and thank you! We'll come back loaded with gorgeous gifts, as costly as Papa's wallet allows!" Bussing both Francie's cheeks, he resettled her and threw himself at his cousins in a welter of arms and legs.

So it went, others chiming in, eager to journey but fearful to go, too busy, a thousand-and-one reasons. Despite herself, Doyce judged a "no" as subtle support for her; a "yes" as a betrayal, desertion. So unfair, so unlike her. Of course Bard longed to go, take Lindy and Byrlyn with him, introduce them to his heritage. Sarrett and Parse declined; Mahafny and Harrap as well, Parm sagging dejectedly, while Davvy agreed, leaving Jenneth elated.

Holly and P'roul, Theo and Khim—Doyce went expressionless, stunned by casual defection, not to mention their lack of authorization. Except, since she no longer served as Seeker General, she could hardly deny them leave. A grumbling but secretly pleased Arras and Harry. And—Honoria Wijnnobel. "My right hand at the mercantile." Jenret's matter-of-factness sounded forced, an effort at self-control. "Since she's survived keeping an eye on the twins, as well, she can ride whip on Byrlyn and Harry, if need be."

Ice and hollowness, cold and emptiness, hurt expanding and cracking within her; no one, not one person had thought to ask if she wished to go! Finally Jenret turned, straining to mold his features into a suitably sympathetic expression. "Doyce, I'm so sorry you can't join us. Still, we shouldn't be gone more than four octs, five at the most."

She stood now, resting icy knuckles on the table for support, the burning warmth of anger kindling within her, filling the void. "But, Jenret, I certainly *do* plan to go. I wouldn't miss it for the world!" Hazel eyes sparked against gentian blue, refusing to yield, give in.

"But, Doyce," a sputtering protest, spurious concern, "of course we'd love to have you along, but can you really abandon the Seekers Veritas for that length of time?"

"For that long—and longer." Stretching across the table, she boldly claimed his half-filled glass of celvassy, raising it to her lips and downing it in one gulp. The only way to drink celvassy—if one craved the sensation she wanted right then. The burning warmth expanded, courage from a bottle. "You see, Jenret, my news is still to come: I'm retiring as Seeker General. Providential timing, isn't it?"

Secretly relishing Arras's silent *"Brava, Doyce! Square between the eyes!"*, she gestured for him to refill her glass, conscious of the stares, the consternation all around her. She raised the glass in toast. "To the Sunderlies!"

Jenneth gazed out her dormer window at the Lady Moon with her eight perfect, full satellite disciples floating serene in the sky, tiny white flakes of icy snow glinting like falling stars. After tonight, the disciples would vanish, only to recommence their cycles of waxing and waning, one after the other appearing to denote the passing octants. From everything to nothing—except for the Lady's eternal vigilance, never-changing, constant, her beneficent, silvered light shining on all.

Why, oh, why couldn't everything be constant, never-changing?—as it had been when she and Dic were small, not so very long ago. A shiver made her snug her pink flannel nightgown tighter over her knees, wish it would cover her feet.

Candle in hand, her brother crowded beside her on the window seat, huffing on the cold window glass to fog it. He sought her bare feet with his free hand. "Glacial! The Tetonords in the dead of winter are warmer!" Wrapping his nightshirt around his legs until his pose book-ended hers, he slipped his feet over hers.

Giving him a wan smile, she abruptly stiffened, feet itching as if she'd run through nettles. "Socks? Wool socks?" Her eyebrows rose. "Bed socks, mayhap? With little, frilly cuffs? From Helwys?" A bony knee cracked hers in warning. "Lady help me, Dic, they itch like a demon!"

"Itch or be cold. You choose." And despite himself, he grew defensive—when all he wanted was to be protective. Amazing how she could unintentionally ruffle feathers, just as Mama did to Papa at times. Tonight, though, had been different. Well, don't dwell on it, Jen was doing that enough for both of them.

"Not bed socks," he emphasized. "High wool hunting socks. They've got wonderful patterns at the tops. Mine are navy. Didn't you see yours?" He hiked his nightshirt to model them, holding the candle close. "Auntie Francie and Uncle Arras brought them down. They're from Addawanna and Nakum. Helwys couldn't knit a fishing seine the way she drops stitches." His brow creased. "Though it doesn't seem very manly to knit."

Still, what did it matter? Anything that the Erakwan Nakum and his grandmother Addawanna did was fine by him, especially when he and Jen visited, went hunting and fishing. Not that Nakum often ventured from his mountain fastness where he tended his arborfer trees. He must have gathered the wool from the mountain goats up there, given it to Addawanna to card and spin. Knitting would pass the time during those long, cold nights—mayhap he should learn.

Forehead pressed to the glass, dark hair curtaining her face, Jenneth whispered, "I wish Nakum would visit. He'd find a way to make Mama and Papa stop bickering." No, she wasn't going to be distracted. Her hand groped blindly until Diccon captured it, wound their fingers together. "Tonight was the last straw! Why do they compete against each other? It seems like all the time lately!"

Though he agreed in essence, he wasn't quite sure what to make of her statement. "But what are they competing over? What do they win?" Somehow he never saw problems as lucidly as Jenneth did. Action, activity was so much easier—find a concrete problem, solve it. On this problem he had no answers, except . . . "Sometimes," he labored over the insight, striving to shape it, "I think they're competing for us—for our love. At least that's part of it—love." A snort at such foolishness. "We love'm both, don't we, Jen?" There, *that* was the problem, had to be; now find a solution, a way to tangibly show them both they were equally loved, appreciated. A warm glow suffused him.

"I can't believe we're going to the Sunderlies! The Sunderlies!" Almost guttering the candle in his excitement, he dripped hot wax on his thumb. "Ouch! Think of it, Jen! What an adventure!"

Jenneth's hand squeezed his in a vise-grip. "Chowder head! They're *not* just competing for us, think about it. Think about it, instead of the stupid trip!" Rapidly swabbing her eyes and nose with her nightgown sleeve, she tossed back her hair, expression defiant in the wavering candlelight as she gripped his hand harder to make him concentrate.

"Ow! One hand burned and you're crushing the other! What, Jen?" Cross, he squeezed back, hard, harder, but she'd trapped him, knuckles pinching, grinding against each other. "What?" He subsided. "Pax." The signal to yield, and the pressure eased.

"It's more than us, though we're part of it." Her eyes peeked over her knees, the rest of her face shielded. "It's like a contest . . . or . . . or some strange sort of combat to convince each other they don't care anymore! To attack, to hurt each other! But I don't know who started the battle."

Diccon bit his lip, leaning his forehead on the cool glass, letting his twin's comments settle in his brain. Fine, mayhap he *wasn't* as perceptive as Jen; he didn't relish marshaling the words, the emotions needed to reveal his deepest feelings. Action came easier. "You're right," and reluctantly, "and you're wrong, Sistwin."

Flexing his jaw, he waited for the words to surface, prayed to the Lady they would. Hated seeing Jenneth fearful like this, was fearful himself, despite stolidly ignoring it, pretending things were fine. "Yes, they're attacking each other. But," he bounced on his knees, unable to stay still, "but they're battering at fortresses, trying to batter down the defenses, rescue the love still harbored inside! Don't you see?"

"Are you sure?" Distinct relief, definite hope glowed in Jenneth's eyes. "You mean they still love each other, but they've forgotten how? Locked it tight inside?"

A wash of exhaustion swept over Diccon, as if his insight had drained everything he could give at that level, and he lapsed into mindspeech. *"They don't work as a team any-*

more. Can't pull in tandem—they each pull in different directions. Not like us." That seemed obvious; each parent boasted his or her own sphere of influence, and they rarely overlapped, except for him and Jen.

"*Sometimes it* does *seem as if the only thing they have in common is us.*" Her matching shift to mindspeech had further calmed Jenneth, as if they shared a womb again, protected from the outside world. Except for a fleeting memory: "*What is fire? Mama scared?*" The growing warmth—too warm, too uncomfortable—the oxygen's now-sluggish flow through their umbilical cords. She pushed the memory away, but the flickering candle flame began to mesmerize her with its seductive, powerful dance.

Conscious where her eyes had drifted, Diccon edged the candle out of reach. "*Think you could go to bed now? Go to sleep?*" He buried his yawn in the crook of his arm. "*Can't hear them fighting, can you? Been quiet ever since they went to bed.*"

"*Too quiet.*"

Swinging his legs from the window seat, he rose, tugging her along in his wake. His bed seemed a long, long way off, his separate room lonely. "*Too quiet's not bad.*" He grinned, winked. "*Maybe . . . they're . . . you know . . .*" and wriggled his eyebrows, rolling his eyes. "*Oh, but that isn't always quiet either, is it?*"

Jenneth cuffed him, frustrated, embarrassed. "*Dic, how dare . . .*" and began to giggle.

As her helpless giggles finally tapered off, he struggled to construct a façade of offended seriousness, but it collapsed at the sheer joy of his anticipation. "*Just think, Jen! We're all going to the Sunderlies! Maybe they'll make up there. The Sunderlies!*"

"*The Sunderlies,*" she echoed, but her mindvoice lacked his conviction. "*The Sunderlies.*"

What was it about the close of an old year, the beginning of a new, that sent people to their windows deep in the night or as dawn broke? The closer it came, the more people stared out, waving farewell to the old, welcoming the new with regret and relief, remembrance and, perhaps, reconciliation. How many other tormented souls stared out their windows tonight at the Lady Moon, just as she did? Too many, Lindy suspected, and all praying for miracles.

Should she choose a different window, a different view for each bittersweet emotion, for each wish for the future, each wistful thought about the past? She wandered, restless, yearning for a view to soothe, make the future right. If not from this window, mayhap from another. If not in this life, mayhap in another. Except that resolving to strive for a new future, a new life glimpsed from a new window, struck her as faintly sacrilegious, and she cast the eight-point star of her faith.

Never did she wish for anything, fearing it might come true. Not that her wishes foresaw the future, but that sometimes she glimpsed it and fervently wished she hadn't. It hurtled her along, willy-nilly, no chance to change it, elude it, halt it. Somehow, somewhere, around some future corner it would rear up at her, leering. And sometimes she glimpsed a "now," kilometers barring her from being there. Had suffered it as a child, shedding bitter tears as she "witnessed" Byrta's death in distant Marchmont. No journey sped fast enough to change it, halt it. Just be thankful the "nows," the "futures," didn't unveil themselves more often than they did, because they altered her perceptions of the people involved. How could it not, knowing their future?

Hair down her back in a braid, ready for bed, she swung the plait forward, gnawing at its tip end. The house creaked and settled, Bard still puttering downstairs, the reassuring sounds of a steady spouse checking the closure of things for the night. Closure! Heart breaking with hopeless love for Bard, she fled their bedroom as he began up the stairs, detoured into Byrlyn's bedroom off the half-landing. No matter how often she'd checked on the child, Bard always did it once more. As quiet as if fleeing an enemy, she slipped into Byrlyn's old nursery, now her sewing room.

Panting as if she'd been chased—and in a sense she had been, by her thoughts—she pressed behind the cheerful yellow draperies, peering up at the stars twinkling high above the few city lights still aglow.

Determined, with a painfully throbbing heart, she stared southward—toward the Sunderlies. A land as unknown, as unknowable, as the dear husband she'd slept beside these past eight years. One octad. The never-ending eight one could trace through eternity yet never reach an end, looping around and around itself. Self-contained, hopeless to break in or break out.

The curtain rustled and she nearly screamed with fright, cramming the dusty liner into her mouth to smother her cry. No sense frightening Bard or Byrlyn with her feverish imaginings. Yes, she'd been envisioning the sea, the waves, for some time now—at least, at last—she understood what that signified. No, the curtain *had* shifted, something grazing her knee. In the dimness, the white forehead star, the white chest blaze glowed, the left foreleg, with its white stocking, stretched up at her, beseeching.

"M'wa! You gave me such a fright," she whispered. He ventured higher, both forepaws on her waist and dug his head under her elbow as if to hide. "Sweet? What's the matter?" Wondered if he'd 'speak her, answer her directly? The ghatti were reticent to 'speak those who weren't Bondmates, or at least Seekers, and she'd respected that restraint from the beginning. Most of all, had respected and loved M'wa's grave ways, his obvious love for Bard, a love that had existed longer—mayhap even ran deeper—than hers for Bard. True, she was Bard's mate, but M'wa was his Bondmate.

Again he slammed her elbow with his broad head, uttering a ragged, anxious mew that seemed to beg for comfort. Cupping a hand over his head, she waited for the warmth, the touch to reassure him. When that didn't work, she squatted, the draperies still shielding them, and shifted his forequarters into her lap, hugging him against her breast. The next thing she knew, he'd scrambled into her lap, wedging himself tight. At about fifteen kilos, a lapful of ghatt tended to spill over, so, with a sigh, she wound her arms around him and awkwardly stood so they could both stare out the window.

It came, unbidden . . . strange greenery, lushly growing plants and trees, mostly alien to her eye . . . Bard confidently slipping through as if he'd been born to do so. Others with him, though she couldn't sense who. Then screams, blood, Bard struggling hand-to-hand with someone, but it floated in a crimson haze except for the naked hatred burning red in Bard's eyes. Now another man appeared, blond hair to his shoulders, a deep-tanned skin, handsome except for the crazed twist to his face. The crazed man looked faintly familiar, but she could not for the life of her—or for Bard's life—think where she'd seen him before. She hugged M'wa harder as the foretelling vanished, gradually dissipating like mist.

The black-and-white ghatt pressed his head against hers in commiseration, tremors rippling his fur. No, *she* was shaking, they both were. "Oh, M'wa, I don't want to go to the Sunderlies!"

He sat high on the beach, far above the tide line, the jagged demarcation that traced the ocean's farthest reach. On the wave-smoothed sand below, the flotsam and jetsam—his pickings, his livelihood—settled, came to rest. Where he had come to rest so many years ago, no longer storm-tossed by mania, able at last to leave it behind him. Or almost so.

Tonight he'd sit and remember, staring at the stars and the unchanging ever-bright Moon, her eight disciples ripely full at this turn of the new year. Shoving bare feet into the coarse sand, still faintly warm on top but chill beneath, he angled his arms for support and cast his head back at the night skies. These were his boundaries now, the sand and reeds and tough sea grape vines behind him, able to thrive on brackish water. The churning ocean beyond his feet, the sky above his head.

Sixteen years! Was it possible? Two full cycles of eight. Oh, another world had been within his grasp, so very near! He picked up a handful of sand, tossed it. No vindictiveness, no anger to his gesture, just the necessity to cast something aside, as he'd been cast aside. So many grains of sand; no doubt one of them thought it was special, just as he'd thought he'd been special, chosen. In truth he'd been just one more grain of sand.

Another handful, and this time he kept his fist closed, letting it trickle out, grain by grain, before unclenching it. The few grains left, their numbers, the patterns they made, their position on his palm, would augur his future. Careful, he turned his hand over to study it in the moonlight. Ah, like tiny diamonds flashing against his skin as the moonlight reflected off each grain, a glint of the future, aglitter. He bent forward to look, holding his breath so as not to disturb the grains. Stared harder at what he saw revealed.

Just at that moment a cloud drifted over the moon, his light, his vision gone. A reminder not to believe in this or anything. With a rueful laugh he rubbed his palm against the side of his pantleg, the only piece of clothing he wore, and climbed to his feet to begin the walk inland to his hut.

No, wait, he'd almost forgotten. Turning toward the ocean once more, he stretched an arm in salute to the moon above, still obscured by the clouds. "Bless Baz," he whispered. Once a year it was necessary to remember, although whether he honored the memory or the man, he wasn't sure. Men believed different things, thought different thoughts, in the Sunderlies.

PART TWO

"Grown-ups never *move very fast."* Diccon strained to catch sight of any following figures, but the roadway remained empty, had been practically deserted ever since they'd passed through the Ring Wall, the basalt wall that guarded Gaernett, just as the sun was rising. Bored, Harry shivered in the early morning cold, pounding his gloved hands together as he continued to watch Diccon fidget. Goddess save them all and—better yet—march the adults along at a reasonable clip. If this balky start foreshadowed their trip, they'd *never* reach the Sunderlies, let alone Windle Port, by the time school began again!

Mirroring his cousin's frown, his impatient shoulder shrug, Harry jerked the sorrel gelding's reins a little too hard, set it ajitter at the roughness. *"We're off! Hurrah!"* he 'spoke Diccon, pleased at such man-to-man camaraderie, relieved, too, that his mindvoice hadn't shattered. Ah, the road ahead beckoned, promised adventures around each curve, but he held his mount to a canter, matching Diccon's, puffed with pride at blazing the way with his cousin. Overhead the sky swiftly changed from a predawn gray to a sharp blue so intense it stung his eyes, and the breeze carried splinters of icy snow tossed by their horses' hooves. A tarp-covered wagon finally rolled by from the other direction, the man and boy on the seat bundled together under a mangy fur throw. At first he furiously waved to attract their attention, then settled for a calm acknowledgment, the mere hint of a worldly smile.

But Diccon now acted glum, slumped in the saddle, unwilling to talk, share his exuberance. Mayhap Diccon'd caught a bad case of adulthood, couldn't move any quicker. Bored, he let his horse fall back to join Jenneth, accompanied by Byrlyn on her barrel-girthed pony.

"What's he frumping about?" Harry mouthed as Jenneth's horse closed the gap. Though he'd have preferred to 'speak her, he didn't with Byrlie present. Resonants shouldn't privately converse, exclude any Normals present; that was ill-bred. Besides, he remembered all too well adults addressing each other over his head, literally and figuratively, until he'd learned to pluck their shining mindvoices from the air. "Hey, Byrlie-Barl, what do you and Dolly think?" She wasn't a bad sort, for a child, babyish in years but pretty serious in her thoughts. Like her papa that way.

Actually, he knew why Diccon acted so grumpy; Jenneth, too, if it came to that, though she concealed it better. Same reason he felt a bit cranky, though actually starting the trip, even with such excruciating slowness, had muted some of it.

Leaning confidentially toward the rag doll belted to her waist, Byrlyn whispered and straightened, mittened hand shoving up her red woolen cap to expose an expanse of wide, white forehead hedged with escaping curls. "S'mad 'bout what he had to leave behind," and nodded once for emphasis.

Despite herself Jenneth's lips quivered, finally twitched in a smile. "We both got thumped pretty thoroughly when Mama and Uncle Arras inspected our packing. Not only *how* we packed, but *what* we packed," she amended. "Did you survive their once-over?"

"Ouch! Practically turned my pockets inside out!" Patting his saddlebags protectively, Harry cast a surreptitious look back, relieved to see the baggage wagon where his small trunk rode. Any smaller and he'd mistake it for a covered lunch bucket. "Light and lean, that's the Muscadeine motto. How much did you have to leave behind?" He was genuinely curious: had he fared better or worse than his beloved cousins? But one special indulgence *had* been granted, one leniency he'd not anticipated from a man who commanded the King of Marchmont's troops, something he'd buried deep in the trunk, praying his father would overlook it. *Was* he a coddled, pampered only child, as Diccon sometimes teased?

As if she'd read his thoughts—and Harry's spine tingled, because he'd sensed nothing of the sort—Byrlyn reached to pat his hand. "Mr. Monkey'll be stuffy in the trunk, won't he?"

His favorite stuffed animal, comrade since infancy, shabby from love and a thousand adventures. Impossible to leave him behind on this real one. Oh, he didn't need Mr. Monkey anymore, not truly, not as grown up as he was now. A good-luck token, that's why he'd smuggled Mr. Monkey into the trunk, burying him beneath his necessities. But wonder of wonders, his father had respectfully laid Mr. Monkey on the meager pile of things to take, not crowning the larger stack of things doomed to remain behind.

"Won't be stuffy," a raised eyebrow, a downward jut of his chin. "He's riding in a saddlebag, up near the flap, plenty of air there." Satisfied, Byrlie's eyes smiled at him.

"Diccon packed an entire armory, or so it seemed." Jen had apparently regained her good humor, much to Harry's relief. "Would've clanked all the way to the Sunderlies— or worse, sunk our ship!" She waved an expansive hand in the baggage wagon's direction, still trundling along behind them. "A bronze breastplate, a helmet, his half-size crossbow—still packs a mean punch." Momentarily she reckoned on her fingers. "Quarrels, naturally. Six daggers of varied and sundry sorts, a short sword and a long sword, plus scabbards, and some sort of knuckle-things . . . knuckle-dusters?" Brandishing a fist, she demonstrated. "Think he slipped those in his waist pouch. A coil of rope, a folding shovel, a trident—for fishing, he claims—and I don't know what else."

"But I do," Byrlyn interrupted. "More clothes than you packed. Right?" The three burst into giggles, Diccon swiveling a disgruntled look in their direction, belatedly realizing he served as their topic of conversation.

"Takes after Aunt Doyce, that way," Harry sputtered, swiping at his eyes with his scarf fringe. "Mama always swears Auntie Doyce is half packrat, pockets stuffed with hoarded treasure!"

Lifting her hair clear of her fur collar, Jenneth pondered. "Hard to be as impetuous as Papa and as loaded down as Mama."

"But Aunt Doyce believes in *portable* odds and ends," Harry emphasized. "Two porters couldn't budge Diccon's stash, I reckon!"

Stung by Harry's good-humored criticism, Jenneth sprang to her brother's defense. "He just wants to be prepared for anything, Harry. You know that. It shows he thinks ahead."

Aware he'd violated a cardinal rule—criticizing one twin to the other—Harry went tactfully mum, taking sudden interest in a crow rising with ungainly flaps from the remains of a cornfield, black wing-beats stark against white snow and bone-white stalks. Diccon could do no wrong in Jen's eyes. Or rather, if he did do wrong, only Jen had license to chastise him. Let another try, and they stood back to back, defending each other.

"Look! They're finally catching up!" Byrlyn had rammed her pony against Harry's leg, tired of his woolgathering. "Dolly and I are going to ride up with Diccon now, 'cause Dolly thinks he's lonely," and at the drumming of her heels, the pony trotted ahead in all his shaggy-coated, wintery glory.

"She's funny, like a little old lady sometimes. Like she knows more than she should for someone her age." Patting the saddlebag and Mr. Monkey for reassurance, Harry drew himself up with adult sobriety, the road too well-traveled now for such childish acts, even if no one could see inside his saddlebag. Too many people coming from and going to Gaernett, passing them with ease! As if they had more important things to do! Midmorning, and already the landscape bored him: rolling hills, stone-fenced fields with haystacks crisped by frost, cornstalk clatter, the remnants of a tattered scarecrow. All so comfortable . . . familiar . . . tedious! Town after little town with their smiths, bakers, and butchers endlessly repeated as they headed southeast, toward the sea. The sea!

Pounding hooves behind him, closing the gap, more travelers—or mayhap Father and Uncle Jenret. His neck chafed against his woolly scarf as he twisted to check; for a moment he clamped a fist over his mouth, tight, then trumpeted through his fingers, "Oh, oh, your Aunt Jacobia and that Nori-person have trotted ahead—they're joining us." Jacobia Wycherley was . . . was . . . just splendid, cracking splendid! His heart crowded his chest with its pounding, making itself known through two sweaters, a vest, and his leather jacket. Her looks—like Jen's, but a *real* woman's—

darkly lush, exotically pale, curvaceous—plus business acumen, too, or so his parents swore. She'd journeyed to the Sunderlies four times already! A shame she wasn't going this time, because he'd stick to her side, learn every detail about the Sunderlies . . . and about her, her likes, her dislikes, everything. . . .

The Nori-person made him edgy, twitchy-like as if he had to anticipate her—edgy-good or edgy-bad, he couldn't unravel. She *was* drop-dead gorgeous, her looks, her personality entirely different from Jacobia's. Which did he prefer? Pale blonde cool or raven-haired intensity? As if they'd fight over him—ha!

"Oh, Honoria's nice enough." Jenneth sounded studiously neutral, giving nothing away, just like Aunt Doyce. Except with Jen, her face spoke volumes, a private language he could only haltingly decipher. "Just takes getting used to is all." So, something about Honoria stuck in Jen's craw.

"Rein in!" Jacobia called. "Do you plan to beat the ship to Windle Port?" She shot past them, a blur of scarlet jacket bent low over her horse's neck, before circling to rejoin them. "You'll cool your heels for days and sniff fish—it's a treat, I tell you!"

"But if the ship comes early, it might sail without us!" Harry raised himself in his stirrups, hands flicking the rein ends.

"It's a three-day ride to Windle Port, even four if it snows. The vessel depends on the weather as well to reach port, plus it needs a few days for repair and reprovisioning. You've plenty of time—even if you walk."

By now Honoria had brought her mount beside them, her horse almost as sleek as she, silvery-white with a darker mane and tail. Glancing at his own legs, spattered with mud and snow, a string of horse drool, Harry marveled at her ability to have ridden this far unmarred, her dove-gray trousers and coat should have been a magnet for mud. A touch of color—a maroon cap and gloves—drew the eye, warming his heart, but Harry fought it into submission.

The contrast between Honoria and Jacobia was emphasized even more by the strong family resemblance between Jacobia and Jenneth, midnight dark hair, the pale, heart-shaped faces—yet their eyes were entirely different, Jacobia's a sparkling, striking violet to pierce the heart, his heart, and Jenneth's hazel, shrewd, yet always slightly troubled. Like his mother's, like Auntie Doyce's, his own eyes, hazel, as well. Always unsure about something, someone. More of a burden than he liked. Better to be decisive, like Nori's light gray eyes, sharp, slicing through uncertainties.

"Come on, move up with Diccon and Byrlie." The cuff fringe on Jacobia's riding glove flickered in the breeze as she waved them ahead. "One reminder before I head back to mind the shop. Easier to deliver it once, not twice." Nori's composed expression subtly mocked Jacobia's enthusiasm, and a burn of indignation flashed through Harry. Let her prove herself as Jacobia had; so far she'd been about as useful as a decorative china figurine, no matter how Uncle Jenret bragged about her head for figures. Jacobia could work shipping calculations in her sleep, he'd bet!

Cutting between Byrlyn's and Diccon's mounts, Jacobia paused until Harry and Jenneth had obediently positioned themselves to either side. Honoria hung back, meticulous about avoiding any hoof-tossed mud. "Now remember, this is an adventure, yes, but it's also a hardheaded visit to improve business. There's money to be made in the Sunderlies, goods to export, goods to import and resell here. Exotic woods, a small but growing glass-blowing industry, spices and medicinal plants, rice and superior cotton."

Almost dreamily, she continued, "I'd love to see us expand beyond fabrics someday, once we're fully established, have ironed out some of our problems." Her forehead wrinkled, mouth tautening in a frown, but just as Harry began to wonder about her secret woe, a sunny grin broke through, and she winked at him.

"The people you'll meet are *not* all convicts; the actual number of unrepentant criminals we've deported through the years make up a *very* minor segment of the population. Regardless of whether they are or aren't criminals, treat everyone respectfully, just as you've been taught. That way you can't go wrong. Still, visitors are a novelty, exciting. Up till recently, ships have been rare—those that came deposited prisoners, or Guardian troops on rotation, necessary supplies. Now ships deliver promise, trade opportunities, new faces. The population has grown enough to make real trade viable, profitable for them, not just for us. In the past we had to import our own labor—folk who were dependable—and that cut down profits, not to mention the difficulty of recruiting enough hardy souls willing to work in a strange new land.

"It's still easier to sail into Samranth, the capital city, than it is to sail out. Three Guardian fortresses are stationed at intervals along the coast, and they conduct rigorous inspections of all outgoing ships to ensure no convicts escape back to Canderis. Usually a semiretired Seeker pair or two are on duty to determine the truth in case someone attempts a new identity. Then it's up to the Canderisian-appointed Governor and the popularly-elected council to determine any punishments meted out."

"We'll be mannerly, blend in—you know us, Aunt Jacobia." But Diccon's response was undercut by the hint of a swagger. And on horseback, no less! Harry was impressed. "I'll keep an eye on the children." His head jerked and he amended with as good a grace as possible, "Jenneth and I will watch out for the children, make sure they stay out of trouble."

"Then I expect I'm along to keep *you* out of trouble," Nori countered from the rear, and Harry started because he had almost forgotten she rode there. "And Jenret as well."

"Just see that *you* stay clear of trouble." Jacobia gave Honoria a long, assessing look. For a fleeting instant Harry caught an identical expression on both Jacobia's and Jenneth's faces—measured and wary. Of what, he wasn't sure, and suspected he didn't want to find out. Women! He'd heard his father, his uncle, so many other males employ the word like a mild expletive, freighted with a sense of long-suffering fortitude. Mayhap women *were* another species. He'd ignored the fact that someday Jenneth would be elected, join the world of women, never suspected he'd so readily recognize their baffling differences. He *was* growing up!

Doyce swayed to her mare's easy canter, Khar on the pommel platform, sound asleep, as usual . . . **"Am not!"** came

her peevish response, the baleful half-masting of an amber
eye.

"All right, not." Best be agreeable, maintain peace, not
lose the gentle, meandering skein of thought that spun her
through the past. Her old sheepskin tabard felt exactly
right: durable, warm, the thick fleece guaranteed to protect
its wearer against rain or snow or accidentally unsheathed
claws.

"And it *still* smells!"

A companionable scratch at the ghatta's neck, a tickle
behind an ear, the gold hoop swaying. *"Some of us aren't
well-pleased to be riding circuit again, are we? Even if it's
only pretend."*

**"Riding circuit doesn't include a parade *and* a marching
band!"** With that, Khar buried her head in her Bondmate's
tabard to blot out the shrieking notes of a fife. Harry had
somehow secreted a tin fife amongst his baggage, and his
inability to play it was outweighed only by his spirited enthusiasm. **"Wouldn't much like it even if he played in
pitch."** Ears flattened, Khar shuddered at a particularly
piercing screech. A demented "vroom-zoom" accompanied
each discordant note, Doyce's eardrums vibrating at the
sound.

Not to be outdone, the twins and Byrlie had improvised
comb kazoos; even worse, Jenret, Holly, and Theo had
joined in, carefree as the children. Doyce wanted to laugh,
though the ear-splitting racket had caused her mount's ears
to swivel, her eyes to roll whitely more than once. They'd
rented livery horses for the trip to Windle Port, and while
her bay mare was reasonably docile, the fife set her skin
atwitch like an assault of botflies.

After a lengthy stretch, Khar sniffed the damp cold, eyeing the surrounding dreariness as they progressed southward. Winter boasted keen blacks and crisp whites, the
pointed greens of firs, not this doleful, hummocky landscape of tatty browns and grays, a girding of dingy white
around each hummock like the precious fringe on an old
man's balding head. Still, slightly warmer weather *was* nice,
except it felt like a perpetual spring thaw underfoot. The
next time she dismounted, she'd jump directly onto Doyce's
shoulders, then spy out a dry place to land. **"Rawn wants
to know what would happen if Harry,"** a delicate pause,

"oh, say, swallowed his fife." Her ears pricked up at the suggestion's appeal.

Doyce considered it as she urged the mare along, anything to escape the strident tootle-tootle-tot. The kazoos' constant "vroom-vroom-vroop-vroop-Vroom-VROOP" had worn like acid on her nerves. *"Actually, I'm afraid that if he swallowed it, Harry would peep with every breath, with every swallow, with every—"*

"Wait!" A single tail-lash signaling her irritation, Khar's head rose, her pink nose pointing skyward toward the descending sun. At this season, the Lady Moon's shadow-presence hung on the horizon, hasty to claim her rightful domain in the night sky. **"I swear, this message had better be more urgent than the last one!"**

Doyce cuffed her shoulder. *"How many have you withheld?"* Resign she had as Seeker General, but the queries hadn't stopped, transmitted onward, ever onward by the ghatti mindnet, zealous to ensure each final transition detail was resolved. Most of the questions were minor, irrelevant, even: Had Doyce truly meant . . .? Did the new schedule require . . .? And where in the name of the blessed havens was the . . .?

Once they had their feet under them, Berne Terborgh and Sh'ar would do a good job, far better than that, but right now they trod with exquisite care. They treated their new position as if it were thin ice beneath their feet, ready to crack at any moment. Still, if Khar could ease their burdens, she would, just as ruddy-furred Koom—so dependable, so dedicated—had lingered behind despite his desire to join the Elders when Doyce and Khar had assumed the Seeker Generalship after Swan Maclough's death.

"I've told Sh'ar twice already what it's listed under in the ledgers!" Batting at her head, Khar pinned her right ear, the tiny garnet rose twinkling below her white paw. It wouldn't block the mindmessages, or the fife's notes, but it helped—marginally. **"Worse than training a ghatten,"** she complained yet again. **"Were we *that* green and twitchy-tailed at the beginning?"**

"Poor love, how quickly you forget," Doyce crooned, cupping both hands over Khar's ears while she relayed a less-than-polite mindmessage to Jenret about combs lodging in noses. *"No, I mean it, Jenner. Now!"* she reiterated,

reins still draped over her wrist as she shifted in the saddle, resting a hand on the mare's croup as she cast a quelling look behind her.

At that moment the mare bucked, and Doyce found herself flung over the mare's neck, grabbing at thin air, blinded by the flying mane, winter-long and coarse. Left hand fumbling for the loose reins as they slid down her arm, her right hand clinging to the pommel platform, she heard an "Oof!" and knew she'd compressed Khar beneath her. Hindquarters gyrating as she kicked at invisible demons, the mare then commenced a stiff-legged dance as if determined to mince something beneath her hooves.

One boot slipped free as Doyce slammed back into the saddle, her foot chasing after the missing stirrup. An impossible task—her hard landing in the saddle had set the mare off as if a burning brand had been lashed to her tail. Whipping the air, the reins dangled tantalizingly beyond reach, and the stirrup bounced and banged against her leg. Yet in the midst of this, a gloating voice slithered through her mind. *"You won't like the Sunderlies. Turn back while you still can. Go home now!"*

"A wonderful idea!" she sputtered, clinging as best she could, Khar flattened beneath her and protesting all the way. "But I think," she swiped at the swinging stirrup, missed, "I'd rather return on foot." Her shiver of fear as the strange message flashed through her was overwhelmed by panic at the mare's inexplicable behavior, not to mention a grudging admission that she had no hope of halting her. She and the mare were strangers, bore no great affection for each other, let alone insight into the other's moods.

Shouts and urgent whoops rent the air, drifting away like fast-moving clouds. Worst of all, the mare spooked and veered when she least expected it, though once Doyce glimpsed something unfurling, waving from a low branch. Both Jenret and Arras peppered her brain with useless advice and misguided warnings. They meant well, feared for her safety, but *they* weren't astride a panicky beast utterly determined to return to her stable, preferably without a rider. *"Jenret, keep following,"* she begged, *"you can't miss the trail, believe me!"* At the end of the trail would be a bruised and battered body—hers.

"**Mine, too, if we don't stop soon!**" Grumbling as she wormed beneath Doyce, Khar's head and shoulders popped clear. "**Clamp my tail between your teeth—hard—no matter how much I yowl!**" Eyes blearing from the whipping mane, Doyce restrained Khar by the scruff of her neck.

"What in the name of the hells are you up to?" A stinging tail-slap in the face was her only answer. Then, an inkling of Khar's plan took shape as the ghatta shook off her hand, began crawling along the mare's neck, legs wrapped as tight as she could without sinking in her claws. Again Khar's tail whipped Doyce's face, demanding, and against her better judgment she bit down on it, fighting a gag reflex at its furriness.

Farther now, across the poll, Khar slithering between the laid-back ears until she'd draped herself over the mare's white-rimmed eyes. At the abrupt blinkering, the horse slowed, finally stumbling to a halt, blowing, shuffling, uneasily tossing her head. For a moment the world stayed blessedly still.

But the crackling of brush intruded as Honoria and her mount came streaming after her, Arras and Jenret at her heels, then Theo, so improbably lanky it looked as if he'd override his horse. It struck Doyce, the way some tangential details do once danger has passed: If you needed a nose to the wire to win, bet on Theo, he'd outstrip his own horse. With a relieved sigh she settled back heavily in the saddle, and the mare gave a final, startled buck that sent Doyce rocketing over her ears. No, the dried streambed and its water-rounded rocks held little promise as a landing site. She gave an experimental arm flap, willing to try anything, but the rocks loomed, looking less and less like randomly-tossed pillows. . . .

Eager to help but unsure how, Theo stretched and bobbed, for all the world like a long-necked crane scouting a flashing minnow. His height worked to his advantage at moments like these, let him survey the scene, see it as a whole. But viewing was *so* passive, especially when he itched to help. Running his fingers through his sandy hair, he gathered it into a peak, tugging at it, cursing his ineffectualness.

The Seeker General—Doyce, he mentally corrected himself—had half the world hemmed around her, including
Holly, always so solidly practical. No room or need for him.
But no, Holly was herding the children away, positioning
herself to block their view as Davvy came running with his
eumedico bag. That didn't bode well, and Theo chewed his
lip in frustration.

Khim slapped his shin, claws piercing the fabric, **"See to
the mare—that's useful,"** and tossed a final thought his way
as she bounded off to join her sib. **"Khar swears something
made the mare bolt, that it was meant to happen."**

"Wha . . . what?" he mumbled, grateful for her suggestion, but perplexed all the same. A fluttering leaf, a rolapin
breaking from cover—anything unexpected might spook a
horse. But those incidents simply "happened," weren't
"meant" to happen.

Still, he felt a bit more cheerful, focused. Horses he could
handle, better than people anyway, especially when it came
to the casual chitchat of ordinary life. With the Truth-
Seeking Ceremony he always knew exactly where he stood,
the rules spelled out, no need to goggle and gasp to find
something to say. No, mayhap the mare didn't need him
either; Honoria was already with her. But, to his surprise,
she appeared to be making a hash of it, fighting the horse,
striving to impose her will on it as she hung on the reins,
her mouth thinned with effort as she sought to subdue the
mare. Better to let the mare believe she wanted to be
calmed, comforted, not engage in a battle of wills.

Ducking the bay's constant, restive motions, Theo stood
beside Honoria, blessing the longer reach that allowed him
to snag the mare's cheek strap, slide his hand down near
the bit. "Sh . . . shsh . . . shsh . . . sh," he commiserated
as he stroked the straining, sweaty neck with his free hand,
the horse planting her head against his chest, whickering
and blowing in relief. Yes, a minor neck scratch or two,
nothing serious; despite her care, Khar's claws had had to
find purchase somewhere. Resting his cheek on her forehead, he rocked with the horse, whispering nonsense words,
and after a few moments she let him walk her in a circle
to defuse some of the excess energy still coursing through
her. "Yes, love . . . hush, love, that's a girl, good girl," he
crooned and gave her withers a familiar bump.

Refusing to yield, though, Honoria had matched him move for move on his other side, mashing him between horse and woman, their body heat enveloping him, perfume mixed with horse sweat. As diffident with the woman as with the mare, he finally whispered, "Th-think I've got her st-steadied. You c-can drop her r-reins."

"No, I'll tie her with the other mounts. Don't bother yourself." Theo fixed his gaze on the top of her head, the part of most people that he saw first. When she tilted her head, she didn't meet his eyes, and a vague hurt welled within him. Instead, her gaze fixed on the mare, refusing to let it out of her sight. Her mouth pinched reprovingly— lovely the way she accomplished it—and finally her eyes met his, flint-hard, prepared to dominate and control him as well as the horse. "I *said* I've got her, just about had her easy when you butted in." Now she strove for a specious warmth, but it was too late, too obvious, even to Theo, schooled as he was to slights and mockery. "Thanks for coming to my rescue, though. I *did* get distracted."

Shamed by his biddability, eternally trusting, he started to relinquish his grip on the bridle. Someday, someday someone would see him, appreciate and cherish him for what he really was—someone other than dear old Holly. "S-s-sorry!" Embarrassment sent a flush that raced up his chest and neck like a heat rash. But Khim had returned from her errand, springing up to sprawl on the pommel platform, amber eyes wide with spurious innocence. Right behind her, her sib P'roul leaped onto the saddle itself, daintily wrapping her tail round her white toes.

"Don't be so tractable." Khim moistened a foot, scrubbed at her face. **"Let's see some starch in those wilting, bashful bones of yours,"** while P'roul chimed in, **"Haven't you noticed yet?"**

He shied, much as the mare had, casting a wild glance along her flank, unsure what to do next, how to retrieve the situation. Except, ignoring Khim meant he'd be in the doghouse, and she'd ensure he resided there with the meanest, most flea-infested dog she could locate—metaphorically speaking, of course. **"It's where you belong when you don't use your head, refuse to see,"** she agreed. And then he saw it, a thin trickle of drying blood that emanated from under the saddle.

Honoria tugged at the reins. "Again, I appreciate your help, but I *can* manage, truly." Her eyes—blue? gray? a hint of both?—held his. The horse took an obedient step forward, Theo's hand lax on the bridle, until he jerked the beast up short. "S-s-sorry," he repeated, conscious of the fine spray he cast. "Seekers are obli-obligated to c-care for the Seeker General's mount, whether the SG's retired or n-n-not."· Plausible—he hoped, hunching his shoulders—because he badly wanted a look under the saddle, already empathizing with the sharp surprise the mare must have felt, had tried so desperately to outrun.

"Honoria! Miz Wijnnobel! I need your advice—if you don't mind?" Bless her, bless good old Holly for breaking the impasse, ending his predicament.

"You might bless me first," snapped P'roul. **"Guess who suggested it to her?"**

With unquestionable reluctance Honoria relinquished the reins and stalked to Holly's side, Theo walking the horse in the opposite direction to a fringe of cedars, their tiny cones crunching underfoot. *"I know, I know,"* he grumped as Khim stretched a restraining paw on his shoulder, *"Without you two prodding us, neither of us would ever manage an original thought. And even if we think we're being original, you probably planted the seeds—am I right?"* Checking to see if anyone watched, he swung the mare 'round so her blood-streaked flank faced him. *"What do you think— a burr?"* Sliding his hand under the blanket's edge, he let his fingers quest, moth-light, until he'd worked just below the cantle.

"Ouch!" He flinched but didn't jerk his hand away. *"Damnably sharp, whatever it is."* Time enough or not? Doing so would make his search too obvious. They weren't likely to unsaddle here, unless it wasn't feasible to move Doyce—and he now doubted that, or P'roul and Khim would be agitated. Easing his hand free, he examined his finger, blood welling bright from the puncture. *"Not likely to be a burr."* Gripping the cantle, he lifted the saddle just a tad, nonchalantly running his index finger underneath the edge. Nothing in that direction. Shifting his grip, he traced the opposite way.

This time something scored a line across his finger pad. Concentrating, he grasped it cautiously between thumb and forefinger, but it refused to yield. An experimental push and the stitching on the saddletop began to bulge in one small spot. The horse shifted, restless under his examination, as if anticipating that the sharp sting would come again. Crowding her sister on the saddle, Khim expertly hooked the seam with a claw and two stitches ripped clear. Theo pushed again, and a long pin with a T-shaped head reared up, no longer trapped by the stitching.

"**Not nice,**" Khim sniffed once at it. "**Land hard on the saddle this far back and it was bound to poke through.**"

With care Theo slipped the pin through several layers of handkerchief before folding the cloth and securing it in his waist pouch. *"Remind me not to blow my nose."* It didn't make sense. *"You don't use pins to mold the saddle cantle. Who put it there?"* From his own saddlebags he grabbed a small bottle of disinfectant, a bit of rag, and efficiently daubed at the four punctures dotting the mare's back, then wiped at his own minor pricks.

"**It seemed random to us at the livery stable,**" Khim's forehead stripes wrinkled in concentration, "**as to which horses got which saddles, I mean. Lucky they had five saddles our platforms would fit. Was it meant for Doyce? Or just a way to harass any Seeker?**" He sucked his own wounded finger, reflective, trading stares with his ghatta, her sib.

True, he was bashful, given to stammering, but he wasn't stupid. After all, the ghatti didn't choose fools, and he cherished the knowledge, let it warm his heart. Inept, insecure, an articulated beanpole, but the comfort of being Chosen overcame those flaws. *"You're ignoring the question, my furlings. Who put it there?"*

No response, nor had he expected one. The ghatti could and would search out the truth in people's minds, but not unless formally instructed to seek. No prying for the sake of prying, even to satisfy their curiosity. Therefore, no matter how much *he* wanted to know—yet didn't—neither did the ghatti. Fine, they were all equally in the dark, except for one thing: even in the dark ghatti "saw" more clearly than humans. What weren't they telling him?

"I don't suppose we could turn back, question the stable hands? Do you think that Honoria planted it there?" Khim and P'roul gave matching falanese shrugs at his stab in the

dark. *"I suppose it's unfair to assume that, just because she's the only one I don't really know."* Two penetrating stares, a whisker-twitch, made him rephrase that: *"The only one I don't know and don't know much about. All of the others are our 'own,' or relatives of our 'own.' "* A puzzlement— a downright worrisome one.

Davvy stood his ground, not an easy task when attempting to face down an irate Seeker General. Ex-Seeker General, he reminded himself, as if that might help. It didn't—not when the boy he'd once been still viewed Doyce as a Seeker whose exploits were the stuff of legend, impossibly adult or, at the least, an elder sister capable of eliciting instant obedience in an awestruck sibling.

"And when did you obey?" Khar-the-Ever-Helpful gave a falanese snicker as she cleansed a minor gash. Overfamiliarity with the ghatti, especially Khar, carried its own perils: no need to ask permission to 'speak her, not when she decided to speak her mind. **"You're the eumedico in charge, tell her it's eumedico's orders."**

Was she having fun at his expense, or would it work? Well, all he could do was try—except that standing lopsided amidst a jumble of rocks and long-dead tree branches at the edge of a dried stream-bed somehow made him feel lacking in authority. Oh, for the hushed, hallowed atmosphere of a hospice, not to mention his long white coat, not just a badge of authority but the armor of eumedico invincibility! Sorely missing it, he jammed his hands into the pockets of his shapeless gray worsted jacket.

"Doyce, as your eumedico, I order you to stay at the inn tonight, not camp out. It's the worst thing you can do right now, sleeping on cold, damp ground." Retrieving a hand, he waved an admonitory finger under Doyce's scraped chin. Actually, there weren't many spots he could point to where Doyce hadn't sustained a bruise or scrape. Absolutely miraculous—aha! Sententiously mention that! "Absolutely miraculous that nothing worse befell you. No concussion, no broken bones. But trust me, those bruises will throb worse than any nice, clean break. And wait till your muscles stiffen up in the morning!"

Supported between husband and son, more for their reassurance than her need (**"Well, you are *too* shaky!"** *"Am not!"*), Doyce Marbon glared at Davvy McNaught. "I believe it's more that I *fell*—not what *befell* me. Don't go all pompous on me, Davvy. I earned my eumedico rank before you were born." Haughty superiority wasn't something Doyce could pull off with ease—especially given her split lip—but Davvy mentally applauded her attempt. "Besides, we promised the children we'd camp under the stars tonight." That sounded like the real Doyce, conscientious to a fault, unwilling to break a promise, even when circumstances changed.

Paper-white from shock, Diccon hugged his mother's waist, protesting, "Mama! There's absolutely no need!" Davvy cocked his head in Jenneth's direction, waiting for her to back Diccon, give her twin time to steady himself.

"Diccon's right, isn't he, Harry?" Arms wrapped around Harry's shoulders from behind, his head tucked under her chin, Jenneth squeezed him hard enough to make him squeak in surprise. The way her eyes rested worriedly on him bothered Davvy. Mayhap it wasn't playing fair to depend on the children to convince Doyce—especially Jenneth, anxious to show him how mature she was. Jenneth rushed on, "We can count the stars from the ship's deck. Besides, we've all camped before." Burdened by the same sense of fairness that dogged Doyce, she emended, "Except for Byrlyn." A rush to include the child, "But Byrlie doesn't mind—do you, love?"

Tightly clinging to her father's hand, Byrlyn peeked out like a downy, ruffled owlet from behind her mother. Knit cap askew, hair falling over her forehead in a fine fringe, she edged out, then reluctantly set her shoulders and stepped away, forcing Bard to relinquish his grip.

Goddess bless and keep her, she was *so* diffident! She stared back at Lindy and Bard—especially Bard—then at him, as if painfully calculating her position. The pain on Lindy's face as she watched her daughter measure a compromise, one that showed no favoritism toward himself or Bard, tore his heart.

"Oh, Lindy," he cried, all too aware he couldn't let her hear him, couldn't share in her pain, *"what have we done to her?—so little yet so dispassionate!"* He smiled tentative

welcome at the child. *"No matter what we've thought—and that's all we've ever dared—Byrlyn doesn't have to choose between Bard and me. He'll always be her father."* But his need for the comfort of shared minds didn't matter; Lindy was resolutely mind-deaf, wouldn't hear his Resonant voice. Mind-deaf to his love as well.

Berating himself for compromising the child's chosen space, Davvy scooped up Byrlie before she reached Doyce, afraid she might try to pick up the child. The fragile weight of her in his arms, her childish smell, left him weak-kneed. "Auntie Doyce?" Tickling her mouth with her braid, Byrlie stared hard at its tail, blew on it. "You hurt, don't you? Hurt real bad?"

"My pride hurts worst of all, Byrlie-Barl." Tilting her head, Doyce received the featherlight brush of the braid against her own split lip. "Like when you fell when we went skating last winter, and you were so frustrated at losing your balance that you cried. Remember?" Byrlyn nodded, somber. "Wasn't the hurt so much, though it hurt, as the feeling of foolishness, being clumsy, falling in front of everyone."

With tiny, thoughtful nibbles at the braid, the child's face swung toward Bard, Lindy, then back to Doyce, ignoring Davvy. "But camping is like falling on the ice, isn't it, Auntie Doyce? You don't want to feel foolish, you?" A half-smile, quirked with mischief. "And it hurt loads, Auntie Doyce, when I fell—more'n I let on. So camping's going to make your hurts hurt more." As if she'd endured too much, Byrlyn began to struggle in Davvy's arms, her cap sliding over her eyebrows as she shoved against his chest.

Panicky the child would fall before he could untangle them both and set her on her feet, Davvy signaled a silent plea in Holly's direction. As she reached his side, Byrlie eeled into Holly's arms as if she'd found a sanctuary between two equal dangers. From the congested look on Bard's face, Davvy feared she'd read it right; he'd not anticipated that his innocent gesture in scooping up the child would set off Bard's overprotectiveness like that.

Shifting Byrlie astride her hip, Holly made a show of rolling up the cuff on her cap, whispering in her ear, then spoke over her head. "Seems we're fussing over nothing.

The reason we planned to camp out is that Schweiker's Inn is too small to hold us all comfortably, right?" Doyce nodded a reluctant agreement. "So Theo and I'll camp with the children tonight while you ancient adults indulge yourself in feather beds, warm baths, and fine foods."

Davvy met and withstood a final glare from Doyce. *"Just so you don't think you've had the last word,"* she 'spoke him.

Despite himself he grinned. *"The only reason you think you can have the last word is because Mahafny isn't here!"* Rolling her eyes in acknowledgment, she also accepted what he said aloud without a demur. "I agree with Holly's prescription, Doyce."

"Oh, so do I," she groaned, holding Diccon close. "Though I think the warm baths might be better *before* the feather beds."

"Well, you decide in what order to dose yourself. Otherwise you'd be mad as a wet hen!" Unable to help himself, he clicked his heels in delight. "I hope someone noticed— because you're all my witnesses—I got the last word!"

With a half-charred branch, Holly raked the coals into a flat bed, striations of red-orange shimmering through the gray ash. That accomplished, she built up the fire at the rear of the pit while waiting for the coals to settle. P'roul— black as her sire, Rawn, but with her dam's bulls-eye stripes—sleeked out of the darkness, skidding to a halt as she furiously nibbled at the soft fur of an inner leg. **"Do fleas go south for the winter, like birds?"** Her ear hoop swayed as she tracked the breathless giggles, sotto voce warnings as Theo played Monster with the children.

"Tired?" Obligingly, Holly sat on the spruce log they'd dragged in front of the fire pit, patted her lap in invitation.

With a stretch, P'roul moved closer to the fire. **"Hardly. Khim and I can run circles round them—in fact, we have been. But it's boring when it's so easy."**

"Just another way of reminding us we lack the swiftness, the subtlety and sagacity of the ghatti, right?" P'roul flashed a ghatti smile, a secretive mien containing just the barest hint of condescension. Or was insecurity to blame for that interpretation? Humans hid surprising facets, as well, and Holly exploded from the log with a rousing "Woo-Aaah!", arms looming, fingers hawk-clawing as she dove for the startled ghatta.

Springing halfway across the clearing, P'roul landed with her back arched, tail fluffed and lashing. At Holly's chuckle she abruptly realized she'd been played for a fool and shook herself, grooming the length of her spine with a distinctly sour expression. **"Point taken. Humans *are* capable of making our hair stand on end. But that was as subtle as a Plumb detonating beneath your feet."**

"Plumbs weren't meant to be subtle, weren't meant to detonate, either, P'roul. You know better." Rooting through the jumbled supplies for the night's camping, Holly finally located the bag with the custables.

Before she could straighten, P'roul landed on her back and began to make herself at home, settling to knead her claws in the sheepskin tabard. **"I won't let you up if you lecture. Plumb—Periodic Linear Ultra-Mensuration Beamer—"** (amazing how the ghatta could mimic like that) **"employed by your ancestors, the first colonists, to chart underground resources. But something went wrong and they began to explode, wreaking terrible damage. Some colonists fled back into space, stranding the rest here."**

Holly rolled her shoulders, but the ghatta refused to budge, continuing relentlessly, **"All gone now. You know *your* history, and *I* know one of the Elders' Major Tales when I hear it. What neither version ever mentions, though, is that without Plumbs, it's very possible we ghatti would never have bonded with you impossible humans. End of tale!"**

Letting her hand creep over her hip, Holly poised her fingers by P'roul's tail. "End of *tail*, if you read my meaning," she warned and grabbed at—

—thin air, P'roul springing neatly down. "Oh, bother!" But it was impossible to stay angry at such a dearly infuriating Bond. "So, how are the children doing?" Arranging a dozen custables around the coals to bake, she sat back on her heels to admire her handiwork. "Frankly, I'm still a bit concerned—especially about Diccon. It's probably the first time they've witnessed such a potentially deadly accident. They think they're invincible at that age—hells, Theo *still* thinks he is! But it's traumatic to realize your parents aren't equally invulnerable, won't live forever." With a mental wince she reenvisioned Doyce's airborne body, limbs loose as a rag doll's, the abrupt downward plunge. Sheer luck—or the Lady's intervention—to miss most of the rocks. Doyce had dryly insisted her flapping arms had provided uplift.

"How ironic—to lose the Seeker General to an accident." P'roul's eyes shifted, settling everywhere except upon her Bond, and Holly knew what that meant. **"There are those who dislike, even hate her, enough to do a more thorough job—if the opportunity arose."**

P'roul wasn't lying—impossible for her to do so—but she *was* skimping on the truth. Exasperating beast! "Well, care to tell me something? Anything? Even a hint—if we're playing Sixteen Questions? After all, Theo and I haven't really talked since the accident." She hunched forward, premonition heavy in her heart. "It *was* an accident, wasn't it, P'roul?"

High-pitched giggles rang nearer as Theo herded the children toward the fire, lurching at their heels with menacing growls. Even the twins, too old for pretending, had entered into the spirit of the game, reluctantly at first, finally wholeheartedly. It offered controlled terror, able to be halted at a moment's notice with no ill effects, not unlike the delicious chills engendered by a ghost story told 'round a crackling fire, the warmth of parent's lap just a leap away. This mock chase would discharge some of the anxiety and fear engendered by this afternoon's accident.

"Hurry up, P'roul," her voice thickened with an unnameable dread. "You know Theo and I can't speak openly until the children are asleep. *Was* it an accident?" For the life of her, she couldn't think why it hadn't been, but seeking truth often meant thinking the unthinkable, accepting unpalatable answers.

Toting Byrlyn piggyback, Diccon wound his way through a stand of scrub oak toward the welcoming warmth of firelight, swinging the child groundward with an elaborate flourish. "We have eluded the fell beast, my lady! Shall I return and slay the brute for you? Make a rug of his cowardly hide?" He dropped to one knee, head bowed. "Just command me, my lady!" From the dirt and damp leaf fragments caking everyone, especially Theo, they had already slayed the fell beast uncountable times.

Hands on hips, a "crown" of running pine straggling over her red knit cap, Byrlyn surveyed her loyal subject. "Arise, brave knight." For a moment she precariously balanced between fantasy and reality, finally whispering to P'roul, "He wouldn't really, you know. Diccon would *never* hurt Holly's cousin." Holly knew she'd been meant to overhear, to be reassured of Theo's safety. The child was too serious by half, still innocent yet achingly introspective, and Holly's heart felt freighted with melancholy for her.

"Well, my lady?" Still kneeling in the damp, Diccon squirmed.

"I don't think the beast's furry enough to make a very good rug, do you?" She tapped Diccon's shoulder with a branch from the firewood stash. "Arise. Besides, it would hurt him." A tear trickled down her cheek, rosy from the cold. "I *don't* like it when people get hurt!"

"Neither do I, love, neither do I!" Diccon fervently hugged the child. "I was *so* scared for Mama and Khar today! And I wasn't quick enough to help them. Papa looked as if he'd die of fright!"

With a triumphant whoop, Harry and Jenneth burst into the light, dragging Theo between them, their captive emitting an enthusiastic assortment of growling, gargling roars. A mock lunge at Holly, and Jenneth and Harry hauled him back. His beanpole form practically glowed with happiness and delight in the game, all shyness banished by the children's acceptance. Ah, if only she could exchange Byrlyn and Theo at this precise moment—transfuse adulthood into one and childhood into the other.

Giving each custable a showy half-turn, Holly intoned, "Lo, observe! This exotic fruit, baked with a magical recipe, shall reverse the dire spell, transform the slavering beast back into a handsome man." A wink in Byrlie's direction. "Beats having to kiss him, doesn't it?"

Apparently deciding to leave the beast on his own recognizance, Harry dropped Theo's wrist, inhaling with exaggerated delight as Holly's knife pierced the first red-gold fruit, the steam carrying its sweet, creamy aroma. "Papa calls them custies instead of custables," Jenneth announced. "Remember the story, Dic?—about Mama and Papa camping that first night as they hunted the people who'd killed Saam's Bondmate, Oriel.''

Holly half-listened as the familiar tale unfolded, the twins interrupting each other to add colorful—often conflicting—details for Harry and Byrlyn. As she continued piercing the custables, enjoying the piping whistle each gave as the steam burst forth, Harry crouched beside her, leaning across her knee. Holding out his hand, he whispered, "Can I?" and Holly passed over her knife at his pleading look. Doubtful, downright unlikely that Harry'd been struck by the joys of a culinary career, but messing around always appealed to boys his age.

The knife's point shimmered silvery-red from the reflected coals as Harry dawdled, knife wavering as he deliberated over the perfect spot. Just as the point pinked the surface, the custable exploded, a wave of scorching heat and blinding light flinging them backward. As she fell, Harry went tumbling, screaming, an arm flung over his eyes. More smoke and a sulfurous reek clogged the air as the next custable erupted, and the next, Holly's ears ringing as she found her feet, diving to interpose her bulk between Harry and the fire. Another explosion, and something smashed her shoulder, hot and hammer-sharp—blossoming pain, the sensation of warm, sticky blood—and she shook her head, perplexed. An overcooked custable shouldn't—couldn't—do so much damage.

"'Ware!" Khim and P'roul had screamed at the first blast, blanketing Byrlyn's small body where it had been tossed, while Theo's long arms scooped the twins off their feet and bore them down beneath him into a crusted crescent of icy, leftover snow. A final detonation as the last custable fragmented, but they stayed prone, hugging the ground, not daring to move.

At last, ears ringing, Holly replayed the explosions in her mind, counting them—twelve, she hoped—and rolled clear, cradling Harry to her. "Theo?" Her voice croaked, phlegmed with fear and acrid smoke as she ran her fingers over Harry's face.

"Fine, I think." Unfolding like a carpenter's rule, he half-rose, deliberately scanning the scattered fire and their surroundings. "Stay down till I give the word," he admonished, his stammer temporarily vanquished. A pause to retrieve a smoldering brand too near the hem of Byrlyn's jacket and to examine P'roul's hip, then Theo deliberately quartered their campsite, grinding live coals beneath his feet. Dead grass and fallen leaves released an overheated, acrid scent tinged with a metallic overtone and the sickish reek of caramelizing, burning custable fragments.

Harry whimpered in her arms, but she kept her thumb firmly pressed against the slice parting his right eyebrow. A custable *could not* be responsible for that, for nearly blinding a child. Oh, a burn, mayhap, the custable bursting, a piece of hot, sticky pulp clinging to flesh, but a cut?

In the light of the lantern that Theo hurriedly lit, she deposited Harry on the log, struggling to restrain his tears. *"May the Lady damn someone to the hells and beyond!"* P'roul and Khim certainly appeared ready and willing to, if the Lady couldn't oblige. *"Ask Theo to check for metal shards. I swear someone cored those custables from the bottom, stuffed them with shrapnel."*

No need to suggest that possibility to the children, anxious for reassurance and, in Harry's case, first aid. Everyone else had emerged unscathed, though her stinging shoulder reminded her that she'd been a casualty, P'roul as well, the odor of singed fur strong in her nostrils. "Merciful havens, I thought we were roasting Plumbs for a moment!" Somehow she gathered a laugh from deep within where it hid and tossed it free. To her relief, it sounded true, didn't falter or quaver. "What your parents neglected to mention, Jenneth, Diccon, is that custables require prompt piercing! I let them go too long without. I doubt there's enough left to eat unless we scrape it off everything."

Byrlie stood gravely inspecting her knit cap, picking at raveled yarn where something had sliced it open. Tiny fingers held something aloft. "Look—custable skin! It's all woolly, though."

"Come on, everyone, pitch in, let's neaten our gear, rebuild the fire." Make them move, bustle around, *do* instead of think. The twins hastily began putting things to rights, Byrlie shadowing one or the other as she helped. Ignoring her own wound, Holly began to patch Harry. "Nice clean cut, bit of sticking plaster and it'll be fine," she chattered, one eye on Theo, methodically scuffing through matted grass and decaying leaves, fingering scars on nearby tree trunks to judge their freshness.

"You might even boast a dashing scar, dazzle the ladies with it." Forcing her hands steady, she crisscrossed bits of adhesive to pull the wound closed. "Bit of a burn as well—no wonder, that custable fragment was scalding hot when it hit. But you must've sliced yourself on something when you went head over heels." A lie—big or small?—and she hoped P'roul wouldn't take her to task. "Still, no real harm done. Davvy'll do a neater job, but this will hold till we get you back to the inn."

"Theo says you're babbling worse than a brook at spring thaw." Khim 'spoke her, teasing as much as chiding.

But Byrlyn had obviously heeded her pointless chatter, because she stomped to Harry's side, mouth set. A furious whisper in Harry's ear, and the child slipped something from under her coat, tucking it inside Harry's. "Don't want to go to the inn. Harry, neither—do you?"

"And spoil our adventure?" Harry added, his stout-hearted nonchalance marred by the toy monkey now peeking out of his jacket.

"If Harry's that tough, we might as well stay. Otherwise the adults will get all dithery when they hear what happened," Diccon contributed, helping Jenneth shake out a blanket, "Why spoil a good night's sleep for them?"

A stormy though silent argument ensued, Khim and P'roul hard-pressed to relay one cousin's words to the other while arguing their own position. At last, reluctantly, Holly and Theo agreed to stay the night. If the ghatti didn't sense an imminent danger, then there undoubtedly wasn't any.

"Whatever happened, happened. Luckily, no great harm done," was Khim's comment. **"Though P'roul may feel a bit drafty tonight, poor sib nearly got her pinfeathers singed off."**

"Besides, Theo has something to show you later—two somethings." P'roul looked down her nose at her sister. **"Forgot, didn't you? The first one, that is."** Equally mystified, Theo finally gave a triumphant grin, patting his pocket.

With the children finally settled in their bedrolls, Theo and Holly at last could confer. "There were enough custables for everyone," Holly pitched her voice low, fighting back a yelp as Theo swabbed her wound clean. The chill of the night air, the icy sting of antiseptic on her bare flesh made her quiver, and she found she couldn't stop. "I mean, enough for the whole group, since we'd thought everyone would camp out—we just didn't roast all of them. There should be almost a dozen left in the sack. Harrap gave them to Doyce the night before we left. Grew them himself—how could they have been safer?"

"Enough to d-damage everyone, you m-mean." Theo stoppered the bottle, patted a dressing in place with finicky fingers. "I th-thought of the l-leftovers." Hooking a thumb into Holly's shirt and coat collars, he eased her garments back so she wouldn't have to shrug them into place. Still shaky, Holly buttoned herself clumsily, Theo holding her tabard, patient as a coatrack.

"T-took the ones you'd p-pierced, p-plus the raw ones out and away . . . b-buried them. Deep!" His determination to spit out the word misted the air. "Fi . . . figured it was safer—in c-case they ex-p-ploded, too!"

"Damn!" Feeling marginally more secure with her tabard on, she collapsed against the log, lacking the energy to care that she leaned against her bad shoulder. "I would have *loved* to dissect them, see what was inside." Concentrating, she tied her sash.

"Eu-medico manqué? And end up f-fingerless, b-blind?" He captured her hand, chafing it between his; she hadn't realized how cold she was—shock, no doubt. Amazing how someone so thin could generate such heat, as if his bones should glow lambent through his skin. He slid something into her hand. "Don't know if th-they were *all* l-loaded, but I *did* f-find a metal s-splinter, s-stuck in the l-log." Patting the log to indicate the spot, he waited while she examined it.

An elongated wedge, almost like a miniature arrowhead, but narrower—about the length of the first joint of her little finger. Only about half a centimeter wide at its widest, though. "Can't all have been like this, Theo. If that had struck me, you'd have needed pincers to pull it out. Whatever grazed me must have been bigger, with rough edges. You saw the hole in my coat."

He nodded. "Also, I n-nearly forgot," and placed a handkerchief in her hand, "this was em-b-bedded in the b-back of the SG's s-saddle. When D-doyce s-shifted back in her s-saddle," he placed a fist on his knee, then dropped his elbow to make his fist rock back, indicating how the contact point had shifted, "s-she c-came down hard on the c-cantle. D-drove it into the p-poor mare—that's why she sp-spooked so."

"What the hells is going on?" Holly challenged first Theo, then the ghatti, one after the other. "Any ideas?"

"Well, whatever it m-means, I'll b-b-wager this isn't going to be a n-nice, quiet trip to the S-Sunderlies," Theo intoned dolefully. "And to wh-whom do we report this?"

Holly ran both hands through her hair until she suspected it looked as disheveled as her brain felt. "I don't see any point in contacting Sh'ar and Berne Terborgh. What can *they* do when we haven't a clue who's behind it all?" Refusing to meet her cousin's eyes, she added softly, "Theo, what if it's someone in our party?"

"I kn-know! Th-thought of that before." Theo subjected the knees of his pantaloons to a minute scrutiny. Damnation! If he'd already considered the possibility, he *had* to know only one logical candidate came to mind, even if he refused to utter her name. Sometimes Theo had more scruples than the ghatti! "But P'roul and Khim *c-can* discuss it with R-rawn and Khar, M'wa—surely?"

"Of course. Can you imagine any better security guards than five ghatti—plus us?"

Theo grimaced, clearly out of sorts. "M-much good we've b-been as guards. L-left the ba-baggage wagon un-g-guarded each n-night!"

It was true, Holly had to acknowledge it. But then, who'd have ever believed such things could happen? Lolling her head against Theo's shoulder, she sighed. "I suppose we've one consolation for being heedless fools. At least Doyce can't fire us! And believe me, she'll want to when she hears what nearly happened to Harry and the others!"

Nervously flexing his jaw muscles, M'wa resolutely stared into the distance, fervently wishing he *were* distant, anywhere distant from here. Mayhap Bard would 'speak him, require his immediate presence, though it wasn't likely. Bard and the other adults lingered over breakfast; the sau-

sage had been much to M'wa's liking. Children—none from
his group, thankfully—played behind the inn, throwing
rocks and branches at a small pond sheeted with skim ice.
From their squawks and honks, the pond ducks and geese
were *not* pleased. Neither was he, for that matter, though
for entirely different reasons.

Neutral observer, mediator, impartial and implacable
presence, referee—none of the roles Khar had assigned him
appealed. One thing he'd known for a certainty since ghattenhood: Never stick one's whiskers in the middle of a family feud, or likely they'd be crimped. Worse yet, this
disagreement wound in ever-tightening circles like a gyring
falcon preparing a stooping attack. Not to mention he was
cold, perched atop the woodpile here on the shady side of
Schweiker's Inn, black tail lapped 'round white toes to ward
off a chill. At least it smelled pleasant, the clean sweetness
of birch, apple, the tang of pine. Blast Khar for dragging
him into this—ghatti determined the truth, but Khar expected him to side with her, regardless.

Khar's white front expanded, her muzzle contorting in a
snarl as she deliberately invaded P'roul's space, pink nose
to pink nose. Both noses pulsed rosy, a sure sign of anger
or overexcitement. "Did you *truly* believe you two could
sidestep the whole thing, *not* tell us, when you've guilt written all over your faces, plain as day?" Impartial, she directed her tirade at Khim as well, reminding her the single
reason she currently escaped direct censure was because
Khar could outglare but one offspring at a time. M'wa'd
already witnessed Khim's dressing down, his skin crawling,
each individual hair shivering as if Khar's wrath were directed at him. That this confrontation was conducted in
their native tongue, falanese, rather than mindspeech, emphasized Khar's utter frustration, each minute twitch of a
whisker, a muscle, an ear conveying ghatti subtleties beyond the scope of mindspeech.

"Yes, guilt—the way your whiskers droop, the way you
side-glance me." Khar's forehead loomed over P'roul's,
forcing the younger ghatta to angle her neck, drop her head
lower to avoid returning the challenge. "I birthed you both,
I should know! There's not a trick I can't match!"

Rawn's glossy black shoulder wedged itself between Khar
and his offspring, P'roul. Only this close would anyone,

human or ghatti, notice how his midnight hue matched
P'roul's. However, her overlay of showy stripes and white
markings instantly tagged P'roul and her sib as Khar's progeny. What Saam, Khim's sire, would make of this spat,
M'wa dearly wished he knew, wanting to whisper his worries to his steel-gray friend back in Gaernett with Mahafny.

With blade-keen precision Rawn forced a passage between them, his bulk driving them both onto their haunches
lest they risk being knocked over. With a consoling brush
of his tail 'round P'roul's neck, he looped to face them
both. "Peace, Khar, it's done, over with—luckily no one
was badly hurt." A long look at his daughter to make her
focus. "Did you notice anything about the bag, the custables themselves? Stains? An off-scent, mayhap? That of
an unfamiliar human? The smell of the explosives?"

Edging to her sib's side in a show of support, Khim
bumped her shoulder, began licking P'roul's cheek to comfort her, give her time to consider. "Wasn't exactly sniffing
around. Never took to custables—or them to me." Her jest
fell flat and M'wa shook his head at her delaying tactic.
He'd turn into a statue out here, not to mention miss the
last batch of sausage!

Nose probing P'roul's inner ear, Khim murmured advice
to her sister. "As they warmed in the coals, they *did* smell
bitter. Not that puckery-sharp scent they have when they
aren't ripe. Not eumedico-stinky, either—that's clean-
sharp." Screwing up her nose, she ventured, "Mayhap it
was the explosives I scented."

"After Theo buried the rest of them," Khim chimed in,
"P'roul and I wanted to dig them up."

Leaping to her feet, each hair abristle, Khar shrieked,
"And blow off your precious paws? Shred your ears, blind
your eyes? Haven't I taught you better? In all the Elders'
tales about plumbs, didn't you—"

Physically intruding once again, Rawn paraded beneath
Khar's chin, ignoring her hiss of annoyance as he barri-
caded her. "Let them be, Khar. We've learned what we
can, and they're old enough to show sense. Let me remind
you, they *didn't* dig them up. They're no longer ghatten,
and they don't deserve this grilling." A ghost of a smile.
"Ladies, make yourselves scarce till your mother's temper

cools. By the Sunderlies she should be 'speaking civilly to
you.''

"I wouldn't wait for a second invitation," M'wa counseled and gave a meaningful glance over his shoulder. By
the time Khar could notice—he hoped—he was delicately
nibbling along his spine, intent on cracking a flea. Good,
this was over, and he could politely meander off on his
own business. Some paw grooming was definitely in order;
frozen sap from the firewood had melted, soaking the fur
between his toes and turning them sticky.

But as Khim and P'roul shot off in undignified relief,
M'wa nearly nipped himself in shock. "Now, Khar," Rawn
sat, his massive shoulders untensing in relief, "it's over,
done. As Jenret would say, 'Soonest ended, soonest
mended!' What we need to consider—"

"Don't you dare quote Jenret at me, throw him in my
face like the eternal font of all human wisdom!" From his
vantage point, M'wa swallowed hard in anticipation as
Khar's tail gave an almost imperceptible flick, the tiniest of
advance warnings, and her white paw buffeted Rawn's
head, hovering to deliver a second blow. "Talk about sharing no more truth than is necessary or agreeable! We both
know where P'roul learned that habit! Always protecting
Jenret, forever ensuring his tender sensibilities aren't trampled—as if every day didn't bring something large or small
to scar the rest of us!"

With wounded dignity Rawn stalked to a safe distance,
settling himself into a mound, his tail straight out behind
him, thumping. "Jenret is *my* bond. He's my first concern,
just as," he noted with heavy emphasis, "Doyce is always,
must always be *your* first concern. That is why we are
Bonded." He swallowed once, his yellow eyes pleading.
"Much as I esteem you, Khar, our Bonds both unite us and
divide us. But surely you must grasp by now that Jenret
would *never* do anything to hurt Doyce if he could possibly
help it."

Eyes rolling skyward in disbelief, M'wa gulped in wonder
at Rawn's utterance. By the Elders—when was the last time
that Rawn had so literally walked on thin ice? From the
pond the shouts and laughter of the children mixed with a
sharp crack. Except if Rawn plunged through, he'd be
bathed in Khar's scalding fury, rather than icy disdain.

"Did you backslide down a spiral of wisdom?" Khar's amber eyes glowed like torches. "He already *has* hurt Doyce, you fool! And *you* won't explain why! Truth is Truth, whatever pain or joy it brings. Selfish, obstinate—exactly like your Bond! Jenret comes first! In your heart and in his own as well! No wonder Doyce and I don't stand a chance! Never have, in fact!" With that she stalked away, her skin rippling as she struggled to resettle her spine hairs.

In perplexity Rawn dug at his shoulder, behind his ear with a hind foot. **"M'wa? Do you understand ghattas at all? I mean, human females or ghattas? I swear sometimes reason is totally wasted on them."**

Flowing from his perch, M'wa stretched one stiff leg after another, eyes resolutely fixed on the frozen ground so that only his white forehead star showed. **"Rawn—did you have a sib or not?"**

Leg frozen in midscratch, Rawn licked his toes, meditatively chewed at a claw. **"No, not to grow up with. My sib brother didn't survive."**

"Ah, never mind." Any explanation he could furnish would still be inadequate to explain how one sometimes learned early on the convolutions of the female mind, as he had with P'wa. Mayhap those windings *did* allow ghattas to climb the spirals of wisdom more easily than ghatts—complexity appealed to them. So very, very like, he and P'wa, and yet so dissimilar in some ways, though they had melded their differences. **"I suppose you're bound not to tell Khar certain things, aren't you?"**

"I'm not free to tell even you, old friend. I gave my word on that. But truth will out in the end."

Skirting Rawn, M'wa went in search of Bard or, better yet, he'd seek solace from Lindy, despite the fact they never shared their minds. Worries could be shared without mindspeech. Things were breaking apart, tiny fracture lines, fissures that webbed the ice when the burden it supported became too great. Was this what maturity brought? Bitterness, distrust, resentment—no one *listened* anymore—truth shoved back, disregarded. No one could hear it, even if it shouted out loud. And he, too, was suffering from it, infected by it, all for the love of his Bond, the fear of hurting him.

Thoroughly shamed by her outburst, Khar summoned what little dignity she retained and stalked inside the Schweiker Inn without looking back. How could she have snapped like that at the ones she loved? Ignoring the alluring clatter of breakfast plates and Doyce's laughter, she slunk upstairs to the abandoned bedchambers to bury herself in the down comforter, still warm and exuding her beloved's scent mixed with Jenret's and Rawn's. Oh, to be cuddled and comforted, but she wasn't worthy of it, would immure herself here until they left, mulling things over in her mind. And that, mayhap, was the problem: she'd been mulling things too long, chasing them in ceaseless circles without coming closer to the truth, let alone understanding!

Crawling deeper beneath the comforter which—she had to admit—did deserve its name, she curled into a ball, forepaw across her eyes, and heaved a whistling sigh. When her self-recriminations peaked, she made a decision: it was past time to contact the Elders, ascend the spirals of knowledge all ghatti traveled throughout their lives. Some gained the spirals early, others late, and some never attained ultimate knowledge, but within the collective Mind Spiral resided all ghatti wisdom and lore, tales of the past, both major and minor, nothing lost, nothing forgotten. The Elders investing its eight ever-turning coils were both universal and unique, some retaining past personalities, others merging with the collective whole. Would Mr'rhah still be there? Khar'd been thinking of her of late, wishing for guidance, but if not her, other guides abounded. Except—she nibbled her tail-tip in annoyance—sometimes the Elders proved as irritating, as aggravating as . . . as . . . fleas! The way they burrowed and nipped, made one's very soul itch— proffering truth without a translation!

Abandoning her frustration like an empty shell too small to house her, she allowed her mind to float, gliding into the first turning, working her way up and around, craving the communion, the connection that linked all ghatti, past and present. Upward—so free and easy, so familiar and reassuring—she hadn't lost the knack! Already mindvoices spangled around her, mindchatter twinkling and toying with her whiskers, hugely enjoying themselves. **"Oh, Khar . . .**

pretty Khar'pern . . . hello!" "Hello, bold-striped
ghatta . . ." "Catch truth . . . by the tail . . ." ". . . would
you?"

They teased, but she refused to react to their blandish-
ments, a polite salute should suffice for now. **"Greetings,
Elders."** Once the spirals had left her daunted and dizzy,
overwhelmed by the shimmering chime of mindvoices, but
now she wound up and around with a certain hard-won
confidence, knowledge attained at great price. Looping, she
sailed through the Fourth Spiral, ascended the Fifth, advancing to her niche in the Sixth Spiral. Would she ever be
wise enough attain the two final spirals? At her age she
thought it unlikely, and mourned her loss. Climbing beyond
one's ability was akin to a ghatten intent on scaling a brass
pole, scrabbling claws lacking purchase, constantly slipping
backward. After this morning she'd feared she'd backslid a
spiral or two, regressing, forced to learn them anew. Ah,
what she'd lost sight of of late!

The mindvoices, the mindcaresses tumbled and jostled
her as she halted, both tired and exhilarated by her ascent.
**"Greetings, Elders. I have come to seek advice, wisdom,
the truth."**

"And when, when . . ." the voices sounded distinctly
grumpy, **". . . have you . . ." "Have you . . ." ". . . ever
sought anything else?"** A distinct coolness to their recep-
tion, as if the Elders were as moody as she'd been recently.
"Take, take, take!" someone mocked, while another wheedled, **"Oh, give me . . . give me wisdom . . . give me
truth . . ."**

Plucks and pinches and pokes sparked all over her body,
and the spiral turned deathly cold and slick beneath her
belly, cold with despair. Would they deny her? What had
she done? Everything and nothing of late, and bent her
head in humility, enduring their taunts. Simply distrusted
her oldest, dearest companion, Rawn, for starters. Because
his Bond came first, she'd doubted his sincerity, his commitment to her and to Doyce. She'd doubted her own offspring, more than old enough and wise enough to make
their own decisions. She'd doubted Doyce's decision to resign, and she'd doubted herself. Confidence in the truth
had given way to comfort.

"Oh, dear Khar, it never becomes any easier, does it?"

came an old, familiar voice, though not whom she'd expected, but then she was hardly worthy of meeting the esteemed Kharm, Ghatti Mother of them all, twice in her
life. It was old Terl, rusty of coat and voice, who'd once
buoyed her ascent to beg the Elders for a signal favor: a
revelation of the past—how humans and ghatti had first
Bonded—to guide Doyce through the present. After all,
ghatti had originally suffered the same distrust, even loath-
ing that now plagued the Resonant community, despite
Doyce's efforts. **"Some penance might be in order, dear
one."**

"Agreed, but what would you have me do?" she asked
meekly.

Terl still possessed his raspy, tickling chuckle. **"Ah,
you've learned so much yet forgotten what it all means,
haven't you? Mayhap some self-flagellation is in order?"**

Without volition her striped tail began lashing, refusing
to obey her commands. By the Elders, it'd snap off if she
thwacked herself much longer! Not to mention how it
smarted, forcing her to open her eyes, her mind to the
stinging truth!

"Oh, enough, Terl!" Mr'rhah's soothing mindvoice rever-
berated everywhere and nowhere. **"She's learned her lesson. Now, dear Khar, what is it you wish? More wisdom,
more memories, what?"**

Relieved her tail had gradually stilled itself, Khar
thought, then haltingly whispered, **"To see more clearly,
please. I think minor problems now loom larger than major
ones, simply because they're closer, right under my nose."**

"And so you lose sight of the true dangers?"

**"Oh, yes, Mr'rhah! Both Doyce and I *have* lost perspec-
tive at times."** Hurtful to admit, but she must be honest.

"Ah, the Sunderlies . . ." **"South to . . . the
Sunderlies . . ."** **"New vistas, new sights . . ."** tinkled the
voices, chiming with excitement, golden dream flecks dusting her fur, setting her whiskers aglow.

**"Ah, yes, you travel to a new land but pack old woes.
So, let us ease your mind. Trust the truth. Some things are
accidental, yes? And others not. Learn which merit your
concern."**

What Mr'rhah advised sounded sensible, almost too
forthright for an Elder response, and that perplexed Khar.

"Yes, true," she cautiously agreed. **"Look for life's larger truths."**

"Don't try to cushion . . ." "Oh, comfy, cushy, cushiony . . ." ". . . cushion your fall." **"Landing hard is truer, safer."**

Now that made absolutely *no* sense—highly reassuring, since the Elders seldom said what they meant. But at some point it *would* reveal truth, and she'd bless them for it. **"I thank you, Elders, for bolstering me in my time of need."** The peals of laughter came louder, stronger, than she expected—not laughing at her, but with her—although she couldn't grasp the humor. Bowing her head a final time, she began her descent, each downward spiral a reminder of how truth itself was not always straightforward, and that ghatti vision, keen as it was, could sometimes be too narrowly focused.

Hood drawn close to shield her hair, Honoria walked briskly through the streets of Windle Port. Strange, she'd fully expected to hear the familiar cadenced clip of her boots striking the cobblestones, but the mist and drizzle swallowed each footstep. It reminded her how totally alone she was in this gambit, despite the many passersby bustling along the length of Staple Street and its row of shops that provisioned sailing ships as well as landlocked working folk, everything from eggs, butter, and beef to fishnets, rigging, rum kegs, and ketches. Nothing like the gaudy bazaar back home, rife with open-air banter and barter.

Seized by an unexpected shiver, she hugged the hood tighter around her neck. Hateful climate! She'd scarcely bargained on a winter in Canderis—and every soul sagely agreed that this had been a mild one thus far. Not exactly a comforting thought! Still, this late afternoon fogginess and cold drizzle did allow her the pretense of solitude, despite the soft-edged, muffled figures squelching along in both directions. Not only that, it had ensured she could venture out alone, not have Harry at her heels, or Lindy offering to help, or Arras's courtly suggestion of an escort. The batting of fog reminded her how she and her cousin Hirby had enacted plays as children—high melodrama transpiring behind a hung sheet, their shadowy forms cast menacing and large.

Alone! No need for numbing small talk, to unobtrusively be what most expected her to be—although that in itself afforded her a certain quiet, superior amusement. What they *believed* her to be! In a land so in love with truth she took perverse pride in being accepted at face value. Oh, some were skeptical of what she was, but not for the right reasons. Misdirection suited her well enough, though, and she'd become adept at it through the years. After all, wasn't that the whole point of her presence here?

As previously agreed, the message had been awaiting her at the harbormaster's office. Reassuring, at least, to have confirmation of where she stood, how matters had progressed. Too bad she couldn't send a return message before they arrived in the Sunderlies, but no ships were set to sail ahead of theirs. Hardly surprising during the storm season. That was the point in acting at long last; with fewer merchant ships in and out, they'd have better control, fewer exigencies to distract them from their goal.

Debating the indulgence, she allowed herself to win her internal argument, making her way into a beckoning chaffay shop and ordering a mug and a cinnamon bun at the counter. Ah! Wrapping her hands around the mug, she hunched over it, letting its warmth seep into her fingers. In just a matter of moments her hands began to throb, and she gingerly gripped the mug's handle and moved clear, conscious how she'd blocked traffic at the serving counter. Yes, that high stool shoved beneath a narrow counter running round the side wall, the only unoccupied space she could spot. Loosening her hood, she let it fall onto her shoulders, eased her heather-toned cloak open. Surprisingly crowded, but the foul weather undoubtedly increased business.

The shop was almost *too* Canderisian for words! Fussy little lace window drapings, starch gone limp from the steam. Oak stools and counter, light green-and-blue paint, neither too obviously masculine or feminine, just weakly neutral. Fragrant pipe smoke curled and mingled with the scent of spices, melted butter, and the bracing scent of chaffay throughout the little shop, its windows misted on the inside. Doubtful anyone could see in unless she wiped the glass. Newcomers—like herself—dripped moisture, depositing puddles on the floor if they'd tarried outside too long. Amazing how much mist could accumulate. Give her a good Sunderlies cloudburst any time!

Congested as the shop was—broad-shouldered men jogging her elbow as she raised her mug to her lips, women laughing, drawing their chairs tight 'round the tiny marble-topped tables, people wending their way to the serving counter—she could still maintain her illusion of privacy. Not a soul here knew her—neither the real Honoria nor the fabricated one—she could be herself without jarring their expectations, their preconceptions. Cultivating a bland civility went against her grain, especially against the cheery jangle of their own guileless personalities. A sigh of happiness as she unwound a piece of cinnamon bun, its glazed sugar icing sticky on her fingers, plump raisins peeking from the dough.

Frankly, she needed these few stolen moments to ruminate over recent events, because she could discern another subtle hand at play. Honoria Wijnnobel did *not* countenance being caught out one little bit, ignorant as to the "why" of something. And if her knowledge proved imperfect, didn't suffice, she must be resourceful enough to anticipate, at the very least. If the rumors about Lindy were true, her foresight would be an invaluable asset in Honoria's endeavors. No—that was wishful thinking. Besides, from she could gather, Lindy lacked control over what she "saw;" the last thing Honoria needed was advance warning about extraneous matters.

Plucking a raisin, she gave it her considered approval before popping it in her mouth. The Tacky Incident, as she'd disparagingly named it, was happenstance, pure coincidence—she was almost positive. Stable boys planning a prank on some customer who habitually ill-treated their mounts, or didn't tip. They'd not counted on the Wycherley party hiring practically every mount in the small stable. Utter bad luck that that particular saddle was a finely crafted, smooth leather, the ghatti platform able to fit over its pommel. Five Seekers in the party—one chance out of five the sabotaged saddle would go to Doyce.

Of course she'd had wit enough to turn the situation to her advantage when Doyce's mount had bolted—or so she'd hoped. Her mindvoice was untrained, weak, a failing she'd dearly love to rectify. Indeed, should have while here in Canderis, except that she'd no desire to expose her ability, untutored or not. Simple enough, though, to project *"You won't like the Sunderlies. Go back while you still can. Go home now!"* Well, if the warning had rattled her, Doyce hadn't shown it.

Ah, if only she *could* reverse time, but it was too late, her legacy destined to be one she'd never coveted. At least she'd had more say in it than poor Hirlbert!

Belatedly aware she'd mashed the next raisin between thumb and forefinger, scowling all the while, she smoothed her face. Fine—examine it as dubiously as if it were a bug, attract people's notice! Bad enough Jenret's obstinacy in lumbering them with the twins, but Doyce's presence could jeopardize everything. The expression on Jenret's face at the party that night had been *delicious,* though—almost worth having Doyce along to cramp her style.

Well then, face facts. And she did so, lightly clucking her tongue. Doyce was entirely too sharp for her liking. Her inclusion forced Jenret to maintain a front around her, convinced she'd discover their intrigues before this affair had run its course. Fearing he'd compromise their plans, afraid he'd hurt her, his distance toward Doyce had become entirely too obvious, too worrisome. Lady help her if she ever involved herself with another man unable to govern his passions!

If Doyce found out . . . she blew on her chaffay. Still too hot to sip, should have taken cream with it. Hmm, if Doyce *did* find out, it was hardly the end of the world. Worth telling Doyce herself, if only to clear the air? If Doyce learned the truth, it would certainly relieve her of one burden, remove part of the handicap under which she labored. A cautious sip. Well, leave it be for now. The option still remained, and she relished having options open to her. So take the unexpected in stride, and she might even contrive a use for Doyce. It didn't mean, however, that she had to like it.

Off track again! Contemplating Doyce distracted her almost as much as she did Jenret! Fine, the Tacky Incident was an accident, but the Exploding Custables certainly hadn't been. Not that any adults beyond Theo and Holly were privy to that charming incident, nor would she have been so privileged if Byrlie's whispers hadn't had that piping, piercing quality children's voices so often possessed. All she'd had to do was lean her ear against the wall to hear her talking it over with her precious Dolly.

The untidiness of that incident upset her. Precisely at whom had it been directed? Explosions rarely showed fine discrimination in selecting victims, targeted or not. Had someone recognized her, taken steps to stop her? Had Jenret's complicity been discovered? Packing custables with deadly explosives and shrapnel was an outright act of vengeance, not a warning, and it explained as well why Holly and Theo regarded her with such unveiled suspicion of late—the outsider, the stranger intruding in their hermetically sealed little world. A wonder, too, the ghatti hadn't strip-mined her brain in search of the truth. If she held the key to the truth all unwitting, she'd almost welcome them into her mind to ensure she remained one jump ahead of danger.

Hardly likely to be Geerat. Staring distantly over her mug, she sipped without really tasting what she drank. Not his style, required too much initiative. Though—she tapped the mug against her teeth—she *did* know someone who boasted bountiful motivation and enterprise, repressed anger aplenty. Would the knowledge he might potentially harm innocent children halt him? Not after what he'd visited on his own offspring! All those years she'd sat on his knee, learning her lessons from him . . . And what she'd learned by heart was the cold calculation within him when he chose to show it. His reach, though, was longer than she'd expected if he'd orchestrated this, but why should that surprise her? Machination should have been his middle name, and he wouldn't even have to change his monogram! Uncle Vaert was cheap that way—two for the price of one—ensure her death, Jenret's, and anyone else likely to know the true facts.

Then again, Doyce Marbon had gained enemies of her own. But why strike now after she'd just relinquished a position of power as Seeker General? Retirement surely diminished influence. A renegade Resonant, even a Normal bent on striking back at her, nursing a grudge that she'd altered the safe, insular world as they'd known it? Very likely, in fact. Setting down her mug, she tore at the cinnamon bun again, but her appetite had fled. No matter how she inured herself to certain things, past pains caught up with her, broke through her self-defenses without warning. Such moments of soul-searching could cripple, kill as incontrovertibly as one of those innocent-looking custables.

Well, on with the game. Forcing down another few bites of her bun, she rose and reslung her cloak over her shoulders like a warrior returning to the front. Smile pleasantly and vaguely, catch no one's eye. She'd awaited this game for so long, and now the chase had commenced, the prize nearly within her grasp. Yes, a lone game as much as possible, Mettha had respected her abilities enough to send her here. But Mettha had also insisted on involving Jenret, giving him a share in these initial feints to drive the prey from cover. One could hunt with a pack or hunt alone, and every piece of her being yearned to assume responsibility for single-handedly stalking and capturing this particular quarry. She'd convinced Mettha that it wasn't mere vengeance that drove her, but that wasn't entirely true. Soon it would be over—and high time, too.

Rehanging a gardening trowel on its peg, Mettha Prinssen absently brushed away the dried soil left behind and unfolded the note, flattening it on her workbench alongside the glazed pots and cut-crystal vases dulled with water scum. The cipher took but a few moments, its code so antiquated yet obvious that some of her younger agents had endlessly struggled to break it, assuming a subtlety that didn't exist. Still, this agent had employed it for nearly forty years, and Mettha saw no need for altering such archaic perfection, small marvel that it was.

The news was as expected: neither earth-shattering nor revelatory, destined to sound invisible trumps. It laconically reported what a competent agent should: facts, both common and clandestine. Noted parallels and connections as necessary, as well as parenthetical comments concerning whether something appeared dubious gossip, a plausible account awaiting confirmation, or firsthand observation. Little of the agent's personality showed through and that, too, was precisely as it should be. While Mettha valued an agent's opinions, applauding those who showed initiative, she'd learned whose views to accept with a grain of salt, even the whole salt cellar. First and foremost, an agent was a *receptacle,* a human container for collecting the world's seamy data and conveying it to her desk. For that they received reasonable—and steady—fees simply for doing what gossips did gratis.

Pouring fine sand into one of the clouded vases, she rolled up her frayed cuff and worked her narrow hand through the constricted neck, polishing inside with a damp cloth and a tiny, stiff-bristled brush. Working with her hands helped her focus while she read a report, burnishing each informational gem, holding it to the light to assess its facets and flaws, where it might enhance a seemingly worthless chain of data from other agents. This particular agent was content with her small "world," never aspiring to any wider reporting realm, aware Samranth's bazaar served as a microcosm. Whether from Samranth proper, the outlying Sunderlies districts, or from abroad, sooner or later every major and minor confidence made its way into the bazaar for barter or buying. What better venue than a bazaar for illicit activities? And this agent was the most powerful trader of all, though few other stall-holders realized it.

She finished the second and third vases, humming under her breath, pleased. The pieces were assembling *very* nicely, the case building, dates and times and amounts recorded. With rapid strokes of her penknife she made a sharp diagonal cut on each stem, grouping the peach-tinted rosebuds in one of the newly-cleaned vases. Mettha Prinssen, Security Chief for Samranth, held sway in a messy cultivation room with a paint-chipped door sign that read "Garden Assistant," and it suited her. Oh, it was no secret around the Governor's Mansion, but this out-of-the-way office ensured that outsiders remained ignorant of her and her activities. After all, Security bore certain similarities to gardening—nurturing, coaxing along "plants" to make them flourish, nipping others in the bud, or routinely extirpating life's "weeds."

The Sunderlies had a more compelling reason for espionage than did most countries. Once Canderis had exiled its most hardened, depraved criminals to this colonial outpost,

someone must discreetly watch them, allow them latitude
to rebuild their lives—as long as those new lives didn't
hinge on crime. The paramount concern of the Canderisian
Guardians stationed here was to ensure criminals never returned; what they actually *did* with their lives was of sec-
ondary interest, even run-of-the-mill lawlessness. Although
the cost of a constabulary more attuned to the pitfalls of
mingling criminals with innocent citizens should have fallen
to Canderis, the High Conciliators avoided the issue—year
after year. In turn, the Samranth city council felt it unjust
to levy an assessment from some of the very souls said
constabulary would be paid to observe! An earlier governor
with atrocious penmanship *did* convince Canderis to approve a budget line erroneously read as "Securities Collat-
eral," thus inadvertently funding Mettha's predecessors. A
covert crew of agents did surveillance, allowing criminals a
modicum of dignity without suspecting that authority constantly peered down its nose at them, alert for the tiniest
misstep.

A tip-tapping knock on two different door boards sent
Mettha hurrying, rose in hand, to slip the lock. Only Erzebet Hoetmer, the Governor, and Baskin, her adviser,
were privy to that particular signal. Clad in a messy gardening apron loosely tied over an amethyst shot-silk caftan,
Erzebet skimmed off her shabby straw hat, fanning herself
and Baskin impartially as she gratefully sank onto a high-
legged stool. The woman carried too much excess flesh to
work in such heat but could never resist stealing time for
her gardens. Anyone impatient to see the Governor had
best hope horticulture didn't take precedence over administrative duties on that particular day.

Hefting a long-spouted red watering pot, Mettha poured
water into battered, handleless china mugs, handing one
each to Baskin and the Governor. "Oh, tush!" the Governor snorted, "can't you spike it with something, dear?"
Baskin's eyebrows wrinkled just long enough to alert her
the Governor still had meetings scheduled. The little man,
brown and wrinkled from the sun, appeared to be some
lower-level bureaucrat proud of a nebulous title and his
officious-looking black caftan, shiny with wear, but it never
paid to underestimate him. While Baskin's title might vary

on occasion, he served behind-the-scenes as Erzebet's right hand.

"I've a lovely new plant food, a heady blend of deliquescent fish heads, calcium, magnesium sulfate, and I don't know what else," she offered.

"Oh, *all* right!" Peevish, Erzebet raised her solid arms to fluff her wispy white hair, wide dark ovals of perspiration marking her caftan. "Just tell me the latest."

"I received a report earlier from my contact at the bazaar—" and was nonplussed to discover both Baskin and Erzebet Hoetmer dissolving in laughter.

"Not old Saucy Sausage?" Baskin regained control first, his spectacles flashing, his eyes refusing to meet Erzebet's. "Still on the job, still on the payroll?"

Taking pity on her, the Governor shifted heavily on her stool to explain, "Saucy Sausage—old Mama Santellena, the sausage vendor at the bazaar?" At Mettha's nod she continued, "Oh, when Baskin and I first arrived here, Mama was quite the looker, charmed Baskin no end. I always teased that he'd abandon his duties and run off with her!"

"Fascinating, I'm sure," and though she was thirty-odd years younger than they, they both immediately sobered, awaiting her news. "More details on incoming and outgoing shipments from the bazaar proper, and a clue as to where their warehouse may be. Janacz & Sons, no less. We'll check it out. The noose is slowly tightening, though Vaert doesn't yet realize it."

"So when do we kick the stool from under his feet, let the noose do its work?" Baskin polished his glasses, beaming vaguely.

"True, Vaert's the mastermind, but unless we can take them all down together, we may inadvertently leave some of their system in place," Mettha cautioned. "Our agent in Canderis should be back here in the next oct or two, depending on the weather, but we need the information she's obtained on that end. I left her a message at Windle Port to let her know what's happened at our end."

"Storm-season," Erzebet mused. "Baskie and I came over during storm-season. Swore I'd never board another ship again. Stayed on here, always reappointed. Good thing, too, wouldn't have wanted to abandon my gardens. . . ." Tranquilly returning to the present, she continued, "Is it confirmed that Jenret Wycherley's accompanying her, rather than his sister, Jacobia?"

Again Mettha felt dubious, distrustful about this aspect of their plan, but that was intuition, not hard facts. All well and good to listen to intuition, but one couldn't run an operation like this on it. "Yes, but there's no guarantee Jenret Wycherley's the man his father Jadrian was."

"I should certainly hope not!" interposed Baskin. "Now come, Erzie, I've reports to write. If I steer you to your council meeting and lock you in, I might actually get some done." And with that, they left, but not before Erzebet Hoetmer further dirtied her fingernails poking around the hibiscum slips she was rooting.

Mettha saw them out and relocked the door with a certain relief. There were moments with these two when she felt she'd unwittingly stumbled into a traveling troupe's slapstick farce, destined to be hit by inflated bladders at any moment. Mayhap she just didn't understand Canderisians. In their own way they'd make matchless agents, adept at misdirection and mischief, their considerable intellect masked by bickering foolishness. Except this wasn't a laughing matter.

"But damn, why Jenret Wycherley?" Mettha'd not been impressed by what Honoria had relayed to her about the man, although Honoria seemed convinced he'd prove useful. If she didn't know Honoria's history, didn't know how she ached to witness Vaert's fall, she'd swear Honoria'd been swayed by a pretty male face. After all, she hadn't thought anything of moving her surveillance of Geerat beyond flirtation if it shook loose some needed information.

Bard leaned against the railing, eyes straining against the soft stringers of mist and low-sprawling clouds that obscured any division between sea and sky. The mist muted sound as well, the slap of water against hulls an indistinct "lub-lub," the heartbeat of the sea punctuated by an occasional, stronger "slap!" as if the sea were as impatient as he to get down to business. A gull mewled, then dove into the mist. The town sounds behind him formed a tedious, predictable background. Beyond the Frisian Sea lay . . . his land, the Sunderlies.

M'wa appeared wraithlike out of the mist, the contrast of his black-and-white markings gradually defining themselves as he came nearer. A sharp sneeze as the mist tickled his nose. **"Funny place for a porch, a veranda—whatever you call it."** He stuck his head between the balusters, stretching his neck, whiskers wide and questing. **"Must be a wondrous view when it's clear."**

"That's the idea." Weight on his elbows, Bard stretched forward as well, eyes sweeping what he could make out of the moorings, the empty dock where their ship would land. "Up here you can spot arriving ships—their topmasts, anyway—long before they put in at Windle Port." An appreciative sniff at the air—salt, seaweed, tar, and oil. The drifting scents of dried cha and spices overlaid the rot and reek of dead fish and shellfish, the uncovered banks at low tide—a heady brew, filled with promise. Promise and a sneeze. "Mmph! Does clear the sinuses, doesn't it?" He dug out a handkerchief, blew, swiped at the moisture that gilded his skin an almost otherworldly gold in this diffused light. "Most of the houses and shops right on the seawall have these porch-things atop their roofs, the houses that march up the hill as well."

Leaping up, balancing on the railing, M'wa thrust his face toward Bard's, urgent. **"Don't want to go,"** he confessed. **"Don't like ships, don't like the sea, don't think I'll like the Sunderlies."**

Uneasy at his Bond's outburst, he cupped the ghatt's face, touching his forehead against M'wa's white star. *"But you'll go, won't you? Suffer it for me?"* Worrisome—M'wa never required constant cajoling, flattery. *"I need to go, need you at my side."* His heart pumped harder with longing. *"My ancestors' land . . . I can feel it calling me from across the sea. It's pulling me, M'wa, like calling to like!"*

Forefeet on Bard's shoulders now, the ghatt crooned in his ear, **"Please! Please don't go! Fate can sleek-foot on you before you know it! I don't know how, I don't know why or what, but danger lurks in the Sunderlies. I sense it deep in my bones!"**

The ghatt broke off as Jenneth scrambled through the roof-trap onto the porch. "Uncle Bard! I didn't know you were up here." Pleasure overrode the momentary chagrin that had first tightened her expression. Nestling close to Bard's side, she gave M'wa a gentle stroke, shook her hand. "Ugh! Soggy ghatt! Sorry, M'wa. Bless the Lady that wet ghatti smell nothing like wet dogs!" A sniff at Bard's shoulder. "Or wet, stinky tabards!"

"Another indication of ghatti superiority," Bard agreed, slipping an arm around her shoulders as she shivered at the mist. So few people with whom he felt truly at ease—few enough to count upon one hand. His sister, Byrta, he bent his thumb, the pang of her loss—even after so many years—worse than losing a thumb. Byrlyn, his precious one, who almost rolled time back for him, *could* roll it back if she weren't so stubbornly herself. Or if he weren't so intractably himself. A disparaging grin at the admission. Jenneth, of course—he'd stood up for her on her naming day— a reason to hope, to tentatively love beyond the grim limits of dispassion he'd used as a shield. Even a twinge of jealousy at her twinship with Diccon, for what she so effortlessly had and he so sorely lacked.

A thumb and two fingers accounted for: Lindy, his ring finger, the connection to his heart. Or his head. Easier to be selfish, scantish with his heart, convinced the remains must be rationed out. And lastly, Doyce, stalwart friend, who pushed and prodded, yet also knew when to leave him be. Strange, he'd not noticed it before, but all the people of his heart were female.

"So, excited about visiting the Sunderlies?"

"I suppose, I guess." She tucked her head against Bard's collarbone, gave a gusty sigh. "It's just . . . I don't know . . . it feels like a detour."

"From what? Where are you rushing so fast that you can't afford a detour?"

"That's what I don't know, what I'm trying to decide." The child, young woman—when had she grown up?—was a walking dichotomy: her father's outward mien, but her mother's prudence, never jumping into anything without thought, too much thought, sometimes. Diccon, on the other hand . . . well, it was a wonder he and Jenret didn't collide, what with leaping without looking. "If . . . if you hadn't bonded with M'wa, Uncle Bard, what would you have been?"

He and M'wa exchanged a look, a look that said it all—
that no other possible fate existed. "You mean, if I hadn't
been Chosen as a Seeker?"

Fisting her hands, Jenneth tapped an impatient beat on
the railing. "Well, there are more people who'd make good
Seekers than there are ghatti to choose them, aren't there?
Whether they're Resonants or Normals."

"Probably." He'd never really thought of it, that there
might have been someone, more than one, out there M'wa
could have Chosen, loved—if fate had been different.
Koom had found Swan Maclough after his Bond had died,
hers as well. Saam had found temporary solace with Nakum
until Mahafny had opened her heart. And Parm had fled
from an unstable Bond into Harrap's welcoming arms, mystifying them both. Each should have been an impossibility,
and yet each had occurred within his lifetime.

"The ghatti aren't known for breeding well." He stared
again at the mist, the cloud swirls, wishing he could pierce
the veil. "I suppose if M'wa hadn't come along," and P'wa
as well, for Byrta, how could he have left half his heart
behind? "that I would've been raising beef cattle, like the
rest of my relatives."

"Only that?" Insistent now, the tempo of her pounding
increasing to match his heartbeat. "*Nothing* else? Even if
you knew—deep in your soul—you didn't fit that life, felt
like a fish out of water, even though you'd grown up with
it?"

She had a point, he had to concede. The child had been
thinking entirely too much lately. If he *had* stayed, gradually hating the monotony of the cattle more and more, then
he would have come to hate himself, perhaps even have
come to hate Byrta. Both of them trapped, each reflecting
the other's mirror-image of despair. "You're right," he
swallowed hard, spoke her name aloud. "Byrta and I would
have been miserable. We would've had to find some other
way to live. Mayhap we wouldn't have chosen wisely the
first time—trial and error—but eventually we *would* have
discovered what we were meant to be in life."

"Eventually!" Face screwed in dismay, she managed a
shaky laugh. "I get so scared not knowing what's ahead—
for me, for Dicçon. Whether it's in the Sunderlies or in
life."

"Don't we all, M'wa, don't we all?" and yearned to cry
out to Jenneth: Be thankful you're not Lindy, that you
don't know what will happen, tomorrow, the next day. Be
thankful you don't bear her burden. Instead, he sought for
the familiar. "Come on, it's almost time for dinner. Best
go down, get dried off." With solemn grace he twirled Jenneth under his arm, making her chuckle. "Well, 'not knowing' can paralyze you, or you can view it as an opportunity.
Don't fret about opportunities until you have to—wastes
too much energy in ones that never come your way."

As they ducked beneath the trapdoor, M'wa turned back
on the steps to regard his Bondmate. **"Was I supposed to
benefit from that little lecture as well? Fine, you've got
your 'opportunity'—but I still don't like it!"**

Doyce scrutinized the entire parlor, a sourly methodical
and meditative examination to ensure nothing escaped her.
Would that it could! They'd had the run of Miz Hasten's
parlor, what with travelers being few and far between in
Windle Port or at the Hasten Inn during the stormy season.
Even the inn's name set her teeth on edge, better to Hasten
Out, not *Inn.* Everything—everything—adorning the parlor
showed appalling taste: an assaultive clash of patterns and
colors that made the very spirit cringe and beat a "hasten"
retreat. (Oh, dear!) So did her back, her posterior, any part
of her anatomy in contact with the furniture decorating the
room. The Schweiker Inn had been an oasis of tasteful,
comfortable simplicity in comparison.

Well, truth be told, not even a deep, downy feather bed
was terribly comfortable, given her recent fall. At the fringe
of her thoughts, the words that had insinuated themselves
into her brain just before her fall—*"You won't like the
Sunderlies. Go back while you still can. Go home now!"*
Her imagination? A part of her brain vocalizing its dismay?
Khar hadn't thought so, but she'd been remarkably reticent
about the gloating threat since then, almost shrugging it
off. All the more reason to pity herself, stalled here in
Windle Port—either go home or go forward! Take the trip,
prove the words wrong! Either have things out with Jenret,

or give up and admit their love was dead. But to even admit that possibility set her shying worse than her rented mare.

If their ship didn't reach port in the next day or two, late from an outlying storm front, she'd go stark raving mad second-guessing herself. "How can you sit, not squirm in that thing?" Stretching a foot, she joggled Lindy's chair, a mahogany monstrosity carved with raised swirls, rococo designs of fruits and vines, an inlay of opalescent shell fragments on any flat surface.

Looking up from her reading, Lindy gave a rueful smile. "Well," she started to squirm, fought the urge, "once the pattern's incised on my bottom, I make sure it matches each time I sit down." A gesture to where Bard, Byrlie, Arras and Harry—a rakish sticking plaster on his brow—clustered on the floor, constructing a card castle. Harry had proved remarkably blasé about his accident, as had everyone involved in the overnight camping trip. His response to the question, "What happened?" had been an offhand shrug and a "Oh, nothing much. Sliced myself." Neither Theo nor Holly had proved any more forthcoming.

"Try the floor. The carpet should be softer," Lindy advised before raising her book like a shield. At that moment Arras shifted one knee, muttered a heartfelt expletive and rocked back. Driving his fingers through the yarn shag, he retrieved a cherry pit, pitching it at the fire in disgust. Merciful havens, had Miz Hasten booby-trapped the parlor for maximum discomfort?

To her right, Honoria and Jenret had sunk into a sofa whose voluptuous softness mimicked quicksand, capable of entirely swallowing the unwary. Who knew what missing guests might be found in its depths? Covered in a demented print of pinks, chartreuse, and a violet shade that blurred Doyce's eyes, she wrenched her gaze to the sanity of the carpet, merely an unmown lawn of tufted green. Theo and Davvy played cards against Holly and Jenneth, gathered 'round some sort of woven rattan table that looked ready to sprout leaves. Whispering unsolicited advice, Diccon hovered behind one player or another, picking at the beading adorning each fan-shaped chair back.

"Aah!" Doyce groaned to no one in particular, but not a soul rose to her bait. Unfair, since self-pity required an audience, and even Khar refused to oblige. Lindy's eyebrows raised, but her eyes never wavered from her page. Rawn, Khar, and M'wa continued to doze, so Doyce attempted that. Aha! Slitted eyes minimized some of the color-clash vibrations. Lady help her, she was acting more immature, more demanding than Byrlie—worse than Jenret!

Egging each other on, P'roul and Khim took turns stalking the strings of translucent shells curtaining the doorway. First one ghatta then another tagged a shell, sending it tinkling and chiming against its mates. Rolling onto her back to put all four feet into action, P'roul gave a coaxing upside-down look. **"Want to play?"**

"What's the goal? How do you win?" She was curious, half-tempted to play, if only to distract her mind. And if she accomplished that, she'd temporarily forget her bodily aches.

Khim's lightning tag swung one strand back and leftward with a clingety-tingety-ping-rattle-ping as it swept across its neighbors, then tangled on another shell strand. **"The goal's simple—see how long it takes to drive you humans mad. Think we're succeeding?"** She cocked her head, looking incredibly like her sire, Saam, but the devilment and the stripings were all Khar's.

"Well, what do you 'win'? What's the prize? Other than having one of us plant a boot on your fanny."

Khim's neck swanned limply, amber eyes dejected. Had her idle threat worked? **"Well, we're bored, too!"** P'roul pouted, **"We've explored Windle Port from head to tail, top to bottom. The one interesting thing we've come across isn't ready—yet!"** The two exchanged conspiratorial whisker twitches. **"So it's either this—or watch women salting herring again!"**

Somehow their querulous boredom restored a trace of Doyce's own good humor. *"How about a walk?"* she offered and began gingerly heaving herself up. *"Khar needs to stretch her legs, too."*

Opening one eye, Khar yawned. **"If you'd listen a bit harder, you'd hear it's raining. Again. I think not."** Stymied again.

A rich aroma beguiled Doyce's nostrils, the scent mellow yet bitter, a savory, invigorating smell. Shell strands swept aside as if comber-tossed, their brittle jangle overwhelming

as Miz Hasten bore down on them with a tray full of mugs
and a massive, enameled-tin chaffay pot. Doyce sat up eagerly: she'd never acquired a taste for chaffay until now,
had preferred cha, as did most inland dwellers. Chaffay was
expensive, a luxury—it demanded skill to properly prepare,
roasting and grinding the beans, filtering the brew so the
grounds remained behind yet left their essence. But here
at Windle Port, everyone drank it, a common Sunderlies
import. Obviously they'd plotted to monopolize it!

Miz Hasten proved as exotic as her parlor, a paisley
shawl in deep jade, crimson, rose madder, and cerulean
blue dripped with saffron fringes that outclashed a swirling
caftan striped with lime green, ocher, and buttercup yellow.
Somehow the plaid, bibbed apron with ruffled edges
sounded the final death knell to the homeyness Miz Hasten
strove for. Doyce ground her teeth, clenched them to hold
her laughter in check, because Miz Hasten was always so
accommodating and pleasant, even if she'd never scaled the
heights of fashion. Without a doubt all this was booty from
Mr. Hasten's voyages south. Shell earrings swung wildly as
she flourished her tray.

"A final chaffay to drive the damp from your bones before bed?" A generous touch, and one that wouldn't appear
on their bill. But the aroma and Doyce's craving suddenly
paled, overcome by the sight of a half-grown ghatten parading at Miz Hasten's heels. Cocking its head, it stared bold
as brass around the room, its long, thick tail raised, the
tip crooked.

"Ach, poor, little dear!" Miz Hasten addressed the ghatten. "You behave yourself if you won't stay in the kitchen."
Her hand rose to her lips. "Oh, I hope I haven't done
wrong. I didn't think your big cats would mind some little
visiting cousins." She gestured toward the ghatten, who'd
plunked its bottom down while it sniffed the air. "We've
had a pair of strays around—adorable little nippers. I let
them into the kitchen when it's rainy like this. The Mister's
been trying find a ship to take them."

Jaw slack with shock, Doyce found speech eluding her.
A ghatten, here?—and well past the age when it should
have Bonded. Floundering from the sofa's depths like a
drowning man, Jenret found his voice first. "Madam, that's
no cat—it's a ghatten, a juvenile." The word appeared to

baffle Miz Hasten. "I mean, it's the kitten stage of our ghatti here." A final surge as he gained his feet, smiling with casual charm to mask his concern. "It hasn't bitten you, has it? I mean, you haven't felt an unusual communion between you two, have you?"

"Land sakes, no! I chatter away at them, but never a word back do I get—just like the Mister!" Miz Hasten halted in mid-pour. "They're sweet beasties, friendly—least-wise this one is. Her sister's bashful as can be."

After passing the mugs, Miz Hasten left the parlor, more than a shade perplexed as to why everyone had acted so distracted, so perfunctory with their thanks. Well, what could one expect from inlanders, anyway? Preoccupied by such thoughts, she never called the ghatten after her.

A low, astonished buzz filled the parlor. Basking in being the center of such awed attention, the ghatten preened, delivered a dainty scratch behind an ear, and began grooming a paw, toes spread wide. Still sitting, it angled its head, taking quizzical measure of each person present. Finally, it stared at the swinging shell curtains and uttered a high-pitched "Pw'eek?"

"What does 'pw'eek' mean?" With Khar now possessively draped across her feet, Doyce trailed a hand on her head to attract her attention. All the ghatti sat alert and motionless, engrossed by the ghatten's antics.

Folding herself into a compact loaf, white forepaws tucked inward, Khar muttered brusquely, **"Doesn't mean a thing."** Finally she relented. **"It's not a 'thing.' It's a 'who'—a name."**

Seizing the initiative, the ghatten stretched, a low front dip followed by a luxuriant extension of each hind leg. A quick ruff lick and it approached Khar, allowing its muzzle to be greet-sniffed. An about-face and it patiently allowed its other end to receive similar treatment. **"A bit rambunctious, but mannerly,"** Khar allowed.

That accomplished, it leisurely toured the parlor, its stride self-assured despite an inquisitive bunching of forehead stripes at each new sight or smell. Hardly a ghatten anyone would impetuously label "beautiful," but Doyce found herself mesmerized by its subtle markings as it continued its survey of the room.

A wee female, colored a warm pewter with just the faintest hint of copper. Her back and sides appeared flocked, but as she stretched, Doyce had discerned definite stripings, a copper ripple that vanished into the gray when she compacted herself. Distinct stripes marked her face, legs, and tail, though the gray became muted, transformed into more and more delicate shadings of gray, buff, and fawn. A tantalizing suggestion of a spotted stomach when the ghatten reared to tag a drapery pull.

Another "Pw'eek," this time more imperious, but still no response or reaction. Tossing a disappointed moue over her shoulder, the ghatten continued prowling, her swaying tail carving sinuous waves in the air. A sniff at Holly's boots, a foray to a chair leg to bat a sparkling piece of inlay, a considering head-tilt as she stared at Arras's mustache, which he obligingly wriggled at her until she leaped in fright.

The little mite effortlessly held center stage, and Doyce felt fraught with anticipation, almost holding her breath. What if . . . what if it bonded with one of the twins? One worry would be lifted from her shoulders. But how would the overlooked twin react—the one not Chosen? An agonizing dilemma—one twin blessed, the other bereft. Twins unpaired. Better in the long run?—each allowed to discover his or her own identity, but oh, what hurt!

A trot to the lawnlike carpet's center, and Byrlie sat stock-still, touched by enchantment. Harry, too, looked ready to explode with excitement, his eyes dancing between the ghatten and his father. Lady bless! She'd never even considered Harry or Byrlyn as Bondmates, so desperate was she to divine the twins' futures. But the ghatten bypassed both youngsters to thrust her head between the shell-strand dividers, exclaiming "Pw'eek! Pw'eek!" yet again.

"You've forgotten, haven't you?" Khar radiated a certain smug satisfaction. **"Miz Hasten mentioned there are two. Providential, isn't it?"**

❖

Frozen behind his sister, one hand on her shoulder, the other clenched on her chair back, Diccon ignored the pain as decorative beads embedded themselves in his palm. His surroundings receded, darkened by desire, his absolute need for the sunny-natured ghatten to be *his,* to be forever Bonded with such an exuberant spirit. A depth of need he'd never before experienced, a desperate gut knowledge of its utter rightness.

A deep, ragged breath, and the world swam into focus again. No, life had been full of infinite possibilities, a rainbow swarm of choices, all equally alluring, impossible to choose just one. He'd not decided, couldn't bear to, yet now he knew that no other choice could shine so brightly that it could eclipse all others. Oh, both he and Jenneth had toyed with the idea of being Seekers Veritas—how could they not? Children played at so many things, assumed so many roles. This—*this* was beyond all playing, beyond childhood, a path straight to his heart and soul, his adult self. And he'd willingly do anything—walk barefoot across hot coals—to ensure that the ghatten Chose him.

Jenneth's involuntary whimper scored him like a whiplash, made him realize he'd gripped her shoulder hard enough to bruise. Or . . . the thought lanced his heart: mayhap *she* felt exactly as he did about the ghatten? Yearned for it with an equal longing, an equally unswerving certitude at the rightness of it all. A sick feeling churned through him, threatening to double him over at the pain. Jenneth? Jenneth—*not* him?

Oh, Lady bless and guide them both! His sister, his own twin whom he wanted to steal the ghatten from! The ghatten cast a flirtatious eye their way, and he honestly couldn't tell which of them it found more appealing. A deep, shallow breath, and he fought to control his racing heart. Jenneth, his soul mate, his other half. Jenneth, often so fearful, so needy, plagued by demons of her own imagining. Of the two of them, she . . . she needed the ghatten far more than he. He could manage, survive, without it. Yes, adulthood meant learning to cope with loss. He could survive without the ghatten, even survive the hole in his heart.

But now it struck, an insight so bitter it burned. If the ghatten Bonded with Jennie, would he lose her as well? Always before the pairing, the sharing, as natural as breathing. What one had, so did the other. Eyes filmy with tears, he stole a look at Bard, tried to *see* inside, understand what it meant to irrevocably lose the other half of one's soul. No answer, no help there, Bard's pain walled tight within.

The ghatten minced two steps in their direction, stopped, tail erect, the crooked tip alternating from side to side. This one, that one, this one, that one . . . Diccon mentally counted it out. Einie, meanie, minnie, mo. . . . Choose me, *me*!

Swiping at his sweaty forehead with an impatient hand, he drove his hair into a peak. Jenneth remained still as stone beneath his hand, eyes closed, lips silently moving. A wild, pleading glance at his mother, his father. No advice, no answer from either, they could not make the ghatten's choice for her.

One mindvoice took pity on him, gruff with love, one he'd listened to throughout childhood: Rawn, so competent, the rational, steady soul who balanced his father's flighty impetuosity. **"It's not her Choice either, you know. Gather all the salt in the sea, and it wouldn't suffice, if it's not meant to be."**

True, too true. No matter what he wanted, how much he wanted it, there wasn't a thing he could do to alter the outcome. "If not in this life, perhaps in another," as Harrap would say, *did* say on many occasions. Now he understood it a little better.

He rubbed his thumb against Jenneth's neck. *"If she picks one of us, Jen, I hope it's you."* This, this must be what being an adult meant, this sacrifice for another's best interests. Now if only the ghatten would realize how much Jen needed her love. Another step toward them . . .

Another step, and the gray-cream ghatten stopped short, her tail snapping as she issued another "Pw'eek!" even more peremptory than before. Perhaps it was the pelting rain, the creak of a shutter, but a hesitant "Kwee?" drifted back in response. Spinning around, the ghatten made a bee-line for the shell curtain, only to drop into a stalking stance as she parted the strands without a rustle. The ghatti in the parlor watched, intent, restive.

Arras Muscadeine's offended whisper broke their silence, "Not a one of us here to suit?" He shook a finger at Khar. "You ghatti are the most finicky beasts—"

"Hush!" As if with one mind, five human Bonds chided him. More kindly, Jenret clarified, "That was the first act, Arras. The second's about to begin."

A crash, a clashing clingety-pingety-ting as shells wildly chimed, rattling in protest as a second ghatten burst fanny-first into the parlor, rolling and stumbling over its own re-treating feet. Regaining its footing, it cast about in all direc-tions, one white forefoot poised to flee if it could only decide in which direction safety lay. But the striped ghatten barreled tight behind, delivering a head-butt to its sib's fanny that propelled the newcomer deeper into the parlor.

She was a butterball gray calico patched with white and butterscotch. The left side of her face was butterscotch, the right, gray, except for a small smear of butterscotch above and below her eye, like a teardrop waiting to fall. Her white upper lip looked as if she'd been caught sipping from the milk bucket. An expansive white chest and stomach, white forefeet and longer white stockings behind, with a bowl's-worth of pudding color decorating one hip. Irregular butter-scotch patches flecked her back, and Doyce wondered if some cook hadn't dipped a comb in the pudding and daubed her here and there.

A piteous "Naaa-oow! Kwee, Naaa-oow-meoow!" split the air as it dashed under a low shelf, barely squeezing into place. Any hope she harbored of being ignored, even forgotten, was marred by a low-pitched grumbling rumble that emanated from deep in her ample belly. Not exactly a growl, but very similar, a forlorn plaint freighted with woe, at the very least.

"Khar, what's the poor thing saying? What can we do? Is it hurt, hungry? Or just afraid?"

"Hungry? With that girth?" Khar's chuckle cascaded into a chain of purrs.

The gray ghatten dove after its sibling, drove her into the center of the parlor again, and Doyce found herself exclaiming, "Lady bless, she *is* ro—" "Bust," Holly finished for her, a commanding look in her eyes. Swallowing laugh-ter, Doyce filed "rotund" with a list of like adjectives she suspected were now forbidden, such as "pudgy," "stout," and "plump." If anyone would be sensitive to the ghatten's weight problem, it would be Holly.

"Naaa-oow!" the calico entreated once more, and this time took frantic refuge in a cupboard, despite the alarming clatter of dislodged pewter. And from there she refused to be budged, no matter how much her sib cajoled or bullied. Crooning entreaties, snarls, hisses, snaps, nothing swayed her to emerge, her plaintive rumbling-grumbling a recital of each and every tribulation she'd encountered from birth to the present.

The striped ghatten stalked away, long-suffering exasperation plain on her face. Throwing herself down, she began a serious belly-groom, each lick sleek and long, until her good humor was apparently restored. Tidied to her satisfaction, she popped up, head cocked as she resumed her survey of available humans.

Unable to seize control of this situation, mold the outcome to his liking, Jenret stood by helplessly, his fingers working. Doyce could hardly fault him, for she prayed for a specific outcome as well. *"Doyce? The lively one for Jenneth—give her a little self-assurance, confidence? Balance their personalities?"*

"And the plump"—blast, it had slipped out despite herself!—*"little scaredy-ghatten for Diccon? Make him look before he leaps? Think things through before he acts?"*

"Exactly!" A confirming nod of relief. *"Mayhap the Lady does work in mysterious ways!"*

Rawn's tail thumped in warning. **"Or the Elders, more likely. Now don't count—"** but Khar broke in, **"Hush! Wait!"**

The tiger ghatten began a tentative sortie in the twins' direction—step, step, sit, paw wash. Backstep, step, step . . . Suddenly gathering momentum, she edged toward Diccon with a sideways skitter, exuberant yet wary. A final mad dash and she flung herself into Jenneth's lap, springing from her shoulder into Diccon's welcoming arms. Needle-sharp teeth nipped his thumb.

"Ouch!" Diccon's face was a wonder to behold, radiant at the sharing of another mind, not human but one now Bonded to him for life. Joyous tears tracked down his cheeks, dappling the ghatten cradled beneath his chin. Then reality intruded as he blurted, "Oh, Jen! *Oh, Jen, I'm so, so sorry, but she Chose me!*"

"Jennie! Give it up, get some sleep." Diccon crouched at the closet door, Kwee draped across his thigh, swatting at a tempting tail dangling on the other side, resolutely refusing to admit it was her own. *"Leave her alone for a bit. It's the best thing to do."* The chubby calico had finally made another break for freedom, going to ground this time in the depths of an overstuffed, oversized closet just beyond the alcove "room" where Jenneth and Byrlyn slept. Besides, when Jen emerged, he might be able to reach his trunk; he'd purchased a few other "necessities" on the sly. Windle Port's shops were crammed with the most marvelous gadgets . . .

"Sissy's scared," announced Kwee, rubbing her chin along his knee. It still gave him shivers when she 'spoke him, utterly intimate yet undeniably alien—and his. **"Both Sissies scared,"** she amplified, **"not brave like you, like me."**

He rushed to her defense. *"Jen is not a sissy! Oh, she gets scared sometimes, more than I do, but she doesn't let it stop her."*

The ghatten's whiskers scrunched in perplexity. **"Not your Sissy? Thought she was your Sissy-sib, just like Sissy and me."**

"Aah," and the comprehension flooding his voice reached Jenneth, who cast a confused look his way as she crouched deeper into the closet, futilely coaxing the ghatten with chicken tidbits. Poor plumpkin must be scared if she wouldn't budge for chicken.

"I know she won't starve, Dic. And I'm not trying to force her to Bond, truly." Shrugging her hair back, she duck-walked under the overhang of a coat. *"But she's so frightened. I want to help, convince her no one means her any harm. I can't—we can't—just leave her all by herself."*

Diccon sighed; clearly it was going to be a long night. *"Can't you make her come out?"* he begged Kwee, praying he hadn't broadcast to both Jen and the ghatten. Each seemingly had her own private mindlink with him, but it left him uneasy. What if he slipped? Being that intimately connected to two different beings could mean he'd make a muddle of it when he rushed. What if he didn't want them to hear the same thing?

"Your Sissy or my Sissy?" the ghatten asked with sweet reason. **"You can lead a Sissy-sib to milk, but you can't make her lap!"** Inordinately proud of her new-minted proverb, she puffed out her chest, but a yawn spoiled the effect. **"Ooh—so clever! I think we let Sissy-sibs go to sleep."**

"Here? In the closet?" After an uneasy wait for clarification, Diccon gave up, sat on the floor with a thump. Another long-suffering sigh, though Jenneth didn't heed him, just kept coaxing, pleading with the ghatten to come out. Filching a scrap of chicken from the plate, he ate it; somehow it didn't taste as good when Jen forgot to slap his fingers for stealing. Tired as he was, he maintained his vigil, Kwee dozily curled on his lap. At first he thought she slept, only to gradually realize she, too, was waiting, at rest yet totally aware of her surroundings.

Tired from holding out the chicken, Jenneth's hand drifted floorward. Stifling a yawn, she shifted cramped legs and dropped onto her hip amidst the dust balls, finally nestling on a forgotten cloak that had fallen off its hook. Diccon listened, absently scratching Kwee behind an ear, as Jen's breathing changed and her eyelids began to droop. No sound from the concealed ghatten, though moonlight reflected in her eyes when she turned just so.

With languorous grace Kwee spilled from his lap, arched into a stretch. **"Time to put Sissy to bed."** A nutmeg-tinted nose nudged his hand.

"And you'll see yours to bed, I suppose?" A wince as he rose, pins and needles exacting their revenge for his crimped position. *"It's a start, and I'm grateful for that."* Hunched low, he threaded through the coats, clambering over parcels and trunks to scoop up Jenneth, her muzzy protest tickling his neck as he shushed her. Still low, so very conscious of his burden, he eased out and crossed the hall, slipping between the heavy maroon draping that separated the alcove from the passageway.

Byrlie tossed, fretful, on the window seat that served as a child-sized bed. Ghosting to her side, Kwee feather-brushed the child's cheek with a velvet head rub until she

sank more deeply asleep. He'd clean forgotten about little
Byrlie, wakeful, alone and wondering about Jenneth and
the ghatten. Child wondered too much for two adults, let
alone someone her age.

Damn! How to turn down the covers while holding Jenneth? This was getting complicated! Snag the coverlet with
his teeth? But the dim white of a turned-back sheet, the
plump paleness of a pillow swam in the shadows where
her bed was stationed. On the pillow, Byrlyn's much-loved,
much-worn rag doll, left to console Jenneth in her
aloneness, on this night of all nights.

Muscles protesting, he deposited Jenneth with less ceremony than he liked and hauled off her boots. That would
have to do. Hands in the small of his back, he stretched,
then leaned to pull the covers over her. *"Dic,"* she fretted,
and he couldn't tell if she were awake or half-asleep, *"don't
go, sleep here tonight."*

"Right enough." They were too old for such indulgences,
he knew full well, but heaved off his own boots and folded
back the coverlet, sliding in as he had so many times before: his feet at her head, hers at his. Gonna be yelled at
in the morning. Don't care. No matter how tightly their
minds melded, the physical contact still mattered. While
they'd been assigned separate rooms at the age of six, he
didn't dare count how many times Lindy, or one parent or
another would discover one twin had migrated to the other,
now spooned together in one bed.

Snuggling in, he felt her settle against him, gave a start
as Kwee sprang up, tucking herself behind Jenneth's knees
and next to his heart. Still unable to believe his good for-
tune, he caressed her—so soft, like duckling down—and
sailed toward sleep, warm with contentment.

"Waow! Wa . . . oow . . . WOE!" echoed from beneath
the bed and a spherical shape launched itself, landing
smack in the middle. A protesting "oomph!" from Kwee
as she struggled and shifted, began to purr. *"Next time your
Sissy decides to join us, ask her for a little more warning.
She's a big girl."* Undraping an errant tail from his face, he
wriggled, elbowing for his share of space as he listened to
the joint purring, one contralto, the other deeper, but hesitant, oh, so hesitant.

"Big Sissies have the *biggest* loving hearts." Head pillowed on her sister's back, Kwee brushed her nose against his and slept.

Not mud; that—at least—would dry, brush off. A circumspect sniff at her hem confirmed it: tar plus that filthy muck tracked by anyone who roamed the cattle mart. Muck was the politest word she could find to refer to it—now that she was a Shepherd of the Lady. Tucking the offensive hem of her wheaten robe well under her, Shepherd Aidannae pasted on a contemplative smile, her sharp gray eyes respectfully downcast. Ah, humility! Ah, service! Ah, obedience! Ah, muck!

The individually-wrapped loaves still warm from the ovens, she unwrapped them, placing each on the outspread cloth, more darned than woven, but as white as repeated bleachings could make it. Show off each golden-crusted loaf to its best advantage—and let the scent beckon to hungry bellies. Six round, herbed breads; six rich with spices and raisins; each signed with the Lady's eight-pointed cross slashed into the top. Bethel bread. A dented begging plate beside the loaves, should anyone care to donate some coin beyond the price of a loaf. Better yet, donate and not buy— the longer the loaves stayed unsold, the longer she could remain in the midst of the market. One learned much about one's fellow man—and woman—by watching (despite the hindrance of downcast eyes) what transpired in Samranth's bazaar.

Gauging the sun's shift, knowing it could burn only hotter and brighter as the day progressed—what did she expect? this was the Sunderlies, after all—she surreptitiously tugged the bread-laden cloth leftward, easing it into the shade cast by Mama Santellena's sausage booth. After all, as a religious group sworn to poverty, no one expected a Shepherd to rent booth space, an awning. Hadn't Governor Hoetmer herself ruled the fee be waived, as long as the space wasn't prime? Except Mama Santellena begrudged anyone and everyone the time of day, a breath of air, let alone squatter's rights on this sliver of space. Aidannae wouldn't borrow her shade, except that her scalp still burned easily, the reverse tonsuring not that long distant.

Striving to act natural, she gingerly touched the top of her head. The sides and back had been close-clipped, the remaining crown hair pulled up, banded tight atop her head. Since it was a riotous, rich auburn, it was highly noticeable, like a round, overweight banty cock flaunting his flame-red comb. Bee-awk! Bwraak, bwraak—she'd be scratching at the dirt before she knew it!

But no, she blushed in vexation, thinking about one's looks—even in less-than-complimentary terms—was vanity. All-Shepherd Cubzac had decreed their tonsure unsuitable for a woman, the first woman in the Sunderlies to take the Shepherd's holy vows. The first woman anywhere, if Aidannae'd guessed right. This was Cubzac's compromise, making her relinquish a portion of her crowning glory for the greater glory of the Lady.

But her thoughts spun 'round to her robe again and the mucky footprint marring its back. Shepherd's robes, or habits, were part of their communal property, belonging to the group as a whole. Hence, it had been decreed that one size would fit all, so that no one Shepherd might take a particular liking to one specific robe, boast a subtly different style or weave—an attack of individualism. Well, that might suffice for the other four Shepherds at the Bethel—no, three, she corrected herself, hastily breathing a remembrance prayer, still unable to believe that Shepherd Nualan had died. But it didn't work for Aidannae.

She was roundly plump, even dumplingy, but her girth came nowhere near matching the men's, nor did her height. The sleeves she could and did roll—actually, it proved handy, she tucked small objects in the folds since the robes lacked pockets. And unrolled, they protected her hands from the oven's heat when it came time to pull out the loaves. No need to guess Shepherd Ergen's new location for the pot holders; it varied each morning, depending upon where Ergen was in the kitchens when the tune for a new Mystery Chant overwhelmed his soul. He'd slid a paddle of fresh dough into the washtub one day, sure it was the oven.

So, hike up the robe, knot the hempen belt tight round her middle to hold it in place. Except at some point each day someone would tread on her hem—accidentally or not. Blithely unaware, she'd take a few additional steps, the material unfurling, expanding to its full length, until she came to a screeching halt, pinned in place. More than once she'd landed with a thud on her bum.

Well, 'twas a small price to pay to be a Shepherd, a woman Shepherd, the order's first. How she'd dared apply, she still couldn't fathom, just *knew* that her rackety, hand-to-mouth existence lacked something—something more sustaining than the basic necessities of food, shelter, and clothing. She felt *right* at the Bethel, not just praying to the Lady during services, but passing the time of day with Her when the worshipers left. Quiet-like conversation so as not to disturb the Shepherds at their own prayers or duties. One day, not sure what drove her, she asked to see the All-Shepherd, asked to be a Shepherd.

To his credit, Cubzac hadn't roared at her to leave, or laughed at her being a simpleton. He'd just made a hmphing sound as he'd studied her strained, blushing face. Not the bad hmphing sound—the sniffy, superior kind—but a contemplative "hmmmph," his eyebrows rising and falling. In retrospect she now realized why Cubzac hadn't dismissed her out-of-hand: Men weren't exactly beating down the Bethel doors here in saucy, sassy Samranth to bolster the Shepherds' ranks. And the four Shepherds who'd remained in the Lady's service had a combined age of just under three hundred years. That said it all.

Mama Santellena grouched, elbows flying as she wielded her broom, dust floating perilously close to the loaves. Turn the other cheek, she instructed herself, and did, rolling on one haunch, eyes still downcast in devotion. The sound and aroma made Mama Santellena drop her broom and curse, while Aidannae displayed a pinched, long-suffering smile, slanting her eyes in Mama's direction when a passerby suddenly gasped and picked up his pace.

So, the day had arrived for the vote to determine if she'd gain admission to the Shepherds, and she hadn't a clue how it would fall. As far as she could judge, Cubzac and Nualan were for her, Conraad stridently against, and as to Ergen, she couldn't hazard a guess. Had she answered every question spang-on, unraveled each knotty problem of doctrine and theory? The nuances of each had left her giddy at intricacies she'd never considered, shadings far beyond the catechisms so arduously learned. She'd had faith in her mystery chants, round and ringing in her untrained alto voice.

"One final question," All-Shepherd Cubzac had asked, mouth straight and stern, but that was but a front, she could tell, his brown eyes dancing. "Why do you—a woman— wish to be a Shepherd so badly? Why, when for all these many years, only men have served our Lady faithfully and well?"

She'd studied her toes, side-glancing here and there, as if she'd expected to find the answer etched in the cool, worn stone beneath her bare feet. Or sparkling in the beeswax-scented air, or burning bright in the honey-toned wood of the choir loft. But at length she felt compelled to look upward, beyond the All-Shepherd, straight toward the statue of the Lady in the niche above the altar. The Lady— with her eight-armed, all-welcoming embrace—gave a se- rene yet beckoning smile, urging her on, inspiring a truth.

"Well, that's just it, don't you see?" Hesitant at first, she'd let her confidence rise and build—was confidence the yeast that caused her soul to expand and rise like bread? A conviction at the rightness of her need and her service, and her voice came loud and true, so that even old Nualan need not cup his ear. "Eight Apostles—all male. Every Shepherd since the beginning—male. Seems to me that the Lady might hunger for some woman-talk. Not gossip, mind, straight woman-talk, the nitty-gritty bits of life we humans struggle with each day—man or woman or child."

All-Shepherd Cubzac's face had begun to simmer redly, mouth pinched tight and cheeks pouching till they'd squinched his eyes. "Oh, Lady, I've failed," she'd thought, miserable and ashamed. "I told them what You told me, but they didn't let it into their hearts! They're Your earthly Apostles, they must know that I heard You wrong, couldn't be expected to understand Your glory!"

A sizzling hiss, and she'd looked around wildly, focusing on Cubzac just in time to see him lose the battle, burst out laughing, roaring, holding his sides. "Oh, child, I'm not laughing at you! But we men *are* pretty poor conversation- alists at times, despite our piety. Sometimes our belief in another, better life to come distracts us from the here-and- now." And so she'd been accepted, street-smart, gutter-wise grundy that she was—and an ardently thankful one at that.

Seven loaves sold by now; despite her ruminations, she'd not ignored her selling, or the plaintive look that cajoled all but the most stingy or truly impoverished into dropping a bit extra into her begging plate. A pragmatic decision, too, to price the loaves at four coppers—and always lack change for a five-cop piece. *Someone* had to see the funds were there to run the Bethel, clothe, feed, and shelter her dear, doddering old Shepherds. Have enough to do good for the many who subsisted on even less than they.

The Lady provided, but She *did* appreciate anyone who'd roll up her sleeves, apply some elbow grease to the world's problems. Mayhap 'twasn't as seemly as Shepherd Conraad would like, but it worked. Prayers said on a starving stomach seldom worked miracles, could barely reach the Lady's ear, besieged as She was by too many souls who couldn't tell "wants" from "needs." That she knew, and they'd lost track of in their introspective holiness.

A flash of faded blue at the near corner of Mama Santellena's booth, and Aidannae flung her arm back without looking, captured an ankle and yanked. A thud followed by an "Oomph!"

"Smir!" she hissed it almost like a curse word. "What you trying that for? Mama Santellena'll skin you twice, she catch you! Todgy, shysty fool, you!" A boy of about twelve slithered on his stomach as she reeled him in. "Didn't snag nothing, did you?" If he had, he'd have vanished, have bitten her wrist to break her grasp. She'd done the same at his age to survive. He poked his head under her arm, keeping her bulk between him and Mama Santellena's booth. "Kasimir, *what* am I going to do with you?"

The only covering the boy wore was a pair of drab blue, threadbare trousers, hacked off high above the knee. From the way they lapped his waist, Aidannae suspected he had a problem similar to hers—communal clothes, and none his size. "Aw, Dannae," blue eyes stared out of a hollow-cheeked face split by a nose prominent as a ship's prow. His skin was an even umber, darker than exposure to the sun would make it. "Siri's hungering agin. All the child does is gobble-gobble-gobble!" His exasperated affection mingled with his worry. "Been jobbiting ev'chance I git.

Nefty hiring, nefty 'cept fer ol' Wrastle-face." Despite the
baking sun, he shivered, his eyes going dark, seeming to
shrink into their sockets like a death skull. He bit his lip.
"Won' do that agin, nefty it's only way ta feed Siri up.
Rotter die! Den Siri'd kill me!"

Aidannae shivered in sympathy. What Wrastle-face demanded was something no child should be forced to give—
nor any adult, unless it was freely given. Sometimes Aidannae found herself and the theological underpinnings of her
faith parting company, ripped asunder like rotting fabric.
"If not in this life, perhaps in another," she sneered under
her breath. "If you starve to death in this life, perhaps you
won't in another life!" Head pillowed on her lap, Kasimir
stared up at her with concern.

"Can you run a loaf home to Siri without someone snagging it?" The Bethel needed the money the bread would
bring, but this was a more pressing need. This was what
she strove to remind the Blessed Lady about in her prayers,
remind Her of true hunger, of perverted souls who preyed
on children. The Lady wouldn't fail Her family, and Smir's
and Siri's lack of food was failure. Plentitude in another
life was too damn late! Taking the biggest loaf left, she
handed it over. "Sirikit doing well, other than being
hungry?"

Scrambling up, he tucked the loaf tight to his side. "Kep-
ping her zin, much as I kin. She's parsing book she barried
fro a do-good lady." His eyes met hers, didn't flinch. "She
bor-rowed," he enunciated, "it, fer true. Didn't finger-lift
it fer her. Honor on it." For a moment he stood straight
and bowed from the waist. "Thankee yed fer this. Blessings
bounce back ta yed!"

"Scoot." Checking that the coast was clear, Mama Santellena haggling with a customer, no troublemakers in the
lanes between the stalls, she slapped him on the fanny to
start him off. "Lady bless and keep." Kasimir scooted, narrowly missed sideswiping three children in tight formation.

Eh! Aidannae tugged at her topknot. Not again? Funny
to see the Oordbeck children in clusters, always a bigger
one herding littler ones close and anxious. Usually they ran
free as they fancied on real or pretend errands, active yet
mannerly children, and all the stall-keepers kept an eye on
them. Something going on there, and she'd dearly love to

know what. Still, she'd learn at some point, she was confident of that. If the Lady didn't whisper in her ear, someone else would.

She yawned, hunching her shoulders and burrowing into the pillow. Reluctantly freeing an arm, she groped for the coverlet to snug it round her neck, but when her fingers found the edge and pulled, it wouldn't budge. "Nnph!" Raised on an elbow, she tugged harder, but still nothing moved.

"I thought you were going to sleep *all* day!" Through sticky-lashed eyes—had she been crying in her sleep?—Jenneth discovered Byrlyn sitting on the foot of the bed, chin propped on knees, a skinny book tented over stockinged feet. "Want me to read to you?"

"Byr-LIE!" Jenneth groaned, closing one eye. Suddenly she sat bolt upright and urgently bent toward the little girl. "Has the chubby ghatten come out of the closet? Have you seen her this morning?" It struck her then that she'd slept in her clothes.

"Not this *morning*." Something about the child's pedantic emphasis focused her attention. Reaching down, she dragged a giggling, squirming Byrlie lapward, arms tight around her waist.

Fingers poised suggestively near ribs, Jenneth growled in her ear, "Byrlie, *did* the calico ghatten leave the closet? 'Fess up, or you're in trouble, deep tickle-trouble." Thrashing in mock-terror at Jenneth's threatening pose, Byrlie capitulated. "Yes, but I haven't seen her this *morning*!" Jenneth's index finger tracked down her ribs. "Saw her last *night*. When I woke up, I could see you and Diccon and Kwee and the t'other one all jammed together. It looked," she sputtered, choking back a giggle, "*very* crowded. And you were snorning!"

"I do *not* 'snorn'!" Swinging the child clear, she scrambled from bed, hunting haphazardly for clean clothes. "Though Diccon does sometimes—snore, that is—when he's overtired. How late is it? Is everyone up? Has everyone eaten?" Lady help her, she was in for it now. Parents never approved of oversleeping, making the cook keep

things warm until laggards reached the table. Where was
Diccon? She let her mind go blank, cast it in search of her
twin, a tiny shudder of relief as the familiar response came.
*"Diccon? Where are you, what's up? Where's the other
ghatten?"*

*"Relax, Jen. It's not late, really. I just started eating. Byr-
lie, however, rose with the birds. Heard her padding around
last night, retrieving her dolly. She probably thinks it's
lunchtime now."* As clearly as if she sat beside him, she
could see him—a rooster-tail of reddish-brown hair sprung
free from his damp combing, his elbows on the table—
sneaking bacon tidbits to the tortie-tiger. Through her own
bond with Diccon she could almost sense Kwee's purring
pride at her Choice, Diccon radiating a similar pride,
though she couldn't detect any flaunting. Oh, he was full
of himself, all right—always was, but he never gloated.

*"The calico's hiding again—though she ventured out long
enough to empty her breakfast bowl, plus half her sister's
bowl. Ferocious appetite, if nothing else."* Pot calling the
kettle black, he stretched for a third helping of pancakes,
turning dejected at discovering he'd already drained the
syrup pitcher.

As Byrlie wandered off to join Diccon, Jenneth managed
to locate clean gray pantaloons and a rose-colored tunic,
after rejecting the green-striped and the navy one. Tossing
them over her shoulder, fresh smallclothes tucked modestly
under her arm—in case someone (such as Davvy) might
see—she scampered to the washing-up room. A quick
knock. Ah, unoccupied! Not as fancy as the porcelain fix-
tures at home, but the tin tub did boast something she'd
found to her liking—a vertical pipe with a perforated disk
at its crooked end that rained water on the bather, like a
flower sprinkled by a watering can. The only problem was
that the water was highly temperamental—"just right"
turning into "too cold" in the blink of an eye—as it did
now. Well, she was entirely awake!

Gasping, she grabbed a towel and hurriedly began drying
off. But as she peered into the mirror mounted on the back
of the door just above a towel bar, comb in hand, distraction struck. She didn't enjoy looking at her reflection that
much—*really*—but she couldn't help but stare deep into
those scaredy-cat, changeable hazel eyes anxiously looking

back at her. Scaredy-cat changeable—Diccon always called them that when he was bent on riling her. Mayhap, mayhap . . . she *wasn't* good enough for the little calico?

What if it were forced to endlessly wander, away from its littermate, away from Windle Port? Always desperately seeking a Bondmate, yearning for that special person who could make it whole, soothe its fears, its loneliness? Oh, she had intimate experience with that emptiness deep within, what she could share with the ghatten about that hollowness, despite her closeness to Diccon. . . . Without that, she'd have faded into nothingness long ago.

Arms resting on the towel bar, she stared straight through her reflection, wandering in another world, so achingly empty. Oh, how she could love and protect the ghatten if only she'd let her! Heedless, her bare feet padded forward, back, running toward . . . fleeing from . . . the door partially closing, nearly opening, like a child swinging on a garden gate. No matter how many people surrounded her, all she ever felt was how powerless, unsure she was deep inside where nobody but she ever looked.

As the door creaked open again, the calico ghatten dove inside in silent desperation at the vastness of the world. Despite its plumpness, it leaped on soundless paws onto the hamper behind Jenneth. Forward again and back . . . running toward . . . fleeing from . . . and the calico ghatten stood poised in an agony of indecision, stretching its neck farther and farther, almost overbalancing the hamper. Forward, back, and the ghatten lifted a white forefoot and stretched toward the flashing white buttocks looming ever-nearer . . .

Jenneth registered a needle-sharp pain as tiny ghatten fangs sank in. "OW! MO-THER!" Screamed it again in astonishment and trepidation, panicking the ghatten into an untidy tumble off the hamper as Jenneth tripped and landed atop her.

"YEOW! NNEE-OOW!" it screeched, scared half out of its wits, but tremulous with delight. So, for that matter, was Jenneth, until the pounding of heavy male feet echoed through the hall, leaving her to belatedly wonder where her towel had fallen. Ample though Pw'eek might be, she still didn't provide quite the coverage that Jenneth deemed seemly.

Jenret drifted to the dimly-lit entryway again, mentally counting the stacked trunks and carryalls. Unsurprisingly, the number remained unchanged from four earlier tallies, and he shook his head in resignation at his compulsiveness. Damn! A wonder he hadn't started dragging things down to the docks, loaded them aboard himself, he was *that* impatient! Should've gone with Doyce and Khar for a walk, instead. Still not too late to catch up with them, mayhap explain, reassure her that once this trip was done, things would return to normal once again. Halfway to the door he faltered. Shoulds, oughts, coulds—all of them tried his patience. Besides, she'd been out of sorts with him of late, and he'd royally deserved it, preoccupied with Honoria as he'd been.

Ah, but tomorrow—this morning, actually—they'd set sail for the Sunderlies! The additional days of inactivity, the prolonged wait for the delayed ship had cost him dear. So much for patience; a spendthrift like him seldom had extra to spare.

Rawn grumbled from his perch on a trunk, **"Patience? You and it can't coexist in the same thought."** When rumpling the ghatt's ears didn't mollify him, Jenret let him gnaw on his knuckles. **"Ha! I've got it!"** Rawn screwed his face pedantically. **" 'Be patient, Jenret will settle down eventually—when he's ninety!' "**

"Certainly I'm the most tolerant of Bondmates, putting up with you." No sense informing Rawn that he'd essentially created two sentences: a command followed by a declarative.

"Tolerant! You're more likely—" but the coal-black ghatt stilled, massive head cocked, eyes narrowing, then widening as he relaxed. **"Look! Over there! And don't laugh, whatever you do!"**

Obediently Jenret eased round as far as he could, studying the semidark to determine what had attracted Rawn's attention among the looming furniture shapes that threatened to leap out. A genuine smile began to play on his lips. Pw'eek, the calico who'd bonded with Jenneth two mornings ago, had at last ventured on a private expedition while his daughter slept. The white "milk" mustache and white front, the white feet floated, disembodied, in the darkness until his eyes gradually adjusted.

Her chunky body fraught with purpose, she lofted one white paw, then dipped it with lightning speed. A screw of discarded paper had captivated her, and she scooped it up, pouring it into the opposing paw. Juggling it from paw to paw, she let it "escape," only to pounce on it, send it skittering to "safety" behind a chair leg before hooking it free. A quick head toss sent it aloft until her deft paws snatched it in mid-flight.

"Hardly Kwee's style, eh?" Rawn chuckled, and Jenret had to agree. Kwee charged everything, harum-scarum paw swoops sending her "prey" rocketing across the floor—and more than likely under something. Any exuberant follow-up sent the ghatten overshooting the object of her desire, unable to alter course before momentum banged her against the nearest wall. In contrast, the calico worked with dainty precision, a tap here, a tap there—control and concentration.

Abruptly the ghatten raised her head, the crumpled paper forgotten as she belatedly sensed another presence. Her whole body tightened as she prepared to retreat to Jenneth and her sib, Kwee.

Relishing such a challenge, Jenret dropped to one knee. After all, he was renowned for flirtation, was he not? **"Khar and Doyce think you're 'infamous,' not 'renowned.' Don't think your looks will help this time, though."** Rawn seemed to find his own humor particularly amusing, and Jenret's face darkened dangerously.

"Hello, sweetheart," he poured empathy into his voice, truly wanting to earn the ghatten's wary regard. "Hello, beloved of my Jenneth, mindwalk if ye will." Kwee rarely required an invitation to tramp through any inviting mind, but from what he could judge, Pw'eek had 'spoken only Jenneth and, finally, Diccon. Even Doyce's efforts had met with little success. Bashful and abashed described Pw'eek's personality—that and a dexterity and keenness that he'd not credited her with, had judged her solely by outward appearance, too self-confident to bother looking within her heart and mind.

"Truly?" She leaned forward but her feet never budged. **"Truly want to 'speak with *me*, with Pw'eek?"**

"Oh, assuredly," he made his tone as gentle, as unobtrusive as possible; be domineering and she'd disappear. *"You're a wise little ghatten, but you must trust, especially other Seekers."*

A hesitant step, another, and her tail slowly rose in a questing, upright position, its tip crooked, a momentarily brave, beckoning banner. **"I am Bonded now."** Her tail waved, then began to droop. **"Don't know what Bondmates do, what Seekers do, get all achy inside, not knowing."**

"Then come and find out, listen, learn." Struck by her earnest mien, Rawn paw-swiped his face to erase a smile.

Abruptly flinging herself at Rawn, Pw'eek nearly dislodged him from his perch as she scrambled on the trunk beside him. Biting hard at his lip, Jenret stifled every particle of laughter igniting within him at Rawn's stunned expression. Laugh with, never at any of the ghatti, he reminded himself. Lady bless, if she grows much more, she'll outweigh any ghatti the world's ever seen. Recovering both dignity and balance, Rawn licked her face, her ears, the ghatten's tail-base aquiver with relief.

Still, she possessed the most beautiful eyes—a soft-tinted yellow-green surrounding a clear chrysoprase center. Exquisite! And such long, white whiskers, too. He held out a hand, let her sniff timidly, take her time. Did he or did he not know how to charm the ladies? She'd be eating out his hand in no time at all!

"May I?" Giving him leave to stroke between her ears, she slid her head beneath his hand. Daring, he let his thumb caress the demarcation down the middle of her face, butterscotch yellow on one side, gray on the other. *"Thank you for Choosing Jenneth. You'll be good for each other."* A surge of relief, of pride, that his offspring had been Chosen, had discovered their roles in life.

"Oh! Oh, dear!" A hand lightly touched Jenret's shoulder, making him start and the ghatten stiffen. The next thing he knew Pw'eek had literally turned tail, running as if eluding the hounds of the hells, her frightened explanation trailing in her wake. **"Oh, don't like that woman, no, I don't! Jenneth needs me!"**

Honoria leaned against his shoulder, peering after the ghatten as she galloped up the stairs to the sleeping quarters. Her perfume enveloped him, suffused with the vibrant warmth of her body. "She'd be adorable if she weren't so fat. A wholesome little country ghatten, forever garbed in calico."

Her offhand remark stung—insensitive, a calculated unkindness about it he'd not expected of Honoria. Not over something so innocent. "Believe me, her heart and mind may prove even larger. It's not your place to judge."

She stepped back, equally nettled yet conciliatory, and again he found himself admiring her skill at smoothing disputes, large or small. "Jenret, I didn't mean any harm. I've no right to judge, I'm not a Seeker. She's a darling little thing," and reached for his hand.

The double front door to the Hasten Inn creaked warning, opening to reveal Doyce and Khar, a breeze of sea air half-blowing them inside, clearing Jenret's head. Tomorrow, the Sunderlies. *That* was what he had to think about now. He was a married man with two grown children, a wife, a business. Enough to guarantee any man's happiness, wasn't it? But there were no guarantees to anything these days, he bitterly reminded himself. Honoria'd reminded him of that.

"Beggin' yer pardon, sir." The sailor set his bare feet on the ramp and waited, shifting the trunk from one shoulder to the other as if it held naught but air. He distinctly remembered that trunk because he and Arras together could scarcely move it, even once they stopped pushing against one another.

"Of course, of course!" As Jenret stepped aside, he heard the warning shout that indicated another sailor still tossed baggage down the hatch. Complain or not about the mishandling their belongings were receiving? In truth, not one telltale crash or hollow boom gave evidence of a piece hitting the lower deck, so someone below must be catching them. With a start he realized that sailor and trunk still patiently loomed beside him as if they'd taken root. "Yes?"

"Sir, there's 'in the way,' and there's *'in the way,'* if ye take my meaning." Again the trunk—Diccon's, he realized—traveled from one canvas-clad shoulder to the other, the only sign of the man's impatience. "You're both ways,

sir." For a moment the trunk teetered on its perch, and
Jenret envisioned it tumbling down to land on his booted
foot. Without a doubt the sailor'd nimbly spring clear to
spare his own toes.

A solid weight pressed against Jenret's knees and shins,
Rawn silently agreeing with the sailor's comment as he jostled his Bond. With a boyish grin the sailor balanced on
one bare foot, his toes stroking Rawn's back as deftly as
a human hand. Much to Jenret's chagrin, the ghatt good-
temperedly accepted the uninvited caress, returning the salute by angling his head to seize the sailor's ankle between
his teeth. Either the man's skin was leather-tough or Rawn
hadn't punctured him, because the man's smile broadened,
turning almost sappy as he gave a loud haw. "Had us a big
bruiser like yourn when I was a tadling. Ran blubbering ta
Mam how the cat planned on eting me alive first time he
pulled that trick!" Unperturbed, he wriggled his big toe
behind Rawn's ear. "Yer bruiser's got the right of it,
though. He's figgered out 'in the way.' One'n most likely
both of them."

Coolly rigid Jenret stood his ground, refusing to budge.
To have Rawn welcome a stranger's touch stuck in his
craw. "And the second 'in the way'?"

Had he not been bent by the trunk, the seaman would
have stood a head taller than Jenret. "T'other kind's the
advice you keep dishing out with such a bountiful hand it's
nigh ta choking us. We ken how ta shift things, how to
stow'em safe'n sound, be it your wee bags or cargo. Don't
be a lecturing us, sir."

"And if I continue?" A certain perverse pleasure in
goading the man, testing his limits.

Two more crewmen now lined the gangplank behind this
one, all three balked at completing their jobs. "Kin stow
you in the bilge or toss you into the harbor." A shrug.
"Yer choice, sir. I'll tell the Capt'n where I put you."

Unexpectedly the whole situation struck Jenret as comical. "You're right. The baggage *is* an excuse, a distraction
to keep my mind occupied." Moving clear, he ostenta-
tiously made room for the sailor to pass, waiting for the
next two to cross as well before bounding back to the dock.
The gangplank jounced, and he strode more heavily to
heighten its spring, give Rawn a taste of his own medicine.

A lacing of pinks and roseate purples reflected off string-ers of mist, expanding and fading even as he watched, the air so dead still that each sound carried with preternatural clarity this early in the morning. Back to the *Vruchtensla*, he lounged against a bollard, digging into his pocket for the remains of a roll he'd purchased from a yawning street vendor, drawn to the docks by the ship's presence, un-nerved yet relieved they'd depart today.

Ripping a hunk from the roll he tossed it beyond the jetty, idly watching its fall. An ugly-looking bird with sooty brown-black feathers paddled below, its eellike neck and head needling the water as the piece landed. An indignant squawk when the bird discovered he'd gobbled roll instead of fish scraps, the roll a lumpish mass in his throat as he convulsively swallowed it. "Well, friend, we don't always get what we'd prefer, not a one of us."

"Damn it all, I wish *Doyce weren't going!"* Throwing the remainder of the roll at the ungrateful cormorant, Jenret dusted his hands against his thighs. The sparrows, at least, seemed appreciative of the crumbs, if not of Rawn's pres-ence. *"I've handled things badly, haven't I? I'm no good at juggling things."*

Reclining on the dock to absorb the sun's first rays, Rawn lazily looked at his Bond over his shoulder. **"Why shouldn't she know the truth? It might help. Once you were partners in heart and mind."** His tail indolently switched. **"In fact, she tends to be very reasonable—unlike others I might mention."**

As a breeze started playing across the water, he turned up his collar, shoving his hands in his pockets to hide their shaking. Kicking at the coiled hawser by the bollard, he straightened the coils with the toe of his boot, fussily aligning them. Some things he could do right. *"I've hesitated to tell her precisely because she's so reasonable."* Shame-faced, he kicked the coils, undoing his work. *"It all harks back to the past. And into the future. It haunts me—wonder-ing what legacy I'll leave my children, what legacy my father left me."*

"Past is past." Rawn's tail quirked. **"You were a child. It was Jadrian's problem to solve, and he did solve it—as best he could. Your father's ways aren't necessarily yours."** Gathering his feet under him, he rose and stretched his

length against the bollard—a black exclamation against its
white-and-yellow span—and began to sharpen his claws,
eyes slitted in pleasure.

"Rawn! Don't whittle it to a toothpick!" Was Rawn
changing the subject, or was he? Reading Rawn as he did,
he suspected a diversionary tactic to allow him to press
home his point from another direction. Bucking Rawn was
no easy feat, not when he still felt distinctly unsettled from
last night. What had possessed Honoria? For a few brief
moments she'd exposed a side of her he'd never believed
her capable of showing. Minor, true, but an insensitivity to
ghatti that he'd not expected. A sort of off-hand contempt,
a sly belittlement. And then Doyce slipping in when she
had—how to explain?

So he'd paced the dark parlor, alone except for Rawn,
planning how he'd tell her, what he'd tell her, enough to
assuage her fears. Had waited and paced so long she'd been
sound asleep when he'd finally gone up. And this morning
he couldn't help himself, *had* to see how the ship fared—
two opportunities frittered away, wasted!

The tide was on the upturn, the cormorant bobbing and
drifting, upending to disappear underwater with a sinuous,
bending dive. More times than not, he surfaced with a small
fish in his beak, already halfway down his gullet. But this
time the fish was large and plump, the cormorant holding
it crosswise in his beak, frantically juggling it so he could
grasp it headfirst and swallow it. The fish flopped and shuddered, head and tail beating the air as the cormorant fought
to assert his control, too stubborn to release it, unable to
consume it.

*"I'm like the cormorant, too stubborn to give up, eyes
bigger than my stomach. What compels me is more complex
than I've admitted—to you or to myself. Mayhap that's why
I hate to tell Doyce. Somehow I have to resolve this, make
a better job of this than Father did with his troubles."* A
helpless shrug. *"This trade problem's crucial, affects more
than just the family. Besides, Now hasn't anything to do with
Then—does it?"*

**"Well, sending Jacobia would have been more sensible—
just between the two of us. She has a steadier head than
you for figures—and family ties don't bind with the same
intensity."**

But Jenret ignored Rawn, still wrestling with his earlier guilt. *"I wanted so badly to spare Doyce—she shouldn't be responsible for my family's flaws!"* "I just can't believe her timing!" he shouted at the cormorant, who nearly dropped his prize in startlement. Barked commands, shouts, hammering, the scrape and shift of cargo momentarily halted aboard the *Vruchtensla,* and he hurriedly switched back to mindspeech, chagrined his voice had carried to entertain the crew. *"And Honoria and I've planned with such care!"*

Jenret's haphazard pacing sent Rawn shooting away; the ghatt had a healthy regard for his toes and tail, but neither he nor Rawn could always judge where safety lay. Humiliating to spin round and discover he'd trod on his best friend's tail.

"Hmph. Vesey was part of Doyce's past, was Doyce's problem, but she was wise enough not to forbid you joining her search—even though she didn't want you. Ever think of that?"

It was a memory highly unlikely to provoke a smile, yet Jenret's blue eyes did twinkle. *"Why, Rawn! I thought my myriad charms were already winning her, even then. True or not?"* More soberly, *"It's not Doyce's battle, it's not Jacobia's battle—it's mine. That's why I insisted I go. After all, the Monitor contacted me directly."*

"And I can't believe you weren't voted down, three to one. Jacobia, your mother, and Syndar each own a quarter share, after all." Cautiously venturing closer, Rawn stretched his paws to Jenret's waistband, hooking his claws over for balance. "Jacobia does the real work—day-to-day managing, the master account books, and setting future plans. She had to convince you to open the Sunderlies branch. She knows it inside-out. Why claim center stage now?"

For a moment Jenret grinned at Rawn as he ruffled his ears—sardonically, to be sure, and he relished every moment—prolonging it, hoping against hope that Rawn would twitch with discomfort, yield. *"Know why I wasn't outvoted, old friend? Because I'm the perfect foil for Honoria! I play my usual role: vain, overbearing, self-indulgent Jenret, ever-prone to rash enthusiasms. The one you love to chide on occasion. As we all agreed, it's a perfect cover! Few souls ever suspect me of subtlety!"*

"Not I," Rawn admitted. "And certainly not Khar. You're making my life very awkward, in case you've not noticed—overbearing, self-indulgent Bond that you are. Those *are* the words you used, weren't they?" Looking increasingly glum, Rawn threw himself on the dock. "Khar knows something's up, but her duty is to Doyce." He let that sink in. "Just as my duty is to you."

Duty—an obligation, a pledge of accountability. With Doyce and the twins, of course, through commitment, love. Surely Doyce didn't require proof of that! And this was a familial obligation! Starting down the deck toward the storage huts, Jenret raised an eyebrow at Rawn. "Breakfast? Back at Miz Hasten's? Extra bacon if you don't tell on me." Rawn moved with slow deliberation, stretching fore and aft, taking his time, ignoring his Bond. *"I did try to explain—you know that. She'll just have to trust me until I can disclose everything. If anything, knowing might endanger her."* He'd not thought of that before, and it deeply jarred him. The more she knew, the more she'd be determined to do something about it!

"Well, she can exercise more choice in the matter than we Bonds can—just remember that," Rawn grumbled, picking his way around the gull splatters on the dock. "Act willfully blind and you'll trip yourself up."

Doyce paced the deck at its widest uncluttered spot. Left, right, left—just shy of a meter. Right, left, right—two shy meters. So eleven sets of "triplets" meant about ten meters across. Leaning against the rail, watching the dance of the waves, reveling in the pure blue of the sky, she noticed that even the few fluffy clouds overhead couldn't outrace the *Vruchtensla*'s spanking swiftness crossing the Frisian Sea.

Deliberately she turned back, thoughtfully squinting across the clean-scrubbed deck: so, ten meters meant it was about three kitchens wide. A homely comparison helped in judging size. Gone were the scents of Windle Port, and the sails cracked and popped like laundry on a line on a breeze-swept spring day. Hm, from front to back took thirty-three "triplets," thirty meters, though she'd fumbled that figure time and again, each mast or hatch requiring a detour. And she'd discovered how to ride out the ship's motion—not unlike learning to canter, it was all in the legs. It was *almost* tolerable, as long as she remained ondeck, not mewed up in the cabins.

From her perch on a hatch cover, Khar drowsily muttered, **"Still the same size it was last night, yesterday morning, the morning . . ."** she yawned, **"before. Hasn't shrunk. What a relief!"**

Walking as naturally as possible, though she suspected she still exaggerated, Doyce dodged a sailor industriously holy-stoning the last of the deck and sat gingerly beside Khar. Stay clear of the crew at work; it had been one of Captain Thorsen's few rules for his passengers. Sometimes sailors converged from all compass points, or abruptly appeared and disappeared, shooting up one of the three masts or dashing down into the hold. *"I don't like being on this boat, not at all!"* she smiled falsely over clenched teeth, striving to appear at ease. It would help if she understood what the sailors were doing, whatever it was that they did! *"Never have liked them. Didn't relish that horrid raft ride across the Greenvald River. You didn't look very happy either, as I recall."*

Khar stretched, all four feet kneading Doyce's hip. **"Ship. It's a *ship*, call it a boat again and Captain Thorsen may cry."** Claws pinking through the fabric warned she'd best pay attention. **"Now, which way did you walk when you checked the width this time?"**

"Starboard to harbor," she blurted, projecting hearty self-confidence. *"I mean larboard! Or port? Blast it, Khar, I wish we were in port, any port. At least I know what to do, how to act on dry land! I don't care how picture-pretty it looks, I feel vulnerable out here!"* Well, she'd certainly been vulnerable on dry land, so why not here? An accident, mishap, whatever she called it, made her feel as if a dark but invisible giant cloud shadowed her, despite the clarity of the sky. Too late to go home now!

And it wasn't just that—as if *that* weren't enough. Jenret was still abstracted, distant. Oh, they were physically close, how could they not be, given the size of their cabin? But he'd gladly chat with anyone before he'd discuss anything with her, unless she counted weather talk, sailing times, the polite but limited talk one made with a stranger. When

had she become a stranger, an outsider to be courteously
tolerated? Blessed Lady, Honoria saw more of him, spoke
more with him, than *she* had of late. Something preyed on
his mind, but what was it? If it involved Honoria, she could
deal with that—not happily, but she would. She firmly
quashed that thought, though it cost her dear. If Jenret
were guilty of something, then so was she; after all, she'd
never mentioned the mindthreat that had almost made her
bolt home.

"Cluttering your mind with what-ifs, that's not like you."
Paw pads continued flexing against her hip, scant comfort,
but comfort nonetheless. **"You love collecting facts, stringing them together—haven't done much lately, have you?
Too busy sitting around feeling sorry for yourself? 'Starboard to harbor. Or was it larboard?' "** she mimicked.
"Shameful!"

"But it doesn't make sense!" And she hated the whine
she heard in her voice. Nothing made any sense, and the
boat—the ship—was but a part of it. *"The stern should be
the* front *of the ship, but no—that's the bow. The stern's the
rear."* Capturing a white foot, she shook it. *"After all, the
sternum is in front, the breast bone. Of course I've muddled things!"*

Khar's forepaw sleeked free. **"Eumedico terminology's
hardly the same. *I* think sailors use perfectly lovely terms
to describe different ship parts—ratlines, cathead."** Arching
her spine, she demanded a scratch.

As Doyce absently obliged, Jenneth came bounding
across the decking, confidently skipping despite the ship's
unceasing motion. Expression intent, Pw'eek trundled at
her side, all her attention focused on her Bondmate.

Somehow the sight stirred a touch of envy in her, as well
as concern. *"Khar, did we do the right thing? Letting them
come along after Bonding? Should have sent them straight
back to Seeker Headquarters for training."* At first Khar's
palpable wince beneath her hand convinced Doyce that the
ghatta agreed, but then realized she'd scraped tender skin.
Jenret had been adamant that the twins stay, continue their
Sunderlies trip. Half of her agreed—the protective, smothering half—because she felt loath to let them out of her
sight. A premonition of trouble?

More likely a mother's futile attempt to gather her growing chicks close, not let them wander! Mayhap it was just the change, more than a sea change, the transformation of a whole way of life—one where she'd known the rules, indeed, had made them. Not being in charge had been driven home to her in both subtle and not-so-subtle ways. Here, every step loomed brand-new, forcing her to labor over each one. Frankly, she wasn't proving a very apt pupil!

"We *do* have five Seekers aboard, some of the best in the land," Khar reminded her. **"Some formal lessoning along the way would hardly be amiss."**

"For me?" Enmeshed in her own plight, she'd momentarily pushed the twins' needs out of her mind.

"Both Pw'eek and Kwee are quick studies, even though they're behind schedule. I'll have P'roul and Khim pour on the knowledge, pour it thick and fast. Ask Holly and Theo to do the same with the twins. They'd feel honored by your trust."

As usual, she had to acknowledge the soundness of Khar's advice. Best of all, it would offer something to discuss with Jenret—she hoped. Jenneth and Diccon weren't solely *his* responsibility, though he'd overruled her on this trip.

Having tired of throwing stale bread over the rail for the fish trailing in their wake, Jenneth now balanced against Doyce's shoulder as Pw'eek plumped herself on the girl's foot. (**"Excellent ballast,"** Khar snickered.) "I think the ginger's finally taking hold." Face flushed from the sun and the wind, her hair an unruly mass, Jenneth caught at her billowing jacket, stilling its flapping. "If it stays down. Poor Diccon, poor Papa."

Much to her surprise, Doyce had discovered her stomach had remained stable, although an occasional queasiness reminded her how transient that could be. The fresh air helped; the cramped, stuffy cabins magnified the ship's every lurch and sway. The others had gained their sea legs after minor discomfort, except for Harry, Diccon, and Jenret. And Harry, she suspected, had been nauseous with excitement, rather than the motion, since he'd recovered enough to shadow any sailor who'd tolerate his tagging along. So much for the captain's request in the face of boundless curiosity.

Jenret and Diccon, however, had been laid prostrate,

each tinged a sea-foam green, hands clammy, body still
quaking after each upheaval. Let them scent food, even
hear the word, and they moaned, faces turned to the wall,
bleakly clutching their basins. Neither Rawn nor Kwee had
fared particularly well either; since seasickness was hardly
contagious, Doyce suspected empathy. The strangled retching of the ghatti was not conducive to a sense of well-being
under any circumstance. Kwee, at least, retained her high
spirits, though they were tattered. This morning she'd thundered after a mouse, only to halt and throw up in
Doyce's boot.

"Air and a bit of nourishment would help. We ought to
drag them abovedeck." Doyce absentmindedly fiddled with
Jenneth's collar. "Which lucky soul's pulled sick duty
now?"

Expertly twisting clear of her mother's meddling, Jenneth
grinned. She'd gained a modicum of confidence over the
past few days, Pw'eek forever at her side, even though Diccon couldn't be. "Uncle Arras huffed at playing nursemaid,
but allowed he could manage. Said it was a gift from the
Lady to be able to needle Papa and not have him retaliate!
He plans to cajole them into sipping some cha with brandy,
then ask Bard to help liberate them from their den of misery." Hand to her ear, she pretended to listen. "Hark, can't
you hear their piteous moans even now?"

The calico interrupted, chastising them both. **"Isn't nice
to mock ghatti or humans with sick tum-tums! I've licked
and licked Kwee, and she's still wretched. Had to eat her
breakfast for her so she wouldn't smell it."**

"That was truly sisterly of you." Jenneth caught Doyce's
eye. "Tum-tums? Where did she learn that word? Byrlie?"

Thoroughly ashamed at breaking one of the cardinal
rules of ghatti etiquette regarding laughter, Doyce doubled
over, praying internal mirth didn't count. "Actually," she
gasped, "that's what you and Diccon used to say when you
were little. Ask Lindy, if you don't believe me."

Pw'eek almost visibly shrank, chin dipping in embarrassment. **"Not right word? Found it in your head, liked it.
Tum-tum's nicer word than stomach—"**

**"Or gut, or abdomen. Now belly depends on how it's
described,"** Khar interposed, casting a baleful amber gaze

at Doyce. **"In fact, Pw'eek, you've a beautiful white tum-tum, an absolute lily belly."**

The ghatten's spine quivered at the praise, her white paws kneading the deck. **"Oh, oh, yes! Want to see? Show you my lily belly if you don't tickle-mash like Kwee!"** Eager, even a touch vain, she flung herself onto her back, all four feet akimbo as she aired her lily belly.

"Very impressive, I'm sure, but come look at this, every-one!" Khim 'spoke them from the foresail yard, looking impossibly small up so high, and Doyce breathed her relief that she hadn't decided to climb to the topsail above. **"Cash or vouchers accepted, but place your bets now! It's a sure thing!"**

"What in the Lady's name are they up to?" Tired of craning her neck at Khim, Doyce finally stood on the hatch cover for a better view. Ten sailors served as crew, five per shift, but six now clustered round Holly and Theo, both of them visible because of their height. Harry dodged here and there, netting airborne coins in his cap, egging on the sailors while Theo mournfully stripped off his Seeker's tab-ard and jacket, rolled up his shirtsleeves. Sympathetic goose bumps rising on her own flesh, Doyce couldn't believe the sailors' canvas britches and shirts were warm enough. It was definitely warmer the farther out to sea they sailed, but it wasn't *that* warm. Theo's scrawny arms were a washed-out white against the sailors' deeply weathered skin.

"Place your bets, ladies and gentlemen," Holly sing-songed, and more sailors abandoned their tasks to join the group. "First one to the top of the mainmast wins. Smart money's on Theo."

Good-natured jeers and catcalls from the sailors, and with good reason. Thin and pliant as an over-whittled stick, Theo hardly looked athletic, let alone coordinated. Doyce had always half-feared his long arms and legs might snarl, knot together, if something distracted him. Somehow, though, he always managed to remain untangled. Empha-sizing the contrast, one sailor, rugged and blond, pulled his blue shirt over his head, muscles rippling as he negligently dropped the garment.

"Can he win?" Bouncing frantically to see, Jenneth scrambled beside Doyce, hugging her waist. A heartfelt, appreciative sigh as she caught sight of the unshirted sailor, and Doyce experienced a twinge of admiration as well.

Even though she hoped Theo would win, Doyce doubted it. No doubt the ropes—what did they call them? Rigging, halyards, stays?—would prove his downfall. They'd snare him and he'd half-hang himself; Captain Thorsen would be less than thrilled if Theo had to be cut down. Still, Theo was a dear and valued friend, so she forced herself to make an act of faith. He'd confounded her expectations more than once, and Holly'd scarcely let her beloved cousin play the simpleton with no chance of success.

"Harry, a golden on Theo," she shouted, and Theo's smile nearly bisected his face as he gave her a thumbs-up sign, his Adam's apple bobbing like a fishing float.

Loyally, Jenneth yelled, "A silver on Theo for Diccon and me. A silver each!" she added with genuine bravado. So, the sailor's impressive physique hadn't swayed her as much as Doyce had imagined. But how Diccon would react to his sister gambling away his money without his say-so remained to be seen.

Waving them to opposite sides of the mast, Harry strutted back and forth, brandishing a small brass whistle. "Exactly like listening for 'on the count of three,'" he instructed and attempted to demonstrate, cheeks bulging as he raised the whistle to his mouth and blew. Khar gave an anticipatory shiver, but the whistle peeped an anemic "twee, twee, twee" like a laryngitic songbird. Shaking spit from it, Harry critically examined the whistle and puffed at the opposite end. "Tweet, tweet, TWEE!"

"Are you ready?" The sailor and Theo nodded. The sailor, compact but with a brawny chest and anchor-cable arms, jumped in place, shaking loose-fingered hands. In contrast, Theo simply stood, half-wilted, in imminent danger of folding in on himself.

"Get ready!" A deep breath, and Harry blew with a will, Doyce envisioning the pipe shooting from his mouth like a projectile. An ear-splitting "TWEET, TWEET, TWEE!" fractured the air.

They were off! The sailor swarmed up the rigging, momentarily in the lead, until Theo abruptly exerted himself, arms and legs a rhythmic blur, confident as a daddy long-legs spider scaling its web. Each long arm reach outstripped the sailor's, sending Theo higher aloft until he'd almost regained the lead. Looking over his shoulder, the sailor quickened his pace, aware he'd been duped.

"What in the name of all the silvery-starred—" Captain Thorsen materialized beside Doyce and, as he did, planted an unwitting and heavily-shod foot on Pw'eek's long, thick tail.

"YE-OW!" she shrieked, and the captain's answering oath frightened her even more thoroughly. "YE-OW! WOW!"

Heart pounding, Doyce could just discern a gray-butterscotch mass rocketing madly between sailors' legs before lunging for the mast. For a long moment both Theo and the sailor hung immobile above the rolling deck, transfixed as the ghatten shot up and past until she'd gained the mast's highest point.

Aghast, hand over her mouth, Jenneth moaned as she strained to see her beloved Bondmate.

"All wagers are void! We have an undeclared contestant as the winner!" And Holly gave Harry a push to send him around the circle, returning the coins.

Pink nose pointed upward at an alarming angle, Khar sniffed in surprise, began to thoughtfully polish a foot. **"Always bet on a ghatten to win."** Another considering lick, a close scrutiny of white toes. **"Now the only problem is how to coax her down."** A pitiful meow echoed in the distance, a plaintive cry for help. **"Up is always so much easier than down."**

Shifting the dripping basket more firmly against his hip, he raised his right hand to resettle his palm-weave hat, jam it lower on his forehead. Wind was picking up, his leg and side distinctly chilly as the moisture trickled from the rock crawdiddies. Other than that—good luck today—enough diddies to steam for dinner tonight and enough to sell for a tidy profit. Too late to make town now, not with the weather so two-faced, come-hithering boats and skimmers with a sunny smile, only to storm-fang them later if they took her for granted. Why risk it? The diddies would overnight in his holding tank. Seaweed-steamed or skewer-broiled? His tongue sliding across his lips, he debated, belatedly tasting the salt spray riming his face and beard with its dried granules.

The sudden, percussive barking sent his shoulders hunching earward, unable to muffle the clamor. Damn! Hirby's mangy Tigger dog, a meddlesome, noisome beast if ever there was one. Much as he hated relinquishing the easier going on hard-packed sand, he veered to the sea's fringes, let the water rise knee-high before trudging on. Dog had a nose on him, had to grant him that. Hm, sea was running harder than he'd supposed, dragging at him, making him fight for each step. Still, worth it. Mayhap something else would distract Tigger, Hirby, too, and he'd not have to tolerate man or beast. The turbid water slapped gray-green, shot with spiraling ribbons of brown sand, the current sucking harder than it should this late, tide not due in for a goodly bit. Greasy white foam lingered, scalloping the beach sand with dirty lacery. The back-drift was rough—imperious tugs—as if it knew what he'd plundered, wanted the diddies restored to their now-submerged outcrops where he'd waded at low tide.

"Yo!" Hirby came hustling and huffing across the beach, bare feet churning sand, the damn dog gamboling alongside, water-drenched and sand-spackled. As inevitable as death, the dog crashed to a halt and gave a mighty shake, for once too distant to do any damage. Too damn big for his taste, too damn big and far too little brain. Let anything move, and the dog chased it, pea-brained. Cannier than Hirby, though that wasn't a heaping peck of praise. A slow smile as he pondered freeing one of the diddies in the dog's path—nice, strong pincers aching to nip a warty snout. "Yo!" Hirby repeated as he came closer, "Pommy, boy! Glad yer headed in. Jes looket it out there!"

With grudging good grace Pommy fought the sea's cling, laboring to turn back the way he'd come, toward the headlands. Greedy, the wind grabbed for his hat yet again, and he reflexively jammed it in place. Despite himself, his jaw slacked; the whole horizon behind him had been transformed into a bruised yellow-gray expanse, weighty and oppressive. The sun had vanished—behind a cloud, he first thought, but no, whatever this was had vanquished it. Abruptly the wind stopped, the air turning thick and dead as he strove to fill his lungs, each breath an effort, nature suddenly stingy and rationing. Despite himself he staggered as the seas snatched harder at his shins, sucking away the sand beneath his submerged feet, the whole bottom shifting and churning.

Hirby waded in and grabbed his free arm, anchoring him as the wave retreated. The dog stayed on the dry sand, dancing and barking, challenging the sea to fight. "Best git ashore, make tracks." An almost visceral concern radiated from Hirby, his usually sunny, vague disposition sharpened by weather fear. Or weather wisdom. "Bad blow tonight, a widder-wowser!" A forearm shoving back lank hair the color of a greasy mouse, he gallantly guided Pommy beachward, skipping ahead of the water surging in again. Stone-wall stolid, yet trusting and playful as a lambkin— what sin, what crime had earned Hirby forced transport to the Sunderlies, Pommy couldn't fathom, and Hirby never outright said. Come to think on it, Hirby might have been Sunderlies-born—made more sense. Didn't harbor the warped, lunatic nature, that mental shadow that blighted whatever it fell upon. Tigger struck Pommy as a more likely candidate for deportation than Hirby.

"Sweet, powerful sweet pickins after a blow like this'un looks to be, Pommy." His face went dreamy-soft, unfocused, like a cloud-filtered Disciple moon. "Kin smell it in the wind." An expansive sniff, nostrils flaring, and his expanding chest threatened to further split his shirt rags. "Gotta be ready, *ready* to harvest the best pickins!" His drumming fist on Pommy's back reinforced his words. Then, a slow, sly peek at Pommy's woven basket. "Rock diddies? Kin hear'm clicker-clacking neath the seaweed."

"Yes, crawdiddies." Pommy kept staring out to sea, uncaring when the wind returned, ripping his hat from his head, sending Tigger after it in a chasing, snapping frenzy. Didn't matter, he didn't care. Yes, there *was* something in the air, something special. An ominous guarantee that this would surpass the average storm, more potent than any he'd ever experienced in his sixteen years here. Mayhap storms like this came once every double-eight, and the implications set off a febrile, answering energy within him, a bone-deep certitude that the flotsam and jetsam the sea would cast on his doorstep would deliver something special.

Something he'd never before experienced, something uniquely different. Something so rare that only someone who'd experienced, transcended the hells of hope and loss he had, could deserve or appreciate it. For a moment a profound sorrow for Hirby's lacks and wants overtook him—except that Hirby could never miss what he'd never had.

The wind whipped his hair, streamering it, whispering promises in his ears. He shook himself, forced himself back to the present, conscious how Hirby's lower lip drooped, his mournful brown eyes watery with longing as he stared at the basket. By the blessed Lady, what made the man so weak-willed? This was the Sunderlies; here you took from those weaker than yourself, fought to protect what was yours. No, he'd never match Hirby's brute strength, but cunning saved bruises and broken bones, protected as well or better than fists.

Oh, it played a smidge different in the towns, in Samranth—a veneer of civilization: Yes, Ma'ams and No, Sirs; sometimes you didn't even have to watch your back, just your wallet. But out here on the fringes of society, anything went—the stronger, the smarter, always prevailed. He never wanted to see a city again, the toxic thoughts that steeped and boiled, the hatreds that brewed. Even when you were right, had justice on your side, the poison set in, things had to be severed, cicatrices allowed to form. He knew it for a fact, scarred by loss from head to toe.

A drop of rain, then another and another began pelting down, stingingly cold. "Kin last two nights an a day, I reckon." Hirby shivered but tilted his face to the skies and the pounding rain, scrubbing his face and beard with both hands, gargling. "Not much chance finding food. Me, least I got a fresh loaf'n budder tucked tight'n dry. Bone for Tigger-wigger." A coy droop of eyelids to assess what effect his confidence had had on Pommy. "See my way clear ta share, I might." A gape-toothed grin plumped the flesh below his eyes. "But Tigger, not likely!"

Pommy laughed at the thought. Two nights and a day? Well, company, even Hirby's, might be welcome. But not in that half-cave, half-hovel clawed into the cliffside that Hirby called home. "So, Hirby? You think you'd relish a mess of steamed diddies?" The man's head bobbed, smile

beamish as the lighthouse-fort on Gander, his hair now
neatly slicked along his skull. For the first time Pommy
glimpsed a massive crescent scar sweeping from the center
of Hirby's hairline to his ear, like a melon smashed by
a rock. Mayhap that explained his problem, his changed
personality. "Then hustle, Hirby! Bring back that loaf and
butter. Can you keep them dry from your place to mine?"

Hirby churned up the dunes, his enthusiastic "yes" floating behind, stocky calves bunching as he plowed along.
Damn! He was a greater fool than Hirby! Hirby's company
also meant two nights and a day with Tigger—dear Tigger,
wet Tigger, demented Tigger! A silent prayer—please let
Hirby remember Tigger's bone!

With an exaggerated sigh meant to disguise a frisson of
fear, Jenneth settled herself more securely against the cabin
wall and levered Pw'eek onto her lap. Each time the *Vruchtensla* plunged and rolled, the chubby ghatten tumbled off.
*"It's all right, sweetheart, truly. This nasty storm just means
we'll reach the Sunderlies that much quicker."* Or so they
said, but she was growing dubious. Every falsely heartening
comment from the captain or a hard-pressed, hurrying
sailor held a subtle undertone, a residue of fear tangible to
any Resonant. Yes, Captain Thorsen had continually emphasized that this was the storm season, but even he
seemed cowed by this one's ferocious arrival out of
nowhere.

"Not scared," Pw'eek insisted, burying her head in Jenneth's midriff. **"Not with you here. Just** *hate* **this humpity-
dumpting-thumping. Wrong! Horrible!"** Her paws ceaselessly worked, but she'd never extruded her claws, even to
save herself from sliding off Jen's lap. **"First I was treed
atop that nasty stick and . . . and . . . when I looked down,
everything but me was swinging in circles, as if you all . . ."**
she swallowed hard, **"were running 'round and 'round. So
I squinched my eyes, sank my claws in, and sang my song—
the one you made up for me."**

"Poor, brave lamb," Jenneth traced a butterscotch patch
by Pw'eek's ear and gave thanks for Khim's good nature

in climbing up after the terrified ghatten. *"Really, truly, magnificently brave!"*

"Really?" A sharp rightward tilt and Jenneth automatically heaved Pw'eek's hindquarters back on her lap. **"And now we're bouncing in this thing's tum-tum, swallowed whole but still kicking."** The ghatten, Jenneth had discovered, possessed a more than vivid imagination. No wonder she was so daunted by her world!

When the storm had first hit earlier that evening, Jenneth had reveled in its power, the ship leaping wild and free across the waves, the wind bellying the sails, shrouds resonating a low, pure vibratory hum heard over the wind. But then the sky had occluded to a weird, jaundiced yellow mottled with purplish gray and constantly severed by jagged white veins of lightning. Then the rain had come, lashing hard enough to muffle the thunder.

At times the *Vruchtensla* almost thrashed through the seas as the skipper tacked, fighting against being blown off course. Even that was preferable to losing the leeward wind, heeling over, for some badly-ballasted ships never righted themselves. The storm and winds proved fickle in addition to their pounding strength, the ship constantly re-trimmed, sailors clinging to the masts and yards, repairing rigging, fighting to furl some sails, raise others. Her father had asked to help, but Captain Thorsen had banished them all belowdecks, tautly civil in his thanks but relieved to have the landlubbers safely stowed away.

Shivering, she wondered anew how the sailors fared abovedecks, if they'd won their battle against sea and storm or if they'd deadlocked? All she could do was sit here, worry with the rest, crammed together more for consolation than from necessity. One cabin held those who'd lost the battle with their stomachs—Harry and her father, Lindy and Theo this time—while the rest gathered here, softly conversing, playing cards to distract them from the disheartening lack of news, involuntarily flinching at each new straining sound that might presage the ship's sundering.

Despite warnings to not stir, Byrlyn jittered from person to person, staggering with the ship's movements, falling once, the floor rising to meet her before she could fall the full distance. Finally, to Jenneth's relief, Byrlie locked her

arms around Bard's neck, contentedly draped along his
back like a cloak, momentarily happy while Bard dealt
cards to Uncle Arras and Holly.

Poised and ready, Kwee waited for a momentary lull between rocking shifts before dashing to her sib. **"Whee!"**
she announced and crashed into Pw'eek, landing athwart
her. His timing off, Diccon followed at an even more pre-
cipitate pace, glancing off the bulkhead, only to land atop
Jen, both ghatten crushed between them.

It hurt—more than she wanted to acknowledge—her
breath smashed from her lungs, the sensation of not being
able to breathe. Alive and, worst of all, knowing full well
how far below the waterline their cabins were situated. For
a moment everything swam black before her eyes, then
blessed relief came as the ship pitched the other way and
Diccon threw himself clear.

"Phew! Sorry 'bout that! Thanks for a soft landing." Diccon scrambled beside her, wedging himself shoulder-to-
shoulder, linking elbows. "I'm *sooo* bored!" Even in the
dim light his blue eyes sparked, ready for action. If that
proved unavailable, he'd gleefully settle for sibling deviltry.
How he'd avoided the seasickness that had felled the others
was beyond her.

Kwee licked Pw'eek's ears, down over slitted eyes, calming and soothing, her rasping tongue lulling. With exaggerated caution she slid along her sister's length, jamming her
nose beneath Pw'eek's tail and began an industrious cleaning. **"Stop that!"** Pw'eek's mindvoice screeched through
Jenneth, hot with indignation. **"I'll scrub there later!
Rude!"**

"Stinky!" And Kwee stuck her nose there again for
good measure.

"Rude, impudent ghatten!" A white paw snapped out,
thumping Kwee in the eye. A return swat and they threw
themselves at each other, Jen's lap their battlefield as they
tussled and belly-kicked, Kwee's ears flat, Pw'eek's tail
anger-fluffed. **"Always bossing, always pushing, whacking
me, planting naughty, nasty, rude nose where it doesn't—"**
Without waiting for a further exchange, Jen dove into the
mass of seething, flying fur, confident Diccon would haul
at whichever legs or tails presented themselves.

"Enough! Both of you!" Heaving Pw'eek's rear end over

her shoulder, she rapped the ghatten's nose. Diccon, muttering about fresh scratches, pressed Kwee beneath his knee, lightly shaking her by the scruff of her neck. A sense of humiliation flooded Jenneth at having the other ghatti witness such unruliness.

"Now behave!" Somehow she half-blamed Diccon for this, Kwee his surrogate, misbehaving a fraction sooner than Dic. Well then, only just that he pay a price for his responsibility—and her lips parted in a devious smile. "I'll see what chance we have of dinner, if you like. The cook fire's been dowsed, so it'll probably be salt pork. But don't worry," she continued, remorselessly warming to her task, "you'll barely notice how the green glistens, almost iridescent, on the red streaks nestled in that nice, fatty white. The bread'll hide them."

Diccon groaned, clutched his stomach. "Jen! Don't! Even hearing about food makes me want to be sick all over again! All right, I encouraged Kwee's mischief. I'm sorry!" So, Diccon'd gained his sea-legs, but hadn't quite mastered his sea-stomach, just as she'd suspected! "Can't even play cards. The pips frolic all over the pasteboard. Then everything starts to spin."

Patting his knee in mock concern, she shared a fleeting smile with her mother, amused and aware what Jenneth was up to to restrain Diccon. But she relented despite herself, "When that happens, concentrate on something that can't move."

"What the hells would that be? There's no horizon down here to stare at." As if to prove his point, a domed leather trunk shucked its lashings and shot across the floor as if greased. Jumping up after it, Arras slammed his head on an underdeck beam, cursing as he recaptured the trunk.

For an interminable moment their world stilled, precariously poised for they knew not what. Instinctively Jenneth clutched Diccon and Pw'eek as the ship lurched into a sickening downward dive, smiting the sea's surface with a sound like a giant open hand against bare flesh. As they guardedly righted themselves, Jenneth caught an oddly triumphant exhilaration enlivening Byrlie's normally somber face, but as quickly as it had appeared, it vanished, composure settling in its place.

Wearily untangling herself, waiting for the next wave,

Jenneth felt Diccon's fear mirroring her own, but more liable to surface, shame him. When no second monster wave savaged the ship, she sought a distraction. "The lamp," weaving her fingers with his, she still kept an eye on Byrlie, curious if she'd be transfigured yet again. "Watch the lamp, Dic, it's stable." The captain had allotted them one oil lamp with strict instructions not to light others, nor to let this one break, start a fire. Below it sat a lidded bucket of sand to smother the flames, if necessary.

Two brass rings, one horizontal, the other vertical, encircled the lamp and sealed oil reservoir, the sphere coupled to a ball-and-socket joint with a wall-mounted base. Strange as the contraption was, it allowed the lamp to tilt and right itself, its flame staying upright even during severe rolls and dips. Although everything around it might shift, the lamp always seemed to know which end was up. A gimbal, that's what the captain had called it.

"Too bad I can't swallow a gimbal, make my stomach self-righting!" Lightly thumping their entwined hands against his thigh, Diccon drew a shaky breath, nestled his head on Jenneth's shoulder. "If I sleep, I won't have to watch everything move. Be my pillow?" Snuggling, he fell sweetly asleep, still possessed of the childish ability to drop off at a moment's notice.

How could he be so resilient, so self-confident? She gave a wry shrug, careful not to dislodge Diccon. Well, in truth, he'd been too busy vomiting the first few days to sleep much. He needed to catch up, she decided, mustering all the charity she could. One of twinship's nicer traits was having someone ever ready to make allowances for the other's frailties. Diccon did for her; she was honor bound to do the same.

But no matter how hard she tried to relax and sleep, she couldn't, though everyone else seemed to have fallen into a doze or a restless sleep. Mayhap the rocking had lulled them to dreamland, even if it had left her wide awake. Slumber would make the time, the storm, pass more quickly, but her body and mind were too alert. Besides, someone should stay awake, on guard.

What was the point? Could she stop the storm from worsening, the ship from sinking? Hardly. And if the worst—the unthinkable worst—should strike, the sailors

would warn them. Wouldn't they? Reluctantly closing her
eyes, she strove to match Diccon's even breathing, her free
hand seeking the solace of the ghatten's fur. *"My very own,
my precious Pw'eek."* A ragged purr rumbled and steadied,
only to wispily fade as the ghatten sank into sleep. Nothing
bad could happen to her with Pw'eek beside her, not to
mention Diccon and Kwee—could it?

Eyes snapping open—uncertain how long, even *if* she'd
truly slept—Jenneth tensed, some subtle difference gnawing
at the bounds of her awareness. But what? She gingerly
stretched her legs, still burdened by the ghatten's limp
form, and surveyed her surroundings, alert for any change.
Diccon now burrowed against her chest, blissfully asleep,
grunting little snorts issuing from him. So that was what
Byrlie had meant by "snorning." *"Dic, roll off. You're
mashing me."* His closeness—usually such a comfort—was
constricting, destroying her concentration.

Muttering, he shifted as she elbowed his ribs. *"Sor-ry, so
com . . . fy . . ."* he apologized and was lost to sleep again,
Kwee indignantly rearranging herself across him. The storm
sounded no worse than before, the creaking protest of tim-
bers, occasionally as sharp as a cracked knuckle, the
shrouds' low-pitched thrum, but something felt different.
They weren't wallowing as badly, the sideways roll nearly
gone, though they still pitched, and she could sense its pattern, anticipate the next rise or dip. The gale-force winds
chased the *Vruchtensla* ahead, the ship driving forward,
running before the storm. She could make out her mother's
sleep-slack face, the white on Khar's muzzle. Arras, Bard,
Holly, Honoria, and Davvy—she could account for them
all.

A blast of fresher, sharper air raised goose bumps, ruffling her hair like a ghostly exhalation on the back of her
neck. But the cabin door stood securely closed by the time
she could check. She looked around more closely. No one
in, no one out, so it couldn't have been the door. Still,
one niggling puzzle piece had strayed. Byrlyn? Where was
Byrlie? Not snugged against Uncle Bard? Had she slipped
out to join her mother? Even though the cabin was next

door, the child could lose her balance, roll down the long passageway like a ball when the ship pitched again.

"Pw'eek, love, wake up! I need you!" With clammy hands she boosted the ghatten onto her feet, her gray-butterscotch face screwed up in groggy bewilderment, Jenneth's plea dousing her dreams like a bucket of ice water.

"What? Trouble? Pw'eek fight! Jenneth safe with Pw'eek here—slash them, bite them! Oh, dear!" Again her tail puffed twice its size with fear-pride, a warning flag of her readiness to do battle—or scramble for cover, terrified out of her wits.

"Byrlie's not here. Just gone next door—I hope. But something tells me she plans to slip on deck, watch the waves." Mayhap she was wrong, borrowing trouble by the bushel, but Byrlie's earlier, unguarded exhilaration had burned itself in her brain. She knew that look—for her, it was fire; for Byrlie, the action of the waves, as if the child must witness such power firsthand, revel in what she, as a child, could never possess.

Rolling to her knees, Jenneth started to rise, but the ship's renewed roll convinced her to stay down, crawl toward the door. Undignified but faster and quieter than bouncing round the cabin. Reassuringly solid, Pw'eek anxiously pressed beside her as she scurried on hands and knees.

At her touch the door swung outward, obviously unlatched, as the ship tilted, tossing Jenneth into the corridor, tumbling the ghatten after her. The sea- and rain-scented air pouring down the open hatch made her inhale greedily. After the cabin's stuffiness, even the damp and saturating spray felt invigorating. As the ship wallowed upward and the door swung shut, Jenneth desperately gripped its edge so that it wouldn't slam, despite her pinched knuckles.

"Wake Kwee? Wake Diccon?" Pw'eek's eyes, so sure in the dark, inspected the passageway. **"Other door didn't open, didn't close. Ghatten-child not in there."** A sniff here, a questing sniff there further reinforced her point as she belly-slunk toward the companionway leading to the main deck. **"Ghatten-child outside. Need others to help? Kwee good nosy-poker, always poking where she shouldn't!"**

Obviously the provoking incident with her sib still ran-

kled Pw'eek, made Jenneth wonder if she'd ever forgive or
forget. Well, not that *she* shared similarities with the ghatten. After all, *she* magnanimously forgave Diccon any number of things—

"And stacky-store twin-sib's naughties in your memory!"
Pw'eek finished for her.

She cast a quelling look at Pw'eek, but she refused to
back down. So this was what it felt like to face the truth!
No time, though, to argue the fine points, not with Byrlie
on deck somewhere. *"No, don't wake anyone yet. Let's see
if we can't find her. Otherwise we'll give Diccon a golden
opportunity to store up one of* my *shortcomings!"* With a
lurch toward the narrow steps, Jenneth grabbed hold and
steadied herself. Steps? Ladder was nearer the mark! *"No
sense upsetting everyone till we have to."* Muttering words
she'd be caned for if her parents heard, she negotiated the
steps, boot soles slick against the wet wood. Pw'eek waited,
then scooted ahead, claws scarring the worn treads.

Stinging rain and spray pelted her as she emerged,
clothes and hair sodden between one breath and the next.
Sometimes the deck stayed where it belonged, other times
it shot up to meet her descending foot, or coyly stretched
the distance. Pw'eek hissed as water swept along the planking, then receded in a rush. Forearm to brow to block the
driving rain, Jenneth circled in place, desperate to spot Byrlyn. What she *did* see stunned her: the deck barren, loose
objects swept away, even some articles habitually lashed in
place had vanished. Shreds of sails, rigging with frayed or
snapped ends, a spar tip swinging pendulously from a
shroud line all hovered intrusively over this empty vista.
The desolation, the casual destructive force made her shiver
at its power. Poor *Vruchtensla*, Captain Thorsen's pride
and joy!

"Byrlie!" She screamed the name with all her might,
"Byrlie! Where are you?" The wind tore her words, tossed
them overboard. A sheltered lamp aft by the compass box
cast a faint nimbus over the forms of two men struggling
with the ship's wheel. A rending, snapping noise, and the
wheel spun wildly, throwing the men onto the deck.
Hunched low and scuttling like a beetle, a sailor dashed
by, pulling himself hand over hand along a lifeline.

Somehow scrambling to a stop, he turned back to her,

soaking hair plastered to his forehead. "Git below, child! Afore ye be swept off yer feet!" At least she thought that was what he bellowed, his mouth a dark cavern in his pinched, white face, his neck cords straining to punch his words through the wind. An emphatic arm gesture at the hatch, indicating she should retreat.

Faltering, his terror more infectious than her own, she took a tentative step toward the hatch until guilt made her bend low, fight her way back, almost clawing at the deck. "Have you seen the little girl? She's on deck somewhere!" But he shrugged and again pointed to the hatchway. When she shook her head, he tossed an arm heavenward to abdicate any responsibility, put his burden in the Lady's hands, and continued pulling himself aft.

Drenched and rat-sleek, Pw'eek scurried forward, determination in each hasty step. A shaft of stabbing light, a rumbling clamor rolling across the sea, momentarily obliterated the wind and the shrouds' anguished thrumming. Half-blinded by the brilliance, Jenneth faltered, blinking as another bolt of lightning shattered the pitch-black sky, striking the foremast with a cracking explosion. The shuddering vibrations seemed to rise through the soles of her feet, tingling up her legs, and Pw'eek's rowl of terror told her the ghatten experienced the same sensation. The mast splintered, yards and cordage snapping free, furled sails falling like shrouded dead men as debris rained down.

"I see! I see her!" Pw'eek's mindvoice jittered. **"Over there!"** and the ghatten began climbing over tangled canvas and cordage, Jenneth trailing after her as fast as she could.

"Byrlie!" A hint of pale hands and face as the child huddled by the starboard bulwarks, just ahead of the foremast, holding on to a rib support for dear life. A soundless shout turned the small mouth into a dark "O," her arm waving, pointing, but Jenneth couldn't spare time to heed Byrlie; not with the ship's prow pointing at the skies, prepared to begin yet another stomach-heaving slide from peak to trough before fighting its way back up again. If she could reach Byrlie before everything jarred loose—otherwise they'd rattle across the deck like dried peas.

But now Pw'eek had turned tail, bounding past her as she screamed **"Back! Back!"** Risking a glance ahead, she went numb at the nightmarish dark bulk sweeping down

on her like a giant bird of prey. A crack of a stayline like
the snap of a whip, and a length of spar, near as long as
she stood tall, dragging a sodden mass of canvas in its wake,
wrapped Jenneth in its smothering embrace and arched her
over the ship's side. Screaming her wrath, ready to rend
and kill, Pw'eek sprang in attack, lashing her claws at the
canvas flying past, and sailed overboard with her Bond. . . .

"Jennie? Jennie? Pw'eekie?" Fingers clenched, toes dug
in, Byrlyn hung limpet-tight as the wave streamed from
stem to stern, surging over her. Gasping, sputtering as the
water drained clear, she screamed again, "Jennie!" sounding like a lonely, piping seabird. The sailors were too far
to reach, too distant to hear her cries, and the child curled
into a ball, sobbing. Her dear Jen—overboard! Pw'eek, too!
Oh, how Auntie Doyce would hurt! Diccon, too! And she
was too small, too insignificant to help, do anything to save
her beloved Jennie. Small fists beat upon the planking until
blood ran from split knuckles.

Sucking at her bruises, she thought as hard as she could.
The one idea revolving through her brain was unpleasant—
but necessary. Papa? Papa could do anything, Papa would
help! Papa loved Jenneth almost as much as he loved her.
And for all the times that she'd yearned, fervently prayed
to be seen as herself, not as a miniature version of Papa's
beloved Byrta, she put her qualms aside, throwing every
scintilla of her being into her cry from the heart—her cry
from the mind. *"PAPA! Help me, help Jenneth! Oh,
please!"* He *would* hear, he'd *have* to hear, and he'd rescue
them, that's what Papas were for, to keep their dear ones
safe.

His dream of Byrta fragmented like a shattered mirror, and
she was gone again—such irony, a mirror! All he had to
do was look into a mirror, squint his eyes, to see Byrta,
see himself, the two shapes overlapping, solidifying into
one. One, alone, always alone now. Without knowing how
or why, Bard found himself on his feet, his heel sliding on
a discarded playing card, tripping over weary bodies. If he
hurried, he could catch her this time! An especially vicious

roll slammed him into a bulkhead. He had *heard* her! He and Byrta reunited in their minds—at last! Except . . .

Resting his bruised forehead against the cabin wall, he dug at his eyes, forcing himself to think, hear the voice yet again. A tremor leached the strength from his legs as he listened harder, certain this time: *Byrlyn* had called him, Byrlyn *needed* him, the barrier between them had torn, she'd fought her way through, a champion just like her aunt! He met M'wa's lingering gaze, exultation evaporating in reality's harsh glare.

"Baby, where are you?" Out the door, down the corridor, a hand on each wall to steady himself, he gained the companionway, unable to sense the direction of her mindvoice. *"Byrlyn, where are you? Are you all right? Papa's coming. What's wrong, bunny?"*

"Jennie and the ghatten—overboard!" Even through her mindvoice he could sense how this effort had drained her, her teeth chattering with fear, with cold, limbs trembling with fatigue. Heard her sudden intake of breath, his own fingers cramping tight as another wave began to wash across the deck, rushing at her. Bound to her feelings and emotions, his own pain caught him off-guard as a shoulder rammed his spine, letting loose a guttural growl as he was thrust aside, shoved clear of the stairs.

Doyce had overtaken him, scrambling up the steps, a heel grazing his shoulder, Diccon hot behind her, his face a set mask of pain. Before Bard could gather his wits, Kwee swarmed up him, launching herself from his shoulder to gain the hatch, while Khar seamlessly flowed up the steps between pounding feet. M'wa, breathless from dodging, darted past as well. **"Stop looking dumbstruck and hurry! Rawn and Jenret just got word. If you want to reach Byrlie, hurry or be trampled!"**

Sage advice, for now everyone belowdecks crammed the passageway, he could see Lindy, ghost-pale with dread—wondered who'd told her—tucked in the sheltering curve of Davvy McNaught's arm. *"I'm coming, Byrlyn!"* he cried again and took the stairs two at a time. Of course—Jenneth must have 'spoken her twin, her parents, as she went over the side.

But just as his head cleared the hatch, he saw a sight that made him retreat at speed, hands sliding down the

side-rails so fast his palms burned. M'wa rode him down,
clinging to his shoulder, springing clear as soon as he could.
Doubled over in a ball, Diccon came flying fanny-first
straight at Bard, as if he'd been bowled down an alley and
Bard was the scoring pin.

Reaching for Diccon, desperate to break his fall, Bard
found himself tumbling backward as Diccon's posterior
slammed his chest. A thud as Diccon's head grazed the
hatch's lip. Doyce must have shoved him with incredible
strength, must have had some logical reason, he told himself, the wind knocked out of him, panic spreading as the
darkness turned deeper, more confining and suffocating.
Like a giant laundry basket overturned, canvas spilled
down the hatch, wet and heavy, folds of it slithering down
to flood the companionway.

An arm 'round Diccon's chest, the other capturing a leg,
he struggled to his knees, passed the boy to other willing
hands. Again he began to climb, burying his face in the
heavy, rough canvas as he fought at it with hands and
shoulders, put his back and legs into the effort, a red rage
burning the peripheries of his vision at his impotence.
Something pinned it, finally ripping through the canvas like
a spear to gouge the lower deck. Arras now wedged himself
beside him on the narrow steps, shoulder to shoulder, as
they both grappled with the spar, trying to heave it up and
out. "It's jammed!" Arras grunted in his ear, but they both
gave one final heave, hoping against hope.

"The aft hatchway!" M'wa had already covered half the
distance. **"Some falling debris struck Doyce! She's entangled in the downed rigging and canvas. Out cold—
according to Khar."**

Those who understood ghatti mindspeech instantly reversed themselves, thundering back down the passageway,
Holly and P'roul in the lead. Bard ached to overtake her,
push her aside and be first out. A minor twinge at having
shouldered Jenret aside, slamming Honoria against the
wall, but they'd impeded him. Byrlie! His Byrlie still lingered out there, needing him, wanting him!

Conflicts warred within him, a dull, burning hatred at the
need to make prudent choices, rational decisions. Fine—
first he'd find Byrlyn, make sure she was safe, then Doyce.

They could be saved. But what could he possibly do for Jenneth?

"Did Jenneth truly go overboard?" Mayhap Byrlie had been frightened, had misinterpreted what she'd seen. For all he knew, Jenneth might have lodged in the scuppers, Byrlie convinced she'd been swept to sea. M'wa would know—always so calm and restrained—would have made order out of chaos. He'd have 'spoken Khar, even Jenneth's new Bondmate, and sorted out the details. His own rage would fade, he'd reassert his self-control. . . .

"Pw'eek was swept away as well. Khar can't sense them anywhere on deck, only . . ." M'wa hesitated, then pressed on, **"beyond. Out among the waves somewhere."**

Now his fingers ached for the captain's throat, wanting to throttle him until he hauled the *Vruchtensla* round, sailed back to rescue Jenneth, pluck her and the ghatten from the devouring seas! But there was no way to halt the ship; landlubber though he might be, even Bard recognized that. Not in the teeth of a storm. A ship couldn't halt like a horse obedient to the reins. With this mother of all storms, they stood no chance at all! *Oh, Blessed Lady, help Your lost ones,* he prayed inwardly. *Don't let the sea swallow them without a trace. I'd forfeit my right arm for Byrlie's safety, my left for Jenneth's. Save them, Blessed Lady!*

It hit him like a bolt, piercing both heart and soul—weak-kneed whining! Begging for something without having given his level-best first. Had he turned tame, docile, so like everyone in Canderis that he now prayed to their mealy-mouthed, sanctimonious Lady? *Oh, yes,* he mimicked to himself, *there's a reason for your anguish, but I cannot explain it to you poor mortals. I am beyond, above all that. But take comfort in knowing you can change your next life for the better.*

Well, he'd pray to whichever gods honored a fairly-struck bargain, even Harharta! He was closer to the Sunderlies, *was* of the Sunderlies, where more ancient, puissant gods expected to be propitiated, honored mortal-god contracts. *A suitable sacrifice—my blood, my life, for Jenneth's! Let her be found, safe. I promise, on my honor.* A murmurous, murderous approbation, the savage joy of distant deities, resounded in his head as he began to scout the decks for his daughter.

Critically inspecting his carved nglonka-wood pipe, Mvelase
tamped the tobacco with a thumb and extended his free
hand, waiting for Dlamini to pass the coal tongs. Expecting
the attentiveness due his age, he shook his head at such
misfortune, his hand remaining empty, his pipe unlit.

"Dlamini!" Swinging his staff in a low curve, he allowed
its horns to prick the lad, the boy nearly levitating, at last
tearing his eyes from the lithesome Kaaseme and the
equally beauteous, round-rumped heifer she so lovingly
curried by the thorn kraal.

"To my sorrow and shame, Uma-Uncle, I've ignored
you." Dlamini fumbled for a coal, finally taking Mvelase's
pipe and reverently lighting it for him, puffing until it
burned evenly. "I've been admiring the heifer, hoping she'd
be one of your choices." Dlamini's features may have been
obscured by falling shadows, but Mvelase recognized his
tone of infatuation too well.

"And which heifer would that be? The two-legged or the
four-legged one?"

To his credit Dlamini chuckled, unembarrassed. "I admire my little cousin, but I admire my cousin's father's herd
even more."

"We shall see," and Mvelase allowed that phrase to
cover a multitude of possibilities. Instead, he leaned back in
his molded leather backrest and sucked at his pipe, Dlamini
settling at his side on the ground, arms wrapped around his
knees and staring at the fire, truly pleased with life. What
he was going to do with the boy, he didn't know—clever,
industrious, but somehow soft, too guileless for all his
twenty-some summers. This long trip had been meant to
temper the lad, make him the man he was destined to be,
not extend his childhood. After all, how many of his other
grand-nephews and great-grandnephews had clamored to
come on this trip?

Rumor had it that Cousin Mbewanga's clan had bred a
superior strain of cattle, stockier, more heavily-muscled
than their own lean, hard herds, but equally tough, resistant
to drought, willing to wander wide for good grazing. Since
Mvelase enjoyed roaming in the old ways of his people,
now less and less nomadic as time passed, he'd offered to

inspect these beasts, decide if clan funds should be invested.

Close to an octant afoot—the addition of a new moon in the sky—it had taken him and Dlamini to reach this little village nestled between the Big and Little Mbujki Rivers. Southeast across the Naukkilari Plains and its succulent, lush green grass, visiting various clans camped at shade-dappled watering spots, young men and boys with their horned staves always on watch for predators. Then through the Uulbora Mountains' middle pass till they struck the birth of the Little Mbujki, cascading waterfalls roaring in delight at running free, unaware it was the junior of two rivers. Ah, how his heart had lifted at witnessing such stirring sights again!

Cousin Mbewanga's cattle *were* handsome, had potential—less than he'd hoped, but more than he'd expected. During his years of wandering, many things in life had matched that description.

"Well, boy. How many do we take—if Cousin Mbewanga doesn't set his price too high on spying your eager face?"

"That's easy, Uma-Uncle!" Throwing the shawl end of his loincloth over his left shoulder where it belonged on a full-grown man, Dlamini set a pebble in place to indicate each choice. "One young bull, no more than three summers old, but proven at stud. Three heifers; eight cows, established breeders." He looked modestly pleased with himself.

"One bull, Dlamini?" Could he shake the lad's confidence? "Just *one*? What if it should break a leg, die on the trip home? Even if it thrives and prospers, sires many calves, do we know whether he'll pass on his breed's best or his worst traits? Those too-short horns, for instance."

"Such things *do* happen, Uma-Uncle." As if he'd lived through a host of trying times, his nephew nodded sagely, and Mvelase considered another jab with his staff to deflate the boy. But Dlamini turned long-lashed, gold-brown eyes on him—so like his youngest sister's daughter, Dlamini's mother—and took his ankle in hand, politely offering it to Mvelase. "You wish to pull it? Yes?

"One young bull for stud, both with the new heifers and mated to some of our best cows—I would check the herd-book first. But each of the eight cows purchased must be with calf, sired by many different bulls. Oh, not all the calves will be male, but very likely some will—consider the odds, Uma-Uncle. *That* will give us more bloodlines to breed." Folding his leg back under him with a grin, Dlamini confidently changed the subject. "Now tell me more about your sister, Lesedi."

Deciding his nephew had earned it, Mvelase complied, losing himself in his memories, pleased someone cared to listen. Ah, Lesedi, his eldest sister! Kwekwenga'd been a lucky man to take her to wife, have her barter for two more bride-wives so they'd immediately have clan enough to strike out with their own herd. But who would *ever* have believed they'd march their herd in stages across the plains, over the peaks, and down to the very edge of the sea, to Samranth—take passage in a huge, canvas-winged, wooden basin sailing the seas to Canderis! Ah, his pretty Lesedi had itched with an even worse wanderlust than his own! No more than nine summers he'd been when Lesedi and the others had journeyed to the ends of the world, but still he remembered it as if it were yesterday!

Occasionally word drifted back, relayed by strangers to friend or kin. Kwekwenga and Lesedi had sent word to select suitable brides for two sons, had even picked one for the third before canceling the marriage-price. A shame to the entire clan for that, especially when all learned the youngest son had chosen his own bride without family approval—a Canderisian maiden. Twins from that peculiar breeding that their lineal records never recorded. A boy and girl, the girl now dead, he'd heard, for he always listened closely for word of Lesedi and her own wherever he roamed. True, he should have no truck with these off-shoots—after all, the Canderisian wife's brothers should help raise them—he knew that should it ever come to pass, he would succor the oddly named Bard, all for the love of Lesedi's memory.

A heavy wind picked up, soughing through the kraal, the cattle stamping and restless, dewlaps atremble as they shook their heads, unable to spy what disturbed them. The roof thatch on Mbewanga's whitewashed mud-brick house and handsome outbuildings rustled and complained. "Storm. Blowing from the sea. Feel it?" Holding up a hand, Mvelase tested the wind on both front and back, uneasiness welling within him. "A harsh one, very strong."

"Someday I will see the sea," Dlamini mused, all dreamy-eyed. Fast as a finger-snap, the sky went dirty yellow like the Plains after a drought, and large raindrops began falling. Believing it wise to take shelter, Mvelase sprang up, retrieving his staff and planting it firmly, its paired horns pointing skyward.

It started then, a tingling within the staff that escalated into a galvanic throb, the paired horns on top etched by a glowing, bloody light, pulsing ever brighter, until Mvelase feared the staff had been lightning-struck. Harsh laughter boomed its doom in his ears, the wind screaming like a hysterical hyena. Ashiver with an uncontrollable sanguinary lust, Mvelase balefully fortified himself to rend and kill, even unto his precious Dlamini when seen through this red-hazed fury! Harharta! Who had thrown his own being aside and called on Harharta, God of vengeance, for aid?

"No!" he cried out, dropping to his knees, clutching the staff to his chest, a slim shield, but all he had for protection. "No! You cannot bargain with a mortal, Harharta, not with someone whose blood recalls but half our ways!"

"Uncle! Uma-Uncle! Art thou ill?" Dlamini's youthful, blood-free hands clasped his arm, and Mvelase fled from his trance, keeling forward on his staff until his forehead touched the ground in prayer. Kneeling at his side, Dlamini sheltered him with his body from the pouring rain. "Uma-Uncle, speak to me! What is it? What did you see?"

"Death," he answered heavily. "The death of one I've never met—yet love, despite his pact for power." Using Dlamini as a crutch, he dragged himself to his feet, the rain turning his ocher loincloth the color of washed-out blood. "We must go. We have a charge of greater import than mere cattle."

"But where are we going, Uma-Uncle?"

"That is the question. And that Harharta did not reveal." Dlamini's eyes went wide with awe. "But since he comes from across the sea, we shall try Samranth first. Mayhap word of him has reached there. His beginning here is not his end, for Harharta will honor his pact." Pressing a finger to Dlamini's lips, he quelled his questions. "My grand-nephew, Bard Ambwasali. Your cousin comes home at last, Dlamini."

Cold! The water was *so* cold—and harshly unforgiving.
Never before had she thought of water in such terms, but
the drenching reality slammed her, buffeting the spar, eager
to pluck her free and consign her to its depths. Hang on,
clasp the spar tight as a fervent lover, refuse to surrender
it. Some waves she had warning of, others crept up on her,
avalanching down like boulders. Just hang on. . . . But at
length the sea tired of its most recent diversion, calming by
imperceptible degrees, though in her battered mind the
waves still loomed implacably high.

Jenneth shook her head, tried to think. Salt burned her
eyes and nose and throat, left it raw and ragingly thirsty,
while her limbs felt leaden, ready to draw her deeper into
the bottomless seas. Clothes, yes, clothes. Her pantaloons
and boots, shirt and vest weighed her down, dragged at her.

It took effort, more than she'd bargained for, but she
kicked, rammed the toe of one boot into the cuff of the
other, gasping as she eased the soaked leather, tight as a
second skin, down her ankle. Kick! Kick again, kick
harder—rest. Worry at it, pry with her other foot. Damn,
her foot'd stuck halfway, the boot's vamp flapping limply.
Intent on her goal, she didn't notice the wave stealing up
on her, got slapped by hectoliters of water for her pains.
Cough, sputter, kick again. Yes! A languid, slipping sensation as boot and foot parted company. Now the other one,
easier but still effortful. Rest, rest! The boots were all she
could muster strength to shed. Well, she wasn't going anywhere special, was she? Or rather, she was . . . she just
couldn't tell where. . . .

Desolate and drenched, Pw'eek crouched at the spar's
shattered tip to allow Jenneth as much space as possible.
Gingerly she claw-tested a damaged segment, a partial fracture held together by long, splintery wood fibers that flexed
and twisted like a joint. Those straining fibers and a short
length of rigging bound her segment to Jenneth's larger
one. Painstakingly easing along, she stretched her neck,
touched her nose pad—half-nutmeg, half-gray—to Jenneth's closed eyelid, began licking. A hateful taste and texture, but she knew how the salty buildup stung her own
eyes, how it stung her Bondmate's. This, this at least she

could do. Jenneth twitched in her sleep, hugged the spar tighter, a flutter of eyelids as she whispered, "Pw'eek, my love!" and the ghatten feared her heart might shatter with joy at being loved.

Creeping backward to her segment, she dunked herself only once, clawing for dear life to regain her perch and huddle in weary misery. **"Sissy-Poo! Sissy-Poo? Where are you, Kwee?"** she pleaded at the night sky above, to the surrounding seas. Her sister's presence hovered somewhere, Pw'eek could sense her, but the presence teased, taunted, refusing to remain fixed. An ache of loneliness, her heart as empty as her stomach. and as if mocking her, her stomach rumbled. Never had she been separate from her sib for any length of time. Who would tell her what to do? Cajole her, bully her into doing it? Who'd be brave for both of them?

Still asleep, Jenneth extended a cramped arm, seeking a more comfortable position. Slowly, deliberately, Pw'eek matched her gesture, right paw reaching until her pads rested on the back of Jenneth's hand. **"I have Jenneth. Don't have Sissy-Poo, but I have Jenneth."** She stared at Jenneth's hand, her fingers. Strange how human hands could be so useful for some things and so worthless for others. **"Love Jenneth. Oh, beloved human!"**

Once, when she and Kwee were little—long ago, not so long ago?—they'd had a mother who spun them marvelous tales. An Elder always appeared in the stories, sometimes more than one. Puissant, sagacious, valiant ghatti with eyes that glowed like the stars and moons, and these vaunted Elders had left the ghatten starry-eyed as well with their exploits. According to their mother, the more a ghatta or ghatt grew, not just in size but in wisdom and courage, the higher she or he rose on the spirals, until someday, somehow, they, too, attained the stature of the Elders. A long, considering sigh—if only she knew what a spiral was! Kwee probably knew, but she'd been too shamed to ask. Kwee knew everything.

Still, whether or not she had a spiral, she had to try. Hadn't the ghatti in the tales 'spoken the Elders, asked their advice? **"Elders, hear me, please."** Staring skyward, she finally discerned pinpricks of light far above, hazed but visible. Was it clearing? **"Help me protect my beloved from harm. I am so small and scared . . ."** Uncomfortable reality struck; ghatti would not and could not lie, nor could she allow her fears to shade the truth. She would start over again.

"I am *not* small, I'm pudgy, because when I'm scared I eat and eat. I'm scared because I'm only a ghatten, and I have so much to learn. Help me, please! Help me be a good Bondmate. And ... and ... if you can, let my Kwee, my sweet Sissy-Poo find us soon!" On and on she went, expanding her story, anxious to explain, ensure no details were omitted.

Such relief in pouring out her heart's fears and hopes, describing how hard she always tried, but at length, exhaustion overwhelmed Pw'eek in mid-story, and she fell into a deep sleep without hearing the Elders' answers. . . .

"What are we going to do? What *can* we do?" Well, at least she hadn't wrung her hands while voicing such obvious questions, the ones already seared on every brain. Biting her lip to avoid blurting anything else, Lindy replaced the compress on Doyce's head. Not that Doyce would notice, still adrift in a drugged sleep, but it represented a constructive task, minor as it was.

"I think we can unleash her now." Davvy pitched his voice low as he began untying the straps that had secured Doyce in her bunk through the storm's finale. A shaved spot on Doyce's head and six neat black stitches—improbably neat, given that Davvy had sutured them during the ship's wave-tossed travails—indicated where the foremast had struck Doyce. What the blanket currently concealed was a giant hematoma running along her right leg from hip to knee. A snapped length of rigging with a massive iron block and tackle attached to one end had swung like a morning star, glancing off Doyce's leg and throwing her in the path of the toppling mast. So they assumed; Lindy couldn't see arguing over which had happened first, Doyce had still been injured.

Lindy wondered at the silence, still wanting to know what they planned to do. A rapid flash of the Lady's eight-point star with her hands; Lady bless that Byrlie hadn't gone overboard. By any logic she could muster, it *should* have been Byrlie, so casually tossed to the seas. Instead, Jenneth floated out there somewhere, her Jenneth, whom she'd loved and cherished since infancy, close as blood kin. Was it a sin to be thankful it wasn't Byrlie? No, she decided, that was natural; after all, she'd prayed the Lady take her in Jenneth's stead, just as she would have prayed to assume Byrlie's danger.

Still, who could marshal strength to think, let alone devise a coherent plan of action? Just remembering last night made her ache all over again, though she'd had an easier time than most. At first she'd sat with Doyce, reluctantly entrusting her to Harry's and Byrlie's ministrations to take her turn at the pumps. Anyone not belowdecks pumping was abovedeck hacking free fallen yards and rigging, draggling sails that left the *Vruchtensla* precariously tilted, vulnerable to foundering.

A hindrance on deck or aloft, they'd all been pressed into service on the pumps, fighting to save themselves before they could even consider rescuing Jenneth and Pw'eek. Backbreaking labor that drove all to a nether region beyond exhaustion's bounds where eyes stared blankly, backs rising and falling like pistons, hands curling like claws with blisters that popped and oozed, split and bled, an existence circumscribed by ceaseless pumping. And still—for an eternity—the water had risen ever higher, mocking their puny efforts. She'd been paired with Honoria, amazed at the tensile strength in the seemingly fragile body, and awed by her slight smile, a smile that became a grimace. Lady grant her serenity to match Honoria's!

Lindy sorely needed that serenity right now. Wouldn't *one* of them venture a suggestion, any suggestion? She knew too little of calamities of this magnitude, honestly didn't know where to start, what to do, but surely any Seeker, Arras Muscadeine, as well, must boast firsthand experience and skill! Finally, to her keen relief, Holly stirred, pushing herself upright by dint of using the wall as a brace, and shoved her tawny mop clear of her face. Overnight she'd shed kilos of weight, unflagging on the pumps.

"We should reach port morning after next—mayhap tomorrow afternoon, if we're lucky. Captain says we're off course and limping along." Hoarse shouts and pounding mallets assaulted their ears, the scent of hot pitch and oakum sharp in their nostrils as some sailors caulked, others hacking and hewing away damaged masts and rigging. "Lady forgive me for saying it, but till we reach Samranth, I don't see what we can do. How we could search for them, I mean." Unable to summon any further words, she made an openhanded gesture to indicate her lack and wearily slid back down the cabin wall, her head lolling.

"I take it we're operating under the assumption they're alive?" Arras rubbed sunken, raw-lidded eyes. "I hate to say it, but someone has to ask the obvious." Choking with anguish, Harry inarticulately slammed himself against his father, his fists pounded Arras's chest at the enormity of his betrayal.

"Of course they're alive!" Blue eyes feverishly brilliant against dead-white skin, stubble dark along his jawline, Jenret's look dared Arras to deny him hope. "Rawn and I'd have felt her death, Khar and Doyce, too—if she were conscious—and most of all," he whirled on his son, "Diccon would know! She's alive, *isn't* she, Diccon?" he appealed. "Tell them!" Could they have survived? Lindy wanted to believe with all her heart, unsure whether or not to be thankful she'd never foreseen this disaster.

Elbows pinning the map ends to stop them from curling, Diccon intently traced a line on the map with his finger, frowning. "'Course she is, Pw'eek, too. I *know* that, so does Kwee." He hung on his father's sleeve to bodily drag him toward the map, his burning eagerness clear to Lindy. "Now look, Papa, if we—"

But Bard and Theo spoke together, voices rising in agitation. "Can't the captain—" "If we sweep—" Their jumbled voices rose, drowning out each other, Bard's face reddening dangerously as Honoria interrupted.

"We can't afford a single side trip, a single detour!" Rising, she placed a hand on Jenret's arm, reclaiming it from Diccon. An obscure relief flowed through Lindy that Doyce didn't have to witness the gesture—compelling, absolutely; compassionate, mayhap. "Understand it and accept it— now! Captain Thorsen won't authorize it. The ship's severely damaged. He has all our lives to consider, plus his crew. We *have* to make Samranth first." A level, almost challenging stare around the room, and Lindy hated the treacherous cowardice that made her own eyes waver, refuse to challenge her. Serenity? Or cold, hard assurance that she—and only she—had the right of it?

"Reaching Samranth's to our advantage, Jenneth's as well. We have time to devise an exhaustive plan, mount search parties as soon as we land, rent boats to comb the inlets, check the beaches."

"But we have no idea where to look! The Sunderlies coastline is ragged as a beggar's coat! If we have to search each bay and inlet, sail around each point, the distance is at least three times longer than the land route from Samranth to Siemerink, the northmost township." Face-to-face with Honoria, Bard shouted as if volume alone could crack Honoria's calm demeanor. Lindy'd rarely seen Bard this passionate, this concerned, but she recognized the potential danger all too well. He'd almost snapped last night searching for Byrlie, and Jenneth's prolonged absence only exacerbated the tension still tight-wound within him. "The longer we leave them out there, the more likely they'll die of exposure!"

"But if we . . ." Although she heard and wanted to acknowledge Diccon's insistent voice, Lindy had more pressing matters at hand. Somehow she had to calm Bard before he exploded into one of his uncontrollable rages. Honoria was standing her ground, and neither looked prepared to yield. . . .

Damn! He'd been *convinced* he'd captured Lindy's attention—she'd *always* listen, hear him out when he was little, an ever-patient audience of one willing to listen to his grand schemes, applaud and encourage, point out pitfalls. "But if we . . ." Diccon shouted louder, praying his father—someone—would heed him. "Listen, Tuck says—" but still no one even looked his way, too caught up in the escalating argument between Honoria and Bard.

Despite his aching head, the spangles still dancing before his eyes when he blinked, he'd learned something *crucial*! Tears of frustration, fatigue, and pain filmed his eyes, made him realize how his mother must hurt if his own minor head bump had left him so wambly and disoriented. *No,* he wouldn't think about her—Mama would be fine—Davvy had said so. What he had to concentrate on now was Jenneth.

Days ago Tuck had shown him how the currents flowed in the Frisian Sea, where strong ones overtook weak ones, shifting from one course to another. The old sailor had spared precious time this morning, hammer pounding all the while, to explain what might have happened in a storm like the one they'd survived. How fast and far things tended to drift—and their most likely direction. And not a soul would listen to hard facts!

Kwee daubed at the map with her paw, looking more like a scruffy alley cat than her usual sleekly insouciant self. **"Oh, want my Sissy! Want your Sissy, too."**

"I know, love." He firmed his jaw, rolled up the map and slipped out. Who'd notice in this ruckus? How disillusioning when adults he loved couldn't make a simple decision to find Jen! A decision meant actively finding, saving Jen and Pw'eek, not merely deciding if and when to attempt it! *"Tonight? When it's dark?"*

"Yes, oh, yes! I can hear Sissy calling me. You, too?"

Contenting himself with a nod, Diccon worked his way on deck, searching for old Tuck again. Everyone teased him about being impetuous, but this wasn't a time to play the fool. So check and recheck, find out every possible detail about where he should mount his search. It wasn't a game; this was life and death, and the thought of Jenneth not existing, no longer a part of his life left him sick and empty. *"I'm coming, Jen! Just hang on, be brave. Kwee and I'll find you both. I'm coming!"* The thought of what he had to do daunted him, but not as much as losing his twin did. Jenneth would do it for him; could he do any less?

As dark as it would get tonight, now that the storm had passed, the Lady moon and her first Apostle hovering bright, their beams reflecting lustrous silver-gold crescents off the chop of the waves. Their light seemed to stretch on forever, a shimmering path beckoning him to travel it, wherever it might lead. Respite at the path's end might mean a watery death, but it would be beside his twin, his Jenneth. Somehow they'd drift together, like calling like.

Uncomfortable with such fancifully morbid thoughts, Diccon shivered, Kwee shivering beside him, similarly moved. *"Keep watch. 'Speak me if anyone comes."*

All pewter-and-silver shadows, the ghatten ghosted into place near the launch, creaking on its davits. Ducking aft, Diccon began consolidating his hastily gathered supplies, swinging them up into the launch, conscious of every noise. Silence was always easier said than done, especially when he rushed. And Jen would tease that that was most of the time, he thought ruefully. Luckily sailors still caulked below, their random pounding disguising any noise he made. *"What have I stowed so far?"* He hoped Kwee kept better track of things than he did; nothing would lodge in his mind, everything flitting in and out, restless as doves settling in their cote at dusk.

The ghatten began to obediently recite, **"Tin of biscuits, tin of cheese, tin of chocolate."** A head bob after each item and Diccon nodded back. **"Lucy-furs,"** she stumbled over the word and he smiled, 'speaking it correctly, *"Lucifers."* Damn! How lucifers reminded him of Jen! Well, they were sealed tight, as were the other supplies, against water damage, and he was proud he'd thought of that. He wouldn't need lucifers on the launch, but if they needed to start a signal fire after landing, he'd be ready. It struck him then that biscuits, cheese, and chocolate made an unlikely ghatti diet, but wasn't sure what else he could scavenge without being caught. 'Twasn't stealing, he'd told himself, stern and cold, but it was.

"Don't worry, Pw'eek eats most anything." Affection suffused Kwee's mindvoice, exploding into an audible purr. Given Pw'eek's girth, he suspected she was right. Now for the next load.

Good! No one had moved the small keg from where he'd hidden it earlier. Two smaller glazed pottery jugs were freshly filled with water as well. A blanket, another jacket and pantaloons—not exactly dry, but then nothing was—the comforting oilcloth cylinder that protected his precious map. In they went. Kwee stared meaningfully at him—or more accurately, at his pocket—and he slapped his hand there, slid it inside until his fingers confirmed the smooth metal and glass of the compass. *"Compass, check."*

The trick would be lowering the launch without the

scream and screech of its pulleys announcing his intentions to the world while he skulked around in his navy sweater and black pants, blending with the night. He'd slapped grease on the pulleys as often as possible each time he'd pretended to nonchalantly wander by, but he hadn't dared stop to work it in. No matter how he sliced it, lowering the launch wouldn't be easy for one person.

Pensively sucking his lip, he ran through his plan again, unhappy with this part of it, but unable to find another way. Start a task badly, and the whole thing would end badly—no, he'd not jinx himself like that. Better to have a person on each davit, simultaneously lowering it so it hung level. Alone, he'd have to play catch-up, lower first one end and then the other in stages. Wouldn't do to dump Kwee and their supplies into the sea. A deep breath and he spat on his hands. *"Best hop in now."* His cheeriness sounded forced. *"Keep watch from there."* Kwee sprang to his shoulder, then into the launch, eeling beneath the gap in the canvas covering and reversing until her head peeped out.

"Ugh! Water in here—sloshy!"

"Well, what did you expect after the storm?" Still, her news made him quickly hunt for some empty container suitable for bailing. Tin bucket in hand, he stood stock-still, reliving last night's frantic pumping, his aching head pounding in rhythm with each downward shove. Was it fair, right, to do this? Both the *Vruchtensla*'s long boats had been storm-damaged. Should anything else go wrong, he'd have stolen the one serviceable launch, dooming the others. On his head, then—so be it. This was for Jenneth and Pw'eek, and he couldn't bear imagining them out there so alone, afraid, the seas surrounding them, awaiting the right despairing moment to swallow them whole.

A high, startled squeak, and the launch's canvas violently dimpled as Kwee almost burst through it. Failing at that, she sling-shotted from beneath the canvas to the launch's bow, her back arched, tail fluffed. A broad black head with a white star popped from under the taut canvas, and Diccon found himself being outstared by M'wa. **"Can't find a decent nap place anymore, forever being interrupted."** The ghatt didn't look in the least as if he'd been napping, but rather as if he'd been patiently waiting for his unsuspecting prey to venture near. And where M'wa lurked, Diccon silently seethed, then surely—

A firm, familiar hand on Diccon's shoulder made him whirl, mouth open in a silent shout. He'd fight if he must— even Bard—because no one could stop him from going! "Think you'd get very far without these?" Bard indicated the two long oars casually tilted against his shoulder. Only then did Diccon notice the small, worn pack slung over his other shoulder, as well as the sword belt girding his waist. "For that matter, think M'wa and I'd let you get free and clear without us?"

"Or without me?" came another voice, and Diccon gulped at the choleric anger that momentarily overrode Bard's normally phlegmatic expression at hearing Davvy's voice. "And a few other essentials." Davvy exhibited a lantern and kicked at a folded square at his feet. "Signal light, a bit of sail, and," he indicated the waterproof rolled pouch at his waist, "my emergency medicament kit." Speechless at the turn things had taken and heartily glad that actions counted more than words, Diccon struggled to lift the canvas packet into the launch. Oof—heavier than it looked! "And more water," Davvy continued in his ear, setting his shoulder under the sail to help Diccon heave it aboard. "Most people misjudge how much water's necessary when you're in a boat all day, the sun baking you dry."

"Wouldn't need as much if fewer tagged along," Bard growled and closed the distance to fiercely whisper at Davvy. Stepping clear of their wrath, Diccon winced as their hissed sibilances slashed like swords, forcing him to consciously admit something he'd resolutely refused to think about: Bard did *not* like Davvy—at least, not anymore. Whether Davvy returned the antipathy, he wasn't sure, wondered what Jen would say. Everyone said Bard and Davvy had been close when Davvy'd been younger, a child—even Davvy'd told him so many a time, had seemingly admired Bard fully as much as he and Jen did. Diccon's heart lodged in his throat as Bard reached, almost without volition, to caress his sword grip.

"Bard, eumedicos heal, that's what we're trained to do." Davvy continued with unemotional yet damning logic, "If my presence improves Jenneth's chances of survival, who are you to deny me? Or to deny *her* that chance? We can fight," he slapped the sheath of his belt knife, aware of the odds against him, "or we can work off our anger—your anger, at least—by finding Jenneth and Pw'eek. Any preference?"

What could possibly kindle such irrational anger? Had the world gone mad while the storm raged? When had Bard turned so unreasonable—almost unreasoning? Stubborn, yes, that always. Did he think being a Seeker made him always right, while Davvy was only a eumedico—if you could use the word "only" to describe a eumedico, especially a Resonant-eumedico. The inside of his nose, his eyes, prickled, as if he might cry. Didn't dare for fear he might not be able to stop, hadn't dared mourn Jenneth's loss. If Jenneth could vanish, if old friends could have such a falling-out, the world *must* be coming to an end!

"Grown-up worlds are different from our world," Kwee soothed, **"Complex rules and codes, but grown-ups still fight over silly things."** Mayhap he didn't want to understand this senseless world after all.

"Argue, fight, I don't care which you choose—*truly***.*** M'wa uttered a harsh, dismissive cough. To Diccon, it was clear he'd meant it, thoroughly disgusted by such petty squabbles. **"If you want to rescue Jenneth, though, best leave now. How long do you think it will take for people to notice you three are missing?"**

Leaving apologies in abeyance, the two men turned as one, and Diccon found himself being unceremoniously hoisted into the launch, the last of their supplies tumbling on top of him as they began untying the launch and lowering it. Too harried to notice he sat in water, Diccon stowed their supplies in the bench lockers. But he wasn't too busy to notice that the davits didn't squeak. Yes, a fine job! The launch slapped against the sea, then settled easy as a swan, and Davvy slithered down, casting off, holding the final rope until Bard made his way over the side. Somehow the rope took a half-hitch around Bard's sword, nearly jerking him into the water between the ship and launch, but Davvy reached out a hand to pull Bard aboard.

"What?" Diccon knew the eumedico's mock-innocent tone too well, held his breath, waiting for the two to ruffle and circle again at any excuse. "Think I'd cast off and leave you?"

Instead, to Diccon's relief, Bard concentrated on setting the oars in their locks. "No." He waited, hand on hip, then picked up the bucket and began to bail. "Let's see you row, eumedico," Bard taunted in a whisper. "You *can*, can't you?"

Seizing the oars, Davvy bent his back into the task, and they pulled clear of the *Vruchtensla* without a betraying splash or ripple, only the stars and moons overhead to guide them. This was *not* an adventure, it struck Diccon with absolute certitude—it was too achingly real—and prone to failure.

Pommy stared hard out to sea, squinting against the brightness that flashed like knives against the aquamarine waves. Already the sea had commenced its offerings to him and Hirby, some acceptable, some not. It all depended on what you waited for, would deem acceptable. Hirby stood knee-deep in the surf, wide smile splitting his face, making chirping sounds, snapping his fingers to entice a piece of planking to float close enough to grab. The damn dog, damn Tigger, carved frantic crazy-eights along the beach, sniffing here and there, lifting his leg so many times he'd gone bone-dry, doggy senses overwhelmed at this release. They were all relieved to be out for the first time, no longer crammed together in his hut for a night and a day and a night.

No sense burdening himself right now. He'd picked up only a few things, choosy, so far: some small pieces of ambergris, more than worthwhile; an old gold coin, its mint marks smoothed almost to oblivion by the sea's tumbling. Amazing it had finally yielded it up, miser that it could be. Faster down the beach, faster now, his tracks stringing behind them, then disappearing as a new wave erased them. Just as he'd been erased so long ago. Most everything in life could be erased, drawn over if you were patient, waited long enough.

Again he looked out to sea, tilting his hat so the brim wouldn't obscure his view. Had had to weave a new one to replace the old one lost. Well, it had helped pass the time, kept his hands occupied during the storm. Patience.

It wouldn't be today, but tomorrow, possibly. Day after, more likely. That decided, he began to look more appraisingly at what the sea'd surrendered, both at the water's edge and at the high tide line. No sense letting Hirby get everything. That keg, for instance. Even if one end were stove in, 'twas still useful. He angled up the beach toward it. Sometimes people stored things in kegs—not just liquids. You never knew. Once he'd found a ring in one. Had ignored the finger it still encircled—the brandy sloshing round inside had preserved it. Sold the brandy, too, just hadn't mentioned the finger.

Pulling the keg out of the sand, he inspected it, shook it. Intact but empty. Tucking it under an arm, he began walking faster, scanning left and right. Two days, most likely, salvage any little worthwhile pickings, and then, then . . . something special.

❖

PART
THREE

❖

The brilliance spangled and sparkled, clashing against the slap of azure and indigo waves, sharp and clear as they struck the surface, others more muted as they lapped against her. One—as errant as her twin, Diccon—reared playfully high, broke over her, showering her with water. A sputter, a groan, and Jenneth came awake, no longer dreamed. The shimmering sight of nothingness, such emptiness, brought tears. The dream had been safe, comforting—and dry. A frond of reddish-green and brown seaweed with limp, battered leaves and bulbous air sacks floated parallel with her spar, apparently had designs on her ankle.

"Pw'eek?" A relief to hear even her own voice, though it was husky, her throat desperately dry. Limpid yellow-green eyes stared back at her, although they seemed more distant than before. Was the ghatta drifting away? Flexing a cramped hand, Jenneth tentatively prodded the wood fibers the held the yard together at its fracture. No, still intact. The ghatten's mouth made silent smacking sounds, drowned out by the rumble of an empty stomach.

Utterly woebegone on her spar-perch, the ghatten looked as if she'd shrunk overnight, wet fur sleeking her bulk. **"Beloved? Breakfast soon? Pw'eek not liking it here."** Clumsily stroking her, Jenneth flinched at the stickiness of salt-glazed fur drying in the warming sun. **"Is this an adventure? Do adventures last long?"** Pw'eek hungered for both reassurance and food—as did she.

Jenneth began to cry in earnest. Stupid, stupid! she berated herself, mouth twisting in anguish, stinging eyes tight-shut. A whole salty sea surrounding them, and she had to add to it! Diccon'd laugh at such an extravagance! Diccon?—of course! If anyone could sense her whereabouts, he could. Just concentrate, keep concentrating on him, let him use her mind as a homing beacon.

Still grinning, nose leaky, she realized that Pw'eek waited patiently for an answer. *"Oh, sweet one, I'm sorry! This isn't exactly the adventure I dreamed of us having together."* The ghatten seemed to contract even smaller at her answer. *"Things will be fine, you'll see. After all, I've the bravest, biggest, most beautiful ghatten in the world with me. To be brave when I can't, clever when I'm dull, resourceful when I'm not."*

A scrabbling as Pw'eek's hind claws dug for balance as she retreated to the tip of the spar. **"Shouldn't have *me*, then,"** she wailed, mouth pale pink against the rippling blue of the sea. **"Should have Kwee, she's clever, so, so brave . . . I'm just . . . big!"**

Impatient, Jenneth slapped the sea with her palm, the sharp crack startling Pw'eek, her ears down-tucked as she scanned for danger. *"Silly! Being loved makes you brave, clever! And I love you! Kwee's nice, but you're* mine—*you Chose me! Did you make the wrong Choice? Mayhap you should've Chosen Diccon—let him be brave for both of you?"*

"Mine!" Half-rising, lashing her tail, Pw'eek cast a baleful look that dared anyone to question her choice. **"Love Kwee, my sib-mate, but love you more!"** A perplexed headshake. **"Am straining to 'speak Kwee, but she's so distant. Diccon distant, too?"**

"Yes, love," and wished the ghatten hadn't 'spoken the truth. She could barely sense Diccon, suspected he strained to pinpoint her as well. *"That's why we have to focus on Kwee and Diccon, concentrate long and hard as we can, so they'll know where to find us."* The ghatten looked marginally comforted, and Jenneth realized how tired her arm had grown: unaware, she'd been clutching at Pw'eek's segment so it wouldn't detach. Could she lash the spar with some dangling cordage, ensure the pieces didn't separate? The cable was heavy, tar-coated, and almost impossible to ply, nor could she find a free end among the tangled coils. The best she could manage was to loop it twice around Pw'eek's segment.

Even that effort left her panting, unable to gain a purchase on anything to work more efficiently. Finally, arms draped over her segment, she let her legs dangle, dimly conscious of their languid swing and sway, the sea currents like a breeze. The sodden fabric of her pantaloons eddied round her legs—pantaloons! Slip them off, use them to bind the fracture! One-handed she fumbled at her waistband. Stripping them off required more expended energy, an almost insurmountable task, the wet material clinging, molding itself to her when she moved. Did she dare release the spar, use both hands? The notion of her head slipping beneath the surface made her heart pound, her lungs already hungering for air, water inexorably pressuring her nostrils, her clamped lips.

Anxiously, Pw'eek ventured, **"Are human teeth as strong and sharp as ghatti teeth?"**

With a gasp, she spat a mouthful of salt water clear and reembraced the spar, a seaweed frond tendriled across her shoulder. *"Why? What does that have to do with anything?"* By the Lady, this was worse than listening to Diccon's babble!

Her thought not as private as it might have been, Pw'eek deflated, dismally embarrassed, and Jenneth bit her lip, ashamed of herself. Diccon ignored her slips, shrugged them off, too secure to be bothered. But Pw'eek wasn't equally assured, nor was she.

With surprising determination Pw'eek persisted. **"Humans have two hands—not four clever paws. Can you bite the rope? Then both hands can pull at silly pantaloonies?"**

Striving to be objective, she contemplated the idea, not especially fond of it, indeed, she absolutely loathed submerging her face like that. Diccon always teased when they went swimming: she cautiously duck-paddling, barely wetting her shoulders, Diccon skimming otterlike beneath the surface. Well, he wasn't here to tease her now! Mayhap he'd never believe it, but she'd do it—show him, prove to herself she could! Stuffing the rope into her mouth, she gagged at its tarry taste, her stomach heaving. Ha! She'd forgotten she could still converse with Pw'eek, even encumbered with the rope. *"And if I drown? I suppose you'll pull me out?"* It never hurt to ask, to check in advance.

Raising herself to her full height on jittery paws, Pw'eek balanced herself precariously, preparing to dive in. **"Can ghatti swim? Don't know, don't care! Pw'eek'll save you!"**

With loyalty like that—blind loyalty, though true bravery—how could she fail? Inhaling a deep and—she hoped—not her final breath, Jenneth allowed her face to sink below the surface. As she guardedly opened her eyes, a tracery of tiny, silvery exhaled bubbles raced surfaceward. Determined, she struggled with both hands to strip her pantaloon. A grab at one ankle and she yanked, ripping downward at the waist with the other hand, and suddenly a leg came free, like a snake shedding its skin. Intent on repeating the procedure with the other leg, she ran out of breath, fighting down panic and allowing the water to loft her upward. Popping up beside Pw'eek, she wetly kissed the startled ghatten's flank before pulling herself hand-over-hand along the rope to her end of the spar. Simple, now! Encircle the spar with one arm, lean back and raise her leg with the pantaloons depending from it like a flag. A very soggy flag. Yes!

Having physically distanced himself to the extent the cramped cabin allowed, Jenret Wycherley spun to face the ghatti, his neck cords bulging, face livid. *"Well, what do you have to say for yourselves?"* Hands on hips, he waited. *"Anything? Anything at all?"*

Reprimanding ghatti was always an unsatisfactory experience; their reactions, so characteristic of their species, did naught to temper Jenret's anger and discouragement. Rawn, Khar, P'roul, and Khim sat lined before him in near-identical poses: each gracile neck contracted until their heads seemed to sit directly on their shoulders, and all eyes slitted, blandly staring this way or that. Occasionally one or another would neck-stretch, evince passionate interest in a ceiling crack, or deliver a fastidious spine-lick.

"Rawn?" A direct appeal to his Bondmate, his other "half" who always endured his overzealousness, their occasional spats and outright quarrels. *Why didn't you—one of you—say something?"* Meaning, "Rawn, why didn't *you*, my oldest, dearest friend, 'speak me, warn me?" *"Tell us Diccon planned to run off, search for Jenneth?"* He splayed his fingers through his hair, savagely pushing an errant lock aside. Unfair to Rawn, the others, perhaps, when in hind-

sight Diccon's actions were so obviously predictable. Now if he didn't vent his frustration and fear, he'd explode.

Yawning full in his face, Rawn fractionally shifted from paw to paw. Heartily wishing patience were a purchasable commodity, and well-aware the yawn represented nervousness rather than an insult or a delaying tactic, Jenret conquered his impulses, grimly outwaiting his Bond. **"Would've, if it had been just Diccon and Kwee."** As he lowered his forequarters to the deck, a twinge of discomfort distorted his muzzle. Ah, he knew how the ghatt's joints ached these days! Declare Rawn old, then he must be as well, and tonight hopelessness ached in every bone. Ancient, anguished, and impotent to save the ones he loved! **"Once M'wa agreed he and Bard would go, we judged that sufficient."**

P'roul, offspring of Khar and Rawn, came to her sire's support. **"Davvy's decision caught us a bit off guard."** Behind him Holly suppressed a gasp; a rare moment when any ghatt or ghatta voluntarily admitted a lack of omniscience. **"But not by much. After all, we grew up beside Davvy and the twins. Jenneth and Diccon are like younger sibs to him."** Though she'd politely omitted mentioning Lindy, the full force of the situation struck Jenret—a permutation he'd not counted on—Davvy and Bard together, with Diccon as a buffer.

Holly's breathless running commentary echoed P'roul's words so Arras, Lindy, Honoria, and the children could understand. Finally, he spoke aloud. "And now we've *both* Jenneth and Diccon in jeopardy—not to mention Bard and Davvy. M'wa, you'll assure me, can take care of himself." Sarcasm rarely fazed the ghatti, though they were prone to practice it on their Bonds. Practice, though, was hardly the word—they'd perfected it long ago.

Rawn stirred. **"Wouldn't have minded going with Diccon and Kwee. I, for one, enjoy the water."** The black ghatt had been a gifted fisher in his day, wading chest-deep into streams or ponds, crooked claws swooping to snag unsuspecting fish.

Those had been the days! *"Well, why didn't you say so? We could have gone—should have gone!"* Had Rawn betrayed him by his silence? Why? *"We can still go! Not sit around here waiting, worrying, wondering! Anything's better than that!"*

"And I will *not* have you dashing toward death with another half-baked plan!" His claws deliberately scraped the planking, a drawn-out rip designed to further set everyone's nerves on edge. Through his anger, Jenret heard Holly's "diplomatic" translation. Bad enough Theo, Holly, and Doyce had been privy to Rawn's retort, but the ghatt had intended it that way.

From beside Doyce's bunk Arras rose to his full height, a hand on Harry's shoulder as if to reassure himself of his son's presence. A perfectly natural gesture, but Jenret ached to be able to touch his own two. "And how do you propose to go after them?" Jenret recognized too well—and heartily disliked—the dangerously-honed sweet reason the slightly older man wielded. "By swimming? Thorsen's already told us the dinghy and the second launch can't sustain heavy use. Diccon knew he'd appropriated the one seaworthy boat." After three days without shaving, Muscadeine's cheeks and chin were stubbled black and silver, his usually dapper mustache tatty as a piece of frayed cocoa matting.

Taking a deep, sustaining breath Jenret prepared to verbally square off against Arras, but Doyce overrode him with a look, and for once he subsided. Her halting effort at organizing a coherent thought raked his soul, driving home his complicity with Honoria, a subtle insinuation she wasn't capable of aiding him, or that he longer valued her help. Blessed Lady! She couldn't have thought—even worse!—that he and Honoria . . . ? No, of course not!

Her pain was his—the throbbing head still faintly mazed by drugs, the ugly bruise on her thigh had left him near nausea on viewing it, purples and maroons, blacks and deep blues, a massive, swollen life to it. His own pain he could conquer; anyone else's sent him fleeing. And he, he'd been the one who'd insisted the twins come, not wanting to admit he'd brought them as cover.

"Jenret, no!" Levering herself onto her elbows, she frowned, hazel eyes unsure where to focus. Did it count, he wondered, if she chided his double-image instead of him directly? "Please, not and lose you, too! I couldn't bear it! Jenneth, Diccon—and now you!" Mouth set tight, he resolved not to let his own fears wash over her, unable to comfort her without losing his self-control.

Damned if he didn't want comforting himself, had always relied on her for that, selfish without even thinking about it. But his offspring floated somewhere on the open seas. Part of him, part of her. A hard swallow, but he managed. And when comfort failed, Doyce knew full well he inevitably took refuge in action, any action, to alleviate his fears. Diccon had done exactly the same.

With a calm, sane reasonability that set his teeth on edge, Honoria bravely crossed into a no-man's-land of unspoken emotions. "I agree with Doyce. Losing you—even being forced to worry about you—is more than any of us can cope with right now." Jenret caught a fleeting disbelief on Doyce's face at this unanticipated ally, wondered if his own revealed a look of betrayal.

Without reacting to either expression, Honoria continued, "We'll make Samranth shortly. Once we land, you can commandeer Oh-Oh—Ozer Oordbeck, Wycherley-Saffron's agent," she interjected in explanation to the others. "He's efficient, knows Samranth inside and out. Whatever you need—guides, boats, supplies—he'll find them ten times quicker than you can, will smooth the way with any officials who might help. We can't make up lost time, but there's no need to squander more precious time once we land. Now's the time to plan, decide who stays or goes, who's responsible for finding Jenneth, who tries to overtake Diccon."

"And I'll be with you each step of the way. Just like the old days, eh, Wycherley?" He wanted to shrug off Muscadeine's hand, stand strong and solitary to reassure Doyce, but Rawn's steady glance warned him to swallow his pride. "She's my niece, Jenret. Between us, we'll find her, and make sure Diccon's safe as well."

"Well, will you settle for that?" Rawn prodded. **"That's the way to do it, unless you still want to swim. I want our ghatten safe and sound as much as anyone."** A slow wink at Jenret. **"Especially now that they're old enough not to pull my tail."**

Reluctantly capitulating, Jenret leaned over to gently tug Rawn's tail, the ghatt swatting back—a love tap.

"You're probably right." Public apologies, let alone apo-

logies en masse were scarcely his forte, but Rawn's poised
paw warned him the next blow might not be as loving. "I'm
sorry. I know you all care about the twins, too. Diccon's
safe as houses with Bard and Davvy along, so let's concentrate on finding Jenneth—and soon!" He smiled at Lindy,
so pensive during all this, Byrlie so solemn on her lap.
Lindy didn't look particularly worried—a positive sign, yet
perplexing all the same. Always so steady, ready to give
solace—she'd been so from her youngest days. Others came
first with Lindy, not herself. Would that he were capable
of that, could do it as naturally as she. But who comforted her?

"Well, at least Bard knows the country." The thought
of Bard at Diccon's side made him feel better, his smile
more genuine.

A minimal headshake rebuked him. "No, he doesn't."
She shook her head harder, brow furrowing. "He's never
been to the Sunderlies, *never* in his life. *Never*," she reiterated. "And . . . and," her mouth trembled, "any stories he
may have been told by his people . . . well, they're inland
dwellers, cattle herders. He has *no* idea what the coast is
like!" Much to Jenret's consternation she burst into low
sobs, burying her face against Byrlie's blonde head.

*"Jenner, pray she hasn't seen something, a vision she
doesn't dare tell us about!"* Doyce's 'spoken plea reminded
him of the harsh truth that Lindy sometimes "saw" worlds
beyond their own.

Flames, coruscating spangles of flame, cavorting around
her, highlighting a molten crimson-orange path toward the
setting sun. Groggily, Jenneth tilted her head to watch,
guiltily wondering when, *when* had she possibly had the
time to light this fire? Be more careful with lucifers, stupid
girl! Let Mama or Papa find out . . . or Diccon . . . she'd be
in serious trouble. Serious trouble, young lady! An invisible
finger wagged in her face, making her hang her head in
shame.

**"Not fire, dear heart. Sun's setting. Water's like a mirror,
reflecting it."**

"Not fire," Jenneth agreed because it was easier than

arguing. If the voice said it wasn't fire, only the reflecting rays of the setting sun, fine—she'd avoid a scolding. It dawned on her then, slowly and with difficulty, that another voice *did* sound in her head. Not . . . Diccon? Gradually the pieces coalesced—the calico ghatten, Pw'eek, the storm-tossed ship, half-drowning, and now this aimless drifting. Eyelids puffy, she forced them open, licking at split lips. "Pw'eek, sweet one. How goes it?" An exploratory shift on the spar left her biting her lip as brine burned new chafed spots.

Peering owllike from beneath Jenneth's white shirt, its sleeves trailing in the water, Pw'eek looked for all the world like an unfortunate cat a child had decided to dress up. Still, it had been all she could devise to protect her from the sun's beating rays; she'd sheltered her own head and shoulders with a remnant of canvas sail. Useless again, she realized, for it had settled beside them like a sunken cloud. **"Harder to hear Kwee in my head. More distant. Can you feel twin-sib?"**

Concentrating, she again licked her lips, tasted blood, the touch of moisture tantalizing if it hadn't been for its saltiness. Speaking aloud hurt too much, so she switched to mindspeech. *"You're right. Diccon's farther away. But somehow . . ."* she cast around the horizon, testing, *"the direction's different. I can still feel Mama the tiniest bit that way,"* a half-hearted wave west toward the setting sun, *"but they've separated."* She absently scratched a raw spot on her inner elbow, specks of blood oozing from each pore.

Pulling her head under the shirt like a turtle retreating into its shell, Pw'eek wilted, chin flat between her paws. **"Kwee and Diccon *will* come for us!"** She poured as much confidence as she could into her 'speech, but Jenneth wasn't fooled. **"Soon, soon. With plenty of food and water!"**

Food! Water! No—block the words from her mind, refuse to hear them, or she'd be forced to acknowledge the depths of her hunger and thirst. The mossy-moist dark circle of the dripping well shaft, a dripping bucket of water bursting into the light, her hands hefting it high, pouring it into her open mouth, letting it stream over her sunburned face and chest and shoulders. Despite herself she opened her mouth, her yearning so intense she could taste the icy water's faint metallic tang. When she caught Pw'eek eyeing her as if she'd lost her mind, she abruptly shut her mouth.

"Of course, Diccon and Kwee will come find us." She didn't believe it, wasn't sure when she'd stopped believing. Mayhap thirst forced you to see reality, not fantasize. But she had to act brave for the ghatten, dared not say they floated lost, alone in the midst of a boundless sea, would drift forever and ever—or until they died, fell off their perches, their shriveled bodies sinking beneath the sea to feed the fish. . . . *"We might even wash ashore by tomorrow. We can wait for Diccon and Kwee on the beach."* Why bother with this subterfuge? Pw'eek recognized the truth more clearly than she.

. . . Or their bones would wash up on the beach, naught but bleached bones to identify them—picked clean by scavengers, bones tossed and strewn, tumbled and churned by the rolling waves until finally . . . finally . . . cast ashore. . . . One certainty remained: the hells of ancient legend weren't fiery, though fire existed there; true hell was watery, consisted of oceans of undrinkable water that taunted and beckoned. . . . Oh, for just one sip! Harrap and Parm swore that wasn't true, that the hells had no place in the Lady's religion, but she knew better—now.

The beaten metallic disk of the sun had nearly extinguished itself in the sea, only a few random sparks and splinters of brightness remained, antic as the fireflies she and Diccon used to chase, their pale fire never burning. Dark would bring a coolness of sorts, except that then the shivers would rise through her body. Strange how water no longer balmed her burns and hurts. The night would be long, too long and yet not long enough to end this torment. Sleep would stop her thinking, but she refused to encourage oblivion for the little time remaining in her. Pw'eek needed her—there must be some courage deep inside her that hadn't evaporated in the sun and the heat.

Pasting a grin on her face, she winked at Pw'eek, not very successfully, given her swollen eyelid. *"Did I ever tell you about Parm? Well, he's a calico just like you, but not as beautiful. Always landing in the most impossible fixes . . ."*

They drifted on, lapped and lulled by the waves, dark stealing over them as Jenneth continued. The ghatten lis-

tened intently, as if only this story in the whole world—
and its teller—mattered.

The swells came rougher than expected, but at least they
ran in a pattern, though higher than he'd like. It took both
him and Davvy on the oars, one apiece, to point the
launch's prow in the right direction, ride the waves like the
sleek cormorant he'd spied in Windle Port harbor. Otherwise they took the waves broadside, half-swamping the
boat. He could bail in his sleep now, that lesson ingrained.
Behind his straining back Diccon huddled at the prow, lantern letting a bare crack of light fall on map, compass.

On the stern seat, tail warped round his feet, M'wa critically observed their efforts. **"Together, together, yes. Don't
fight the rhythm, don't try to row faster, Bard. Teamwork,
please."** Glaring at the ghatt, Bard ground his teeth and
set his pace to Davvy's. No one except Byrta could ever
match him perfectly—heartbeats, strides, thoughts. Still, if
he fixated on the here-and-now, not the past, he could
mimic Davvy's stroke pattern. In reward M'wa sought a
pleasant subject. **"Doesn't Kwee look like a little figure-
head, angled over the prow like that? Prettier than that
fruit salad cornucopia on the *Vruchtensla*."**

Stealing a glance, Bard grunted assent, fighting a smile—
fruit salad! **"Misses her sib something fierce. Ah, I know
what that's like . . ."** Guiltily, M'wa broke off. The ghatt
knew to his cost how few moments were right to bring up
the subject of Byrta, let alone his own long-dead sib, P'wa.
A familiar sense of emptiness tugged at Bard. And when
he hurt, ached with loneliness, he turned cross-grained miserable, remote enough to nearly drive away the one other
being who knew him, mind and soul alike.

"It's all right, M'wa. I know, I understand. Who better?"
But his tight grimace signaled his distress all too plainly: his
oar missed, slicing air instead of water, the launch slewing.

Davvy's elbow rammed his ribs, threatening to topple
him after the muffed stroke. "Concentrate, man. Want to
spin us sideways, catch another wave?" He blew an exasperated breath from a jutted lower lip, his bangs feathering
in its breeze. He'd taken to wearing them pushed back,

baring his forehead, but they hadn't grown enough to stay
in place; it frustrated Bard that he'd not noticed before.

For no reason and every reason, Bard harbored a bitter
longing for the boy Davvy, rather than the man. A spoiled
and stubborn child, but brave and funny as well, a child
who'd defended a smaller, too-trusting child—Lindy—
saved her from death at the hands of Bazelon Foy and Tadj
Pomerol. The scene in the pit came back, haunting him.
For such bravery Bard would always love Davvy, and because of that, he now feared—nay, almost hated—the man
the boy had grown to be. Davvy's claim on Lindy's loyalty
went back near as far and even stronger than his own.

Bending into his work, he matched Davvy's stroke, content to let him lead, at this, at least. From behind their
smoothly flexing backs, Diccon called out an occasional
course correction in a voice soft as the surrounding night.
At least Diccon hadn't remarked on the tension threatening
to swamp the launch as surely the waves. Tension wasn't
bailable.

"Why hate him now?" M'wa's tail flicked, its tip moving
with metronomic anger. **"You have what he wants, though
he's too honorable to take it from you. Besides, you don't
want what you have—always yearning after Byrta. The only
being you've truly dared love. Hardly fair for Lindy. Or
for Byrlyn."**

"Shut up, ghatt!" Even now the pain sliced scalpel-deep,
that sundering so long ago. Each time he deceived himself
that he'd recovered, he instead discovered he was raw
anew.

With a final tail-switch, M'wa twisted away, his spine announcing his rigid reproach as he addressed an invisible
horizon. **"Let it eat at you like acid, corrode till nothing's
left inside . . . if anything at all remains by now."**

Stroke after stroke in silence, arms and backs working in
unison, cadenced. At length Davvy whispered, "Diccon
does know how to read that compass, doesn't he?" Bard
nodded. A pause. "And that map he's so proud of?"

Somehow his throat clogged, probably the mist, he told
himself. "Give Diccon his due." The words rasped, but he
choked down the lump of mist. "He's Doyce's and Jenret's
child, after all. Yes, he's young, needs seasoning, testing,
but he's older and wiser than you were when you rescued

Lindy. Diccon'd do anything in this world or the next to save Jenneth. And that's why I—why we—came, to help him do exactly that."

Oar end cradled to his chest, Davvy slumped, finally straightening to restrain Bard as he lofted his oar for the next stroke. "I stand rebuked. Diccon's a good lad, canny, but he needs your guidance. Just as I did once—still do."

"Port!" Diccon called. "No, starboard! Damn it all, I swear we should go left and Kwee says right! Now what do we do?"

Swinging round, Bard fervently wished he'd turned the other way, not encountered Davvy's pale face. A kind, compassionate face, intelligent brown eyes with a silvery glint of moisture. Jealous? Of course—youth, strength, determination, a man with a future opening wide, beckoning him, not plagued with a past to carry like baggage. The past was hardly Davvy's fault, even though he comprised part of the burden. "Diccon. Align your map to match compass north, make sure we're aiming toward land, not back to sea. Jenneth and Pw'eek must be somewhere between us and the coast."

The coppery glow of lamplight burnished Diccon's reddish-brown hair, made his features stand out in stark relief as he cracked the lantern's shade a bit wider. Brow furrowed, he traced a finger along the map. "No, we're on course. Headed toward Haringa, just as Tuck swore we should."

"Good. Now you and Kwee can continue your argument."

"I don't suppose ghatti can row?" Blowing on a blistering palm, Davvy trailed his hand over the side, wincing at the sting. "They do so many remarkable things that I've been half-hoping . . ."

Bard stood cautiously, slipping his oar from its thole pins and standing it upright in a hole bored in the center of their rowing bench. Fumbling, muttering, he finally set it firm in the matching collar bolted to the keel. "Mayhap it's time to unfurl your sail, Davvy. You brought it, after all. Just don't expect M'wa or Kwee to fill it, though. Up to you to provide your own hot air." The gibe left him faintly pleased with himself. *"Always too serious, too bound up in the past to appreciate what I have now, to make jokes, am I?"* he tossed in M'wa's direction.

"Ah," muttered M'wa, opening one eye. **"What sort of Bondmate would you be if you allowed a mere Resonant-eumedico to make light of a ghatt's abilities?"**

Again, the dazzle of sun-shards splintering on the waves bored through her eyelids, piercing the darkness she'd wrapped about her, invading her mind. "Damn shun still shetting," she groaned around a tongue that crowded her mouth, her lips splitting in new spots as she spoke. *"Pw'eek? How much longer till sunset?"*

A disjointed memory of reciting tales about Parm made her mind stutter, falter—so many tales, often droll, sometimes brave—Parm saving Auntie Mahafny from the poisonous snake. That had been brave, daring even, and Pw'eek had been awestruck. *"Pw'eek?"* No answer. Hadn't the sun set *before* she'd told that story? Prying open eyes that bleared in the light, she scanned the sea, saw only emptiness, her limbs going limp as string, panicky enough to almost fall off her spar. Pw'eek's end had been only loosely attached to the main spar segment, and it tended to sway and flex, the partial break making it seem jointed.

No Pw'eek! A pantaloon remnant wafted against her, a single leg, sundered from its pairing. Not night but morning! A new morning—and alone, oh, so alone! To confuse night and dawn as she'd done. . . . How long had Pw'eek been missing? Why hadn't she said anything, cried a warning?

"Jenneth? Beloved?" Pw'eek's mindvoice trembled across the water. Thank you! Oh, thank you, Blessed Lady! The ghatten hadn't drowned during the night! **"Was so sleepy . . . so tired . . . didn't know our Bond had broken."**

"Our mental bond, never!" she projected with all her strength. *"But my pantaloons weren't as strong as our Bond. Beloved, which way are you?"* It wasn't easy, she was so weak, her skin burned raw, but she sat upright, locking her legs around the spar as if it were the barrel of a horse. Raising both hands to shield her eyes, Jenneth scrutinized the sea's flat expanse, except it never held steady. Always

waves, a constant roll and toss, a tantalizing dip, then a
rising swell would block her line of sight.

"To your left . . . I think." Pw'eek resonated more
strongly than the faraway twinges she still received from
Diccon, but the ghatten's 'voice definitely wasn't nearby.
**My spar's moving. Almost like sailing, not just floating.
Fast. Oh, so scary!"** A pause. **"No! Pw'eek scared but not
afraid—Pw'eek brave! Brave 'cause Jenneth loves her!"**

"Oh, love, that's right! So brave! I'll find you." With a
deep breath and a prayer Jenneth rolled off her spar, hooking her arms over it and kicking, the water flurrying white
behind her. She moved, but only sluggishly. Harder, kick
harder! Harder! The pounding in her heart, the pounding
in her brain increased, each throb a mockery of what she
needed. Already her legs had turned to lead, her feet twin
anvils weighing her down. Exhausted, gasping, she clung to
the spar, let her legs sink, wanting so badly to follow them
down and down. . . .

Something brushed her knee and she screamed, scrambling from the water onto her perch so quickly it rolled,
depositing her back into the sea with a splash. She completely lost her grip and flailed wildly to the surface, the
spar nudging the back of her head like a curious horse as
she broke the water. Blindly, she clung to it, chest heaving,
her whole body wracked by shudders. Water jammed her
sinuses, her ears, made her heartbeats emptily echo in her
head. **"Oh, beloved! Climb back on, please! Not wanting
hungry fishy tasting you! Don't worry about Pw'eek."**

Slowly, painstakingly, she swung a knee over, cautiously
easing herself in place again. *"Pw'eek,"* sea water burned
and churned in her gut, and she retched, her whole body
spasming, *"I don't think . . . don't think I can reach you."*

Slumped full-length, she began to weep, but had no moisture to spare, her body rung dry. What? What was she
going to do? Die out here in the middle of the Frisian Sea,
alone, bereft of everyone she loved? How much longer
could the Lady taunt her like this? If she had to die, let it
be clean and quick, not shriveled with thirst, scorched by
the sun!

"Not going to die! Pw'eek won't let you die!" Her 'voice
came fainter now, the ghatten still apparently drifting,
caught up by a different current? Near, far—what did it

matter? What could the ghatten do about whether she lived or died? Pw'eek faced the same fate as well. Still, it touched her to know how much Pw'eek cared, and she cherished it in her heart. Finally, cheek pillowed against wood, she drifted into a current of unconsciousness. Her last thoughts . . . drifting, drifting. . . .

Hiking her robe and recinching her hempen belt, Aidannae started down the stone launch-ramp, each step an adventure. The storm had battered Samranth and the coastal towns longer and more fiercely than any storm had ever held them hostage before. Dirt, leaves, branches, roofing tiles, and assorted debris—including the carcasses of small animals and birds, fish and shattered shells—caked the rampway, overflowing the center gutter that protected a ship's keel when it was hove ashore for major repair work. The ocher mud plastering the ramp was lushly thick, slippery, and smelled like—she sniffed; yes, exactly as she'd thought—a didie-clout full of baby quat. Not a pleasant comparison.

Hard at work, cleaning crews scraped, shoveled, raked. Others bobbed up and down at the four-hand pumps that pressured sausagelike canvas hoses for spraying down the streets after the worst of the mud had been carted away. Leave it, and the sun's rays would bake it brick-solid until passing feet and wheels powdered it, reddish dust lodging in nostrils, clothes, food.

Idly she wondered what they did with the debris they removed, had never considered it before. Knowing the city council, they probably ordered it dumped in Middentown, Samranth's eastern quarter, the city's "backside," so to speak. Here the poorest of the poor, Samranth's less savory citizens congregated in hovels, desperate to eke out a living. The next storm would sweep it all down again, along with Middentown's own richly ripe garbage, a veritable stew of reeking refuse. A wonder the city council hadn't assessed them for walls to dam in the debris, instead of merely damning their presence.

Eyes narrowed, she examined the flag-topped copper dome and the three watchtowers of the limestone Guardian fort on Tarango Island in the bay. Being trapped there, surrounded by the sea, had to be worse than hunkering down on the mainland to wait out the storm. Part of her snickered "good," but she automatically formed the eight-point star to bless the island fortress and Canderisian Guardians stationed there, insuring exiled criminals didn't escape. It was their duty, their obligation, and it was unfair not to wish them well. Most were kind, conscientious souls, reluctant to impinge on the rights of the average Sunderlier.

While clambering over the Bethel roof at dawn to repair the storm damage—the only Shepherd young and agile enough to dare the venture—she'd heard shouts that some of the fishing boats had ventured out. A whoop of joy at that, and she'd tossed her hammer in a circling arc, caught it again. Fish! Just mayhap she'd be lucky enough to cadge some fresh fish. Rations had been slim during the storm, wind and rain sweeping through the Bethel as if shutters, doors, and roof hadn't existed. Keeping the ovens fired for baking was impossible; no bread to eat or sell once they'd shared out the remaining loaves, even their stale, rock-hard heels. Well, at least Conraad had had no reason to complain how tough and dry they were; rainwater was a marvelous softener.

Now, while Ergen worked at cleaning the ovens, starting small fires to drive out the moisture so they wouldn't crack under the heat, she'd ventured harborside, a palm leaf basket clutched under her arm. Given the mess and muck underfoot, the clean, rain-swept shakes of the Bethel roof seemed preferable. Still, there had to be some virtuous soul, even if only one, who'd take pity, offer up a fresh-caught fish or two. So what if they were the scrawniest, the boniest, grudgingly given to honor the Lady? Even noffals—generally disdained as garbage fish by any but the most empty-bellied—would please the Lady, though less so Aidannae; she'd made do too often with them as a child. Noffals were notorious scavengers, eating everything from putrid refuse that seethed by the sewer gates to the bodies of dead sailors floating homeward.

"Dannae!" Kasimir slither-slopped to her side, a broad grin plastered on his face. A critical, head-to-toe survey showed that wasn't all plastering him. Mud, the hated mud, caked and coated him, legs gaitered with it clear above his

knees; dull, dried strips and drips decorating his chest and
back, his face, matting his hair. Apparently his worn blue
trousers had been saved for better occasions, for a faded
print loincloth wrapped his skinny hips, its tropical bird and
palm design hinting at its former glory. A real bird sporting
that much mud on its plumage would drop from the sky
like a stone, she decided. Hm, not a bad thought: all mud-
coated like that, she could bake it in the coals. Crack it
open and the hardened mud would pluck the feathers from
succulent baked meat. The Lady's shame on her for ob-
sessing on food; if she were hungry, no doubt Kasimir was
doubly so!

"Dannae! Yef woan bulief it!" A mud-sticky grab for
her arm, and she fended it off by shifting her basket. "Ah,
sorry! Muckety-mucked, ain I?" Reaching up level with her
tonsured topknot but careful not to touch, he jerked his
hand downward, uneasily checking for loiterers. Obediently, she bent to let him whisper close. Wouldn't be long
till she'd have to make him stoop, the way he was growing.
"Gaddess love and pertect me, I got five cops! Five! All
earned!" he added fiercely.

"Smir! Honest? Earned square'n fair?" She yearned to
believe, but few would hire a boy that size. Earning honest
money took far greater effort and persistence than stealing.

A vigorous nod sent mud pellets flying. "Sez I were too
wambly-weak fer the muck-up crew, so I hipped the foreman a hefty, serious stare—not rude ner nudding—and sez
back, 'N I slave-slog hardern most all, cuz a that. Yef try
me 'n see.' " An extravagant stretch, arms wide overhead,
back arched, set his ribs marching under his skin. " 'N I
did, Dannae, *showed* me wurf. Same pay as de rest! 'N
more work afder meal break, if'n I want it." He side-
glanced her, trying not to stare at her pitifully empty basket; he'd copped to why she was here—begging again.
Though she'd never said a word, he knew how she hated
it, even though the Lady smiled on such blessed humility.
She'd begged as a child to hold body together, since she'd
not yet found her soul. "Yef kin werk my muck-up crew
dis afdernoon." His chest puffed out. "Foreman'd hire yef
on my sez-so ifn I true-vouch yef a hard slogger."

"Smir, you're a true friend, offering to do that for me."
Lady bless the lad, she knew how good it felt to be able

to return a favor, especially when one was poor. But mud-stained fingers now grabbed her arm, smearing the wheaten fabric, while Kasimir's sharper eyes turned seaward, his free arm pointing.

Squinting, Aidannae could make out the striped lateen sails of two of the larger fishing boats and, limping a short distance behind, a three-masted merchanter bearing just a skimp of sail, its hull slightly listing as it followed round the island. Obviously the storm had savaged it, and now the fishing boats were towing it in. Closer, a skipjack skimmed the waves, racing toward the beach, a skip from one of the fishing boats. Curious despite herself, she let Kasimir tug her down the ramp, leaning against each other to remain upright in the treacherous footing. So much for staining another communal robe. All-Shepherd Cubzac would swear she'd stied with the pigs! Even worse, he had laundry duty this oct!

The skipjacker judged the combers, dove for the beach, willing hands hauling the rider ashore against the pull of the ebbing wave. His news passed quickly, reaching all the way up to them—the *Vruchtensla* and Captain Thorsen, her cargo, and the name Wycherley, excitedly repeated several times. A tug at her topknot to help her think. Why did the name sound familiar? She tugged harder. Of course! Ozer Oordbeck was their agent! Twelve children the man had, and still he contributed to the Bethel, though the family seldom attended. For that she could forgive him, suspected the Lady could as well. The Mystery Chants were glorious, moving—and rigid, with scant room for infant improvisations. The Lady wanted joy for all Her children, to let them run and sing and shout with abandon, not immure them in adult impenetrabilities.

"Smir!" Aidannae took him by the shoulders and swung him to face her. "How bone tired are you? Truth?"

An upthrust lower lip, a dipping frown as he decided how much truth was required. "Got me wind back." But beneath the flaking mud his normally rich umber skin peeked grayish with fatigue. An afternoon's labor would drive him into the muck.

"Still as fast as ever?"

" 'Course!" His eyes flashed indignation. "Better be!

Even wid an honest job!" Anyone with coins on him had best be quick.

Aidannae pointed up the sloping ramp. "Know where Ozer Oordbeck's office is? The pinky, square building with the long, louvered windows?"

Bafflement at first on hearing the name, but the building's description did it. "Yef mean Oh-Oh's?"

"Aye." A push up the grade to give him a running start. "Fast as you can, take word a Wycherley's on board the *Vruchtensla*. Likely Oh-Oh's employer. Be first, and there'll be coin for you. Mayhap enough to skip afternoon muck-up. Oh-Oh's generous."

Hoped she had the right of it. About who was arriving on the *Vruchtensla* and the connection to Oordbeck, about Oordbeck's kindness—even if she were wrong about the first two. The cleanup labor was brutal, hard work, too much for Kasimir for a full day.

With a final inspection of the cabin to ensure nothing had been forgotten, Honoria tapped her teeth, ruminative, faintly fretful. Lost or misplaced articles were hardly her concern, but she could play-act about their importance. It was their arrival here—and its aftermath—that concerned her, and already she'd been forced to improvise, play by ear. That talent, an unflappable tenacity, and an ability to guarantee results had earned her this assignment. Composing herself, smoothing her face clear, she lightly hurried up the companionway to watch the *Vruchtensla* come to wharf, storm damage on shore evident wherever she looked.

To Thorsen's chagrin, the crippled *Vruchtensla* couldn't dock unassisted; two fishing smacks towed her toward her assigned pier. Soon, she knew, a capstan would grind, eight men or more leaning into it, feet digging for purchase as they repetitively circled, winching the cable meter by meter. She always relished ogling the broad, sweating chests, the bulging arms, the play of light off bare, glistening backs ranging from milk-white and scorched pink to deep, blackish-brown. A harmless habit, especially when she'd repressed so much else to keep her goal in sight. Any bonus she received would definitely be blood money, but she'd expected from the start that betrayal was a requirement.

Damn! Whether through cajolery or bullying, Jenret Wycherley was swinging himself into an extra pilot boat, urging them to shore. Not a chance of slowing him, distracting him. That meant she'd been involuntarily assigned another distasteful task, ensuring Doyce and the rest safely disembarked. Let Jenret take her for granted once more, and she'd pin his ears back, remind him who was in charge. Leaning on the rail, she waved with false gaiety after him, only to discover Theo and Holly flanking her—entirely too near for her liking. Disliked in equal measure their ill-concealed side-glances as they ostensibly peered toward the bustling port. Obviously subtlety and misdirection weren't highly prized as Seeker skills—except in their damned ghatti.

Theo's mouth worked, silently rehearsing his words. "D-do you ha-ve any i-dea," he bit down on the final syllable, "idea where we're to s-stay?"

"Some inn, no doubt." Holly pivoted, checking on Doyce where she semi-reclined in a canvas sling serving as a temporary chair, Lindy and Byrlie by her side.

Clearing her workaday twill divided skirt to avoid brushing the ghatti, Honoria gave a final look back at the island fort, emphasizing the innocent curiosity of a newcomer. "Once Ozer Oordbeck hears what's happened, I'm sure he'll find a house to rent. We need something more private than an inn. Besides, most inn sleeping rooms are upstairs—too hard for Doyce to climb." Demurely tilting her head to look up at Holly, her eyes widened. Damn—it came so automatically, but batting eyes and a soft smile were wasted on Holly, better to shed them on Theo. "We don't need strangers' prying eyes weighing our sorrows and losses, avid to see how we're coping with this tragedy."

Tragedy, yes, but a tragedy bound to benefit her. Hard-hearted, hardheaded, yes, but not yet as cold-blooded as it might sound. She pitied the twins' fates, but compartmentalized her sorrows. Each passing day diminished the chances of Jenneth being found alive, but it provided a distraction, as did Diccon's half-witted scheme to rescue her—unfortunate but providential. More players would be swept off the board—out of her way—when the others set out to find the twins. Sometimes there *was* justice in this world, just as she was prepared to howl, berate the skies over the constraints she labored under. Yes, just give her free rein and justice could be served—without requiring ghatti intercession to determine the truth.

"What?" she shook her head. "I beg your pardon, Holly. Thinking about what to take by hand, what the porters can bring later. Details, always details!" Again she raised guileless eyes to Holly. "This is *such* a responsibility, you know. I'm constantly afraid I'll forget something." With calculated nonchalance she linked arms with Theo. "Of course, you'll both go with Jenret and Arras, won't you?" A buh-buh-bah from Theo. "Looking for Jenneth, I mean? Seekers are *so* competent in crises."

"Hasn't been decided yet." Honoria tried to gauge if Holly's brusqueness was directed at her or at the fact this major detail remained unsettled. Interesting, if so. She'd been counting on both of them—and their ghattas—politely exiting. That sort of assumption smacked of carelessness. Ah, at last! Holly strode off on some ill-defined errand or, more likely, fleeing the cloying sweetness that had left Theo dazed as a nectar-drunk bee. This was one game Holly hadn't a hope of mastering! And Theo, her poor, lanky lamb, was slouching, knees awkwardly bent, so she could easily clasp his arm! Heavenly Lady, he was tall! Long all over—and made no effort to curb the mantling blush flooding her cheeks.

"How do the forts function? I'm so hazy on that." Slowly sliding her hand into the crook of Theo's elbow, she hoped against hope he knew, could explain without stuttering. He was hardly a lackwit, might as well discover precisely what background he—and undoubtedly Holly—had. Khim gave her a long, speculative stare, and she matched it, had the sensation of her own ears folding back, her spine hackling. No, she'd not hiss at the ghatta.

With an expansive wave, Theo related, haltingly, then with more confidence the little he'd gleaned about the Guardians at the fort. Yes, the fort. She wanted to contact Geerat Netlenbos, the Guardian Captain, but that could wait. Time for that later, when things settled. Let Geerat harbor a touch of anticipation; it would make their meeting that much sweeter—love, revenge, and justice were always sweeter after an absence. Waiting did that, and she'd waited so long for the coming day of reckoning. Once, revenge would have sufficed, but it was too short and sharp. Justice took longer, let anticipation build. Had she mellowed? No, hardly. Just grown more realistic in choosing her causes.

From behind his desk Ozer Oordbeck watched anxiously as Jenret Wycherley paced the office like a caged beast. Except that Ozer felt as if he were the one trapped, caged. "I understand, I understand fully about mounting a search," he placated, and his heart ached, because he truly *did* comprehend the torment of his loss. Even the thought of one of his twelve chicks vanishing so made his eyes moisten in sympathy, but other reasons oppressed as well, reasons he must damper, ignore for the time being.

"—So you'll make arrangements, order whatever equipment and supplies you deem necessary? Good, good. Buy or hire mounts? We'll leave tonight." An abrupt halt in front of Ozer's desk and Jenret Wycherley leaned full weight on his knuckles, face thrust too close for Ozer to feel comfortable. Of course he'd do everything in his power . . . "She's been lost so long, but I know—*I know*—she's still alive! I can feel it—here!" He struck his head. Odd, Ozer would have sensed it deep within his heart.

Try again, make the man listen to reason. "I can and will do that, Wycherley. But you can't chase off after her tonight. You'll get lost yourself. You're not familiar with the lay of the land, the—" And found himself unwillingly levitating from his chair as Wycherley clenched a double-handful of caftan and lifted upward, blue eyes intently boring into Ozer's. The darker, larger man and a woman of imposing size intervened, seizing Wycherley's arms, breaking his grip on the material.

"Sorry, Oordbeck," the larger man apologized.

"Oh-Oh's fine, everyone calls me that," he automatically emended. Well, everyone *did* call him that, though he disliked it, yearned to block his ears to the tones that often warned of an onslaught of "amusing" japery. The man possessed a lovely lilt, a foreign cadence to his speech that appealed to Ozer, though he found comprehending it difficult until he unraveled the rhythms in his head. Muscadeine, Arras Muscadeine, *that* was his name, the Marchmonter. First time he'd ever met anyone from there. Fingering the red streak round his neck where the caftan had chafed, Ozer extended his arms, shrugging the ruckled garment into place.

Patiently he reiterated the facts of Sunderlies life: the best the Guardians could do, spread thin as they were, was to keep a sharp lookout. They had their orders, and rescue missions weren't generally part of them. Ozer could almost hear Geerat Netlenbos's incredulous laughter at such an idea. At least Wycherley hadn't met laughter, only bureaucratic obstruction at the first Guardian post he'd charged into upon landing. The most Governor Hoetmer and the city council might authorize would be a token search after this much elapsed time. The sea stole too many—a fact of life—for anyone to constantly mount futile searches. Needles in haystacks were easier to retrieve than a lone soul adrift in the wide seas.

"Jenret, listen," Muscadeine urged, "think things through. We need the best available help. Is there," he appealed to Ozer, "someone we can hire to guide us? We'll pay handsomely for someone familiar with every nook and cranny of the coastline."

His papers sat unregarded, all the meticulously arranged records and ledgers he'd compiled to show Jacobia Wycherley, once he'd heard a storm-tossed ship had limped into port, a Wycherley aboard. Had rewarded the lad with the news a half-silver, his relief so great. How could he have guessed the *Vruchtensla* brought Jenret, the hotheaded brother, not Jacobia Wycherley, his sister? And now this tragedy outweighed his woes. A sigh as he scrubbed both palms across his cropped head, ordering his muddled thoughts. "Rudy," he shouted, and his nephew peered round the door. "See if you can run Bullybess to ground. Try the docks first, then up to Middentown, then the Riff. Tell Bullybess there's solid coin for an urgent guide trip." A two-fingered salute, and Rudy shot off.

"Don't worry, Rudy knows Bullybess's haunts. Wish he didn't know some so thoroughly." Rising, he fiddled with the swamp cooler, refilling the water, adjusting the vents, winding the weights tight to turn the blades as they dropped. Daring a liberty, he took Wycherley's elbow, guiding him over to receive the full benefit of the cooler's efforts. "Stand here, let the coolness bathe you. When the body's cool, the mind thinks better."

A single, disbelieving snicker from the tall, broad woman, and Ozer swore a smile ghosted across her face; not at him, he surmised, but at the idea of Wycherley acting cool and rational. Her large cat with the rich brown-gray striping against black, sauntered toward the cooler and gratefully threw herself in front of it, exposing her stomach. The solid black cat, the one who'd glared at Wycherley, also positioned himself in the faint breeze, sitting with lambent eyes half-shut.

Ghatti, they called them, or so the woman'd said. Oh, he'd *heard* of them, but had never expected to view one up close—let alone have two make themselves at home in his office. Should he send Rudy for milk? No, he'd already sent Rudy after Bullybess. Closest he'd come before was a glimpse or two when he'd had business at Tarango Fort. Usually a retired Seeker and ghatt served at one fort or another to determine the facts about any exile apparently escaping. How the beasts accomplished that, he had no idea, wasn't sure he wanted to know. Too many tavern tales about human brains being turned inside out, emptied like pockets.

Uneasy at continuing to stare at the ghatti; Ozer busied himself pouring cha from a condensation-beaded pitcher, handing glasses around. "Some swear hot cha's best to cool you, but I prefer letting it sit till it's tepid."

Dubious, Wycherley took a long sip, wiped the sweat from his face, then sipped again until he'd emptied the glass. "Minty," he belatedly pronounced, pressing the glass against his forehead. "I *have* to find her, Oh-Oh! My son's somewhere out there as well, searching for his twin. Don't know exactly where he is. Both of them, gone!" Setting down his glass, he drifted to one of the louvered windows like a lost child himself. Nearly as despondent, Ozer stared after his retreating back.

Carefully blotting his mustache, Muscadeine finally broke the awkward silence. "So, who's this Bullybess?" Hardly a question—or answer—Ozer wanted to dwell upon, though the man was attempting to toss the conversation his way.

"Bullybess? It's not Bouillabaisse, is it?" He pronounced it "bwe-jabez" as close as Ozer could determine. "You've someone here named *fish soup*?"

Lady give him strength! Massaging his eyelids, Ozer slumped, miserable, helplessly fighting a bubbling surge of laughter that threatened to spurt cha out his nose. "So that," his voice whooped so high he scarcely recognized it, "*that's* what it means? Truly?"

"I don't know," Muscadeine confessed, eyeing Ozer as if the agent were demented. "Mayhap it's spelled differently, mayhap it just sounds similar, but where I come from, bouillabaisse is a fish soup. Is it a common name here?"

Here. The Sunderlies. They had no idea, couldn't possibly realize how dissimilar the Sunderlies could be from their own sedate lives in Canderis or Marchmont. Some sort of formal spear-clattering they'd called a war some years back; unrest among Resonants—and bless the Lady they didn't harbor such creatures here; criminals were enough, thank you! Elbow firmly on the papers he refused to mention in deference to their loss—no matter the cost to him—Ozer pondered where to begin. Pondered to the depths of his soul if *he* might be forced to sacrifice a child if he dared inform Wycherley about the misleading entries, the falsified invoices, payees with less substance than shadows. . . . Hold his tongue, and his children, all twelve precious ones, would be safe. Wag it, and who knew what perversity might transpire?

"Not everything's as it seems, here in the Sunderlies," he ventured, diffident until Arras Muscadeine's almost imperceptible nod signaled him to continue. Of course, talking about something, anything, would pass the time until Rudy located Bullybess. "In the old days, exiles often adopted a new name—sometimes fanciful—to denote starting a new life. One of our more upstanding families—now, at least—calls itself Gloryrot. Short for the curse their ancestor always muttered, 'Glorious Goddess rot them all to hell!' " A deep breath and he warmed to his task. Whether he edified or entertained was all one to him if it soothed Wycherley, made him amenable to reason. Still, reason and the Sunderlies seldom walked hand-in-hand, despite superficial similarities to Canderis. Well, they'd comprehend shortly; experience was a powerful teacher. Double damnation! Which house could he short-lease for the rest of the Wycherley party? Talk about a hefty debit against the mercantile!

Ever appreciative of well-told tales, Arras listened to the thin business agent with the profoundly pale hair and nearly invisible eyebrows, the look of perpetual surprise on his face. Small wonder he'd been called Oh-Oh! Between them, he and Holly peppered Oordbeck with questions, begging for details while Jenret sat, sunken with dejection, dark hollows swallowing his eyes. The most obvious indicator of his state of mind was his jawline; forever fastidious, always shaving—no matter the circumstance—Jenret had botched his last attempt. Clumps of stubble and dried soap vied with nicks clumsily coated with patchy white alum. After his failure with the Guardians, he'd squandered the last of his energy ranting at Oordbeck, wasting it on the wrong soul. Only Rawn's bulk across his feet solidly anchored him in the room.

Unable to help, Arras sighed, keenly aware of the passage of time from the sun's changing height. Dusk soon. Not that the time had been spent idly listening to Oh-Oh's stories. All the while the agent had recounted his tales, he'd also been scribbling notes, lists, calling in one child or another—son or daughter, nephew or niece—and sending them out in tidy pairs on errands. Further, Oordbeck'd conversed with his sister-in-law, Gelya, pressing lists into her hands, assigning her the unenviable task of renting an abode for them at a moment's notice. At least, Arras reflected, Doyce and the others could contain their grief—or shout their joy, Lady willing—in a homey, private setting.

Doyce—how could she endure the uncertainty, bottling it inside? How could she cope, wounded in body and spirit yet again? Oh-Oh's flow of conversation began to sputter and falter; he'd left Holly to coax Oordbeck along, and now it was time to stop musing, shoulder his share of the distraction. "Why is that, do you think?" Why what, he'd no idea, just thrown it as a lifeline to Ozer. Legs stretched in front of him, Arras concentrated on the agent. Something was eating this man, something beyond the trouble they'd piled on his doorstep with no warning. Like it or not, repress it—ample time for new problems later. He hoped.

What to do about Jenret? He liked him well enough, found him intelligent, witty, but couldn't always stomach his impulsiveness. Ought to be used to it by now, but Jenret's rashness gave him a rash, made him itch . . . to slap Jenret down. Might as well acknowledge the truth, though he'd not acted on it—yet.

Again his mind wandered along its own chosen path. Lady be thanked that Harry was a dependable, levelheaded boy. Except . . . except, what had he dragged Harry into, bringing him here? Harry was sharp, young yet—too young, his mind cried—but maturing. The lad'd be fine. Yes, fine, but the paternal part of him stayed on guard, vigilantly sheltering his one chick. Well, Harry didn't take foolish chances—that was from *his* side, no doubt. A clucking, commiserating sound to quicken Oh-Oh's newest chapter . . .

Francie, Doyce, Jenneth—the Marbon women, he always inwardly referred to them, despite Jenneth's resemblance to Jenret. Cautious, careful, too—what?—squeamish of others' feelings, too convinced their own feelings and fears betrayed their weaknesses. Sure any fault was theirs, deserving of blame if something went wrong. Despite that, they felt obligated to shoulder the world's burdens; if Doyce hadn't done so in Marchmont, Eadwin'd be dead, uncrowned, Maurice on the throne and himself hanged as a traitor.

Oh, Francie boasted fewer self-doubts; her infirmities had taught her what she could accomplish despite them. Jenneth harbored the most doubts, cloaking herself in them, so typical of youth. And Doyce, ah, Doyce, landed smack in the middle. A smile quirked his lips—such thoughts! Always the secret womanizer, though not in the manner most employed the word. He loved and adored women's minds, prized their difference from men's, preferred their company, truth be told. And him a soldier, a Defense Lord! *"Ah, Doyce, Jenret's not worthy of you, never was. You deserve the best, but who am I to say, as long as you're happy."* But was she?

Jolted from his reverie by a brisk flurry of knocks, Arras wondered what the hells Oh-Oh'd been talking about, prayed he'd not be quizzed on it. Darker out now, louvered shadows banding the floor. "Come in." Oh-Oh broke into a smile at whomever stood behind the door. "Ah, Bullybess! Thank you for coming."

So, Oh-Oh's renowned Bullybess had arrived, despite a bashful entrance. Rising to greet this man who'd serve as their guide, he prodded Jenret to rouse him from his lethargy. Mayhap it was the shadows' fault, obscuring details, but he swore Holly wore the oddest expression, surprise and . . . and what? Anticipation? Amusement? No, almost as if she'd partaken of some delicious secret. She was as large as many men, stronger than most, and he almost considered her a comrade-in-arms. But . . . ah, he had it! She displayed the exact same expression the ghatti showed when silently gloating over something only they themselves discerned. But what? Something about Bullybess?

"Glad ta see yef, Oordbeck. Leastwise I'd better be. Had better ta do than be dragged down here for naught." The voice grated like gravel-clogged phlegm as a runty figure materialized from around the door, slamming it shut. "Best be wirf my while."

Already striding forward, hand outstretched, Arras consciously fought to keep his jaw from dropping to his chest. Whatever he'd expected, it had hardly been *this,* and cursed his dreamy musings about appreciating women, his pleasure in their company, his trust in their abilities.

Hands on hips, bare foot tapping, Bullybess glared up at him, cocky as a bantam rooster or, more accurately, hen. A worn, scarred woman lurking somewhere—anywhere, he had no idea—between forty and sixty, her short, sandy hair was liberally peppered with gray, coarse and wiry, springing in all directions. Skinny and ropy with muscle, that much was obvious, her dirty white singlet and baggy black shorts showing off her arms and legs, one bowed as a barrel stave. A shiny, jagged scar wove ivylike along her neck and windpipe, while another, narrower one, darted across her right brow and eye before taking refuge in her hairline.

"Enchanté, madame." His politeness dropped like a shafted bird at his feet, and she reared back, giving him an affronted once-over, eyes nearly flaying skin from his flesh. Grasping her hand in both of his—hard, horny, and (Blessed Lady, preserve him!) perfectly capable of applying enough pressure on a sensitive knuckle joint to make a strong man sink to his knees in agony. "A pleasure," he wheezed and prayed she'd proved her point, would release his hand before his bones were ground to dust.

"Doan hold wid falootin names nor fancy manners." Warningly she slapped his hand as she released it. "Ent time fer that. The lost'un yern or," her shoulder jerked in Jenret's direction, "hissen? Ah!" and read the answer on Wycherley's face. "Call me Tildy, short fer Matilda, er Bess, short fer Bullybess. Just don't faloot me. Doan faloot an I woan flirt, got that? You wid the shrub sprouting outa yern nose."

"Yes, Ma—" he stoppered his mouth, tried again. "Point taken, Bess." Rubbing his hand, he tried to realign his knuckles. "You're well-versed in the territory we need to cover? And you're capable of a good pace? We've little time to waste." Her bowed leg concerned him, that lurch and dip as she'd entered the office. He'd not hire anyone—man or woman—who couldn't keep up. Somehow, somewhere, Oh-Oh'd find them another guide, disappointed at Oordbeck for attempting to foist Bullybess on them. The agent hadn't seemed the sort to take advantage—not with lives at stake. But then, mayhap this was one of the things Oordbeck'd meant in contending that the Sunderlies were unlike anything they'd previously encountered. But how to inform Bullybess her services weren't needed? That was the rub.

"Been up'n daun the coast fer years, all seasons. Interior, too, more times'n I got fingers fer counting. All the way to Carvajal, over the mountains and onto the plains, seven times." Narrowed mud-gray eyes held a heat like glowing embers. "Been wandering since I got here, plan ta wander till I die."

Arras cleared his throat, paused. Ask her why she'd been sent here, what crime had exiled her to this wandering existence? The furtive warning on Oh-Oh's face made him reconsider. Perhaps the woman still ran from her sins, her past? If so, who was he to judge, since judgment had been passed.

"So—what, what? Yef tinking Bullybess slow, maybe? Weak? Wambly woman-weak? That one over there," she indicated Holly, treating her to a gap-toothed smile, "be big'n solid, strong as a man. Women always able. Bullybess not as big, but yef wait, see." An imperious hand shoved Arras's knees apart, stinging swats until he spread his legs, bewildered and not a little unnerved at what she'd do next. Oh-Oh and Holly offered no guidance, and Jenret wore a faintly mazed expression, still inhabiting his world of loss and pain. Loss and pain, Arras winced at its literal nearness, refusing to look down.

Measuring him with a tailor's eye—or a coffin maker's—Bullybess made a half-tour round him, halting behind him and humming to herself. Never had he felt so vulnerable! Sweat formed on his upper lip and draggled his mustache, his spine going icy-cold. "Keep yer back straight, balanced. Let Bullybess do all the werk." Without warning her head popped between his legs and her shoulders suddenly heaved against his buttocks, lifting, lifting. As his feet skimmed clear of the floor, she tucked an arm around each thigh, pinning his legs to her. Desperately flailing his arms for balance, his mouth open to shout a protest, he heard Jenret erupt in a crow of startled laughter.

The next thing he knew, Bullybess trotted toward the door, shouting "Duck!" as they passed into the anteroom. "Duck!" she instructed again as they lumbered outside, Bullybess picking up speed, trotting him down the street. In the twilight men, women, and children stopped dead, gawking at the dark foreigner, arms violently waving as he fought for balance. At the end of the street she stopped and deposited him with surprising gentleness.

Legs quivering as if the labor had been his, he sucked in a whooping gasp, her breathing entirely normal. With a shaky swipe of a handkerchief across his streaming brow, he began to roar with laughter at the spectacle he'd made. "Bess, I'd be honored if you'd guide us. We need you badly." Someday he might dare ask why she'd named herself after a fish soup, but not today.

"Absolutely not!" Shaking free of his son's imploring hand, Arras glowered at Harry until the boy stepped back, still wrestling with his emotions. "Lad, we've no idea where we're headed, only that we'll travel as fast as humanly possible. Of course you're worried about Jenneth, but you're too young, bound to hinder us without meaning to."

"Can swim like a fish," Harry muttered. "Ride. Addawanna taught me how to paddle a canoe." Brows beetling, he stared pointedly at his father's midsection, grown more generous and soft of late. "How long since *you've* ridden hard all day? Done a forced march carrying full gear like the troops you command?"

Ignoring their bickering, Jenret sorted through the first lot of supplies Oh-Oh had delivered, selecting a runt sack and passing it to Byrlyn, who obediently trotted with it to a smaller pile she guarded. Some might haphazardly paw through the pile, intent on specific objects, but he concentrated on inspecting each item, considering it for the group as a whole.

In this matter of life or death he'd not be caught wanting, nor would he be flighty, fickle in his choices, despite people's beliefs. The reject pile loomed larger, threatening to overspill the yellow-and-blue-tiled entry hall of the house Oh-Oh'd hurriedly rented for them. Come to think of it, he'd not seen much of it beyond the entry hall and the kitchens on one hurried visit. No point, since they'd leave at dawn. Rawn prowled, twitchy, uncomfortable at being idle.

On her knees across from him, Holly examined a canteen, frowning at a hairline crack before discarding it, its thud nearly unnoticeable. "Poor Harry! It's miserable to not be taken seriously," she muttered at the pile.

"Harry has the right of it, though." Valuing her opinion, he leaned to show her a heavy belt with tabs and lacings, musing, "Arras *has* a bit of a paunch. Too much soft living at the castle."

She tested the lacings, nodding to herself, and handed the belt to Byrlyn. "And neither of you want to own up to your age." Undeterred by his scowl, Holly pressed home her point. "Theo and I'll ride with you and Arras." Wonderful, she'd assigned each doddering charge a personal keeper! "Sensible, I think—if we have to split up for any reason, each party will have two members."

Unable to restrain himself, he asked, "Planning to divide Bullybess in two, are you?" The wrangle between Harry and Arras had escalated without him noticing it, Harry teetering on the brink of a tantrum. No question the boy was distraught, not merely upset, sulky at not having his way. Harry'd outgrown such outbursts early, and such distress only underscored the depths of his love for his cousins. Loyalty, too. Bless the Goddess for loyalty and love— Arras's, Harry's, Holly's, Theo's. And Doyce's. If only she weren't so blindly stubborn! Hadn't Honoria warned him there'd be repercussions if she came?

"But, Papa, I *don't* expect an adventure! 'Spect it's gonna be a miserable trip—finding Jenneth, finding Pw'eek is *serious* business!" For a moment Jenret wished Harry's Resonant skills hadn't skewed, gone erratic with the coming of puberty. If the boy were a full-fledged Resonant, he'd have been tempted to overrule Arras, bring the boy along. Fine, expose another child to danger!

As for Holly and Theo, he 'spoke Rawn, asking for confirmation. It made sense, the more competent, experienced people they could press into searching for Jenneth—and most likely for Diccon and Bard and Davvy—the sooner they'd find them. Oh-Oh'd promised to mount search parties, but Jenret had read the doubt radiating from Oordbeck. Any other aid would likely be quick and cursory at best, even with the promise of a handsome reward beyond the daily stipend he'd instructed Oordbeck to offer.

But Rawn stood stock-still, one forefoot in midair as Khim answered ahead of him. **"Oh, I don't think so. Theo and I'll stay here."** Theo registered a surprise to match Jenret's own, his provisioning list fluttering from his fingers.

"W-we *do*?" His knuckles cracked as he wove his pencil between them, not daring to look directly at Holly or Jenret. "W-why?"

"Someone should protect the ladies," and Khim winked at Rawn.

He'd have expected such a comment from staid old Rawn, but hardly from Khim! *"The day Doyce becomes a delicate, shrinking violet requiring masculine protection—at least once she's recovered from her mishap—then the hells will freeze solid. Don't worry overmuch about Lindy or Honoria, for that matter. After all, the female of the species—"*

"—is perfectly capable of surviving and thriving without male muscle or ego around," Khim finished for him.

Rawn gave a little cough of paternal pride and amended, **"Ahem, er . . . perhaps Theo and Khim should remain. One fully fit Seeker pair can work miracles until Doyce is up and about with Khar. They'll comb Samranth for any word, any hint that might help us."**

Although unsure why, Jenret suspected Rawn of genteelly coercing him into altering his plans, just as the ghatt had found himself surrendering to Khim and P'roul. The ghatti radiated some private signal, a falanese conversation he wasn't privy to. How galling to be talked around, talk floating over his head, like being a Normal in the midst of Resonants. Still, one ignored ghatti machinations at one's peril. "Theo, would you and Khim mind terribly? Staying, I mean."

Expression lugubrious, ears scarlet, Theo pointed his chin at Harry, a question in his eyes. What was he driving at? Surely Theo didn't expect him to take Harry in his place! But Holly immediately caught Theo's intention, smiled encouragingly. "H-Harry!" Theo called, beckoning Harry to him, the boy still petulant and protesting under his breath, on the brink of unforgivable behavior. "D-do you th-think you could a-s-sist me?"

"Saving face." Rawn's tail swept approvingly across the polished hall flooring. **"Neither you nor Arras thought of that."** No, women hardly required male guidance and direction, but Harry certainly could, though Jenret surmised there was more to Theo remaining behind than that.

"I n-need," Theo's chest swelled as he inhaled, expelling the words in a gust, "a strong second-in-command. S-someone to s-speak for me, be my right h-hand."

Everything looked unfamiliar because it was; one night in a new house did not a home make. The stables, at least, seemed familiar—stables were stables, after all—stalls and lofts, hay and oats, leather and manure scent, even if they'd not been recently occupied. Clad in a worn cotton dressing gown over hastily donned pantaloons, Doyce absently tucked her crutch higher under her arm as she surveyed friends, loved ones readying to leave without her, leave her behind. Her internal hurt at this leave-taking pained worse than her physical infirmities, and together they promised to lure her across the threshold of despair. "Please, Jenret—don't go!" she whispered, but he had to, *must*, if they were ever to hold Jenneth in their arms again.

A daunting woman, small and bandy-statured, was directing the horses' loading. Their guide, Bullybess, Jenret had said she was called. Under other circumstances she'd have been curious about this woman, someone who'd clearly "lived" life, not passively let it swirl around her. But now all that mattered was having Bullybess stand guarantee for Jenret's safe return.

Fisting a yawn, Doyce leaned against the stable wall, letting the sun slowly seep into her bones. Sleep had eluded her last night, her pain and fears too great to allow slumber. She'd lain silent beside Jenret, refusing to toss and turn so as not to disturb his slumber—though he'd not garnered much rest either. They'd both lain separate yet parallel, each stranded with private thoughts. Except to her surprise she'd apparently dozed, awakening to discover she lay in Jenret's arms, her crown resting against his bare chest.

"Doesn't that tell you something?" Khar wove her way to Doyce's side after her own farewells to Rawn and P'roul. What admissions and admonitions had Khar given her old companion and partner, her offspring? And what could she say to Jenret?

If her yawn were any indication, Khar appeared equally subdued and sleepless. **"You say what your heart holds, beloved."** Except Doyce was none too sure what her heart held right now, beyond a surfeit of dread.

Pairs sundering to go seeking: Arras hugging Harry, tousling his dark hair, the boy torn between relishing such overt affection and shying away from such demonstrativeness. Theo and Holly, Theo hovering close, towering over her, his smile too crooked to be genuine. He dropped a glancing kiss atop her head, and Holly hugged him hard enough to make him yelp, lacking the padding to cushion himself from such strength of emotion. Even P'roul and Khim pressed close, engaging in a final mutual grooming.

"Here, love." Out of nowhere—she'd been too engrossed by envy—a mug of fresh chaffay was thrust into her hand, Jenret standing to block the sun so she needn't squint. Even so, a shimmering halo outlined his somber, black-clad form.

"You need to get your blood flowing, grumpy bear. Bless Lindy for learning how to brew this nectar." The handsome face whose contours she so intimately knew had gone gaunt, the gentian-blue eyes red-rimmed.

"Doyce, I . . . I swear to you I'll find Jenneth, bring her back to us." Deadly serious, he clasped her mug-hand and raised it to his lips, sharing a sip as if sealing a vow. Her own hand warmed between his and the mug, a part of her coming alive again. "I love you, you know that—*have* to remember that over all else. Things have been . . . difficult lately. My fault—per usual."

She lifted his hand and the mug until his knuckles grazed her cheek. "Some's been mine, as well." Only just to acknowledge it. "My resignation caught you by surprise, I know. Somehow I thought things would be better if I spent more time with you and the twins."

Fond yet frustrated, he shook his head. "Oh, we *are* a pair, aren't we? I've been . . . well, I've been involved in some things that sent us in contrary directions, almost set us at swords-point. But it's been necessary, believe me— I'll explain, I swear, once I return."

Making impatient grumbling noises that carried all too clearly, Bullybess pointedly stared at the laggard, and Jenret squared his shoulders, heeding her command. Leaving the mug in her hand, he kissed Doyce's forehead just below her six neat stitches, and let his lips linger for a too-brief moment. Straightening, he added, "No doubt you'd have thought of it on your own, but personally visit the Guardian Captain Geerat Netlenbos, mayhap even the Governor. I've already made a hash of things, but you're more diplomatic, can smooth things over—mayhap convince them to officially aid our search. Not to mention keep an eye out for Diccon."

"Of course." Frankly she was glad for his suggestion, had been so sunken in depression that nothing had seemed to matter. Of course she'd do her share—and more! "Jenret, take care! I'm selfish—I want the twins, and I want you as well! You know I—"

But before she could voice her love aloud, he moved away as if drawn by a magnet, kissing her hand as they separated. "Honoria! Nori!" he called with feverish intensity. "Please, a moment . . ." as he hurried to her, standing confidentially close, whispering in her ear.

What intimate secret Jenret shared with Honoria Doyce never heard, wheeling herself on her crutch and limping as quickly as she could toward the kitchens. Damn the man! Such a casual betrayal, shunting her aside like that! Well, Honoria would be bored here in Samranth with her. But if she thought she could claim Jenret without a struggle, she'd best think again!

Eyes cracked a whisker-wide, Pw'eek resettled her chin on white-tipped paws, listening to her heart's lonesome beat, yearning to hear the echoing throb of her Bond's heart. Better yet, to *feel* its pulsing rhythm when Jenneth cradled her in her arms. The hot sun throbbed, red-gold ball expanding and contracting like the sky's heartbeat: the sparsely furred strip running between each eye and ear had sunburned, the insides of her ears, her nose pad, as well. The water's glare hammered as brightly brutal as the sun's.

Nostrils dry and itching, salt-rimmed, she sneezed. Almost a full day since that greedy current had snatched her, sundering her from Jenneth. Idly, she wished her spar would lodge in the sea's watery throat like a bone in a dog's, thoroughly scaring herself at such temerity.

Alone! Oh, so alone! No Jenneth. No Kwee. Jenneth's fading mindtouch, tantalizing as a distant bowl of rich, cool milk, heightened her thirst. Kwee's mindtouch hovered even farther away, their sibling linkage shredding, a dimming memory. Paws sore, she shifted, permitted herself to flex one set of claws, then another before hanging on tightly again. She would *not* slip, would *not* roll off as she dozed!

Without quite knowing when, she sensed the sea's motion had subtly altered, each extended forward glide now followed by a faint backward ebb, as if a big dog and a little one gently tugged her between them. Strange. Scrubbing her eyes with a roughened paw pad, she strained to see something new, something different, something not tinted watery-blue. Water—bleh! Except how she craved it, pure, clear water, deep enough to bury her muzzle in, soak her dry-rasped tongue! Her tongue curled, making lapping sounds despite herself. An enticing scent come-hithered by her nose, the breeze taunting her as it tossed it away. She drew the air deep into her nostrils, snuffled, let it flow along the roof of her mouth. A hard, searching sniff confirmed it, and she strained, head raised, nostrils wrinkling rapidly, eagerly. Land! The scent of land, of dry earth, sand, growing green things. Land! Yes, there! She could see it, not a low gray cloud hugging the horizon, but a dark smudge of solid land!

But how, how could she reach it? A longing cry warbled deep in her throat. Swim? No, she was still unsure if she could, felt too tired and weak. Would she float past it? Near but not near enough? She rowled her hopelessness. So thirsty, so hungry, so tired and lonely! Canny, clever Kwee'd discover a way to reach shore, but she was only cowardly, chubby Pw'eek, such a *useless* ghatten. No, *not* useless, Jenneth needed her! She'd find Jenneth again, somehow, somewhere. She would!

Determinedly shaking her head to cast off her woe, Pw'eek noticed her spar cruising faster now—a speedier forward glide, then a minor retreat, forward and back. The sea undulated like a wavy satin ribbon—lapis on one side, ultramarine on the other—twitched by an invisible hand, luring a ghatten to play, then teasing by pulling back out of reach. Frothy curves of whiteness edged each ribbon of waves, sometimes she and the spar crested a ribbon wave, sometimes they slid behind. And the distance closed, the land rising higher, larger, more solid. Not a daydream dangling from a sunbeam.

A fork-tailed tern wheeled to slice the cloudless sky, then dove, both curious and hungry. Pw'eek reared back, hissing defiance, twisting to lash at the air as the bird rose clear with one confident pump of its wings. Bite your neck, pluck your feathers out! I will, I will! Will eat you, bad bird! Don't beak-poke me—Pw'eek's not dead yet! And as the spar bobbed, then swiftly shot ahead, Pw'eek realized her folly. Ghatten couldn't climb through air, chase after birds, even taunting terns who so richly deserved chastisement. The sea and the spar leaped ahead into a foaming, lace-lather of activity, the wave tossing and breaking on a submerged coral reef.

Tumbled, tossed, submerged, Pw'eek clawed against

nothingness, mouth wide in a silent, bubbling scream. But the blue-white surface shimmer, luminous as a moon-pale beacon, proved fickle, eluding her, her round, furry body tumbling like a ball. A precious lungful of air once as the water tossed her high, a false welcome, like the cheery light shaft from an open door suddenly slammed in her face on a sodden night. Legs madly scrabbling, tiny bubbles trailing from her nostrils, she fought, striking out blindly, screamed precious air as her right forepaw slashed a spiny coral outcrop. OOOW! Within the churning blue-green wateriness, a narrow ribbon of red blood spiraled upward, her body chasing it.

Air! Waa-OOOW! The sliced toe-pad burned and bit at her nerves, galvanizing her. Despite the excruciating hurt, she somehow coordinated her legs, treading water. The combers still rolled strong but less playful, intent on reaching shore. Strong, furious kicks to fight against the undertow, not lose ground, somehow she learned to gauge the swells, ride them when she could.

Hurts, hurts, hurts! Oh, woe! Woeful Pw'eek, a part of her brain dolefully sang, but the ghatten snorted water, kept paddling, eyes locked on the beach. Pw'eek swimming! Pw'eek is being brave, clever. Pw'eek *can* reach shore, *can* find Jenneth, *can* find Sissy-Poo! Oh, Pw'eek so brave! And her heart swelled with pride.

A new wave, and her scrabbling feet touched sand, only to find it jerked away in the next breath. Oh, no, nasty water, not winning over Pw'eek! Gathering herself, she let the next wave lift her landward as far as it could and drove herself forward, staggering against the sea's efforts to reclaim her. A step, another step, and yet another. With a limp and a swagger, she dashed up the wet, hard-packed beach, throwing herself onto the hot, dry sand, rolling on her back, her white, wet lily belly exposed to the sky, the sun. Oooh, lily belly, beautiful lily belly! Beautiful land! Legs splayed, she fell asleep, a tiny smile of ghatti satisfaction etched beneath her white mustache.

"That should be," Diccon licked a finger to trace a course on the map, "Gosling, Goose, and Gander. Islands, I mean," he added in case Davvy or Bard required further clarification.

"**Goosie,**" Kwee confirmed with a yawn and blinked to drive the sleep away. "**Clever Diccon. Gos-ling, Goo-sie, and Gan-der.**" M'wa concealed a fatuous smile, faintly abashed at having succumbed to Kwee's wiles. Ghatten could be infuriating—utterly literal one moment, all dreamy fantasy the next—yet astoundingly delightful little beasts. As long as her silliness didn't rub off.

Bard trimmed the sail to catch the breeze rising with the sun, while Davvy shifted the tiller—one of their oars, actually, doing double-duty—until the launch pointed toward the smallest of three islands dotting the sea. "Which one first?"

"Doesn't matter, we'd best check them all." Ignoring Diccon, Bard sat back, elbows propped on splayed knees, gold-toned hands dangling loosely. "Jenneth and Pw'eek could've washed up on any one of them." The boy's over-eager words buzzed and bumbled in Bard's ears, the endless night, the rowing, had taken their toll, physically exhausting but leaving him too much time to think.

Looking as singularly relaxed as if a sleepless night at sea in a cramped boat had been nothing to him, Davvy sprawled on the stern bench, steadying the rudder-oar. "Sail or row round, do you think? Check the shoreline that way—or should we land?"

"Ashore." "Around." The answers collided, the silence leaden as Diccon and Bard scowled at each other, Bard unyielding, his face emotionless despite the fact his blood was racing, the land, the Sunderlies coastline beyond the islands singing so seductively in his brain. Yes, he *had* to find Jenneth, *would* find her, but she couldn't be here on these paltry islands, not the way the land cried its welcome to him! Couldn't the boy understand, feel it?

"We *have* to land, scour the beaches, check each inlet and cove, work inland if necessary. What if they're hurt and crawled into the undergrowth to hide, then lost consciousness? I'll shift every pebble on each island myself, if I have to!" Diccon's imploring hand on Bard belied his steadfast insistence.

Taking his time, moody without his morning cha, Bard snagged a water jug, unplugging it and drinking deep.

Raised a questioning eyebrow at Davvy and passed it along. On its return Bard hefted it assessingly before wordlessly passing it to Diccon, who sipped almost daintily, not throwing his head back so he could keep his eyes on Bard. When Kwee nudged his hip, Diccon blindly fumbled a little pannikin from a belt-loop and poured water for her. Misjudging the depth, she sank her nose too deeply, her muzzle screwing up in surprise, water beading her whiskers.

"Thing of it is, Diccon," Bard studied the launch's ribbing as if each curve might hold a special and singular secret—if only he could learn it. When had he given up—after Byrta died? "If they *were* there, don't you think Kwee or M'wa would sense it? *You* as well, even with Jenneth unconscious? Your twinship would shout it loud and clear!" Envy thick as syrup clogged his throat. Byrta—gone. Never again, except perhaps in death, to revel in the paired beat of hearts, the twinned minds. At least . . . at least he had Byrlyn now, unfurling like a bud just beginning to bask in the sun's smile. Ready to let him in, let him share a fraction of what he'd had so ruthlessly snatched away from him before.

Early morn radiance gilded M'wa's white markings with a wash of peach and pink, rosy gold, turning him almost raffish, though his speech was anything but. **"He has the right of it, Diccon. I can't sense them, Kwee can't. Can you?"**

Reluctant to admit defeat, Diccon finally shook his head. "So we do nothing at all? Just sail by? Not even row round—just in case?" He clutched his map hard, the stiff paper crackling protest beneath whitened knuckles. "Tuck swore the currents sweep round here, deposit things on the islands' lee sides. This would be the first place they'd wash ashore."

"And Captain Thorsen couldn't plot our location when Jenneth and Pw'eek went overboard. He had other things plaguing him—like keeping the *Vruchtensla* afloat. Without that as a starting point, Tuck's made an educated guess, nothing more, nothing less." He hated to damper such hope and enthusiasm, but better the lad should taste disappointment, stare reality in the face. Then a full dose of disappointment might not destroy him later. "None of this means we won't succeed, Dic, just that we're unlikely to

find them first try. Somewhere on the mainland's *my* bet."
What possessed him to use Diccon thusly?

But Davvy took pity on Diccon. "How about going
ashore on one island? Never hurts to replenish our water
while we can, or add to our supplies if there's something
better to eat." He rapped a sea biscuit on the gunwale for
emphasis. Fresh hope eased some of the tightness that had
made Diccon's face a death mask of lost innocence. "Who
inhabits these islands, Diccon? Fisher folk? Ship builders?
Shepherds?"

Diccon giggled, and Bard found he had to smile as well.
"No doubt Harrap was birthed here."

"The sheep kind, not the religious kind," Davvy hurriedly amplified, unamused. "Even Gosling looks big
enough, hilly enough to support a grazing flock. Besides,
we can ask any islanders to be on the lookout. Can't hurt."

His humor departing as rapidly as it had come, Bard
inspected the bailing bucket, turning it ceaselessly in his
hands. Bail himself out? He wasn't precisely angry at
Davvy for siding with Diccon but was ill-pleased, all the
same. When had it become Davvy's place to intrude, inter-
vene like that?

**"Ever since you fell into this foul mood. What's ailing
you?"**

As if M'wa didn't know, hadn't worried from the beginning about his strange attraction to the Sunderlies. Fine,
tell M'wa that both feet had been cramping all night and
he truly wanted to walk on solid land—not some puny island—to work the kinks out of his legs, his whole body.
Say that and the ghatt would instantly know he shrouded
a greater truth from himself. *"M'wa, I'm trying. I beg you,
don't. Give Davvy time to make me look the fool before
you harp at me."*

He and Davvy had known the twins forever. This trip
wasn't about assessing whom Diccon respected the most,
was it? *"Is it?"* he 'spoke M'wa, not expecting an answer
but determined to cover all fronts. Had he misjudged every
thing, every action, every person since that festive night
when he'd made the one impulsive decision of his life—to
visit his ancestors' homeland?

The ghatt gave him a sorrowing look, head imperceptibly
shaking, but that was all. Bard cleared his throat. "Fine,

then. Let's land on Goose—I yield to middle ground, at least." With a salute to Diccon, he announced, "Captain, chart our course."

Rumble-gut, grumble-rumbling, belly-knotting agony! So very, very hungry! Thirsty! Pw'eek awoke with a start, panicky at no longer swaying to the sea's rhythms. Shook her head, shook sand out of her ears and whiskers, unable to determine if this were a new day or the old one still. Remaining as motionless as she could to avoid detection, she took in her surroundings, pupils dilating at so much newness, gradually recalling how she'd gotten to this place. Just then a wavelet tugged wet and cold at her tail and sent her bouncing to her feet with a shriek, shrieking even higher as her right forepaw ground into the sand. Whimpering and hobbling, she dragged her exhausted, empty body higher up the beach, fleeing the encroaching high tide. Never-ever want to see the sea again!

Shadows, lovely coolness higher up, the sun dropping lower. Green frondy things reaching down, green-fingers tickle-tracing the sand when the breeze ruffled them. Clearly the sand had fought back, won in isolated instances; some of the frondy things had fallen, littering the ground, turned the same color as the sand. Would they tickle her, green-fingered grab at her? Tweak at a ghatten tail? Oh, dear. Oh, woe! Nervous, she licked an inner leg, made a sudden face, tongue still half-extended. Oh, ick! Salty salt all over fur, sticky fur, caked with scratchy sand! Her nostrils flared, catching the scent, the seductive smell of water deep within the greenery.

Steeling herself, she dashed through the low-hanging fronds that caressed but didn't snatch as she followed the bracing scent. Big-leafed things with stinky-soft purple blossoms drifted pollen on her, but she didn't care, ignoring the myriad insects darting into the smellies, listening to the secret sounds of the greenery but hearing nothing to fear. Oh, water, water! She labored, shoving and butting against twisted, thick vines knotted by the storm, too tired to leap them, her right forepaw shooting arrows of pain. Finally, she dropped to her lily belly and slithered beneath them,

choking back a sob when a tendril snared her. Rose and
limped along when she could, staggering against ridged
trunks of trees so tall their tops hid in the sky when she
braved a look up.

The alluring water scent engulfed her, nearly driving her
mad with desire, promising unheard-of-delight. Squishy
moistness underfoot, bubbling, gentle plashing, and the
scolding trill of a bright-hued bird nearby. A velvet, moss-
banked brink, a profusion of plants, a tiny rodent with
bead-bright eyes raising its head from the water—her
water!—and skittering off in chittering dismay. A swirl of
convex stone with rippling sides carved by the spring's flow,
an oval swirl nearly as big as a human washtub, sweet water
brimming over its lip. Casting aside ghatti fastidiousness,
Pw'eek sank muzzle-deep into the water, let the coolness
lave her open mouth, her tongue, finally pulling clear to
breathe, then licking in a pink-tongued blur. The crisp chill
salved her hollow stomach and she decided to immerse her
whole head. Yes, aaah! Hateful being wet again, but this
was balm, soaking the salt from her sore eyes, pleasantly
numbing her sore spots.

Coming up for air at last she tossed her head, water
droplets flying, and began to drink once more. Do it, not
do it? Get wet all over? She debated between licks, slow
now and savoring. The thought of thoroughly grooming
every bit of skin and fur made her shiver, her tongue want
to shrivel. Nasty sand, nasty salt, and her tongue was *so*
small! With a final shudder she scrunched her eyes and
threw herself into the spring basin, submerging herself
again and again, thankful her paws could touch bottom.
Clambering out and vigorously shaking herself, she felt her
beautiful calico coat clumping, spiking in wet quills. Clean
clumps, at least.

Groom now, she ordered herself, and gingerly commenced. Her slashed toe cried for attention, for a thorough
cleansing, but her stomach writhed at the thought of such
pain. Gathering her courage, she worked down her right
foreleg, slower and more cautious as she neared her white
toes. A hideous cacophony of squawks and shrieks made
her startle, even that done improperly, well-nigh impossible
to fluff her tail in fright, ridge the fur on her spine. Too

wet. Danger! Though the longer she listened, the more it
sounded like a raucous argument or squabble of some sort.

Crouching on her belly, slithering between drooping
branches and bushes with improbable foliage, she edged
back until she could again view the beach, eyes glowing
chartreuse amongst jaggedly notched leaves larger than any
human hand that had ever stroked her. A white gull with
black wing-tips and feet dove downward, a gray-winged gull
rising to meet him, the two clashing in midair while others
swarmed and swirled just above the waterline, all of them
fighting and yammering, clacking their nasty beaks, one faction intent on driving off the other. Nasty birds! Her tail
switched at the memory of the tern who'd taunted her,
made her fall off her spar. Beat each other up! Beak-stab
and slice! Settling on her belly, she avidly watched the confrontation, front legs extended so her bad paw didn't bear
any weight.

A change in the breeze, and she inhaled long and hard,
her mind whirling. Aah, so ripely rank, so richly rotted! The
enticing odor swirled by her, and she cracked her mouth to
inhale the scent, smelling and tasting it simultaneously.
Those days with Kwee, scavenging around the docks and
along the shore at Windle Port hadn't been wasted, she
recognized that come-hither scent all too well. Fish! Old,
perhaps, stinking, surely—but wondrous, tasty fish! If the
sea had a purpose, it was to nourish fish—finny, scaly,
toothsomely tantalizing fish!

By an act of will she ignored her sore foot and readied
herself, leg muscles coiled to spring, hindquarters elevated
and switching to gain momentum. With a low, predatory
growl Pw'eek charged across the sand, scattering gulls,
slashing at razor-sharp beaks, ducking drubbing wing-blows.
Foraging sand crabs scuttled, buried themselves eyestalk
deep as she straddled the fish carcass, growling in triumph
as a cloud of gulls took off. Mine! Pw'eek's fish! Food!

Its eye sockets empty, the fish was skeletal in parts, its
remaining flesh sickly white, stippled with festering, iridescent color. It tasted divine, simple to strip from the bones
with long, burr-tongued slurps, dainty ripping gestures,
powerful jaw-crunches severing the spine when she greedily
dug deeper. Nothing in her few brief ghatten octants of life
had ever tasted so good! Its comforting bulk swelled her

belly, made her warmly happy all over. Beautiful, succulent fish!

At length, with a waddling, limping gait she stepped away from the remains and sat staring out at the waves as she groomed, scrubbing tiny flakes of fish from her whiskers, her cheeks. The secondhand taste on her paw was almost as delicious as the first bites. Wash, scrub, remove all food scent—danger came if another could smell you, smell what you'd eaten. Behind ears, yes, under chin. Downward licks on the white bib. She stopped, blankly staring seaward again. The longing, the loss hit with such force she nearly toppled on the sand. Jenneth! Kwee!

Still, a vague sense of them in the distance, two different directions, each far away. Her heart and mind cried out to them, but they weren't close enough to truly hear. What to do? Finally, as the sea slowly swallowed the sun, she limped past cast-off seaweed streamers crackling in the heat, continuing toward the sheltering finger-fronds. Patiently she worked herself deeper until she hunted out a spot free from the scent of other, larger animals, hoping her calico markings would camouflage her. Circling, circling, clumsy at the tight footwork required, she finally settled with a thump, pillowing her chin on her curled tail. Tomorrow. She'd decide what to do tomorrow, and fell into a bea-yoou-ti-ful belly-full sleep. Ah . . . fish . . . !

As the keel scraped the shingle, Diccon stripped off his boots and jumped into thigh-deep water, struggling to beach their launch. With a trill of enthusiasm Kwee leaped for his bent shoulders, a convenient stepping stone in her race for dry land. Unfortunately her "stepping stone" found himself first off-balance, then facedown in the water. Breaking the surface and grasping the launch's gunwale, Diccon levered himself upright, water coursing off him. "Don't," he warned with dire emphasis, "even think about laughing."

In perfect accord for the first time, Davvy and Bard both tightened their lips, Bard jumping in to help ground the launch on the pebbled beach. "Laughter never hurts, especially if you can laugh at yourself first." Together they strained, hauling higher, until Bard gave a critical nod, satisfied.

"I know. The whole family's famous for it—sometimes I swear humor's the only emotion we dare show, safer to keep the more serious ones under wraps." Diccon rough-combed his fingers through sopping hair, burrowing his toes in the wet sand. "It's just that nothing's very funny with Jen lost out there somewhere." If anyone should—could—understand, it would be Bard.

Stowing the rudder-oar beneath the benches, Davvy jumped out to join them. "So this is Goose?" They'd agreed to land on the middle island first, then move on to Gander. Arms extended, he twisted at the waist, bent first backward and then forward to loosen stiff muscles, taking in the terrain with quick glances all the while. Disembarking in one long, fluid leap, M'wa joined Kwee, sedately chaperoning each curious sniff, each darting move as she reconnoitered the beach. A finger-long lizard, exactly shaded to mimic the sand, captured her attention when it dashed up the dunes, and she trailed it, nose practically touching its swishing tail.

"Ahem," M'wa lifted a forepaw, looking back to the figures on the beach. **"The youngling and I'll do a bit of . . . exploring, if you don't mind. Of course we'll stay within mindcall."**

As comprehension dawned, Diccon recognized a problem he'd blithely overlooked in his gathering of necessities. There was exploring, and there was "exploring," as M'wa had so diplomatically called it. The ghatti lacked a way of relieving themselves while at sea, short of actually soiling the launch, and they were far too fastidious for that. At least he and Davvy and Bard could pee over the side, though it was wise to check which way the wind blew—Tuck had taught him that. *"Of course. Just keep Kwee out of trouble if you can, M'wa."*

Retrieving his boots, Diccon trudged higher, determined not to wince or yelp at stubbed toes or ankles threatening to roll on loose stones. What the rest of Goose offered he couldn't tell, but this particular beach boasted more than its share of stones, from ones smaller than the ball of his thumb to cobble-sized, all rounded smooth from aeons of the sea's constant churning. White mostly; intermingled

with some of pale reddish tan; a few glistening black ones
threaded with silvery-white stripes. Wiping his feet on the
dune grass, he pulled his boots on.

For a few moments he simply sat, one of the streaked
black stones in his hand, too overwhelmed and tired to
decide what to do next. At least Bard apparently had a
plan in mind, packing food and water into his haversack,
buckling his sword 'round his waist. But Davvy just continued with his strange exercises, a distant, thoughtful expression, almost a frown on his face, and Diccon nearly jumped
at Davvy's unexpectedly call. "What's that tower thing over
on Gander? Couldn't really see it before, the mist was
hanging too low."

Scooting on his bottom, Diccon looked; Davvy *had* spotted something! A tower, mayhap more than one, as best
he could judge, and imposing compared to the low, rolling
hills it surmounted. Its very top glinted sharp enough to
blind as the sun struck it—a mirror? Behind it he could
make out a large, coppery-hued cupola. Shrugging on his
pack, Bard joined Diccon. "Lighthouse, I'd say. Good news
for us. Means Gander *is* inhabited, and the lighthouse
should provide a view in all directions."

Diccon clapped a hand to his head. Aunt Jacobia and
her interminable history lesson . . . the lantern symbols
scattered on his map. Lighthouse, yes—but Gander also
hosted one of the Guardian forts built to ensure no exiled
convicts escaped from their new and enforced homeland.
Guardians! After all, they were "breaking in," so to speak,
not "breaking out," fleeing the Sunderlies. Of course the
Guardians would help! "Better than that, Bard!" He sprang
up, his heart light, ready to run clear across Goose, signal
to Gander. "It's a Guardian fort! They'll help us find Jen!"

More sensible to take the launch, sail on to Gander, but
Diccon had already sprinted up the dunes, the others at
his heels. But their swift start soon faltered as they found
themselves enveloped by Goose's inhospitable vegetation.
Toiling through tough, tall grasses and sinewy vines, they
fought to bend back the drooping branches of twisty,
gnarled trees festooned with foliage like a cross between a
leaf and long fir needles. The most recent storm left a mute,
wounded legacy: snapped branches with pitch weeping from

their white stubs, and uprooted trees sheltering crumbling caverns at their tilted bases.

Mostly they toiled upward; what appeared an easy rise was instead rawly terraced, nature having sliced slabs of stone into craggy outcroppings. Disturbed by their intrusion, nesting seabirds protested, flinging themselves skyward with noisy wing-claps, plaguing them with stealthy dives, soot-colored wings buffeting their faces and heads. Another thing plagued them: birds in plenty meant guano in plenty—underfoot, on the outcroppings they grasped, and wetly whizzing through the air to strike them.

Heaving himself atop the escarpment, Davvy inspected himself, scraping first one boot sole, then the other on the grass to clean them, wiping his hands on his pantaloons. A large, irregular splotch decorated his right shoulder, another smeared the small of his back. "In some places guano's considered quite valuable as fertilizer," Bard slyly commented as he plucked a handful of sawgrass, held it out to Davvy. "Given what you've collected, you're well on your way to riches." He pointed to the top of his own head, then to Davvy's.

Ignoring Davvy's disgusted groan of comprehension, Diccon wildly waved his arms, jumping up and down as he halloed at the top of his lungs. Yes—there! Distant dots of color hurried antlike, converging at a splinter of dockage across the bay at Gander. "Come on, hurry! We can slide down here!" Without waiting for an answer he began a jouncing descent. "Hurrah! They're launching a boat to meet us!"

Goose Isle did not live up to its name, was hardly soft and downy, sleekly feathered. Only a bit over a kilometer at its widest, the actual distance they traversed proved considerably greater. Up, down, and around; backtrack when the growth turned impenetrable, either thrusting them back or snaring them. But even Bard's and Davvy's ongoing catalog of curses couldn't dampen his excitement as Bard sawed with his sword to untangle him yet again. The only thing Diccon begrudged was the loss of time, but the launch would wait.

At length, hot, weary, bruised, they reached shore exactly opposite their landing site. Some exotic bird with sweeping, scythelike tail feathers of gilded emerald green flared out of nowhere, its screams so chillingly effective that Diccon reversed in midstride, only to smash into Bard and topple him. Apologizing, he decided this mishap was minor compared to the scare Davvy had given them when he'd nearly grabbed a snake as thick as his forearm, taking it for a vine.

"Next time, we definitely row or sail round." A raindrop struck Diccon dead-center as Davvy spoke. "Come on, Bard, call it!" and dug into his pocket for a coin to flip. "One of us can enjoy the scenic coastal tour, bring the launch round."

"Mayhap Diccon's new friends will take us back," Bard suggested.

The rain intensified, drops increasingly larger, drumming on the leaves, dimpling the sand, stinging their tired flesh. As the boat from Gander drew closer, Diccon didn't care who retrieved the launch—let them argue it out. Guardians! In Canderis they lent a hand at anything, from sandbagging a flooding river to their normal duties of warding the citizenry and protecting the land. Of course they'd help! They'd alert the whole coast—why hadn't he thought of it before?

By the time the *Vruchtensla* limped into port, he might even have rescued Jen and Pw'eek—Mama and Papa would be so relieved! But a lingering shame still burdened him— at slipping away as he had, and at having ignored their anxious mindcries until he was too distant to clearly receive them. His willful silence—unlike Jen's—had been a way to avoid distractions, fix his mind on his task.

The larger launch sped along, six pairs of rowers in tan-and-blue summer-weight uniforms plying their oars in unison, a helmed Guardian at the bow with a telescope, scanning the shore. Grand—especially compared to Davvy's and Bard's efforts at the oars! Diccon gave a friendly wave. "Come on, let's give a hand beaching the boat," he urged, sliding down the final sandy slope.

"Guardians, ahoy!" he shouted, cupping his hands around his mouth. "Bless you for coming! My sister's lost at sea," he continued, struggling against the surf, readying himself to catch their bowline. Had they heard—or had the waves muffled his words? With practiced ease the bowman cast a grapple anchor, its flukes whizzing perilously close to Diccon's head before burying itself in the hard-packed sand. "Hey! Have a care, there!"

With practiced rhythm the Guardians shipped oars pair by pair; the bowman and the first three sets of rowers springing over the side, forming a compact wedge as they waded ashore. The six left then disembarked to drag the launch clear of the surf, Diccon noticed as two men abruptly and efficiently pinioned his arms behind him. It hurt. "What's going—" A meaty hand cuffed his head, his question disrupted by the ringing in his ears.

Jaw dropping, then clenching in anger, he tensed every muscle, struggling to twist away far enough to give Bard and Davvy warning, but a foot hooked his ankle, styming his efforts. A shove to the center of his back sent him plunging down, knees pinning his hips and shoulders in the lapping surf. Desperate, he arched his neck back, waiting an eternity for an ebbing wave to inhale a shaky breath, frantically glance up the beach. Rain beat at him, more water to blur his vision, but he could just make out Davvy and Bard fighting as the Guardians' closing circle swallowed them, subdued by punches and the press of bodies.

"What's the meaning of this?" Bard shouted, his sword jerked from his hand and tossed away. Diccon's stomach heaved at the seething passion in Bard's voice, anger that would build to rage, build to an unappeasable red-hot wrath, and ultimately unleash a berserk strength surpassing all normal bounds. "I'm Seeker Veritas Bard Ambwasali! The boy's a Novice, a Seeker-in-training, son of the Seeker General!"

The incoming wave caught Diccon unprepared, sweeping into his mouth, pouring up his nostrils. Gagging, he fought the sensation, desperate to cough, swallow, but forcing himself to fight the urge. "Bard, don't—" he burbled underwater, finally had sense enough to hold his breath, 'speak Davvy. *"Don't let him go wild! You've got to control Bard—for his own good!"*

Davvy's only comment was a brief, bitter expletive.

Again the water receded, replaced by blessed air. The Guardian on Diccon's back shifted, belatedly removing Diccon's knife from his waist sheath. "If your friend's a Seeker, and you are, too, where're your ghatti? Answer me that! Colossally stupid lie, if you ask me."

Colossally stupid, but not a lie. Wearily, Diccon spat sand
and furiously mindspoke Kwee and M'wa as the next wave
came at him.

"I'm perfectly able, thank you!" Flinging her elbow to dislodge Honoria's hand, Doyce stumped ahead, threading her
way along a street already alive with activity, though the
workday had just begun. After the stately Esplanade and
adjacent, tree-lined avenues, all equally subdued, this
crooked commercial street with its jostling, bawling dray-
men, its handcarts and ricks unnerved her, her energy expended on simply reaching it. All because she'd refused to
put on airs by engaging a chair or carriage!

Voices assaulted her from second- and third-story veran-
das where merchants and dealers shouted quotes back and
forth, tossing samples to their street runners. A hectic,
shabby prosperity to the place, despite gimcrack buildings
with peeling paint or chipped stucco, as if people had other,
better concerns, better ways of employing their money.
Throwing her shoulders back, she called to Honoria, "Why
not join the others at the bazaar? I don't need any help—
you've done more than enough for me!"

**"You forgot to say 'thank you' again, the kind where
sarcasm drips off like honey from a comb."** Unobtrusive at
her leg, Khar gave her a slanted look, two parts exasperation, one part discomfort. Out in public like this, Khar provoked a certain consternation, speculation, and downright
anxiety in most folk.

"Doyce, to the right." Honoria steered her from behind
with a light touch. "See? That lane over there." Doyce did
see the sign—after the fact. Would have missed it on her
own, its colors dulled to match the paint-scabbed wall on
which it hung.

"How do you know where to look, where to go?" Already damp from exertion, Doyce wanted nothing more
than to dig her fingers into her scalp, give her stitches a
good scratch. How they itched!

"More or less than Honoria makes you itch?" Khar
wanted to know. **"At least she was up at first light, asking**

directions, even walking partway here to make sure she knew the route."

"Are you defending her?" Dressed in elegantly-cut black serge pantaloons and a crisp white shirt with a high, confining collar and long sleeves, Doyce came to a halt, neatly rolling her cuffs, delaying until Khar answered. A blessing she'd worn her formal tabard instead of the sheepskin, though she'd not yet added white to its purple-and-gold trim to denote her retired status. Already her shirt had wilted, its pleats listless. *"Well? Are you?"* "No, Honoria, I'm fine—just rolling these cuffs clear."

Narrowing herself to squeeze into a sliver of shade cast by an upper veranda, the ghatta took her time as well, craning to see the overhanging carpet samples in jute, woven wool, braided cottons. **"I'm defending this morning's actions: she's concerned, helpful. I'm not defending whatever else she may or may not do—or be."**

Without a word Doyce resumed her pace so swiftly that Khar, caught off guard, scampered to catch up. **"It's not a question of whether I approve or disapprove of her. I simply comment on her current activities."** Sometimes Khar sounded absurdly pompous, but Doyce refused to be baited, too preoccupied with her reason for her visit to this section of Samranth.

Finally wavering, her leg complaining at the pace she'd set, Doyce grimaced at the sweat streaming down her neck, soaking her collar. Grudgingly accepting the handkerchief Honoria pressed into her hand, she astonished herself by limping biddably toward the shaded bench the other woman indicated. It had nothing to do with Honoria, it was her decision—she needed to sit, recover her wind. If only it were as simple to recover her equanimity!

Arranging buttery-yellow skirts with her habitual precision, Honoria opened her reticule and extracted a burlap-wrapped bottle moist with condensation. "Just water," she noted, taking a sip as she handed Doyce a toweling square. "Drink some, then wet this and wipe your face and neck. Have you a comb?"

Curious against her better judgment, Doyce asked, "What else have you stashed in there? It doesn't look as if it could hold more than a few coins and a lace hanky."

"Deceptive . . . isn't it?" Tapping her lips, Honoria considered. "Oh, let's see . . . an emergency flare, half a cheese, a snood . . . a soup spoon, three quarrels and a spare bow string. That's all. Theo said you'd likely bring the bear trap yourself."

Her deadpan comment caught Doyce off guard—or was she mocking Doyce's well-known penchant for carrying every conceivable odd and end? Combing her hair, springy from the damp, and secretly pleased she *did* have a pocket comb, she muttered, "Left the bear trap in my other trousers." The jest gave her spirits a minor lift.

"Ah, isn't that what they always say?" Rising lightly to her feet, she inquired, "Ready? We're nearly there."

"Yes." With a rush, Doyce added, "You needn't accompany me, you know. I've dealt with Guardians for years, and I don't become as overwrought as . . ." somehow she resented uttering his name in Honoria's presence, "Jenret."

"I know," Honoria replied with cool sincerity. "But Jenneth's plight is an emotional subject. Even the strongest of us need support at times. Jenret certainly does. Besides," she appraised Doyce's crutch, "play up your invalid status—bereft, injured mother, consoled by a devoted friend."

Whatever tenuous goodwill might have accrued from their few shared moments of rest vanished at Honoria's calculating attitude. Some gained what they wanted that way, playing for sympathy, but it had never come naturally to Doyce—a crutch she refused to use. *"Well, what do you think of her now?"* and felt a certain smugness.

"That she *can* be useful—has her uses." Padding by Honoria's skirts without brushing them, Khar muttered, **"After all, I never said I wanted to Bond with her!"**

"I heard about the horrid fuss at our Guardian post just as the *Vruchtensla* was landing—I'm so very sorry!" Escorting Doyce and Honoria into a pristine office with spare but highly elegant furnishings, Captain Geerat Netlenbos, commander of the Guardian forces in the Sunderlies, efficiently seated them, even pulling up a footstool and piling gaily-coordinated silk pillows atop it for Doyce's bad leg. She prayed he'd be equally solicitous about her real problem—and as charmingly practical.

Returning to his black-lacquered desk, he sat, leaning forward on his forearms as if to invite her confidences, and Doyce froze, found she literally didn't know where to begin, all her fears suddenly swelling within her. Raising her hands to forestall his comments, she sat back, resting her head, collecting herself for the ordeal of explaining Jenneth's loss again.

"Give yourself time, beloved. He'll wait." Khar sat as far from Geerat's desk as possible. While he'd greeted her cordially, he'd immediately started waving a handkerchief in front of his face, either allergic or indifferent to ghatti.

To restore her calm she furtively studied Netlenbos, fixating on details but unable to form a coherent picture of the man. His crisp blue short-sleeved shirt showed no sign of perspiration, as if he stored a boundless supply of fresh ones in this harborside office. Inconsequentially she wondered if he had his laundry done over here or at Tarango Fort? His hair was expertly barbered, but when she looked away, she almost forgot its sandy color. Vaguely handsome, she supposed, just as he was faintly anonymous-looking both in face and disposition, unlikely to stand out in a crowd.

As her composure returned, Doyce began unfolding her story, succinctly explaining the situation, telling Netlenbos what had been done, why they so desperately needed his aid. "Please," she concluded, "can the Guardians assist in our search? The longer she's lost, the less chance we have of finding her alive." Though her voice had grown husky with hurt, she'd maintained control, hadn't fallen weeping and wailing across his desk, or forced him to run for smelling salts. Well, she'd gladly attempt any and all of that if it would ensure his help! Mayhap Honoria had had the right of it. Shame was too costly a sentiment when begging for help.

"Ah, I can well understand your husband's dismay and anger, how his expectations must have turned leaden." A look of mild sympathy in her general direction before he returned to studying a crested rattan helmet he'd begun toying with during her plea. (**"That's *not* a good sign, you know,"** Khar muttered.) "Do you think it suitable for this climate?" He eagerly displayed it. "That the wicker-weave will be airy, yet still offer protection?"

"Khar, did he hear one word I said? Did anything register?" Mouth agape in stunned shock, she pushed the helmet aside, almost with revulsion.

"Oh, I'm so sorry!" Setting the helmet aside, he adjusted it once, then reluctantly ignored it. "So sorry about everything, of course. What I *hate* about this job," he pounded lightly on the desk to emphasize his words, "is that it's nothing like Canderis! Can you believe that? It's an absolutely impossible job sometimes!"

"In what way do you mean?" Doyce had an idea where this was so circuitously leading, and her heart ached nearly as much as her head. *Oh, Jenret, I tried!* she cried to herself.

"We're here to guarantee no hardened criminals ever flee back home. We patrol up and down the coast, we track outbound harbor traffic, inspect passenger lists, search merchant ships, though the only contraband we're interested in is human. Amazing what some criminals will try—highly inventive!

"There are too few of us as it is. Worst of all, we generally have a hands-off policy regarding local issues—unlike at home. Of course I feel a civic responsibility, but I can't lend everyone a hand. Would you prefer we shovel mud after a storm while criminals escape? Only on rare occasions do we become involved—one has to be diplomatic regarding orders from above, the Governor, you know." The man cast a better beseeching look than she! "I *hope* you understand, can appreciate my anomalous position here. Of *course* we'll watch out for your Jenneth, your son as well—Diccon, did you say? But that's about all this visit will avail you, I fear. Regretfully, we can't offer any active participation. Again, I'm so sorry!" Although he addressed her, his eyes continually strayed to Honoria, demurely seated against the opposite wall, attentive, occasionally daubing her eyes with a ladylike hanky. At this moment she'd gladly let Honoria work her feminine wiles on the captain!

"You *do* see, don't you?" he pleaded again, starting to rise from his desk, preparing to escort them out.

"I thank you for your candor." Leaning back wearily, Doyce suppressed an urge to pick up her crutch and splinter his precious helmet with it. "Some advice, if you'd be so forthcoming? Do you see any harm in my visiting the

Governor, asking if her office can do anything constructive? You wouldn't feel as if I'd gone over your head, so to speak?" Such unthinking slights were best avoided. Do it right, follow the rules and procedures, and he might be willing to provide some surreptitious assistance.

"Oh, dear! Governor Hoetmer?" Starting to laugh, he sat back down, visibly restraining himself. "Miz Marbon, Seeker General—hasn't anyone told you? The poor Governor's a bit loony, ga-ga, you know." Netlenbos was waggling his fingers beside his head in emphasis. "She's practically an antique. Been stationed here so long the Sunderlies have turned her brain to mush. Oh," he added dismissively, "she's spry enough, sometimes she's moderately lucid for short periods of time. But little's accomplished through her offices nowadays—her advisers' hands are tied. I don't know why no one's reported the situation to the Monitor."

Rising, all hope bitterly dashed, she fled Netlenbos's office as quickly as she could, wanting to slink away, shamed at her failure. It was up to Jenret, to Diccon, now, if they were to have any hope of rescuing Jenneth.

Doyce scarcely registered Honoria's hand on her elbow until she realized how close she hovered. Except for a certain grimness about her mouth, Honoria looked collected, contained. "What an utterly pretentious little prick!" she pronounced with icy disdain. "Though he's rather attractive in a way—so regulation!" Doyce goggled, and Honoria drew her along, still speaking soft and soothing words. "Don't dwell on it, it's over, done. You *had* to try, would have despised yourself if you hadn't." Doyce nodded, wordless.

More briskly she continued, "What we urgently need is some temporary distraction. Better than brooding about this, I should think? Let's join the others at the bazaar." And Doyce let herself be led away, glad someone—even Honoria—had taken charge.

"Well, one can't fault her assessment," Khar noted as she trailed after them.

Blinding colors, myriad scents—mostly unidentifiable—and a cacophony of sounds all busily conspired with her throbbing head to convince her stomach to treacherously roil. When she saw Lindy had doubled, two of her just ahead at identical stalls, two of Honoria beside—her? them?—Doyce announced, "Would all four of you sit me down, please? Now!" The weight of the oven-hot air, the clammy-cold moisture sheathing her skin, set goose bumps rising all over her. Loosing her crutch, she hastily covered her mouth, refusing to allow anything more than a faint retching sound to escape. She would *not* disgrace herself, foul the place like some gullible visitor who'd unwarily sampled too many unknown local delicacies.

"Auntie Doyce!" A thin arm sturdily encircled her waist, a shoulder planting itself beneath her arm, exactly where the crutch should have nestled. Strange, in the midst of a wave of nausea, to realize how Harry's strength matched his new height. "Byrlie!" Calling the child to him, he jerked his chin at a booth with a red-and-white striped awning. Doyce groaned as she followed his gaze; the awning shaded piles of boldly vibrant, often conflicting prints. So this, this was where Miz Hasten's husband bought his wife's beloved home furnishings! "Byrlie, go ask the man there if the lady might rest for a bit?

"Come on, Auntie Doyce, just a few more steps. I'll count them off, just like I did for Mama when she exercised." With grave concentration Doyce clamped her teeth, listening to the cadence, so very distant now, despite Harry's body pressed against her.

"Beloved, can you? A few more steps, just a few more," Khar cajoled. Ghatti were *so* prone to pester one at times. Left, oh, yes, left steps *were* easier, her good leg. A strain on the right leg as she swung her left, but not so terrible; she could weather it. But each right step strung a new bead of sweat along her hairline, across her upper lip, as she ordered the traitorous right leg along. Upper thigh muscles protested from the depths of her bone to her skin, distinctly displeased at stretching and flexing. Still, the pain was good. Something to distract her, instead of the two likenesses of Khar floating ahead, those weaving ribbons of striped fur making her stomach lurch.

"Too many stripes," she grumbled, *"fixate yourself, beloved, if you please."* For a moment Khar froze, two sliding into one, looking utterly perplexed before cleaving in two

again. *"Yes, dear double ghatta. Again. Twice as many of you to love."* Step, step. Just a few more. Harry'd promised, Khar'd promised.

Hands—Lindy's, Honoria's, Harry's—lowered her into a giant stack of cushions, and her head limply tilted back, leaving her staring at the red-and-white awning's underside. A repressed shudder—a few more or less stripes, what did it matter? Where'd Theo wandered off to? And Khim? A damp cloth gently molded itself across her forehead and eyes, blocking her view. No more stripes! Her stomach grudgingly considered stabilizing.

"Don't throw up on the man's pillows, Aunt Doyce," Byrlyn whispered. "He's being very nice, and it would be very rude." She could feel Khar sliding and bouncing as she ascended the heaped cushions to settle at her side. Ah, that was better—not perfect, but better. Deep, slow breaths, relax the facial muscles, now the neck. Yes, the pounding in her head *did* minimally ease.

How long she lay perfectly still she wasn't sure. As she tentatively climbed from her well of pain, it struck her— even with the cloth masking her vision. "Are you all just standing there, staring at me?" She'd failed, and now she was falling apart—that's what they were thinking. She could feel it, their worry washing over her, anxious eyes pinning her against the cushions. Two heartbeats later came the abashed foot shuffles, discomfited throat clearing.

Lindy's hand on her shoulder, its coolness penetrating her shirt's sticky fabric; it had been as crisp as her hopes when they'd set out. How could Lindy remain fresh like that? "Doyce, sorry. Think you could sit up? I've a nice drink here." Pushing the cloth away, she managed a narrow smile. An interesting scent, minty, invigorating, wafted toward her, and she reached for the cup. The Sunderlies offered surprises when it came to food and drink, best not be taken unaware. A sip. Mint and cha—not hot, mayhap the same temperature as the air. And so invigorating! She sipped, the mint cleansing her mouth, settling her stomach.

The stall-owner hovered, hands clasped over his chest, an oft-washed caftan of soft yellow-and-ocher stripes plotting their course over his mounded belly. More stripes? A gray-black beard, clipped short, and a mustache more extravagant than Arras's shadowed an anxious, broad-

cheeked face. "Sir, thank you for such a generous good
nature."

"Not 'sir,' just Momsvaert, Momsvaert the pillow-
merchant." He smiled then, mustache rising until she feared
it might crook his ears. "To come from another land, a
different clime, can be stressful," he noted diffidently, rubbing his pate, methodically polishing it. "Light, airy clothes,
little meals taken often—until you adapt." Throughout his
recommendation he eyed Khar, not precisely with concern,
but a vague perplexity.

"She's a ghatta, a ghatti female."

Bending over his paunch, he stretched a hand until Khar
grazed it with her pink nose. "I thought as much." A finger
tickled Khar's chin; she suffered it, then politely eased
away. "I'm just not sure . . ." he trailed off, continuing to
study Khar, "if you should consider shaving her. Against
the heat, I mean. We clip our dogs so they won't suffer
as much."

Backing with indignant rapidity up the pillows to distance
herself as much as possible, Khar gave a sizzling hiss. Momsvaert held up his hands in appeasement, clearly unaware
that the ghatta had understood him. "Merely a suggestion,
though I could swear she doesn't approve."

**"Ooh! Bad enough when Parm feared Harrap might
have him tonsured to match! This one, this one . . ."** she
sputtered, **"my precious satiny coat, my gorgeous stripes!
May his mustache fall off, may fleas nest in—"**

Doyce intervened as mildly as she could. *"It was* just *a
suggestion. He's attempting to be helpful."*

"If he attempts anything on me, so much as touches . . ."
Trailing off, Khar reflectively groomed her shoulder before
grudgingly conceding, **"Well, mayhap I overreacted."** A
lick to the other shoulder to avoid meeting anyone's eyes.

Blessedly ignorant of his brush with danger, Momsvaert
sleeked his mustache, pressing it under his nose as if he
feared it might detach. Or, Doyce wondered, did he somehow have an inkling of ghatti wrath? "You, dear lady,
should tarry at my humble stall while your friends complete
their shopping. Just two close lanes over, my cousin-in-law
tends his stall. A parrot-green awning marks it. He sells
caftans, airy trousers and loose shirts, swirling gauzy skirts

that let your body breath—the ideal attire for a woman of
your perspicacity and subtle charms.''

Sitting straighter, not taken in by his flattery but relishing
it just a little, Doyce allowed, "You've a point, sir. At least
regarding my resting here longer." Her head *did* feel better,
but profound lassitude had stolen over her; she simply
didn't want to move. Or maintain her stoic front before the
others. "Why not run your errands?" she appealed to
Lindy. "Look around, check on the clothes. No sense me
hobbling after you, hampering everyone."

"Yes, stay and watch the world go by." Momsvaert's
white teeth flashed against his weathered skin. "My sales
will be brisk, my competitors envious as buyers flock to my
stall, realize how luxuriant my pillows are when they observe you graciously lounging here. Ah, such sales I will
have!"

The cushions *were* comfortable, Doyce admitted as she
verged between drowsiness and awareness. The bazaar resounded with a hurly-burly of bustling folk intent on bar-
gains, vociferously arguing over the ripeness of a fruit,
clanging a copper pan to test its sturdiness, tossing thin
strips of spice-peppered meat on a grill, the sizzle and scent
tantalizing. Slowly she forced herself to take the time to
isolate one sight or scent or sound, study it with appreciation, rather than question or worry it to death.

"Worry it to death"—bad phrasing, to say the least, and
she fought to briefly set her fears aside because there wasn't
a thing she could do about most of them, as she'd just
found out. Such helplessness gnawed at her. Jenneth? Her
faint mental signature indicated that she still lived, somewhere—and for that Doyce felt gratitude. Diccon? Almost
equally distant, adventuring after his sister, confident or
willful enough to ignore her mindvoice.

Jenret? The closest, geographically-speaking, her mindvoice could touch him—if she so chose. But if there were
anything to report, he'd have 'spoken her. Wouldn't he?
She'd thought they'd begun to heal the breach between
them when he'd taken leave of her yesterday—until he'd
raced to Honoria's side. No message of love and reassur-

ance from him to her, either, and sadly she let her own spontaneous message falter and fade. Blessed Lady, she was acting childish, worse than the twins! Marriage wasn't an equitable proposition; at certain times one mate needed the other more, and then the roles might reverse. Contact him! she told herself. But then she'd have to admit she'd failed at convincing the Guardians to join the search.

But to her mortification, she yearned to 'speak Arras more. To mentally do what wasn't physically possible—rest her head on his shoulder. Shame gnawed at her, made her want to beg Jenret's forgiveness at how she'd so nearly compromised herself and Arras that night on the *Vruchtensla*. Oh, to feel the comfort of his arms clasping her close, his warmth melting her fears, the solace of his broad chest! At this moment she hungered for Arras's steadfast presence, an emotional crutch to match her real one. Jenret's mutable nature guaranteed their love was unpredictable, gave it a spontaneity she'd never attain without him. Right now, though, she wanted something—someone—she could count on without reservation.

"You promised not to fret about things. Stop working yourself into a pother." Cuddling close, head propped on her hip, Khar's amber eyes grew huge at observing a bevy of flittering birds just to the side of Momsvaert's booth. **"Look at those cheeky things!"**

Obediently she did, the corner of her mouth quirking. In size and shape the birds resembled sparrows, the same alert, cocky look, unimpressed by the ghatta's presence. A strip of bright sunshine angled between two stalls, baking the earth, and here at least ten of the feathered creatures had burrowed out tiny dust bowls, industriously rubbing dirt into breasts and bellies, dusting their wing-pits, fluttering to toss it on their backs. The saffron yellow of their breasts and backs, the emerald green of their heads, and sapphirine blue of their wings momentarily dulled as they powdered themselves, immensely satisfied with their lives.

"Why do they do that?" And why hadn't she wondered before—too busy? *"I mean, I've seen birds do it, but never really thought why. All that icky dirt in their feathers."*

Motionless except for a quivering tail-tip, Khar chattered a chk-chk-chking sound deep in her throat before reluctantly subsiding. **"What? Oh, sorry. More hungry than I'd**

realized." A pink tongue briefly swept her nose. **"It's not
icky dirt. The dust kills mites, keeps the little gem birds
from itching."**

"Ah." She liked Khar's name for them—gem birds—because they resembled fiery jewels with their feathers ablaze
in the sun. And as far as she could tell, the females boasted
plumage as gaudily cheering as the males, had resisted the
drab, dingy shading that cloaked many female bird species.

Momsvaert pressed a freshly filled mug in her hand, set
a plate of tiny meat pasties beside her. Khar licked her
chops, past plaints about the stall-owner forgotten, and
Doyce broke several pasties in half to cool for the ghatta.
"What do you call those little birds?" Pointing to the sunny
margin, she tossed a few crumbs their way, the birds vora-
ciously squabbling over them.

The older man beamed as if she'd praised him. "Bijou
birds. Alas, their voices don't match their markings.
Squawks, rusty-hinge screeches, scolding—no melody.
Think they own the place, they do." With fond exasperation he flashed the eight-point star. "The Lady painted
them most extravagantly when She made the Sunderlies
and its creatures. Mayhap to compensate for their clamor,
who knows?

"But look, over there!" He gestured down the hard-
packed path that ran behind his stall, and Doyce craned to
see. "Watch them strut! Soon someone'll discover they're
loose, come looking, but till then we'll enjoy the show."
What had caught Momsvaert's eye were chickens—roosters, more accurately—though they were the strangest she'd
ever seen. One was almost pure white with a broad, imposing breast. Long, wispy black feathers trimmed his throat,
fringed the back of yellow-scaled legs to his feet, while
white-and-black sausage-curl plumes adorned his tail.

His preening, posturing competitor tossed his head back,
throat ballooning, orange eye baleful beneath his strawberry comb, his head and throat flaring fiery red and yellow, his tail as well, with the addition of metallic green.
Each sleek, black body feather was edged with iridescent
bronze. No wonder he strutted!

They paraded back and forth, glaring at each other, then
circling, a sharp wing-snap or lightning-fast beak jab
broaching an invisible boundary. "They're not going to

fight, are they?" The image of those long, lethal spurs stabbing flesh, ripping and gouging, upset Doyce more than she
wanted to admit.

"Cock fights are common here," Momsvaert allowed
with a shrug, "but not for those two. They've already
proved their worth as champions and will be auctioned for
breeding, make their lucky owner rich by nightfall. Oh, they
may fight—on their own, for the love of it—just as humans
do at times." Another shrug. "The Lady put them on Meth-
uen to breed, to protect their hens. If it means killing a
rival, so be it."

Finally having taken each other's measure, the two cocks
took up positions, their necks snaking and wings cocked as
they edgily tested for an attack advantage. Beauty and
blood—were the two inseparable? But as they closed with
a loud snap of wings, a scrawny pig barreled between them,
snout wriggling as he dashed for the leavings he'd scented
in the gutter. Knocked on their tail feathers, the roosters
squawked their indignation, simultaneously diving at the
unlucky pig.

With that, two young boys came running, baskets in
hand, and recaptured the unlucky fowl over their strident
protests. Abruptly the boys froze, even the roosters uncannily silent, as three young men with proud, brutal faces and
odd attire arrogantly swung along, yielding to no one. One
kicked at a basket, crowing mockingly as he sliced a finger
across his throat.

Momsvaert's chuckle died in his throat, the stall-owner
hastily turning away to look for customers. "Momsvaert,
who're those—" but Doyce never completed her query, the
stall-owner drowning her out as he shouted, "Soft pillows!
Downy dreams!"

Puzzled by his seeming nervousness, Doyce looked at
her plate of meat pasties, where one remained in solitary
splendor. *"Khar, did you eat the rest, you inconsiderate
beast?"* Abruptly Doyce felt famished, her stomach settled
but protestingly empty, her headache still there but surviva-
ble. *"At least if I were seeing double, I'd think you'd saved
me two."*

An indignant chin-tuck emphasized Khar's protest. **"I ate
my share. Two for me, four for you. Two's enough, they're
very spicy."** A burp confirmed her assertion. **"You might**

consider who else might relish a snack." Before she could expand on that, her eyes went big as gold coins as she suddenly began sliding backward, clearly not under her own volition. Extending her claws, she desperately dug into a pillow, but it slid right along with her as her hindquarters inexorably disappeared into the mound of cushions. Doyce glimpsed two small, red-brown hands clamped just above Khar's hips.

"Khar, what are you doing?" Intrigued but not precisely worried since Khar didn't appear to be, Doyce didn't know what to make of the ghatta's unexpected retreat.

"I'm not doing anything!" Khar protested. **"I'm being abducted! Will you ransom me before I become the main ingredient in a pot of stew?"**

"Flattering to be wanted, isn't it?" Holding her breath, anxious not to disrupt the cushions, Doyce slipped her arm among them as gently as possible and made a sudden grab. A squeal of frustration and fear as she yanked, along with an avalanche of cushions that dislodged a small, disheveled girl from her den.

"Catnapping, were you?" Having sacrificed the pillows' support, Doyce lay flat on her back, clinging to her captive. Taking advantage of the child's tensile resistance to sit up, she hung on while the child struggled, writhing and preparing to flail and kick until Khar expertly bumped her. Landing with a thump on her bottom, she glared back, eyes blue-green as the sea swimming with tears, her mouth screwed as disparagingly tight as an old grannie's.

"Well, now, what do we do with you?" Frankly Doyce wasn't sure, had already been dizzied by the sight of street urchins pelting through the bazaar, often hotly pursued by outraged cries and—in some cases—the speedier shopkeepers. Any pursuit here in the Sunderlies was bound to be warm work. The child's birdlike wrist swiveled in her grasp, and Doyce aimed a wary gaze at the brown feet. If the child kicked her bad leg, she'd never rise, let alone chase after her.

"Lemme go!" The girl's shift floated on her, its pastel plaid leached away by many washings, the darnings and patches neat and unobtrusive. Her cropped hair—coarse, tight curls all over her head—had been enthusiastically, though not perfectly trimmed, and appeared clean. The rest

of her appeared clean as well; no grime embedded in neck
or knee or knuckle creases. Someone, somewhere, had a
care for this scamp, had done the best possible.

Suspicious of the prolonged silence, the unflinching top-
to-toe inspection, the child gave an ingratiating smile, hon-
eyed her tone. "Lemme go, lady. Thought yed finished wid
the pasties." The gape of missing front teeth. "Things spile
fast in zis heat, not wannen ta let'm go a wasting. Dannae
sez tis a zin."

Doyce returned the smile. "A good point. But my ghatta,
Khar, wasn't in danger of spoiling."

A negligent wave of her free hand. "So big an so
satisfied-lookin', looked pamper-spoiled ta me."

Sniffing at the child's bare foot, Khar sneezed once and
the child skittered, giggled. **"Child's good at rearranging
the truth—may have a bright career ahead of her as an
advocate."** Only then did Doyce notice how the bazaar had
fallen eerily quiet, even the bijou birds no longer scolding.
Nervous sweat trickling down his pate, Momsvaert sidled
beside her, cudgel in one hand, a knife in the other. She'd
not noticed him wearing a knife, suspected he'd stored both
beneath his counter in case of need.

"What is it?" she whispered in deference to the crackling
tension in the air. A glance showed her other stall-keepers,
customers and browsers, too, had begun prudently gliding
away, sheltering behind stalls, or simply freezing, trying to
appear—if not invisible—at least unobtrusive, unthreat-
ening.

He wet his lips, mustache working furiously. "Dagga
boys. Down the lane, heading this way. Too damn many
dagga boys—those we spied before and more. The bashing,
the smashing, the stealing, all'll commence soon. Most folk
daren't stand in their way."

She could see them now, a dozen at least, youths between the ages of perhaps fourteen and twenty. Rags and
tatters for clothes, by proud choice, she decided, because
the rips and tears, the fringes seemed almost uniform from
one to another. Studded leather belts cinched slim hips,
ready to be whipped off and swung as a weapon. Weighted
buckles on some, unless she missed her guess. Others
flaunted studded armlets jammed tight round their biceps.
Easy to slip down, grasp in a pounding fist.

The leader, or so she deemed him, looked no more than seventeen, whipcord hard, scarlet feathers braided into his jet black hair. It belatedly struck her that the child had edged round behind her—so mesmerized by the sight that she hadn't registered any pain—pressing tight as a second skin, absolutely still.

Doyce drew a shallow breath as they gained reinforcements, more dagga boys strutting through the aisles to swell their numbers until now she counted twenty. *"Khar, I hate to prod, but don't you think you should 'speak Khim? Let her and Theo know what's up?"*

From a perch on the display shelves that positioned her to scan the widest perspective or to launch herself at danger, Khar murmured, **"Done that. On their way."**

What had seemed a brilliant idea brief moments ago shriveled into stark reality. Calling Theo, Lindy, and Honoria to the rescue hardly improved the odds—laughable, almost. She prayed they'd found someplace safe to leave Harry and Byrlyn, insane to bring children into the midst of this—bad enough she'd become suddenly responsible for one. Swinging back to look at the lane, she realized that six dagga boys now crowded in front of the stall, idly butting shoulders like young rams, insolently staring, vehemently talking amongst themselves as they pointed at Khar. The clinging child transformed a groan into a feral, throaty growl.

Treating Doyce to a beatific smile that never touched his eyes, the red-feathered leader snatched up a plump, tasseled cushion and daintily pierced it with his knife, then jerked down the blade. Its rip tore at her eardrums, the pillow protesting in anguish. A brisk slap against Red-Feather's thigh and feathers erupted, began to drift. Momsvaert's teeth made a grinding sound, but he said nothing, never raising club or knife to object.

Negligently tossing away the gutted casing, Red-Feather stared at Doyce. "Ho, la-de-dah lady! Kinda stringy, but not 'alf bad fer an oldster. What yef be here fer? Not seen yef 'zaarin afore. Jes off da boat, Sunderlies-shipped? Prove yer past, badder'n bad, la-de-dah lady an mayhap we'll pass yed—zis time. Like a blood-gutty tale, we do, doan we, boys?"

From the corner of his mouth Momsvaert whispered,

"They want to know why you're here, what crime you committed to be exiled."

"Gentlemen." A step forward, and her bruised leg cramped on her, nearly buckling. Lady help her, she'd stood too long, muscles tense, and now her leg had decided not only to disobey, but to betray her as well. She gasped—good, let them think it fear, rather than pain. Well, if the Lady's grace wouldn't extend to her leg, she *could* command her voice, the byproduct of years of Seeker service. "Is this how you obtain your vicarious thrills when parricide palls?" No evidence they'd murdered their parents, but she allowed herself some latitude.

A pouting sneer, a tightening around icy blue eyes warned her she might have overstepped herself in taking blind ignorance for granted. "What's zat mean?" Ah, temperamental, suspicious—and curious! His mates shifted uneasily, glowering their support.

Another step, another, closer now, the child behind her remaining in place, slowly exposed. "Something like victorious crossed with vengeance, a perfect description of stalwarts like yourselves. I'd no idea you gentlemen were such connoisseurs of sanguinary tales of carnage, should have realized how you'd relish hearing a tale, even if it's but a pale shadow of your own presumptuous pusillanimity."

"Pusilla-what? When did you learn to bamboozle like that?" Khar's astonishment tickled her. **"Ask them to sit down. It'll slow them by a few steps if your story doesn't captivate them."**

The rest of the band had drifted down the lane, taunting and yelling, snatching at goods in stalls, tossing them down upon their owners' heads, genially roughing up any who dared protest. Draped with exquisite lace tablecloths, one dagga boy sashayed along, sweeping the ends over his shoulder, gyrating his hips to hoots of laughter. The crash of pottery, the splinter of wood, the tearing of canvas sounded farther away.

Her six remained behind, awaiting their promised entertainment—either a ripping good tale or the chance to punish her, should she fail. Sapling thin but with a mean look in his mismatched eyes, one blue and one brown, a dagga boy with white fringe on his trews pounded on RedFeather's arm, gesticulating at the child. "Massie Man, zat rat-child be sister to zat rat-shit Smir! Shite who doan wanna be dagga-chose! One who laughed in yer face, scamping off afore we could larn'm respect. Wan we should larn'm by 'zampling her?''

As nonchalantly as she could, Doyce rested a hand on her hip, her fingers searching out the dagger sheath that had worked its way behind her back. "You'd harm a child for her brother's mistake? Six strong, clever men against a child? It's like ripping the wings off butterflies!"

A bark of laughter. "Doan bodder wid zat much now. Still," Red-Feather, now called Massie, indicated Khar, "if we bored, chazzas chase the doldrums away, specially a big'un like zat. Trow'm in wid dogs, mayhap." Bringing his hands together, he methodically and lovingly cracked each knuckle. "Easy way ta frolic wid both. Finda burlap sack, stick baby rat-sister innit wid da chazza." His curled fingers suggestively clawed the air.

As Khar responded with an ominously rising growl, Doyce breathed a sigh of relief that the dagga boys couldn't understand her rumbling invectives. However, Massie's animus equaled the ghatta's; without taking his eyes off Khar, the dagga leader snagged a follower's wrist and snapped him forward. "Corly, boy—proving time!" he bantered with evident relish. "Gotta be man ta run wid us, not a blubby babby-boy belongin home."

Neither Massie's comments nor the hand clamped on his wrist seemed to penetrate: the boy called Corly totally unaware of his jeopardy, so engrossed was he in flirting with Khar—making eyes at her, coaxing sounds issuing from his lips. Little rolls of baby fat rippled below Corly's painfully-new scarlet leather vest, emphasizing how childhood still clung to him. Inexpertly peroxided a streaky blond, his pomaded hair sported a fuzzy cluster of blue and yellow feathers threaded into his hair just above his ear. Improbably, he looked like a chick who'd just pecked through his shell, downy feathers damp and sticking in all directions, wide-eyed at the world beyond his shell.

"Corly!" Massie's patience wearing thin, he clamped the boy's wrist in both hands, twisting in opposite directions. "Deef are yed, now? Dumb I knew!" Violently flinching as the voice finally penetrated, Corly shook his head as if he'd just awoken. "Doan stan liker lumpa flabby suet. Snag us zat chazza—now!"

Despite the soft plumpness padding his olive-hued face, Corly's jaw set firm, though his downcast eyes showed a pleading deference. "No, Massie, can't! Doan make me—pleez! I doan hurt nanimals, chazzas, whateffer iffen zey doan hurt me." So snake-fast that Doyce saw not the incident, but its aftermath, Corly's head snapped back, feathers bobbing wildly from Massie's openhanded blow, a palm-print livid on his face.

"Then git! Do someting useful—iffen yed ken!" Rolling his eyes at his mates, mournfully shaking his head, Massie shooed the boy away. "Blezzed Lady! Iffen he wern Chopper's babby brother, I swear I'd . . ." Rounding on the boy again, he snarled, "Git! Yed got one more chanza be dagga-chose, an next time . . ." As Corly slunk off, he muttered, "Wuzzy-puzzy mama's boy, lil suck-teat!"

"Lemme git chazza, Massie!" Slinging off his belt and rethreading its tongue through the buckle to form a noose, a taller, darker boy bounced on the balls of his feet, eager to obey.

"Nah, nah," Massie soothed absently, "leave'a chazza be—jest not in mood no more. Tooka savor outa it, Corly did. Hoist the rat-child, Wafer, and we be off. Too small fer much pring-prongin' joy, splits too easy, but we find ways. 'Joy ourselves till she wear out, or rat-boy buys'er back."

Although Corly's defection had momentarily heartened her, Doyce's blood ice-splintered through her veins as she caught the lewd intent within Massie's slang-filled speech. They planned to take the child, molest her, and casually discard her. Obediently Wafer shoved his way into the stall, kicking at cushions to clear a path, even scooping one to playfully toss at Massie's feet. Trying to watch both Massie and Wafer, Doyce pivoted just in time to see the girl raise her fist, a large, rusty nail protruding from it. She slammed it into Wafer's groin, ripping with all her strength as her shrill scream of defiance shattered the air.

As if at a signal Momsvaert smacked his cudgel against Wafer's skull as he doubled over, clutching himself. Setting her feet, Doyce shouldered the rickety counter and its contents into the four remaining dagga boys' path—a frail barricade at best, but the uncertain footing might hinder them.

"Torc!" Massie waved the pie-eyed boy forward. "Go do fer Wafer." White fringe swaying, Torc leaped the overturned counter, losing both balance and leering smile in the welter of pillows. Khar chose that moment to spring, her claws busily scoring Torc's back and his shaved scalp until his center-braided white feathers turned rosy red with blood.

"Oh, fer a mate who ain a soddering toddle-foot!" Massie shook his head in slow disgust, pursing his lips. "Come on, Gilp, Chigger, lez clean up afore Wafer and Torc soil themselves." A comrade book-ended on each side, Massie high-stepped the counter with slow, arrogant grace. While his flankers flourished their studded armbands on fists, Massie contented himself with swinging his belt in whistling circles, its studs flashing in the sunlight.

Fighting against being sucked into the vortex of its repetitive, relentless spin, Doyce concentrated on its whipping sound, with no time to assess what Gilp and Chigger planned. How to break Massie's whistling defense with a mere dagger? Snagging a cushion, she used it to buffer her forearm, but any further ideas eluded her. And still the belt kept whispering its danger in her ears, the whirling pattern seductively drawing her. . . .

"Toss it! Take another for a shield!" As Khar broke her impasse, the circling lost some of its enticement. Furiously swiping at Chigger, Khar forced him to retreat from the child, while Momsvaert harassed Gilp, feinting with his cudgel, Gilp impotently swatting back at it. Torc, the dagga boy Khar'd first scored, circled in again, back and scalp streaked with blood.

In sync with the belt's spinning Doyce lobbed the cushion with an easy underhand. Had she'd timed it right? Simple enough to bat it away if she'd misjudged. But Massie's sneer was replaced by a look of consternation as the belt, weighted by its heavy buckle, wound itself round the pillow. Seizing that brief opportunity she threw herself inside Massie's guard, dagger aiming for his ribs.

But someone else reached Massie ahead of her; a scrawny, umber-skinned boy with a prowlike nose slammed a slat of wood with an embedded nail into Massie's lower

back at kidney-level. The dagga boys' leader screamed and
crumpled. As if reacting to an unspoken signal, the girl-
child swung Doyce's crutch by its tip, landing a blow on
Massie's temple exactly as if she were driving a ball. "Siri!"
the boy shouted, "Always underfoot! Now git back!"

She drifted clear but refused to relinquish the crutch,
cocking it over her shoulder, ready, as Doyce and her new
ally turned in tandem to bear the brunt of Torc's attack.
"I prick low first, yed spike high," he breathlessly advised,
angling his wood slab toward Torc's vulnerable feet.

But now the bazaar rang with shouts as Theo and a hastily gathered crew of townspeople and stall-owners—including an elderly lady waving a string of sausages—came
charging down the lane. As one, the remaining dagga boys
turned tail and ran. More stall-owners abandoned their hiding places, raining blows on them, tripping them, willing to
get their own back at last.

"Thankee kindly fer 'tecting my sister fra that scum."
With a curiously quaint bow from the waist, the boy
scooped up his sister, who clung to his waist like a monkey,
murmuring in his ear. "I be Smir. Kasimir Motipersad. Little'un's my sister, Sirikit."

"Siri," the child insisted.

"We be at yer service. Ull serve yed if yed need it, wan
it. Alla rich b—" he choked down the word, " 'uns have
sarvants here. No charge cuzza we owe yed." Again a frantic buzz at his ear. "An acuza Sirikit's fair smitten wid the
big chazza," he admitted.

Explosively crimson above and below the rag wadded in
his mouth, Diccon waggled his eyebrows in Davvy's direction, his mindspeech so harried it pummeled Davvy's mind.
Did everyone have license to beat him today, physically
and mentally? Hands bound behind him, he shifted as best
he could to cradle Bard's limp form against his neck and
chest and let Diccon's grievances whiz by without registering them.

"Leave it be, Diccon." He stared back at Goose Island
as their captors stroked through light chop toward Gander.
"We'll sort it out soon enough—an unfortunate misunder-

standing." How many more times, how many more ways could he say it? Bard's paleness left him uneasy—his normally tawny-gold skin now a dingy white tinged with a jaundiced green. Shock, for one thing, a bad blow to the head for another. Eumedico training had never covered this: Was a berserker adversely affected if his raging mental state was involuntarily curbed before its climax? Well, put that aside for further study, because he had no idea what the answer might be.

"From their perspective we probably do *appear suspicious."* Why did he bother to reason with Diccon?

"Treated like common criminals! Wouldn't even listen, let us prove we're ghatti-Bonded!" The fact that Diccon alone was both gagged and bound was no wonder, even Davvy's self-control sorely tried as Diccon ceaselessly berated the Guardians, calling them everything except imbeciles for not recognizing Seekers—with or without their companion ghatti. Bless the Lady for mindspeech—at least now only he had to suffer. *"Kwee's too little to swim this far, and M'wa despises getting his feet wet! If we don't sort this out— as you so charmingly put it, as if the butcher'd mixed up our order with someone else's—how'll we ever rescue Jen and Pw'eek?"*

To Davvy, mindspeech's main drawback was that it could be delivered faster than the tongue could wag and with no pause for breath. Still, the boy needlessly borrowed trouble. They *would* sort it out; eumedicos were rational, logical beings, unswayed by the unruly emotions of the moment. A sensible, frank explanation to the fort's captain, mayhap a corroborative message from the mainland, and things would be fine. How long could it take?

He reflexively shivered at a memory of Jenneth so long ago, when she and Diccon'd both been toddlers. How he'd pretended to be a gently bucking horse for a little girl who'd screamed with glee, only to turn panicky pale as fear caught her up, froze her limbs. Neither he nor anyone else who loved her could accurately gauge when such a transformation would occur—except for Diccon. It might happen between one instant and the next, catching everyone unaware and immediately ruing the hurt they'd inadvertently caused her.

Jenneth was a part of the family he'd constructed for

himself during his own boyhood. Let any outsiders harm
her, harm Diccon, and they'd answer to him. Only *he* was
allowed the imaginary joy of dunking Diccon overboard to
silence him. Little brothers often richly deserved an elder
brother's correction.

Momentarily cheered by the thought, he sought to comfort Diccon. *"Mayhap this'll be a blessing in disguise—let
us obtain more accurate information about the currents here-
abouts, borrow a faster boat."* And please, please Lady, let
it be so! If only Harrap were with them; if the Lady granted
anyone's prayers, it would be his. Eumedicos hosted too
many doubts, always pondering life's knots to comprehend
how they'd been originally tied. And despite their best intentions, they undoubtedly tampered with life and death,
thwarting the Lady's desires—at least on a temporary basis.
He wanted Jenneth to gain confidence and courage in *this*
life, this here and now, and if it took his meddling as eumedico, as a friend who was almost family, he'd meddle—
even if the Lady herself refused to grant him impunity!

Ah—he'd been deep in a brown study, had no inkling
what Diccon had been babbling about while sequestering
himself there. But Dic sat blessedly silent, facing the bow,
staring toward Gander. The oarsmen rowed with a mind-
numbing unison that he and Bard could never match in a
hundred years. Too bad Bard wasn't well enough to observe, pick up a few pointers. Diccon hurriedly warned,
*"Steady! Once we catch this wave, we're there. They'll drive
us in hard as they can—now!"*

A pause at the rise, and then a powerful stroke brought
them in. Stomach catapulting, Davvy braced himself as best
he could, hoped Bard was secure. No way to hang on to
him with his hands tied, but he'd scissored Bard's leg between his knees, hooked his chin over Bard's lolling neck.
The keel grated—so, they'd not docked at the piers Diccon'd spotted—and the launch jounced and bobbed as men
jumped overboard to beach her.

Now, new strangers lifted Bard clear with a rough tenderness he'd not expected them to exhibit toward prisoners,
especially convict escapees. A corporal, not one of the boat
party, swung into the launch, grimacing at the water staining his boots. "Out we go, gentlemen. Not everyone gets
carried." Helping Davvy to rise, the corporal held his elbow

as he stretched a leg over the side, conscious of the awkward straddle that could spill him. A stumble, but he righted himself, turning back to track Diccon's progress.

Catching Davvy's eye, the corporal winked. "Leave the gag on this one? I've heard tell he's powerful noisy."

Diccon's nostrils flared, his eyes casting near-combustible sparks of outrage. "Don't tempt me, Diccon, or I'll say leave it in." Setting himself in the most commanding stance he could muster with his hands tied behind him, he fixed Diccon with a compelling, level stare. *"If you so much as open your mouth, Diccon, I swear I'll—"* he couldn't decide on a dire enough threat, but prayed he'd made his point. *"Things aren't as bad as they could be—as they* will *be if you run off at the mouth. Don't muck things up."*

A terse head bob, although Diccon refused to meet his eyes. So, either the boy was shamed by his previous behavior, or he had no intention of obeying. *"Well, Diccon? Gag in or out?"* The corporal seemed content to wait, equally practiced in contests of the will.

"Pax," he sounded as surly as he acted. *"Truce till this's settled."*

"I'm Corporal Luykas," the corporal introduced himself, a good-humored smile on his broad, wind-chapped face as he gingerly tugged Diccon's gag free. "You don't bite, I hope. Now, let's see about your ankles."

As Diccon rolled over the side, landing on his knees, Davvy decided the time had arrived for two adults to rationally discuss the situation, reach a mutual accord. "Corporal Luykas, thank you for your patience. I'm Resonant-eumedico Davvy McNaught of Gaernett in Canderis."

"Of course," Luykas blandly replied, "and I'm Miss Lily of the Valley, so tiny, silver-green thin. Ring-ching, ching-ring."

Davvy's rosy assessment of their predicament faltered, crashed to the sand at his feet.

Liquid warbles, sleepily murmurous chitters, the flap of night-stiff wings, pecking and scratching wove through her dreams. Slithers and sinuous rustlings, scampering pitter-pats, loud gnawing nearby. Pw'eek yawned and smacked her jaws, reburying her head beneath a hind leg as she resettled, sleep stealing away as the day began. Needed Kwee-cuddling, sissy scent, and she rolled, drowsily reaching for her sib.

It battered her senses like a booted foot to her ribs—foreign scents, alien bird and animal noises, Kwee's absence—and she startled, her upflung head smacking the dense leafage overhanging her like a canopy. Water spattered as each leaf—the size and shape of a cupped palm—dumped its night dew on her fur. Still torn between fear and the growing certainty this was no ghatten nightmare, she peered gingerly amongst the scalloped leaf-lobes, jerking back at spying a scarlet-throated yellow flower big enough to be a bowl. Tiny insects tramped in and out of the flower's maw, wove between dangling things like white, furry fangs. Her heart pounded and her foot hurt—real, all of it. And water whooshed, ebbed and flowed at the sand's far edge. Water, the sea, ugh!

No Jenneth, no Kwee, just Pw'eek—alone, oh, so alone! Oh, woe! For solace she lifted her right paw, began to cleanse the deep slice in a pad that left her unable to flex that toe. Her stomach growled, peremptorily announcing its need for food. The urge to eat, to gorge, was overwhelming. Food made her happy, let her forget she was afraid, unloved, alone. Food made up for a lack of so many other things. But there was no food—unless . . . unless some of that wonderful dead fish remained. Hope rising, she wedged between the scrolling vines that had sheltered her from prying eyes all night, and limped down the beach, hesitating, watching. With each step, grains of sand packed her wound, salt and sand smarting.

What to do, oh, what to do? Her song of woe filled her ears as she scanned the beach for the fish skeleton, for anything else that might prove edible. A pat at a shell that appeared to be moving; she threw herself on her fanny when six jointed legs extended and darted off with the shell atop. Ah—the fish remains! Breaking into a hobbling run, she mewled in anticipation and startled a buff-breasted bird with stilt legs and a needlelike beak. Bones, nothing but bones! A fin, now dead gray, the empty, staring eye sockets—all picked as clean as clean could be. No! She thudded on her belly, forepaws stretched to avoid pressure. Not a

scrap! No food, no Jenneth, no Kwee! Oh, woe! No love for
Pw'eek! An empty, echoing shell of wretchedness, bereft!

Head pillowed on paws, she crooned her dirge of sorrow,
heart aching, belly miserably hollow. Ah, if only the sea
had swallowed her, if only the sky would open, or the beach
beneath her belly—engulf her in all her unworthiness! How
long she lay, blankly staring out to sea, she didn't know,
except that slowly, surely, she felt it: Jenneth's faraway call,
her words indistinct, too far for 'speech to carry, but her
love caressed Pw'eek. And from yet another direction, the
impression of a distant Kwee, who held her sib in her heart-
song, crooning of tender licks, the nestling warmth of fur,
of protection.

Two loved her, two truly did, no matter how far they
roamed! They believed in her, loved her from afar! Could
she do less? With a sigh, she gathered her feet under her,
nosing the air as if to scent their calls. Kwee stood closer
than Jenneth, so much easier to turn, travel south and east,
their sib-love attracting like a magnet. Trembling with indecision, Pw'eek let her head swing back, now testing northward and slightly to the west. Went still, concentrating for
all she was worth, abruptly determined. She was Bonded,
she had Chosen—to sever that Bond meant shame and loss.
Kwee? Jenneth?

The sun ascended higher, warming and drying the sand,
but she turned her back on it and on the east. Hurriedly
limping toward her shelter and the spring, she drank deep
and long to assuage her hunger, the thirst still burning
within from her privations at sea. Then, sniffing, testing a
spot here, a spot there, she steadied herself and laboriously
scratched a hole with her good foot. Squatted over it, let
loose a stinging stream of urine, strong and acrid from her
lack of liquids. Again she balanced, scuffing dirt and leaves
over the evidence and marched along above the tide line,
sheltering beneath the storm-tattered scrub and winding
vines.

**"I'm coming, Jenneth. I Chose you. Don't worry,
Pw'eek'll find you!"** Her pudgy sides swayed as she trun-
dled along with a rolling gait, like a land-locked sailor.
**"Pw'eek's afraid, terrible afraid, and terrible hungry, but
she'll be brave for you. Won't let you down, you'll see.
Make you proud of brave Pw'eek, calico wonder of the**

world, ghatten so brave and bold." If she thought it hard
enough, she could almost believe it. She was needed—a
novel feeling! Mayhap being needed made you brave and
bold instead of being greedy-needy.

Doubled over, arms clenched against her lower abdomen,
Holly shuffled to the small fire and dubiously eyed the distance between her bottom and the windfallen trunk before
she gingerly dropped. "Aah—no!" she groaned as the
cramping recommenced. Invisible, vicious hands wove
turk's heads, slip knots, and hanging nooses with her intestines, and she prayed for sufficient strength to dash behind
a bush. Why the hells had she sat down? Instead, to her
profound relief, she broke wind, a prolonged explosion that
practically propelled her off the trunk. "Phew!" She
mopped her sweaty brow, relieved it no longer felt feverish.

"Phew and pee-yew is more like it!" P'roul's screwed-up
face informed her the smell was as noxious as she'd suspected. Problem was, she'd grown accustomed to it—as had
Arras and Jenret, still feverishly stretched on their tarps,
bunches of dried grass and reeds packed under them to
absorb diarrhea that had flowed like water, the vomiting
that now produced only sour, stringy bile. **"Feeling any
better?"** P'roul rubbed anxiously against her shin, her nose
wrinkled with concern or by the residual smell, and Holly
didn't care to know which.

Poor, fastidious ghatti, to be encumbered with such feeble, flimsy humans! Rawn and P'roul had been near crazed
with worry, but there wasn't a thing they could do to help.
**"Well, we dug holes, but you wouldn't even *try* to reach
them."** Best to ignore P'roul's faintly disapproving tone;
ghatti and humans simply didn't react in the same way
when struck down by illness.

Swallowing a belch and wishing she hadn't, Holly laboriously stretched to snag the tin pot with its pungent herbal
brew. Every muscle in her gut felt sore, strained beyond
endurance. *"Would've loved to, P'roul,"* she remonstrated,
*"but we didn't have much warning, let along the strength to
trot over to your excavations. It was thoughtful, though."*

Mouth crimped in anticipation of the taste, she sipped at

the pot, finally held her nose and gulped. "Gur-ahh, yugh!" A cough almost carried the vileness right back up, but she refused to let it travel the same path twice. Still, it was a near thing.

"I know something that'll make you feel better. Two things, in fact." The ghatta cocked her head in Arras's and Jenret's direction, where they lay, drowsing, still too weak to move.

As the horrible brew coursed through her, Holly could sense knots untying, or at least loosening. Bess's brew could cure shoeleather—or dissolve it! Not a heartening thought. *"What?"* she asked absently, still caught in a vision of lique-fying intestines. Well, hells, that'd already happened and she'd survived—then caught where P'roul was looking. *"Dosing someone else, sharing the pain, so to speak?"* She exchanged a complicitous grin with the ghatta. *"Yes, shar-ing can be so . . . satisfying."*

Yes, satisfying—especially given Jenret's propensity to be a proper pain in the posterior. Didn't he think they were equally anxious to locate Jenneth and Pw'eek? She under-stood his gnawing fears, had held her patience in check, but the illness had drained her of emotional resources.

"What's the other thing that'll make me feel better?" Hold-ing the pot by its bale, hoping it wouldn't slosh, she pushed off against the trunk, grabbing at her gut as she came up-right. Lady bless, anyone seeing her'd think she was a right fool!

P'roul circled, examining her from top to toe, eyes wide with wonder. **"That I've never seen you so slim and svelte. Shapely."**

Holly fought an urge to blush; in truth, part of the reason she clutched her midsection was to hold up her pantaloons. *"Slim and shapely, eh? I know you worship me, P'roul, but best of all, I know the ghatti can't lie."* Svelte! Shapely! Oh, if Theo could see her now!

Convincing Arras and Jenret to dose themselves was hardly easy, but Holly succeeded by winning a brief glaring match with Muscadeine. Finally he held out his hand, toasted her with the pot, and tossed down his dose. But Jenret literally fought the idea, flinging his arms out any time the pot approached his lips. "Two choices, Wycher-ley," she grated, patience fraying as splashing brew soaked her pants, "I sit on your chest, pinch your nose till you open your mouth—pour till it's full. You'll *have* to swallow sometime. Or you can voluntarily take it. Assuming you truly want to get back on your feet, find Jenneth."

Something—whether it was her threat or her sober assessment—quelled his defiance, and he swallowed the brew like an obedient babe. "Sorry," he muttered, scrubbing at his mouth with his sleeve. "Can't always tell which are fever dreams and which aren't." Even in the midst of her own misery she'd registered his thrashing, his screams and piteous pleas to invisible people surrounding his pallet. A severe attack of guilt brought on by the fever, she'd concluded and blocked her ears. What he'd confessed to was none of her affair, though she could list some likely ones.

Frankly, she didn't understand many things lately—that griped her nearly as badly as her gut had been griped. What was the matter with Doyce and Jenret? Why did they act almost like strangers to each other? Their marriage was hardly standard issue, but it had worked well for them till now. Far as she could judge, Doyce shouldn't have bothered coming to the Sunderlies.

Wiping Jenret's brow with some grubby toweling, she eased away the dark lock that always curled over his forehead, had seen Doyce do it so many times. No, she wouldn't want to be a part of this marriage, wasn't sure she wanted to be a part of any. "Don't worry. It's just the fever talking," and in moments he fell asleep again.

Sitting back on her heels, she held the pot in her lap, still pondering. If Doyce's and Jenret's problems were so obvious, she fervently wished some of her other quandaries were as forthright! The tack Theo'd found under Doyce's saddle hadn't just floated off some cobbler's bench and decided to take up lodging there. A pettiness to it, almost a childish stunt—the sort children play without fully realizing the possible consequences. Luckily Doyce hadn't been severely hurt, though the potential for far worse had hovered there.

But turning the custables into shrapnel-loaded grenades had a viciousness to it she couldn't fathom. They'd been meant to maim or kill, the perpetrator lacking the courage to murder face-to-face, content to stand back at one remove and await developments. As if that left one's hands unsullied! Not a childish crime, but a cold-blooded, conniving one. Not to mention overkill. Holding the pot so tightly her fingers ached, she reconsidered. The tack incident had a single target: Doyce. But the custables? The whole group or one particular person, even if other innocents had died?

Mayhap the danger was past and gone, hadn't tracked them across the sea to the Sunderlies? Still, that was why she and Theo had split their forces, leaving Theo in place with Doyce. Frankly, Theo was his own best stalking-horse; his perpetual stammer, his lanky, unimposing physique, and unassuming personality all served as decoys for the subtle, convoluted, and courageous mind within. She was too bluff and forward, intimidating, too likely to send trouble scampering, while Theo would gently coax it near to better examine it. Well, she'd begged Theo and Khim to stay behind, but it didn't stop her from missing them.

Still pensive with unresolved questions, she temporarily abandoned her two charges and managed an unwavering path back to the fire. Rawn had returned, belly-fur wet, the rawhide loop of a waterskin slung across his neck and chest, the skin itself dragging between his legs like a rolapin carcass. **"My thanks for not sitting on him,"** he gruffly remarked, attempting to dislodge the loop with a hind foot. **"Wouldn't have blamed you. Thought you could use some fresh water."**

Freeing him, she slid the bulging waterskin from beneath him, the ghatt's habitual bluff exterior only partially camouflaging his advancing age. *"Bless you, Rawn. I couldn't have walked that far, and I don't know how much longer Bess'll be gone."* A cautious, small sip—ambrosia! Fresh, tasteless ambrosia! The dregs of the herbal brew sluiced from her mouth. Pouring water into a cupped hand, she splashed her face, then drank a little more. She'd pay an oct's wages for a good wash—kill for a bathtub!

"Don't drain it," he warned. **"You need it, but P'roul and I'd both prefer it didn't race right through you."**

An accurate though unpleasant assessment. Reluctantly she stoppered the waterskin and sat, rummaging in her pack for trail-mix for the ghatti. At least someone still relished a hearty meal! To a background of munching purrs she reclined against the log and calculated how much time they'd lost, the distance to be made up.

The swamp fever had struck them two-and-a-half days out. Once Jenret had grasped that Jenneth would likely drift ashore up the coast, he'd adamantly refused to follow the shoreline until they were farther north. Nor would he consider the Coastal Road which—despite its name—sometimes wandered away from the sea in spots, especially just above Samranth where it swung wide to avoid the swamplands. Bullybess had noted much of the lower road was shallowly flooded, the nearby rice paddies turning the area into a morass, unable to handle drainage from both the Stent's increased flow and the storm's deluge. So, over Bess's loud protests, he'd insisted on cutting straight through the interior. Bess might be their guide, but Jenret hadn't let that deter him; once his mind was fixed, nothing could be debated along the way.

"Bayint too soft, not Sunderlies enow fer that," Bess had argued, stomping round them as if critically inspecting them for hidden weaknesses and flaws. Holly'd half-expected her to pry open their mouths, check their teeth. "Took Bullybess years ta not be laid low by swamp fever, be tough enow to snap fingers at it. Gif yed bout one full day afer yer sorry, spewing both ways so fast and furious yed woan know which way ta go first." A prophetic statement, but Jenret had scoffed, nagging and bullying her into submission. "Oh, fine," Bess had finally snapped, "Bullybess not signed on ta play nursey-maid, clean up quat, swab yer spew!"

In retrospect Bess's warnings had been as understated as saying a ghatt was a large cat. Holly winced at remembering how the swamp fever had struck. The air had hung thick and fetid, cloyingly close the deeper they ventured into the swamps. Stagnant water oozed around their feet, emitting bubbling, squelching sounds as they dragged their boots clear of the muck, each footstep unstoppering more rank smells. They fought through dense reed beds, each reed wrist-thick and crowded tight against its neighbor, only to encounter giant broad-leafed trees whose trailing branches rooted to create tangled clusters of offspring, their foliage so profuse they formed a shifting green canopy that obscured any light foolish enough to try to penetrate. Each time they'd halted to rest, they'd wrung out their shirts like wet laundry, vainly hoping their spares had dried. Bess had screwed up her nose at the scent of their stinking wet sheepskin tabards, able to distinguish that odor amongst the others.

Yet worst of all, Holly decided—a veritable connoisseur of discomfort—were the insects. Swarms, veritable clouds of minute midges, visible only because of their sheer numbers. Somewhat larger, buzzing cousins lodged in ears and eyes and nostrils, bit bare flesh with jaws larger than their bodies, each bite begging to be scratched, releasing blood that sang a siren song of feasting to even more insects.

"Don't drink the water," Bess had reminded time and again, unless it originated from a fast-flowing stream. Anything stagnant posed danger. And with muttered curses for her bad luck, she'd driven them through the swamps as fast as humanly possible, begrudging any prolonged rest, scanning faint trail markers only she could discern in the dimness. Both Holly and Jenret had carried P'roul and Rawn on their shoulders as well as their packs, the ghatti traveling through the trees when they could. By the end of the first day even Jenret had been exhausted, mayhap even humbled by their experiences.

Holly'd felt miserable first—or so she judged—joints achy, muscles screaming in a way that went beyond overexertion. Then the cramping had begun, wave after wave rippling through her. Without complaint she'd grimly kept the pace; Bess swore another three kilometers would bring them to a dryish spot, a rise suitable for a short rest and a meal. Start off again tomorrow at sunrise (How the hells Bess could tell, Holly would've loved to know!) and they'd emerge by the next day.

But at Bess's mention of food, Holly'd shamed herself by losing the contents of her stomach, barely in time to bend and retch, convinced she'd turn herself inside out. Poor P'roul had been pitched clear with no word of apology. Weak, wobbling, she'd slowly straightened—avoiding everyone's eyes—only to double over again as agony twisted through her lower gut. Except this promised a worse humiliation; a panicky glance showed her Arras already fumbling at his waistband, stumble-bumming for privacy behind a purple-blossomed shrub scented like rotting meat. Shortly thereafter, none of them could muster embarrassment enough to care if a bare bottom luminesced in the sickly green light.

Somehow, like staggering sots they'd reached the rise Bess had chosen for their campsite. That had been two full days and nights ago. Despite her brusqueness, Bess had bustled like a mother hen—an irate mother hen, Holly amended—doing what she could to make them comfortable. Her herbal potion muted some of the cramping but couldn't halt it, and the fevers and chills simply had to wear themselves out. Now Bess was scouting more herbs, their supply perilously low. In short, Bess *had* turned nurseymaid, caring for three oversized, puling infants, cleaning up their messes, dosing them, and offering not one word of reproof. That accounting, Holly strongly suspected, loomed nearer as Jenret recovered, and hoped she'd be allowed a ringside seat!

Bless the Lady for gifting her with a less-severe siege than the other two'd endured! And if hers had been middling miserable, she'd no desire to contemplate how Arras and Jenret fared. "Blast it," she said to no one in particular, needing to hear a human voice, even her own. "I hope Diccon and crew are making better progress than we are."

If she felt rag-doll limp and miserable—what of poor Jenneth and Pw'eek, adrift and alone at sea? No food, no water, nothing but endless waves around them. A shiver, an honest one of compassion, not a warning chill that'd accompanied the fever. "Wish Bess'd get back." She needed someone to talk to, now that she'd wrestled some of the self-pity from her system.

Both Rawn and P'roul came bolt upright, their fur ahackle, low warning growls rumbling in their chests. Surging to her feet so fast she went dizzy and weak-kneed, Holly snatched up her sword. *"Wonderful. Swamp monsters now? Or human predators?"*

"Hallo?" A male voice rang from her left and she wheeled, gauging whether she could position herself between the invalids and the unfamiliar voice. A second voice, younger-sounding and faintly exasperated, added, "This she-man," Bess stumbled into view, hands bound, mouth gagged, and gray eyes like furious pits of wrath, "this she-man very rough. Not wanting to converse, only wanting to fight. You untie, you make sure she not harm us. Uma-Uncle and I already bruised."

Unsure how to respond, but suspecting the strangers had discovered firsthand Bullybess's tendency to employ her fists ahead of her ears, Holly hastily removed her gag. "Bull-seggin' scum! Cow-pronging preverts! Are yed bung-fu? Piffled? Snagging an honest woman sarching fer herb simples. What? Lonely off yer plains? No cows ta satisfy, makin' do wid Bullybess? Come out an I'll cow yed, I will!"

Rawn, gruff ghatt that he was, looked disapproving at such language, while P'roul muffled a ghatti snicker. **"Nothing to fear, love, sorry if we startled you. They're not dangerous, though I wouldn't say the same for Bess."**

Baffled, Holly tucked her sword under an arm and cut Bess free with her dagger, the task taking forever because Bess continued to bob and dodge, kicking at invisible opponents. "Thank you for delivering her safe and sound," she called to the unseen voices. "Would you care to join us, talk, perhaps?" Wrapping a hand in Bess's collar, she hissed, "Stop it! They may know something useful." And what Bess had meant by satisfying cows would have to wait for a later explanation.

Two men, both a dark-complected, deep umber, one no more than twenty-five, the other in his seventies, hesitantly stepped into view, and Holly took a twist in Bess's collar as she growled. Lady help her, if Bess decided to break loose, attack, she hadn't enough strength to stop her, could barely hoist her own feet! "Lemme go! Kin behave even if they doan." Releasing her collar and narrowly watching Bess for a moment, Holly finally dared devote her attention to their visitors.

Both stood tall and lean, clothed with ocher drapings that swathed their loins, the loose end tossed over the left shoulder. Each carried a sturdy staff surmounted with a pair of cow's horns, and a sheathed machete rested on the left hip, its mate slung across the back beside a bulging leather drawstring sack. "We are lurking," the younger one gravely offered, cocking his head at her puzzlement. "It is lurking, yes? When not finding someone, one goes lurking?"

"Looking," she automatically corrected.

"Ah, *looking*." An enthusiastic head nod, and his words

tumbled out. "Yes, yes. We are *looking* for my uncle's sister's grandson. You know him, yes? Everyone knowing of him—you and many others for his fame. He shares life with large furred creature being like yours, I am thinking. He is in the way of being named Bard Ambwasali?"

"Oh." Wonderful! Misplace Bard for an instant and longlost relatives materialized! "Well, I hope you've time for a lengthy, involved story."

He studied the clouds ambling like contented sheep across the sky, fleecy underbellies tinged rosy lavender from the fading sun. As if daring the clouds to lie, he wet a finger to test the breeze, opened his mouth to taste the air. Although the redness of the setting sun presaged fair weather, he suspected there'd be at least one shower during the night. The freshening wind, the moisture told him that. Still meant fair weather, not another storm; in the Sunderlies, showers cleansed the air almost every day.

The stronger breeze with a driving rain tonight might do it, coax the sea to speed its delivery of his unknown gift. Resounding, hollow woofs in the distance, rapidly closing. Damn! Tigger came crazy-eighting across the beach, sand spewing beneath his paws, his coat a matted disaster, tongue lolling long enough to noose his neck. Oh, didn't he wish! Running circles round him, Tigger finally arrowed in, planting his wet nose in Pommy's crotch, his doggy grin intensifying as Pommy ungently shoved him clear.

And Tigger's presence meant—joy piled upon joy, was there no end?—Hirby. "Ye-ow! Pommy-lad!" Hirby windmilled his arms as he canted down the sand dunes, steeper and more deeply indented from the storm, as if the sea had taken a considering bite out of them. Feet shooting out from under him as he tilted for balance, Hirby went sledding down in a slither of sand, yelping with delight. He sounded uncannily like Tigger.

Blissfully sand-caked, he jogged to Pommy's side, panting, flapping his overlarge waistband to shake the sand free. "Fun, but chafes fierce," he confided, somehow engaging in an internal jig within the confines of his trews.

His innocence touched a chord within Pommy, momentarily overrode his repugnance at Hirby's simpleton ways. As disruptive, as annoying as he might be, it was hard to hate Hirby, better to accept him as one of nature's irritants, like the sand within his trews that set Hirby squirming. But Hirby was no pearl. "The sea gift you today, Hirby?"

Opening his burlap sack as coyly as if he were displaying fragile, exotic blooms for a fair maiden, he let Pommy peer inside. Three sand biscuits, unbroken by the wave action, a branchy piece of pink coral, and half a pair of pantaloons. It took time to identify them as Pommy turned the fabric in his hands, not quite able to make sense of its singular state. Good fabric and weave, but small, hardly man-sized. Still, you never knew when a piece of fabric could have a use, mending or whatnot. Reluctantly, though he hadn't a clue why, he passed it back to Hirby, kicking at Tigger when the dog reared, desperate to seize the pantaloon piece in his teeth, play tug-of-war.

"Good dye job," Hirby offered proudly. "Been in the sea and sun so long and nary any fading. Fresh water wash and dry in the sun—good as new!" Touching the fabric to his cheek, he furrowed his brow, considered. "Mayhap if we goes looking tamarra we'll find the other half. Stitch'em up good as new an sell'em to Widder Roemer." A pleading guilelessness plus a hint of calculation in his limpid eyes as he clutched Pommy's arm. "Help me hunt'em, Pommy? Start when the sun cracks, trot the inlets both ways . . ."

"Can't oblige, Hirby." Much as he pitied Hirby, Pommy'd run short of patience, supremely tired of the odd man's drag on his arm, on his life, always trailing after him, hindering, not only in body but in spirit, often as not. But what to say, how to explain it? Suggest he awaited something momentous and Hirby'd demand to know what, sure he was being shut out. It was his, *his* alone, that Pommy knew to the depths of his soul. Something he'd been anticipating for so long, like that state of grace those robed religious folk nattered on about.

Inspiration struck. "Promised Cooes I'd pluck a mess of crawdiddies to sell him. You know you hate feeling round the rocks with your toes or sticking your fingers in the crevices—flat won't dive under to fetch'em." Mouth downturned, lower lip moistly outthrust, Hirby looked ready to cry. Save him from weepy loons! His big hands nervously worked the sack, kneading it, and Pommy forced himself to pat Hirby's arm. "But I promise, Hirby, I'll keep a sharp lookout for the other half of those pantaloons—if I snag them, they're yours, honor bright."

Hirby's head bounced loosely on his neck as he nodded happy agreement. Then, scanning the shore for possible interlopers, he pulled Pommy's head close, whispering rapidly in his ear, "Tancred Rock? Crawdiddies dancing real fine there, Pommy, Nought knows but me—an you." With those parting words, the disheveled man whistled up Tigger and trotted off, earnestly watching each footstep splash. Once he halted, jumped at a receding wave with both feet.

Despite his relief, a weight of loneliness settled over Pommy as Hirby's broad form grew smaller in the distance. He was companionship—of a sort. But oh, the time was ripe, the sea would willingly yield its promise to him, if only he remained worthy of it! Tomorrow at first dawning he'd start searching. Now, home to eat, attempt to sleep. Impossible, but he'd try, play by the rules, not rise nor stir till the false dawn turned true. False turned true—it could happen thusly, it would. After all, all too often true turned false.

PART
FOUR

Strike the lucifer against the stone wall, watch the flame blossom blue and yellow, almost tear-shaped. More quickly than a caterpillar devours a leaf, the flame consumes the sliver of wood, the char-black remains curling upward. A vulgar joke about that, one she'd heard the older girls tell but hadn't understood until recently. Now, purse your lips, snuff the flame, light another lucifer, watch it burn. . . .

Each pretend pinprick of light could be counted, concentrated on, something to clutch at through another dark night, the sea lapping at her. A momentary wistfulness at the loss of her pantaloons and shirt, but to think on that gave rise to reality, and she refused to face that any longer. Fire, nice bright fire, blazing warm and dry, dry and warm, radiating heat, light against the consuming darkness, the outer dark of night and the creeping dark within her mind.

Ignite something with the lucifer? Yes—oh, yes, why not? Build a fire, light a pyre to burn through the night across the seas. Seas . . . someone sees me. . . . Diccon would see, wouldn't let her light it, nor Mama or Papa either. Always snatching lucifers from her, slapping, naughty, no! Hurting, when all she desired was to watch the flames blaze and flicker, let them burn away her fears. Always that fear, that longing drawing her closer to the flames, fearsome, cheersome flames. Something within her kindling as she struck the lucifer, careful not to snap it, just a brush of the tip against roughness, and from that wooden stem bloomed, bloomed such a lovely blossom, unfurling shimmering petals, burning embers in its throat, pistil and stamen sparks.

What to ignite? Candles, a torch, a lantern? Something with more crackle and spark, like a haystack? Never had she dared, though she'd longed to many times. Why fire? Why not? From the womb it had haunted her; why it didn't similarly haunt Diccon she couldn't judge. In her blood, mayhap, because Mama respected flames, what they could do. Mama'd had another life, another family once. But someone called Vesey had burned it clean away, clearing the way for Jenneth and Diccon to rise from the ashes. Once, in their floating, interior world she and Diccon had become aware of a fierce energy lurking outside, surrounding Mama, fire again. A beckoning brightness streaming through Mama's flesh, growing, expanding with the oxygen it consumed, their lifelines within Mama scanted of oxygen.

Jenneth writhed on the spar, so very weary of its unyielding shape, its rasp against her raw flesh. Nothing to do except hug the spar, let her legs trail, flex a cramping arm so tired of embracing lifeless wood. How much longer until she simply slid off, meekly acquiescent to the sea's seductive whispers or simply rolling off in her sleep? Cold, too, the breeze building, smoothing itself over her wet back and head.

Then a gentle pounding, pleasant at first, as if nature massaged her tired body. A reviving trickle of moisture teased her, and she opened her eyes—rain! Yes, rain! Turning a stiff neck, she opened her mouth wide, greedy for each droplet. Oh, more, faster, please! Let it pour in, enough for a true mouthful, a real swallow, and she'd never think of fire again, ever! But no, it teased and tantalized, compelling her to extend her swollen tongue to catch each one, the blessed wetness promising so much more life than the sea's waters.

A dull grumble in the distance. Annoying, come to think of it. Think, ha? Probably nothing, another version of the watery echoes within her ears, the sepulchral sounds inside her head. So hateful having water blocking your ears, the pressure, the hollow, dum-thrumming of sounds around you when you knew things didn't really sound like that. Cocking her head, she slammed the heel of her hand against her temple, hoping to dislodge the water. No luck, the tumbling grumble still resonated within her. Tumble her long enough and she'd break—

Break? Breakers? The pounding of waves as they crash and foam on shore? Pounding and churning to dash objects on the beach? Jenneth propped herself up just as the wave slammed her, ripping her from her spar, entombing her in a mountain of water, churning her down and flicking her up. Fight! she commanded herself, find the surface, breathe! As her body began rising, she kicked feebly, struck out with her hands. A lightening shade at the surface, a shimmering entrance to life. Breaking through, gasping, spewing water, she sucked fresh, rain-drenched air into her lungs. . . .

And went down again, tumbling and rolling, shaken like a rat in a terrier's jaws. Barnaby? Barnaby, are you waiting for me? Sweet old Barnaby! Something, someone else on that other, shimmering side?—waiting anxiously for her—not like Barnaby waiting to welcome her on this dark, devouring side. Plushlike fur, calico-cuddly? Air and life again, too quickly snatched away by a sudden sinking and tossing, the bruising scrape of the sea's churning bottom. Lungs bursting, crying to breathe in, desperately inhale, the need so primal that everything else was obliterated from her mind. Not going to . . . not going to . . . damn! The waves rolled her hard against the bottom once more, and she reared, discovered her head clear of the water, her hands planted in the sand.

Crawl, drag yourself ahead, do it! As if to finally oblige—or perhaps tired of toying with her—an exceptionally powerful wave lifted Jenneth ashore. Rivulets of water trickled along the length of her body, carving branched trenches in the sand.

With an ear-shattering shriek Kwee streaked up the rise that led to the wildly overgrown heart of Goose Island. Startled, his own mind caught in a cascade of emotions from Bard's mindcries of rage, M'wa froze, blankly staring into the distance before shaking his mind clear and bounding after Kwee's fluid gray blur. Settling into a lope that ate up the distance in less than twenty strides, he shoulder-butted Kwee, but she acted oblivious to his presence. **"Kwee, stop! Wait!"** He leaped a saw-leafed, sprawling bush strewn with star flowers and prayed for an easy landing. Kwee, however, barreled through and under the prickling leaves, but his spring put him a pace ahead.

"**Stop, youngling!**" His legs ached; he'd run like a grey-hound if danger or need pressed, but knew his body'd make him dearly pay for the effort later. Breaking stride, he aimed an awkward swat at Kwee's head, but she dodged him, single-minded in her pursuit, while he stumbled, wrenching his shoulder. Ouch! He pressed on, scanning ahead. Yes, right there—before the path turned so narrow they'd be forced to travel single-file. Pincer her between that mica-specked boulder and his own solid, black flank. . . .

Matching her stride, he leaned into her, harder and harder until he'd pinned her. Twisting, he caught hold of the scruff of her neck before she could wriggle free, spring over him. "**Enough, youngling! Think before you harum-scarum off like a rolapin seeing a hawk's shadow! Do you want to help or not?**"

He'd not bargained on this responsibility, his concern divided between his Bond and this bumptious little beast. His brain still jangled with Bard's crescending fury, and then abruptly cleared, no longer hostage to his Bond's madness. A blessing—Bard still lived, someone had reined him in before his frenzy escalated any further, endangering himself or others.

"**Diccon!**" the ghatten moaned, "**Diccon needs Kwee— poor, poor Diccon!**" Fear-dark, her eyes showed just a scant hint of green rim, her heart pounding so fast he could sense a wild, building resolve presaging her intent to pull free, even if it cost her fur and skin. Smooth and sleek as a snake, M'wa shifted his grip to sink his teeth into her ear, allowing her to realize how close he came to shredding it if she pulled away. How could he have expected her to react sensibly when this was the first real mental cry of danger and anguish that she'd ever received from her Bond?

"**Yes, Diccon needs you, and Bard needs me. But think, little furling, fluff-fur-for-brains, think before you dash into danger.**"

As best she could she tucked her head against his throat, little mewling snuffles ruffling his fur. "**Lost Sissy, not going to lose Diccon!**" she hiccuped.

"**Don't want to lose Bard either!**" unaware his 'speech revealed more trepidation than he cared to display. "**Will**

you behave? Not make me chase you up and down this island? And around it?" Releasing her ear but not straying far from it, he gave her a rough lick as if aligning her forehead stripes. **"May be old and crotchety, but I'll run your legs to stubs if you cross me."**

A purring worry vibration tickled his neck, for purrs arose from varied emotions, not only utter security and comfort. He sleeked her again, scrubbed his chin across her head. **"Like to see you try, Granther-ghatt,"** she chortle-purred before turning solemn once more. **"How can we save them if we don't hurry, find them? Fight the bad men, whack and slap them, scratch and gouge, oh . . . give them such bites!"**

Ah, the glory of youth—he dimly recalled it, refusing to picture it too closely. Youth . . . Bard so loving, yet strong and brave, and M'wa, lithe-limbed black-and-white, the mirror-image of P'wa, beloved sib, beloved of Byrta, the mirror-image of his Bond. . . . Ah. . . .

"Use your energy to think, little one. Where're Diccon and the others now?" He already knew, even with Bard unconscious, could sense what his Bond's body felt, the rock of the waves, the smooth glide of a boat. That plus the message of reassurance Davvy had labored to send. Although he might be a superlative Resonant, Davvy lacked finesse when it came to long-distance mindspeech with ghatti. Still, enough of the message had been clear to allow M'wa to be grateful yet concerned.

Plunking down, Kwee vigorously dug behind an ear with her hind foot. **"Boat, water-beetling to the big island. Diccon's sooo mad!"** Her hind foot hovered, then fell, her scratch unfinished. **"Boat? M'wa—boat! Hurry!"** A striped blur as she reversed herself to shoot down the slope, and M'wa gave a convulsive lunge, sinking his teeth into her tail-tip. **"Ooouch! Yee-ouch!"** Her verbal screech pierced M'wa's eardrums.

"Fine, wake the dead. Or any other bad souls on the island." M'wa spat a mouthful of tail, aggravated anew by her overreaction.

Undeterred by the momentary pain, she side-skittered, pringle-toeing in excitement. **"Chase after them in launch! Catch them, scratch and bash them!"**

An inward sigh as M'wa scoured his memory for how

many times he and P'wa had required a strenuous repetition of lessonings. Probably more often than he liked to acknowledge, not that that made this any easier. **"Yes, you're a clever ghatten, but can you row?** *I* **can't. Can you hoist a sail?** *I* **can't. Mayhap I could work the tiller, but not much more. Would you have us float out to sea, lost and alone forever?"**

"Pw'eek!" Wailing her sib's name, Kwee collapsed at his feet. **"Oh, Pw'eek, oh, Diccon! Woe! Woe is Kwee, no sib, no Bond!"**

"Well, you have me—be thankful for that." Boosting with his broad head, he prodded her to her feet, set her marching to the beach. **"Come along. We need to explore."**

"Along the beach? Around to where the bad men snatched Diccon?" She trotted tight beside him, mottled pewter with copper highlights flashing against M'wa's black flank, his white stockings.

"Mayhap. Best you learn, youngling, how to mindsearch for one of our own. Methodically seek, search farther and wider to find if any will answer, will help." And pray to the Elders that a few ghatti resided in the Sunderlies. Casual talk had told him some *did* live here, semiretired, but for the life of him he couldn't recollect who'd volunteered for duty right now. Old age creeping up on him, turning him forgetful, or mayhap it was worry. Should anything happen to Bard . . . how to explain to Lindy and Byrlie? And what would his life be worth without Bard?

Well, time enough to dwell on that, that final decision he'd adamantly refused to contemplate. Because if Bard had been privy to his resolve, it might have tilted the scales one way or another, destroying the illusion of "balance" he'd projected for so long, the "balance" that had convinced Bard to live all these years. . . .

"You're *sure*?" Aidannae clutched old Mama Santellena's arm, further creasing the sagging skin. "Swear-by-the-Lady sure? Not just a large cat, but a *stealther*? One of those mind-stealing ghatti beasts?" For once Mama Santellena hadn't shunned Dannae or begrudged her the site for selling her loaves, indeed, had run panting to greet her so she

could spread her gossip ever further, ever wider, even this
early in the morn.

Mama nodded vigorously but with decidedly less enthusiasm; Dannae tardily loosening her grip, giving Mama's arm
a conciliatory pat. Aaee!—she'd clung too tight! "Told'ee,
Shep Dannae, big as life—two ov'em. Big stripety one with
white on its chest and face, an later, nudder one, same
stripety sides but grayer neath'em." Licking her upper lip-
bristles, Mama gabbled on, "If they daun be stealthers,
mayhap tis jungle wildcats slipping into the Samranth bazaar!" A delicious shiver coursed through Mama's hunched
body, and Dannae calculated her thrill at another way to
enhance her tale. Should one bit of gossip not pan out,
save another tidbit to spread. Dannae didn't want to believe—but didn't dare not unearth the kernel of truth
Mama invested in most of her gossip, like a starter bud of
yeast that made them swell.

"And Kasimir and Sirikit went willingly?" A cold finger
of foreboding trailed along Dannae's spine, and she prayed
to the Lady that it wasn't so. How the Motipersad clan
courted bad luck! Who knew better than she, being distantly related? "No one forced them to accompany the
strangers? Not taken against their will?"

An indignant sniff, then a longer one as the aroma of
fresh-baked bread wafted to Mama Santellena's nostrils.
"Kin ask Momsvaert, the cushion-merchant, if yed want
nother witness. Siri-child was fair taken with the dark-
stripety one, and Smir were playing 'gen'mun wid debt
o'honor,' offerin ta sarve'em."

Dannae knew what *that* meant. Siri'd been reading aloud
to Smir again, tales where well-born gentlemen disguised
themselves as common folk and engaged in high adventure
and derring-do, aiding the downtrodden in the bargain.
Books too old for Smir—let alone Siri. Where was the child
finding them? That, however, was a far-distant and minor
worry compared to the one now confronting her.

"Mama, have you heard word where these strangers and
their stealthers are staying?" Mayhap, if she were lucky—
or if the Lady smiled on her endeavors—she could extricate
the children before any harm was done, their night amongst
the stealthers fading like a bad dream. But it might already
be too late, their brains snatched, and she didn't know what

she'd do then. After all, she no longer was Dannae the
Avenger, terror of the streets. That misguided soul'd been
replaced by Shepherd Aidannae, whose mission was to succor the poor, the sick, any who'd strayed from the Lady's
path. And most of all, to ceaselessly murmur the prayers,
sing the mystery chants honoring Her and Her Disciples.

" 'Twould ha been a sweet sight seeing wee Siri wid her
arms wrapped round zat stealther—if it hedn't made me
blood run cold." Virtuously casting the eight-point star,
Mama heaved a sigh and folded her hands on her drooping
bosom. "All cuddlesome close'n sweet, Siri a whispering in
zose beringed ears. Two sets. Earrings," she amplified, "not
ears. Four ears'n ev'rywan'd see they's dealing wid a monster. But a handsome gold hoop in one ear, an a red rose
in the other, just like her human slave-bond's. Ruby, less'n
I miss my guess!"

That added detail, too accurate for Mama to have con-
cocted, panicked Dannae even more. Swinging her wrapped
bundle of bread from her back, she thrust it into the old
woman's arms. "Take it, please. Sell it if you will—for the
glory of the Lady, for the aid of the Bethel. If not, eat,
enjoy, be blessed."

With that she spun 'round, her walk speeding into a
forceful trot as she navigated the aisles of the bazaar, rolling her sleeves up tight until they stayed above her elbows.
Her oversized sandals slapped puffs of dust as she hiked
up the hem of her robe, twisting the excess round her hempen belt. Unseemly, to say the least, displaying so much
broad, bare calf, but now Dannae the Avenger took precedence over Shepherd Aidannae. As she'd planned, her path
took her by Eckholm's stall, her old childhood friend,
Eckie.

Barely slowing her pace, she shouted, "Eckie! Begging
the borrow of your toughest broom—short, thick handle,
bristle-twig, if ye can." Eyes puzzled under his shaggy, dark
hair, Eckholm commenced a frantic inventory, holding out
a broom as she whizzed past, snatching it without breaking
stride. "Thankee! Lady'n I owe ye." Groaning, Eckie shook
his head as he always did at her demands. Poor Eckie expected the worst, envisioning his precious broom in splinters, no coin to cover it. She supposed it *was* her fault the
Lady wasn't over-prompt about paying Her earthly debts.

Hefting the broom, working her hands along its handle, testing the twig binding, Dannae single-mindedly marched along, shouldering aside any obstacles in her path. How, how could Ozer Oordbeck, generally an honorable man, have arranged to rent a house to such outlanders, such scum? Allowed them a base from which to work their evil wiles practically in the midst of town? Had they already sucked *his* mind clean? Or was this but an example of the typical mercantile mind: money to be made, even from an unsavory source? Either way, she mourned the loss of a good man.

Broom on her shoulder, stride grimly determined, Dannae turned up Frais Street, unconscious of the titters and stares following in her wake. Here the upscale merchants had their hoity-toity shops, assisted perfumed, pomaded ladies in and out of litters. Use the likes of her as a mounting block, they would—and not even notice! Already huffing with righteous exertion, she swung over to the Esplanade, the broad, tree-lined boulevard running up the easy slope of Traders Heights. A pleasant stroll and guaranteed not to raise any sweat to dew their brows. Most of the well-to-do made their homes here, high above Samranth's squalor, removed from its port smells and the earthy tang of the town's lesser inhabitants. More—an affected sniff—salubrious. Free, too, from the raging torrents of mud and debris that clogged streets and homes after a torrential storm.

Now a curb-set marble dolphin plaque indicated a winding, private path with prycanthius crowding each side, its pale-green blossoms' honied fragrance enticing butterflies, bees, and tiny, darting humbers with needlelike beaks and wings that beat so fast they blurred Dannae's vision. An amethyst one hovered as if to probe her red topknot, two rubies with emerald throats looped and chased each other. The prycanthius encircled the house, offered pointed protection, gardeners laboring for years to foster it, prune and direct it. Gardeners earned prime pay, didn't always live long enough to enjoy it, despite their care. Thorns long as her little finger stood guard in all directions.

Even if an intruder were foolhardy enough to risk shredded, punctured flesh, he'd best outfit himself with a heavy, cured leather jacket and gloves, pants and hood. And have alcohol at hand, for even minor scratches festered, went infected. Some swore 'twas better to excise surrounding flesh, not just pluck out the spike, hope the poison hadn't spread too far. Others pulled and poulticed. A long, silvery scar threading along the underside of Dannae's arm made her wince at the memory of having tested the prycanthius's defenses.

Impressed despite herself she stood stock-still as the house came into view. Dolphin House looked more imposing than it truly was, for its core was a central courtyard, almost every ground-floor room opening onto it. What more safety or seclusion from the squalid life of downtown Samranth could any desire? As much as she scorned such luxury, Dannae experienced a twinge of wistfulness. She'd been welcomed within years ago—or at least welcome as far as the kitchens. Her mother'd served as undercook for two octants—longer than usual—before bad luck and drink caught up with them again. Had Ozer Oordbeck *bought* Dolphin House? 'Twas far grander, more expansive than his own domicile, but then, a dozen children guaranteed even the grandest house would quickly be run-down. Maundering again—Lady guide her straight and true to her task!

Shifting the broom to her other shoulder, Dannae pushed up her sleeves and knocked, hammering the shell-shaped knocker against the iron gate harder than she'd pounded each nail into the Bethel roof. There! Take that for Smir! And that for Siri! Ears ringing, she paused, sure she'd waked the dead—or driven some innocent soul to an early grave. But no, nothing. Again she hammered, impatient and increasingly fearful, poised to berate any who answered. Would rudeness gain her admission? Hardly. *I'm the Lady's Shepherd, meek and mild, but I'll poke out your eye if you get me riled.*" A nervous grin at such sacrilege, but she felt marginally calmer.

A dark-haired boy with a pale, outlander complexion—twelve, mayhap—tidily dressed in baggy navy shorts and a loose white overshirt, hurried out, a half-smile of query dimpling his cheek. What? Had they coerced, seduced other innocents, wiped their minds blank? An inward groan, not only Kasimir and Siri, but another lamb to save, Lady help her! "Yes? Good morning . . ." a considering pause as he took stock of her attire, "Shepherd. May I help you?" Unruffled, perfectly composed, the boy stood a discreet distance behind the gate. Such sedate patience in a child was preternatural to her mind—especially compared to Smir . . . oh, poor Smir, was he already like this lad?—but apparently he'd not unlock the gate till she'd stated her business. "I've come for the Motipersads—Kasimir and Sirikit." A flash of inspiration! "They're wanted—elsewhere." Elsewhere, *anywhere* but here! Knuckles white, she clutched her broom, not wanting to threaten unless she had no choice. Broom? No wonder the child looked askance at her! Smile, she told herself, smile, but suspected she'd bared too many teeth, falsely hearty. Mayhap she could resolve this without conflict. "I'm the Shepherd Aidannae."

"How do you do? I'm Harry Muscadeine." Reaching to unlock the gate, he hesitated. "I hope Smir and Siri won't be away long. They like it here, and it's fun having them." Finally he turned the lock, pulling open the gate and gesturing her inside with a little bow of greeting. Too, too mannerly—clearly the stealthers had gotten him! Murmurously commending her soul to the Lady, Dannae stepped inside, wondering how deep she'd have to delve inside this den of depravity to rescue the children? "This way, please." A sweep of his arm, and the boy escorted her along the brick walkway to the front door.

"Lady grant me strength, grant me courage," she whispered, lips soundlessly moving, her immortal soul as frosted with fear as the rest of her. "Mayhap I can spirit the children away before *they* even realize I've struck a blow for Her cause. . . ." Still mouthing silent lauds, Dannae at last raised her eyes to see—to her everlasting horror—a tall man, gaunt as an oct-old cadaver, hurtling down the passageway toward them, frowning. "H-Harry? W-what does he—" Taking a second, more assessing look, he corrected himself, "s-she want, this Shepherd?" But what sent Dannae near witless with terror was the apparition of a stealther at his feet, a huge, dark-striped cat whose eyes bored into her very mind and soul as if sponging up her every thought, wringing her dry.

Petrified hands locked on the broom, Dannae yearned to cast the Lady's eight-point star, but her traitorous hands denied her even that protection. Well, Aidannae might need such solace, but Dannae the Avenger depended on her wits, her strength to survive! First rule: Attack first,

without warning. She who struck first, fastest, hardest,
turned advantage into victory. The only cheek she'd turn
would be the one she'd flash this skeletal man when she
and the children hightailed it out of here in triumph!

Broom up—and lunge! Stabbing the twigs at the man's
face, his eyes, Dannae confidently anticipated his backward
leap to safety. Yet despite his gawkiness, he adroitly evaded
her, grabbed the handle as well, his large-knuckled hands
crowding on either side of hers. With a grunt he lifted upward until Dannae found herself dangling, sandaled feet
kicking air. Ha—thank you! She'd been unsure she could
kick that high, but if he insisted—

Just then, an inquiring nose and set of whiskers tickled
her foot, her calf, and she frantically frog-legged, vainly
attempting to draw them out of reach. "No! Back, beast!"
Her upward stretch had unfurled her robe from her belt,
the excess length draping the stealther's head. A sneeze
and the stealther tangled in the clinging fabric, mole-
mounding along until it popped free.

Dizzy with fear, still hanging on for dear life, Dannae
fought to bring a knee into play, drive it where it would
do the most good. "P-please don't," the man implored,
swiveling so the blow struck his hip. "Th-that tends to s-
smart." To her amazement, he shared a glance with the
stealther as if exchanging a message, and he cautiously lowered her without relinquishing the broom. A canny adver-
sary! Expelling a deep breath that ruffled her topknot, he
gabbled, "It's only a g-ghatta, you know. Nice beasts." A
lopsided smile failed to warm her heart. "N-nicer th-than
you! S-Shepherds don't—"

Heaving back on the broom with all her considerable
weight, Dannae swiftly reversed herself, jabbing the handle
up and catching the man a hard blow under the chin. His
jaws snapped together like a nutcracker, a gratifying trickle
of blood leaking from his mouth. Good! Either he'd bitten
his tongue or driven his teeth through his lip! "The children!" she roared, standing on tiptoe as he dropped the
broom to cover his mouth. "Release the innocents now!"
Another menacing broom thrust at the foe, then one at his
stealther, who hissed and swatted at the twig-ends.

Too intent on tracking the stealther and its familiar, Dannae'd lost track of the boy who'd greeted her, Harry what-

ever-his-name-was. Hadn't given the poor, lack-witted child a second thought until first Siri's high-pitched voice, then Smir's, registered. "Doan hurt the chazza-ghatta!" "Dannae, what yed doin? Fightin's a zin! Siri'n me be debted to these folks! 'N like'em, too!"

Too late! The children had turned on her! The strangers'd made the children theirs, snatched their minds! The beast hissed again, back arched and menacing. At the risk of her own life, she tore her gaze off it for a moment, shouting over her shoulder, "Run, Siri, Smir!" Mayhap the Lady's smile hadn't completely passed them by, would shine on them, release them from the spell. Too intent on her own fears and the pressing need to thoroughly whip the foe in front of her, Dannae never noticed her new adversaries until it was too late. Without a word or wasted motion, two women efficiently pinioned her arms, wrenching her precious weapon from her grasp.

"The lovely thing about fighting woman-to-woman," someone hissed, and Dannae quailed, fearing she heard the beast's insinuating voice, "is that being gentlemanly doesn't pertain."

The voice on her other side oozed false compassion. "You've no experience with ghatti, have you? Don't tell me you've never heard of the Shepherd Harrap and his ghatt Parm—back in Canderis?"

Bucking with all the strength in her stocky frame, Dannae tried to throw them off, found herself held tighter. The woman with the coolly hissing voice boasted an intimate appreciation of the body's vulnerable pressure points, information that left Dannae writhing, while the other contented herself with containing Dannae. Breath shuddering in her lungs, Dannae blinked back tears of defeat as the more kindly, less-menacing outlander said in exasperation, "If you wish to speak with Kasimir and Siri, you're welcome to without wielding a broom. We're hardly holding them prisoner—"

"You're not?" Dannae blurted, the torque on her shoulder joints marginally relaxing. "Of course, no need to imprison them once you've snatched their minds for your baneful rites!"

"Lady save us! The ghatti don't steal minds! Did you drink in that tired tale with your mother's milk? And in

this day and age!" Dannae couldn't decide whether the
woman sounded more scandalized or sorrowful at her
"error"—if error it was! "You mean you've *never* heard of
the Seekers Veritas and their Bonds?"

"*That's* what a Bondmate is?" Half-incredulous, Dannae
stared at the striped stealther, only to discover it had split
into two entities! She closed her eyes to blot out the sight,
then forced herself to sneak a look. No, it'd been joined
by another, older, she thought, and the unstriped fur was
darker, a rich brown-black. This one looked bemused and
more than a little uncomfortable draped across Siri's narrow shoulder, its hindquarters an ample armful for the
child. "*Those* are Truth-Seekers?"

Well, who *hadn't* heard tales of the Seekers Veritas?
After all, they were the reason most Sunderlies exiles were
here! No, that was wrong, backward—the reason people
were exiled here was because they'd committed a heinous
crime, and the Seekers Veritas had determined that truth.
Rumor had it that some were stationed at the forts, though
she'd never run into any. Hadn't relished visiting the same
scabby haunts as she, clearly! *Had,* however, heard tales
of mind-thieves and suchlike, scare-tales for children late at
night. Which stories were true, which false? The disso-
nances crowded her mind, jogging her sense of fair play,
her resolve flagging as her curiosity grew.

Judge not, least ye be judged—and what had she been
guilty of doing? But her faith in the Lady had come hard-
won, and these beasts would have to work equally hard to
gain her trust. As a Shepherd, the Lady's goodness flowed
through her, through her touch. Right, then—if she could
touch one, if it didn't flinch or flee, yowl and madly spit,
mayhap it wasn't so loathly dangerous after all. "Let me
touch one—if you dare!" Recklessly she threw the challenge at their feet.

Through a puffy lip the tall, scraggly man asked, "Khar?
Khim? Would you, please?" Ha—mayhap the fat lip had
stoppered his stammering.

The beast in Siri's arms blinked amber eyes, craning her
sinuous neck to look at Dannae. "Nice Khar," Siri cajoled,
"Come meet Dannae. She's a Shepherd, the kind that doan
keep sheep." Awkwardly burdened, unable to see her feet,
Siri guardedly closed the distance, obviously protective of

the animal. When Dannae's arms were released, quick as a flash she formed a shaky eight-point star in front of the ghatta's face and, steeling herself, reached a tremulous hand to touch its satin-sleek head.

"Not easily convinced, are you? A Doubting Dannae." Goddess bright! They *did* speak—inside your mind! How to shut it off? She jerked her hand back, sure her touch had set it off, but no . . .

"We prefer being invited to mindwalk, but regardless, what we read in your mind remains, intact." Forcing herself to reveal no expression, Dannae cudgeled her brain to think how she'd greet an ordinary cat. Alley cats—and her fingers acted without her volition—enjoyed an ear scratch. A rumbling purr greeted her fumbling. **"Chin scratches are nice,"** the beast hinted. **"We've something in common: 'Judge not, least ye be judged.' We seek out the truth, but it's not our right to judge. By the way, I'm Khar'pern, Bondmate of Doyce Marbon. She's resting, but I hope you'll meet her later."**

"What is going on here?" Winded and white, caftan ruckled in his fist like an old lady crossing a muddy street, Ozer Oordbeck shook the gate, Harry at his side. "Shepherd Aidannae, please! I hope even the Lady considers the ghatti blessed by her hand—er, hands? Whatever." Giving a "well-done" nod to the boy, the puffy-lipped one opened the gate and Ozer entered, still expostulating, "If you'd *only* asked, I would've brought you straightaway, showed you the children are fine."

A flush traveled from her toes to her face, and over her shaved pate until it reached her topknot, flaming red against red. Jumping to conclusions again, Dannae! When, oh, when would the Lady see that she mended her impetuous ways?

"Ma'am, as Jenret Wycherley's wife, as Jacobia Wycherley's sister-in-law . . . naturally I assumed . . ." Ozer Oordbeck slumped in the canvas sling chair, sliding lower each time Doyce gave a vigorous headshake of denial, each question more and more mystifying. "And everything I've said has been absolute *news* to you? You haven't a clue, an inkling, about the Wycherley-Saffron problems?" Morosely he peered over his knees, eyes blankly wide, trapped in his own private disaster.

Restless on the wrought iron bench—why had she chosen it, knowing how her thigh muscles would cramp?—Doyce levered herself up and stumped to the perimeter of the courtyard's central plot. The surrounding garden beds had run riot, needed pruning, weeding, sturdier stakes to support the profusion of heavy-headed blooms each plant sported. Hardly an auspicious time to inquire about gardeners for hire. Even allowing herself to be sidetracked by such things told her how she attempted to postpone the inevitable.

Plucking a storm-ripped branch from the graveled path, she raked the grass with it, truly yearning to give something or someone a good drubbing—like her husband. "By the Blessed Lady, not one whisper about financial woes has reached my ears." Of course, even if rumors *had* been rampant, she'd likely have ignored them, shrugged them off, too wrapped up in her own world as Seeker General. An honest answer, but one she didn't especially fancy. Contenting herself with poking the branch, she continued, "Just as I've no inkling who that Shepherd was yesterday morning—hardly standard issue—or why we upset her so. Truly, Oh-Oh." Dagga boys, demented Shepherds of the female persuasion, financial woes—all on top of missing children. What next? And did the financial worries explain part of Jenret's distance of late?

As he scrubbed his face in dismay, Doyce caught the agent's faint recoil at being addressed as Oh-Oh, the sort of slight reaction that Seekers automatically noted. "Don't really care for your nickname, do you? What do you prefer being called? At least it's a start, something I *can* rectify." And also convince the poor agent someone was on his side, even if she felt she'd become "It" in a game of blindman's bluff.

"Hate it!" Startling himself at his own vehemence, he gave a weak, apologetic smile. "Absolutely loathe it! And each and every time someone calls me that, I smile, don't let on. . . ." Struggling from the sling chair's embrace, he hiked his chambray caftan clear and knelt, attacking the encroaching weeds, belt knife gouging the soil, levering roots free as he yanked the intruders. "Ozer. Even Ordy'd be fine," he mumbled, then in a louder appeal, "Call me anything you want if you can solve my problems." With a groan he sank back on his haunches, his round face, round eyes and mouth skewed in anguish. "I hate to further burden you . . . I know how you . . . what you're . . ." Doyce could sense real empathy in his halting speech. "Whoever's fleecing us, trying to ruin the mercantile, is willing to threaten, even harm my children to succeed!"

In complete startlement at his confession, Doyce jammed her crutch too deep in the sod, abandoning it to take a hobbling step toward Ozer, her hands outstretched. "What do you mean?"

Clasping her hands, Oordbeck rested his forehead against them. "I just *don't* know! I don't know if it's mere scare tactics . . . if they'd truly do it, or . . ." he swallowed convulsively. "But when you've twelve children in your care, that multiplies the worry!"

Mounting frustration made her unjustly want to box Ozer's ears in lieu of the culprit who deserved her blows. Damn Jenret for holding all of this so close to his chest! "Did you mention this to Jenret?" she asked while she 'spoke Khar. *"Beloved, quickly, please! Bring Theo and Khim, too."*

Still clutching her hand like a lifeline, Ozer Oordbeck rose, wiping his eyes on his sleeve. "Hardly seemly to wail about my problems, the company's problems, when your husband was suffering, his own children lost or strayed." He stood marginally straighter now, striving for control. "If I can't keep Wycherley-Saffron solvent, protect my own family, what sort of agent am I? But it would be a relief to feel I'm not alone in the struggle."

Banded tail quirked in question, Khar came at a trot, Khim and Theo hurrying along by another path, curious and anxious. Theo's lower lip was still swollen, giving him an almost voluptuous, kissable mouth—totally at odds with his bashful demeanor. "I th-think I s-set things right with the S–" and plucked a simpler, less treacherous word from his mouth, "with Dannae, sir, with your help yesterday. It's n-not that," a deep breath, "that she's credulous, it's just she's had so lit-tle ex-POSURE." He greedily inhaled.

"In other words," Khim interjected, **"Theo won't be de-**

prived of his giblets or the family jewels, as you humans call them. Means Khar and I are safe as well." Khim endured a quelling look from Khar as their paths joined. **"That's not your current concern?"**

"Well, it's a distinct relief that friends, human or ghatti, won't be dissected or disassembled, but you're right: bigger trouble's afoot." Limping to retrieve her crutch, she smiled at Oordbeck. "You've already met Theo Morheuser, know he's been at the receiving end of Shepherd Aidannae's broom. When not protecting himself and Dolphin House against misguided beliefs, he's a Seeker Veritas. I, by the way, held the office of Seeker General until very recently." With a neat bow, Theo took a seat while Doyce quickly outlined Ozer Oordbeck's revelations about the mercantile's financial woes and his own intensely personal worries.

The more deeply Theo involved himself in an assignment, the less he stammered; indeed, those who'd encountered him only at a formal Seeking ceremony had no idea how his words often bottled themselves inside. Still, it temporarily confounded her when Theo changed modes. "Can't say Holly or I've heard any rumors about that. But then, we couldn't raise three coppers to invest. Wish Sarrett were here—she'd know the gossip." Did Sarrett know something? Had she known and not intimated a thing to one of her oldest, dearest friends? A sting of betrayal at the thought.

"Or you're betraying your friendship by doubting her," Khar chided. **"I'll tell you this: T'ss never breathed a word of any such thing to me."** Momentarily Doyce felt better.

Engrossed, Theo stroked his lip, gingerly fingering its new dimensions. "Except the night of the twins' party, there was something in the air, some sort of tension with Jacobia and Miz Wycherley, er, Miz Saffron." An apologetic shrug. "Can't always remember to call her that. Not between Jacobia and Miz Saffron so much as between Jenret and them. Ask Lindy? I think she saw them all arguing outside just before you arrived. Jacobia still seemed upset about something when we spoke later that evening."

Anxious to help, Khim added, **"Doesn't Honoria go over the bookkeeping with Jenret? They review the records after Jacobia sends them over."** An unpleasant reminder of an ongoing problem that Doyce had pushed aside, but she was more surprised by the fact that Khar's amber eyes slitted and her tail swished dangerously. So much so that Khim evinced a sudden fascination in a bijou bird hopping across the grass.

"Oh, I doubt we need involve Honoria." Khar's white foot tapped Doyce's knee, reclaiming her attention. **"Rawn said Jenret has piles of paperwork in his trunk. Mayhap we could start there, see what clues they hold?"**

Forcing herself to be fair, she debated with herself over Khar's suggestion; not being overfond (a slight understatement) of Honoria didn't mean she couldn't ask her for help. Honoria had experience with the ledgers, and Doyce refused to allow Jacobia's and Jenret's venture to fail if she could help it—especially because of sheer pettiness on her part! Why hadn't she confronted Honoria the morning Jenret had left, had it out with the woman? Was she afraid she'd appear a jealous, vengeful old crone?

"Theo, why don't you and Honoria review what Jenret brought with him? Mayhap he or Jacobia scribbled marginal notes, saw something Ozer didn't." Unblinking, she returned Khar's stare, too proud to ask the one question she truly wanted answered—or did she? Khar always 'spoke the truth, was incapable of lying; ask, and Khar'd be obliged to answer, very likely with a truth Doyce might find unendurable. Then what would she do?

As Theo obediently rose, already speculating over what he might find, Doyce halted him with a hand. "Ozer, if you don't mind. It's not that I disbelieve you, but would you allow us to perform a Seeking on you? I want to search out any little thing that may strike you as unimportant, unrelated. Moments where your rational side discounts those niggling intuitions that arise at odd moments." And she'd been listening too hard to her intuitions, not her rational nature which reminded her how much Jenret loved her.

With a martyred look intimating an interrogation involving whips, racks, hot coals, and pincers, Ozer shuddered, the skin around his mouth going a delicate green. Surely Ozer was a more worldly person than the Shepherd Aidannae, someone who'd understand the basic workings of the Seekers, but his reaction didn't bode well. If he fainted on her, she'd feel like a torturer.

"Wh-what do I h-have to d-do?" The agent had more pluck than she'd given him credit for. More eagerly now, "I don't care—*do* it! If it'll protect my children, seek, find whatever you can!" He stood swaying but resolute, and she admired him for it. He might not know what a Seeking entailed, but he was brave enough to risk it.

"Ozer, it's not *that* bad. Please," she soothed as she forced him down, made him put his head between his knees. "This isn't part of the ceremony, but I'll be damned if I'll have you faint dead away on us." Sure at last he wasn't about to collapse, she turned to Theo. "Bring your tabard, your staff, and sword—and a stiff drink for Ozer."

Black formal tabard flapping, Theo came back in short order with everything except his staff. Cinching his sash as Doyce handed Ozer his drink, he indicated the broom, apparently left over from the Shepherd Aidannae's crusade. "Don't think a one of us thought to bring a staff. Figured this would serve. And remove temptation from the good Shepherd's hands, should she visit again."

An explosive choking and hacking muffled Doyce's laugh. They both spun, panic-stricken, to discover Ozer had downed the drink in one swallow, his face crimson as the setting sun, his sinuses flooding. As Doyce patted him on the back, Theo rolled his eyes, dug a peppermint pastille from his pocket for the agent. "Celvassy—I didn't think! Jenret had a flask in his room."

Reassured that Ozer would survive, Doyce seated him on the bench, her handkerchief in his hand to blot his watering eyes. "Ozer, it's much simpler than you think—not hurtful in the least. The Seeker—Theo—will ask you a question. Answer as well and as fully as you can. As you answer, his Bondmate—Khim—will examine your mind, weaving together any facts you're ignoring or overlooking.

"You may feel a slight rummaging sensation in your mind, but no more. Khim won't directly mindspeak you, but will transmit what she discovers back to Theo, who may fashion it into a new question for you. If you outright lie—she'll catch it. She can also tell if you've lied to yourself, rewoven the facts to support your wishes or wants. But anything she discovers, big or small, will remain in your mind—my oath on that."

It sounded deceptively simple but wasn't, a certain innocence forever lost after that first Seeking, the niggling sense that nothing—not even one's own private musings—was sacred any longer. Long before she'd become a Seeker, she'd had direct experience with a Seeker Bond-pair who'd questioned her regarding the circumstances surrounding the fire that had destroyed her husband Varon, their daughter Briony, and her stepson, Vesey. What had most unnerved her was the way the ghatt had brought to light the "lack" she always felt within herself. Sometimes she still felt obscurely wanting in certain ways, faintly inadequate. The feeling swept over her again in this sunny, petal-strewn courtyard where the bijou birds pecked and scolded and flaunted their jewellike feathers.

As Theo marched to the lawn's center and knelt with dignified grace, Khim continued another four steps before turning to sit and face her Bond. Laying the broom beside him lieu of his staff and unclipping his sword scabbard, Theo balanced it on his palms before ceremoniously laying it horizontally between him and Khim. He drew the sword a hand's breadth from its sheath, the rasping sound making her shudder as it always did, as it always should.

"The sword's position indicates the separation of Bondmate and Seeker," she explained, "that they're individual beings. Partially drawing the sword reminds everyone involved that it can be fully unsheathed in pursuit of the truth, should it be willfully hidden or obscured in any way. Likewise, so can Khim's claws." Ozer nodded, although he didn't look especially reassured.

Theo's clear tenor intoned the reason for the Seeking ceremony. "Ozer Oordbeck, we are here to determine the truth in the matter of theft or possible embezzlement from Wycherley-Saffron. Have you, Ozer Oordbeck, ever made false entries in the accounting ledgers?"

So faint it could barely be heard, Ozer gave his answer. "Yes, I have. I *must* have."

Subduing a smile, Theo amplified, "Have you ever *knowingly* made false entries?"

"No. It would be a sin and a crime." Ozer seemed determined to adhere to each particle of truth he could find, flagellate himself with it, but at length he settled down.

Or did until Theo asked, "Are you the only person who posts entries in the ledger? Who else has access to it?"

"Well, of course I'm the only one! It's up to *me* to determine if each invoice is correct before it's paid—to know, in turn, how much each client owes us!"

Thoughtfully brushing the grass with his knuckles, Theo let the silence lengthen, Doyce wondering what Khim had found, what she was telling Theo. Eyes flickering from Theo to Khim, Ozer knotted the handkerchief between his fingers, physical evidence something was amiss. He acted very much as if he were attempting to cover up something, whether big or small, she couldn't judge.

"Of course you checked the invoices, the receipts. That's what a good, thorough agent does." Whatever Theo was after, he probed delicately. "But once you inspect them for accuracy, are you the *only one* who posts the actual ledger entries?"

"I told you I'm *responsible* for the—" Ozer's wail was cut short by Theo's next question.

"We know you're responsible for the figures entered, but do you enter each and every figure yourself? Don't obfuscate, Ozer."

Bending his head into an upraised arm, Ozer shielded his eyes. "Some . . . sometimes one of my eldest writes the listings for me. I can't do everything, not with the work piling up everywhere I look! Always more to be done, more and more—if the ledgers aren't up-to-date, I won't know what I can or can't afford for expenditures!" The reminder of his heavy, often unrelenting workload, made Ozer wail even more. "You're *not* suggesting a nephew or niece, a son or daughter has been . . ." the rest drifted away as Ozer literally stifled his anguish with Doyce's handkerchief.

But before Doyce could worry that he planned to swallow it and end his misery, he railed, "All right! *All right!* Not just the children, but sometimes, mayhap a half-day every oct, Momsvaert the pillow-merchant helps when the bazaar's closed! I pay him out of my own pocket, just so I won't fall farther behind! My reports to Jacobia Wycherley have *never* been a day late! I pride myself on timeliness and accuracy!"

But now the import of what he'd reluctantly admitted had finally sunk in, making Ozer aware of who else might be at fault. Practically tripping over the bench, Ozer made to dash out of the courtyard, out of Dolphin House, only

to be faced with Khar smack in his path at Doyce's signal.
Anticipating his every move, the ghatta herded him back
to the bench, Doyce's heart full of pity for the man.

"I'll find Momsvaert, kill him!" he groaned over and
over. "Known him for years, and he's been tricking me,
cheating me, threatening my children!"

How to calm the man? But Theo wasn't finished, not by
a long shot, and he and Khim brought Ozer back to himself
by asking him another question. "No, Momsvaert makes
figures in a hand much like mine," he told Theo. "Even
my children mimic my hand, know how I prefer things to
appear uniform."

Theo smiled encouragingly. "Isn't it also possible someone's substituting false or altered invoices to you—either
you've approved an incorrect one when you've been in a
rush, or the real invoice has been replaced with a false one
in the stack to be entered? Those are two other possibilities. Someone—anyone—could make an honest error,
transpose digits when the entry's being made. How often
do you have the leisure to double-check, match invoices,
receipts against the actual entries?" Ozer's chin sank to his
chest. "Not often, eh? Hard enough to find time to enter
them without rechecking them, isn't it?"

If Wycherley-Saffron's financial problems were that
great, Doyce pondered how a man who worked an occasional half-day an oct could do that much damage? All in
all, she'd rather liked the pillow-merchant—without him at
her side in the bazaar when the dagga boys'd attacked . . .
She caught Theo concluding, "It's possible, Oordbeck, but
we can't question Momsvaert because he hasn't been
charged with anything. Are you ready to press charges,
have any hard evidence? Too bad we can't do a Truth-
Seeking with your ledgers!" A hysterical giggle leaked out
of Ozer.

Time to call a halt, despite the vague dissatisfaction that
shrouded her. "Well, we've discovered some new angles
and leads, perhaps gotten a better grasp on the problem,
but," she concluded, resentful of the wasted time, "nothing
earthshaking."

Hunched over, staring at the gold tip on his scabbard,
Theo pressed his hands against his temples as if determined
to make something pop to the surface. "One more ques-

tion," his self-deprecating glance told Doyce he'd lost the scent. "Probably because I don't know a great deal about business and I'm curious." Yes, as curious as any of the ghatti. Tight-lipped, tired, Doyce nodded at him to continue, though she badly wanted to call a halt. All she needed was for Theo to discover something else wrong, something more she couldn't solve or resolve!

"When . . ." Theo waved his hand vaguely to encourage himself, "Jacobia and Jenret set up their trading company . . . I mean, it's a large one, isn't it?" Oordbeck nodded. "At least by Sunderlies' standards—very large, yes? Well, is there business enough to go around with this new outside company barging in? Has business expanded so everyone still has a piece of the pie? Or did littler companies see their slices shrink? Find themselves forced into failure?" Wonderful—Theo wanted a lesson on supply and demand! How unlike Theo to let a formal Seeking wander, though Khim apparently still kept zealous track of Ozer's thoughts since she hadn't been officially instructed to desist. What was Theo after?

"No, really," Oordbeck protested. "Wycherley-Saffron's presence is benign for the most part. You're right, Theo, business *has* expanded, times are *good!* We've opened up new markets, new products for us. Plenty of opportunities to go round, no one driven to the poorhouse because of Jacobia's business acumen."

As the whisper of a long-forgotten name flashed through Oordbeck's mind, Khim nudged Khar with her shoulder. **"Livotti?"** Khar nudged her daughter back. **"Livotti and Rutenfranz,"** they both 'spoke to their Bonds.

Preoccupied, speculating on things she shouldn't, the names came as an intrusion. It sounded like a third-rate comedy team never invited to repeat their routine in any town. But clearly both Khim and Khar found it relevant. "What happened to Livotti and Rutenfranz, then?" She tossed out the question casually, not particularly caring but determined to be thorough, show Theo she was on top of things. Somehow she'd developed a pounding headache, just a garden-variety one, nothing to do with her injury. Just the usual bilious mix of uncertainty, tension, and frustration—for her own loved ones, for Oordbeck's loved ones.

Frowning, Oordbeck looked from one ghatta to the other. "I'd not given them a thought for years! A sad tale—even a cautionary one—so I've been told, but it hardly pertains. They went out of business long before Jacobia set up the agency. Blessed Lady, it happened before I was born—that's how long ago it was! Mayhap fifty years past.

"Livottis have lived in the Sunderlies forever, one of the first to be deported here. Actually set up a new life, prospered. The partner, Rutenfranz and his family, emigrated down here about . . . oh . . . oh," a spot of color dotted each cheek as he realized what he'd said, "mayhap seventy years ago. Voluntarily emigrated. Both families were notably standoffish, but they had fine contacts with some of the smaller weavers."

"So what happened?" Theo looked about to pounce.

"Two things, though the first I'm not positive about. Supposedly their bankroll dried up. Major investor from Canderis—Rutenfranz's contact—stopped pouring in money. Without it they were overextended, had grown too fast to sustain it on their own." Financial gossip, even from years past, worked like a reviving tonic on Ozer. "Pieter Rutenfranz, the eldest son, was sent to 'prentice with the investor, came back home with his tail tween his legs. Never knew the hows or whys of it—doubt anyone does now."

But Ozer's round face slowly lengthened, his eyes taking on a haunted look. "Other thing that happened was swamp fever—nearly wiped out both families, most of their staff. Reaped young and old alike. The few who survived couldn't keep the company afloat, especially without the money to hire new help. It's a brutal illness—my Evangie and Willem caught it, nearly lost them."

A sad story, to have diligently labored for so many years, only to have it all swept away by a fickle investor and by illness. Fate, not the Lady's fault, just one of those quirks that bring the high so low, and the low so high at times. Nothing to do with this, not with the problems plaguing Wycherley-Saffron. Funny, how she'd used "plague" without even thinking about it, influenced by Oordbeck's story, no doubt.

❖

One step, two, three, ouch! And again. One step, two, three, OUCH! Pw'eek flung herself on her stomach, white paws outthrust, mouth cracked in pain. A bird with ruffled azure throat feathers and a trailing, lyre-shaped tail dove to a lower branch, its crested head swiveling to let first one bead-black eye and then the other scrutinize the ghatten. A hiss and a whizzing slash with her good paw, weight on her sore one, made her crumple and whimper, the bird shrieking madly as it flapped to a higher branch.

Too many feathers, all feathers and practically no flesh for such effort. Not worth it. Her stomach responded that meat, even a meager amount, would be welcome. Rolling on her flank, she lifted her throbbing paw, licking at it, cringing between each lick. Hurt, hurt, hurt! She rested her bicolored nose on the paw pad beneath the offending toe and sensed the fever heat had risen higher, nearly into her leg; the pad itself swollen, red-streaked, while the slash festered and oozed. Night soon—what would she do for food tonight?

Limp toward the beach again, despite the way the sand caked in her wound? The sea spread its cast-off bounty on the sand—were she the first to claim it, she might feed well. Hunting was out of the question—unless she literally plumped on top of a foolish creature, just as she had on the half-grown rodent last night. Popping from behind some scree, it had made a crazed dash for freedom right between her legs—but Pw'eek had been quicker, dropping on it and trapping it beneath her.

Up, again. But before she began marching, she held her head high and questing, giving a sudden squeak of excitement. Yes, oh yes, Jenneth *was* closer, definitely nearer, their Bond stronger! The Bond always linked them, whether she concentrated on it or not, but several times a day she purposely searched it out, gauging if she'd traveled true, if Jenneth felt closer. The worst times came when the Bond grew fainter; sometimes she had to detour, find land suitable to navigate. **"I'm coming, Jenneth! Pw'eek is coming! Hurty foot not stop Pw'eek the brave!"**

An unanticipated thought struck with such intensity that she sank to her haunches, pupils dilating. Ghatti didn't lie, *couldn't* lie. Mayhap, just mayhap she *was* braver than she'd believed, could be a true Bondmate after all. Stout-hearted Pw'eek! Oh, to share that with Kwee! Yes, knock Kwee right off her furry feet—*fat,* furry feet—she would, sit on her till she cried "'Nuff!" and admitted how brave and true Sissy was!

With almost a spring to her step—in her hindquarters, at least—she hobbled beachward, the wave sounds rumble-swishing comfortably in her ears. It had rained last night and into the early morning, but the sky had turned silky blue, the sun warm but not scorching. Eyeing the tide line as she approached, she spied a low, broad rock dragging itself along the packed sand. Rearing on her haunches, eyes wide, she wondered how a mottled yellow-brown rock could do that, saw, to her relief, olive-toned, flipperlike limbs churning through the sand. Turtle? A very, very big turtle!

Thoughts of food momentarily driven from her head, she lumbered along in its wake, intensely curious, only to hear a whistling, grunting snort from behind her. Oh, woe! Always look all around before dashing after something! Wheeling as best as she could, she turned her back on the turtle, confident it presented a lesser danger than what she'd heard. Another menacing, grunting rumble, a frenzied stomping of horny forefeet, and she froze, her own warning growl dying in her throat.

Diminutive red-rimmed eyes glared above flamboyantly curled tusks, a second, shorter and more lethally-sharp pair pointing in her direction. Deep grunts thundered again, followed by a high-pitched squeal of defiance. Trimly dainty legs supported a barrel-shaped body tufted with coarse gray hair, a stubby neck connecting it to an equally massive head boasting delicate, cocked ears with drooping tips. And between the lethal tusks, a flat disk of a nose, nostrils wrinkling in suspicion. Whatever it was, it didn't smell very appealing, Pw'eek decided. Smelled like . . . smelled like . . . and sniffed at her own sore foot, scenting a similar but stronger taint of infection in the tusked beast.

Another stamp of the beast's neat hoof, then a pawing motion that shot sand in all directions. Canting its head, the beast shrewdly examined her all over and, apparently satisfied she posed no threat, began to paw more eagerly. Phew! It was intent on unearthing something, not charging her! It looked like . . . Pw'eek considered it, cataloging its

features, like a . . . pig, she decided. Pigs had rooted in the
back alleys and down by the docks back in Windle Port.
But this beast was more . . . more of everything! Mayhap
it bore the same relationship to a pig that ghatti bore to
cats? Similar—but obviously superior!

Now the pig-beast frantically dug with both front hooves,
sand flying, and Pw'eek heard cracking and crunching, followed by ecstatic slurps. As the pig-beast raised its dripping
snout to regard her, Pw'eek scented and saw the deep yellow
drip of egg yolk. Eggs! Food! Raw eggs, so slurpy good!

Limping forward step by step, she dropped to her belly
appeasingly. Again the wary, red-rimmed eyes regarded
her, and the pig-beast gave a muffled snort, a bubble of
egg blossoming from one nostril. It looked, dipped its head,
crunched another egg with a satisfied smack. Did she dare?
Would it work? Could she speak with pigs? She and
Kwee'd spoken with cats and dogs, sometimes in mindspeech, more often by finding rough similarities with their
standard falanese. Cats were simple to speak with, dogs
more difficult—though all Kwee ever did was mock them.
Call them slobber-tongues, stinky-rollers, flea-mats, dribble-
droolers, and bum-nosers. Then she'd laugh high and gay as
they gave chase, never catching her, while Pw'eek shivered,
fearful in a safe, high refuge.

**"Piggy? Dear Biggy-Piggy, are you willing . . . would . . .
would you let me share your eggs?"** She mustered her most
mollifying voice, harmless, humble, helpless. Not that that
was difficult, she'd been that all her life. Still, best pretend
she hadn't a clue where pork chops and bacon originated.
"I'm a *very* hungry ghatten, and I truly need some food."

A belch, and the flat nose wriggled, the head swinging from
side to side to more closely examine her. It has rather nice
eyes, she told herself, hazel. It was just that the red rim unnerved her. **"Why?"** He possessively straddled the nest of
turtle eggs. **"I find, I hungry. Neck hurts,"** he complained,
tossing his head, rippling his neck. **"Not Piggy. Me Wart
Hog!"**

An ugly red spot glistened at the center of his neck, the
hair rubbed away, the surrounding flesh blood-encrusted
and torn where he'd tried to dig at it with a hoof, scrape
it against rocks and trees. Something protruded, short and
thin, at the very heart of the rawness. **"You've something**

lodged in that ripply flesh on the back of your neck." Mayhap if she were helpful . . .

"Dumb . . . dumb . . . whatever you are—what are you? 'Course I got something sticking in neck! Humans shoot nasty darts, arrows. Want to kill you, roast you! You any good roasted? Ha! You fat enough!" Pw'eek quivered with insult. "Aargh! Neck hurting fierce. Wartle—being me—sooo discouraged! Prime of life, joy to gore and tear at other boars, romancing many sexy, lithely rotund sows as possible . . . and now, can't fight. Squeal like little hoglet if I tear into 'nother boar. Humiliating for Wartle!"

"That must," Pw'eek consoled but wasn't sure what would make Wartle feel better, "make life very difficult. Miserable all over when you hurt—my toe sick-hurts, too."

"Too bad, but so?" Wartle scooped a leathery egg, rudely crunching it in her face. "Wartle not care. Not care you hungry."

Her stomach rumbled, her mouth watered as the egg vanished down Wartle's gullet. *She* cared that she was hungry! She *needed* those eggs! If she didn't stay strong, how could she locate Jenneth? Could she, with her short front teeth, fix her grip on the dart's stem, pull it free? She could try—if the wart hog would let her. "Could I eat eggs if I tug out the dart?"

"May . . . be," he grumbled, rumbling some more. "Can do?"

"Can try!" Ooh, she'd turned so bold and daring! Bargaining with a wart hog, no less, one with curved, razor-sharp tusks and horny hooves ready to slash. "Bend so I can reach?"

Reluctantly abandoning the eggs, Wartle bent his front trotters, awkwardly keeling forward, discomfort twinging his bristly, tusked face. Clambering atop, Pw'eek winced at the seeping, abraded wound. Wartle had no way to reach it, pull the dart. Gingerly setting her teeth on the stem, she clenched her jaws, pulled. Nothing—except for a squeal of pain from Wartle. No, front teeth too dainty. The egg smell wafted by her nostrils, mocking her efforts. Cocking her head, working with deliberation, she locked her back teeth like a vise around the stem and set her feet, heaving with all her might, and—

She was airborne in a soaring somersault, no time to

twist, realign herself for landing. Come to think of it—
oomph! as she plunked down flat on her back—just as well
she hadn't landed on her feet or she'd have squealed like
Wartle. Wartle ran in crazed circles, snorting and squealing
"Woo-woo-woo!" until he gradually slowed his pace and
his complaints. **"Phew! Like pulling out tusk—sunk deep!"**

Rolling clumsily onto her feet, stealing one surreptitious
slurp of runny egg, Pw'eek stretched to examine the wound.
"Wash clean, feel better," and began to lick as tenderly as
she could. Wasn't as pleasant as grooming Kwee, but it felt
good to be needed, having someone want her ministrations
here and now. Almost as good as the turtle eggs would
taste when she finished.

"Now hold still, concentrate!" Despite the admonition,
Kwee fidgeted, sleeking her muzzle along his cheek, whiskers tangling with his. Ghatten! Might as well attempt a
mindmeld for distance with a . . . a . . . M'wa stood, baffled,
unable to conjure up another innocent creature with a mind
more scatty than Kwee's. He truly needed the additional
mind energy she generated with such profligate ease but
couldn't control with any accuracy.

In appeasement Kwee licked M'wa's nose, rumbling a
plaguesome purr, further rattling his focus. Which worked
best—discipline or love? **"Come, pretty one, clever one.
Show me how clever you are."** Chinning a circular pattern
atop her head, he surprised himself at how pleasurable it
felt. **"We want to help Diccon and Bard and Davvy, don't
we?"** Allowing that to sink in, he continued, **"And if we
help them, then we can find Pw'eek and Jenneth."**

"Diccon!" she trilled, the emotion radiating from her little body sweeping over M'wa. **"Pw'eek! Sissy-sib!"** With
that crooning trill of loneliness, M'wa found himself nearly
undone, overwhelmed by the aching loss of P'wa. **"Try
again! Send my mindspeech far! Let everyone hear me!"**

He'd already reached Khar and Khim in Samranth, but
the solo effort had cost him dearly. What he needed without further delay was a Seeker-pair with authority, someone the Guardians at Gander would believe. **"Good
ghatten! Steady, steady, now!"** Buoyed by her energy his

mind swept through the quadrants, questing, questioning, seeking. A touch, a hint? Pull back slightly, fine-tune, keep Kwee steady.

"Hallo? This is M'wa, Bond of Bard Ambwasali of Canderis. Who are you?" A faint, familiar tang to the mental signature, but nothing that set him vibrating, immediately identifiable.

Hmm, a sinuous sensuality to the responding mindvoice, obvious enough to make his nose pad steamy, his inner ears flush. By the Elders! If he didn't rejoin Bard soon, he'd be way overdue for his 'script, could already feel a reckless amorousness. Oh, to find a willing female and mate, fight off all interlopers to prove his masculinity! What a titillating distraction from his dear Bard! Come to think of it, Diccon probably hadn't started Kwee on the related prescription that ensured ghattas didn't come into heat. And here he was, alone on a island with a nubile adolescent ghatten! Mind over matter! Ignoring his loins' answer to his brain, he concentrated on the tingling mindvoice now homing in on him.

"Well, hel-lo there, yourself! How delightful to have visitors, even at one remove. I'm Mew'ph, Bond of Dymphna Lindevald. Under the auspices of the Seeker General we're serving as Truth Seekers for the Guardian contingent at Gander Fort."

Well of course she served under the auspices . . . ! "But where are you?" Clearly not on Gander, or he'd have encountered no problem in reaching her! Stifling his impatience, M'wa struggled between Bard's predicament and the come-hither tone to Mew'ph's greeting. To be struck by lust on all fronts at his age! "We need you to verify that Bard and his companions aren't escaped convicts. They're being held prisoner on Gander."

"Ooh! How absolutely dread . . . ful!" Ah, yes, memories of Mew'ph poured fast and furious now—a teasing little flirt, capable of wrapping any self-respecting ghatt 'round her lovely, sinuous tail! What had Mem'now called her once . . . ? "Alas, we're in Verhagen, upriver on the Calcanis—visiting friends. There's no one at Gander to receive our message—best we can do is contact Tarango. No, wait! Tarango's without a Bond-pair at the moment—due on the next ship, we hope. We'll travel back quick as we can. Be patient, handsome, we're on our way!" Was that the barest hint of jealousy insinuating itself in her final query? **"And who's that ghatten, that precious little minx tangling the mindmeld?"**

An urge to chuckle rippled from whiskers to tail; falanese humor seldom respected boundaries, found little off-limits. Amusement at Mew'ph's lustily proprietary tone redounded back on himself, and doubly so. **"This is Kwee,"** he began the introduction, **"new-Bonded to Diccon Wycherley, son of Doyce Marbon and Jenret Wycherley."** Hardly necessary to further identify Doyce, the magic of her name should suffice. It did.

"Ah, oh. I see." All business now, Mew'ph smothered her chagrin. **"Still young. *Very* young,"** she emphasized, as if reminding him of the pleasures of experience.

"But very clever, so jaunty and adorably striped," he added as Kwee gleefully wriggled, tickling him to distraction. A whisker flick against her ear stilled her. **"We thank you, Mew'ph. Do please hurry as fast as you and Dymphna are able. I yearn to be back at Bard's side only a fraction more than I pant to renew my acquaintance with your lovely self."** Amazing how he could pour on the charm, as if he were two octads younger and eager to court. Ah, that subtly romantic, keenly erotic dance of minds and souls and bodies, sensuous as the twining of tails . . . By the Elders, were those teeth busily gnawing at his jugular? That scamp, Kwee!

The mindlink broke, shut down almost rudely as he pried Kwee loose. Well, so be it if it meant Mew'ph would entreat Dymphna to hurry. Kwee sat on her haunches, eyes atwinkle as she stared up at M'wa. **"A very elegant ghatta."** Almost a sigh of envy. **"Smart and sooo elegant. I want to be just like that when I grow up."**

"No doubt you shall." An expansive yawn masked his expression. **"Now, shall we try catching dinner again?"** They'd cadged a few supplies from the boat, but there were too many they couldn't open, despite ghatti guile with claw and tooth. Now they had no choice but to hunt.

Wreathing herself around M'wa, rubbing enthusiastically, Kwee pounced, a lightning-fast paw sliding off his nose and jamming his eye. **"See how quick I am! Catch dinner this time, I shall!"**

Yes, but more probably he'd die of old age—or starvation—before that happened. A born speedster, Kwee dashed right over their prey, leaped higher and more zealously than needed, swept paws through the grasses too wildly. Rodents and birds startled but had the last laugh as Kwee overshot and reversed, speeding back to where their paths should have crossed. His stomach pinched, reminding him how truly hungry he was. **"How about you observe, serve as backup to ensure no tasty morsel eludes us? Fast doesn't always fill tummies, slow and cautious does."**

"Whack'em, smack'em, bite'em!" Kwee chanted until he glared her down, her abject crouch betrayed by only a flickering tail-tip. **"Watch you whack'em? Economy of movement? Oh, yes, Kwee can remember—this time! Learn how clever M'wa does it."**

Please let her behave, let her watch and learn. If she flushed one more dinner right out from under his paws, he'd whack and thwack her! She seemed to sense that. And she'd better—unless she relished dining on ship's biscuits tonight! Putting up with a youngling, no matter how appealing, was brutal, unrelenting labor. If she pounced on him once more and attempted to wrestle him to the ground, he didn't know if he could contain himself.

Convinced sleeping flat on his back was a lost cause, Davvy rolled onto his side, fumbling to rearrange his blanket. However long this blanket had languished in the cells had obviously been too long, the dampness had shrunk it to laprobe size. Then again, mayhap Sunderlies prisoners were considerably shorter than he. Certainly when he lay on his back, either his feet froze or his neck and shoulders goose bumped. Curling up on his side reduced his length enough to cover it, except then protruding knees or butt bemoaned their drafty exposure. The warped plank bed-shelf that unfolded from the wall was also abnormally short, but long on creaks and pops whenever he shifted. The reason the bed lacked legs, he was sure, was because they'd grow barnacles. The cell *had* to be below sea level!

Above him Diccon muttered in his sleep, his dangling arm brushing Davvy's face. Bard slept at right angles to Davvy against the adjacent wall, leaving them nearly head to head. Or rather, he assumed Bard slept, but then he was always contained whether awake or asleep.

Much as he hated it, Davvy found his actions and reactions to imprisonment of interest—equally so his comrades' reactions. Something to study, a way to pass the time. Pumping his stockinged feet, he worked the corner of the blanket over and beneath them, then straightened and smoothed it to ensure the corner diagonal to his feet stretched to his ear. Yes! The diagonal was the longest of the three sides of a right triangle. With luck—and no squirming—the two opposite corners just might remain in place to warm his knees and bottom!

Pressing his inner wrist against his brow he detected a telltale heat—a slight fever, without a doubt. Hardly surprising. Well, odds were they'd be released before it could develop into something worse, bronchitis, perhaps a pneumonic ailment.

What most perturbed Davvy about imprisonment had come as a surprise. The sense of enclosure, entrapment, the loss of control and freedom was obvious and expected: he'd avoided succumbing to it, retained his equanimity. Except for one thing, something he'd always taken for granted—his mind was equally constrained. The cell's thick walls weren't the culprits, blocking or baffling his Resonant skills. The oddity had registered once they'd landed on Goose Island, then been so ignominiously hauled to Gander. He gave a silent whistle just recollecting it.

Resonant that he was, he'd let his mind sail free in search of other Resonants to hail. Bound hands, a dingy, damp cell held fewer terrors when one's mind freely roamed, conversed with others of a like mind, a Resonant mind. In all innocence he'd expected to encounter some, cheerfully assuming that once he'd established his credentials with a Resonant of standing on the island or mainland itself, the Guardians' mistake would be quickly rectified.

What his mind had encountered had been nothingness, a bleak emptiness, not a single Resonant within mindhail. Oh, he'd sifted through unconscious exclamations crackling like heat lightning from some Normals, had obliquely touched the mental signatures of his scattered friends before veering away to avoid upsetting them. Even found a few fragments of mindspeech projected from latent Resonants ignorant of their abilities. To contact them might shock their systems so severely it could imperil their sanity, even their physical integrity, should the person have a weak heart.

At first it had felt peaceful to call his mind his own. Almost like being a Normal, blissfully oblivious, deaf to the mindvoices whizzing by one's head. After all, they survived perfectly well without Resonant ability, and he refused to consider himself superior because they lacked what he had. Certainly his Resonant abilities enhanced his eumedico training, enabling him to "hear" a patient's innermost thoughts, subconscious ruminations about the body's functions, its ailments, that too many were incapable of verbalizing. Still, he'd had to learn to interpret what he'd "heard," how it pertained to illness or disease. In all frankness, he'd met, been taught by Normal eumedicos who made diagnoses identical to his. True, they relied on different clues, had to interpret what they observed, what their fingers palpated, but their skills equaled and ofttimes surpassed his own.

Never before had his mind been left solitary like this, solely dependent on his own inner thoughts. A salutary lesson, one doubly reinforced by physical restraint; a lesson he should have taken to heart from his childhood, those days in Gaernett while he nursed Swan. During those times any wise Resonant buried such skills deep, camouflaged them to survive, only one's nearest and dearest sharing such a dangerous secret. And should that dear one be a Normal, any Resonant would think twice and thrice before revealing such a secret, ceding the power of life and death to someone like that. Reveal that to the wrong soul . . . A shiver made him pull the blanket close, not chills, he hoped. Darl Allgood, constantly in the public eye as a High Conciliator, walking his self-controlled narrow line in the Normal world; Faertom venturing from his family's isolated island, eager to taste the real world. They'd been the courageous ones, constantly protecting themselves and yet participating in life.

Lindy. Ah, Lindy, no Resonant she! Her farseeing spells boded an entirely different ability, worthy of eumedico study. Had those skills been passed along to that lovely, solemn little girl of hers? Lindy's talent had to be an unrelenting burden—"seeing" things as they happened in distant places, sometimes seeing them even before they occurred. If you knew your life would cease in one brief octant, forty days to live, would you live those remaining days more fully or miser them? Interesting thought . . .

"Davvy, you awake?" Bard eased along his plank bed until his head almost touched Davvy's.

For a breath-stopping instant his whole body wanted to levitate, plaster itself against the underside of Diccon's bed to escape the unexpected voice. Mayhap his own random thoughts had congested the very air around them, poking and prodding at Bard, disrupting his sleep. Hadn't contemplating Lindy and Byrlie turned him into a trespasser—worse yet, a poacher? "Er-ah?" The strangled sound finally left his throat. "Yes."

"Scared you. Sorry. Thought either you'd heard me stirring or that you youngsters slept like the dead." His voice sounded tight with pain and fatigue.

"Diccon, yes. Not I, alas. A certain innocence is needed to sleep that soundly." Why had he said that? "The older you grow, the more likely experience tempers innocence. Or crushes it."

Folding his arm under his head, Bard wrapped his hand around the back of his neck, cradling it. "Miserable headache—where you thumped me. That, and my mind keeps running in circles about Lindy, about Jenneth, about Byrlie, about Byrta. . . . Swear I'm fair dizzy with it."

Flipping onto his stomach, he stared across the darkness at Bard. "This sounds silly, but here's what you do. First, construct a doorway in your mind, escort each person to the door and across the threshold. Tell each good night. Then smooth out the wrinkles from any other worries cloaking you, fold each one and pack it away, let your mind empty . . . so empty you could float . . ." With slow deliberation he stretched his arm, let his fingers drift behind the point of Bard's jaw, checking his pulse.

Bard's breathing calmed, evened, "Can't fold . . ." he whispered, "never could fold . . . Sunderlies . . . so special . . ."

Biting on his blanket, Davvy tasted its woolly dampness, permeated with salt from sea spray and from human perspiration, ordering himself not to cry. He deserved to suffer, rousing Bard from needed sleep with forbidden thoughts about Lindy. He couldn't apologize, but he could do penance, focus himself, forcibly occupy his mind to make sure he didn't impinge on Bard's rest yet again. Name every bone in the human body. After that, a long list of muscles and ligaments, veins and arteries to label. Avoid mentally dissecting the human brain—it was too frail.

Pink sand inviting, glistening white sand, rock-toothed jumbles impossible to thread, secluded spots, rock pools, catchbasins known for the flotsam and jetsam they attracted . . . Cove after cove, inlets large and small, the sweeping crescent beaches lining the bays, he'd checked them all, obsessively scanning just above and below the tidemark. All for naught! The sun stood well past its zenith now, glancing off waves and sand, its dancing coruscations turning his vision spotty, unreliable. He slit his eyes against it, tilted his hat over his brow. Slowly the radiant specks and motes floated and faded away.

Had he been wrong? Had his intuition failed? He'd been so *sure* that something awaited him, promising to fulfill his need. The intimation tantalized and taunted him—can you guess what I am, can you find me? Will you even *know* when you find me?

Frustration, an acute sense of loss and longing swelled within him, his chest aching with pent-up emotions. Ripping his hat from his head, he slammed it down, kicking it, sending it skimming across the beach, racing after it, kicking it again and again. Then stood stock-still, lungs heaving, the absurdity of it washing over him. Lady bless—worse than Hirby and Tigger combined!

So, what had he expected? A touch of magic and mystery? Redemption? And if so, redemption from what? It had been an accident, fate conspiring against them, the time not ripe. Despite himself his mouth crooked, frown upcurving into a smile at one corner. Well, the best way to turn this squandered day around, make it palatable, was to do what he'd told Hirby he'd do: search out some rock crawdiddies. After all, hadn't Hirby told him how they danced real fine at Tancred Rock?

Sweeping up his battered hat and slapping it against his leg, he settled it on his head. No harm in beachcombing as he walked, mayhap he'd stumble on a surprise after all. Some little thing to amuse, prove useful—no expectation of uncovering anything dramatic or dumbfounding. He strode down the beach pretending he was lord of all he surveyed. After all, he was—for the moment, at least—since no one else was present to challenge his title.

Umph! Later than he liked for plucking crawdiddies, tide coming in, not heading out. Harder to keep his footing, not get face-slapped by the waves. Best cut cross the neck of Penalty Point to the bay twixt it and Perdition Point, 'stead of marching full around. Save time. A shake of his burlap sack and the reassuring rattle of wooden claw pins, latch them on and the crawdiddies couldn't snap at each other or at him through the bag.

Up, up, over Penalty's spine, navigate the jumble of brine-stained boulders, jumping from one stone to another. No wonder Hirby loved wandering here. Snatch-grass bearded the boulders, clusters dotted in crevasses, its tough blades a deep green with purplish edges, stems heavy with burr pods that hooked in flesh. His soles might be horny with callus, but he wouldn't willingly walk on burr pods. Now, jump to the high point of the dune, rubbery runners of manza vine snaking down it, each vine heavy with furled blossoms that opened into pink trumpets each dawn and dusk.

Damn! The sun's angle nearly sliced his eyes, tricking him with wavering afterimages. Something up ahead or not? Long, pale, not very wide, mayhap a piece of spar? If so, some salvageable rope, a block or deadeye might be attached. Even a shred of sail. Whatever it offered was fine. Don't expect much and you might be pleasantly surprised, that was his new motto. Think the other way, as he'd let himself for days, spending all this morning and early afternoon on a fruitless quest, and see what it'd gained him? —nothing!

He scuffed along, refused to hurry, delaying the surprise—whatever it was—his shadow skimming beside him, not raising his eyes. Finally glanced ahead to gauge his progress and stopped short in shock, began sprinting, bare feet pounding across sand. Damn all! A body! Distorted by the shadow it cast, a pale arm stretched above the head as if it—she? he noted long, dark hair . . . or seaweed—had attempted to crawl higher but failed. Alive? Dead? Almost he hoped for dead: whatever the corpse bore on it was deemed fair salvage, especially if reported to the authorities. Up to the family, then, to pay a finder's fee, buy back the person's personal effects. No boots far as he could tell, nor trews, either, so no pockets holding hidden treasure.

Breathlessly tossing down his sack, he knelt and placed a hand on the body's upraised shoulder, rolling it toward him. A whispered moan of protest issued from burned, cracked lips. Ho! Live one! And so . . . so . . . Hastily sitting back on his heels, he cradled his hand as if the contact had scorched, burning him clean of the old desires and woes, the bitterness. No longer Tadj, no longer Pommy, but a new being, worthy of this woman-child, long-legged, lovely despite the bruises, the scrapes and abrasions, the prolonged exposure that had turned milky skin a flaming scarlet, as radiant with heat as if she were the sun. Not the Lady's moon-silver coolness, but the life power and passion of the sun.

Unsure what to do, he balanced his hat against the side of her face to shade her. Her face smoothed with relief, the sun's rays no longer scorching, and she moaned again. "Wa'er?" As diffident as he'd been so many years ago when he'd first met Bazelon Foy, appearing like a god, the first sight he'd seen after the sailors had beaten his body almost beyond redemption.

"Wa'er?" Swollen, reddened lids parted to reveal bloodshot eyes that wandered in their focus. "Real?" A chafed hand rubbed her lips, dropped to pat at the sand.

"Yes, real. Not a fantasy, not a delusion." He scrabbled in his sack for the wooden canteen with its shredded canvas cover. Seductively shook it beside her ear, let her hear the sound of sloshing water more mysteriously beautiful than the echoes within a sea shell. "Stream-fresh this morning." Unstoppering it with his teeth, he eased a hand beneath her neck, her matted hair sticky-moist against his palm. "Just a sip now."

Her abrupt grip on his wrist, the hand holding the canteen to her lips, reminded him of the claws of a delicate bird fearful of falling off its perch, ready to trustingly cling forever. "No," he chided as he gently unwrapped each finger. "More later, I promise." He could almost hear the water hitting her empty stomach, she was so hollow. "Do you have a name? Who are you?"

"Wa'er!" Feeble but insistent, she repeated her demand.

"No, your name's not 'water.' Tell me who you are, perhaps I can contact someone."

"Doan . . . know . . ." Her eyes gleamed hazel, hinting at a changeable medley of ambers and blue-greens at the center, the mutability heightened by her pain. "Should know . . . fun . . . ny . . ."

Another small sip calculated to coax, yet let her discover he was in control, and she sucked at it greedily. "So, what am I to do with you?" A fair question; he had no idea. Too far to take her to Verhagen while the light held, especially since he'd have to waste precious time seeing who'd lend him a skiff or a skimmer. Doubted, too, that she'd be comfortable near the sea again, even being *on* the water, as opposed to *in* it. Too far to lug her overland without help. Hunt for Hirby, ask him? No, better Hirby didn't know right off. This prize was meant for him alone—someone to pamper, simply be with, talk with, an eternally grateful companion, the glow in those eyes, like sunlight dancing on pebbles in a dancing stream . . . entirely for him. . . .

Besides, the way her body was sun-scoured, pickled by the sea, she'd not be happy being moved any distance. Just looking at her abused flesh made Pommy flinch, sent a shiver up his spine. Much as he wanted to cradle her in his arms, springing from rock to rock with a dead weight would prove awkward. He'd fall, sprain or break an ankle, crush her if he landed atop her. She'd fallen asleep now, or unconscious, but a tiny smile hovered on her lips—smiling for him, trusting in him. So long, how long since anyone had done that—short of Hirby? This time he wouldn't fail at his trust, no accidents. Let Fate turn her face away now that she'd united them.

After careful thought he scooped her up and carried her into the shade, laid her down respectfully, straightening her limited clothing as much as possible to make her decent. Much as he hated leaving her, he'd have to, for just a bit. A freshet bubbled up at the base of the point, deep in the undergrowth; he could locate it with a bit of hunting.

Velvet-leaves thickly surrounded it, their heart-shaped succulent leaves dense with soft furriness—gather a sackful,
soak the bag and the leaves, refill the canteen.

He did so, working quickly once he found the freshet,
willing the water to flow faster, turn even cooler and
sweeter. Sack dripping, he hurried back to her side, pulling
out his knife and cutting the bottom corners off the sack,
mourning their loss. Inserting her limp body into the sack,
legs dangling through the new-cut holes, posed a greater
effort than he'd thought, her limbs uncooperative and so
very fragile he feared bending them. He arranged the
velvet-leaves around the sack's interior to cushion her flesh
from chafing. With that accomplished—plus a prayer that
the velvet-leaves would stay put—he heaved her upright,
fumbling to keep the sack from slipping down her torso.

Damn! Of course she couldn't balance on her feet—what
had he been thinking? Tall and slender, almost gawky, and
as utterly supple as string. A stagger at her dead weight,
and he faltered, righting them both, turning her so her back
faced him. A deep breath and he hefted a fistful of sack in
each hand. Count of three: one, two, three—spin! Duck
under his arm and pull the sack over his shoulders. Now
her front nestled against his back, her legs loose but not
touching the ground, and he sensed her resettling into the
sack cocoon.

"Off we go. Going home," he told her, exhorting himself,
pleased with how wiry and strong he'd grown after all these
years of hard living in the Sunderlies. No longer was he
weak, defenseless, eager to be someone else's tool. "Have
to call you something, you know, leastwise till you can remember your name. Water, eh? How about Aqua?"

She didn't answer, so Pommy decided it would serve.
Liked the sweet assonance of it flowing across his tongue.
"Come on, Aqua, we're going home."

By letting her head loll and barely cracking her eyes, she
could watch the charcoal glowing in the clay-lined fire pit
that protected the packed-dirt floor. The red-orange glow
of the coals comforted her, peeking back through their
white skin of ashes, an occasional air current ruffling them.

At those moments, if she stared intensely, a seeking finger of flame might rise and writhe as if to taste the breeze. It smelled like . . . morning, clean dew-scent and earth-cool mingling with the first beams of the sun.

Still afraid to look, she placed her hand palm-down beside her, encountering dryness, solidity. So, she'd only dreamed of the constant rocking of the sea . . . and dared drift off to sleep once more. Yes, sleep was preferable to puzzling out this new—and perhaps tenuous—pleasantness, becoming too attached to it. . . . What guarantee did she hold that what she'd just viewed wasn't the dream? That in truth she still rocked and bobbed among the waves, the endless sea stretching out to the horizon in all directions. *That* she distinctly remembered, the way the blue sky arched down to kiss the changeable blue of the surrounding sea, sealing her within its hemisphere, no escape. Sleep . . . she hurt so much, her skin all-over sizzling, crawling as if insects tunneled just beneath the surface. It made her want to shiver, cast off the enveloping heat. A smack of lips, so dry, mouth cottony, throat rusty . . . sleep . . .

Mild noise, the whispery pad of bare feet circling her, the subdued chink of a pot lid, the smack and plop of bubbles against a congealing surface and . . . the scent of food, boiling rice. When she attempted to open her eyes, blackness still blanketed her and she panicked, whimpering, thrashing, frantic to see, to identify—in all certainty—where she was.

"Hush, Aqua, my Aqua Vitae, I laid a damp cloth over your eyes to loosen the crustiness." An arm slipped under her neck to prop her head, and the cloth dabbed, easing away the stickiness so that her lashes parted. Now the light hurt, its slant different, wider and higher, brighter than before. . . . Something eased behind her back to angle her upper body . . . whatever it was felt dampish, a mildew scent enveloping it. A sniff—mildew . . . and dog? Mayhap a pillow, a bolster . . . accidentally left in the rain and not fully dry?

A water-beaded tin wafted before her, and she lunged for it, afraid it would drift away, her hands and arms shaking as she jammed it, rattling, against her teeth. She drained it in one voracious gulp, hardly a feat since it hadn't even been half-full. "Mo . . . re!" she growled, the rasp in her voice startling, as if she hadn't used it for a long, long time. "Please?"

The man stood with his bare back to her now, she hadn't really seen him before, his presence peripheral compared to the tin cup. "In just a bit, Aqua. First, a little food, just a bite or two. Understand?" He turned and walked toward her, but again she couldn't bother with him, more intent on the shallow panikin, the aroma issuing from it. She *did* notice his hands as the panikin came closer: tan crisscrossed by white scars, long-fingered, the nails clean but ragged. A flat wooden spoon dipped into the pannikin, and she grabbed the handle, discovering to her mortification that even the simple act of propelling the spoon was beyond her. The food spattered, dappling the sheet draped over her, and she wailed her frustration.

"Hush," he comforted, gaining control of the spoon. Redipping it, he daintily wiped it against the rim and held it to her lips. She let it rest there momentarily, quivering with anticipation, with the heat radiating from her body. Whatever it was, it wasn't hot, had been allowed to cool. Opening her mouth, she allowed the spoon to slide in. A rice gruel, thinnish but so richly textured on her tongue, a taste of the sea to it as well.

"Rice is ni . . . ce!" she informed him, utterly serious, after she swallowed.

"Yes, rice *is* nice, especially when it's boiled in a light fish broth." She gazed upward at the face, determined not to be distracted this time, saw golden bristles aglint on cheeks, chin. Pretty, like gold dust. The whole face handsome, blue eyes laced at the outer corners with white squint marks, longish hair blond-bleached by the elements to gold-and-silver threadings. Old, but not as old as . . . as what? As who? A shiver as she realized she lacked comparatives, had nothing, no one to match him against. Why not? What had happened?

"More?" The spoon teased toward her, hovering, and despite her anxious rummaging for memories, she wanted it, badly.

Like the water, it wasn't nearly enough to satisfy, and she squinted at him, petulance building at such stinginess. His smile was small but very proud, as if he'd just invented her—and mayhap he had. "M . . . more!" she implored, her voice stronger, but still foreign to her ears, as if her vocal cords had been vestigial until very recently.

"Uh-uh," his finger wagged, distracting, as his other hand produced the tin mug. "Here, another sip or two to wash it down."

Greedy for the liquid, its concentrated clarity, she forced herself to swallow slowly, reveling in its blessed wetness. Leaving her alone with her thoughts and the near-empty cup, he went to ladle a dish for himself, hunkering down and eating with neat, economical motions, no slurping. Hunting behind him, he produced a lidded tin, retrieved a heel of bread from it to dip in his gruel. Lady help her! If she possessed the strength, she'd jump up, snatch that bread from him! Cram it into her mouth, suck down water with it, let the bread swell and soften like a poultice! Then a new pain struck; her belly suddenly felt distended, crammed full. She gave a bleat of surprise and belched, sweat breaking out on her forehead.

"You see?" he admonished with his spoon, "that's why you can't have any more right now. Your stomach's shrunk, can hold only a little at a time. But I'll feed you again shortly. A bit more, and a bit more after that." An annoyed frown as another belch rose from her depths. "You're supposed to say 'excuse me.' "

" 'Scuse me." It made her feel foolish, babyish, to be so instructed. A sense of chagrin at being lectured on manners.

Restless, too embarrassed to look at him, she pawed at the sheet covering her, hating its itch and drag against her skin. Plucking the fabric between her fingers, she tented it and peered beneath it, only to discover she lay there naked, her clothes vanished. A residue of ointment coated her skin, leaving white lines in the creases of her flesh. What? Where were her clothes? Had he—this man, this stranger— removed every stitch of clothing, scrutinizing her nakedness, slathering every part of her body with salve? Shame coursed through her, made her want to cry at the violation, but she had no moisture to spare for tears.

Somehow he discerned the alarming drift of her thoughts and worked at distracting her. "By the way, I'm Pommy. Pommy at your service." Rising, he sketched a quick bow that revealed sun-freckled shoulders, a flat stomach as he unfolded. "I'm glad you . . . dropped by," his eyebrows rose comically, "but how did you arrive at the inlet? And what did you say your name was? In the hustle and bustle of carrying you here, I forgot. Never was good with names, myself."

Pinning the sheet tight to her sides, flattening it across her chest and protectively crossing her arms on top, she glared at him, sensing a trick or test in his questions. "By boat . . . I . . . I guess." Wracking her brain, she struggled for some recollection, could only assume she'd sailed on a boat, a ship, whatever. Then prodded the assumption a step further, her brow wrinkling with effort. But then, somehow, she hadn't been aboard a vessel—or so she gathered. Pommy's conversation intimated he'd discovered her on a beach, and she giddily recalled a sensation of sand, solidity, her impression growing stronger. "I don't really . . . know."

Her news—or the lack of it—didn't perturb him the way her bad manners had. Indeed, he cocked his head as if sagely verifying something in his own mind. "All ships leave from somewhere—don't they? Can you remember where yours left from?"

"Can't remember!" Even to her own ears, she sounded shrewish, mean-spirited and obstructive.

"And I suppose the tag with your name on it vanished with your baggage?" he countered mildly, rinsing his dish in a bucket of water.

"No! Of course not! I'm . . . I'm . . ." Sounds flittered across her tongue, struggling to form themselves into a word, a name. "J-j-d-d-" They sounded right, familiar, but refused to coalesce. Flailing with frustration, kicking her legs free of the sheet, she clumsily clasped it to her as she gained her knees. *Get up, flee!* her brain told her. *If you lack a name, you're nothing, you can't "be!" Nameless nothing! Run, hide, till you find out who you are!* Legs tangling, she toppled, whimpering, her internal anguish as keenly raw as her outer pain.

"Oh . . . now, oh . . . dear," he singsonged, pressing her against the pallet with such delicate concern that she almost relished her invalidism, shyly welcoming the touch that had soothed her singed skin, scabby and rough and itching. "Well, since you can't remember, I'll just keep calling you Aqua. Everyone needs a name to answer to."

Hut, two, three, four, Jenret instructed, clutching the side
rails for dear life and shambling ahead, eyes fixed on the
back of Arras's dirt-encrusted, sweat-stained shirt. It
boasted an array of blotches and streaks, enough to map
in his mind, create his own country. Holly walked ahead of
Arras, the three of them the middle—the filling—of an absurd human sandwich. As part of the filling, he suspected
they all smelled like rank, overly-aged cheese, though his
nose no longer noticed.

"Some of us still notice." Rawn strolled beside them,
P'roul on the opposite flank, blessedly upwind. **"Pumper-
nickel bread?"**

"Rawn, don't!" His plea encompassed a multitude of
needs: don't make me laugh, my stomach muscles hurt from
retching; don't insult our new friends, Bard's distant relatives; don't distract me, it's difficult enough lifting one foot
in front of the other as it is.

After an appraising lick down his black flank, Rawn
stared behind Jenret at Dlamini, the younger man, nephew
to Uma-Uncle, or more accurately, Mvelase. **"I'm darker
than he is any day—or night."** Mvelase led off with the
poles, while Dlamini carried them at the rear; they formed
the "bread" of their human sandwich. **"And you're not as
stinky as before; nobody's . . ."** his whiskers bristled as he
primly screwed up his nose, **"in quite some distance now."**

But at that moment Arras froze, every muscle rigid as
he fought for control and finally lost. " 'Ware, it's coming!
Cork didn't hold!" A sharp report and the air hung heavy
with a ripely rotten stink that overwhelmed the swamp's
fetid bouquet. "Sorry!"

"Faster, Uma-Uncle," Dlamini laughed, "Hurry us from
this cloud-stink!" Mvelase's medicaments, plus Bess's latest
herbs had served to bind their bowels, reduce their fevers.
What it couldn't do was provide them with the stamina to
leave the swampland behind.

Short of letting time take its course, Mvelase's solution
was not dissimilar to a walker for steadying infants taking
their first steps. Supporting a stripped sapling on each
shoulder, Mvelase and Dlamini propped up the weakened
trio, letting them balance on or drape their arms over the

rails. Tumbles occurred with regularity, and Jenret suspected they resembled a spastic centipede. The last time they'd toppled, everyone had fallen in a jumble of limbs, Bess chuckling and cursing as she righted them. Still, childish though it might be, they kept marching, and Jenret was grateful for that.

Once out of the swamps—the supposed "shortcut" he'd insisted upon taking—Mvelase'd promised they'd ride, rest while renewing their search for the twins, not to mention Uma-Uncle's errant nephew, Bard. Locate Diccon, and they'd find Bard as well. Relieved that their goals were thus far compatible, Jenret allowed himself to contemplate Bard's so-very-alien relatives.

Dlamini, tall and ropy-muscled, with a handsome face of soft curves and strong planes, strode along cheerfully, chattering with each step, pleased and proud to be on this adventure with his revered uncle. His body and features more sharply honed by age, Uma-Uncle acted pleasant but distant, thoughts of Bard seriously weighing his mind. A playful poke between the shoulder blades made Jenret turn his head to determine what Dlamini wanted.

"The Holly-one, so strong, so lofty, so, so . . ." Dlamini sighed, limpid, dark eyes admiring. "How many cattle must we offer? A prime breeding bull and how many cows?"

"What? Cows for what?" Stubbing his toe, Jenret cursed under his breath. "What do cows have to do with Holly?"

Rawn sneezed three times in rapid succession, ear-hoop bobbing until he brought himself under control, only a hint of good-humored dismay tinging his 'speech. **"Bride-price, I believe. He wants to know how many cattle it will take to acquire Holly as his bride."**

"Holy, blessed . . . Damnation! Are you sure?" He opened his mouth, intending to query Dlamini, but Rawn smoothly interrupted.

"Not too loudly! Do you want Holly to hear? P'roul's already suspicious. I, for one, would prefer to march on, not halt while Holly practices a crochet pattern with Dlamini's limbs!"

When his eyebrows reached their zenith, Jenret pursed his lips, mind still aboggle. It could hardly be true, could it? Yet in the recesses of his mind he recollected Doyce once telling him how Bard's and Byrta's grandparents had

sent to the Sunderlies for wives for his first two sons, had
paid a handsome sum of gold and the new beef cattle he
was raising in Canderis. But the youngest son, Bard's and
Byrta's father, had disobeyed, fallen in love with a Canderisian woman, blonde and fair and taciturn. No, that wasn't
right or, more accurately, the story was true, but Oriel Fal-
tran—Doyce's love, Saam's first Bond—had told him the
tale over a beer at Myllard's. How he'd nursed the beer,
much preferring wine. . . . Strange, once he'd never have
given Doyce a second glance . . . and now . . . and now . . .
even the memory that she'd once been Oriel's . . .

**"Marvelous! Did Oriel own her? Do you? That's how
you make it sound. Not so different from Dlamini, are
you?"**

"I don't think I'm the one to ask," he whispered to
Dlamini, conscious of how his voice shook at Rawn's reproach, at those memories he hadn't dusted off and examined in years.

"Ah," a serious nod, "it is Arras-friend who will barter
as a male of Holly's clan, yes?"

The situation was *not* improving, complications mush-
rooming, and a horrific urge to laugh almost drove Jenret
to his knees. "Where we come from, the man asks the lady
directly." Or the lady asks the man—as Doyce had done,
proposing to him. . . .

Beaming, Dlamini almost visibly expanded with delight.
"So, so! How wondrous clever! I give Holly cattle, she
wives me, and we keep the cattle in the family! And if she
already possesses many herds . . . How do I ask? Is she a
shrewd bargainer?"

Swinging along beside them, determined not to miss a
thing, Bess's scowl broadened as she dropped the sledge
line. A fierce backhand across Dlamini's ribs staggered the
whole procession as Bess jumped up and down, fists
cocked. "Ye doan buy a wife, dolt! She'll have yed or no—
fra free cherce an love! She's na a cow ta be traded or
bought!"

All clumsy solicitude, intent on mending his gaffe, Dlamini reached to pat Bess's shoulder before Jenret could cry
a warning. Purposely interpreting his gesture as an attack,
a provocation, Bess found the excuse she'd longed for.
Slamming her heel behind Dlamini's knee, she sent him

staggering into Jenret, Jenret dominoing into Arras, and down the line. Jenret eeled clear in time to see Bess swarming openhanded blows to the back of Dlamini's unprotected head, stinging slaps driving him down each time he tried to rise.

Having had the presence of mind to sprint clear of the wall of flesh toppling toward him, Mvelase leaned on his staff, impassively watching. Shoving Arras off, Holly arose—glorious in her wrath—impartially kicking at anyone in her path. Planting her hands on her hips, Holly towering over Dlamini, crouched on the ground, arms wrapped 'round his head to ward off Bess's blows. "A woman grows tired of being talked about as if she weren't even there." Stepping over her potential future mate, she took advantage of her height to stare down Bess. "And you, don't damage the merchandise! Haven't decided if I'll buy it or not!"

Hugely unrepentant, Bess grinned. "Nary a fist did I lay on him! Slaps serve fer silly, stupid boys, na matter their size." The look they exchanged made Jenret realize how little he understood the rituals of women.

Extending a hand, Holly hauled Dlamini to his feet, where he gazed adoringly at her while brushing himself off. "Uma-Uncle, Mvelase. Your nephew does me great honor to consider me a suitable wife, but I don't wish a husband right now. I've a job, a calling that honor-bonds me to serve. When that life is done, I'd be happy to consider your nephew—if he'll still have me."

Dlamini radiated a sober joy, but Jenret suspected he wanted to caper like a puppy, would wag his tail if he possessed one, Holly's tact defusing but not destroying Dlamini's dream. Helping each other clamber up, Arras whispered, "Ah, isn't love wonderful?" The bracing sarcasm Jenret'd counted on was lacking; Arras's longing tone spoke of dreams of Francie, of Harry, of home.

And Doyce, what did she dream right now? Did she long for him? Each time he strove to fix her features in his mind, Honoria's face overlaid it . . . those blonde tendrils curling around her brow, those eyes, so penetrating and assessing. . . . Yes, together they'd solve the puzzle, and he'd be free to . . . A spasm of guilt more severe than the physical spasms that had so recently wracked his body, knotted within him. Duty first—Doyce, if anyone, would understand duty.

" **'Speak her, tell her what's happened,"** Rawn urged, his needle claws purposely provoking.

At first he misconstrued Rawn's advice, actually believed the ghatt meant Honoria, Nori, and nearly lost his composure.

"Utter fool!" His disgust patently clear, not just to Jenret but to the rest, Rawn stalked away, deserting him. No matter how well Rawn knew him inside and out, any explanation he offered would sound lame. Lady help him conquer his stupidity, his refusal to shift gears, put first things first, not stubbornly grind away at a problem that truly didn't matter in the greater scheme of things. Whether he was rich or poor, Doyce would love him!

Of course the ghatt had meant Doyce, but he'd been so enmeshed in his worries . . . Hadn't taken time to discover how she fared, if her injuries had healed, what word—if any—she might have received from Diccon, any news concerning Jenneth. Doyce, the mother of his children, the woman he'd loved hopelessly and from afar for so long. . . . *"Tonight, Rawn, when we've settled in. I swear, my promise on it."*

As they resumed their journey, Bess hauling their supply sledge, the others tottering between their baby rails, Jenret struggled to analyze his relationship with Doyce, his relationship with Nori. What made such bonds work . . . or not? Why, why, couldn't it be as simple and uncomplicated as his Bond with Rawn usually was? How far could a bond stretch before breaking? How did one reknit it—pick up the dropped stitches, the lost moments?

Slogging along, planting his feet firmly in the spongy, oozing earth, obdurate as always, he searched his mind and soul and heart. Much of what he found there was worthy of respect, but he also unearthed aspects that weren't as pleasant. Oh, not that Rawn hadn't tried time and again to alter his ways . . .

Needing to distance himself, he half-listened to Arras and Dlamini talk of the native's life and land. Of the Naukkilari Plains where they grazed their cattle, wandering with the herds, living with them, protecting them, the cattle a part of their extended family. Of the dangers of marauding beasts who brazenly cut down calves, who stampeded whole herds, picking off the weak, the young, or old. The hazards of the weather, too little or too much rain, lush grazing or barren, overgrazed land. Of lameness, disease, or calving woes. It sounded comforting, a connection with the land, abiding with its rhythms, both good and bad.

"And I have seen our city, Mkjinka, even," Dlamini's enthusiasm threatened their poles. "We have learned that while we travel with our herds, we must also have one central meeting place for trade—not just cattle or goods, but information. Learning is a commodity to be traded, too. We have buildings, not tents, we grow things from season to season and beyond. Some of the old ones do not approve, turn their backs on us for settling in one place, call us lazy sinners, even jest we are now *too* lazy to sin! But Uma-Uncle honors old and new, has visited Mkjinka many times—is that not so, Uma-Uncle?"

"Ah, I like to wander." Mvelase shrugged, shifting the saplings more comfortably, still apparently fresh and vigorous. "Missing my cattle when I wander, though. Have crossed the Uulbora Mountains three times, to Mkjinka seven—even to your Samranth, once. So bustling strange, so many distant hearts."

"Then you enjoy exploring, comparing old ways and new things?" Arras asked. "Enough to visit Samranth again, anyway. You said that was your original destination until you ran into our party."

Mvelase's slow smile warmed his face as he glanced back at them. "Get old, need to see new. But this time blood calls."

"Because of Bard?" Sounding charmed but curious, Holly doubtless hoped to learn more from Bard's relatives than any of them had ever learned from his lips. "Because you want to greet your nephew? How could you know he was coming to the Sunderlies?"

The suddenness of their halt caught them all by surprise. Shifting his hold on the saplings, left hand now grasping the right, right gripping the left, Mvelase smoothly righted himself to face them without disturbing their balance. His brown eyes wet with suppressed emotion, his voice went husky. "Not to greet, but to bid farewell. He is drawn home for farewells."

With that, he turned his back and began walking more slowly and deliberately than before, a burden beyond the weight of strangers on his shoulders. What it truly meant, Jenret couldn't fathom. What farewells? How could you say farewell before you'd greeted someone? For a moment a cold apprehension cloaked him, but he shrugged it off. Bard was capable of coping with his own problems, made a better job of it than Jenret did with his. Jenneth, Diccon, Doyce, Jenneth, Diccon, Doyce . . . he paced to the drumbeat of their names . . . Jenneth, Diccon, Doyce . . . Honoria . . . missed a beat and tripped.

"Hun-gry!" An extravagant stretch and Theo's long arms nearly swept the ceiling beams, colliding with strings of dried chili peppers, garlic, and onions. "Abso-lutely s-starving!"

Giving him a distracted smile, Lindy continued stowing packets and parcels from her afternoon's shopping. Plagued by a vague guilt, similar to what struck when Byrlie teased for something just before a meal, she relented, tossing a fruited biscuit in his direction. For a moment she feared he'd capture it in his mouth, swallow it whole, and choke to death in front of her eyes. To her eternal relief, he didn't devour it in midair, but he did cram half of it into his mouth. "So, did you and Honoria find anything, any clue among Jenret's papers?"

Adam's apple rising and falling as he gave a mighty swallow, he shook his head and stuck it under the half-keg of ale as he gave the tap a turn, letting the ale flow into his mouth. "Theo, you've got disgusting manners. How does Holly put up with you?"

An exaggerated look over his shoulder. "Wouldn't dare if Holly were here!" So the absence of Holly's wrath made his stammer lessen, even disappear. Sometimes Lindy speculated that Holly's presence made it more pronounced, her dominance versus his passivity. "Answer's no, scant joy for t-two days' effort. A few things we c-can't make heads nor t-tails of, though." He munched the remaining biscuit in three bites, chary of his still-swollen lip. "Mayhap Oh-Oh can make s-sense of th-them. 'Nother?"

"No, you'll spoil your dinner." This was uncannily like a late-afternoon in her own kitchen in Canderis, Theo acting out Byrlie's role. A silly thought, but she craved the commonplace, explicable rather than inexplicable goings-on.

"There's something," Theo snatched at an invisible word, "h-hinky 'bout the figures, though. They all add up, b-but they don't. If you know wh-what I m-mean? I like numbers, th-thought I'd be an accountant, mayhap." Slinging a hip on the counter, he interwove his knuckles, staring at them. " 'Cept Khim had other p-plans. What's for din-ner?"

Finished unpacking the kitchen supplies, Lindy dusted her hands against her apron. "Don't know." Couldn't resist a certain smugness. "It's your turn to cook. What's Honoria doing?"

Melodramatically reeling as if struck a mortal blow, Theo moaned, "Oh, no! Not my turn a-gain? What have we s-servants for, if not to c-cook?"

"Might I remind you that our servants are eight and twelve, as close as we can judge? Wonderful for errand-running, sweeping, and occupying Byrlie and Harry. Cooking? I don't think so." Come to think of it, where were the children and what were they up to? That strange Shepherd woman had come to visit them before she'd gone off to market. The last she'd seen they'd been playing some game in the courtyard, tossing pebbles across rudely scratched lines on the gravel pathway. Best go see what they were doing.

Morosely peeking into cupboards and bins, prying off canister lids, Theo took stock of what was available for dinner. "N-nori, Nori," his eyes brightened on speaking her name, "s-said she'd wash up, n-nap before din-ner. She'll have a n-nice long rest, t-takes me forever to make a meal. Did you buy ch-chicken?"

Mind still absorbed with the children's whereabouts, Lindy fought to focus on Theo's question, her vision blurring, face paling as she battled to think about the concrete, the here-and-now. Deep breaths, nice and easy, but her voice still seemed to belong to someone else as she responded, "Of c-course I bought the ch-chicken," saw Theo's offended start, sure she mocked him, "it's promenading 'round the p-patio, c-couldn't b-be any fresher!" Everything spinning now, present and future colliding and melding, clouds drifting, lifting, the vision tenuously solidifying. *Oh, Lady, take a hand, paint something pleasant, something we can rejoice in, not weep over!* But whatever would come, would come. She could see but never alter bad to good.

"Mama?" Byrlie skipped into the kitchen, stopping short to eye her up and down. She could see her daughter's reaction, yet was incapable of calming her fears, had relinquished control over body and mind. Theo grumbled as he hunted for a cleaver, muttering about wilting women who preferred chickens as pets instead of dinner. "Mama, what are you seeing?" Byrlie clutched her hand now, the child's so alive against her chill flesh.

Lindy heard herself shriek, eyes tight-closed to blot out the vision. But it didn't halt, it never did, the vision relentlessly playing itself out against her inner lids. "Bard! No, Bard, take care! Davvy, don't! Look out!" Registered with utter certitude and a breaking heart that Bard was dead—or would be shortly—while Davvy lived. Bard! Davvy! Two loves—must she choose between them, sacrifice one for another? Had she unintentionally willed this to happen in her heart of hearts?

"Mama, he's *not* dead, he's *not*!" Byrlie latched herself around her waist, but Lindy went sinking, slipping through her embrace, her apron slithering up, riding over her face. "I can *feel* Papa, he's *not* dead!" Theo had her now, swinging her into his arms, sending her soaring wondrously high, to the Lady's havens almost. Mayhap she could visit Bard there. No, Byrlie was right, Bard was *not* dead—yet. But soon he would be—her visions never lied.

"Go get Auntie Doyce," Theo instructed Byrlie, sweeping parcels from a bench with an elbow as he laid her down. "Run, child, Auntie Doyce will help."

She could hear each word, weigh its falsity: Doyce couldn't help, no one could help Bard or Davvy—it was too late for help. Always too late. But what the vision had obscured was whether Bard and Davvy struggled at each other's throats. That crucial aspect remained stubbornly veiled, shrouding something, someone from her view. She'd sensed Bard's rising, seething frenzy, a red haze enveloping him in an aura of blood, and Davvy, equally and adamantly angry, but showing mental restraint. Like Theo and his columns of figures, something didn't add up, but the sum total never varied: Bard would die.

Hurried, limping footsteps, Doyce bursting into the kitchen, frown lines wrinkling, her eyes wary. Ah—what Doyce had seen through the years! Poor thing, to burden her further when she had so much to bear. As the tatters of her vision dissipated, her control returned, and she swung her legs off the bench, managing to sit up, shakily smile. Because she truly *had* viewed something worth smiling over in those final, fraying moments: Jenneth. "Doyce, Jenneth's alive! She washed ashore a few days past. I don't know where, but she lives!"

Whatever her farseeing was—or wasn't—it strove for evenhandedness: bad news offset by good. One woman weak with relief, the other rehearsing widowhood. And since she loved Jenneth, Lindy found pleasure in her revelation as her eyes drifted shut and she dozed against Theo's bony shoulder. Her final coherent thought was an outpouring of sympathy for a black ghatt with a white forehead star and a high white stocking on its left foreleg. The ghatt's grief as wrenching as her own—worse, perhaps—for the many years shared. Poor, dear M'wa!

Aidannae paused, absently hitching up her robe as she slipped out the door. Had overstayed herself, still craving reassurance that Siri and Kasimir truly prospered in such strange company, their brains untouched. Her relief had made her linger longer than manners allowed. Crouching among the children—the two she knew, the two she'd recently met, Harry and Byrlie—all too vividly evoked her own childhood, the street games, the whispered secrets and moments of camaraderie. And for newcomers to prove ignorant of a simple game like "Scale the Ladder"—of course she'd had to remedy that lack! Show off her prowess, too, if truth were told. Such maturity, such Shepherdly decorum!

The Lady would have played a mean game of "Scale the Ladder," had She manifested Herself. If one hand couldn't accurately toss the pebble, She held another seven in reserve. Mayhap an unfair advantage? Not that the Lady would cheat, but how could She not help but win?

Dannae had planned a proper and timely adult leave-taking, but she'd dallied to take Byrlie's turn when the child set off in search of snacks. But such a commotion, such emotion, had erupted inside that she'd thought twice before encroaching to say farewell. Better to leave quietly, not intrude. She'd return another time since the tall Theo was still owed a more measured apology. Several loaves of bread, too, in earnest of her sincerity.

Tarrying just outside the front door, hand still on the knob, she pondered the cries of happiness and woe she'd inadvertently overheard. They weighed at her soul, almost pinning her in place—wasn't it a Shepherd's duty to succor such anguish? To share such woe at the very least? Should she go back?

But as she hesitated a figure came slipping from around the side of Dolphin House, soundlessly unlocking the gate and silently passing through. Following the figure's lead, Dannae unobtrusively opened the gate and departed, easing it closed to avoid disturbing anyone. Or alert them, part of her whispered. Now she had no choice but to discreetly dawdle behind to circumvent any semblance of spying on the hurrying figure. Pure happenstance they'd both left at the same time. No shortcuts off the path, either, not with those blessed prycanthius thorns so sharply vigilant.

Dannae impatiently lagged along, anxious now to return to the Bethel, especially once she realized whom she followed. The woman ahead was the harsh one, the blonde who'd been so painfully subduing when she'd pinioned Dannae the other day. Honoria—wasn't a common name, not here. Hadn't thought of it in ages, but one of the remnants of the Livotti-Rutenfranz clan had borne that name, apparently died during the last major fever epidemic.

Leastwise, that was the gossip her Mam had shared with her, waving her bottle, then drinking deep to ward off the fevers. Shared not just the gossip but the bottle, too, with Dannae. Funny, the woman *did* have the look of a Livotti, come to think of it, the same snooty arrogance Mam had mimicked till they'd both rolled on the floor, weeping with laughter. Not that anyone had many dealings with them, kept themselves to themselves, they did, 'specially the few that were left. Silly rumors from that, and she was old enough, wise enough now to discount them. Rumors settled thick on bad-luck families like flies on a corpse.

Onto the Esplanade now, Dannae continuing to follow, not out of choice, but simply because this route was quickest. At least the deeper dusk under the overhanging trees concealed her presence. Still, she felt embarrassed and out-of-place, the houses too luxurious, guarded by granite retaining walls on both sides of the Esplanade, not to mention the high prycanthius hedges defending privacy and privilege. Trailing behind, she fervently wished she could scurry to her Bethel, leave such lavish extravagance behind.

Then the sound of a gate, not a lamplit, well-oiled, main gate, but a tradesman's entrance, its rusty hinges screeching. Fine, now what did she do? The gate remained open, Honoria conferring with someone, the bars between them a spurious protection. Cross the Esplanade? Any way she chose, she'd be noticeable as tits on a trout—Mam's favorite expression—a Shepherd's robe, let alone a woman Shepherd so out of place here 'twould stick in people's minds.

Just ahead, an unpruned crepe myrtle's branches cascaded over and down the wall like a waterfall, nearly obscuring the decorative half-column that broke the wall's monotony every five meters or so. Well, just wait there in its rustling dimness, pray her tummy didn't curve out farther than the column. Hum a mystery chant so's not to eavesdrop.

Except she *did* overhear some, couldn't help it. Despite their low-pitched voices, their vehemence carried. ". . . not waiting much longer," came a man's voice, overconfident and drink-slurred.

"You'll wait till you're told, Geerat!" The ice-tinge of Honoria's tone made Dannae shiver. "It's dragged on longer than any of us expected, but in another few days . . ." Then murmurous intimacies flushed Dannae red with memories, nearly making her miss the next sentence. ". . . Oh-Oh's precious offspring—they'll be . . ." Honoria's voice rose, "Wycherley has no choice . . . bound by the contract . . . way I want it. If he suffers . . ."

A sick certainty invaded Dannae. Evil, palpable and real, and she cast the eight-point star. But what did it mean, this half-heard evil? And what should she do with such knowledge? Most of all, she wanted to escape, to flee from such filth, a feculence threatening to stain her soul. She *had* to move, now! Hand shaking, she fumbled in a rolled cuff for her lucky stone, momentarily unwilling to relinquish a token of childhood. With an expert wrist snap she cast it across the avenue to skitter against the opposite wall, bounce and rattle down the sloping boulevard.

With an oath, the man pulled Honoria inside with him, slamming the gate behind them. Heart in her throat, Dannae stealthed up to it, rushing by when she saw no one lurking to catch her. Once past, she began to run, her robe billowing. Roly-poly? —yes. Fast on her feet? —absolutely! A neat turn of speed had been a childhood necessity, preferable to letting other urchins roll her like a barrel. Praying to the Lady for guidance and wisdom, Dannae took to her heels in earnest.

Khim sat patiently on the marble window ledge, alternating between staring outside and eyeing a frustrated moth fluttering against the upper corner of the pane. Sometimes it settled on the glass, its feelers feathery, its wings mottled gray with ivory and minute gold speckles. Yearning to pat it, Khim forced down her wandering paw, checking outside again. The moth was a way to wile away time, and her amber eyes, so like Khar's, flicked toward the bedroom door.

At last Honoria slipped out of her room, scorning any eye contact with Khim as if the ghatta were invisible or didn't exist. Waiting while she turned the corner and went down the stairs, Khim listened until the outside gate lock gave its distinct click. The unruly prycanthius obscured her view of the gate, but if Honoria took the path, Khim could be sure. Ah, interesting. Her absurd topknot jouncing, the Shepherd followed Honoria, her sandals swish-slapping on the path, no louder than the moth's wings.

Well, it didn't matter, but curiosity was hard to conquer. Why had the Shepherd chosen to follow? Feisty as she was round—and safely broomless today. But Honoria—and her absence—preoccupied Khim more. With a pat at the moth's velvet wing-dust for luck, Khim flowed off the ledge toward Honoria's room.

The doors in Dolphin House were old, easy to open for the most part, except for a few so stubbornly stuck that even Theo applied a hip or shoulder to open or close them. Since Honoria never made any racket, this must be a loose-fitting door. Stretching on hind legs, Khim leaned against the lock plate, listening as she bounced against it. Hm— something in between. The door wasn't hung square in its casing, its lower edge scraping the floor, the latch itself wedged against the bottom of the strike plate opening. Rattling it, working it a bit farther each time, wouldn't do. Honoria probably lifted up on the knob as hard as she could before opening or closing the door. Well, she'd find a way.

Angle, have to do it at an angle, she counseled herself as she backed down the hallway. Apply upward pressure right below the plate and at an angle—should pop the latch, the force swinging the door open. Simpler to 'speak Theo, let him do it, but he wouldn't approve. Besides, he had his hands full in the kitchens—or would have soon. She could feel the convergences, a gathering, a realigning of energies that presaged the visions Lindy often had.

A nervous whisker-lick as she considered it. Lindy's ability to foresee the future unnerved her, upset most of the ghatti, primarily because they were unsure whether or not it presented a preview of the truth. The problem was that Lindy couldn't be counted on to interpret what she saw as clearly as any one of the ghatti could. M'wa believed in Lindy's foretellings, but some called him credulous behind his back.

Well, no matter what Lindy did or didn't see, she had a job to do. Backing farther, Khim checked her position, then crouched, slowly raising her hindquarters, purposely tethering the energy welling within her. *Pretend you're chasing P'roul, just as you did when you were both ghatten!* Her eyes went huge, dilating as she spooked herself. *Tag her!* At "tag her!" she made a mad dash and went airborne, front paws careening off the door as she flexed in midair to reverse and speed off in another direction, both hind feet slamming below the lock plate. Skidding on the tiles as she landed, she battled the urge to continue her careen-

ing flight down the stairs, over and under furniture, up curtains. The skreek of her braking claws—oh, how humans
hated that!—brought her to her senses, and she heard the
door pop open.

A modest ruff-lick for calming purposes, convince herself
that P'roul truly didn't lurk behind the door, ready to
pounce, and she sedately walked into Honoria's room and
sniffed. None of the ghatti particularly relished the scent
she used, dabbed behind ears, at the hollows of her collarbones, on each wrist. There was something entirely too ag-
gressive to that scent that made them all want to hackle
and hiss at her implied challenge. Since no one was there,
Khim gave in to her urge, let the hairs along her spine rise,
hissed, and gave a violent sneeze. For a finishing touch she
attacked the carpet, back-kicking with all four paws, fibers
raking under her claws.

Satisfied, Khim padded and prowled, the semidarkness
no obstacle as she nosed about. Humans loved hidey-holes,
would never fathom how easily ghatti could find them.
Truth be told, were a human a mouse, complacent at the
safety and security of its newfound refuge, a ghatta or ghatt
could find it every time. To be fair, reaching inside was
sometimes a more difficult matter. Under the mattress? No.
Not inside the pillowcase. The point was to methodically
search, stalk each clue. Although the ashes in the grate
were an obvious spot, she left them for later. Never be
untidy unless necessary.

Ah, yes! A square of paper with a ragged edge lodged
in the cranny between floor and whitewashed wall, virtually
disappearing, blending white against white. An oversight on
Honoria's part; the woman hadn't realized it had drifted
free when she'd torn up the paper. Claw-carefully easing it
out, Khim patted it this way and that to study it. Skidding
it to a safe spot where it wouldn't blow away, she continued
her hunt, jumping on the mantlepiece and finding an empty
envelope tucked behind a vase.

Now for the fireplace itself. As she'd suspected, the fire
had been small, the weather too hot for any real need of
it. The ashes cold now, Khim stirred them with a front paw.
The moth had been softer, more pleasant to touch, but
equally dusty. Frustrated, even a little fretful, she turned

her back, briskly lashing her tail to loft the ashes, let them sift down.

Lindy's cry that Jenneth lived, was safe, made Khim sit heavily, eyes squinting in relief. Jenneth and Diccon had been the first humans she and P'roul had ever loved—ah, those milky-sweet, cuddle-warm days of ghattenhood. A sad truth that human-ghatten never grew as quickly or as wisely as their ghatti counterparts. But much as she loved the twins, Theo stood first in her heart—his uncomfortably narrow, bony lap, his stammer, his mournful looks. Hers, all hers!

Dismayed by her maundering, she quick-scanned the sifted ashes, saw her tail breeze had uncovered three scraps of paper that hadn't completely burned, only their edges scorched. Honoria had apparently been too pressed to make a thorough job of it. Hooking them clear was not appealing, and Khim shivered fastidiously as she snagged the first two. The third refused to comply, eluding her each time until she was forced to stretch inside the firebox, pincer it with her teeth to pull it clear. Ashes on her nose, ugh!

Four pieces, counting the one by the wall. How to carry them—one at a time? All at once? Sooner or later Honoria'd return, would hardly be amused at finding a ghatta in residence in her precious room. The envelope on the mantlepiece? Why not? Just as Khim prepared to jump, it struck her that her paws were coated with a fine layer of ash, might leave tracks. Best wipe her feet first. Ah, yes, that strange, peachy-pale undershift Honoria had hung from the peg. Stretch and hook that slinkily enticing strap. How it pooled in front of her as it fell, so sleekly smooth under her feet, sensuously soft on her paw pads! *Tsch, tsch, naughty Honoria, to get your undershift so streaky dirty! Dirty Honoria, stinky Honoria!* And gave vent to all the hostility she'd so nobly quashed for several octants now. *Don't even think about flirting with* my *Theo,* my *bond!*

A relaxed jump to the mantle, knock the envelope clear, and float down beside it. Awkward to open, to cajole the pieces inside. Having four agile paws helped, but she still suffered a paper cut on her nose. Satisfied, she picked up the envelope in her teeth and scurried off to find Khar.

Moments later in a storeroom off the kitchen the two sat, striped shoulder to striped shoulder, skidding the pieces of paper into a row, rearranging them, checking first one side and then the other.

"Anything? It must have been important if she tried to burn them." Khim glanced from the paper fragments to Khar and back again.

Sweeping her chin just above them, Khar's whiskers brushed the ragged squares, shifting them. **"Did you notice?"**

"Notice what?" Baffled, Khim mimicked her mother's head movements. She'd intimately touched each piece before in Honoria's room, so what could Khar have noticed that she hadn't? A faint shame in admitting she didn't know, couldn't guess, so she tried again, harder. **"Jenret scent . . . underneath?"** Given the heavy-hanging scent in Honoria's room, Khim would have been hard-pressed to notice anything else.

"From him to her? Sappy letters?" Khim ducked, aware too late of her impertinence, Khar cuffing her.

"No, his papers, records. A leathery smell from his trunk."

"Think she stole them?"

Restlessly shifting her weight from foot to foot, Khar bent her head in thought until Khim couldn't endure the wait. **"What do they say? Is there enough to read?"**

"I . . . can't read." Her head scrunched tight on her shoulders, her ears back-turned, Khar shot Khim a defensive look.

Her admission shocked Khim beyond belief, but was the truth, pure truth. Had to be. **"Thought you could master anything!"**

Circling the scraps, Khar eyed them from all directions. **"Can read my name. Doyce's name. The word 'ghatti' and a few others. Know my numbers. Can you do better?"** she challenged.

At Khim's miserable headshake, she continued, **"These are numbers, long, tangly strings of them. More numbers than words."**

"We could ask Doyce or Theo what they say!"

Easing the envelope to her, Khar sat, pressed its bottom against her hind feet, squeezing each side with her front paws until it gaped open. **"Push them in. I need to think. You know how humans are—even when we do something** for their own good. Doyce or Theo might be mad at us for finding these."

Diffident, almost not daring to suggest it, Khim whispered, **"Harry? He'd enjoy deciphering these."**

"No, I've a better idea!" But beyond that Khar remained smugly mute, Khim seething at her mother's unfairness. After all, who'd braved Honoria's stinky lair to salvage these scraps of intelligence?

Uneasily kicking at a pebble, Bard succeeded only in jamming it into the sand instead of lofting it over the water. Toying at it with the side of his boot, he made himself examine it—so round, so perfectly smooth from the constant tumbling. Pale salmon, veined with a fanned tracery of gray like a fern frond—a gift for Byrlie? He pocketed it; children were easier to please. What Lindy would want from this trip was more ticklish to fulfill: she'd want him whole, safe, and sound, prepared to devote himself to her and Byrlie without Byrta eternally casting her shadow between them.

Lady help him, but his body ached abominably—three days and two nights in an eternally damp, kelp-scented cell hadn't helped. Neither, he ruefully admitted, had his aborted berserker spell. Hand in his pocket he clenched the pebble in his fist. The urge to fight, maim, rend limb-from-limb, kill . . . and now the residue of that compulsion protested its caging as vehemently as he'd disputed his jailing. Uncage it, let it roam, and he'd be near whole again because it was impossible to call it forth and then casually cancel it. He'd been lucky that night aboard the *Vruchtensla*, the storm giving him something to battle. Davvy'd meant well this time, taking quick but primitive action to stop him from breaching that invisible boundary, inflicting unimaginable damage, but Davvy boasted no cure to eliminate the residuum of such an intense state.

Finally he dared raise his eyes toward Goose, trying to determine if the launch were any closer. Diccon, silent for once, pointed and he followed the finger, caught the flash of white-bladed oars beating like a gull's wings. The Guardians at last were retrieving M'wa and Kwee and their

launch so they could resume their journey. A companionable shoulder-bump from Diccon, still holding his peace.
And best of all, in the distance, M'wa's occasional comment
lofting over the water, the ghatt laconic in his relief at
their reunion.

"Magpie-chattering, I suppose?" Unexpectedly breaking
the silence, his remark caught Diccon off guard, made him
blush as badly as if Bard teased about a comely lass. "Quite
an adventure for a ghatten." Then, because he couldn't
help himself, had to know, "You can still feel her—Jenneth,
I mean?" Please, by the Lady, by the spirits of his ancestors, so near at hand, let Jenneth live! Reassure him of that
and he could die happy, his duty done. Dying, why was he
so obsessed with dying the past few days? Well, when the
berserker urge raced through his blood, something, someone, had to die. Stopper it, he supposed, and the death-lust
bored inward. *"Oh, M'wa, how I need you!"* he thought
but didn't dare 'speak it for fear the ghatt would deem him
oversentimental.

The sharp peal of a whistle, the rowers' signal for one
final stroke, then ship oars. Diccon already crowded the
water's edge, ready to snare the ghatten in his embrace
when she leaped. Deliberately hesitating, Bard spared the
time to strip his boots, toss them on dry sand before stepping beside the boy. As the bow grounded, he and Diccon
both reached out, heaving until the keel scraped and
lodged. **"Would've wet my feet for you,"** M'wa growled.

"Well, yours didn't need washing. Mine did." Poised on
the bow, M'wa sprang onto Bard's shoulders, the prick of
his claws painfully, gloriously familiar. *"Missed you,"* he
admitted as the ghatt gave one robust rub across his ear
and temple before subsiding. *"This youngling,"* he lifted a
shoulder to indicate Diccon, face buried in Kwee's flank,
sounds suspiciously like sniffling muffled by her fur, *"has
been driving me wild."*

"Tell me about it," M'wa gave a dry cough, **"or better
yet, don't. I'm worn to a mere shadow, practically youngling'd to death."** Still, Bard could hear the fondness in his
plaint.

"Old sober-sides, that's us." He stroked the length of the
long, black spine, basking in the ghatt's nearness, wanting
to hug him close, unrestrainedly bury his face against

M'wa's fur. Before he could throttle the impulse, he scooped M'wa into his arms, let his lips trace the firm shoulder-line, retreat for a moment behind the ear, bereft of an earring.

The ghatt shuddered with reciprocal passion before they were overtaken by habitual reserve. **"Good . . ."** M'wa swallowed hard, **"good news. Khar and Khim 'spoke me to say Lindy had one of her farseeing spells. Saw that Jenneth's alive, has washed ashore—though Lindy can't judge exactly where."** M'wa's announcement shrouded something deeper, darker, but Bard refused to pry.

"Has Kwee told you, Diccon?" He hugged Diccon's shoulders, not caring for once if his emotions showed. "Jenneth's alive!"

"I know! Isn't it grand?" But his giddy grin warred with a sadness that dulled the brilliant blue of his eyes. "But Pw'eek's not with her. Kwee's worried sick. We have to find her as well."

The crunch of shingle beneath many feet distracted Bard as Davvy, hair swept off his forehead by the sea breeze, rattled and skidded to their sides. With a broad smile he offered a down-turned fist to M'wa, and the ghatt rubbed his knuckles, pleased to see him. "There's someone here you should meet—our saviors, in fact. They're the ones who vouched for us!"

He already knew someone had, or they'd still be languishing in their cells, measuring the high-water mark on the wall that indicated what happened to the cells during a storm. Erasing that image from his mind, Bard obediently looked where Davvy pointed. There, perched on a rounded beach stone was one of the most striking ghatti he'd ever seen. Ghatta, he assumed, from the delicate build, the narrow, triangular face. Large blue eyes, a blue that outshone Diccon's, twinkled from a chocolate-colored mask, examining him with sly humor before her gaze slid to M'wa, the blue transfixing him. The ghatt quivered in his arms, then subsided by a visible act of will.

The chocolate tint continued over her ears, trailed down her spine to her tail, her legs as chocolate as if she'd landed in a confectioner's vat of the stuff. The rest of her was pale taupe with a lavender tinge. The overall impression was of length and sinuosity, as if she'd been drawn with sweeping

cursive strokes—except for a little pot belly peeping between her front legs. *"Mindwalk if ye will,"* Bard formally
'spoke her, although he wondered if she'd respond—she
seemed to have eyes only for M'wa.

Lightly leaning on an ebony cane, obviously more acces-
sory than necessity, an older woman presented her elegant
and equally angular profile, her bearing as regal as Mahafny's in her prime, yet entirely different—a desire to flaunt,
attract attention, arresting all eyes despite her years. Her
tabard bore a crimson trim, the sign of semiretirement, the
crimson echoed in the piping on her trim navy trousers,
and the cuffs and collar of her crisp white jacket. Damnation! For a moment the years fled and Bard relived the
burning, yearning futility of his adolescent crush on
Dymphna Lindevald.

"Greetings." As Dymphna broke her pose and started
forward, the ghatta sinuously flowed off her rock, curvetting
down the beach to give a saucy shoulder-roll at Bard's feet,
cocking her head over her shoulder to ensure her blue eyes
never left M'wa. **"I'm Mew'ph. And this is Dymphna Lindevald—in case you've forgotten us."** Her arch emphasis
indicated that only the dead were likely to expunge this
duo from their minds and loins.

**"The human-youngling does bear a striking resemblance
to the Seeker General—or should I say ex-Seeker General?
Precision's so important."** Now she figure-eighted around
Diccon's shins, staring upward at Kwee with an insincere
expression of interest in those azure eyes.

"Dymphna, Mew'ph, it's always a pleasure to see you
again. One too-long denied." Forcing himself to give a
short bow, Bard refused to click his heels, not barefoot like
that, though males lost in Dymphna's equally blue gaze
seldom felt pain. "It's so kind of you to vouch that we're
not escaping criminals." With a touch of muted sarcasm,
he added, "It's just unfortunate it took so long. Bad luck
on all our parts."

Dymphna's cane traveled his arm from shoulder to wrist,
hesitated. "All good things are worth waiting for—like
Davvy McNaught here." Now the cane's gold knob tapped
under Davvy's chin. "To think the last time I saw him he
was an obnoxious child playing dragon-nursemaid for poor,
dear Swan. Look at him now!"

Not about to be eclipsed by her bond, Mew'ph's undulating roll in the sand, the languid extension of one hind leg, then the other in a pleasurable stretch, drew everyone's eyes from Dymphna to her, much to Bard's relief. **"We were due leave, but we hurried back as fast as we could."** Her forepaws were fetchingly curled over her chest. **"I hope someday M'wa earns an equally peaceful semiretirement. But then, M'wa's dedication mutes any enjoyment life might hold for him. Doubt if he has the temperament to luxuriate in a life like this—not the way Dymphna and I do. He needs to relax, sun himself, let heartache and weariness flow away. Find new . . . interests."** Folding herself, she rolled onto her haunch. **"Oh, dear, I'm monopolizing the conversation, aren't I? Retirement's sooo pleasant, but it can be boring without fresh blood, fresh interests."**

To Bard's relief, Davvy appeared willfully immune to Dymphna's and Mew'ph's wiles beyond his first enchantment. Pounding Bard on the back, bringing him to himself, he crowed. "More good news! The fort commander bent the rules—we've the loan of Corporal Luykas till just beyond Owl Head Point. After that we can likely hire a local called Hirby. Not terribly bright, but he knows the beaches and the currents like no one else. Except for one minor thing," a dimple showed as he ducked his head in M'wa's direction, "apparently wherever Hirby goes, so goes his dog Tigger. Genially known in those parts as the 'hound from the hells.' "

"Bless Davvy, if you never have before." Doggedly casting his eyes skyward, M'wa ignored the ghatta still at Bard's feet, the imploring seduction in her blue eyes. Interestingly, Kwee was growling at her.

Sitting on a bambusa stool with a woven palm-frond seat, she glanced at the fire, took heart, and began twisting the broad pods to pop the beans inside. The pods were incredibly tough and fibrous, her hands still tender. But it felt good to do something, anything to earn her keep, show Pommy what she could accomplish. Not that he'd complained—never. It was just that with so much vanished from her brain, knowledge of what she could or couldn't do . . .

who she was or wasn't . . . It left her feeling empty, horribly
useless. The beans would be part of tonight's supper; she
thought she could remember how Pommy had cooked them
two nights ago.

That and the flowers she'd picked earlier, crammed in a
milk-glass pitcher, were her contribution. She still felt so
weak, good for nothing. With a sigh she peeled a layer of
dead skin from a finger; between being immersed in the
sea and being burned by the sun, her skin was sloughing
like a snake's. At least now she could bathe herself, rub
the aloe cream all over her body. The thought of Pommy
doing it before, tending her body like a helpless babe's,
made her blush. Her ability to care for herself proved she'd
gained strength, autonomy enough to feel humiliation.

Now she could sit outside clad in Pommy's outsized spare
shirt, worn so thin its blue was but a memory. Watching
the fire helped lift her spirits. Fire always cheered her,
she'd discovered, but it tantalized as well—momentous
answers dancing at the flames' tips, crackling and snapping too quickly for her to even ask the questions. Shadowy faces also took momentary form in the flames.
Shadowy faces materializing everywhere she looked, crying that she must know their names, say them aloud, before they'd assume solid flesh. Angry, frustrated, she set
the beans aside and built the fire higher, savagely jabbing
at it to drive away the faces.

Aqua, she was Aqua. Good to possess a name, even
though it didn't sound precisely hers. Pommy loved it,
loved the way it flowed off his tongue. Whatever intimacies
she'd accepted as ordinary in her other life, being stared at
with adoring, yearning eyes wasn't one of them. Wasn't her
body, obviously, that Pommy worshiped and wanted—he
could've had that any time he'd chosen while she was so
weak—but something beyond that, almost like her soul.
Some sort of melding or merging. He treated her as if he'd
been given a precious gift, his precious Aqua. And that
frightened her more than the fantasies playing across her
own mind, left her body aching with want at the memory
of his hands sweeping across her flesh, every part of her
welcoming, open to his touch, praying his hands might linger here . . . or there . . . or . . .

Struggling to drive such sensual, unbidden daydreams

from her mind, she jabbed, beat at the fire, coals and burning branches scattering, smoldering, catching elsewhere. "Who am I—who, who, Who?" Such emptiness hurt, and she doubled over to catch her breath, whimpering. Beat it out of the fire, beat it out of her head! Catching sight of the smoldering spots, a lick of flame here and there, one perilously near the hut, she shakily retrieved the palm broom from the hut and began pounding them out. The refrain came out of nowhere: "Naughty child, bad child! Mustn't play with fire, mustn't play with lucifers!" Mustn't! She knew that. But then, didn't every child?

Voices on the path and she quivered, poised to flee, take shelter in the hut. Pommy'd warned her and warned her. Without a name, without a past, she was like flotsam from the sea—anyone could claim her. Be thankful he'd been the one who had. Yes, safe with Pommy. But it was Pommy's voice, someone else's as well, high and chattery, Pommy answering, his irritation clear.

A low woof and a whine, and she spun to encounter a huge dog, sodden and sandy, gamboling at her. Rearing, it slammed mud-caked paws on her shoulders, licking wetly and enthusiastically at her face until she shut her eyes to block it out. Lady help her, the dog stank like an oct-old dead fish! Worse, even! "Down, dog!" she cajoled and tried to peel him off.

"Tigger!" Pommy anxious now, rushing, the man behind him laughing, pointing—at her or the dog? Grabbing the dog by the scruff, he yanked him away, but the dog nipped Pommy and threw himself at her again. She landed flat on her back, the dog astraddle her, nose juicily snuffling under her chin, working downward to where he shouldn't. "Hirby, haul him clear," Pommy shouted, picking up the stool. "Swear I'll brain him otherwise!"

With kicks and coaxing Hirby lured Tigger clear, and she sat up, Pommy's clean shirt slimed with dog drool. A seaweed strand—Tigger's contribution—lankly adorned her shoulder. "Now I'm sure why I like cats better," she said without thinking.

For the first time since she'd met him, Pommy's face went stiff and still, his blue eyes ablaze with hate. "I'd take a dumb mutt like Tigger over a sneaking, stealthing, mindstealing cat any day! Conniving beasts crawling into

your mind, sucking it dry—any ghatti or Gleaners deserve
to be killed outright! No mercy shown!''

Puzzled, she nervously twisted a shirt button, wanting to
smooth things over but unsure what to do. No further evidence was required to prove that Pommy believed what
he'd shouted with every fiber of his being. Had endangered
herself, revealed something, though she didn't know what.
Scooting backward on her bottom, she prudently increased
the distance between them.

At last he focused on her again, his eyes now brimming
with concern. "Don't worry, Aqua. I'd *never* let anything—
anyone—like that come near you, hurt you. I promise!''

"**You are *chunky beastie-cat!***" Wartle trotted along, sharp-
hooved feet hammering a staccato beat that devoured the
distance—except when a succulent plant or a ripe, fallen
fruit piqued his interest. Once Pw'eek had almost cata-
pulted over his head when he'd stopped short, enthusiastically sniffing and rooting. Sinking her claws in had
somehow seemed impolite—until she'd landed in a rude
heap one time too many. "**Ver-y chunky, ho-ho!**" A red-
rimmed hazel eye rolled back at her almost flirtatiously.

Despite her initial misgivings she rather liked Wartle. He
was crude and boisterous, ardent and impatient for female
companionship to stroke his ego and elsewhere. But he also
exhibited a keenly clever, kind side, and trotted far faster
than she could with a sore foot. She glanced at her mending
foot, a deep indentation now marring its scalloped shape.
"**Thank you, I think.**" On top of such suffering, it hurt to
be called "chunky," drove home how much fatter she was
than Kwee, so trimly slim, even her subtle striping further-
ing her sleek appearance.

"**Roundly firm, firmly round.**" Sensing her discomfiture
he slowed, let his round nose search out her dangling foot.
His snout with its disked nose still struck her as absurd,
large and flat, a naked, fleshy pink—not to mention two
moistly snuffing nostrils constantly sampling the air. "**Wartle *likes* his lady friends chunky, roundly firm, and beautiful. 'Course they never have fluff-soft fur like you.**" His
snout flexed, twitched as if tickled. "**Toe be fine,**" he con-

soled. **"Only way, nip-snip toe, you know. Better than losing whole foot. Maybe even leg."**

She licked the healing wound on his neck, wishing his fur were as soft as hers—it prickled and scratched no matter how she tried to tame it with her tongue. **"I know. I'm not brave like you. Lady Wart Hogs will love you—even with your scar—but I'm afraid Jenneth won't love me because I lack a toe."** After removing the dart from Wartle's neck and being rewarded with a share of the turtle eggs, she'd trailed along with him, sore and lonely, even his rough companionship a relief. Until the past few days she'd had someone beside her all her short life, guarding her, teasing her, loving her—first Kwee, then Jenneth.

Finally, uneasily bedding down together that first night, Pw'eek had curled tight against his scrubby flank, and he'd bent his head round, staring nearsightedly at her foot, that disk of a nose nudging, nostrils puckering and flaring. **"Smelling bad."** A grunt of relief as he rearranged himself, wrinkling his hide with pleasure now that the embedded dart no longer dragged. **"Infected. Just like my neck. Not good."**

She'd known he spoke truth, couldn't ignore it, hide from it or the pain any longer. Planting her head flat against his flank, burrowing against his firm warmth, she mewled. Never find Jenneth now—never could she travel fast enough, far enough, not with her foot afire like this. **"Let Wartle see."** The alarming curved tusks bracketing his snout pushed implacably closer, capable of ripping and tearing with casual disdain. **"Phah! Can't see right under my snout, eyes can't roll enough. Ah, well, good scenter means good sense."** Despite the tusks, she innocently assumed he planned to lick her toe, just as she'd ministered to his wound, so she was hardly surprised when his mouth opened, his tongue nudging the offending toe. **"Ready?"** he'd asked, all solicitude.

What had happened next still sent shivers through her, the skin along her spine uncontrollably rippling. With a snap of his jaws, his sharp, short front teeth neatly severed her toe. Her precious white toe! Emitting a curdling shriek, she'd launched herself over him, floundering and crashing through the deceitful, tripping branches and vines like a ghatten possessed. Oh, to outrun the hurt that ran like lightning up her leg, invading her brain! Burrowed deep into the forgiving ferns and moss that overspread the raised roots of a tree, she'd whimpered and wailed, her whole body ashudder.

Amazing how he'd so silently tittupped after her, tenderly shouldering aside vines and branches rather than ripping through them. **"Pw'eek come out. Toe be better now."** "Toe be gone!" she'd wailed.

"So? Got others. Just a scrawny toe." A moist snort resounded like a gale in her ear, half-deafening her.

It welled within her, a panic more awful than before, a need to know, be sure. **"You didn't . . . eat it, did you?"** Mayhap Wartle planned on consuming her a toe at a time, working his way up!

A grumbling grunt rolled from his chest, his head bouncing up and down, tiny ears flapping. **"Oh-ho! That good one! Beetles taste better! Anything taste better than scrawny toe!"** Bending his trotters he'd crashed beside her, ugly head rakishly draped with fern fronds as he wedged himself near. **"No, soft-fur, chunky one whose blotchy-beautiful markings blend with shadow and light and leaves. I spit it out. Now come, Wartle wanting sleep, wanting cuddle first."**

Reassured, she'd slunk out, ungainly as she balanced on three feet, and they'd nestled together for the night. Sleep came only after she'd thoroughly licked and cleansed her pitiful toe stub.

Wartle'd been right; her foot improved, though she still mourned the loss of her toe. For three days now they'd traveled together, Wartle content to amble or trot in the direction she wanted, the mental beckoning she felt ever stronger, ever clearer. Eager and willing now to challenge any boar who crossed his path, Wartle cheerfully confessed how he enjoyed exploring, the chance to claim new turf, perhaps romance some chunky sow who'd relish his debonair good looks, his strength and bravery. To demonstrate his readiness, he ripped at the turf with his tusks, jabbing left and right, twisting and ripping, tossing dirt over his head and back, panting victoriously. While it was only a pretend victory over an invisible foe, it *had* unearthed some succulent grubs. And each day Wartle insisted on piggybacking her to atone for snipping off her toe without warning.

"So, humans kind to you? Not hurt you, hunt you?" As

always his head swung alertly, his ears perked, nostrils questing.

"**No! Never! My Bond, my Jenneth loves me inside out, and I love her. Pw'eek loves Jenneth even more than Kwee, my Sissy-Poo!**"

It struck her that Wartle was almost imperceptibly slowing, taking more time to sniff for danger, looking for movement, hearkening to strange sounds, though his nose provided his strongest confirmation. "**Hard believing. 'Course Wartle not zactly love his littermates, either. Greedy, pushy, steal my dug if I let'm. Twelve of us, that litter, Mama so proud.**"

"Oh . . ." was the best Pw'eek could manage, unable to envision enduring eleven siblings, all as clever and sharp and jaunty as Kwee. "**But** *you* **were the strongest, the best—yes?**"

"**Damn daisy right! Wartle best boar ever!**" A stop now at a small copse rising above them, shielding them. A path scarred its flank, worn enough to indicate people or animals regularly traveled it. "**But Wartle no fool. Not wanting 'nother dart in neck or spear 'tween ribs. People thicker here, thick as flies on dead boar. Can scent too much people stink.**"

Naturally there'd be people smells if Jenneth were near, her scent and other human scent as well. But Wartle abruptly sat so that she found herself coasting down his back. "**Need to snuffle sweet nothings to adoring little sow or two, set up my territory. Be Wartle over all. But not here, little one. This good-bye.**"

No more Wartle? Be brave all on her own again? Shifting her weight tentatively onto her bad foot, so much better but still tender, she stretched up, licking Wartle's nose, working along his snout toward the amiable hazel eye with its stubby lashes. "**Love Wartle! Pw'eek thanks you!**"

An explosive gust of air tenderly ruffled her fur. "**Hope I find sow so tenderly caring, as clever and chunky as Pw'eek! Hope you find your Jenneth-human and your Kwee-sib, too. May Nature treat you well!**" A decisive turn and he trotted off, hindquarters side-jouncing, her last sight of him a farewell flirt of his short, stringy tail. His desertion could have hurt more, but the sensation that Jenneth was somewhere, somewhere near, thrummed through her, set her heart pounding. Pw'eek sooo brave to ride ugly, dangerous Wart Hog, yes! As long as no one ever discovered what a truly sweet beast Wartle was.

Like so many Guardians, Luykas, the corporal unofficially assigned to them, relied on a bluff professional cheer to hide any doubts he might have about their success. Content to speak when spoken to, he expertly guided the little craft along the coast, every obscure bay and inlet, bluff or point crystal clear in his head. Much to Diccon's relief, at least now they sailed instead of rowing, or he'd have disgraced himself. For some reason he had the blazes of a headache, his mind as muddled and confused as an overshaken melon. His brain was ripe, all right, and ready to ooze. Too many thought fragments that wouldn't cohere or connect, while others had gone missing, stowed somewhere for safekeeping. Either that, or mayhap someone had stirred his brains in the cauldron of his skull. Probably should beg a headache powder off Davvy, but the idea of swallowing it made his stomach go even queasier.

"Poor head still hurting?" A soft paw touched his temple and he fought not to flinch away.

"Yes, sweedling." Lips compressed in case his stomach did rebel, he debated hanging over the side just in case— not disgrace himself by decorating the launch. Having Kwee near made the nausea and percussive accompaniment near-endurable, his relief at their reunion still overwhelming. To distract himself he began to enumerate her markings, delineate where each soft shade began and left off, where the stripes ran, how many she sported. Manage that and his brain wasn't as muddled as he'd feared. Let's see, how many tummy spots, each like a smudgy fingerprint against the pale buff belly-fur? Two, four, six, eight—then what?—four smaller, more indistinct ones?

Charmed by his attempt, she preened, then flexed and began to wash her stomach, exposing just enough soft belly fur to let him count. **"What's a sweedling? Is it good? I'm good, so it must be good. Not a weedling? You didn't call me a baby weed, did you?"** Indignant, her head swung up,

a slip of pink tongue peeking from her clamped mouth.
"Tummy spots *not* smudgy!"

Cautiously shifting his head on the runt sack, he prayed
he wouldn't forget, overstretch, and kick Davvy or Bard.
Better to let them think he still slept. Everyone was fine
without him and with him, well, the way his head pounded,
he wouldn't be much use. *"Sweedling's an endearment, a
secret one between just the two of us."* By the Lady's starry
crown, framing a coherent sentence was hard work! *"It's
sort of a contraction of 'sweet darling,' because that's what
you are to me."*

Purrs avalanched beside his head and, surprisingly, the
steady, breathy vibration of her love slowly reknit his shattered thoughts, stopped them from fragmenting further.
**"Head hurt because of sissy-twin? You feeling what she's
feeling? Confused, lost, afraid?"** Her sonorous purrs rolled
on, soothing. **"My head thrums sometimes when Pw'eek's
upset. Does sissy-twin do that to you, too?"**

Bolt upright now, his flailing leg caught Davvy in the
ribs, scooting him off the bench and into the bilge. Head
held tight between his hands, he struggled to weave together every nuance of Jenneth's mindpattern, compare
them to what he was experiencing. Disciples guide him,
they were nearing her! What was ailing him was the
overspill of her mind, the way her frightened mind began
to slam down barriers when she longed to play with fire!
"Luykas! What's up ahead, where are we?"

Davvy and Bard had spun round, staring at him as if he'd
lost his mind, Davvy fumbling for his medicament bag. But
Luykas seemed unfazed, didn't take him for a raving loon.
"Owl Head Point. Been planning to put in there anyway.
Current sweeps debris into the inlets. If we can find Hirby,
we can ask him what he's seen since the storm." Easing the
rope, Luykas let out more sail until it bellied in the breeze,
the launch fairly leaping across the water's surface. "Way you
looked, I figured you'd either seen a ghost or felt your sister's
touch. Reckon it's so? Not wishful thinking?"

"I *know* it's so," Diccon answered stoutly and promptly
heaved his stomach contents over the side. "Uncle Bard!"
Head hanging, he swallowed, hating the sour taste. "I think
Jen's planning on playing with fire. And I can't seem to
reach her mind, convince her to hear me!"

Suspecting he must appear as prissy as an old maid crossing
a cow patch, Oh-Oh dexterously avoided the papers pro-
fusely ornamenting his office floor as well as spread across
two trestle tables he'd borrowed. A mincing step-turn and
an extended stretch brought him to Rudy's side to peer
over his shoulder. His six eldest—offspring, niece and nephews—plus his sister-in-law Gelya, had been pressed into
service, each and every one blessed with a retentive memory and a level head. The younger ones stayed home with
his wife, safely abed if Zandra had any say in it, because
it was late, candles burning low, oil lamp chimneys soot-
stained, wicks in need of trimming.

A touch to a young shoulder here, an encouraging pat
on a bent head there as he surveyed them scrupulously
checking and rechecking records, receipts, bills of lading
from as far back as he could gather. If a paper trail existed,
his accounting "bloodhounds" would catch the scent. Hopping, stretching precariously, he took an indirect path back
to his desk, like a water-skimmer shooting between lily
pads of pages. Once there, he sifted through files until he
unearthed what he wanted tracked next. "I want you to
match invoices from Janacz & Sons, Wismeer & Co., and
Hoddersen, Geyer," he instructed. "Especially around six
octants back. Check number of bolts versus total price—
invoice price against ledger entry. Sing out at anything
odd."

Damned if he'd let down Wycherley-Saffron, and at least
now he had a glimmer of what to look for, how things had
been disguised, altered. Damnall on his insistence that
Rudy and Momsvaert ape his penmanship, it made it well-
nigh impossible to decipher who'd entered what—not that
his own entries were entirely without flaw. He'd been too
damned prideful, hadn't wanted Jacobia to notice other
hands in the records, fearful it would imply he had too
much to handle, not enough time to personally pen each
line. Of course he should've asked permission to hire help,
but somehow he couldn't acknowledge his workdays had
been so crammed that he hadn't properly checked the
reports.

Bald-faced clever cheating, though he still couldn't figure

out why or who. Caressing his chin, he thought about what he'd set in motion, how it might end—his loved ones endangered, even dead. No—those threatening letters were designed to make him quake like a leaf, intimidate him until he backed off, but his stubborn professionalism plus the lure of a complex puzzle overrode threats penned on cheap paper. Doyce Marbon hadn't demurred at sending over her husband's papers (and it warmed his heart how she called him Ozer), even though she'd warned that Theo and Honoria had discovered little out of line. But then, they were amateurs, had nothing to check against.

He'd do his best to see Doyce's trust in him wasn't misplaced, though the two ghatti's afternoon appearance had come close to fanning his insecurities to incendiary levels. Not one but *two* ghatti sent to read his every thought, every move as he methodically worked through the papers. The lack of trust had crushed him, a brutally explicit reminder that he was a Sunderlies bumpkin and no match for savvy Canderisians determined not to be fleeced, defrauded. So, they were on different sides after all—all his protests and pleas had added up to naught, a zero tally.

But Khim had laid an envelope at his feet, its corner faintly dimpled from her teeth. "For me?" he'd asked, guilt piling upon guilt, wishing it and its bearer would vanish. Two pairs of amber eyes stared up at him, made his stomach go queasy, his palms sweat. They looked so beseeching and yet implacable, ready to bore through him. No, not through him, but delve into him as they had before, rifling thoughts he didn't even know he had.

Gingerly picking up the envelope as if the thin paper disguised live coals, he opened it, deathly afraid of what he'd find. Could ghatti write? Politely pen a note when they deemed it ill-mannered to enter a human mind? Although he was less susceptible to rumor than many, Oh-Oh wouldn't put anything beyond their abilities, especially after experiencing them firsthand. Except . . . how did they hold a pencil or pen? Did they dip their tails in ink, broad brush strokes laying out their demands?

After working himself into a lather, it was an anticlimax of sorts—four scraps of paper covered with fragments of words and figures, some torn at the most tantalizing places. Writing on both sides of several pieces, along with faint

oval prints from ghatti toes. Fingers clumsy, still distracted
by their stares, it took time and effort to sort them on his
desk, reorder them, flip them over, before he began to suspect what they contained. Oh, for the complete sheet or
paper!

"I don't suppose you've any more?" he'd asked, abashed
at addressing such a question to animals. They'd dipped
their heads, eyes half-shuttered in apology. "No, I guess
not, or you'd have brought them, wouldn't you?" he'd consoled. "But if you come across any more, bring them to
me, please!" For the scraps, in handwriting that clearly
wasn't his (or Rudy's or Momsvaert's), were the first real
"skeletons" he'd uncovered—just a bone here, a bone
there, but all building a body of information that told an
informed accountant that any invoices from Janacz & Sons,
Wismeer & Co., and Hoddersen, Geyer should be dou-
ble-checked.

With that they'd risen and stalked out, tails serpentining
oh-so-polite regrets. A desk candle guttered in the breeze
created by a passing child, and Oh-Oh shook himself, forcibly yanking his mind back to the present, eyes burning
tension monkey-climbing his neck and pounding at his temples. "Gelya? Anything for that period?" A grumbled "no"
from his sister-in-law, so he worked through the roll call of
children, eldest to youngest. At Talalay, his thirteen-year-
old niece, he struck pay dirt. Her freckled nose wrinkled
and she scrubbed at it as if it itched. He knew the trait too
well; it indicated she was hot on the trail. Tugging at a
mousy blonde braid, she scanned the numbers again, made
a check on the paper in front of her, two checks on another
sheet to her left.

"Uncle Oh-Oh, could be just a slip on the summary
sheet," she warned, but the corner of her mouth quirked in
self-satisfaction. "A figure transposition under Hoddersen,
Geyer. But 54 plus 117 equals 171 golden, and the quarterly
sheet shows it as 117—an easy mistake to make." Knuckles
white against the table's edge, she arched her back, then
shot forward until her nose almost touched the paper. "But
that 54 also shows as a debit. Can't figure out for what
Sundries can be anything!" She sounded distinctly miffed.

"Lovely, Talie!" and meant it, rubbing his hands together. "See if you can find any more. Mayn't be as obvious

a slip as turning 171 into 117." A commotion outside distracted him, reminding him how late and hushed the streets were, the Lady's two moons sailing high, overseeing the sleepy world below. Well, couldn't be dagga boys—no rocks through his windows, no jeers and japery, no sound of a drunk emptying bladder or stomach on his doorstep. Best send the children off shortly or Gelya and Zandra'd have his hide. Take them home and rest, start fresh at the crack of dawn.

But as if she'd heard him think her name, Zandra burst into the office, shepherding four of the little ones close, tiny hands dragging at her waistband, her face tear-streaked, jaw trembling. He counted heads automatically, convinced the "doubles" had hidden themselves behind Zandra's shadowy skirts. Or crawled under them, prepared to pop out and terrorize their siblings. His and Zandra's four-year-old Vannie and her cousin, Treet, one day younger. They made a matched pair, a team, mixing mischief and mayhem with bouts of meekness.

Raising his caftan and pinning it against his thighs, he stretched and leaped as fast as he could to reach her side. "What's the matter? What's wrong?" Yet he somehow knew, their absence glaringly obvious, a gaping void engulfing his heart. Across the room his sister-in-law's face had turned more pallid than the papers around her, and he read apprehension but no condemnation for his arrogance at risking the children in a game of numbers.

Wordlessly, Zandra thrust a note into his hand, the paper sticky-crumpled, tear-damp, imbued with the scent of her muger hand ointment. Couldn't bring himself to open it, willing Zandra to tell him the bad tidings. "I went to check . . . make sure everyone was asleep . . . not hiding under the covers, playing games." The children's bedrooms resembled dormitories, twelve children stacked like cordwood and apportioned between two bedrooms, the old nursery his and Zandra's domain, while Gelya made do in a kitchen alcove. "Ozer, they're gone—not a trace! A note on Vannie's pillow, and the others heard nothing!"

Forcing his fingers to obey, he opened the note, smoothing it against his hip before looking at it. A fine, cursive hand to it, despite the fact the writer had attempted plain

printing, unable to break the habit of swirls that connected
one letter to the next. It read:

> You were warned to turn a blind eye. A shame you didn't.
> Perhaps the children will grow used to blindness—unless
> you stop puzzling over the figures. After all, Wycherley-
> Saffron has money to burn. Perhaps your ledger books
> will burn bright enough to guide the children home. Say
> tomorrow night at Janacz & Sons old warehouse? If not,
> the children can stumble home in the dark.

With all his waning self-control, he refrained from crumpling the paper, throwing it as far from him as possible
before it poisoned him. It had already contaminated his
hand, sick dread crawling up his arm, invading his entire
body, infecting his mind. Or was he the source of this con-
tagion, blighting those he loved with blindness, death? Willing his hand steady, he reached to Zandra for comfort,
tucking her under his sheltering arm and beckoning for
Gelya, willing to spend what little courage remained to support them. For a moment the printing had looked familiar,
but whatever bell had chimed had been silenced by the
note's threat.

"Ozer, what . . . what are we going to do?" As if he had
a ready answer, any answer, obligingly waiting to be
plucked from thin air! His beloved office had turned from a
familiar, friendly place to a desolate, shadow-haunted cave,
fantastical shapes writhing and rising, ready to snatch and
devour. . . . All of the children—no, not all, only ten—had
gathered 'round in a protective circle, larger ones cradling
younger ones, others holding hands. *He* was supposed to
protect *them,* shield them from harm—not the other way
'round! Hide behind children, blithely assume no one
would dare strike at him through them? Had he truly been
so naïve, so blind? A shiver at the word.

"First—" when had a frog slimily lodged in his throat?
"—we're going home, put the children to bed." His raised
hand forestalled Zandra's protest that that had begun their
troubles in the first place. No sense reminding her it was
his fault—she'd remember soon enough, her blame bom-
barding him each time she looked his way. "All together
in the dining room, wherever we can bed them down. You

and Gelya will stay up, stay awake and on guard. Rudy and Jaz as well, one at each window, while I wake some city councillors, alert them to the kidnapping. Mayhap the Guardians could post guards around the house, start a search." A slim chance, practically nonexistent, but he'd try anything he could!

"No!" Gelya shook, her vibrations traveling up his arm. "Our answer's in the note. Follow instructions, do what they ask tomorrow night! Call in any officials, and we've condemned the children to blindness—or worse."

Why, why couldn't things be simple, straightforward, like numbers? Except numbers weren't always straightforward—look at the figures he'd been chasing. Right or wrong? Mayhap Gelya was seeing more clearly than he? "You're right." A reluctant admission that he'd already failed once. "We'll wait, do exactly as they ask." Except the night promised to be very long, an even longer day after it to endure. Long enough—with a little luck and dogged persistence—to crack the puzzle the numbers presented. And mayhap even to gather his courage, contact Doyce Marbon, pray that that ghatta of hers could winkle out the truth, discover where the children were secreted. With that, they could attack, seize the culprits and free his babies! To cover other possibilities, mayhap a trip to the Bethel, alone, for prayer. It might not help, but it couldn't hurt.

Leaving his family in a huddle just within the office door, Oh-Oh meticulously snuffed candles, turned down wicks, shuttering and locking the long windows. Leave the papers as they lay—a reminder, a reproach, mayhap a redemption. Oordbecks were figurers, not fighters, but he'd fight this assault on his family any way he could, break every rule to win. As each adult scooped up a small child, protective and close, the others held hands as they marched home through the dim streets, shying at shadows, panicky at the pound-ings of their own hearts.

Reflexively slapping at his neck, Arras Muscadeine plucked the offending insect between his fingers, pinching it dead before flicking it aside. An automatic gesture, one he no longer noticed, especially with his attention fixed on the

two massive bovines that Uma-Uncle and Dlamini were
proudly parading in front of them. "Worse comes ta worser,
plenty a good eatin on them beasts." To emphasize her
hoarse comment, Bullybess swatted his upper arm, hard
enough to make him wince. His wince turned into a shudder when he saw she'd mashed a large insect with a darning
needle-sized stinger against his sleeve.

Scraping away its remains he studied the beasts again.
"Think you could carry one, Bess?" But his remark didn't
provoke a rise from her; instead, she examined the beasts
with greater care.

Reluctantly she conceded, "Nah. Too awky-bawky.
Shoulderns tain't wide nough." Gnawing a thumbnail she
pondered. "Lessen I git some sorta wide support . . . Whad
yed wanna bet—"

He interrupted, uneasy at the shrewd look in her eyes.
If she stood ready to bet, he'd more than likely lose. Besides, why encourage her in an antic that would upset Mvelase and his nephew?

They *were* magnificent beasts, though he'd never seen
quite their like before. The closest similarity he could find
was a passing resemblance to oxen, but they made oxen
look almost delicate, petite in comparison. Broad, with rippling muscles under shiny black hides, each boasted a short,
thick neck, and an expansive head crowned with horns that
grew outward from a center ridge and then took an extravagant downward swoop before concluding in an upward
point that left him fingering his own mustache. Their
hooves were the size of dinner plates.

Holly stood next to one, dwarfed by it, energetically
scratching its shoulder while Dlamini beamed like a proud
papa. "Are these the cattle you raise at home?"

"Ha!" A rolling chuckle from Uma-Uncle. "Too big, too
slow, too mild for our plains. Even old Uma-Uncle walks
faster—though they walk longer without rest. Cousins and
cousins," he added as if that explained everything.

Slowly circling the beasts, Jenret scrutinized them from
all sides. "Cousins to your beasts?" Holding out a hand,
still tremulous from the effects of the fever and their swamp
trek, he let the beast sniff it. It turned an impish gentle eye
on him and swung its head to rub against his hip, Jenret

only just evading the horn sweeping by his ribs. Restless, he wandered off a few meters, staring northward.

Kneading along the spine with both hands, massaging the beast, Dlamini raised his eyebrows at Arras. "Our coast cousins loan us these. Good for plowing in swampy land, dragging timber. Strong, steady, never tire—and make their own paths!"

"But not exactly fast, according to Uma-Uncle," Jenret added over his shoulder. "Is there a cart or wagon somewhere?"

As she listened to the exchange, Bess scrubbed the horny sole of her foot against her shin. "Huh! Temper-fuss broke wid fever. Relief!" Elbowing Arras to make him bend, she whispered, "Reason ta' be upset, daughter lost'n all. But he allays so driven?"

A fair question, one worth pondering. What perplexed Arras more was the change that had overtaken Jenret since the previous night. Without a doubt Jenret had 'spoken Doyce, he'd sensed the resonances in the very air, and been left feeling lonely, even envious. But had Jenret mentioned a solitary thing about their conversation? No! Worst of all, he'd calmed, cloaking himself in a steadfast resolution that reminded Arras too much of a drunkard who'd sworn off drink. Easy to pledge, hard to achieve, hard for even the strongest of souls to break such dependency. But what had Jenret sworn to vanquish in himself? Jenret pensive, introspective was guaranteed to make anyone nervous.

It made Arras rue even more that dusk on the *Vruchtensla* when he and Doyce had been abovedeck together, half-mesmerized by the ruffling wake behind the stern, saying their final farewells as Canderis slipped out of sight. A single gull still followed, hoping for a final handout, then gave up, extending a wing like a scythe-blade to swing round, return to Windle Port.

Pointing, he'd started to mention the comparison, had halted, thinking better of it—Doyce and sickles or scythes weren't words to be mentioned together, not after Bazelon Foy with his henchman Tadj Pomerol, and that poor misguided fool, Hylan Crailford. Faertom, dead. Darl Allgood, dead too. But at least that same silver sickle had sliced Baz Foy's throat as well. Something to be grateful for, and Resonants across the land certainly rejoiced. It had marked a tangible beginning of the end of the troubles fomented against them.

A shiver, and she'd huddled close to him, "Gulls scythe the air, don't they? Absolutely slice through it," almost as if she'd read his thoughts, her voice barely under control. "And for all my vaunted Resonant skills, I couldn't stop it."

Without thinking he'd pulled her against him to comfort her, stop the quivering that had overtaken her body, a coldness of spirit surging within. "You had other matters on your mind," he'd remonstrated as he wrapped his cloak around them both. "Birthing the twins, finding the will to survive the bleeding that almost drained you dry. By the Lady, you'd no more power to expend."

"I *always* fail, Arras. I try so damn hard and nothing ever comes out quite the way I want it to." He could see the fine threadings of silver in her hair, the tracks of her tears silvery as well as she tilted her face as if to beg forgiveness.

Could he make her understand? "Doyce, we're *all* doomed to fail in big and little ways because we aren't perfect. If we were, we wouldn't be struggling through *this* life, or the next and the next lives the Lady gives us to work toward that perfection!"

Proud of his rebuttal he'd leaned forward, fully intending to kiss her brow, console her, his dear friend, his beloved Francie's sister. Except she'd stretched on tiptoe to make her lips meet his. Fire, fire! Not fire meeting ice at that moment. Stunned, shocked to his core and—truth be known—both shamed and thrilled, he'd lifted his head to part their lips. "Damn it, Arras, you were a better match for me than Jenret! Another failure!"

Stiffly he'd let go, and she'd sighed as if expecting it. "Please, don't tell Francie that for a brief moment her sister was even more of an utter fool than usual," she'd groaned, staring out and away from him, refusing to meet his eyes.

"Only if you promise never to reveal that I lost my head as well." A gallant answer and a truthful one. "*Will* lose my head if she finds out."

A strained silence, fraught with the newborn knowledge of what they were both capable of doing—betraying those who loved them. He'd thought he'd heard her whisper, "If not in this life, perhaps in another." But there were opportunities for second chances in each and every life.

He hoped she'd remember that, that Jenret had discovered the truth as well. To dare too greatly courted failure; to not dare enough meant another kind of dereliction. What forces drove them all through life? Not simply the outside forces, the exigencies of daily living, but the internal furies that spurred them, sometimes whipped them bloody?

"Driven, yes. What?" Hardly an answer to Bullybess's question, but she patted his back, her brow furrowed with an odd tenderness.

"Yed dig eny deeper, Bullybess need shovel ta catch up." She had the right of it—stop digging so deeply. Let Jenret and Doyce work things out between them—or not. "Ho! Lookee, even shipping crate bigger!"

Head high, a smile dimpling both cheeks, Dlamini planted each foot with care, a wagon tongue under his arm. Behind him, like a children's toy on a string—and not much larger—a high-sided cart jounced into view. It did look amazingly like a shipping crate, although its red-and-yellow-painted sides sloped outward. Each wheel was solid wood, constructed from two slabs of timber, held together by iron butterfly wedges and the iron rim itself. As Dlamini hitched the . . . the . . . Arras shook his head, dismayed he still didn't know what the beasts were, and shot Bess a helpless, questioning look. "What *do* they call them?"

"Nauki 'n Taubi," Bess helpfully supplied. "Taubi's one wid right horn canting at angle. See?" He glared, the glare that had cowed hundreds of Marchmont's finest soldiers, made them quail at the wrath of their commander. Its effect, however, was minimal on Bess. "Bubalus, they be, if yed not bain woolgathering."

While Mvelase supervised the loading as his nephew finished harnessing the team, Bess and—belatedly—Arras pitched their gear over the high side while Holly arranged each piece as best she could in the cramped space. Jenret simply stared off into the distance, his mind obviously thousands of kilometers away. As Mvelase arranged himself on the cart's narrow seat, more like a bracket than a seat, Arras joined his old compatriot, shook him by the elbow. "Jenret, we're off. Come on, man, look lively!"

"I don't know what to do anymore," he confessed, blue eyes dark with the pain of self-discovery. "Each responsibility drags me in a different direction. . . ."

Tired and disgruntled, yearning for a hot bath, a soft bed, and an uncomplicated, bland meal, Arras propelled Jenret to the cart. Responsibilities, eh? Did the fool think he was the first adult to ever have to balance them? Still muttering under his breath, he gave Jenret a leg up and wedged a boot on the wheel-hub to raise himself, careful on landing not to plant a foot on any ghatti tails or paws. Draped across the packs, P'roul made little whistling snores, already half-asleep. Unsure if he dared intrude on their long years of acquaintance, friendly yet politely distant as protocol demanded of a ghatt and a human non-Seeker, Arras 'spoke Rawn. *"Can't you snap him out of this mood? It's more than fever-weakness that's turned him into a walking automaton. Ghosts exhibit more presence than he does!"*

Rawn, black fur lightly dusted with rust-colored mud, looked spectral himself. **"You've my permission to shake some sense into him. Right now he's enjoying suffering."** Draping his head across P'roul's flank, he heaved a sigh. **"Well, 'enjoying' isn't right, but 'wallowing' might be."**

"Too bad Mahafny's not here to snap him out of it."

A wistfulness to those yellow eyes. **"I wish she were, too. But she's not, so bear with him, please."**

At a gleeful shout from Dlamini and a snap of Uma-Uncle's reins, the cart jolted off, Bess and Dlamini escorting it on each side. Within the cart, only Mvelase sat, the others had scant room to stand. "Jenneth's alive, you know," Jenret continued, staring at the back of Uma-Uncle's head as if memorizing it.

"But that's wonderful news!" Arras exploded, crushing Jenret in a bear hug as Holly whooped with joy.

"It's just that so many other things are dead . . . or will be soon." His mood blacker than the clothing he was notorious for wearing, Jenret finally met Arras's eyes, offered a final thought in mindspeech. *"Arras, doesn't wisdom come with age?"*

"I don't think so." Shaking his head, Arras wondered how to explain. *"I think you're born with a finite amount of wisdom—it's up to you how to use it, whether you hoard it or spend it like a prodigal. Everything in life depends on*

*how it's used—wisely or for ill. The Jenret I know always
has his enthusiasms, dares greatly, sometimes falls short.
Without that gift—or curse—he might as well as be dead."* All
too true, Jenret without his enthusiasm would be deadly
boring, predictable, flat. The bubalas's large hooves sank,
sucked clear of the mud at each step; sometimes the cart
almost plowed through the soft, oozing earth instead of
rolling across it. Yet this was clearly the cart path, two
beaten-down parallel tracks firmer than the marshy land on
either side, with its jointed reeds clattering and whisking
by each other. From the deep jade green and taupe reeds
myriads of insects soared up to light on the cart's inhabitants, eager to sample foreign flesh.

"We *are* heading in the right direction, aren't we?"

A tight nod from Jenret. "Yes, Mvelase senses Bard's
pull, just as I feel Diccon's. They haven't reached Jenneth
yet, but they're on her trail, well ahead of us."

"Yes, I'm sure! Why does it have to take so long?" Diccon
glared at Luykas at the tiller, then shamefacedly studied
his palms with their puffy mounds of blisters. He and Luykas had just traded places with Bard and Davvy, the two
older men now bent at the oars.

Affable as he might be, Luykas's face revealed his tiredness and the heightened strain to which they'd all been
subjected ever since Diccon's discovery that Jenneth was
somewhere nearby. "The current's against us here, and the
wind's still blowing from land. We've fought for every boat-
length we've gained." Diccon wanted to ridicule Luykas's
even neutrality in stating the obvious! "Easier to tack up
and around the point, come down overland. Faster, too."

"But we're right *here,* blast it! Practically on top of her,
she's that close!" Hating his own whininess, he coughed,
praying he wouldn't throw up again. Once the reason behind his illness had dawned, he could almost master it,
though he couldn't completely counter the jumbled, pent-
up emotions still emanating from Jenneth. All through their
childhood she'd grow upset, never outwardly show it, and
he'd be the one running to lose his lunch. Anything that
affected him, overenthusiasm, grief, pain, was writ plain on

his face for all the world to read. He exploded; she contracted. He suppressed nothing, while she interred her hurts in her heart.

Abstractedly stroking Kwee, his searching fingers kneaded her overtaut muscles, tickling a little purr from her as she licked his hand. She'd been quiet in his mind of late, mayhap realizing how Jenneth already crowded and confounded his own thoughts.

The intrusiveness of Bard's question on their separate silences caught them unaware. Face obscured, he angled forward to set his oar. "How deep is it," his dip and pull evenly matching Davvy's, propelling the launch ahead a scant meter, "here?"

Helm tucked between his knees, Luykas scrubbed at his short-cropped hair, cogitating. "Not that deep, tends to be shoaly here—unless the storm rearranged things. I'd guess, oh, in landlubber terms, mayhap two, two-and-half times as deep as I'm tall. Call it four, mayhap five meters. You could tell if it weren't dark—the blue should be lighter, brighter."

"Too deep to wade ashore," Davvy stroked grimly. "Given the current, swimming doesn't seem advisable."

"How much rope do we have aboard? The anchor line plus the rigging, any other pieces?" A dour amusement touched Bard's face. "Wasn't thinking about swimming, Davvy. Thought we might try a different tactic. More like a tug of war. Fancy it?"

Throwing his leg over the tiller to hold their course, Luykas began to calculate the rigging's length, while Diccon measured off the anchor line. From nose to the end of his fully-extended arm should be a shy meter—or close enough. The coils left a slimy residue as they peeled through his hands. Rummaging, Luykas hauled out another short coil secreted in the bench-locker.

"Shy twelve meters," Luykas announced.

Adding that figure to his anchor length, Diccon called out, "Sixteen meters, close enough—mayhap even seventeen." Was Bard simply trying to distract them? If so, estimating rope lengths didn't seem the best way to do it. Still, Bard seldom asked illogical questions, would suffer silence in lieu of stupidity.

"So?" Davvy shared a blank stare with Diccon and Luykas.

Sputtering figures under his breath between strokes, Bard murmured "Yes!" sounding almost pleased. Another few strokes as they awaited enlightenment, Diccon mutely tapping Bard's shoulder and claiming his oar, willing to split blisters to hear Bard's idea.

"Don't know if it'll work, but it might. Anchor's light, right? A grapnel—all sorts of nice hooks, flukey things, whatever you call'em. Meant to hook into the seabed or the beach—just like M'wa's claws—right?" After a long drink from their water jug, Bard wiped his sleeve across his mouth. "Oh, ye of little faith! Think of it as the equivalent of scaling a wall with a grappling iron and a rope. Some imagination, please, gentlemen!"

Luykas gave a whoop, slapping his thigh. "Think we can warp her in?"

"Don't know, you're more a sailor than I."

"What he means," Luykas cast an almost pleading look at Bard, rushing ahead at his permissive nod, "is that we throw the anchor as far ahead as we can, hook it firm, then—as you landlubbers say—haul the boat after it. We should gain ground instead of more sweat and blisters just struggling to stay in place. Especially if two of us row as if the hounds of the hells snapped at our heels while the other pair does the heave-hoing!" Luykas's enthusiasm was unfeigned—and almost contagious.

"And how," Davvy countered with deceptive mildness, "do we unanchor the anchor—once we catch up with it?"

Diccon burst out laughing, fluffing his stroke so badly his momentum pitched him off the bench. Action, yes! Any action, any effort that dangled the hope of reaching Jenneth—faster, sooner! "You brought up swimming, Davvy. Don't mind diving down and hauling it up, do you?"

Humming as she marched Dolly across to meet Mr. Monkey, Byrlie admired the deft way Sirikit controlled his movements, didn't make him overeagerly flop at Dolly. Except for her ability to read bigger words than she, Siri was a nice friend: she stayed comfortably close but never crowded, didn't talk much at all, left Byrlie to her thoughts—and that was fine. Frankly, she had entirely too much to think about. Papa was in trouble—or going to be in trouble—that much she'd learned from Mama, from what she guardedly didn't say as well as what she did. When Mama got tangled in one of her farseeings, Byrlie took care of her, because the near, the present could trip her up, hurt her, while she was busy seeing so far ahead.

She shook her head, unsure how to unpuzzle all the problems lodged in her brain. Papa talked in her head now, had done so several times since sailing off with Diccon and Davvy to save Jenneth. Actually, she didn't think he meant to 'speak her, kept saying things she couldn't understand or answer. Like overhearing someone talking to himself. Disquieting that her three favorite men—not to mention dear M'wa—had gone off without her. And Papa sounded so weary, strung thin, vibrating like a plucked string. Auntie Doyce had described him like that when she'd tried to explain Papa's spells. She'd never been around Papa when one of his rages struck, and Auntie Doyce said 'twas just as well 'cause Papa hurt others and himself when the rage took him. Where it took him she hadn't asked, because she suspected it was far, far away. Hard for him to get home again.

Siri smiled, brushed her arm with Mr. Monkey's paw. So kind of Harry to let Siri play with Mr. Monkey, and she'd promised to faithfully watch Siri to ensure Mr. Monkey came to no harm. Unlikely since Siri played nice and polite—'cept when she wrestled with Smir. Same as she tackled Harry sometimes—when you were littlest, you fought the best you could, any how, any way—or risk being tickled to death. Death. She cringed, threw a wobbly smile at Siri, waiting for Dolly to dance with Mr. Monkey.

Stifling a yawn, she bent Dolly into a curtsy. Early, no grown-ups yet, only she and Siri wide awake, even the boys slug-a-beds. No breakfast yet, 'cause she wasn't allowed to light the fire. Didn't matter, she and Siri had taken fruit from the bowl, a yesterday's biscuit apiece, all spread on a pink paisley kerchief Theo had bought her at the bazaar. Hadn't even teased for it, just admired it. She smoothed it with her free hand, pleased with its pattern against the green grass. Pleasantly sunny but not hot, settled here beside the walk that led from the kitchens to the courtyard. Insects making scraping sounds as the sun reached them, birds busily chirping and hip-hopping, not squabbling yet. Soon as anyone else got up, they'd know. Dolly danced with Mr. Monkey, sweep, swish over the grass. Oh, dear! Mr. Monkey tripped, took a tumble! Bad Dolly, naughty to stick out her ankle like that!

A rattle from the front gate, not clangy enough to indicate the gate had opened and shut. The breeze? Mayhap Khim or Khar slipping between the bars? Or just the way old things creaked and rattled and groaned all on their own sometimes. Auntie Doyce said she did as well. The ghatti liked to prowl, had already meandered around the yard, stopping for a friendly morning chin-rub. As usual, Siri'd dragged Khar into her lap, but the ghatta'd unwound herself after licking Siri's chin. Siri's face'd gone all scrunchy 'cause Khar's tongue was raspy rough.

Ah, good, footsteps now, decisive and light. Honoria from the sound of it, an adult to light the fire, start breakfast. 'Cept that Honoria didn't have much use for children, 'specially when they were the only ones around. Let an adult be watching, and she was nice as pie to Byrlie and the others. Easy to peer into the kitchen from this angle, see when Honoria started breakfast, not disturb her till then.

"Ha, Livotti!" Siri muttered against Mr. Monkey's head.

"What's a Livotti?" Byrlie whispered back. "Dolly wants to know."

"It's a . . . a," Siri hung Mr. Monkey's tail over her wrist, let him dangle, "a . . . name for some people."

"A name name or a word to describe'm?" Dolly didn't have a tail, couldn't swing like Mr. Monkey.

Rubbing Mr. Monkey's muzzle against her mouth, Siri's brow wrinkled. "Kinda both, I reckon. She is, too. Think she's one by name—or should be. Otherwise, yed call some'un a 'livotti' an it means they be . . . oh, standoffish, you know—'loof."

A longer explanation than Siri generally volunteered, but what she said fit Honoria. No sense asking about " 'loof." "Livotti, Livotti." It slid along the tongue, then snapped sharp on the ts. Ah, good, the crumple of paper, the rattle of kindling being stacked in the iron stove, the scratch of a lucifer. The cheery chatter of flames made the kitchen sound full of life. Honoria stood in front of the stove, reading a note.

When Khar's fur brushed her arm, Byrlie nearly jumped, hadn't noticed her silent-padding along as she busily stared kitchenward. Mayhap she and Khim were hungry, too, but Auntie Doyce and Theo would remedy that shortly. Doubtful Honoria'd offer them a treat, not the way Mama pampered M'wa or the other ghatti. Siri stretched an arm as if to restrain Khar from entering, but Byrlie shot her a look. Ghatti did as they wanted, and Honoria wasn't about to hurt them. Not receiving a snack was hardly hurting.

But Honoria acted unaware of the amber eyes studying her—and then she was. Had no choice as Khim prominently planted herself between Honoria and the stove, Khar flanking Honoria's right, between her and the door. A crunch as Honoria fisted the note into a ball, tossing it at the open stove lid. "Goodness, I didn't realize you two were about!" but she didn't sound happy at seeing them. The balled paper arced through the air and Khim sprang, batting it aside. It shot in front of Khar, and she began skittering it, one neat white paw and then the other tapping it ahead, snatching it back.

"Ah, playtime, is it?" Honoria stooped, hawk-swift with fingers clawed to snatch back the discarded note. "Well, find something else to play with, if you please." Her tight mouth worried Byrlie, even her neck muscles were tense, corded. Another grab, and again Khar evaded her, scooping and flipping the ball to Khim, who neatly blocked it and then picked it up in her mouth, trotting off, tail erect.

"Damnation!" Honoria started after Khim, but Khar wreathed round her ankles, always underfoot no matter which way Honoria went. Once Byrlie swore that Honoria purposely slammed her shin against Khar's middle. "Double damnation!" and threw up her hands dismissively. "Well, if anyone finds it, they'll throw it out like the trash it is."

Abruptly—too late for Byrlie to pull back—Honoria sensed other eyes on her, her audience larger than anticipated. "Good morning, Byrlie, Siri! Care to help mix cornmeal muffins?"

"She doan usely like us helping," Siri-the-suspicious muttered behind Mr. Monkey, but rose obediently, nudging Byrlie, who scrambled to her feet. Siri was right, it might be wise to distract Honoria, let her get annoyed at them and forget the ghatti's antics, silly ghatti!

"I'll get the eggs," she announced, sidling into the kitchen, hating to leave the sunshine behind. "Can Siri stir, please?" Khar gave her a look of amused thanks and padded off without a backward glance.

Khim and Khar padded along the streets, slipping in and out of shadow as the sun swung higher, the new day truly begun. While neither slunk nor hid, they instinctively selected a route designed not to call attention to their presence. One of the ghatti—with or without its Bond—about its business in Canderis provoked no alarm, a fact of life. Here in Samranth, however, they felt more alien with each finger-pointing exclamation, each quick intake of breath. A minor detour down an alley as a baker's 'prentice's eyes widened, his tray tilting, fresh muffins tumbling onto the street.

Khim carried the balled-up paper in her mouth as carefully as if she held a raw egg. **"Makes you know how Kharm, Mother of us all, felt each time she heard someone gasp 'larchcat,' "** Khar sniffed. **"Shall I tote it a bit?"** Khar knew the discomfort of gingerly holding something like that and only hoped the paper didn't taste of Honoria's scent. Paper never tasted especially appetizing, anyway.

"S'fine," Khim gave a snort, picking up her pace as someone shouted, "Will you look at that?" **"Through the bazaar? Faster?"** At Khar's almost imperceptible nod, she swerved down one of the narrow, cluttered dirt lanes that separated the backs of the stalls. A few stall-owners were unpacking their wares, collected at first light from shops, docks, or farms, but they were too occupied to pay the ghatti much notice—except for one man.

"Hallo, my striped beauties! Out alone so early?" Momsvaert, the cushion-seller who'd helped fight off the dagga boys, peered over a pile of pillows rainbow-stacked to his chin. In fact, his chin-wedge kept the plump cushions from falling. Khar and Khim each dutifully rubbed a bare shin in passing, crisscrossing to repeat their greeting on opposite sides and then made an about-face. Both battled a powerful urge to peer inside his mind, check if he bore any blame for Ozer's accounting woes. Besides, his cushions gave off an aura of delectable comfort, fluffy and generously-sized to accommodate a ghatta curled tight or limply sprawled in the depths of sleep.

"Stay awhile," he urged, dumping his load inside the stall, standing back to admire the riotous commingling of color and texture before rearranging them by size and hue. "Smoked fish for breakfast."

Khar had already scented it, hadn't needed his reminder. Eyeing her, Khim swallowed suggestively; neither had breakfasted this morning. **"No, straight to Ozer Oordbeck's office."** Smoked fish, beckoning pillows—shameful bribery to make her lose all willpower. The next thing she knew, she'd be sunk in decadence, reading Momsvaert's mind without permission! It was more than that, though. The man made her restive, something discomfiting emanating from Momsvaert, rather like Honoria, but more pronounced. Butting Khim ahead, she refused to look back even when she heard the crackle of paper as the fish was unwrapped.

Avoiding a half-dozen hissing, snappish geese, each staked by a leg, they scampered on, weaving, shifting lanes until they reached the bazaar's far edge. **"What if he's not in his office yet?"** Khim sounded anxious. **"It's early."** But before Khar could answer, she sneezed, a wafting confusion of scents from an herb-seller's booth—dried herbs, decocted oils and seasoned vinegars—clashing in her nostrils.

"Lady bless." A borrowed saying, courtesy of Parm, who'd absorbed so many religious snippets from his beloved Harrap that there were plenty to share among the ghatti.

And Harrap's adages naturally turned Khar's mind to Aidannae and her broom, but she forced it back, concentrating on Ozer Oordbeck. **"Think he'll be in, he's been cat-curious,"** a high compliment, **"to find how the figures were tampered with. Besides, people here start early, then go all sleepy after lunch."** A fine idea as far as she was concerned, but then ghatti devoted as much time as possible to sleeping or dozing. Oh, those pillows. . . !

Dropping the balled paper and putting a paw on it to secure it, Khim pointed her nose skyward, flexing her jaw. **"Are there numbers on this? Like the scraps?"**

"Don't know." Khar's forehead wrinkled, her stripes merging. **"Couldn't resist when Honoria crushed it like that. Mayhap it's a love note. Or a market list. But someone should see, check."** Giving her daughter an admonitory look, she scooped up the note, trotting ahead, confident Khim would catch up. Love note—what'd possessed her to say that in front of Khim? It could hardly come from Jenret, he was too far distant. Besides, given the chance, Rawn would've shredded it. She appreciated Honoria's usefulness—indeed, her disparaging comment about Geerat Netlenbos had been on the mark—but she still couldn't bring herself to like her. Doyce was her sole concern: whatever touched Doyce touched her, happiness or sorrow, love or betrayal.

They'd reached Ozer Oordbeck's office now, only to discover all the long windows still shut and draped. **"Ho, mayhap they aren't here yet."** Khim sat and scratched her chin, surveying the building. **"No, I hear people inside. A whole crowd—children, too."** Slipping round, she checked the shady side, rearing up to press at the side door, only to find it securely bolted. Bounding back, she gave a troubled sniff. **"Doesn't feel right, does it? That intensity that's louder than a noise when humans struggle to be oh-so-silent. Fear's loud that way."**

"Scritch-scratch at the window," Khar instructed. A fusion of fear and worry leaked from within, no need to seek to determine that—it was near-palpable. Obligingly Khim drew her claws across the glass, her scratch producing an obscene, tooth-grinding shriek no human could bear, would be compelled to respond to such a sound. Yet not a curtain quivered. **"Vocalize. Politely insistent."** Well, see what response that generated. Khim began an interrogatory, "Raow? Raow? RAA-OOW?" and continued scratching, varying her pace, allowing a spine-quivering anticipation to build.

At length a curtain shifted whisker-wide as Ozer's troubled face appeared and vanished, the window opening a crack as he squatted to match their level. "Bless the Lady and Her Disciples!" his whisper was barely audible. "To the side door! Quick! The Lady's sent you to me in my need!''

Bolting round, Khar and Khim fidgeted as the locks snapped back, the door opening a scant hand's breadth. One after the other, they slipped inside, Ozer blocking the door with shoulder and hip, anxiously scanning the walkway and patch of lawn. ''Please, where is she? Doyce Marbon, even that Theo fellow? Didn't anyone accompany you?''

Both mystified and miffed by his greeting, Khar emphatically shook her head. Grappling with the realization that the ghatti had come alone, Ozer double-bolted the door in anguished silence. ''A note for me?'' As he fell to his knees, Khar dropped it in his hand. ''Oh, please, please, listen to me, ghatti—I need your help so much!'' Tears slow-tracked along his cheeks, though he paid them no heed as they dripped, splotching the wood floor. ''It's passing strange to talk with you, as if you understand—that you *do* understand—but I have to tell someone! Share my burden!''

''I'm going to 'speak Theo!'' An impatient lash of her tail as Khim slanted a look at Khar. **''Want him to bring Doyce?''**

Comfort, that Khar could give as she rubbed against Ozer, stretching her front paws onto his bowed shoulders, butting under his chin, uncaring at the dampness soaking her fur. **''No, wait. Doyce has so much on her mind. First let's find out what's bothering Ozer.''** All the Sunderlies offered in abundance were problems and more problems— enough to make her wish they'd remained home, that Doyce still served as Seeker General. Blast the Elders for insisting she'd been too comfortable, complacent!

Three blue-patterned china plates, all with chipped rims and assorted cracks; one soup plate with a scrolled ivy edging; four everyday wooden bowls; two crockery chaffay mugs, one lacking its handle; two wooden tankards, rims and handles smooth-polished from use; and one delicate glass goblet set way back on the flimsy shelf. Each day Aqua washed and dried them whether or not they'd seen use. If they came directly off the shelf, she followed a subroutine before washing: first blow on them to dislodge spiders and other insects, thatch splinters; then rub off any peculiar growths blossoming in the damp cracks of the wooden bowls and tankards. Most of the time it was damp.

Trickle the wash water on the sickly starflower plant so painstakingly transplanted. Restake it, and speak encouragingly to the yellow flower buds, most hanging dejectedly. Swish the palm broom across the packed earth floor inside, sweep up any ashes. Toss her sheet over the bushes outside to air it—if it weren't raining. Wipe the planked table that leaned against the wall—oh, she should have done it before sweeping. Now crumbs littered the floor. Take her spare shirt—Pommy's, really—down to the steam to scrub, then spread it on another bush. The borrowed short trews she wore needed a wash, but they were her only ones. And for the last few days, discreetly check to ensure no one—Pommy, Hirby, even Tigger-dog—could see, and rush streamward to surreptitiously rinse the bloody rags left soaking in a large, hollow gourd. A burning shame at this, though it came with womanhood. That much she remembered.

Tired, she sat by the fire pit outside the hut, brow in hand. Her head had ached abominably of late, and Aqua couldn't understand why, not when the rest of her slowly recovered from . . . from whatever it was that had brought her here. Wherever here was. Agitated, restless, she lightly drummed at her temples, longing for some new activity to temporarily distract her from the throbbing, banish her bad mood. Something in her head wanted out—or in. What it might be she hadn't a clue; the harder she thought, anxious to capture it, the more it fled from her.

Picking up a fallen palm frond—it didn't seem to matter how often she neatened things inside or out—she stripped off a long leaf and thrust it against a coal. Waited for it to catch and burn. Then she could hold it near, observe it twist and shrivel. Unsatisfied, she lit another. No, Pommy didn't like it when she played like this. Somehow instinct told her it wasn't wise to rile Pommy, not after she'd seen him threatening to kick Tigger when Hirby wasn't around. Lips pulled back in a snarl, Tigger'd growled. Let Hirby kick or beat him, though, and he whined and whimpered, tail between his legs. Would she cringe, belly-slink back to

lick the hand that had beaten her, like Tigger did? Mayhap.
She wasn't sure, didn't want to find out. Pommy had saved
her life, he'd told her so many times.

Much as the fronds cried and begged to be thrust on the
coals, she tossed the cluster behind her to avoid temptation.
If she couldn't play with the fire, what to do, what to do?
Way too early to start supper. Try to weave a basket? Her
last lopsided, loose-woven attempt leaned against the hut,
mocking her, more like a fish-trap than a basket. The
pounding in her head intensified . . . let me out, *out*! Let
me in, *in*! Would that she could, because then mayhap
she'd learn who she was. But mayhap the inside Aqua
wasn't as sweetly docile as Pommy's Aqua—was bad, unruly, a minx? What Pommy said, and didn't say, intimated
that. Except . . . how was he to know—unless he'd learned
where his gift from the sea really came from, who Aqua
really was?

Wanna play with the fire! No! Bad Aqua or rather, bad
person who's now good Aqua. Yet again, that skin-crawling
sensation of being spied on, even though Pommy and Hirby
scavenged south of Owl's Head. Round eyes touched with
the green of new leaves unblinkingly peering from here or
there, boring into her as she washed or swept or sat outside
by the fire pit. Even at night they pierced her dreams, such
sad, yearning eyes, so prettily green, wanting something
from her. Everyone craving something from her—and she
couldn't guess what that something was!

It was all too much! With a muffled curse Aqua leaped
up and grabbed the discarded palm frond, shredding its
remains, ripping and tearing, feeling it slice her fingers.
Blood. She licked, tentative, overcome by an urge to rub
her bottom, as if something had nipped her there. Oddly,
the thought of being nipped brought an all-encompassing
joy.

Do something, anything—quick! Run down the dunes to
the beach, hunt for clams, for shells or driftwood? No, the
sun was still too high. If her freshly healed skin burned, it
would hurt worse than searing hot coals. Stop hammering,
head! Stop staring, eyes! Stop, stop, stop! Aqua—her name
meant water, fluid, liquid . . . aqua quenches fire.

Tossing her hair to shield her face from those prying
eyes, she sank to her knees. Was water more powerful than

flame? Fire could make water evaporate; water could quench fire. Fire burned through the dross, cleansed, cleaned—a forest fire meant new life springing up afterward. Water was birth as well as death, capable of patiently eroding most anything over time.

With a squall of pain she scrambled into the hut on hands and knees, taking refuge in the corner, huddling in a tight ball. Ah, marginally safer, better inside, diffused light, the earth beneath her cowering flesh smooth and cool, the hut containing yet not constricting. Breath shuddery, she stared blankly at the floor, let her restless fingers scrabble in the dirt, scratch out tiny stars, squiggles, a chubby cat. A single deft swipe erased it all—just as her mind had been erased—and she began to draw anew. Intent, absorbed in her handiwork, she uncurled herself and knelt, debating whether to use a fork to make her patternings, how it would serve. The dirt lodging under her nails disgusted her, and her fingertips felt sore, but with the fork she could . . .

The eerie impression of staring eyes washed over her, threatening to drown her, sweep her away, even within the hut's safe confines. Watching, watching her! *No! Don't move, don't look over your shoulder till you're sure. Yes, it's slinking closer, staring, oh, Oh, OH! NO!*

Spinning on one knee, she confronted the eyes but found herself blinded, squinting in the brightness streaming in the doorway. "Stop staring at me!" And something, something large and furry scrambled madly to safety outside. By the time she cleared the door, all she could see was a branch swaying from a hasty passage, and hear a crackling crash in the distance.

Tail like a bottlebrush, ears back-folded, Pw'eek slumped against a tree trunk, trembling. **"Oh, Jenneth!"** she inwardly sobbed, even though mindspeech did no good, her dear heart batting it away like an annoying fly. Sinking onto her belly, she washed between her hind toes, chewed at a rough claw, debating whether to return to the hut, reveal herself to Jenneth.

Why, oh why wouldn't she listen, answer? What happened if their Bond dissolved, was lost? Chin on her paws,

Pw'eek gloomily realized she had no idea, still uncertain what Bonding encompassed to begin with. Did Jenneth hate her, want nothing more to do with her? Parasoling a piece of leaf over its head, an ant marched in front of her nose. Soon another and another marched by, the diversion making her feel a little better.

"Get out, cat. Shoo!" Doors and shutters slamming in her face and Kwee's in Windle Port. No one willing to let them in, except for Miz Hasten—Kwee'd charmed her, she had. Flirted, rubbed, and purred. She thought about it, about shutters and doors, of being outside when you wanted inside, and inside when you wanted out. How did you make a door open for you? Stretching her neck, she daintily nipped a leaf promenading by her nose, lifting it and its clinging ant, setting them both down farther on. Leaf and ant tumbled, righted themselves, quick-marching back to their line, shoving their way in.

Should she nip Jenneth again? Would that work? So tempting to start all over, fresh and new. Two whole days since Wartle'd left her on her own, and she'd been constantly watching, hidden but observing her beloved from every vantage point she could find. Had neglected finding food, water, in favor of remaining near, even as her hope dwindled. Her stomach reproached her. Last night, greatly daring, she'd slipped inside the hut once the man's breathing went deep and steady, her Jenneth's whisper-soft. Had pressed against Jenneth's hip in such ecstasy that she'd feared her purr rumbled loud as thunder. For the briefest instant a sleep-tossed hand had brushed her back—rapture! But touching had semi-wakened Jenneth, and Pw'eek had fled as fast and silently as she was able.

Did ants taste good? Plunk right in front of their trail, open her mouth, let them march into her tummy? Her lovely lily belly! Oh, those moments when Jenneth's hand, her lips would caress her lily belly! Now, no matter what she 'spoke, how much she pleaded and begged, professing her love, Jenneth wouldn't listen! Left her crying at the door, begging to be invited in. Slowly it came to her, Jenneth wasn't being rude, denying her; she literally could *not* hear, understand. But how to reteach her that language, the special, private language of their Bond?

A sniff at a passing ant—no, they smelled sharp and bit-

ter, too strong. Now . . . mayhap sprinkled on fish . . . or
mutton . . . or fowl, they'd offer a nice contrast . . . Food!
She had to hunt soon, must. If she wasted away to a mere
shadow-ghatten, Jenneth wouldn't recognize her. A shiver
rippled her spine. If she revealed herself, she had to be
sure that man didn't lurk somewhere near. A visceral sensation that he despised cats, loathed ghatti. Some folk literally
had such animus oozing from their pores, positively stank
with hate. At least that scent didn't emanate from Jenneth.

Tonight she'd remain outside the hut, stay hidden while
she whispered to Jenneth of their love, their Bond, bathe
her in such love that she'd remember, have to recall it. In
the morning, once the Pommy-man had left . . . And if that
Tigger-dog came bouncing along, she'd rip out his eyes,
gouge and slash and bite, send him packing! Jenneth had
hugged Tigger, she'd seen it, and that place in Jenneth's
arms belonged to *her,* to Pw'eek, Pw'eek the brave and
true! Pw'eek, the brave and true . . . who couldn't even
figure out how to knock so Jenneth would open the door
of her mind. The space around that door was stained, cluttered with festering, jumbled emotions, turbulent confusion,
and an aching emptiness. But she could fill that emptiness—would!

A scarlet bird burst from the foliage, diving low and zig-
zagging to avoid some hawklike predator hot on his tail
feathers. Without thinking Pw'eek launched herself, paw
swooping, smashing the bird to the ground, stunned. Grabbing its head, she shook the bird, let her teeth slice through
its spine. Dinner! Forcing herself under control, she began
licking the feathers, her burred tongue rasping and plucking. A downy, salmon-shaded feather stuck to the bridge
of her nose, left her staring cross-eyed, bobbing her head
to dislodge it. Eat now, think more later, true sleep instead
of half-nap. And tonight, find the words, the tones, the
knowledge to touch Jenneth. Show her the truth.

Why did Jenneth call herself Aqua? It set Pw'eek
aquiver, remembering the rocking, colliding storm waves,
her salt-encrusted fur, her thirst. After so many days adrift,
water was the last thing Jenneth should want to think
about!

PART
FIVE

Cradling one knee, the other leg extended—she harbored no intention, thank you, of checking how much her abused muscles would flex without complaint—Doyce watched as the sunlight crept up the trellised wallpaper pattern, making the stenciled flowers bloom brightly. A part of her wished the insect netting hazily draping her bed were capable of blocking the noises outside that indicated a waking world. A locust sawed its wings, buzzing a long, drawn-out note that seemed capable of continuing until dusk. Muted traffic on the Esplanade, the chatter of children in the kitchen below, and the clank of a cast iron stove lid. Good, someone was up and had started breakfast.

Contentment at basking in her own private, netted universe alternated with supreme grouchiness, a legacy of the preceding night. Sleep hadn't ameliorated it, had instead bequeathed the residue of a headache. A yawn and a stretch before she thumped against her propped-up pillows. Diccon and Davvy'd 'spoken her last night, apparently laboring under the misguided belief that a joint communique would be doubly reassuring. As if belatedly discovering your son and two dear friends had been falsely imprisoned was reassuring! Especially when she'd believed them busily searching for Jenneth! That had been irritation Number One.

Irritation Number Two involved her growing suspicion that Khar, dear Khar, oh, we didn't want to disturb you with the news, had known this. About time for a talk with the ghatta, and she debated 'speaking her, dragging her from the kitchen where she undoubtedly sat, keenly supervising breakfast preparations and cadging handouts.

Against her better judgment she smiled, the corner of

her mouth quirking. So much for Davvy setting a good example for Diccon, guiding him! She'd have thought Bard . . . Bard! Her fingers knotted the sheet . . . Bard! Lindy's foreseeing couldn't be, mustn't be true! A misinterpretation, a mistake, Lindy was no seer, was far from infallible. Unlike the ghatti, the truth of her visions often proved ambiguous. That *had* to be it! Just because she foresaw something didn't make it literally true. Dropping the sheet, her fingers sketched the Lady's eight-point star, too late perhaps, but still superstitious enough to try to ward off fate. After all, nothing was inevitable . . . Except death.

And then Irritation Number Three had struck. Just as she'd fallen asleep, Jenret's mindvoice had hesitantly interrupted, subdued, filled with a·tension that left her fretful that one of them—him or her?—was in more parlous straits than she'd realized. Yet he'd been oddly circumspect about his own problems, shifting the focus to her again and again, overly earnest, almost too considerate. He'd always been heedful of her concerns and needs, but never to such an exclusive degree. The more tactful and even-tempered he became, the more she wanted to rail at him, ask what he'd done with the real Jenret—or was he feeling guilty about something? Even after a night's sleep, it still baffled her.

Hiking her nightshift, she pinched the extra flesh around her waist. Enough to make her want to join Jenret in a bout of swamp fever; he'd informed her in passing that his pantaloons hung off his hips. Silly to wish that, but hardly silly to wish she stood by his side, her hand in his, sharing their fears over Jenneth. Jenneth! Alive, she sternly lectured herself. Lindy *swore* she lived; and in this Doyce firmly believed Lindy had seen true. No matter the distance, the uncertainty, the essential cord binding mother and child had not been sundered, simply stretched.

The chaffay aroma seductively curling up the stairs finally caught her attention, left her weighing whether to swing both legs out of bed and rise. But no, she deserved a little more solitude—needed it for her soul's sake. Should she tell Lindy that Bard's relatives were looking for him? Jenret had held back something during that telling, exhibiting the same scrupulous consideration she'd evinced in not mentioning Lindy's foreseeing about Bard. She wanted to know more, learn everything she could first.

One way to find out, at least some of it. *"Khar, beloved. Come snuggle, we need to talk."* She wriggled a foot, adding, *"I'll let you attack my foot under the sheet."* Bribery, but so what? Khar still adored the game, as did she, as long as Khar's claws remained retracted.

No immediate response, so she broadened her mindvoice, let it range more widely. Hmph! Rambling again, or off sunning herself somewhere? Khim had become fascinated by the tiny sand-tan lizards that turned green to match lawn or leaf; Khar was fond of them as well, though she pretended she merely kept Khim company. Still no response, so she pressed outward more forcibly, beyond the grounds of Dolphin House. Not exactly worried, but concerned. A concern that had expanded as Khar aged, the sick, lurking certitude that someday there would be no response. Gone, forever. She dashed a tear from her eye.

An arm bearing a yellow mug of chaffay made a disembodied appearance around the door, finally followed by Lindy's head. Haloed with sun she looked pale but cheerfully resolute, as if no darkness had shadowed her heart yesterday. Except that Doyce knew Lindy too well, the solemn child had become a solemn woman. "Come on, sleepyhead!" Lindy came closer, still teasing her, holding the mug beyond reach.

"I've been awake for some time—believe it or not!" she grumped. "If you don't release that chaffay into my custody forthwith, you're in deep trouble."

But at that moment Khar's mindvoice homed in on Doyce. **"Good, you're awake. Can you wash quick, pull on some clothes? We need you. And bring the others, too. Ozer Oordbeck's in enough serious distress to make him truly 'Oh-Oh.' "** Scrambling clear of the sheet and batting away the netting Doyce snagged the mug.

"Grab me a clean shirt and pantaloons, Lindy." Half the chaffay went down at a gulp as Doyce sloppily poured water from the ewer into the washbowl with her other hand. "Tell the others the ghatti want us. Ozer's in some sort of trouble."

Impatiently toweling off soap suds at her hairline, Doyce rough-combed her hair and dragged on her shirt before her nightshift hit the floor. **"We're at Ozer's office, in case you**

didn't realize. Bring the children," Khar emphasized,
"whatever you do, don't leave them behind, alone."

Repeating Khar's admonition, Doyce shouted after
Lindy, already halfway down the hall as she called for Theo
and Honoria, began repeating the children's names.

Harry stuck his head inside, eyes rolling ceilingward upon
discovering his aunt not fully dressed. "What's up, Auntie?
Are we having an adventure?"

"I sincerely hope not." The new, gauzy pantaloons hung
like limp, overcooked string beans, tangling as she thrust
her legs into them. "But I'll tell you what, Harry. Find my
sword for me, and you can carry it, be my weapon-bearer."

"Supremo!" he crowed and shot out.

"Well, Khar? Are we having an adventure?"

"Not sure if that's the word I'd choose." Her mindvoice
took on a meditative quality. **"Crisis is more like it. Best
let Ozer tell you."**

Distinctly recalling Jenret's mention of how spacious and
airy, uncluttered, Ozer Oordbeck's office was, Doyce wondered if Jenret's critical faculties had totally deserted him
under stress. Obviously he'd been distraught over Jenneth,
anxious to start his search, but he was usually an acute
observer. . . . Stepping over a child stacking blocks, Doyce
grimaced as her thigh muscles registered the unaccustomed
stretching. No room to swing a crutch, though she'd
brought it from habit more than genuine need now. Still,
it gave her confidence, took the place of her absent Seeker's staff, as suitable a substitute as Theo's borrowed
broom.

Although adult voices were pitched discreetly low, the
constant babble of childish cadences, pure and high, assaulted her ears. Towhead to strawberry blonde, toddlers
to adolescents. Nor were they all still enough to number,
though she reached ten, only to decide she'd missed some;
Ozer's brood totaled twelve, so he'd said. Now her own
temporary brood—Harry and Byrlie, Sirikit and Kasimir—
intermingled with the throng. "Mercy," Lindy breathed in
her ear, "you'd need a full-time Seeker-pair on call to un-

ravel who did what to whom first! I only had seven
siblings!"

A foxlike bark of amusement from Honoria at Lindy's
comment, though her gray eyes never wavered from a little
one whose dirty hands ached to stroke her powder-blue
divided skirt. Scooping up the offender, Theo tucked him?/
her? against his chest as he surveyed the crowd. The older
children, those perhaps twelve and up, all sat or sprawled
on the floor, intent, almost transfixed by the papers spread
around them. In the background a whiz-hum, clickety-click
as abacus beads zipped along their wires, while other children mumbled as they rolled and tapped their knuckles
against each other. The whole scene boasted an air of unre-
ality, children patiently laboring in the semidarkness at
some arcane task.

"You didn't miscount." Khar wove among the children,
her tail tickling a neck, her shoulder rubbing an arm or
knee as she made her circuitous way to Doyce's side. **"Two
are missing. Ozer's been left with ten instead of twelve."**

For a moment the significance of Khar's comment didn't
register, left her still assuming that two of Oordbeck's
brood were elsewhere. Two women, highly similar in build
and coloring, kept vigil at the long windows, slipping from
one to another for a fresh vantage, feathering the curtain
for the briefest of views. Doubtless Ozer's wife and sister-
in-law. And Ozer was here, had brusquely hustled them
inside, staying behind to lock the door. *"Are two of the
older ones out on errands? Delivering messages?"*

Khar's response, an almost supercilious head-to-toe scrutiny of her Bondmate, set Doyce's insides writhing with
frustration. Blast the ghatta! **"Aren't you completely awake
yet?"** It was so unfair! True, her one hastily gulped mug
of chaffay hadn't been nearly enough—but it wasn't the
residue of sleep that clouded her mind. All she'd accomplished with her early waking was to battle her personal
problems into submission, not solve them.

A hand on her shoulder from behind, large-knuckled and
long-fingered. "Khim says," Theo gulped and his Adam's
apple scampered up and down like a mouse inside a snake,
"that two of Ozer's children have been kidnapped. Someone's no longer content with anon-anonymous threats, has
taken action." Only his near-flawless enunciation and the

peremptory clutch of his hand revealed the iron discipline
that overrode his insecurities at such moments.

But now Ozer had sidled into the office proper, making
a circuit of the room to confer with his wife and sister-in-
law and an older lad who also stood guard. Overnight his
tan had leached to a cottony-paleness, more pallid than his
sun-bleached hair. The stubble on his cheeks glistened like
translucent grains of sand in the subdued light. "Come in
here, it's more private. Fewer children underfoot, too." A
ghost of a smile wobbled but remained in place as he beckoned them. "Though I'd rather have more."

The private office to the rear of the large, open room
could barely house its safe, two rattan chairs flaking green
paint, and a table with one leg leveled by a wheel from a
child's toy. The far wall bulged with shelves and pigeon-
holes crammed with loose receipts and invoices, rolls of
ledger paper, yet office supplies stood stacked with finicky
exactitude on adjacent shelves, each necessity alphabeti-
cally arranged and labeled. Ozer might have lost his battle
with the constant onslaught of paperwork, but the supply
shelves showed he hadn't been conquered. The room bore
a faintly forlorn air, the repository of too many minor de-
feats resolutely shunted aside, clearing the way for the newest crisis.

Two oil lamps cast grotesque shadows as well as unwel-
come heat, and the crowded closeness of their bodies emphasized the rising temperature outside and within.
Dejectedly leaning against a wall covered with fanciful children's drawings, Ozer slid down until he folded at hips and
knees, his body forming a chair of flesh and bone. His va-
cant gaze roamed the water-stained ceiling, finally focusing
as he forced his mind to not only confront his predicament,
but to admit it to outsiders, strangers.

"The worst has happened. 'Twasn't a bluff." Thigh muscles bulging, he held his position, brow filmed with sweat,
sweat pooling in the hollows of his collarbones. "Somehow
Evangeline and Altreetus were snatched away, plucked
from their beds while the others slept."

"Precisely when did you discover them missing?" But
before Doyce could ask any more, Lindy chimed in, earnest, empathic. "And you all came here for safety? To be
together?"

Ozer nodded, his mouth rounded. "Discovered it before the Lady's moons were high. Zandra had to rouse the others, bring them all here so she could tell me. Didn't dare split us more, give *them*," he nearly spat the word, "another chance. We hurried back to the house, searched again, then tried to sleep. Feels safer here, somehow—they haven't violated this sanctuary yet."

"Was there a note? Any indication what to do to reclaim the children?" Doyce knew the "short" answers already, Khar had informed her. Still, better for Ozer to repeat it, the more oft-said, the more tangible it became, not simply a nightmare but a harsh reality to be faced. And with each repetition, seemingly inconsequential, previously unmentioned details often surfaced. Theo watched and listened with the quiet, encompassing intensity that marked a good Seeker, sorting facts, comparing and analyzing them in different configurations. And all the while Khim was poised to pounce on any discrepancies he might miss.

"They—damn it, if only I knew who *they* are!" He pressed the heels of his hands against his temples. "They ordered me to bring all the paperwork, every record I have on Wycherley-Saffron to the old Janacz & Sons warehouse tonight. It's not used anymore—cheaper to let it fall down than pay to demolish it. Rudy and Jaz and I combed through it at first light. Couldn't get the Guardians to help—didn't surprise me. They said the note indicates possible foul play, but that it's more likely the children wandered off, became lost on their own. Until I have further proof . . .

"Anyway, we're to deposit the records there and leave. With luck Vannie and Treet will be returned safe and sound. If we're unlucky, blinded or . . . or dead!" His hands pounded his anguish against his head.

"Then why," Honoria radiated a brisk but-me-no buts attitude, "are half your offspring poring over those records as if they were reading an adventure tale? Why aren't they busily gathering every scrap of paper they can lay hands on, stacking it, packing it for tonight? Combing the files to ensure nothing's missed?" She'd risen as she spoke, edging round the table to stand over Ozer, clenched fists hovering over his head as if she'd willingly pound further sense into him. "Don't tell me you're not surrendering your precious papers? That you'll simply father two more children to fill the gap?"

Never had Doyce heard Honoria's voice so richly rebuking—Lady bless, she showed emotion, after all! While she agreed with Honoria's sentiment, if not her censure, Doyce had to protest. "Honoria! Hear the man out. Yes, the records *are* valuable to Wycherley-Saffron, but scarcely in the same league as the lives of two children. You know that. Ozer knows it far better than you. Let's hear his reasoning."

Wearily sliding upright, Ozer tugged his sticky caftan clear of his chest. "Oh, I'll give over the papers—willingly—never fear! I'd give my eyes, my life, for those two, for any of them out there!" Leaning close and intimate, practically nose to nose with Honoria, he spoke with deliberate emphasis. "But I will be *damned* if destroying the papers destroys their trail! I aim to find every trick, every falsehood those ledgers hold, lodge them in my heart and mind. Recreate every scrap from memory. That's why the children are cramming away. I'm not planning on packing especially neatly." He gave a little giggle before recovering himself.

An inky finger hovering near the lace on Honoria's placket, he prepared to drive home his point. "I take *pride* in my job, in doing it to the *best* of my abilities! And my best is very, *very* good! People depend on me. And I will *not* fail them—neither my children nor my employers! I am *not* like some . . ." his burning eyes forced Honoria to glance away, "some sniveling, spineless scion of Livotti-Rutenfranz, the feeble vestige of a once-proud family, fleeing all responsibility. Do you understand me?"

To Doyce's surprise, Honoria backed clear, pacifying, "Fine. I'll not hinder you. Indeed, I'll even help."

"Khar, what's this about? I feel as if they're conversing on a different plane than I'm hearing." She'd never particularly pretended to understand what motivated Honoria—they shared too little common ground, except for one thing—but Ozer had fixated all his anger and resentment on the woman. Had sounded as if he issued a challenge or a warning. Even stranger, Honoria had taken it with reasonable grace, more than Doyce could have mustered.

"I know! Want me to Seek?" Khar's suppressed eagerness took Doyce aback.

"Didn't Khim sufficiently plumb Ozer's depths? Is there more to uncover? Other than guilt at failing his children?"

"I meant Honoria."

"No! Absolutely not. There's no need." The speed and passion of her response startled Khar, startled Doyce herself. There wasn't any need, *was* there? Allow Khar to winnow through Honoria's mind, discover things she didn't wish to learn about Jenret, about Honoria's and Jenret's relationship? How could the ghatta have suggested such an unpalatable idea, mingling personal with professional concerns? To use Khar's gift for personal gain, private reassurance was to take unfair advantage of another human being, just as Resonants had been so accused in past times.

Khar flinched, lowered her head. **"Fine. I shan't."** Whiskers spreading as she yawned away her embarrassment, she relented enough to add, **"Livotti. Heard Byrlie and Siri use the word this morning—means stiff-necked, snobbish, aloof. Strange, Ozer was convinced in the Truth-Seeking Ceremony that the Livotti and Rutenfranz folk were long-gone, dispersed or dead."**

"I remember. But he seemed to be intimating something when he made his point." But they could scarcely debate such details, not when children's lives hung in the balance. "Ozer, any objection if we send Khar and Khim out to explore? Say, around the warehouses and anywhere else they might wander?" Both of the ghattas rippled with muted anticipation, their pupils dilating until only amber rims showed. "While you and your family may feel safer here—and I don't blame you—the rest of us should be out and about, keep our eyes sharp and our ears pitched for anything relevant, from rumor to fact. Kasimir, I think, should be good at that. Siri, too. People often discount a child's presence, don't check their speech when they're near."

Ozer's defensive argument with Honoria had brought near-normal color to his face, almost affirming his membership amongst the living. "The ghatti, yes. Adults, too. Besides, I can't control your actions, nor should I. But please, *please* don't send the little ones out to do adult work. They may be street-bred, clever and quick, but if anything should . . ." he couldn't finish. "I won't save my children's lives by sacrificing someone else's child!"

His sense of honor was finer than most. As Ozer rejoined his family, stalked by an irrational fear something horrible might have transpired during his absence, Doyce began to outline their plans, determine meeting points for passing word back. Anything to make the day spin faster, night visit sooner. "Any problem if we bring in food?" Doyce stuck her head outside and caught Ozer's eye. "We've a long wait before evening, and the children will be hungry long before that." She already was, for that matter.

Under her breath, Honoria added, "And some extra diapers." Her nose wrinkling, "I don't think the youngest are fully trained yet." Well, Honoria was nothing if not practical and pragmatic. Somewhere in her past she'd obviously dealt with little ones.

❖

Staring at the arched ceiling—silvery stars afloat on deepest blue—Doyce swung her heels, avoiding the curved teak legs of her tapestry chair. Obviously a new level of meaning to the phrase, "cooling one's heels," and frankly she'd cooled her heels long enough! Leave? Grit her teeth and stay? The delicately veined marble walls offered no advice, nor did the reed carpet with its artful imprint of lily pads and lavender blossoms, fat orange carp feeding and feuding around each floating leaf. Very clever and very expensive.

What had possessed her to seek an audience with the Governor when she could be doing something useful: devising a strategy, combing the back alleys for clues, wringing a confession from . . . With an openhanded smack to her thigh she disabused herself of such daydreaming. Ozer's two little ones were missing, and the odds of finding them happily squabbling over a toy wagon in the halls of the Governor's Mansion were *very* small. What she hugged to her heart was the hope that the Governor, Erzebet Hoetmer, might be reasonably lucid, today of all days. Lucid enough to perform a minor miracle—decipher the intricacies of Sunderlies intrigue, send men to scour the town, nip danger in the bud by arresting . . . Enough! When the explicable failed, one had to consider the inexplicable, acts of faith, more or less.

Craning around first one chair wing and then the other, she frowned at the chain of anterooms receding in each direction and then curled deep into its cushions. Each, as far as she could judge, was inhabited by people impatient to importune Governor Hoetmer for some special privilege or favor. Interesting. If the Governor couldn't be counted on, a good many people apparently hadn't yet been apprised of that sad fact.

Though it flew in the face of logic, there were always some who believed themselves deserving of a special privilege or dispensation. She'd suffered through similar pleadings during her years as Seeker General, and despite herself she felt a twinge of sister-sympathy for the Governor, even as her wait lengthened.

"Oh, hullo—didn't see you denned up all cozy in the chair." Like a child caught out, she removed her feet from the upholstery and sat primly, hands folded in her lap, speechless at seeing who stood before her, a crested bronze-and-leather helmet balanced on his hip to display its high polish. His dolman artfully gathered at one shoulder to reveal its crimson lining, Geerat Netlenbos gave a charming, self-deprecating smile that revealed even white teeth. "Mind company? The other anterooms are packed, people about to spread picnic luncheons while they wait." A polite pause, and when she neither granted nor denied permission, he continued, "That is, if you'll allow the intrusion?"

"With your rank, I suppose you'll gain the Governor's ear right away. For whatever good it does you." Hardly a gracious response—after all, he'd shown courtesy at their meeting, even if she'd despised him for his rigid interpretation of his duties. Now her frustration made her sound as if she were zealously numbering those who succeeded in seeing the Governor ahead of her.

"Sorry! No, of course, please—join me." A certain level of manners was called for, she supposed, giving him a wooden smile. All polished and sleek, boots glossy, every burnished detail about him annoyed her more than she'd have believed possible. Sitting on the chair's edge, he shrugged a shoulder until his dolman fell into place, then balanced his helmet on his knee like a pampered pet.

His refined contrast to her own rumpled looks set her to internally inventorying her flaws. Her missing tabard distressed her—utterly unprofessional—but she'd not wanted to waste time retrieving it, had begged the loan of a biscuit-colored, polished cotton jacket from Zandra. At least it didn't clash with her green-bean pantaloons, already as dispirited as her mood. No sword—she'd left it with Zandra to make her feel safer. No staff. And most of all, no—

An overloud throat clearing ended her litany. "Actually, no," Netlenbos murmured, and she hadn't the foggiest notion what he meant by that. With a self-conscious stroke to his sandy hair, he amplified. "I mean, no, I'm not waiting for an audience with the Governor. The Detentions Registrar has offices here as well." Rising smoothly, helmet retucked under his arm, his other hand expertly shifting his sword so its curved sheath didn't mar the chair legs, he gave a short bow. "Geerat Netlenbos, Captain in charge of the Guardian forces stationed here in the Sunderlies. We also serve who only sit and wait . . . and wait."

By the Lady! Apparently she'd made so little impression on him the other day that he'd totally forgotten her—as well as her plea! But his wry assessment hit the mark. "Doyce Marbon, former Seeker General. We've met previously."

Miming surprise, he pressed his hand against his forehead. "Forgive me! I should have realized! But somehow, without," an exaggerated glance round the room and beneath her chair, "the great Khar'pern present, I was remiss in recognizing you. My apologies." Well, that confirmed that he'd barely taken his eyes off Honoria.

"I'd say I was incognito, but that's hardly the case." However tempting it might be to berate him for his bureaucratic obduracy, it would gain her nothing. He did, however, seem like a man who'd enjoy complaining, perhaps some badinage about their respective woes, see if shared commiseration would further her cause? "Retire and you fall apart. Your ghatta wanders off, your tabard's stored in the back of the closet." Her sigh sounded more heartfelt than she'd intended, "Even my pantaloons have drooped. Not that I'm sure they ever stood to attention!"

"Ah, in the Sunderlies," he reseated himself, "they refer to that as relaxed. It simply shows you're fitting in." His

knuckles thumped his breastplate. "How would you enjoy
trudging around in this . . . this carapace? It's a wonder
turtles don't suffer heat stroke! On full-dress occasions at
high noon the bronze on the helmet or plate blisters your
fingers!" His knee touched hers, ingratiatingly. "So, any
word about your son—I mean, daughter?"

Tell? Not tell? Her fingers paled as she clenched the
chair's cushioned arms. True, the Guardians weren't running a rescue service for people lost at sea. She didn't like
it, but could understand it. But what about children lost—
kidnapped—here in Samranth? Wasn't that an exception
even a rule-bound person would make—a crime involving
innocent children? Didn't their lives matter?

"I don't know if you can help, but I've come to report
two missing children, the four-year-old daughter and
nephew of Ozer Oordbeck, the Wycherley-Saffron agent
here. They've been kidnapped, may even be murdered if
Oordbeck refuses to conceal some financial chicanery involving—"

"Captain Netlenbos?" An aide in a knee-length white
caftan over narrow-legged, knife-creased navy trousers
beckoned, and Netlenbos hovered beside him before she
could blink. "Registrar Aalders will see you now, if you
please."

Netlenbos swung back to her, dolman gracefully asway.
"But how horrible! Has this been reported? Bring all the
supporting evidence so we can commence criminal proceedings, fill out the forms to authorize a search. I guarantee
our men will keep an eye peeled for them! Now, if you'll
excuse me—" and Doyce found herself abandoned, angry
anew at how Netlenbos managed to avoid being a true
Guardian. Did he interpret his orders so rigidly that he'd
never discovered when and how they could be bent or
swayed? Or had bureaucratic necessities totally constipated
him, blocking all fellow-feeling?

In retrospect his cavalier attitude came as no surprise,
but she still found his lack of serious concern odd. Well,
count to two hundred, then count backward from there,
and mayhap she'd forgive or forget or, better yet, someone
would escort her to Governor Hoetmer. If not—she'd
leave. Whatever she could accomplish beyond these over-

decorated rooms would have more impact than this tor-
menting, interminable wait!

. . . Thirty-nine, thirty-eight, thirty-nine—no, damn it,
thirty-seven! Glaring at the goldfish on the carpet, she continued her countdown, forcing herself not to rush. Thirty-
six, thirty—

"Seeker General Marbon?" A bored-looking aide stood
in the doorway, his caftan and trim trousers topped with
an abbreviated vest of moss green. Actually, its armholes
were larger than the bits of fabric comprising the vest itself.
Not a bad compromise between ventilation and an indication of status, she suspected, and didn't know whether or
not to be relieved. Had Netlenbos been right about the
Governor's waning grip on reality? Conceivable as well that
he simply didn't want anyone going over his head, disrupting his routine. "The Governor's so sorry to have made
you wait, but it's been a trying day. If you'd come this
way, please."

Snapping her jacket into place as she rose, she composed
herself to decorously follow, but instead nearly outpaced
the world-weary aide. "The Governor's stealing a few moments to relax in the gardens, but asked that you join her
there. Otherwise I doubt we'd have found an opening for
you today." A reproving little cough. "Without an appointment, it's so difficult . . ." he let his rebuke trail off, eyes
modestly downcast.

Quick-pace, reverse! Take maximum advantage of the
Seeker-trained voice and jab an admonitory finger in the
aide's sternum, then flick a vest button. "Young man, I *do*
regret my lack of foresight in not making an appointment."
She snapped the button once more as he stared down his
nose at her offending finger. "But kidnappings are spur-of-
the-moment—no appointments in advance, either." At that
he deigned to bend his head and meet her eyes, brow creasing as he assessed what she'd said, promoting her from
"merely bothersome" to "possibly of interest."

Taking the aide to task was sheer pettiness, but she
couldn't stop herself, especially after Netlenbos. "You see,
two children were kidnapped from their beds last night,
and I doubt that was noted on your events schedule. Crises
can't be neatly organized to fit a slot. Astute aides check
the sign-in register, ask a pertinent question or two, juggle

things accordingly. Otherwise their superiors waste time on unimportant things instead of paying heed to more serious matters."

"Oh!" The dawning light of reason and the desire to protect his position set the aide to emphatically nodding. "Then I'm sure I could escort you much more quickly if you removed your finger . . . ? My apologies for assuming this was a routine courtesy call."

"Excellent!" As the aide's hand locked on her elbow, Doyce found herself kite-tailing behind as he swooped along corridors, her legs double-timing to keep pace. It was worth it and, besides, she deserved the satisfied smirk he gave as she huffed up the final flight of white marble stairs.

With a stiff bow of thanks she crossed through the double glass doors that opened onto a geometrically arranged garden of artful curves and angles, ellipses and polygons. The garden's seamless unity bewildered her, entire unto itself, without seeming to have a beginning or end. At least she could concentrate on the plashing fountain at the garden's very center, aware that she viewed the unique expression of a labyrinthian mind. This self-contained paradise might put Dolphin House's courtyard to shame, but at least she knew where she was within its confines.

"Seeker General Marbon, over here!" A pair of hedge clippers wagged from behind a glossy-green bush lushly ornamented with ruffled flowers speckled sunny yellow and flaming orange. Giving up on charting which path would take her there, she guiltily cut across an incredibly plush lawn, stopping short as she heard the snip-snip of enthusiastically-wielded clippers. "Come along, I haven't much time, and I must trim this hibiscum-heliothalus!"

A stout woman in her late sixties held the clippers aloft, blades separated as she gauged her target and brought the wooden handles together with a brisk snap. "Have to prune the daylights out of them, you know. Too much foliage and all the vital energy goes toward that instead of to the blossoms. Look how paltry these are." A sleeveless, sacklike dress in a pale blue and lavender floral print did its best to conceal her bulk, and her tanned arms bulged with muscle. A man at her shoulder ducked beneath the frayed brim of her hat to whisper in her ear, pointing as he spoke.

"No, Baskin! Just because you potter around in your

own little plot on your infrequent days of rest doesn't make
you expert enough to advise *me* about *my* hibiscum-
heliothalus!" Swinging round, the point of her clippers
pinking the brim of her hat, Governor Erzebet Hoetmer
stared at Doyce, mouth screwed in puzzlement. "Can't recollect—have you met Baskin, my adviser? Obviously not
my gardening adviser."

Hastily Doyce stepped forward to shake the older man's
hand, found her own eyes met by a pair of shrewd brown
ones in a wrinkled face. "And Mettha, there, gathering the
clippings. A shame to waste hibiscum-heliothalus blossoms
after their noble sacrifice, growing on a branch that requires
lopping. Don't you agree?" Only then did Doyce realize
that a younger woman in her late twenties unobtrusively
scurried about, tenderly rescuing the fallen blossoms and
placing them in an open-ended, flat-bottomed carrier.

The sun's percussive beat on her head left Doyce dizzy,
detached from this bizarre yet bucolic scene. Snap, snip!
"Shouldn't venture out like this without a hat, you know.
I was stubborn myself, like you, when I first came here—
silly weakness to need a hat, I told myself." Governor
Hoetmer passed the clippers to Baskin and clung to his
caftan as she precariously tilted him between two boughs
where her stouter form wouldn't fit. "No! To the right,
Baskin! Good man!" Releasing the double-handful of fabric she'd clutched so suddenly that Baskin nearly tumbled
into the hibiscum-heliothalus, she rammed her hat back on
her head, vaguely perplexed by Doyce's continued presence. "Yes, yes, pleasure to see you, welcome, all that. Paid
your respects, thank you very much. Duty done, yes,
what?"

Was she mad, or had the Governor gone mad, turned
senile by the sun or simply by the Sunderlies themselves?
Netlenbos had *not* exaggerated, after all. "Governor
Hoetmer, please hear me out! I desperately need your help.
Two very young children have been kidnapped—"

"Oh, yes . . . of course, your poor twins . . . missing,
what?"

"No! I mean, yes, they're missing, but that's not what
I'm here about. You see, two children, a four-year-old girl
and boy, have been snatched away—"

For the briefest instant blue eyes shrewdly assessed her,

and Doyce glimpsed the powerful, politically-adept woman Erzebet Hoetmer had once been. "*More* missing children? Awfully careless, aren't you? Wouldn't trust you with *my* little ones if you keep losing them!"

By the Lady's heart and hope, if only Khar were here! The temptation to allow Khar to seek inside the Governor's mind, determine what remained and what was irrevocably lost, was overpowering. "Ma'am, kidnapping is the most urgent aspect of the problem, but I've reason to believe that Sunderlies trade is being compromised, merchants here and in Canderis cheated out of their hard-earned profits, money being illegally siphoned off. . . . Do you countenance outright theft here? Is this the Sunderlies way? Should the Monitor find out . . ."

Voice dwindling, she looked helplessly at Baskin for some show of compassion or concern, swung her gaze wider to gauge Mettha's reaction. Head demurely bent, the young woman continued arranging her flowers, making sure each showy blossom hung unbruised over the basket's lip. The flowers' fragrance suddenly seemed cloying, so thick she could taste it, and she fought the urge to sneeze.

"Now, my dear, things *do* take longer to accomplish in the Sunderlies than they do in Canderis," Baskin hugged his scrawny elbows. "If you'd just begin at the beginning, and explain everything slowly and distinctly, Governor Hoetmer—"

"No! Never mind! It's very kind of you, I'm sure!" Turning on her heel, she raced from the gardens, blindly stepping over and into swaths of flowers, leaving broken-necked and dangling blossoms in her wake. With each blundering step she prayed she could find her way out of the garden, as well as the mansion and its mazed corridors. Taking one final, disillusioned look behind her, she gave a mighty sneeze and, appalled, discovered pink petals fluttering from a now-denuded blossom. Laughter fought with tears as she hurried on. Madness, absolute madness—that's what the Sunderlies supplied in abundance. She and Ozer and the rest were on their own.

♣

"That," commented Mettha Prinssen with a certain clinical admiration, "was downright cruel, Erzebet!"

Holding the hedge clippers at shoulder height, Erzebet Hoetmer let them drop, their points piercing the grass beside her foot, where they quivered but remained upright. "Damn it, I know. I simply didn't see any other choice. Her visit was spur-of-the-moment—as was my response, and you followed my lead beautifully." The Governor twisted the clippers deeper into the lawn. "We'd expected she'd come earlier, had devised a suitable cover story, but things have changed too rapidly."

Hands in the pockets of his caftan, Baskin absently scratched his ribs. "If she fouls things up, we'll have lost our advantage. Did you know, Erzebet, that Geerat Netlenbos was speaking with her while they were both waiting?"

"Hmph. That was close! Be thankful her ghatta wasn't with her!" With fussy fingers the Governor selected a blossom from the basket, stripping the leaves from the stalk, working her way higher, ruthlessly plucking petals that fell in a golden drift. "Any word from our operative?"

Liver-spotted hand over hers, Baskin stopped her. "No, don't. Destroying a flower won't save the children. Yes, we've heard from our operative." He rolled his eyes, thinking back. "Yesterday morning. Feels longer. Everything's going according to plan."

Cupping the mangled blossom, Erzebet gave it a rueful look. "And someone's keeping an eye on the bazaar?"

"Several, as agreed. Mama's set up shifts." Mettha Prinssen, Security Chief, now sat on the grass, tearing at clumps with angry little jerks. "I keep rotating staff. Might be too obvious, otherwise. It's not been easy."

"Good girl! The Monitor and I have worked so long on this. Thank the Lady our operative is flexible, takes things in stride. That reminds me—Mettha, make sure we order out our best agents," her raised hand forestalled Mettha's response. "I know they're all good. But see that the best of the best look for those babies."

"Of course, ma'am. They already are." Mettha hesitated, finally gathered her resolve, and challenged, "I must ask, though—wouldn't it be wiser to tell Doyce Marbon the truth?"

"What, Mettha, scruples? Such a burden in a Security Chief." Baskin reached a hand to pull her lightly to her feet. "The more she knows, the more likely she'll involve herself even more. With everything set, it's safer to leave her in ignorance a little longer—for her sake and for ours. Your operative said Vaert arranged for exploding custables before our friends arrived—think what he's capable of with them right under his nose here."

"But she's *already* involved—more deeply than we realized, has been since this morning!"

"Blissful ignorance!" Erzebet snorted, overriding Mettha's objection. "I swear the Sunderlies rots, corrupts everything! Don't ever let me be buried here, Baskin, pickle me in a rum cask and ship me home—promise!" Pulling her clippers free, she rested them on her shoulder. "Now come on, we've so much to set in motion before tonight. Then, for good or ill, it will be over—finished."

Despite her fear, Pw'eek climbed higher in the twisty-limb tree, parting its silky fringes of whispering leaves. It was worse than the day she'd shot up the mast because her only thought then had been to outrace the pain in her tail. How could ghatti possibly descend when their claws curved the wrong way? Mayhap she should throw herself from the tree's silvery-green crown, crash to the ground, miserable, no-good, cowardly ghatten that she was! Except—ghatti landed on their feet. That might hurt, and she wailed just imagining it. Her delicate white paw with its amputated toe had healed well but was still tender.

Wedging her butterscotch-dappled rump into a crotch, she hung on for dear life, head listlessly propped between her paws. Stinky-poo, rotten ghatten, fear-stink, spineless coward, mama-whimperer! Bad Pw'eek! Hadn't dared 'speak Jenneth, piddly coward! All night she'd hovered near, twitchily awaiting the perfect moment. Had she ever once dared seize her chance? No! Jenneth was distracted, the blond man was due back for his evening meal, oooh, was that that mangy dog ambling by again?—excuses piled upon excuses. But the truth was crystal clear: Jenneth unnerved her—exactly the same outside, but so different within, so bleakly empty, except for the moments when her brain seethed and raged. Tapping that had almost over-whelmed Pw'eek—writhing fire images dancing through Jenneth's mind, banked but shimmering when something diverted her, flaring higher when new fears fed them.

On Bonding, Pw'eek had bustled through every corner of Jenneth's mind, discovering her need for fire, attracted to it just as moths fluttered round lanterns and candles. But Jenneth had kept her need under strict control, mindful her compulsion was wrong, must be damped. But this, this was all-consuming, powerful enough to devour, and Pw'eek dreaded pressing close to Jenneth's mind—Aqua's mind—sure that internal fire would burn her to a cinder. What to do, what to do?

Blankly watching the clouds, she shivered with the tree boughs as they tossed in the wind, though they weren't as restless as she. Storm coming, her tingling skin, her crack-ling fur told her that. Good. She deserved to be drenched by pounding rain, soaked to the skin. Mayhap she should throw herself into the sea again, coward that she was. She was too familiar with the sea's vastness, its rippling expanse usually empty except for a small boat or two near shore, or a larger one venturing farther out, fishing. A wind-borne shout made her swivel her ears, determined to capture it before it wafted by her. Ah—there! That boat had hooked a big fish, the water exploding whitely as it lunged, bursting into the air midway between the shore and the boat.

No, that was no fish, that was a *human,* struggling now in chest-deep water, falling and floundering but pulling the boat after him! And, and . . . her mind reached out, subtly inquisitive as her nose, to touch a mind she'd slighted over the past few days, too lost in her woe over Jenneth. Kwee! Yes, yes, Sissy-Poo had come! There! Bouncing on the stern seat, ebullient at a brand-new world to explore and conquer!

Too overwrought to send even a minimal message, Pw'eek wriggled her rump free and reversed herself, look-ing down for the first time. Whoa! Woe! Everything had shrunken to teeny-tiny size, and the branches below were sooo slender, sooo far apart! Her tail twitching as indeci-sively as the rest of her, she wavered, ordering her legs downward. No, no, no! Finally, eyes tight-shut, hanging on for dear life, she let her fanny slither down the rough bark. Better—not much—but a little.

Down, down, down she went, adamantly refusing to look, her claws scarring the bark, curling threads of it tickling her nose. I am climbing down, I am climbing down—all by myself! At last, when she could bear no more, she opened one eye and tremulously let her forequarters lead, kicking off against the tree trunk. Flying? No. Floating? No. A crunch, a bounce, followed by a slither-twist as she extracted herself from the depths of the squashed shrub that had sacrificed itself to break her fall. Extending each limb to test it, she shook her head vigorously, dislodging a twig rakishly draped over an ear.

Now she sprinted helter-skelter down the worn beach path, all caution cast aside. Sand spewed behind her as she hit the shore, her flashing white feet absolutely flying. The boat had almost landed . . . oh, lovely, friendly people in it! Kind people with food, mayhap! Diccon, Kwee's Bond and Jenneth's twin-sib. Cheerful Davvy, and the silent Bard. And dear M'wa, too! Squeaking with eagerness, Pw'eek lost her footing as she angled too hard, her feet skidding out from under her, but she righted herself in an instant.

Jittering at the stern, Kwee spotted the flash of gray bursting from the dune's shadows and leaped over Davvy, springboarding off Diccon to fling herself on Bard, now knee-deep in the surf. Unnoticed, upstaged by her sib's antics, Pw'eek wanted to hide as everyone pointed at Kwee, cheering and shouting. Kwee's high trill tickled her ears, **"Pw'eek? Pw'eek?"**

"Kwee? Kwee?" she sang back, just as they had to reassure each other ever since they'd been the tiniest of ghatten, eyes not even open yet. A sound of homecoming, of safety.

Yet no more than a meter apart, they simultaneously slowed, sidestepped, circling, hedging each move, alternately challenging and defying. *"My beach, my territory, interloper!"* Pw'eek spat, reluctant to share. **"Not here when I needed you, didn't help me hunt, didn't comfort me when toe hurt! Useless Sissy-Poo!"** Standing rock-solid Pw'eek slanted a disdainful glance at Kwee, who sniffed but refused to break off her equally unwavering stare.

Edging sideways, Kwee stretched her neck to sniff her
sib's rump, and Pw'eek uttered a cautionary growl.
"Rude!" she grumbled deep in her throat. **"Sissy-Poo always rude!"**

"Sissy always stinky!" Kwee retorted, retracting her neck
and giving her shoulder a glancing lick to show how little
she cared.

"Sissy-Poo deserted me!"

"Didn't want to! Couldn't help it!"

Like a quarrel from a crossbow Pw'eek closed the distance, bowling over her sib and sending her tumbling across
the sand. With a wrenching twist Kwee halted on her back,
anchoring herself with a hind foot as her other paws lashed,
taunting her sister to attack again. **"Sooo scared, I was!"**
yowled Pw'eek.

"Sooo brave, Sissy was!" Kwee encouraged, but Pw'eek
had already launched herself, swatting and kicking, biting,
determined to take a stand. The new Pw'eek—Pw'eek the
Brave!

"Lady help us! Should we separate them?" Running up
the beach as the ghatten kicked and battered and thumped
each other, clumps of fur floating like thistledown, Diccon
gaped at the seething mass, unsure where or what or whom
to grab. "What if they kill each other?"

Going limp under her sister's weight, half-again her own,
Kwee whimpered, **"Nuff! Nuff! Ooh, Sissy whipped me!"**
Working her head free, she delivered a lingering lick up
her sister's throat and under her chin, and Pw'eek began
mutually grooming her, both of them rapturous with delight, sleepily replete.

" 'Course I whipped you! I am Pw'eek the Brave!" Her
burrowing tongue rasped inside Kwee's ear, Kwee frowning
at the intrusion but not flinching or fighting back. **"But
wish Kwee could help . . . ?"**

Bemused, Kwee's purr rolled louder. **"Sibs always help."**

Gawking and gawky, Theo wandered with seeming aimless-
ness through Samranth's upper streets where minor bureau-
crats and major business combines had their offices. The
outsider, the foreigner, stopping here and there to stare,

ask questions, look lost, reveal innocent pleasure at sighting anything new, different. At moments like these he thanked the Lady for making him as She had: his stammer, his ready blush, his angularity, all combined to make him stand out, yet be complacently perceived as utterly harmless, an innocent marveling at the novelties this new land offered. Strike up a conversation, ask naïve and not-so-naïve questions.

"Well, guileless one, how goes it?" Although intent on her own search, Khim 'spoke him whenever she could, sharing his enjoyment in this odyssey in quest of answers. **"Anything?"**

Head back so far his neck cracked, his jaw slack, he stared at the carvings above the lintel of a large, official-looking building. Farmers threshing grain, or mayhap whacking snakes to death—hard to tell. *"Bits and pieces, but nothing adds up."*

"Well, don't leave your mouth open too long, or you *will* convince the citizens you're witless." Embarrassing how she could discern his expression when she wasn't even present—was he that predictable? Regardless, he hastily clamped his mouth shut.

Finding a convenient cedar bench, he folded his legs under him like a giant grasshopper as he continued craning his neck to survey the carvings. Grain, definitely—unless snakes were gathered in sheaves. Pulling a scrap of paper and a pencil stub from his many-pocketed new vest—dapper black, even though he knew it absorbed too much heat—he sketched away.

"I keep wondering. Do you think Ozer's problems are meant to involve Doyce? Strike at her through him?" How he missed Holly, her incisiveness, no hesitancy or doubt when she discovered a solution. A lick at his thumb, a scrub at the paper propped against his knee and he put his pencil to work again. *"This could be a continuation of the problems from right before we sailed."* He sucked the end of his pencil. *"But if so, it's awfully indirect, more subtle, convoluted, I guess."*

"Rats!" He could almost hear her tail lash, visualize her hindquarters rising, settling into a gentle sway to propel her pounce. The ghatti didn't need to hunt, rarely did so, even for the pleasure of the chase, but a rat dashing directly across their path did reawaken old instincts. **"Sorry.**

They're a distraction, to say the least. But I suppose if you have warehouses by the waterfront, you have rats." A pause while she groomed herself under control. **"Well, striking at Ozer is also a strike at Wycherley-Saffron. Someone's set on ruining them. Or at least stealing enough to make them dearly feel the pinch."**

"True, but Jenret and his family have other trading interests. It'll pinch, but not bankrupt them. Humiliate Jenret and Jacobia in front of the other mercantiles, yes. Jenret'll be livid."

"Have you . . ." Khim paused, her reluctance setting off little warnings inside Theo, **"have you ever considered the dagga boys' attack as anything more than a chance encounter?"**

Agitated, Theo unfolded himself, crumpling his sketch paper and attempting to saunter along, shaking hands buried deep in his pockets. *"I'm not sure I follow. The dagga boys spotted Siri, knew she was Kasimir's sister, decided to cause a scene."* Doyce and Siri had looked so small and defenseless in the midst of the violence that he'd been near-sick with trepidation—and sicker still at seeing how ably they'd coped. Physical violence made him want to run the other way.

"They could have killed Doyce. Did someone tell them Siri was there? That Doyce was resting there? Stall-keepers that you or the others spoke with while you shopped? Something about the whole incident sat wrong with me, even though most of the fun was over when we arrived."

"Fun?" Bloodthirsty little beast! He struggled for perspective. *"Mayhap. But Khar's a little overprotective, you know."* Just as Khim was with him, and he'd not have it any other way. *"Let me think on it. I suppose next you'll say it's connected with Resonants. Frankly, I've not encountered a one here in the Sunderlies, have you?"*

"As if you'd notice a slow brain-leak!" she scoffed, but sounded distinctly pettish.

He quelled a triumphant laugh; when Khim retreated into a snit, he'd gained the upper hand. But laughing alone would encourage bystanders to suspect lunacy. *"Blessedly peaceful without them, isn't it? Must be a few. Mayhap they're all trailing after Jenret and Arras? Rowing after Diccon and Davvy?"*

Khim hadn't relished his one-upmanship, would be staring down her nose, full of injured pride if she sat beside him. **"Must Khar and I explain *everything* for you? Look, I've scouting to do, so do you. Put your brain to work, mine's tired from trying to pour sense into yours."**

"Fine, fine. Don't be grouchy, please!" What had gotten into Khim? Worry over Doyce and Khar, the whole gaggle of Oordbecks? *"Back to work again."* Hadn't he seen a stand selling fruit drinks just around the corner? The last thing his bladder needed was more liquid, but it offered a way to chat up people and, best of all, to listen to people chatting. Not to mention asking where he could relieve himself before he floated away.

Having accomplished both goals, he found himself fighting the current of people returning from their after-lunch rest, so he bought a paper cone of steamed crawdiddies and ambled with the flow, alternately blowing on scorched fingers and waiting for the crawdiddies to cool enough to peel. Late afternoon, now, and he'd not succeeded in uncovering much information, other than confirming his new sandals had blistered his heels. How he wanted to help Ozer! The thought of little children being used as pawns, expendable if need be, made his skin crawl, his brain seethe. Unaware, he scowled, passersby scurrying clear of the tall foreigner with the limping gait and the sudden, cruel expression.

His sore feet had carried him away from the administrative center down toward the wharves, and he halted, lost in admiration at the picture-perfect scene: the rippling blue crescent of the bay stitched with the white wake of passing fishing boats, barges, ferries. Peaceful, too, because he was too far distant to hear the constant clamor of rolling barrels, crashing shipping containers, the bawls and yells of docksiders. The *Vruchtensla* was still docked, repairs nearly finished after the pounding she'd sustained from the storm. Out farther he could spy Tarango Fort, idly wondering what the view into the harbor looked like, if it were lonely out there?

Well, where to now? Honoria'd volunteered to canvass the docks and warehouses, pretending an interest in loading and unloading costs, storage fees, since she already possessed a working knowledge of such topics. Lindy's search area encompassed the bazaar and its environs, while Doyce had planned on presenting herself at the Governor's Mansion, or at least leaving a message.

Back to his assignment, he supposed. Time to venture into the lower class clamor of Samranth, check out Middentown where the Bethel was located. Ozer'd pulled him aside, whispering to him man-to-man that no well-bred ladies should wander there. Frankly he'd not had the heart to tell Ozer that these "ladies" were very capable of defending themselves. With his sorry luck, that female Shepherd would accuse him of trespass! She'd wielded a mean broom, and despite her copious apologies, he harbored no real eagerness to meet her on her home ground. That decided him. Folding the crawdiddie wrappings, he hunted for a place to toss them, heard a plaintive meow at his feet. A scrawny cat peered 'round a plaster urn topped by a stunning crop of dying, unwatered flowers. All he could see of the cat were oversized black ears, the glint of its eyes, and a pink tongue longingly licking its chops.

Squatting slow and easy, he spread the wrapping, poking amongst the folds for scraps. "Not much, little one. Mostly shell pieces, but . . . ah . . . wait!" One he'd missed, hadn't cracked open. With a quick look each way the cat sidled out, dashing at the paper and scattering shell fragments in its haste, wolfing down the crawdiddie meat. Disappointed there was no more, it licked the discarded shells, the wrapping, determined to find the last scrap.

"Poor little kitty." The cat, white with black patchings, ventured a lick at his fingers, began to chew on them; Theo experienced the familiar wrench that always came upon viewing a hungry or hurt cat, so very like their ghatti-cousins, yet often so disparaged or ignored by humans. Mayhap Ozer's children would like a pet? No shortage of friendly laps in that family! With a basso purr louder than it was large, the cat ardently rubbed against Theo, lifting its chin and cocking its head for an ear-scratch.

"Flirting, are we? Deserting me for another?" Khim's teasing mindspeech collided with a voice at his shoulder, "Here, give the little thing this." Sea-scent, the brine-fresh scent of fish made him start, rub his nose. Basket balanced on hip, Aidannae stood dangling a skinny, silvery-sheened fish not much larger than a minnow beside Theo's ear.

Sharp claws pricked his knee, his shoulder as the cat swarmed up him, quirking its paw to snatch the morsel. "Impolite, rude!" he chided, detaching the beast's claws from his new vest as he set it down, a muffled growl of complaint directed at him through a mouthful of fish.

"But I apologized!" Dannae tugged her topknot in dismay, scowling. "And you kept the broom. Now I owe Eckie five coppers for not returning it, even if it was a wee bit worn!"

Worn, indeed—on his lip and other parts of his anatomy, no less! Knees and ankles popping like snapped twigs, he shot upright as if to outrace the color rising from collar to hairline. Still faintly cowed by his height, she leaned back to look at him. "Here, give the cat another. It's our supper, but I'd not flout the Lady by letting one of Her own hunger." As Dannae selected another fish, Theo saw how meagerly they covered the bottom of her basket. Not a good day for charity. The cat sprang, snatching it from Dannae's fingers.

"Ah . . . I know you a-apolo-gized. And I ac-cepted. Was s-scolding the cat!" His mind whirled for no good reason he could analyze. Although loath to admit it, something about this female Shepherd tickled his fancy: her firecracker defense of the children, her short, round—delightfully rounded—build, that ludicrous knot of flame-red hair like a mushroom cap atop her head. Probably wasn't proper to indulge in such thoughts about a Shepherd, even a female one. Frantically combing through his limited store of conversational gambits, he found himself awed by his own inventiveness: ask about Kasimir's and Sirikit's past. Mayhap she could shed some light on whether or not the dagga boys' attack was coincidence?

Did he dare mention Oordbeck's problems, the children's kidnapping? If it wasn't safe to confess their problem to a Shepherd, then it wasn't safe to confide in anyone. And she might, just might have some ideas. After all, Samranth was *her* city, she must know its ins and outs, its habits and expectations.

Tugging at his earlobe, mentally rehearsing the words so he could uncage them before his stammer trapped them, he blinked, "I don't suppose (joy, the "p's" hadn't budged, obediently stayed in their place!) you'd w-walk with me a bit? I need your ad-vice as a," deep breath and push it out, "Shepherd. It's important."

She shifted her basket, hitching at her robe. "I've one more stop to make—if you care to walk along." Suiting her actions to her words, she started off. "I've a question for you, as well."

Unsure whether to take her arm in a gentlemanly fashion, the street here roughly cobbled, he started after her, only to halt, indecisive, before finally scooping up the cat. It sniffed his chin, yawned full in his face, a fishy blast. "F-fine. Here." Catching up in two long-legged strides, he thrust the cat at her, claiming her basket with his other hand. That was mannerly enough—and would serve as a defensive shield if she took a dislike to him yet again. Best of all, she was marching toward the dock area. No matter how thoroughly Honoria had covered it, it never hurt for someone else to have a look-see. Not that he didn't trust Honoria . . . Well, to be honest, the scales never settled when she was weighed in his mind . . .

"Leggo! Git outa da way!" Kasimir's face warped in a horrific grimace, eyes bulging, lips rolled back and teeth snapping at his sister. "I got charge a yed, an when I say 'git,' yed best git!" Back planted against the wall to shield the loose plank she'd shown them earlier, Siri yawned in her brother's face. Clutching the back of Harry's belt, Byrlie simply hung straight down, legs dragging. Despite the fierce expressions, the anger thick as smoke in Ozer's private office, they'd consciously muted their argument to avoid adult intervention. Finally Kasimir knelt, appealing to Siri on her level. "I bet I ken where the liddle'uns are hid. Got an idea, Siri, check it out, help ol' Ozer find the tykes!"

Twilight, but a weary, wearing time still loomed before they left for the warehouse to exchange the records for the children's lives. Harry wasn't sure if he could stand any more waiting, each moment an eternity of growing doubt. Gelya and Zandra had put the youngest children down for naps, even the older ones nodding over their tasks, the air stale and still with the windows shut tight. To be honest, he and Smir were bored to tears and beyond, edgy with untapped energy and eagerness. "S'my door," Siri insisted. "Byrlie'n me 'scovered it. We say who uses it." True enough, she and Byrlie *had* discovered the loose plank in the tiny back office wall. Not exactly a surprise, the constant heat and moisture, the driving rains and winds aged things before their time here in the Sunderlies. Smir'd showed him how things warped, swelled, or buckled, rusted and rotted, even though they sometimes looked whole on the surface. "We all go, or nobody goes!" How anyone who looked so adorable (especially considering she was related to Smir with his pointy, prominent nose and his slat-ribbed sides) could prove so defiantly stubborn, Harry couldn't imagine. Their personalities, if not their looks, proved their relationship.

"Gotta find Khar and Khim," Siri insisted. "Need'em!"

Red with exertion, his waist sore from Byrlie's tugging, Harry finally gave up attempting to pry her free from his belt. Good belt, too, thin, supple leather in a rich chestnut shade, the gold buckle engraved with his initials. "No use, Smir. Can't make her let go less I do each finger separate, and then I'd darn near have to break them." Would Smir think him weak, babyish for being stymied by a little girl? Not that Smir was having any greater success with Siri.

A tap to Harry's middle and his eyes traveled to his friend's impatient finger. "Yed *could* unbuckle it, knothead!" Mortified, he complied, both the belt and Byrlie slithering to the floor, Byrlie now busily attempting to lash his ankles together with the belt. At moments like these Harry gave thanks to the Lady for making him an only child. A threatening wriggle of fingers at Byrlie's ticklish stomach, and he snatched the belt clear.

Arms wrapped protectively around her stomach, she lay looking up at him. "If you go, we're going, too. Siri needs to ask Khar something. And besides, Smir's wrong. Tell him, Siri."

Tugging at Harry's third-best vest, the tattersall one Smir now wore in place of a shirt, Siri regained her brother's attention. Finger to her lips, she pulled him down for a whispered conference, kicking his shin for emphasis. "Yed sure, Sirikit-cat? Tell the grown-ups, yed should." The whites of his eyes were visible all around the dark-blue iris, and Harry realized his friend was afraid, the first time he'd

ever seen him that way. More harried whispers, Siri's
breath whistling and hissing like a cha kettle on the boil.
"But only if we find Khar-cat-friend, yes? No find, scarper
back quick."

Sticking out her hand to seal their bargain, Siri beckoned
with a shoulder for Byrlie to stand beside her. Together,
the two girls shifted the board, gasping as they struggled to
hold it steady, not let it squeak or bang. Inspecting it, Smir
cautiously worked a nail free and laid it at the bottom of
the gap to keep the plank from completely closing once the
girls released it. Smart if they needed to get in from outside.
Only a bare crack showed, enough for Siri or Byrlie to
hook with a finger.

Out popped Siri, Byrlie poised to follow, and for a moment Harry guessed she'd turned scared, changed her mind.
But no—darting to the shelves she grabbed a ball of twine
and scooted back. Seeing Dolly and Mr. Monkey on the
floor, he handed Dolly to Byrlie, tucking Mr. Monkey safe
in his belt. Who cared what Smir thought, so there! Besides,
Siri'd be mighty glad he'd remembered. If not, how he'd
chide her for leaving him untended, liable to be loved to
pieces by too many Oordbeck offspring!

Full of urgency Smir waved him through the gap, so he
doubled over, duckwalking out, not straightening until he
saw what awaited him outside. Behind him, teeth sunk in
lower lip, Smir eased the plank into place, pinching his
finger and silently dancing the pain away. Outside at last,
a chance to help! Mayhap he couldn't save Jenneth, but he
could help find the two Oordies. Save folk time and trouble
and panic, protect Jacobia's and Uncle Jenret's investment
as well, if they found the babies before the moons rose
high. They'd divvied up assignments earlier—Smir was the
tracker, the finder, while his charge involved inventing
plans to free the Oordies from captivity. Brawn and brains.
Now he reckoned the girls'd insist on assignments. Mayhap
Pest One and Pest Two.

From behind the office down side streets, alleyways, up
and over fences, a bit of a roof scarper and a ridgepole
walk, while Harry followed silent and sure, vastly proud of
himself. Mayhap he'd spent most of his life in a castle,
but he'd also spent time aplenty outdoors with his father,
sometimes even with King Eadwin. And twice, the times

too short but wondrous, with Nakum in the woods, aiding
in the arborfer survey. Yes, he knew his way around, could
match the best of them. Knew that Smir's ridgepole walk
was show-offish. What if someone'd looked up at the wrong
moment—seen them silhouetted against the last of the setting sun? 'Sides, even Siri and Byrlie had tippy-toed across,
no trouble.

But for all that, his nerves prickled, skin ready to creepy-
crawl. Sure, he'd yearned for adventure and excitement,
but the Sunderlies wasn't his homeland, lacked the familiarity of Marchmont or even Canderis, practically a second
home what with family visits back and forth. Running his
hand under his collar, he wiped away the nervous dampness. The air here constantly felt too damp and heavy, clogging his nostrils not just with moisture but with oppressive
scents, sometimes pleasant and ofttimes vile. Even with
night falling, the heat still set his temples throbbing. And
every soul here different from the norm, or *his* norm—even
though Papa always insisted that people everywhere were
alike. Well, Marchmontians and Canderisians were, even
Resonants and Normals. But Sunderlies folk let their emotions surface more readily, their attitudes more casual. As
if . . . life were casual and death, too, happening easier,
more frequently here, and people just . . . expected it . . .
just shrugged it off. Look at what had happened to Aunt
Doyce and Siri in the bazaar! Either or both could have
died!

A shiver, a goose stepping over his grave. Mayhap because he was eldest, he felt responsible for what this outing
accomplished, whether he led it or not. Not that Smir took
this as a game: he'd lived here, surviving on the margins,
raising Siri as gentle and sweet as could be. But if something *did* happen to the Oordies—made them sound like
wee birds, calling them that—Smir'd be sorry, sad for a
trice, but then return to the immediate business of survival,
had no choice. Somehow it made him feel older, wiser, yet
infinitely less prepared. Damn-all-dark now! Smir and Siri'd
better know for sure where they were leading! Better yet—
that he knew where he was following!

A small hand slipped into his, Byrlyn's. Despite the need
for haste, he swung to face her, his free hand smoothing
the top of her head just as his father had done with him

when he was small. "You fine?" he whispered, unable to decipher her expression in the pale blur of her face. Even when he *could* see her face he couldn't always read her, like her Papa, Bard, that way, and perpetually solemn like her Mama. "Scared?"

A further blurring of the pale oval as she shook her head. "Nope. Not 'bout this, other things—mayhap." Her fingers wove between his. "Thought you looked nervous, nibbling on your lip an all." Up ahead Siri stuck her head beneath an overhang, murmuring, "Khar, Khar, Khar. Kitty-Khar, please come to Siri!"

Swinging forward, still hand-linked, he started ahead, not wanting to admit the truth of her words. Heard Byrlie sniff, realized he could smell the sea, the overpowering scent of fish alive and dead, olive oil and salt. Ha! Near the fish-monger section down by the shore. A relief at discovering where they'd come, the vast, surrounding emptiness dividing into manageable portions—shops, streets, homes.

"Can't be nervous, got Mr. Monkey with me." Touched his belt for the lump underneath, only to realize it had vanished. "Oh, damn!" and the hot prickle of tears threatened to flood his eyes, his nose. "He's lost, Byrlie. Dropped him someplace." Too old to need Mr. Monkey—what was he, a little crybaby? Even if he were too old, still no call to treat Mr. Monkey so casually. Lady strengthen him— were the Sunderlies rubbing off on him?

"Here." Byrlie thrust something into his hands, and his fingers touched the familiar stocking material with its darned spots, the wool stitching that marked eyes and nose and lips. "Stepped on his tail, I did, and he yelled. Picked him up and brought him along." She shook Mr. Monkey's paw. "Easier to find him than it is finding my Papa, or yours."

Horrifically dark now, too early for moonlight, no twinkling starlight except straight, straight overhead as they edged between two fishmongeries, one so old and warped that its upper wall buckled outward, practically leaning upon its neighbor. Don't think about what they tracked through, what scampered and fled between their legs! Don't think about Papa, except to pray he found Jenneth. Something more bothered Byrlie, Harry was sure, but this wasn't the time or place to wrestle a secret from a child who guarded them tighter than oysters did pearls.

"Here, Siri?" Smir halted, squatting to confer with his sister. Harry could tell because Smir's voice dipped to knee-level, became more muted instead of bounding between walls like before. Apparently 'here' wasn't here, because Siri dragged Smir a few paces ahead, and again Harry heard the grate of old boards, the wrench of rusty nails. Sirikit apparently had a knack for creating her own private doors. A final, cajoling, "Khar, kitty-Khar, Khar-kitty, please!" as she vanished within, Byrlie and Harry following, Smir bringing up the rear. Clove, cinnamon, cardamon, bay leaves, peppercorns, spikenard—such a mix of homey cooking scents that he almost sneezed. Nose itching, still lost in darkness, Harry felt as if they were all rats, skittering about, slipping through the night on secret errands. Rat-silent, rat-canny, rat in a trap, oh dear!

Dannae tossed and turned on her thin pallet, all too wide-awake. The Shepherds allowed for a moderate, restorative sleep, time allotted between the evening's concluding Mystery Chant and the First Praise Chant of the dawning. Except that assumed one proceeded directly to bed, fell into a righteous slumber unstained by guilt. Flopping on her back, she pillowed her head on her arms and stared at the ceiling, the plaster between the oak beams stained and yellowed—from leakage or guilt? Recite the Lady's Mysteries again, the eightfold way? Ha, she'd already told them backward, forward and nanny-goat crosswise, with no disrespect meant to the Lady!

Guilt? What had she done—or not done—to cause guilt? It hadn't been her fault—truly! Oh, guilt was always to be found, free-floating as pollen in the spring. Giving an exasperated huff, she took stock of her day. Mayhap she should have let Theo give the stray to the Oordbeck offspring, instead of deciding the Bethel kitchen needed a mouser. That could hardly be it—there were strays enough to go around. Give her a half-bucket of fish guts and heads and she'd round up one stray per child and still have more rubbing at her ankles—cats, that was. But she'd touched on her connection with Ozer Oordbeck and his missing children.

No guilt pertained, she'd had naught to do with it, but she did feel—what? Obscurely responsible? As if in the tally the Lady scrupulously marked, she, Aidannae, were accountable for them, the Shepherd accountable for the lambs. Of course the Lady protected lost lambs, but only to a point. The wheel of life always turned, and each soul would come around, come forth again. Cold comfort to Ozer, his wife, his sister-in-law. Now counted more than the next life. Funny, strive to change, to grow, yet if that failed, to fatalistically accept that a distant future would offer another chance. Not necessarily a better or a worse one—just another one.

Wriggling her toes, she tried to relax her muscles, forcing herself to yawn, trick herself into sleep, but knew it wouldn't work. No, best admit her guilt, her shame. Blast Conraad! Blast him and plague him with bedbugs to gnaw at his milk-sour, mean-spirited, primly prudish soul! So there!

Just thinking about it made her seethe at the injustice of it all! Somehow in her growing horror at hearing Theo haltingly tell what had happened to Ozer's little ones, she'd neglected to tell him how she'd overheard Honoria and the man called Geerat. The man's voice, slightly slurred with drink, in counterpoint to Honoria's crispness. ". . . Oh-Oh's precious offspring . . . they'll be . . ." They'll be what? Bad enough to eavesdrop on two strangers she'd never seen and would never see again, but Dannae could not deny Honoria's presence. What did it mean? Who was Geerat? She'd hoped Theo might know. But the whole thing had flown spang out of her mind, much to her shame.

She'd remembered just after they'd parted, and she'd rushed off after him in an absolute lather, bellowing his name, sure she'd never catch him at the rate his long legs worked. Screaming like a fishwife, robe kirtled in one hand, basket full of cat instead of fish (a nice point to debate— the fish resided inside the cat which resided inside the basket), she'd gone hurtling right into Shepherd Conraad! Rocked him out of his sandals and made him irrevocably lose his place in a Mystery Chant!

Before she could explain, he'd hauled her off to the

Bethel, cataloging her sins in such extensive and vivid detail that she'd quaked with terror, fearing her automatic dismissal. How could she possibly explain it to All-Shepherd Cubzac? And that meeting had absolutely driven everything else clear out of her head as she argued against Conraad's malicious, ill-founded charges. Well, she'd not been dismissed, but Cubzac had ordered her to remain in the confines of the Bethel for an oct to meditate on mending her ways. And meditation required the emptying of one's mind. . . .

Well, sleep be damned! Her rightful penance didn't involve sequestration and meditation; it involved, at the very least, telling Theo what she knew. Better yet, she'd find the children! If she interfered, intervened, it might set the children's souls back, but they'd still be alive to enjoy this life! If Cubzac dismissed her from the Shepherds, so be it—the Lady wouldn't turn Her back on her!

With a grunt Dannae heaved herself off the pallet, groping for her robe. Splash water on hands and face. Pull the Lady's Medal from beneath the robe so that all could see, be guided by it. Tighten her topknot high and tight like a Guardian's crest. Ready! Sandals in hand, she tiptoed from the dormitory down the stairs and into the kitchen. A final pause as she fumbled amongst the kindling, hefting and discarding pieces until she found a billet of wood to her liking.

Out the door and into the night, drinking in the sounds and smells, recalling all too clearly her nights as a child, an adolescent, wandering the streets for entertainment, mayhap even finding or earning a few coins. Always something to notice and remark on—or not—for a price. Sometimes an adventure waiting to be found. She tucked the billet into her hemp belt, solid against her side, comforting. Crack a shin with it, a head if need be. Not exactly Shepherdly behavior, and she grinned. Sometimes things required cracking to allow the Lady's Word to penetrate such density. (Ah, to run into Conraad now!) Still, she'd do her best to confine herself to shin-cracking, teach them a lively jig in praise of the Lady's name.

Slipping on her sandals, she let her feet carry her through Middentown's hovels, circumspectly passing the few Guardians who policed major intersections, ensuring shops remained safe, taverns rowdy but not excessively so. What they could do if they truly exerted themselves! No question, she was heading to the wharves. She'd not forgotten her night prowls of yore, hiding spots, hidey-holes, the places smugglers stored their wares till they were ready to ship or sell. Hardly an honorable profession, but a longtime one. Always ways to bypass any law, just or unjust. Please, Lady, let her be right!

With a low-key greeting, a joke, a friendly wave to other denizens of the night, Aidannae made her way toward the docks as fast as she could. Amazing how the old days still clung to her, comfortingly familiar as a second skin; it didn't mean the Lady hadn't claimed her, though: that layer went deep below the surface, heart and soul. Still a few old comrades who trusted her for what she was and what she'd been, secure she'd never 'fess on them, game to share any oddling gossip they'd dinked out. What they'd sussed, surmised, meshed too well with her own misgivings.

Deuced near pitch-black down this path behind Ceddar's Emporium, tenement overhangs blocking the Lady's unchanging light, mocking it. But it was faster, less trafficked, less time lost from bumping into old friends—now that she'd discovered her goal. Lady knew what the inhabitants had dumped into this footpath, rank as a sewer. Drains stopped up again, most any storm did that. A baby cried fretful and low, a repetitive wail; an argument soured further between husband and wife; the residual smells of overcooked, greasy meals; the skitter-scurry of rats' feet and a shrill, indignant squeal. All too sadly familiar, yet something she'd thought, prayed that she'd left behind for good. Even the Bethel's walls couldn't hold the real world at bay.

Tucking the billet of wood under her chin, she tightened her belt, bunching her robe till its hem brushed her shins. Wonderful, another fold round her waist! If she'd had the habit of being sticky-fingered in the bazaar, the roll of fabric at her waist would provide a place to stash her takings. Dannae kept the wood in hand now, easy and ready. The twitch 'tween her shoulder blades told her she'd been spotted, tagged as more than a curiosity back by Sock-eye's

Tavern; it grew, a prickling sensation zinging up her spine until she suspected her topknot would stand and salute. That was the other reason she'd shifted to this back route, to see if she had the right of it, if anyone *did* follow. And the footsteps had, though she'd not yet glimpsed who came padding in her wake.

Quick, yes! Swing 'round the corner, a temporary blind spot to conceal which of two possible lanes she'd chosen. Now run like the wind, gain enough distance to lose whoever followed, let them guess which way she'd taken. Fifty-fifty odds, beat a dead cert—or dead Shepherd. Dodging, backtracking, rolling under a rotting fence, her breathing came faster but still even. Not that far to the warehouses, and if she gained them undetected, she'd lose herself in their anonymous emptiness.

A pause, take a few extra breaths without straining. Swiveling her head, she examined the looming building shapes just ahead and, most of all, strained her ears for footsteps. Damn! May the Lady shrivel your nuts and bolt, rust them to dust! Fine, fine, but she lacked leisure for that occurrence, so she'd best take charge. Up ahead, yes, the alley where it narrowed so much a broad-shouldered man would be forced sideways. A protruding stone door stoop she could just make out, should be an indented door. Go, go! Belatedly wishing she'd greased herself in case she got stuck, she dashed down the alley, throwing herself in the doorway, hoping it shielded most of her as she flattened against it.

Lady—and All-Shepherd Cubzac—forgive her for what she was about to do, but children's lives hung in the balance. Not like the larky games of old, sprinting from one dagga boy gang or another, or serving as a lure to entice them into an ambush. The footsteps still pounded along, as quick and confident as if her trail glowed in the dark. Damn, whoever it was was good, knew the back ways as well or better than she, could almost ken her mind!

Wait, wait, she admonished, clamping the billet tighter. Rather than holding it like a club, she'd reversed its span so it extended the length of her inner arm, bracing flesh and bone. Gonna hurt—her pursuer more than herself, she prayed. Listen, listen hard, and . . . Now!

Lunging, she thrust her arm straight across the narrow

gap, her knuckles grazing the opposite wall, hoping she'd gauged the height correctly. "Psst! Dannae!" a voice hissed, a familiar childish voice, and she convulsively jerked her arm upward.

"Shee-it, Dannae!" sputtered Kasimir, huffing from shock and the long pursuit, "Yed plan on clotheslining me er braining me?" Relieved but overwrought, somehow sorry there'd been no definitive, crunching conclusion, she compensated by delivering an admonitory tap atop Smir's head with her billet.

"Why're you roaming so late? Sneaky-snickering after me?" She could just make out his scrawny body's shape in the darkness, the tattersall of his vest more texture than pattern. "Trouble always travels this late, and you shouldn't be racing it. Ought by rights to be home with Siri! Asleep— both of you!" Then, intuitively, she grasped the situation. "Siri out wandering, too?"

Sidestepping her final question, Smir grumbled, "Been trying ta tag yed haf da night!" Hands resting on nonexistent hips, his foot tapped an impatient tattoo. "Din wan no-un ta see. Yed skim flitter-fast fer an ol' lady! Kent take da streets outa yed, eh?"

Old lady? At the ripe old age of twenty-two Dannae's temper threatened to rise, but she throttled it. "So why've you been trailing me? For the fun of spooking me?"

Practically prancing with urgency, Smir dragged at her sleeve, hustling her along. "Cuz we spied the Oordies, we did! Kin bundle'm up safe'n sound, but we need help. Thas why I skinned off lookin fer yed! Kin hidey'em in the Bethel, belikes no-un'd look neath the Lady's skirts!"

"Who's 'we'?" A perverse pleasure in forcing his pace, treading on Smir's heels as they trotted along. Show him "old," she would! Then, more casually, "Siri out this late?"

"Aye. Siri kipped it out! Harry an Byrlie along, too—fer reinforcements. 'E's not tough as me, but e's tack-sharp an taller. Good ta haf along." Reaching back, he fumbled for her hand, anxiously squeezing it. "Kin stash the Oordies wid yed?"

She gave him a reassuring squeeze in return. "Of course we can hide them at the Bethel till we find Ozer and their mamas. That's what I planned to do."

"How'd yed kip where zey stashed'em?" His chagrin was obvious.

Rub it in—forbearance, forgiveness could come later. "Near thrice Siri's age and at least half as smart. What's your excuse?"

But Kasimir stopped short, his palm soft against her lips, warning her to silence and deliberate slowness. His reason was obvious as soon as she let her senses reach free: a squad of Guardians surreptitiously approaching the old Janacz & Sons warehouse, two buildings over. Other shadowed forms mingled with the Guardians, the sort who looked as if they should be arrested, not consorted with. Slivers of light trembled and shifted between gaps in the weathered siding. Regardless, let the Guardians rescue the babies! Better than four children and a Shepherd confronting who knew what—who?—to save them!

But before she could communicate that to Smir, he shook his head in an emphatic negative, still hushing her as he pulled her after him, angling toward a dilapidated boathouse half-under the pilings that supported the warehouses. "Some Guardians haf turned." He gave her a somber, searching look, and she wished she could see his face better. "Turned," he said again and spat, "curdled sour as milk. Doan wanna toddle up 'side'em till I see which're sour, which're sweet. Compré?"

"Compré," she agreed, but she didn't—not entirely. Lady help her, she *had* been off the streets too long if she couldn't believe that Guardians could turn against the laws they upheld!

With an encompassing look outside the office's side entrance, Doyce waved the children to where she'd stationed Theo, Honoria, and Zandra, the women with lanterns in hand. Out they marched, two by two, the larger ones loaded with satchels and bins of paperwork, medium-sized children lugging the smallest on hip or back. Ozer, Gelya, and Lindy concluded the procession. Quietly fuming, Doyce wondered if Samranth required parade permits, what the penalty was for disturbing the peace so late at night with this cavalcade of children? And were she to meet Governor

Hoetmer tonight in the streets, the poor, dotty woman would probably lead their parade, hedge clippers waving the cadence! It was still too painful to contemplate how that discovery had dashed her last naïve hope that someone else would care, would willingly help.

To top it off, she hadn't a clue where her own child crusaders had gone. Finding that Harry and Byrlie, Kasimir and Siri had vanished without a trace (except for a conveniently loose wallboard that created a child-sized exit) had sent Ozer into a stampeding hysteria, totally convinced they'd been snatched from under their very noses. His sobs and wails had alternated with an incandescent anger and a desire to comb every centimeter of Samranth. Given that contretemps, leaving the other children behind while Ozer, Theo, and Doyce ransomed the babies with the records was no longer an option. They'd all go, or no one would go!

Much as she and Lindy were appalled that the children were gone, they'd both suspected that loose plank had set them on the path to adventure. Not that that protected them from harm; indeed, their unsupervised presence made them a wild card, vulnerable to the kidnappers and to any predator with no qualms about taking advantage of defenseless youngsters.

"Well, not exactly defenseless." Khar always insisted on clarifying things, positively enjoyed it. **"Kasimir and Siri are street-bred and street-wise—you've seen him in action, and Siri shows potential with a crutch. Harry and Byrlie may lack their savvy, but neither are they foolish, just overprotected in comparison."**

Counting heads, Doyce stepped into the street, hand on her sword hilt. *"Thank you, Khar, that reassures me no end!"* Khar let the sarcasm float over her head, refusing to puncture it, but Doyce didn't have time to wonder why.

Forcing herself not to shout hut-hut!, she herded them along, making sure the children stayed protectively ringed by adults, and checking that none straggled. They were amazingly good-natured children, unfussy and steadfast all this day and night, all too aware of what one mistake or mischance might mean for a sibling or cousin. *"Can't you find our missing lambs before they stray any farther? Think how M'wa'll react if anything happens to Byrlie, not to mention Bard and Lindy. Francie's guaranteed to skin you alive if anything happens to Harry."* She wasn't above brandishing a threat or two if it would help. *"That's assuming there's enough of your carcass to receive her tender ministrations after Arras finishes with you."*

As she padded along without responding, Doyce was abruptly struck by how exhausted Khar appeared, head and tail drooping, almost a drunken roll to her gait. After all, both Khim and Khar had already put in a full day hunting for Ozer's two, to no avail. At last she 'spoke with slow deliberation, as if each word were too heavy to share. **"Beloved, you're my first concern, much as I love the children."** A slight stumble as she misjudged her footing, and Doyce held her breath. **"Khim's sure they'll pop up near the warehouses, and I agree. Don't you suspect that's where they've headed? We'll scoop them up then."** Casting a wry look at her bond, Khar's eyes glowed a dull green-gold in the lantern light. **"Don't forget Francie will also knot my tail and pluck my whiskers one by one. Poor me!"**

Awkwardly Doyce scooped Khar against her chest and shoulder to let her rest and, most of all, to hold her close. If anything happened to Khar . . . she couldn't . . . didn't dare finish the thought. Of those she loved so deeply and dearly—Jenneth and Diccon, Jenret and Khar—the ghatta was the only one near enough for her embrace. Yes, you were supposed to spread your arms, let them go, run free— but not toward what awaited at the journey's final end! *"Never, beloved!"* Nuzzling the softness behind an ear, she inhaled the talclike scent that always emanated from Khar. *"I've been saving those torments as a treat if you should rile me. Not that you ever could!"*

On they marched, seven adults ringing ten children, not exactly slinking through Samranth's streets, but moving as unobtrusively as possible with a party that size. A few night-owls hung from upper windows, watching and whispering; others on the near-deserted byways went panicky at the prospect of dagga boys on the prowl and huddled in dark doorways clutching their purses, only to turn perplexed on discovering a pack of children streaming by. Theo walked with her now, and Gelya had moved nearer to guide them. Despite the fact that one of her children was missing, she managed a bleak self-control, tears longshed, her plain, freckled face shiny from too much scrub-

bing, and her strawberry-blonde hair rigorously banded
back. Unexpectedly wrapping his arm around Doyce, Theo
gave her a rough hug, his height plus Khar's bulk threatening to tilt her off-balance.

"I ran into that S-Shepherd today, that f-female one." A
sigh that sounded as if it rose from his toes gusted against
her crown, ruffling her hair. "Haven't had much ch–" another breathy blast, "chance to tell you, what with coming
back to find our crew had scar-pered."

Leaning so far toward Gelya that Theo's fingers were
mashed between the two women, Doyce extricated herself
from Theo's too emphatic embrace. "So what did Aidannae
have to say?"

"It was strange. She kept . . ." he rubbed his forehead,
ransacking his brain for the word he wanted, and finally
whispered at her, "fulminating about H-Honoria, how un-
necessarily rough and cold s-she'd been when she and
Lindy rescued me. That was in-between talking about Smir
and Siri, and more abject apol-ogies. That Shepherd wields
a mean b-broom!" Theo's grin practically lit up the night—
he was smitten.

Did Shepherds ever marry? She didn't think she'd ever
heard of any who had. Not that the opposite implied celi-
bacy, she'd just always assumed . . . Too bad Harrap wasn't
here to ask, except that it was a delicate question to pose.
Certainly she'd brooded over what Harrap's and Mahafny's
relationship encompassed all these years. Friendship, a pla-
tonic love and respect, or something more—something they
both needed?

She almost missed the rest of Theo's news. "Dannae kept
calling her a 'lost Livotti,' and what could you expect from
a Livotti except cruelty, unkindness?" When she didn't respond, he prodded, "Don't you remember? Ozer's story
about Livotti-Rutenfranz? How that company went
under?"

Still busy envisioning Mahafny and Harrap from a new
perspective, Doyce finally answered, "Swamp fever,
wasn't it?"

Giving a skip to close the distance, Gelya chimed in now,
her freckled face momentarily animated. "Didn't Ozer explain? We heard him yelling at her. Honoria's a Livotti,
through and through, Zandra and I are positive—the family

looks to a 'T.' That chilly, 'don't touch my hem, I'm superior to you' look. The other thing everyone in Samranth recollects about both families—even after all this time—is how they always carried a grudge, never could let a past slight or wrong die. They may have just about died off, but I doubt their grudges died as easily."

"So what's that got to do with Honoria? Besides, as far as I know, her last name's Wijnnobel, not Livotti, not even Rutenfranz." Doyce hated this sense of bafflement—weren't there puzzles enough to work out, problems to solve? If she chose not to like Honoria—fine. She had sufficient reasons without blaming the woman for being a Livotti.

"Well, it wouldn't be Livotti, would it?" Gelya said reasonably as she cast a look over her shoulder at the children. "Her mama was one of the last Livottis, forget whom she married. Wijnnobel's not a common name here. I just wish she weren't with us. Still, I'd dearly love to know how and why she went to Canderis, though I can't blame her for fleeing her past. But why come back now? Ask Ozer when all this is over—for better or for worse. Mayhap he knows more than he's saying." A shiver rippled through her, and she hugged her shawl tight. "Oh, Blessed Lady, please give us our little ones back!"

They'd nearly reached the warehouse area now, Khar heavy in her arms, exhausted, dozing but still absorbing every word, she hoped. Let her beloved regain her strength, and mayhap they'd unscramble this mess. Khar abhorred puzzles even more than she.

Harry sat back on his heels, spine pressed against the roof drainpipe that ran down the loft wall before jutting outside to finish its journey along the warehouse's exterior. Truth was—pure and simple—he was twitchy, and being pinned in position like this, always in contact with the blasted pipe, gave him no way to release his nervous energy. Even if he *could,* he wouldn't dare pace, though they'd all removed their sandals.

When Smir returned—with help, if they were lucky—he'd smack the iron pipe three times to signal he was joining them. Harry's response: two slaps for "all clear," or three for "hold, danger above," would determine their next move. So here he crouched, tethered to the pipe, forever making sure some part of his anatomy touched it, alert for its vibration. An impatient wait, especially given the drama soon to unfold two warehouses over. Hard to miss *that* parade, even in the pitch-dark—two lanterns plus a herd of children and adults meandering along the deserted back streets.

If only he were younger or older, his Resonant skills would be trustworthy. Being twelve, going on thirteen meant that puberty muddled his mindspeech. Hormones, the eumedicos said with lofty condescension, as if they'd never suffered it themselves. Skills he'd taken for granted from babyhood, could tap without thinking twice less than a year ago, had soured on him, turned flighty and undependable, swooping like a voice indecisively choosing between soprano and baritone. Humiliating to lose confidence in his own 'speaking and receiving abilities.

Finally dropping to the floor and resting a shoulder against the unyielding pipe, Harry pounded his knee in frustration. Ever since he'd spied the parade, he'd been attempting to 'speak Aunt Doyce, every fiber of his being aware of her nearness. Worst of all, enough of her random mindthoughts sifted through for him to surmise that she and Ozer had agreed to the exchange. It was all so *unnecessary,* even dangerous, because she didn't know what they'd discovered. He and Smir and the girls had *found* the Oordies, stashed right here in this old spice warehouse! Better yet, only two guards watching to make sure they didn't wander, ensure someone didn't stumble on them. And if Aunt Doyce only knew what he knew about those guards!

Harry glanced in Siri's direction where she'd nestled in a jumble of burlap, chin propped on hands while she observed the guards dicing below. Somehow aware of his gaze, she turned, gave him a cheery thumbs-up, bent Mr. Monkey's stockinged arm so he gave a "paw up" as well. Too bad he'd handed Mr. Monkey back to Siri, he wouldn't half-mind cuddling him for reassurance. With a roll onto his belly as he planted his bare foot on the drainpipe, he stretched toward Byrlie where she sat shadowed by a crate, arms wrapped around jiggling knees. A soft finger snap, another, and she looked his way, pale eyebrows furrowing an inquiry.

"Nope, not yet," he half-whispered, half-mouthed the words. "Soon, I reckon. Oordies still asleep?"

"Boy baby's tuckered out." Was that the hint of a superior grin on her face? "Little girl's trotting around, poking and peeking. They roped her round the waist, tied the other end to a . . ." she gestured, "thingy what holds up the beams. You know."

He did, but couldn't think of the word either. "Whatever," he added to fill the space.

Her mouth went all prim again, her voice sounding shamed. "We gonna be much longer, Harry? I gotta pee something fierce."

Damn! That was something he hadn't taken into account: girls *always* had to pee five times as often as boys, seemed to him. "Can you hold on a little longer?" Gave a wild, casting glance, praying he'd spy a bucket, something. "Just don't let loose all of a sudden. Don't make it rain on their heads!"

"Wasn't planning to!" She gestured behind her. "Big old scoop-thing over there, better than nothing."

Something merchanters used to funnel spices from larger to smaller containers, just like a flour scoop. "Sure, just be quick," and waved her off, politely averting his eyes.

Onto his back now, rubbing his arch up and down the pipe as he stared hard at the roof, pretending he could see right through it to the moons, Lady and Disciples alike. Ride their beams to Aunt Doyce, flag her attention, clear everyone out before someone got hurt. A jumbled discordancy—Aunt Doyce, the overspill of other people's agitation, even the tantalizing though weak echo of another Resonant, though this new mental signature felt unformed. There—he overheard Aunt Doyce loud and clear, fretting over Kharpers! Good old ghatta!

A tear seeped down his cheek and he swiped it with his sleeve. Wasn't good for much, was he? Couldn't make Kharpers young again, couldn't devise some audaciously grand deed to make everyone proud of him. If Papa were here, he'd know what to do—even Mama, in her own, very different way. But he was neither boy nor man, awkward at either role these days. Being an adult meant things like

admitting good old Kharpers *was* old, wouldn't live forever.
And by extension, neither would Mama or Papa, Aunt
Doyce . . . Only then did the rhythmic pounding on the
pipe register; he'd ignored it as a distraction. Response: two
slaps, a pause. Repeat, in case Smir'd been woolgathering
as well, though he doubted it.

Giving the girls the high-sign, he scrambled on hands and
knees to the loft opening, its door panel propped open just
a crack with a crate slat. This wasn't a game any longer,
this was real, dangerous—people you loved could be hurt,
mayhap die. Adventures weren't all fun and games, camaraderie; they required scary feats of courage to save little'uns
who couldn't save themselves. Was he brave enough to save
the people he loved, those he'd always depended upon to
keep him safe? No, Aunt Doyce and the rest would be fine,
Theo and Khim'd see to that. Theo might not look like
much, but he was brave as houses—all Seekers were. Smir
had known how to be brave for a long time, despite his
carefree airs. He and Siri laughed in danger's face but
stayed alive. What Smir knew came natural as breathing,
beat all Harry's schooling, his courteous demeanor, his soft-
handed ways.

Taking a deep breath, he unsheathed his belt knife, set
it between his teeth. If he needed it, he'd be ready—wasn't
going to be any, "Wait, can I have another try at that?"
time. Edging the door wider he stuck out his head and
shoulders and almost lost his knife, jaw slackening at the
sight of the female Shepherd Aidannae shinnying up the
drainpipe, Smir on guard below. Diddly-damn! Wasn't what
he'd expected in the way of grown-up help, but he'd take
it and be glad! After all, hadn't Uncle Jenret and Papa told
outrageous stories about the Shepherd Harrap in his
prime? Had sworn that Harrap and Aunt Mahafny had
made an awesome duo.

Nearly level with the loft's sill, Dannae paused to rest,
feet balanced on the narrow lip of a drainpipe bracket.
Couldn't climb much higher since the pipe popped inside
just above her head. Nervous, aware how visible she must
be, even in the dark, pale wheaten robe a giant light splotch
against darkly weathered wood, Harry urgently waved her
within. She wagged an admonitory finger back, stretching
her arm to her fullest to grasp the door casing but couldn't

reach it. Bracing himself as best he could, he stretched, grabbing for her hand.

"Don't be daft, lad," Dannae yanked her hand away as their fingers brushed. "My weight gainst yours and I'd snatch you out of the loft so quick you'd leave your britches behind."

Her remark stung, but it was true. Retrieving his knife from his mouth before he gagged on its metallic taste, he thought hard, saw Smir gesturing at them to hurry so he could swarm up. Except, he now gathered, Smir had never actually employed this entry route before or he'd have known full-well the gap couldn't be bridged. Well, he was in charge of devising plans, so he would. "Can you shinny a little higher, swing your leg over? Legs usually reach longer than arms."

She did, hugging the hump of the pipe. "Right, and leave me with a leg inside—if I'm lucky—and my hands out here, hanging on to the pipe for dear life. Keep thinking! I can't hang up here forever—I'm not a bat!" A foot slipped on the bracket, and she clung grimly until she regained her foothold.

Oh, Blessed Lady, grant him inspiration! What would She do to him if he let one of Her Shepherds fall? Couldn't rescue the Oordies because of that? He was too young to wait around for a second life, a second chance! Eyes cast to the moons in supplication, he froze, discovering his answer. There might be better ones, but this was the only one She'd vouchsafed him for the moment. Directly centered above the loft window was a wooden beam, the remains of an old hoist dangling from its end.

"Dannae! Can you undo your belt, hand it over?" An unexpected tug at his shirttail nearly toppled him, made him squeak with fright until a small hand crammed itself over his mouth.

"Harry, you gotta hurry!" Byrlie jittered with impatience, arms waving. "I think the guards are getting ready to leave, take the Oordies somewhere else!"

"Fine. Go back with Siri, keep watching. One of you play kitty-mouse with them if you have to. Got me? Mousey-squeak, skitter-run and hide?" With a nod and a pat on his arm as if she were his mother, she soft-stepped back to her post.

"Give it over, Dannae!" he commanded and thrust his arm out, hand beckoning. "We haven't got much time!"

"If I undo my belt, this blasted habit unfurls till it's longer than I'm tall—I'll tangle my feet, kill myself!" But despite her protests she was unknotting the rope belt one-handed, holding it together until the last possible moment.

"Just give it here, then grab the hem and stuff it twixt your teeth. Then hold on the pipe till I say, 'Ready.' " Dannae snapped her arm, the hemp belt unfurling like a whip, and he caught the free end, encouraging her, "Drop it now." A panicky giggle at the sight of Dannae cramming her robe between her teeth, cheek muscles bulging with effort. Wondered suddenly what Smir could see by looking straight up at Dannae—didn't want to know, didn't dare ask. He'd heard *that* story about Harrap, prayed that lady Shepherds had different rules about what they wore under their robes!

But as that unseemly thought tumbled through his mind, it collided with mindthoughts leaking warning, resentment, anger, confusion. No choice but to ignore it all as his hands busily made a big knot at one belt end, then three more one after another up the remainder, like spaced beads on a string. Blasted blivet-rivets, Disciple doo-doo! Just a tad shorter than he'd hoped, the knots taking up precious length that he needed. His belt, his favorite, a soft, supple leather that wrapped around him twice before buckling—would it hold? Well, at least it would stretch before breaking. Square-knot Dannae's belt to the tongue end of his, tug, pull it taut, the leather molding itself into the knot.

Quick now, Dannae's face tight with anxiety, the muscles in her hands and arms distended, Smir's sharp whistle from below: "Someone coming!" it warned. Stretching on tiptoe, refusing to think how his upper body precariously poised over empty space, he knotted his belt round the beam, yanked to test it and tossed the end to Dannae. She wrapped it around her thick, no-nonsense wrist, made a grab with her free hand as she kicked away from the wall to swing across. Bea-yoo-ti-ful! Bang on perfect! As Dannae's feet caught him in the chest, he managed to fall backward without landing with a betraying thump.

Back at the doorway now, Dannae's broad frame blocked his view as she encouraged Smir. Before he could whistle a "Hurry" note, Smir swung into the loft, grinning with relief. "Sharp plan! Yed did it, Harry!"

The praise, the way Smir regarded him, new respect in his eyes, gratified Harry. "Got more needs planning," he whispered gruffly and led the way toward the opening at the loft's center. "Byrlie thinks they're going to move the Oordies soon."

Hanging back in the shadows, Dannae studied the warehouse floor, the position of the two guards and the children. She was *not* in the best of moods—too bad for the guards! With both hands she hauled her robe to one side, then bunched the excess material and crudely knotted it above her hip. It'd have to suffice since she'd not retrieved her belt. Actually, it was similar to the way the young women at the harbor markets hiked their skirts when they helped their fathers and brothers haul in their throw nets. The freedom made them more carefree than she felt right now.

Passing strange—the guards wore Guardians' uniforms, but if they were truly Guardians, they'd have reunited Oordbeck and the children. More going on here and outside than met even her skeptical eye. One little Oordie—she'd taken to calling them that herself—slumped in a pile of rags, crying in jerky bursts, not loud yet, but it would be when he went at it in earnest. Treet kept raising his arms for someone to pick him up and cuddle him, but neither Guardian obliged. Vannie, the little girl, sat fingering the rope around her waist, intently plucking at the knot.

The hardly-Guardians had swung open the double doors on the warehouse's waterfront end, one man or the other stepping out, trying to judge what transpired two warehouses over. According to Theo, the children were to be ransomed for all Oordbeck's files on Wycherley-Saffron, but she wasn't holding her breath on that happening. Pouching her lower lip, she considered how to best snatch the Oordies, make a quick, unobtrusive exit. Monkey-swinging on her belt and then sliding down the drain pipe lickety-split wouldn't work; bad enough for Siri and Byrlie to accomplish, absurd for the Oordies. Impossible to carry

432   *Gayle Greeno*

them, either, and pull off such a feat. A set of wings
wouldn't be amiss.

Leaving her vantage point, she huddled with the children.
"Anyone got any ideas? I'm fresh out." The lad Harry had
been resourceful before, mayhap he'd hatch another.

"Drop sonthing on their heads?" offered Kasimir with a
cheerful bloodthirsty relish that would have dismayed her,
except that she knew him. "Fra dis height, blam, smash'em
like melons!"

"Fine, if they faithfully promise to hold still, not move a
centimeter while we do it." Harry worried the idea back
and forth. "And likely we'd make noise moving whatever
we push off the edge."

"I kin go down, ask'em stay put!" Smir grinned, undeterred that neither his plan nor his choice of weaponry had
won approval.

A soft, muffled sneeze, Siri burying her face in the crook
of her arm, eyes wide as she tried to stifle the explosion.
Dannae sympathized, rubbing at her own nose, oddly itchy
and tingling. "Ground chilipeppots," Siri raised her head
experimentally, quickly reburied her face to block another
sneeze. "Whole barrels over there, leaking out. WHA . . .
a . . . a . . . phew," she trailed off as the sneeze receded.
"We stirred up the dust'n all scuffing over here."

"Chilipeppots?" Dannae rolled the pungent word on her
tongue, an idea burgeoning as Siri repeated it as well, the
corners of her mouth impish, blue-green eyes shrewd,
"Chilipeppots!"

"Woan hurt'em bad, but it'll sting'em—nose, eyes, lips.
If'n they're all sweaty, the powder feels burny-itchy on
the skin."

Patting Siri's head, pleased at her insight, Dannae mused,
"Fling it with some of those giant scoops we found, just
let it sift down. Doesn't have to be accurate, not once it's
airborne." Kasimir shuffled his feet in delight, silently
smacking his fist against his palm, but Harry, she noticed,
acted unconvinced, already foreseeing something they
hadn't. "What? Spit it out, lad." The inner workings of
Smir's mind were no mystery to Dannae, but she couldn't
read this boy in the same way. Well, she'd listen, not only
for courtesy's sake, but because of his ingenuity in bringing
her inside.

"Sneeze it out, not spit it out." Both hands swung lazily above his head, his fingers wiggling the way little'uns fitted motions to words when they sang about rain. "Whatever powder we toss, it'll float, work against us as well as the guards, make the Oordies sneeze, too. Got to cover our mouths and noses, tie cloth over them, shield the Oordies' faces."

It made sense; no quibbling with his logic. "Anything else? Such as how we make a graceful exit, thank our hosts?"

"That's what I wanned atell yed afore!" Escorting her to the edge, Smir made her lay on the floor, her head uneasily extended beyond the brink. His brown, ropy arm pointed and she followed his direction, unsure what she was supposed to see. Queasy at being suspended over such emptiness—somehow worse than shinnying up six meters or so of drainpipe—she shook her head, her topknot thrashing the air. "Look again," he breathed in her ear, angling her head, "fourf post, den count five planks in, foller my finger."

Feeling like a turtle extending its head too far out of its shell, she counted it out. Four over, fifth plank in, so? Index finger under her nose, Smir sketched a square, placed his thumb against his first finger and raised his hand as if lifting something. "Hatch," he mouthed.

With a nod she shimmied back, relieved to press her cheek on the solid floor. Lady help her, she'd cricked her neck! "Why not just say so before? Instead, I had to lean out like that, balance my life in the Lady's palms. . . ." Sputtering, she stopped.

"That's why yer Lady's got eight hands!" Smir teased back. "Wanned yed ta see 'zactly where i'twas."

The hatches served to load or unload small boats whose decks didn't reach the warehouse's level even at high tide. Meant they'd drop right into the water, though not all that deep if she'd judged the tide right. Could be a long way down, though. "Ladder still there, half-decent?"

"Yep, zat's how I userly nipper in and out."

Again she gathered them away from the high open area so they could converse in low voices, Dannae assigning roles. "Harry, Kasimir—scarper down to the main level. Once we start dusting, you two'll grab the Oordies. Dodge behind the crates and barrels, keep hidden till I'm down. Girls, you'll follow soon as I signal."

Strategy, strategy. "Siri, right here with the chilipeppot; Byrlie, the far side. We'll set scoops along the edge, anything that'll hold powder, let you sift it over." The girls nodded.

In the midst of her directions, Harry bobbed up, slipping off without a word of apology or explanation. So much for the politeness she'd deemed innate. But he returned as swiftly and silently as he'd departed, a pole over each shoulder. At least that's what they looked like in the semi-darkness. "I've procured your favored weapons, Madame Shepherd, obtained through great cunning and derring-do by that mysterious Marchmontian gallant, so loyal and true!" An uncontrollable giggle spurted from Byrlie, and Siri stuffed Mr. Monkey in her face.

Her sense of humor frayed, Dannae planted her hands on her hips, praying for enough inner strength not to swat the lad, no matter how richly he deserved it. "Pre-SENT Arms!" he barked, soft but intense, snapping both poles forward to slide through his encircling fingers. Without warning his mouth opened in a silent howl, eyes widening as one pole tip speared his bare foot. After a heartfelt but silent string of oaths, he regained his composure.

"Your weapon, Madame!" Balancing on one foot, he shook the other as he handed her the pole. "Brooms are your weapons of choice, I believe."

The handle's smooth sleekness caressed her palms as she brought the broom-head beside her to examine it. To her boundless delight she discovered it was a push broom, its wooden head expansive with bristles, perfect for sweeping dust—or chilipeppot—from wide swathes of floor. The second was more traditional, twig, the sort she'd menaced Theo with . . . how many days ago? "Pour out a line or a nice pile of chilipeppot powder, and sweep away!" Harry instructed, miming the actions to match his words. She considered kissing the boy, but hated to embarrass him in front of Smir like that.

"One other thing." As he knelt at Dannae's feet, his belt knife at the ready, he added, "Remember? We need cloths to cover our faces. Thought you might oblige with your excess fabric."

"Leave me a tail in back," she instructed as he hacked away. Reaching between her legs, she brought the tag-end of material up until she could join it with her side knot, her legs bare and free as a girl's! Bless the lad for shortening her robe! And this time Dannae *did* kiss him, a resounding smack on his cheek.

"No, don't—not yet," Doyce cautioned as Ozer started to signal the children to pile the records in the center of the warehouse floor. "They're our only bargaining chip. Don't hand them over till they've fulfilled their share of the agreement." Handed over Treet and Vannie—alive, unharmed. She wouldn't say it aloud, fearful Ozer'd shy at the mere mention of their names. As long as he treated this as a business compact, he could function.

Even with the lantern shutters fully open, the light they cast only minimally lessened the pall of the long, echoing warehouse with its high beams and rafters. From above roosting bats and birds rustled, made protesting squeaks and murmurs, followed by the sharp splat of droppings. It not only felt cavernous, it was—mayhap forty meters wide and twice that long, the space broken only by skeletal shelf-frames on stilted legs in lieu of separate floors. Toward the front of the warehouse where it balanced on pilings, the sea lapped and murmured.

Little was stored here now except stale, baked dust, leftovers not worth the effort to claim and move, she'd assumed until she noticed a few wooden crates with fresh-stenciled markings, canvas-wrapped bales with cording. A whistle of surprise almost escaped her at reading "Wycherley-Saffron" in block letters on their sides. Heaps of splintered crates and pallets canted at odd angles gave the impression of a ravaged village whose houses had just survived a hurricane.

A rat squealed, its dark form skittering madly through the cluster of children, and some of them shrieked before clapping hands over mouths. Lindy and Gelya circulated amongst the children, reassuring and hushing them. "This isn't one of the warehouses you rent, is it?" Despite the

presence of the marked crates she suspected it wasn't, but
waited for Ozer's answer.

"I should hope not! Even Janacz & Sons gave up on this
rattletrap." No matter how preoccupied, Ozer's business
side never lurked far from the surface. "Look up," he
waved the lantern as high as he could reach, "look to the
sides. They'd pay more for repair and renovation than they
do renting elsewhere. It's a family leftover." Doyce immediately saw what he meant, shingles missing on the roof,
patches of starlight peeking in, wallboards with spaces between them, some loose and flapping in the evening breeze.
Weatherproof it was not. For that matter Doyce didn't care
for the way the flooring felt underfoot; boards would creak
and give but not rebound. She'd not recommend holding a
dance here to celebrate the children's return!

Khar and Khim slipped back into the light, the whites of
their muzzles, their chests visible, their stripings all shade
and shadow. Exhausted as she was, Khar's determination
and discipline hadn't deserted her, but her whole stance
revealed how near the edge she walked. Even Khim's usual
chipper attitude was subdued, and she definitely favored
her right forepaw. **"Splinter,"** she confirmed after examining her curled foot. **"Can you pull it? Theo's busy inspecting the back."**

Dropping to one knee, she probed between Khim's toes.
"Not much to get hold of, is there?" Khim nodded woeful
agreement. *"So, I take it you ladies saw no sign of the
children?"* she asked to distract Khim while she fumbled.
Had the ghattas nosed out any trace of Vannie and Treet,
they'd have 'spoken her instantly.

Fussily mounding herself, Khar sagged with relief, her
amber eyes drooping. **"Not a trace. No one in or out since
we checked earlier. They must plan on bringing them when
you make the trade."**

With a jerk Doyce freed the splinter and, just as she did,
both ghatta went alert, Khar painfully springing up to scan
the dark, Khim already focused, a low growl announcing
the presence of strangers. A rumblous screech as a door
trolled along its rust-pitted track, exposing the night sky,
the surging of the sea beyond. Honoria slipped to her side,
"Someone at the back door as well. I'm not inclined to
invite them in unless they have the children." A reproving

headshake. "That door won't stop them for long, even though we threw the bolt from the inside. You can hear the clink of keys."

"Who goes there?" Sword drawn, Theo'd hurriedly stationed himself ahead of Doyce and Ozer. "I said—Who goes there?" His carrying voice sounded pitifully small and lost within the empty confines of the warehouse.

"Ooh! I'm sooo skerred! He's sooo tall and bonny . . . I mean, boney, it jes makes my heart flutter!" A mock falsetto quavered from their left, followed by a raucous jeer and the thud of bare feet as bodies dropped from rafters and spidered along the shelf-framing, more bodies blocking the patches of sky that had shown through the roof.

"Shut up, laddy-buck! Toe the line—you're not here to provide entertainment." The snap of a flint lighter, sparks like fireflies, but nothing caught.

"Tain't me, Geer!" The voice was Massie's, the dagga boys' leader; Doyce hadn't heard it since the incident at the bazaar, but somehow felt convinced of it. "Stupit Ragva acting girly-girl." The smack of an open hand against flesh, and Doyce's own face stung in sympathy.

"Well, they're your crew, so control them. Or I will." Again the flint struck, its flame creating a small halo before a lantern beam glowed larger. Still not enough to see over such a distance, but Khar and Khim certainly could with their superior night vision.

"How many? Who? Can you tell?" Overcome, Ozer moaned beside her, fist thrust over his mouth. Well, they'd made contact—just as promised, complied as instructed. Now hand over the records when Treet and Vannie were led out, and leave. As simple as that, she told herself. Don't let the dagga boys' presence threaten you.

Khar's lower jaw shifted as if she worked at something unpleasantly tough. **"Four in front—Guardians, no less. Or dressed as Guardians."** Ears pivoting, catching and identifying individual sounds, she didn't spare a glance left or right. **"A dozen of our friendly dagga boys, boys being boys. Six a side. Sorry, Khim tried to tell me, but I was just so—"**

"But they can't be Guardians!" Preposterous! Guardians would never— Had the Sunderlies corrupted them? What

joy—more puzzle pieces, except she'd have sworn they'd
been borrowed from another puzzle.

Poised near Theo's knee, Khim held herself ready to attack. **"And no fresh child scent around. The children aren't
with them. I doubt they intend to abide by their own rules."**

Theo grunted agreement, and Doyce gave thanks that
Ozer couldn't hear Khim's bleak assessment. More light,
wavering, dancing, shivering tongues of flame as torches
came to life, passed hand to hand until light girded them.
For one disjointed instant Doyce became one with Jenneth,
rejoicing as the flames sprang alive, curling fiery, clutching
fingers toward the high ceiling. Jenneth and fire, drawn to
it, obsessed by it . . . A child cried, was hushed, and Doyce
knew they huddled behind her, the knot of bodies contracting until their breath was practically squeezed out of
them. The Guardians moved closer, their brass-and-leather
helms tinged with ruddy glints, their curved swords unsheathed but riding on their hips, each a burnished crescent. Worse luck, she caught sight of Geerat Netlenbos
from Tarango Fort, Guardian Captain in charge of the Sunderlies detail.

"Seeker General Marbon." A sketchy salute, the flames
turning his face florid as a drunkard's. "I'm so sorry you've
accidentally intruded in this little quandary of mine. I'd
much rather your husband, Jenret Wycherley, were present.
Even better, his late father, Jadrian." A dismissive wave of
his hand. "But then time passes, children grow older. The
desire for revenge grows and matures as well, some say. I,
myself, discount such fixations, but they do obsess some."

"And the lust for money?" That, she suspected, compelled Netlenbos more than any festering desire for revenge. The furnishings in his office, the perfectly tailored
uniform from this morning all indicated a man pleased to
spend money on himself.

An agreeable laugh greeted her question, though it
sounded a bit forced. "Well, money *is* the universal axle
grease, isn't it? Nothing rubs when money smooths the
way." He motioned to the three Guardians just behind him,
two Sergeants and a Corporal, from the markings on their
leather half-armor and helms.

"You've no idea what a bloody boring assignment the
Sunderlies can be. Ensuring no convicts escape—and be-

lieve me, very few try. After all, we've exiled very few in
recent years. Watching the merchanters sailing in and out,
confident there's money to be made, money that could line
your own pockets as easily as it does some investor's, whose
only risk is the coin invested." Indignation made his voice
shrill. "You never see *them* living in this Lady-forsaken
place—hot, humid, strange diseases ready to cramp your
guts or worse, storms and hurricanes that sweep out of
nowhere—"

"Doing one's duty seldom reaps worldly riches—or at
least not that I've noticed. We've all mourned missed opportunities, Geerat, but if you're going to regale us with
your life story, let's do it around a tankard later tonight.
Haven't we a business transaction to conclude?" An elbow
to Ozer's ribs, and he jerked convulsively before holding
out the folder of papers he carried. His shaking hand set
them aflutter, and she prayed his nervous fingers wouldn't
drop them. How much longer he could continue, remain
under control, she didn't want to test.

"Ah, you're right. Just as well to conclude our transaction." Another step nearer as he gestured with the crescent-
shaped sword he carried. "Neat and tidy counts, follow the
regs and you can be a captain, too. Protect my trading
partners' identities and their investments."

A hand to his forehead, the age-old gesture of 'How
could I have forgotten?' making Netlenbos appear the win-
some child enchanting indulgent adults. "Oh! Of course!
We *must* discuss how we conduct business in the future,
now that the structure's been laid and tested. No reason in
the world I can't head one of the richest mercantiles in the
Sunderlies." The curved sword's point tapped the timbered
floor. "Pile everything right over there, if you'd be so kind.
My apologies—I'd no idea it would be such a load! Did
you hear that floor creak!"

"Well, claim them, then." No point in arguing, mentioning he'd be tried and convicted not only for betraying
the Guardian uniform he wore, but also for kidnapping and
extortion. Come to think of it, what would his punishment
be—banishment to the Sunderlies? Hardly, since he was
already here. "Aren't you forgetting one thing, though?"
His eyebrows rose in genuine perplexity. "The children?
Oordbeck's little daughter and nephew?"

"Khar? What's wrong with all this? It's all too petty, too ordinary—garden-variety greed."

"That's because you're hearing only half the story, its surface, and Geerat's all surface. Unfortunately truth can be petty, too. Little people like Geerat serve as cogs, servants. Ask him who else—"

But Ozer, half-mad with despair and longing for his little ones, could stand no more. Throwing himself on the nearest dagga boy, Ozer wrestled for the torch, crooking his arm around the boy's throat. As the torch hovered threateningly near the dagga boy's head, Doyce smelled the scent of singeing hair. "Enough! I want Treet and Vannie now!" Tears poured down his face as he squinted though the flames. *"Now,* do you hear me!" He squeezed his arm tighter and higher, levering the dagga boy onto his toes. A muffled screech as his bare feet ineffectually kicked at the floor, backward at Ozer's legs.

"Ozer!" Lady help her, of all the dagga boys he could have grappled with, Ozer had a strangle-hold on Corly! Doyce could see the pitiful yellow-and-blue downy feathers woven into his hair, the rolls of baby fat at the waist and armholes of his precious new leather vest. Corly, the one dagga boy—or would-be dagga boy—who'd dared disobey Massie, refused to abuse Khar! Sprinting to Ozer's side, she ignored the crack and pop of a floorboard. Worse, as justified as Ozer's actions might be in his own fevered mind, he was jeopardizing the children's recovery!

Shouts and torches hemming her in, clubs and knives ready and eager to strike as the dagga boys massed to defend their own, more and more weight straining the already overloaded floor. "Ozer, let him go!" Both hands on his arm now, trying to pry him loose, Khar darting round their feet, assessing points of vulnerability. *"Do something, Khar! We'll peel them apart someplace else if I can shove them clear of this crowd."*

Tiredly gathering herself, Khar backed off, came running full-tilt to ram her full weight behind Ozer's knees, buckle him. Without thinking, she shouted out loud, "No, Khar! Don't—" but her cry was overridden by louder screams, shouts of shock, outrage. "Leave the children be!" Geerat Netlenbos shakily ordered. "Vaert! That wasn't part of our agreement!" Lady help and protect them! Either Treet and

Vannie were here somewhere, being blinded or worse—
except . . . they'd never arrived, had they? The dagga boys
must be attacking the other children! Oh, hells!

Before she could ascertain what—or who—had instigated
this budding chaos, Khar crashed into Ozer and he tottered.
Someone slammed into her back and she teetered off-balance as well, united in an embrace with Ozer and the dagga
boy, Corly. Stepping on, tripping over each other's feet,
they faltered, began a precarious tilt that could defy gravity
only so long. And damnation, she was destined to end up
on the bottom!

The floor slammed her from head to heels, the others'
weight crushing her ribs, knocking the wind from her. The
strangest vision swam before her eyes, that charming fat
man from the bazaar, the one with the mustaches that put
Arras's to shame. Momsvaert, the pillow-merchant. Had he
come to her aid again, ready to fight off the dagga boys?
How very . . . nice of him. . . . The pressure marginally
yielded—how, why, she couldn't judge until a final, ominous crack resounded in her ears as the floor gave way—
and she was falling . . . dropping into darkness . . . Khar
clinging to her leg, Ozer and the dagga boy clutching at
each other, at her . . . down . . . the world dropping out
from under them . . . and then nothing. . . .

Flat against the wall, one foot high, one foot low on the
stairs leading to the main floor, Siri waited, mouth and nose
swathed with a piece of Dannae's robe. "I am a bandit, sir,
a gracious gentleman, and a refined robber of the road-
ways," she intoned to herself. The flowery words were wonderful, though they didn't do much good in this life. A
scrumptious book it had been, 'citing and all that, and colored pictures, too. Had Harry read that one—gotten his
idea for their masks from it? She'd planned to show Smir
the book—he'd have enjoyed the pictures—but the stall-
lady had snatched it, tucking it on a higher shelf before
she'd read more than a chapter. Had tendentiously sworn
Siri was too young to read such racy things. *That* had been
mendacious on her part. Sumptuous, sophisticated words,
exquisitely fine, that the lady probably didn't even know!

Awaiting Dannae's signal, she hefted the crate slat, ready to send it skittering and—with luck—send the guards investigating as far away from the Oordies as possible. She hugged Mr. Monkey to her chest. Then sweep the chilipeppot and aa-choo, Aa-choo, ACHOO! Dannae's broom waved in the air, and Siri gauged where the men stood, sent the slat spinning as she dashed back to her post.

By the time she'd taken her position, ready to pour more trails of powder, Dannae was driving the wide broom forward with long, steady strokes to the lip of the loft. Each stroke cascaded a cloud of chilipeppot into the air, a reddish-orange haze that both sank and swirled, drifted like silt. Byrlie, taller and with longer arms, had been assigned the other broom, much to her private dismay, and swept her edge, swip-swap, swip-swap, with the same tidy concentration Siri'd seen her give the kitchen floor at Dolphin House. Scurrying after Dannae, then Byrlie, Siri laid out more powder, threw a few scoops of her own for good measure, pretending her arm was a catapult. She clapped her hands, couldn't help herself.

The sounds from below were richly satisfying: sneezes and wheezes, coughing and gagging. She caught sight of the taller guard running half-blind, crashing against one of the posts. Not a dead-on hit, but solid enough to further unnerve him as he rebounded, shaking his head stupidly, eyes streaming. Ooh! She clapped again as the two guards stumbled into each other, finally righted themselves. "Head for the back—there's a hand pump outside!" The taller one shoved the other guard in the right direction. "Stick our heads under the pump!"

"WHA-choo! about the AA-aa-aa chool-dren?" the other sputtered, swabbing at eyes and nose with his sleeve. Not very bright, it just ground in more chilipeppot powder, his uniform all dusty with it. The Oordies were crying now, high, whooping shrieks. They'd tried not to sweep their way, but the powder floated wherever it wanted.

Grabbing the broom when Dannae handed it to her, Siri took her turn, handle over her shoulder, leaning into it to shove it ahead. Phew, it dragged fierce! Thundering down the stairs, Dannae checked in all directions as she ran, leaving a trail of footprints, dark, stained wood showing through the orange powder. Once Dannae found the hatch ring, she motioned for the boys to retrieve the Oordies, Smir and Harry dashing from their hidey-holes, masks in place, extra masks for the Oordies dangling in their hands. It had been Smir, not Harry, who'd thought of the burlap sacks from toting Siri during her baby days: each boy had one knotted over a shoulder to drape across his chest and opposite hip. Each Oordie would have a nice little sling seat, and Harry's and Smir's hands would be free.

The boy Oordie popped in slick, relieved at being rescued; but Siri predicted trouble when Harry grabbed for the girl Oordie—a handful, Vannie was. Trust Smir to take the easy one! Hoisting Vannie, Harry held her at arm's length, frustrated, reluctant to bring her any closer while the child kicked, tiny fingers pinching and twisting flesh. At Dannae's whistle, Siri and Byrlie joined hands. Despite being longer than she was tall, its brush segment as broad as Dannae, Siri resolutely brought the push-broom, bumping it behind her as they ran down the steps. Dannae might want it.

By the time they'd scooted down, Harry's face was scowly red as he scarpered for the trapdoor, his extended arms aquiver, what with Vannie being a chunky handful and battling all the way. Without a word Siri skittered to his side, loving how the powder felt silky under her bare feet. The masks had sent Vannie into a pother, fussing her, so Siri momentarily jerked hers down to reveal her face, one the child should recognize. "Vannie! Hark'ee now!" she wheedled, raising and lowering her mask again, doing the same with Vannie's. "Boo!" Arm muscles straining, Harry squatted, balancing Vannie on his knees while Siri slipped his mask down and back into place. He flirtied a kiss at Vannie while it was off. "Gonna switch yed fanny, if yed keep bellowing," she warned, and Harry cast a reproachful look at her. Why, she wasn't sure; after all, Smir threatened her with that and worse eight times each day. Didn't mean he did it, though. Didn't mean she'd do it, either.

Spreading the sack, she helped Harry pop in Vannie. Half-in, half-out of the trapdoor, Dannae circled her arm, urging them on, Byrlie and Smir and Treet nowhere in sight. Down the ladder once she'd left the broom with Dannae, deft as Mr. Monkey, Harry slower, the baby quiet but

squirmy, batting her eyes, coy as coy could be. Ooh, she
was mashing her masked face against Harry's cheek now,
making smacking, kissy sounds! Siri giggled.

At the last rung, Smir grabbed her round the waist and
swung her down into thigh-deep water, all sorta ick things
floating—fruit peels, an old shoe, vegetables nearly new,
others rotten-soft and squishy. Wrinkling her nose at the
stinky-sour smell, she splashed at the green, trailing things
that slimed her skin. Dead fish and live fish, busy noffals
glupping little fishy-nibbles out of carcasses, a bailing tin
from somebody's boat—that she snagged, might want a tin
for something. And . . . and . . . a dead cat, half-submerged,
bumping against one of the ooze-green pilings. Poor little
chazza! A lump clogged her throat because Khar hadn't
come after she'd called and called. Busy, belikes. Still, she
sent a call of silent yearning. 'Twasn't weakness to wish a
special friend by your side, but she'd lief as soon the others
didn't know.

Probing with her broom handle, Dannae took the lead.
"Can you boys tote the Oordies a bit longer?" she asked,
and Siri was charmed to see that Harry was just taller
than Dannae.

"What we doin nixt, Dannae?" Smir splashed to her, left
arm wrapping Treet's burlapped-bottom. With his free
hand he stripped off his mask and swooshed it through the
water, wiped the wet rag over Treet's screwed-up, protesting face to scrub off any powder residue. No sense reminding him the water was dirty. Smir made a good mama,
she'd known that for ages, better than the one who'd
birthed them—showing up whenever Smir'd cadged food,
vanishing otherwise, 'long with whatever they had that she
could sell. Byrlie's mama, Lindy, was the sort of mama
children were sposed to have, curvy-soft in spots, something
Smir couldn't manage no matter how he tried.

Since Dannae wasn't answering quick, taking her time,
looking round as if hoping the Lady'd send an island floating by, Siri figured it was time to say her piece. "Gotta go
water-side," she pointed to the medium-darkness at the far
end, a deep-blue rectangle slashed by pitch-black pilings.
"Guards dashed out road-side, means they'll bring help that
way. Somebody's gonna fanny-tan them fer misplacing the
Oordies."

"I know, I know." Dannae sighed, tight-clutching her broom. "Water's already deeper. May have to swim for it before we're done." She swallowed hard and sicklike, and Siri wondered what ailed her. "Work our way back to shore, hide behind the pilings till we're clear." Her topknot hung all draggly, her face grayish, and not from the lack of light, Siri thought. Could Dannae be scared? "Don't know if we can with the Oordies."

"Byrlie and I can swim." All mannish concern, Harry laid a hand on Dannae's arm, comforting-like. "Least we can in ponds, lakes, even. Same in the sea, I'd guess. Smir? You and Siri?"

Smir grinned. "Flipper-feet, me. Siri's half duck—paddle, spladdle!" She swatted him, but not as fierce as she could have. Wasn't the time nor the place for it.

"Yes . . . but there's . . . one thing." Clinging to the broom as if it were a lifeline, Dannae's face crumpled in shame. "I can't!"

"Cor! Yed jestin' us?" Smir's eyes went wide, the whites showing. "Livin' here all yer life 'n yed neber swimmed?"

Shrugging free from his load, Harry handed Vannie to Dannae, who near-squashed the breath out of the child. "No bladders down here that I've seen," Harry dismissively splattered a piece of trash, "but darn-all everything else. Just stay easy, don't panic. Kinda wanted something for the Oordies myself. Don't know how they react to baths, let alone swimming."

"Hey! Wait up!" Smir yelped, grumpy at being left behind. "I ken dis hidey-hole bedder'n yed!" Siri could see how he wanted to unload Treet on someone, but didn't think the girls were big enough, not in water up to their waists—nearly armpits on her.

"You were the tracker, the finder, and find'em you did," Harry argued. "I'm the planner, this part of the adventure's mine." His face went all solemn and serious. "I'm *responsible* for this part, so let me do my job." While Smir grumbled even more, still burdened with Treet, Harry waded off, and Siri heard more splashes, grunts, the squawk of rusty nails and rotted wood parting.

Something low and wide with a nose pointy as Smir's surged through the water, barely exposed, scaly gray with green splotches. As Dannae shrieked, Siri almost followed

suit until she recognized what it was and transformed her
scream into a scornful "ha!" In a lather, Smir dumped
Treet at a surprised Byrlie, who juggled him as best she
could above the surface. Knife unsheathed, Smir readied
himself for a shallow dive as Siri thrust her hand down atop
the thing's point. The plank's rear end rose dripping, and
she released its jagged "nose" to let it land with a flat slap.
"Siri, yed liddle shite! Thought it was a mowery!"

"Didn't snakey-bend, did it? An slow as last year's zin."
She glided the plank beside Dannae, Vannie now tummy-
down across her shoulder, broom pinched under her arm
while her shaking hands struggled to form the Lady's eight-
point star. If it had been a mowery, Dannae'd have been
better off busting it with her broom. "Nice piece of board."
To demonstrate, Siri rested her chest on it, gripping the
edges as she began a gentle, even kick. "See, Dannae, jest
kick your feet."

Herding something large and round in front of him—an
old, wooden washtub, no less—Harry cheerfully patted his
find. "Prayers *do* work!" Gripping the tub's lip, he spun it
around as it floated on the water. "Thank you! Figured I'd
find something other than that board, but never expected
anything this good." Smir looked distinctly jealous.
"Propped on a ledge, dry most of the time, junk in it. Pop
the Oordies in and it's a boat. Mayhap even have room
for Siri."

Siri glared. "I kin swim!" Hand cocked on hip, her fingers explored a wet, limp bulge. Mr. Monkey! Mr. Monkey
was all wet! "But Mr. Monkey *hates* the water, he could
ride with the Oordies."

Clad in a loose shirt and trews of faded blacks, navies, and
browns—the result not of patchwork but of meticulous effort to mingle night's different hues—Mettha Prinssen, Sunderlies Security Chief, peered intently from the cupola's
westerly embrasure. So far it had all gone according to
plan, and that left her nervous as a cat. Narrowing her
eyes to stare beyond the row of wharfside warehouses, she
checked the harbor for the running lights on the two boats
she'd positioned there. One rested at anchor, its bow and

stern lanterns describing glowing parabolas, while the other cruised aimlessly, a small smack packed with "revelers" waving bottles and tankards, a fiddler sawing frantically to be heard over laughing, arguing voices. Better be pouring fruit juice, or the demotions list would lengthen. Again she sought out the Janacz & Sons warehouse, reassuring herself nothing had changed. For no reason she worried that her face and hands stood out, a disembodied whiteness, tipping off anyone scrutinizing her perch. Likely not, she was dark-complected, though she'd made some of the others coat faces and hands with a mixture of soot and grease to shade them to a night tint.

Mouth dry, she debated taking a sip from the small water-skin at her waist, but refused herself the pleasure. The Lady knew she'd already spent half the night in place up here with no inkling how much longer this mission would last. A full bladder would set her ajig, and she was edgy as a razor without that. Besides, it wasn't thirst as much as craving a diversion, a way to make the time spin by. "Anything?" she queried the night air, but the murmurous responses from the north, south, and east embrasures all tolled a negative, minor chord.

Still, near midnight now, something *should* happen, and soon, or all her careful plans had been for naught. Not that long ago the brisk whisper of feet, the bobbing of shuttered lanterns, had alerted her to the convoy of children and adults reaching the abandoned warehouse. She'd not anticipated the flock of children—shortsighted of her. Considering that Oordbeck had already had two snatched away, what else should she have expected him to do? Still, it reminded her to exercise due caution over apparently insignificant aspects of any chancy assignment.

No further strangeness from the warehouse two over to her right, where she'd glimpsed a most peculiar apparition—or thought she had. Large and light-colored, it had rippled and swooped across the warehouse's loft door like some giant bat. Then nothing, and not a soul stationed nearby who'd seen it. But then, they concentrated on movement in streets and alleyways, at doors and windows, would have been reprimanded for gawking at the upper stories. Mayhap a "floater" in her eye coupled with an overactive imagination, nothing more.

Neat footsteps, each thoughtfully muffled, sounded in the stairwell, counterpointing her thoughts. Four flights and not a pause at any landing. No panting, either, so the climber was clearly fit. A deprecatory "hem" behind her, followed by a hand on her elbow. Baskin, of course, hardly a surprise. Fully expecting to be apprised of how the night's mission fared, Erzebet Hoetmer probably paced the gardens at the Governor's Mansion—without her pruning shears, Mettha hoped.

But before she could formally acknowledge Baskin's presence, something new riveted her attention, leaving her pointing and whispering, "There! Look lively as they slip over the rooftops!" A dozen figures, mayhap more, mostly silent, though a few balked, skittish at launching themselves from one roof to the next, a hastily stifled shriek as one figure abruptly became airborne, arms windmilling. Without a doubt that one had required extra impetus, otherwise known as an unexpected and expert boot to the backside.

"Dagga boys?" Propping his elbows on the casement beside her, Baskin comfortably shifted his weight, his sparse frame clad in the most ugly olive-toned caftan and brown vest that Mettha had ever seen. Fading had given parts of both garments a jaundiced tinge, and fraying threads marked the creases, as if they'd spent too long in a trunk. Noting her appalled interest, he preened, a musty scent rising from him as he raised his arms to reveal the darns and patches. "From my 'prentice days." His head reached her shoulder, his pate as deeply browned as his face. Obviously he didn't follow Erzebet's advice about hats either.

"Had you expected them?" He made it sound as if he maintained an intellectual, rather than an interrogatory interest in the proceedings. "Ah, the flexibility of youth! Throwing themselves into thin air like that!"

She liked Baskin, respected him more than most of the other tight-lipped advisors, afraid to venture an opinion without registering the prevailing breezes on their buttocks. He'd resided in Samranth so long that Mettha nearly forgot he wasn't Sunderlies-born. Never made her feel inferior the way Erzebet could—and did—without any ill-intent, that condescending, measuring look that showed all Sunderlians exhibited a defect in ethics, a moral laxity, each and every one gauche, louche, low even, until proven otherwise. That rankling inferiority had driven her up through the ranks until she'd come to the Governor's attention as being, quite simply, the best, confidently and competently proving to all—native-born or Canderisian—that Mettha Prinssen represented the true essence of the Sunderlies.

"So, did you? Expect the dagga boys?" Baskin repeated, and she realized she'd swung back to watch empty roofs. That was Baskin, ask a question and stick with it like a limpet till he received a solid answer, even a distasteful one. He was as single-minded as she, hence her grudging respect and love for the old man.

Comfortably bumping his elbow, she gave him a solemn wink when he cocked his head in her direction. "When you give a party, gate-crashers often arrive. I didn't *know,*" she emphasized, "that there *would* be, but I thought it likely. Vaert always goes to great lengths to keep his connection with the dagga boys a secret—hence the scuffle in the bazaar the other day. But he wants the dagga boys on hand to offset Geerat's followers, thinks Geerat has been entirely too uppity of late." Hardly unexpected, Geerat Netlenbos was a fool, but he was Canderisian and a Guardian to boot, the natural inheritor of greater acumen and superior cunning compared to some Sunderlies pillow-merchant!

"What I can't fathom is how Netlenbos can betray the Guardians like that!" Damn! She'd not intended her aversion for the man to reveal such a shocked innocence, not when her professional standing revolved around greater goods, lesser evils. No doubt Baskin had noted the parallel between Geerat as Sunderlies commander and herself as Security Chief. Treachery, deceit, betrayal were part and parcel of her job—necessities that would horrify an honorable Guardian—but never wielded for personal power or financial gain.

"I suppose we all have concealed flaws, weak points," she added unwillingly, "but you'd think his would have been exposed before now, before being named commander!"

The wilted hibiscum-heliothalus in Baskin's buttonhole, its yellow-orange petals crumpled but its scent still sweet, reminded her of Erzebet's horticultural homicide in the gardens earlier, how she'd butchered Doyce Marbon's hopes with equal efficiency, sent the woman fleeing. Erzebet's stubborn refusal to share knowledge was a flaw, though she often did it to ensure any blame stayed rooted to her, not to the underling who carried out her orders.

But Baskin was frowning, eyebrows bristling as dangerously as a prycanthius hedge, while he considered his answer. "Yes, we all have our flaws, Mettha. Many times we—and everyone round us—are happily oblivious to them. It requires·the right key—a person, or incident, or place—to unlock them, release them for others to see." Jerking back as to physically distance herself, angry at him, irate at herself for such oversensitivity, she started to protest, but he held a hand to forestall her. "Mettha, Mettha, stop carrying that chip on your shoulder! I'm hardly implying that the Sunderlies corrupted Geerat, or even Momsvaert!

"Usually it's a concurrence of things, 'place' doesn't have to mean a specific country. Don't we all joke of 'being in the right place at the right time,' or 'being in the wrong place at the wrong time'? Mayhap fate moves our feet. Had Geerat served on the Monitor's staff in Canderis, it might have happened with equal ease. Something would have touched him, made him conclude he deserved better, was worth more. But if the flaw doesn't exist within, then the outer stimuli have no effect."

"Am I *that* transparent?" Resettling her shirt, fussing with its sleeves, she realized she was performing the human equivalent of settling ruffled feathers. He'd baited her like a hawk, only to snatch away the lure, leaving her with nothing to pounce upon. "I should think you'd wonder how I managed to attain this position!"

"No, dear—not when I watched you rise every step of the way. Watched you stumble, fall a few times, too. You earned it by being the best at what you do, handling repugnant tasks that would easily turn lesser souls into Geerat's equals. You're," his mouth quirked, brown eyes twinkling, "well, what they used to say on Earth in the old days was 'sea-green incorruptible.' Or mayhap it was," he rubbed his lower lip, dredging up the phrase, " 'pea-green incorruptible.' Dashed if I can remember which!"

Laughing at herself as much as at his words, Mettha stood at mock-attention. "Invest me with the Order of the Pea-Pod, if you please!"

More footsteps on the stairs now, pounding more urgently than Baskin's had. One of the runners, no doubt. Good news—or bad? As Kendell burst through the hatch, his fingers danced, snatching at thin air, hands constantly gesticulating. "Guardians haven't the right key for Janacz's back door, Chief! And things are heating up inside, from the sound of it! Should I let Lieutenant Vanderloo break down the door or not?"

Already fumbling in his pouch, Baskin retrieved a rusty iron key longer than his hand. "If I may, Chief?" It touched her that he scrupulously sought her permission, refusing to undercut her authority in front of one of her agents. "Had a constructive talk with Janacz Senior before dinner. Suspected he was hindering us in mingy little ways since he boasts a mingy little mind. And lo—"

At her clipped nod, he handed over the key. "Try that, first. You've oil with you?" With an enthusiastic nod, Kendell mimed an oil can with his free hand, thumb serving as the spout. "Stealth's always preferable to breaking down doors—louder than knocking." Without waiting for dismissal, Kendell dove for the stairs. Or at least she hoped he planned on descending them, rather than leaping straight down the stairwell to speed things along.

"Erzebet and I harbored a feeling about Janacz Senior," Baskin shrugged, tush-tushing under his breath. "Didn't mean to intrude on your patch, but you've had on-site problems to occupy you."

True enough, but they couldn't resist meddling either. But without Baskin's and Erzebet Hoetmer's aid and diplomacy, she wouldn't have dared include any Guardians in tonight's action to augment her own limited forces. As long ago as last spring they'd opened delicate negotiations with the Canderisian Monitor and Guardian General, well-aware that pointing out a traitor could provoke instant disbelief and denial. In time they'd even succeeded in having a "replacement" sent over, a lowly "private" who'd sounded out his fellows to pass along word as to who'd been "bent" and who'd remained honest—the vast majority, to everyone's relief. Their sense of duty and honor guaranteed they'd obey, but how they'd truly feel about it, she didn't know. They felt as foreign, as alien to her as she must to them—and a woman, to boot!

From their vantage point at the embrasure, they watched Kendell shoot off with the key, Guardian shadow-shapes massing round the door, working at the lock, oiling hinges, the door reluctantly—and silently—swinging open just as another runner sprinted into the cupola. "Seized the two privates—Ritsma and Hanuman—at the warehouse two over from Janacz's!" Tabbico was one of her best agents, snapping out a crisp salute but not pausing with her explanation. "Lady's lungs and liver—begging your pardon, ma'am—if we know what happened to them. They fell right into our arms, eyes blearing, sneezing their heads off. They're totally covered with chilipeppot! Warnowwer's stuck their heads under the water pump and sent for a hose. We've a team combing the warehouse for anyone else, but it's sheer misery in there, like being in a chilipeppot dust storm!" She held out a child's wooden cow. "Found this. Looks as if the kidnapped children may have been held there."

"Keep searching, then. Check everywhere. You've all tied wet rags over your noses and mouths?" She'd send an offering to those silly Shepherds if it would ensure she'd comprehend what had set the thing in motion without her! Someone had stepped in, apparently on their side, but who? And where were the children?

"Of course, Chief. Doesn't protect our eyes, though, and seeing's our biggest problem. Want to question Ritsma and Hanuman, or leave it to Warnowwer and me?" A distinctly hopeful look brightened Tabbico's squat, plain features.

"Start the questioning. I'll be along momentarily." At Mettha's dismissal, Tabbico clattered off.

"Chilipeppot?" Striding around the cupola, Mettha passed instructions to her crew. "Of all the things to use as a weapon! Effective, though, I'll wager."

"It sounds like something a child might do. Clever enough to view the commonplace as a weapon we adults would overlook."

"Coming?" Already halfway down the stairs, she threw the words back over her shoulder, confident Baskin would follow.

❖

The problem with unexpectedly falling, Doyce constructed
the thought with care, only too aware it might be her last
coherent one, *is that it distracts you from determining if and
where you've been hurt.* Yes, that made sense. *Mainly because your mind's preoccupied with figuring out how and
why you fell.* Did she need a "who" somewhere? No, she
felt reasonably sure she knew "who" she was. The floor
was *above* her now—interesting. And a tearing big hole
in it, too. Someone insistently jostling her arm, blubbing
something, splashing around. It sounded suspiciously like
Ozer . . . or Oordie . . . or Oh-Oh repeating, "Doyce,
Miz Marbon, please! Can you move, can you get up?" His
constant plucking annoyed her, like having to deal with a
whiny, clingy child. Lady bright! Damnable Disciples all!
Her inhaled breath hissed between clenched teeth.

She feebly flicked at Ozer to drive him off, annoying fly
that he was. "Let me be!" But something on the periphery
of her inner senses claimed her attention. *"Khar? Beloved?
Are you all right? Are you hurt?"* Movement at the small of
her back told her she lay atop something, more specifically
someone—Khar. Unsure if she could, she tried to roll to
her right, ease the pressure on Khar. Her muffled scream,
just centimeters from Ozer's face, sent him staggering backward, cradling his left arm. For some reason her feet, most
of her legs, were bobbing, floating. "Khar—under me,
Ozer! Hurry!" Worst of all, Khar hadn't answered her.

Splatting, squelching sounds came at her from the other
side, the dagga boy, Corly, looking scared and as young as
he truly was. "Spiked her, spiked'em both, I reckon. Poor
ol' chazza! Poor, poor ol' . . ." Despite his aggressively
masculine scent of wet leather and raw alcohol, patchouli
and pomade, a boy's tears hovered near the surface.
"Spang on lift gears an dey bit dem." Squatting, he eased
an arm beneath her until he supported her shoulder and
head, his other arm slipping under her thighs. "Ozer-Mon?
Ken do same-o wid twiggy arm? No? Least help with
hand?"

Glowering, Ozer waved a fist, ready to renew his fight
with Corly while the boy was crouched helplessly, cradling
her body. Amongst the other smells she'd noticed clinging
to him, the sweetness of childish flesh still remained. "Ozer,
leave him be!" Dear Lady, how had she become the boy's

champion in the midst of chaos? "I think Corly's about to
be stripped of his feathers, expelled from the dagga boy
ranks."

But she had no more time for such frivolous things, berating herself for wasting time intervening when Khar so
desperately needed her. *"Khar? Khar, sweetheart? Can you
speak? Are you hurt?"* She didn't care how Corly and Ozer
moved her, how much it hurt, as long as Khar was alive.

"Aaoow! Chewing at my vitals!" The beloved mindvoice
was thready, breathless with pain. **"Such teeth—giant, rusty
nightmare teeth!"** Her raving words, the absence of jest,
petrified Doyce.

"Ozer, come on! Chazza hurt bad!" Corly's still-juvenile
voice finally worked on Ozer. "Counta dree," the dagga
boy instructed. "Raise her much as yed ken. I'll scoop her,
yed grab fer chazza—gentlelike, yes?" Ozer nodded, ducking as another floor plank loosened, fell beside them with
a smack. Not the havens echoing overhead, but battle,
oaths, falling bodies, blood seeping between the boards.
The children! Oh, Blessed Lady, the children up there!
How had she forgotten? "Whan . . . due . . . DREE!"

Up, metal gear cogs tearing fabric and flesh as they
exited, blood streaming wet-warm down her back, almost
pleasant. Why? Was she cold? *"Khar!"* The dagga boy
swayed, pressing her against his leather-clad chest, only to
stumble backward and sit in the water.

"Got her!" Ozer, breathless, struggled with a mound of
wet, slick fur, Khar's wet tail dangling beneath his elbow,
a rivulet of water finally tapering into individual drips.

"Solider than yed looked." Grunting, Corly struggled to
rise, only to plop back down. "Lousy dagga boy I make!
Soft on chazzas, little'uns, all sorta feeblings like me!"

Absently patting his sodden feathers, Doyce shoved off
against Corly, almost capsizing him as she fought her way
to her feet. The pain was bad, but would be bearable if she
could only reach Khar, embrace her. Sliding each foot, her
stance wide, she waded through murky water, fearful she'd
trip, fall headlong. "Give her to me!" Knees wobbling, she
clutched Ozer's arm as she wavered.

"Oh, my babies!" Ozer sobbed to himself, cocking a
shoulder to direct her. "Platform, behind me. Crawl on and
I'll hand her up."

Groaning as she boosted herself up, Doyce hooked a knee on the edge and rolled onto the debris-laden platform. Curled on her side, she indicated the curve of her body as Ozer slid the sodden mass to her. Hard, always so difficult to determine where the hurt was, so dark here, Khar's fur so wet and plastered . . . part the fur, stroke and lightly probe, move to the next section. Her little finger glided knuckle-deep into a raw puncture, and she sucked in her breath. The next two—farther along the flank, one just shy of the hip joint—she located with just her finger tips. *"Oh, Khar! Not like this, not now!"*

"If you stick in your finger like that again," Khar weakly licked her hand, **"I may bite it. Hurts! You've got holes, too."**

Too overcome to speak, she pressed her lips against Khar's neck. But such intimate communion was cut short as two small, pale shapes cut through the air like a comet-streak in the semidark beneath the warehouse. Doyce came bolt upright despite the pain. Too small for dagga boys or Guardians, who? **"Strategic retreat . . . says Khim. Littlest Oordies first."** Ozer caught the first child one-armed, hugging it tight to his chest, while the dagga boy fielded the second, grinning with relief. With scarcely a pause, two more came flying after them to be caught as well. Finally a rope snaked through the opening; it didn't reach all the way, but anyone slipping down it had control until it came time to drop free. More of Oordbeck's brood came whizzing down with a splash.

Honoria surged by, halted as if taking an inventory. "Well, you're both alive, I see." A quick hand skimmed Doyce's back. "A bit crude as a pincushion, but the effect's similar. The ghatta?"

"We'll make it. Always have, always will." With grim perseverance she sat up, refusing to let pain win, and hoisted Khar in her arms. "This way to the retreat?"

A hand on her ankle effectively stalled her. "Invitation, please? Wait till I call. There used to be a boat moored down here—not much, but better than nothing. Fancy a moonlight sail?"

"More than a moonlight swim."

Skirts billowing in her wake, Honoria waded on, effi-

ciently surveying her surroundings as she went. "If there's
no boat, just follow my trail of bread crumbs!"

"Damnably chipper, don't you think?" She'd cherish any
extra private moments with Khar that the world would
grant her. But the longer the delay, the worse their pain
would grow, the more likely infection would set in their
wounds. It struck her with the force of a blow. *"Khar! What
of the children? Harry and Byrlie, Smir and Siri, I mean."*
Fear cramping her gut, she tensed, sending a flood of pain
through her back. *"And the kidnapped babies!"* Failure,
every step of the way, failure! Not a thing righted.

"Siri's been coaxing me half the night. She'll find us."
The softness of a paw against her skin. **"Touching. Touch
me, makes it feel better."** A hint of light from above re-
fracted in Khar's eyes, cloudy amber now. **Lick . . . my
wounds for me?"**

*"No, but I'll rub your ears, whisper sweet nothings into
them."* An agony to refuse Khar anything, even when she
asked in jest. If only she could erase the wounds, the hurt,
the speeding time that etched age deeper with every passing
moment. For no reason and every reason, a vision of Chak
and Rolf filled her mind, and she let her tears flow. Would
they wash wounds? Staunch time?

As she waded toward the derelict boat beached beneath
the seafront entrance, Honoria grimly ticked off her options. Her preference involved deserting this motley crew,
abandoning them to slip back inside and finish off Momsvaert, dear Uncle Vaert! Geerat lacked both the brains and
the resolve to run things, and with Momsvaert dead the
whole scheme would crumble beneath its own weight.
She—and only she—harbored the drive and deliberation to
reassemble the scattered pieces, direct the game to its ultimate conclusion—winner take all.

Amusing to contemplate, and she stopped short, staring
blindly into the fog-shrouded harbor and beyond. Oh,
Uncle Vaert *had* raised her well, an amoral, pragmatic up-
bringing guaranteed to set her on a criminal path at a
tender age! But she hadn't trod that path for years, had no
inclination to return to it, not when she could match her

own deceptions against these deceivers. With a shrug at how deliciously easy it would all be—criminals derived more pleasure out of their crimes than their dogged pursuers—she shoved aside slimy net fragments, broken crates with an impatient hand, clambering to where the boat lay half-beached on a mud bar, its bow breaking above water, its stern sunk in the mud.

Doubtless many of Samranth's children—some now adults—owed their conception to this craft. Wilf Janacz and his friends had seduced scores of susceptible young women with their moonlight sails, cheap wine, and lavish promises. Her strongest urge that night when she'd grappled with Wilf was to throw him into the harbor, commandeer the craft and sail somewhere, anywhere but Samranth. Well, she'd gotten somewhere on her own, made something of herself. From the looks of the boat, Wilf had grown too staid and slothful these days to put it to its intended use. Still, a new generation of courting couples, children playing at adventure, knew this secluded and legendary site, free of prying eyes.

Hands on hips, she dubiously examined it, straining in the dark and shadows to assess its seaworthiness, testing it with a kick. Hmph, best not try that again or she'd stove it in, scuttle their chances before they'd begun! What other choice did they have? Not much with Geerat and Vaert and his dagga boys up there, more of Geerat's Guardians bursting through the back door. She'd sworn Geerat had inflated how many of his men were with him on this venture, and now she was paying the price for being wrong. Still, Mettha should've warned her, unless she'd encountered complications herself? Best lie low till things sorted themselves out, see if Mettha were still Security Chief.

Should cut her losses, escape on her own; an agent worked most effectively when he or she had the freedom to operate alone, and that's what she was compromising by remaining. She had no desire to see Doyce Marbon, nor anyone else remotely related to the Wycherley clan by blood or friendship, in Momsvaert's perverted hands. Most of all, she'd not jeopardize the children. Better a sweet death by drowning than becoming Momsvaert's chattel, subject to his whims. Old hatreds died hard, if they died at all.

The children, so many sizes. but all so blondly fair, boys and girls both, little replicas of herself and her cousin Hirby at so many different ages. But so loved, so trusting. Funny how Hirlbeck had darkened as he'd grown older, hair finally turning a mousy brown, rather sweet in its own way, matching his meek, mazed personality. Not that Hirby retained much personality, not the last time she'd visited him at the point, blissfully ignorant how his life had been circumscribed, content to play with his giant mongrel dog and wander the beaches to collect the sea's gifts.

A gentle soul who'd drifted as far in mind as some of his precious flotsam and jetsam had traveled—and all because years past Uncle Vaert had lost all patience with Hirby once too often, stinging blows raining down on the boy's head as Vaert berated him as a numeric dunce. "Why can't you be like your cousin Honoria? Quick as a flea with figures, and she's but eight—half your age!"

Scarlet, mortified, Hirby'd risen, hunched against the blows that pelted him from all directions. Ducking an open-handed slap, Hirby'd stumbled against the desk, upending the inkwell, a blazing black trail of shame pouring across the ledger. His attempts to mop it up had created a giant smear that had reminded the little Honoria of a map of the Sunderlies, though she'd wisely not pointed that out. Mumbling apologies, bumbling, Hirby'd busily enlarged the smudge, so intent on rectifying his sins that he'd made one crucial mistake—the one he'd warned her against time and again: "Never, ever, take your eyes off Vaert, don't turn your back on him. He'll store up all the madness, all the rage, unloose it when you least expect it."

She'd seen the blow coming, her scream wasted because Hirby was already sailing across the parlor, his head striking the andiron, blood on the brass, a red track like the mate of his black ink. Red—for debits, debts owed. Red—for Vaert had bankrupted his son, cracked Hirby's brain coffers. No wonder Hirby'd wandered as far as he could once he'd healed, though the dent in his head always remained, hidden beneath his mousy hair. . . .

Theo stork-legged it through the lapping water to join her, keep a wary eye on her, more likely. Poor Theo, wouldn't his illusions shatter when he learned the truth about her! "Will it float?" He sounded suspiciously like a boy eyeing a new plaything.

"With luck, the water will swell the planking, tighten the seams." With luck, indeed. "It needs to float long enough to leave those charming dagga boys, that turncoat Guardian and his crew far behind." To utter Momsvaert's name would bring more ill-luck, even thinking it had been tempting the fates. Now, setting her shoulder against the prow, she began to push. "You *could* give a hand," she suggested, bending her knees into the effort, the blood hammering at her temples as she strained to shift the boat into deeper water.

Scarpering sternward, Theo crouched in the stagnant water, his face nearly submerged as he struggled to pry it free of the muck. A reluctant sucking sound, then a weak plop like a cork exiting a bottle of sparkling wine that had already gone flat. Worthwhile to let Theo think himself in charge? She needed time to think, plan for contingencies if they *did* manage to flee their pursuers. There might be in-fighting now between Geerat's and Vaert's factions, but sooner or later, someone would come after them. Geerat she could handle, but Vaert wouldn't be easily thwarted. She shivered.

By the Lady, she'd row the damn wreck clear to Hirby's if she had to in order to ensure the children didn't fall into Momsvaert's hands! Too bad there weren't any oars, just the mast segments. Reality, pragmatism, killed off the best fantasies, but then she'd not allowed herself the luxury of harboring any for many years. Best utilize what she had: her wits, a derelict boat, and Theo.

Indistinct shouts, the muffled clang of metal against metal filtering out of Janacz & Sons unnerved Mettha, made her want to reshuffle her priorities, delegate the questioning of Hanuman and Ritsma to someone else. But they offered the first concrete lead they had as to the children's whereabouts. What sorry examples of Guardians they were, hair and clothes sopping from their immersion under pump and hose, their skin red and puffy-looking after a rough scrub with a burlap bag. Eyes still teary, nose watery, Ritsma's continual snuffle had driven Mettha to the tag-end of her patience.

"What happened to the children after you left?" Ask it often enough and mayhap she'd receive an answer, a supposition, even! The sporadic noise of fighting took on a softer edge, swallowed by the mist and fog rising from the harbor, bent on a reunion with the fine drizzle now leaking from the sky. Typical Sunderlies weather, hardly a handicap but definitely a hindrance. "You simply took to your heels, abandoned them?"

A particularly juicy sniff from Ritsma shredded her composure. Stalking so close he cringed, she snapped a bandanna from her pocket and applied it to his nose. "Blow, dammit!" Hands pinioned behind him, he heartily obliged, obedient as a child, a comparison that did *not* sit well with Mettha. How could they have forgotten their duty, too intent on saving their own skins to worry about the children? And where could two four-year-olds go?

"But doan you see?" Ritsma whined. "That's precisely what we couldn't do—see, I mean. Hanuman and I wuz lucky to get out when we did, literally found the door by crashing into it, way our eyes was streaming."

"Sneezes near shot us outa there," agreed Hanuman with a certain morose relish.

"Was gonna retrieve the tykes soons we could see our way—"

What lovely specimens of humanity—and Canderisian, no less! The sort hired when one needed a strong, willing body topped by a moderately empty brain, easy to lead into trouble's path because they'd never grow canny enough to see it coming, step out of its way. Behind her Baskin gave a compressed sneeze, apologetically waving the fine lawn handkerchief in his hand when she whirled as if under attack.

But what she viewed behind Baskin did improve her mood. Tabbico and Lieutenant Vanderloo, the Guardian now in temporary command of the troops, roughly escorted Momsvaert and two Guardians, now relieved of helms and swords. One, a sergeant, had been wounded, and the other wore the marks of close and vicious fighting. Further back, a dispirited crew of dagga boys was being briskly marched along, some supporting others and all looking strangely

naked without their studded belts and arm bands. From her
quick count at least three would haunt the bazaar in spirit
only, as the remainder went on their limping, moaning way,
overgrown boys digesting the unpalatable fact they could
no longer play the bully with impunity. "Very nice!" she
congratulated Tabbico with just the smallest smile of satisfaction, a matching one brightening Tabbico's stolid countenance. "Where's Netlenbos?"

But as Tabbico started to answer, Momsvaert spat at
Mettha's feet, tossing his head with a prideful arrogance
totally at odds with his captive status. "I regret to inform
you that I skewered dear Geerat myself. Panache, yes, he
had it aplenty. But sorely lacking in savvy, not to mention
sagacity. A vapid dreamer, sure that money should sprout
beneath his feet in homage to his passing across the face
of the land—isn't that a Canderisian for you!"

Despite the octants she'd invested in prying into Momsvaert's shrouded past, haltingly taking the man's measure,
gaining a wary respect for his patient, merciless cunning,
his sudden candor about his cohort took her aback. This
was the man who'd spun a web of deceit that had allowed
him to divert trade moneys into his own pocket, anony-
mously purchase smaller mercantiles outright, and create
shadow monopolies on certain goods. Illicitly-shipped
goods that never appeared on manifests, were never
charged harbor duties, cost both Canderis and the Sunderlies thousands in lost revenues, as well as syphoning profits
from legitimate mercantiles. He hardly looked the mastermind behind a trading scandal; he still looked like Momsvaert the pillow-merchant, paunchy, pleasant, a minor stall-
holder at the bazaar, his greatest extravagance his sweeping mustache.

"Why, Momsvaert? Pieter Momsvaert Rutenfranz," she
let his full name roll off her tongue, wondering how many
knew it, knew the man who bore it. As Security Chief, her
duty was to dredge up evidence, enough to imprison him.
The whys belonged to Baskin, who'd extract such details
from Momsvaert at a more suitable time. Still, she yearned
to know: understanding the whys of human behavior helped
her see through criminals' eyes, anticipate their actions.

That, and the urge to contrast him against his niece, Honoria Wijnnobel, her top operative, who employed a similar

strain of efficient guile in regulating felonious activities. Honoria was so rarely wrong that Mettha derived a momentary glee from thinking how chagrined she must have been this morning to discover how Geerat had grossly exaggerated the number of Guardians loyal to him. And that she now owed Mettha three goldens! A relief for her to know that the Guardians so quietly entering the warehouse by the back way were there to support and protect her and the others.

"Because I deserved to be born Canderisian, not stigmatized by a Sunderlies birth." A baleful pride burned in his eyes. "Oh, the Rutenfranzs were never exiled, they voluntarily emigrated, courtesy of my father's cowardice. A touch, just the smallest touch of Resonant ability in our lineage, and he fled like a cur with his tail between his legs after The Fifty!"

The Fifty sounded suspiciously like history past and done—Canderisian history, at that—but Baskin breathed an "Aaah" of enlightenment. "I've often thought," Baskin paused, pensive, "that that one moment of collective murderous folly has had repercussions to this very day. It loosed wave after wave of hatred and distrust; sometimes the waves almost dissipated, lost their power, only to reform and inundate Canderis with enmity yet again. A ghastly time, though Momsvaert wasn't born, and I was but three."

Baskin as a three-year-old was more than Mettha's imagination could encompass, hard as she tried. Noting her scowl, Baskin took pity on her, reading it as bafflement. "A group of mayhap fifty Resonants, most barely into their twenties, secretly gathered one evening for a night of music and dancing with their own kind, free to be themselves, to argue if and when—if ever—they could openly live with pride, take their rightful place in Canderisian society. Townspeople surrounded them and slaughtered them. None survived."

For all its brevity, the tale was poignant, but Mettha refused to wander history's ambling paths, intriguing and sad as they might be. Canderis was *not* her concern! "So, coward that he was, your father and family escaped to the Sunderlies?" Throwing her insult at Momsvaert's feet, she let her disdain imply that he, too, was no better than his father. "And he formed a mercantile with the Livotti clan, correct? You could easily have headed up the company—after all, there couldn't have been many left after the swamp-fever epidemic."

Her Sunderlies history, Samranth gossip and innuendo she could reel off by chapter and verse, her intricate knowledge its own reward as well as an indicator of various predilections on the part of certain members of society. Nothing like a long-term vendetta or two to keep the blood flowing—in the veins or in the streets to this very day. Mayhap the Sunderlies' near-perpetual heat let every wound, imaginary or real, fester, never heal. Was Canderis different—more temperate folk for a more temperate clime?

"Oh, yes, what a legacy! Inherit a dying company, one built by convicts, exiles! Mayhap my father was willing to stoop that low in his associations, but not I, even if there'd been anything worth stooping for! Cushion-selling offered more dignity than that!" After each admission Momsvaert's body acted as if it had been seized by a palsy, quaking so hard it nearly shook free of restraining hands. Chilled by the damp and rain, or gripped by deep-seated emotions? His constant jittering set his shadow dancing in the lantern-light, the gathering puddles like silvery mirrors, going quiescently dark as his body blocked the light.

"Yes, ship the dregs of humanity here to build a new society! Dregs, do you hear me? And what dregs produce is a Samranth, its progeny! You should know, Mettha Prinssen, granddaughter of the esteemed Beckett Prinssen! The poor, misguided man grew sick and tired of a wife and whining children—perpetually crying for food, for clothes, for shelter—while he needed every coin for drink and dice! Murdering anyone with a shovel, not to mention a woman and four children, is a hideously gruesome act! So he was transported here, wasn't he? And married a Sunderlies native—a good thing, too. No need for much in the way of shelter or clothing, food plentiful, hanging from every tree, practically jumping from the sea. Let him concentrate on his gambling and drink. Amazing *you* were born with any scruples or aspirations at all!"

Hands rigid at her sides, she fought the urge to slap the smug, gloating smile off his face. Hated Momsvaert and pitied him as well for scapegoating the Sunderlies. No shame in being who and what she was, but somehow shameful for him to flaunt her heritage in front of Baskin, who now needn't ponder what had driven her to scramble after respectability, cloak herself in it. Did a touch of Momsvaert's shame reside in her?

"It's the person, not the distant past, that counts. All of us have relatives we'd rather not acknowledge, pieces of our own past we'd prefer never see the light of day again," Baskin soothed, striving to convince her, Momsvaert, mayhap even himself. "But, Momsvaert, your stay in Canderis so many years ago must have been glorious! The ideal opportunity to prove your worth to your own kind in the very land where you should have been born, had your roots." Caftan limp with damp, a sheen of mist gilding his face and crown, Baskin stepped closer, aglow with fellow sympathy.

But Momsvaert's reaction wasn't what Mettha had expected, nor were Baskin's next words. "One thing we take pride in is record-keeping—who enters or exits the country. Years and years of records." With a fastidious wipe at his nose, Baskin gave a mock-shudder. "Dusty, moldy records that listed how one Peter M. Rutenfranz set sail for Canderis in the autumn of 206 AL and returned early next summer. Your work must have been of flawless caliber for you to have proved yourself so quickly—especially to someone known as a hardheaded merchanter, a man who'd had enough faith in Livotti-Rutenfranz to invest in it, offer you a job and training." A gentle cough. "Or disillusionment, mayhap? A burning desire to commence your career as a pillow-seller?"

An ugly little smirk played beneath Momsvaert's mustache, aquiver with the vibrations still shuddering through him. "Tell us about it, Baskin! Or do you require coaxing, the brilliant yet modest student urged to recite? It gratifies me to find a soul who's searched out my noble history. I'll happily amplify on any details you may overlook!"

What was Momsvaert's game? Why drag it out like this and, for that matter, why was she letting him? His deft manipulation vexed her, made her cast over what had—and hadn't happened—thus far. Did he simply crave an audience, someone who'd appreciate his audacity? A part of her listened, but another part of her worked at the puzzle, tenacious as ever. The tremors that continually racked his body obscured his outline, left her apprehensive that nothing was to be easily discerned this night.

Patting the rain from his brow with his handkerchief, blotting his mouth, Baskin appeared fearful that Momsvaert—mayhap even she—weren't hanging on his every word. Would he concisely wrap up this tale or lovingly relate every detail? If he pontificated, padded his story, she swore she'd charge him with obstructing justice and guarantee he spent a night in the same cell with Momsvaert! But to her eternal gratitude, Baskin chose brevity. "As recorded in affidavits obtained from Damaris Wycherley Saffron and others, Jadrian Wycherley hired you to clerk for him at his mercantile." His breath swirled with the mist floating around them. "After only two octants, he found evidence of embezzlement, and he turned you out. Gave you a lashing for good measure."

"Right in the middle of the roadway, so that every passerby could see and comment," Momsvaert cheerily contributed. "Further, he divested me of every copper in my pockets—reimbursement, he deemed it—despite lacking concrete proof of my culpability. But then, his other three clerks *were* Canderisian.

"A pox on them all! They're all alike—intolerant, smug, self-righteous! Unwilling to listen to anyone different! Luxury all round, taken for granted, while I'd watched my father scrimp, make do! The money Wycherley'd invested would have to be paid back—I knew my father would insist! And would Wycherley listen, let me vindicate myself, show him how I'd saved his mercantile on overbilling, put the money aside for him!" The change in Momsvaert was overwhelming, the years fleeing to reveal a callow youth, innocent of life's ways and burning at the double injustice his unorthodox accounting system had wrought. Proud of serving his employer so zealously, shattered at being so misunderstood.

"Oh, yes, so there I was, cringing around Gaernett—earn a copper here, beg another there to pay for passage home—steerage, no less! Made me a better man, can't you see! Taught me the value of honest labor! What a joke on me—it has no value and never had any!

"My one rewarding moment during my exile came from hearing he'd killed his elder son, Jared, for showing Resonant abilities—a Gleaner taint, they called it then. Best of all—the son'd had the last laugh, swept every thought, old and new, clean out of Jadrian's head!'' His own head back, Momsvaert roared his laughter to the skies, the rain pelting down on him, on them all, in earnest now. A single growl of thunder resounded in the distance. "Swept his brain so clean not a single thought ever adhered again!"

An obscene performance, as if he'd stripped naked and exposed not his flesh, but his mind. It, more than the rain and thickening fog, made Mettha shiver inside. To wait so long and patiently for vengeance, a subtle vengeance at that, didn't seem Momsvaert's way. As if . . . she pursed her lips, considering, it should be more public, more obvious to ensure suitable fulfillment. Damn, she'd give a year's pay to have Doyce Marbon and her ghatta here at her side to seek out the truth embedded deep in Momsvaert's twisted mind!

Slapping her forehead in disbelief, she watched Momsvaert smile, triumphant at the length of time he'd sidetracked her. His smile wavering, he worked to purse his lips, fling a globule of spit at her feet. This time she *would* slap him for such insolence! As she raised her hand, the spittle caught her eye, oddly dark, almost black against the pale cobblestones. "Tabbico! Did he take any wounds in the fighting?"

Shaking her head in the negative, Tabbico nonetheless began to run her hands up and down Momsvaert's sides, around his midsection, jerking away with a hissing intake of breath as her hand slapped a sodden bandage that immediately saturated his caftan with blood that began to stream down his side. Delay, deceive—gain time to die on his own terms—and mayhap ensure that Doyce Marbon and the others would die as well. What a passionate disappointment for him that Jenret Wycherley wasn't suffering his wife's fate too! That had been Momsvaert's end game. Slowly bending at the middle, knees sagging, Momsvaert slid through his captors' hands, collapsing against the cobblestones, blood and water swirling between them.

So, he'd proved true to his own sense of honor—or cowardice—she could contemplate which later. Spinning on her heel, leaving the body for Tabbico to deal with, she headed for the Janacz & Sons warehouse at a trot. Each footstep drove home the fact she'd been played for a fool, mesmerized by Momsvaert's unfolding of troubles past. How could she have forgotten! How? No wonder Momsvaert had been quivering—with suppressed laughter at her for being so obtuse!

From the splashing behind her, Baskin followed, equally mortified at the oversight. After all, he'd been the one baiting Momsvaert. Something had gone badly wrong, or Honoria'd have gathered them all here, safe at last. Doyce Marbon and the ghatta! Where were they? Where was Oordbeck, his family? Marbon's other friends? Hardly surprising Momsvaert had been so content to let Baskin spin his tale. Had Honoria failed?

"DeSouza! Where the hells are the folk we were supposed to be rescuing? All those children? And what word on the two missing children at the other warehouse?" DeSouza came to abrupt attention as Mettha shook her sleeves and hair, a fusillade of water droplets dappling him. Chafing under her own forgetfulness, it irked her beyond reason that DeSouza stood dry and comfortable just inside the door, while she'd been standing out in the wet, lulled by a false complacency that she'd completed her job. At least DeSouza'd boasted sense enough to come in out of the rain!

But the three other agents and two Guardians who hurried from deep within the warehouse appeared far the worse for wear, sopping and stinking, smeared with mud and rotted garbage, fish scales that sparked luminescent in the lantern-light. "We were about to inform you, Chief." Rubbing wearily at his mouth, Gelnsbrock scowled on discovering his filthy hand had merely rearranged the muck on his face. "We wanted to sweep the place clean, look everywhere—other warehouse, too—before reporting. Best we can figure is they all dropped beneath the warehouse to escape. According to a couple of the dagga boys, floor collapsed 'neath some of them. There's blood on the gears of the old hoist system, the ledge down below, so some took hurt. Then they must've waded or swum out, but not a sign of them on shore either. Can't make a passel of children disappear easy as that."

"No . . . you can't," she agreed with reluctance. So it wasn't over yet—Momsvaert might be dead, but his handiwork endangered other innocents. "Did you sight that old wreck Janacz always moored down below?"

Gelnsbrock laughed, white lines radiating along his face as the dirt cracked. "Wilfie's floating love nest? Pretend pirate ship captured by every child in the city? Chief, a fishnet boasts fewer holes than that wreck has these days, I'd swear it!"

"Regardless, signal our craft to search the harbor, grid it as best they can. If they're adrift in that, they're in dire need of rescue. If they *do* manage to stay afloat in this storm, Honoria may try to sail up the coast." Honoria rarely dropped any chance remarks, scrupulously avoided her personal life. But one offhand comment years past had stayed with Mettha, mayhap because Honoria rarely expressed affection for anyone, most especially those comprising her limited family. After visiting with a cousin, she'd mentioned how he'd humored her by playing pirates with her when she was little and lonely. "If we don't catch them now, we'll sail north, storm or no storm."

Baskin shook her elbow now, demanding recognition, practically standing on tiptoe. "But my dear, isn't Honoria Wijnnobel a bit old for pirate games with those children? Why's she running now when anyone endangering her is either in custody or dead?"

It came to her all too clearly: Honoria'd never confirmed the coded note she'd been sent early this morning, may never even have received it! It explained why she'd sought to escape, flee, convinced the forces against them were too strong. "Honoria's rarely foolish or foolhardy, and she has no choice but to assume Momsvaert's after them. By her way of thinking, any risk, even sailing an overloaded, damaged boat in a heavy rain storm, is better than letting Momsvaert catch them."

Claws hooked deep in the age-splintered bow, Khim hunched forward, muzzle and whiskers beaded with sea spray, her eyes squinting against the rain that had begun pelting down. Water above and water below. Out of nowhere a misty fog had stealthily crept in to veil the moons above, even Tarango Fort's tower lights only a hazy glow.

A child trod on her tail, murmured a lisping "Thorry!" and Khim lashed it clear, constantly scanning for floating debris, boats at anchor or, worse, moving ones.

Another ship might carry pursuers or total strangers whose larger vessel could ram them, unable to spot their lightless craft in time to yield. For now they "sailed" at the harbor's farthest reaches; it offered more room to maneuver and kept them as far as possible from prying eyes. With her superlative night vision Khim had been entrusted to serve as lookout. Spreading her whiskers to flick off more moisture, she sampled the shifting air currents that might also tell of approaching danger.

Theo manned the tiller, instantly alert to her least command, except for one major sticking point: their stolen craft wasn't capable of reacting with Theo's alacrity. "Floating sieve" was a more accurate appellation than "boat." Honoria, Rudy, and Gelya had the long yard nearly joined, while Corly cursed in a vivid, fluent monotone, the simple slipknot for the parrel looking more like a piece of crocheting. There'd been a brief but heated debate over leaving Corly behind with his fellow dagga boys. Only Theo's intervention, prompted by Khim, had allowed him a place in the boat. Khim recognized outcasts when she saw them. Ozer, she knew, would gladly throw him overboard if need arose, a symbol of the loss of his babies.

Bad arm in a rude sling, Oordbeck high-stepped over a child here, a child there, offering unwanted advice to people too busy to listen. Ozer felt disregarded, and so did Khim; each time she tenderly let her mind reach out for Khar or Doyce, she roamed through a maze of private pain and apathy, each so preoccupied with the other that no room existed for another being. She and Theo were on their own.

Well, truth was straightforward, simple to find this night: Theo trusted her to chart their course. With the sail not yet in place, Theo made way slowly, dependent on riding the tide and the currents, the wind helping or hindering as it chose. **"In, in toward shore a bit, then steady."** Something there, the blunt butt of a submerged log? Hit that and it'd stove them in. **"Rudder right! Shift weight!"** As the boat heeled to one side, the log rubbing along their length but doing no damage, Theo motioned for the large children to shift over, redistribute the weight. Ten children, eight adults, and two ghatti loaded the boat to the gunwales. If the sea didn't slosh over the side, it rose through the planking, ankle-deep in an eyeblink.

"Sorry. Not the most elegant escape ever planned." She sighed; Theo loved apologizing, blaming himself for things beyond his control. *"Or the most watertight craft."* The silent reproof she cast at her Bond spoke more eloquently than words. *"Honoria did the best she could. If we hadn't found this, I don't know where we'd be."* Wonderful, now he was apologizing for Honoria!

Honoria still troubled Khim. What was she—truly? She'd been kind to the children throughout their long wait, had shown her worth tonight, but always Khim suspected her of being manipulative. Hunching lower, Khim contemplated the harbor, ever-alert but still bothered. Rain plinking and plunking, dimpling the water, now splattering harder, and behind her the steady slosh of water being poured overboard, the children passing the bucket and bailer from one to another. They were compliant ghatten-children, pitching in without complaint, each secure in his or her place, loved and wanted. Sweet but rather unnerving, as if they contravened the very nature of childhood!

But again doubts about Honoria plagued her, left her unrepentant for the wreckage of the silky nightshift under her paws. What to make of her? What of the papers she and Khar had salvaged and taken to Oordbeck? Honoria wore two faces, but which was real? Humans undoubtedly struggled with similar contradictions when they tried to weigh truth without the ghatti. Proof on this side, disproof on the other, the scales forever shifting, never settling. And here she sat, honor-bound not to explore Honoria's mind without permission! Even contemplating such invasiveness made her shiver. But oh, she desperately wanted to know! If only she could ask Khar's advice. **"In to shore more."**

As Theo leaned on the tiller, the craft sluggishly responded. *"I can barely see the shore with this mist! Can't we swing in closer? Each time I think we are, you edge us away again!"* Theo's mindvoice dripped with sour exasperation—a rarity. Finally passing the tiller to Talie and Rudy, he picked his way forward to help set the mast, using his height to stabilize it until Gelya locked in the crosspiece at

the base. Dodging children, he checked on Doyce and
Khar, both sheltered by an inadequate scrap of old canvas.
Doyce reacted enough to give Theo a tight-lipped smile,
but Khar remained adrift in her own world of pain, the
bandage round her midsection wet with rain and blood.
Khim had begged to lick her wounds clean but been forbidden; germs, they'd said in ominous tones, germs from stagnant water already attacked Khar from within, and Khim
should *not* ingest them. By the Elders, she'd lap poison if
it would ease Merowmepurr's pain!

Doyce grasped Theo's hand for a moment before turning
her attention back to Khar, one finger ceaselessly tracing a
stripe on her forehead. Blinking rapidly, Khim glanced
away, wishing she'd not witnessed such tenderness, struggling to uphold ghatti decorum at any cost. Oh, poor, beloved Merowmepurr! If anything happened to Merowme,
how would her dear sire, Saam, ever find joy again?

As Theo wedged himself beside her, Khim went rigid,
trembling at how the boat jerked and dipped at the weight
shift, the waves licking the gunwales. **"Back love, or we'll
scoop up the sea!"** He had his duty, and she had hers, no
matter how she longed to be by his side.

Folding himself tighter, he pressed his face against her
wet fur. *"Sorry I complained before. The little I know about
boats I learned on nice placid lakes, not threading my way
through a harbor without a sail. We'd best have it in place
before we reach open sea."*

**"But you've been angry because I let us go so far out in
the harbor you couldn't see the shore!"** Her skin rippled
beneath her wet coat, cold with mounting anxiety. **"I've
been guiding us 'round the harbor so the younglings
wouldn't have far to wade when we sink."** Half-jest, half-
truth. **"Now you want to head out to sea?"**

He sighed, toying with the hoop in her left ear. *"I think
so. I'd love to reach dry land as soon as possible, but let's
slink by Tarango Fort before we do. I don't trust any Guardians right now. Are there just a few gone bad? And Lady
protect us, that fat pillow-seller urging on the dagga boys!
How did he get involved?"*

Her brief glimpse of Momsvaert laughing, encouraging
his dagga boys to attack had chilled Khim. Had Khar distrusted him in some indefinable way? She'd offered bare

politesse but no more this morning in the bazaar, had even refused his beguiling smoked fish! **"Should we sail to Gander? Could we—if the boat stays afloat?"**

"Safer to hug the coastline, hide wherever we can. How do we know the Guardians at Gander aren't involved?" His brown hair was plastered down his brow, dripping in his eyes, giving him a hangdog look. Khim momentarily wondered where the expression had come from, the thought of hanging dogs repugnant to her.

"Dymphna Lindevald and Mew'ph are back on Gander. They're authorized to perform formal Seekings, determine the truth—oh!" She goggled as badly as if she'd snapped at a fly and swallowed it. **"It doesn't matter what Dymphna and Mew'ph find, does it? If the Guardians are all like Geerat, nobody'll care what she says, won't support the truth."** Never in her life had she envisioned such an impasse, the truth there for all to see and hear, but not a soul to care! Oh, Khar!

But Khim jerked her ear clear of Theo's tender fingers as she strained over the prow, ears aswivel to scoop up the elusive sound. Yes, she *had* heard it. Not just the sounds of the sea and the rain, not just normal harbor noises. **"Back to the tiller, love. I've a surprise—a good one for a change!"** Yes, again! Her mind had heard it before her lazy ears had even noticed! An unfamiliar tickling, a singsong, childish voice! Fix on it, don't lose it, she ordered herself as Theo clambered sternward, lifting children as he went. As the weight shifted, the bow rose higher, improving her vantage point, but the grayness of mist and rain and sea blended and shifted, almost deceiving even her keen senses.

The wind had picked up, not steady but fickle, gusting from one compass point to another. Honoria shouted, "Heave, dammit, heave!" and Khim sensed something looming behind her—with any luck Honoria had them raising the yard. A snap, a whump, and the boat leaped and yawed as the sail dropped, billowing with the wind.

"Theo, swing us right, back deeper into the harbor—now!" Yes! Something floated just ahead, bounding atop the waves, two sleek heads beside it, a flurry of white just behind, the trail of kicking feet. Other churning spots as well, two small ones, one large, an odd, lumpy shape mounded just above the water. One of those strange sea mammals she'd seen cavorting in the harbor? **"Now, right just a bit more!"**

Despite the wind, despite the rain, her voice rang clear. "Here, Khar-kitty! _We need you!_ Here, pretty kitty. _Khar-kitty, can you hear us?_" Though Khar was too enveloped in pain to hear, Khim had caught the persistent childish voice calling to her friend. If children believed deeply, there was always hope.

"Prepare for boarders!" Excited, Khim turned in a tight circle. No space to dance with glee.

"Khim? Are we being attacked? What boarders, where? I don't see another boat! I can barely see the sea!" Humans! She adored hers, but they had terrible eyesight and even worse imaginations! Ghatti knew how to _see,_ to seek with hearts and minds.

"Washtub with passengers preparing to board. Oordie's little ones, ours, too—Byrlie and Harry, Kasimir and Siri." Blinking in shock she identified the mound—not a balk of timber, nor a bobbing mat of debris. **"Don't know how the Shepherd'll board, though."** A daunting thought and a far more daunting task. Mayhap tow her behind, like a dinghy? The last thing they needed was ballast!

Early, daybreak on the horizon, and Holly shivered at the false chill of the breeze. A brief illusion—the day had already turned oppressive, humidity thick enough to carve into blocks, a prickling, staticky charge building in the air. Lightning? No, more likely Jenret, not lightning. The rising sun had a murky red cast like a clotting wound, threatening the low clouds trying to consume it, even the bubalus team stamping and restless as Dlamini and Arras curried them.

Equally edgy, she slapped her extended legs on the ground to release some of her tension while she stared into her tin cup, warning herself not to drain it. Brewing chaffay in the rough meant throwing several handfuls into boiling water with no strainer in sight; the final swallow was always loaded with settled grounds. Bullybess lay propped on her elbows, uncomfortable with enforced idleness when she'd rather have been breaking camp, packing supplies. Mvelase'd realized early on that the more Jenret had to do, the less insufferable he proved to be. Distract the mind, improve the temperament, a shrewd assessment on Uma-Uncle's part. Willing to see if the concept was applicable to Bess, Holly'd been recounting the suspicions she and Theo harbored about someone plotting against Doyce Marbon, mayhap the whole Wycherley clan.

Missing her accustomed chores, Bess had discovered other distractions than Holly. Canting her eyebrows at Arras, she murmured, "He be married? Extra-va-gantly handsome man!" A lip smack. "Kerry him off 'n work my wiles on him, Bullybess would!"

Stunned, Holly drained her cup, cheeks bulging, suddenly determined not to swallow. A grimace and she spat, missing Bess's wink. Chaffay grounds sprayed P'roul's feet, and she looked highly miffed as she lifted a paw fastidiously. Tongue probing, Holly scraped more grounds from her gums, averting her head and wiping her tongue with her handkerchief, determined to be more mannerly. "You *are* joking, aren't you?" With Bess she found it wise to proceed with caution: Sunderlies ways were *not* Canderisian ways. "Arras Muscadeine *is* married—to Doyce's sister, Francie."

Concupiscence in her eyes, mouth leering, Bess openly ogled Arras again, then swiftly kicked Holly's knee. "Yed big girl, that mean yer mind dense? 'Course Bess having joke! Daydreamin' some. Good'uns allays taken." Hugging her knees, she resembled a bleached, craggy stump, her hair like the air moss that festooned the swamp trees. "Now, enner-tain Bullybess like good liddle-big girl." A thumb waggled. "Tack unner horse's saddle." A finger shot out at right angles to the thumb. " 'Sploding fruit."

"But nothing happened aboard ship," Holly reiterated. "Doyce's injuries were an accident. Given the storm, it's a wonder worse didn't happen."

"An Jenneth-child oberboard, that accident, too?"

Much as she hated to admit it, "Most likely. We'll know for sure when we talk with Jenneth. Once we find her, that is."

"Incident in bazaar, *that* jes chance agin?" Her logic was relentless, and embarrassment swept through Holly—mayhap she and Theo *had* been reading too much into a string of bad luck, weaving connections where none existed. "At Momsvaert's stall, the piller-marchant, right?"

She nodded, eyes downcast. "Yes, according to Theo. Or rather, that's what Khim told P'roul. I mean, I know nothing of dagga boys, but it sounds a stupid prank, a prank that gets out of hand, escalates until someone's hurt, even killed. Rogues and rascals who suffered the consequences when they found they couldn't intimidate someone."

But as Bess's middle finger shot forth, P'roul quivered, almost ready to pounce, watching intently. " 'Cepting Momsvaert runs dagga boys. Musskle if he need'em."

"But why would a pillow-seller need 'muscle'?" Although not precisely sure what the term meant, she had her suspicions: moving pillows didn't require much muscle in the traditional sense. "You mean he needs . . . protectors . . . protection? Hires them for that?"

"Not jes hire, he in *charge* of dagga boys," Bess's mouth crimped as if she'd tasted something bitter. "He brains 'hind brawn, eben if mos' dagga boys half-grown cowards, runnin' way all scaredy-pee-pants if someun balks'em."

"But, wisdom of the Lady, why? It sounds so improbable—he sells *pillows*!" It burst out before she could restrain herself.

Surging to her feet, fists cocked, Bess stalked close, too close for Holly's liking. "Yed doubting Bullybess? Cleber Canderisian know eberyt'ing, *eberyt'ing* 'bout Sunderlies? Huh?"

Bess on the defensive was worse than battling a swarm of hornets in a blazing fury. Striving to appear harmless, Holly smiled appeasingly. "It's just that I don't understand. When I don't understand, I *have* to ask. Why would someone who makes and sells pillows need protection, his own armed force? I mean, I'm sure they're lovely pillows . . . but do people steal that many?"

Frankly, she felt as if someone had crammed her head into a pillow, the fibers filling her eyes and nostrils, clogging her brain. Worst of all, P'roul caught her mental image and snorted, belatedly adding by way of apology, **"No, I don't understand why either. Khim didn't suspect anything. And if *she* didn't, likely Theo wouldn't."**

"Dense, big and dense!" Bess dropped her fists in disgust. "Yed neber sneaky-snik special t'ing inna pillow when yed liddle? Many t'ings conceal inna pillow, all sorta t'ings fer piller filling, not jes feathers, batting." Her knuckles lightly tapped Holly's head to drive home her point. "Now yed *unnerstand*?"

P'roul strung together Bess's insinuations more quickly than she. **"It could work! Who'd rip open pillows to check the stuffing? Ideal for smuggling!"**

"Momsvaert's smuggling something in his pillows?" She stood now, towering over Bess. Damned if she'd allow Bess another such liberty, rapping her head as if she tested a melon—even Theo wouldn't dare that, or get away with it! "More questions, Bess. You're right, I *don't* always understand the Sunderlies, your ways. But with the right edifier—one such as you—I could learn." Folding her arms across her chest, she broadened her stance to denote an equal implacability. "What's he smuggling? Where do the pillows go? Does he ship to Canderis, Marchmont, or both?"

"Ol' Bess hears many t'ings, bits 'n pieces. Answer is bits 'n pieces—liddle stole here, something vanish from there—spices, fine weave fabric, whatever." A dismissive wave of her hand to indicate the unimportance of what was stolen. "Duty on pillers—what, you t'ink? Not much. Cheaper'n spices? Cheaper'n silk? Profit eben higher if goods 'free' ta begin with."

Smuggling on top of everything else? Could it explain Wycherley-Saffron's apparent problems? Accidents that weren't accidents to protect a lucrative but illicit trade in stolen goods? By the Lady, dishonest merchanters could siphon off some of their own goods, ship them that way! The whole idea was energizing, gave her a new perspective. *"P'roul, can you 'speak Khim? Ask what she thinks? She and Theo've been closer to the whole situation, may hold puzzle pieces and not even realize it!"*

"I'm not sure, I've pretty much reached my distance. If Rawn mindmelds with me, we can cast a mindnet. Shouldn't be a problem."

But Rawn already picked his way toward them through the tussocks, tasseled grass stroking his flanks and tail, depositing silvery-beige seeds along his coal-black length. Sitting close, he leaned his forehead against his offspring's neck before raising his head and staring off into space. Though Holly's ears heard nothing, a basso vibration played its undernote deep within her mind, Rawn's solid, rock-steady contribution. The strain showed, though, in his narrowed eyes, his muzzle screwed so tight his lips peeled back from his worn teeth.

Rawn's sudden snarl deepened into a rasping growl as he broke contact with P'roul, his eyes sparking, furiously lashing out, clawing some invisible enemy. *"Blessed Lady, what's the matter? What's wrong?"* Holly stared dumbstruck at Rawn as Jenret and the others raced to the ghatt's side.

Rawn too enraged to coherently 'speak, Khim sank to her belly and haltingly explained. **"Couldn't find them at first, had to cast our 'net wider, check each segment. Found them in the very last one we expected—at sea, no less!"** Holly rapidly repeated her words for Arras and the others. **"They're in deep trouble! When they all went to ransom Oh-Oh's children . . ."** ("What? Where at sea? Who was kidnapped?" Arras twisted his mustache, grappling with each new revelation.) **"dagga boys attacked them, rogue Guardians, too. Doyce and Merowmepurr are hurt—seriously!"**

P'roul's baby name for Khar indicated how distraught she was, as did her constant chop-licking and the rapid swallowing that often presaged a bout of nervous vomiting. Still, she delivered the rest of her message. **"Rawn wants to go to them! So do I! Oh, Merowmepurr!"** At this moment she so resembled Khar that Holly feared she viewed Khar's specter, a ghost whose amber eyes glowed with bleak determination.

Rawn in his arms, bound by their commingled pain and fury, Jenret unsteadily rose, his glance distant, unfocused. "Can't touch her at all, just the raw outline of their pain!" Feeling as sick as P'roul, Holly yearned to reach out to him—for his sake, for hers—but knew better than to interrupt while he sought Doyce's mind. Face buried in Rawn's neck, he mumbled, "We *must* go back! She's in such danger. If . . . if . . . anything happens to her, I'd . . . she'd. . . ." Lifting his face to the cloudy skies he shouted, "I am *such* a fool! Such a consummate fool!"

Unceremoniously swinging him round, Arras wrapped encompassing arms around Jenret and Rawn. "I agree, but that's beside the point. What's happening? By the Blessed Lady, be specific!" As his command sank in, Jenret tortuously added what details he could while Arras clutched his brow, sorting things.

"We're closer to Jenneth than to Doyce, yes?" Arras inquired, and Bess nodded confirmation. "You can't rescue both, Jenret." The wrenching admission already reflected on Arras's face. "Which is it? Turn round for Doyce and Khar? Push ahead after Jenneth?"

"No, wait!" A glint of hope, or mayhap that was too strong a word, struck Holly. "Isn't it likely Diccon's close to Jenneth—mayhap closer than we are? Might even have found her already?" Unlikely—Diccon's jubilation would have echoed from one end of the land to the other—without ghatti mindspeech or Resonant powers.

Laboring free of Jenret's embrace, his fur ruffled, his head sagging, Rawn plastered himself against P'roul's flank. **"Go on, daughter—do it! I'll hold you steady, let your mind-voice soar! Reach out for M'wa, ask what hope they have of finding Jenneth."**

But P'roul broke away, white paw raised to score Rawn's muzzle and nose. **"No! You're too tired, too grieved and vengeful! Don't drain yourself! Let me spare you!"**

Rawn's ears swiveled, his ear-hoop flying, distracting Holly from the fleet paw lashing the bridge of P'roul's nose. Four perfect parallels, four thin red lines of blood, and for the first time in their Bonded life together, Holly saw P'roul cower. P'roul warily retorted, **"I deserved it, don't judge."**

Slowly replanting himself, Rawn waited as P'roul subserviently edged into place, flicking a placatory lick on his muzzle. **"Rawn wants that old countdown you and Theo do,"** she beseeched Holly.

Still fuming at Rawn's offense against her Bond, the bridge of her own nose smarting in sympathy, Holly gritted her teeth and counted aloud, "One wasn't funny, two made more woe, three turned it steady, and four made it GO!"

Mindspeech always traveled more swiftly than she deemed possible, but then she supposed the ghatti rarely spared time to chitchat when confronted with a crisis. Still, as she watched Rawn go rigid with strain, Jenret kneeling beside him, hands poised to strengthen and sustain him, she viscerally sensed the cost of the black ghatt's effort. Without warning Rawn slumped, Jenret gathering him onto his lap, cupping Rawn's broad head in his hand, stroking his brow with his thumb.

Unable to sustain her anger at the old ghatt who'd given

his all without stinting, Holly cuddled P'roul against her as
she recapped what they'd learned from M'wa. Arras, she
knew, would have faith in M'wa's counsel, but the others—
Bess, Dlamini, and Mvelase—would have to be convinced,
made to accept how crucial the situation had become, the
narrowing choices.

"There's *some* good news. M'wa says that Diccon and
Kwee are sure they're almost on top of Jenneth, should
locate her by tomorrow, even today—with a little luck. Jenneth's shut out Diccon's mindvoice, so it's not as simple as
it might be. But Pw'eek's safe and sound, so it's mainly a
question of when they feel they can intrude, bring Jenneth
to her senses."

To say that she'd only very lightly sketched in certain
parts was putting it mildly. P'roul stared up at her, confounded. *"Didn't think I could choose which truth, how
much truth to tell, did you? Well, I learned it from you.
Bard's there, Davvy, too—not just Diccon. We can't ask any
better than that."* Gently blotting her handkerchief against
P'roul's nose, Holly brushed a kiss on the striped forehead
and rose.

"Bard's word is good enough for me. We turn around,
go back." A sense of relief at not being sundered in half,
worrying which goal had the greater urgency. She'd already
made her choice: Theo needed her, and she'd do anything
in her power to ensure his safety. It wasn't a bond as strong
as twinship, but she had an inkling of what that must encompass. Theo was dearer to her than her brothers, had
been a part of her life for . . . forever, it seemed.

"I am sorrowed to say this," Mvelase bowed his head,
seemingly intent on his callused, dusty feet. Slowly he
raised his head, looking them in the eye one by one as he
butted his staff once against the ground. "Alas, Dlamini
and I, we must journey north. Our goal is my nephew,
Bard. Our path was carved long before we began to walk
it."

✤

PART
SIX

✤

Purring with happiness, contented as a cat, she forced herself to concentrate on each chore so she'd be finished when Pommy returned, all ready to go. Oh, she wished she had a little kitty to play with, a chubby little calico one with plush-velvet fur . . . Yes, think of kittens, don't recall the eyes that had so wanted to consume her soul yesterday, even invading her sanctuary within the hut. Knock, knock—let me *in*! Knock, knock—let me *out*! Those eyes had better not stare at her again! This time she'd charge right after whatever it was, punch and punch at those spying eyes until they vanished! A shiver rippled up her spine, freezing her stomach, making her hands shake—as if she'd thought something bad, something she'd sense was totally unjust if she only *knew*.

The shiver made her hands lose control of a thick crockery mug, the one with its handle already broken—and a good thing, too—as her fingers fumbled and let it fall. Clumsy, clumsy, breaking up housekeeping! A self-conscious giggle, the mug hadn't been dashed to smithereens, only rolled and spun to rest under the rickety table. Get it out, wash it off, finish her chores.

It wouldn't storm today, it *couldn't,* because Pommy'd promised to take her to pick asimina fruit this afternoon if the weather held, mayhap even picnic by the grove. She'd never visited the grove, had never seen an asimina tree or its fruit, but Pommy swore they were delicious, even if they looked like nothing much. Just a brownish, curved cylinder about the size of two of her fingers put together, but soft and pulpy within, and custardy-sweet. And with Pommy beside her, the eyes never ventured as close as they did at other times. Picnic!

Crawling under the table, she glanced around for the

mug, surprised it wasn't in plain sight. Odd, really, to disappear like that. Not really, she'd only scooted the broom under the table as far as she could easily reach, hadn't ever made the effort to stretch all the way back. More space there than she'd thought. Ouch! Rubbing a tingling elbow where she'd smacked it against a canvas-draped object, she considered its lumpish shape, the fraying ropes wrapped and knotted round it. Cobwebby, mildewed on the bottom, water stains, too. Ah, she should definitely have moved the table and swept properly. She'd have discovered this, not to mention this discarded mouse nest, the hollow exoskeletons of three giant beetles, and this little sluglike creature with a jointed, chitinous coating that rolled up in a tight little pellet when she pushed a broom straw at it.

But the canvas package—what was it? What had Pommy bundled up for safekeeping? Pommy hid little on the outside, trusted her around the hut; it was inside himself where Pommy hid, that much she'd puzzled out. Past? He must have one, but he never said much about it, though she yearned to hear. His present appeared equally nebulous—except for the form she gave it. Knowing—how, what, why someone was Who he was—would have helped, reassured her that she too possessed a past, even if she couldn't remember it. The rope began to unravel, its fibers shredding as her fingers idly picked at it, the mug momentarily forgotten.

Back against the hut wall, shoving with her bare feet while she steadied the bundle with her hands, she scooted it into the center of the room, ignoring the tracks she'd scored in the dirt floor. Bigger, more solid at its base than at the top. Whatever the top was, it felt fragile, unwieldy. Metal clink-chinking, rattling. Ouch! Damn! Hugging her bruised knee, she tumbled backward on her bottom. Already blood suffused under her skin, black-and-blue in no time. Oh, damn again! Despite her care a handle of some sort had poked through the rotting canvas.

The canvas beyond salvation, she tore and ripped at it, its destruction strangely satisfying. Have to find something else to wrap it up again. Curious, even more curious—what, glass? Big, bull's-eye round and dusty, insect remains lodged inside—no, between—two glass plates. Protruding metal bits here and there, curved armatures topped with

darling little balls. At last she uncovered the base, freeing
the crank, and she spun it in an excess of energy—fast,
faster! Yes! The mournful flap, flap of a beltlike strip of
leather told her something had broken, the spinning crank
no longer engaging its gears. A petulant slap at the crank
for failing her, and it went wrup-wrup-wrup as it halted.

Chin propped on her good knee, she sat and regarded it,
disgruntlement growing at being balked like this. It had
been new, different, mayhap a reminder of something from
her past. But no, she'd never seen anything like this before—whatever it was. Oh, well, what had she expected—
music? That would have been nice.

Belatedly remembering the mug, she discovered it back
against the wall, rolling onto her stomach, straining to reach
it. Scrambling out to deposit it on the table, she hunted
through Pommy's neat pile of canvas bits, sorting them,
shaking out their folds, mentally measuring each against
what she needed to rewrap. Light-weight, not sail-weight,
and not too good or he'd miss it all the sooner. Wrapping
and tying the bundle posed a greater trial than she'd anticipated, splicing bits of twine with the rope fragments. Sometimes the rope ends disintegrated when she firmed up the
knot and she had to start over again.

"Aqua, what are you doing? How dare you touch that?"
Eyes glaring, staring, but this time they belonged to
Pommy, turning her inside out, witnessing how she'd pried
and poked. Had those other eyes seen it all, rushed off to
betray her to Pommy? She wanted to get up, but she'd
half-slipped beneath the table's edge, would bang her head
if she tried to rise. And he wouldn't yield any space, just
kept stalking nearer, his hands balled, his face suffusing
with color as he shouted and shouted. . . .

Oh, bad Aqua! No picnic for Aqua today! *What* had she
done? Oh, what *had* she done? Somehow the storm had
already loosed itself within the hut, Pommy's eyes
thunderous-dark, his hands lightning fast, bright bolts exploding inside her head. . . .

"I don't blame Jenret, but I doubt we can reach them in
time to be of use." Damn it, it was too soon to feel so

discouraged, but he was. Bess responded by wrapping her arms around Arras's waist from behind and giving him a heartening squeeze. Inhaling cautiously, he determined his ribs remained intact. Straight ahead his view consisted of Taubi's dipping horns and Nauki's broad, black posterior, Jenret and Holly astride his back. P'roul crouched in Bess's lap, while Holly held Rawn in front of her.

"We do jes fine," Bess reassured him. "Bubalus clumpety 'long, get there jes fine. Mvelase good man ta loan us strong beasts like these." They'd lacked time to argue or plead, convince Uma-Uncle Mvelase and Dlamini to continue traveling with them. Arras had understood: Bard was their concern, just as Doyce and Jenneth were Jenret's responsibility. "Road good, jes not string-straight, more viney-windy."

Experimentally he clipped his heels against Taubi's ribs, the massive head swinging round to nuzzle his knee. Did a bubalus have differing gaits, like a horse? Walk, canter, trot? Damned if he knew.

Settling P'roul firmly against the small of his back, Bess swung her leg across Arras's thigh, toes aiming at Taubi's ear and missing. "Tickle 'hind ear, one side er other ta turn beast. Tap neck ta hurry him." Her other leg flew up, her heel thumping Taubi's neck and the bubalus began a gentle jog-trot, splayed hooves plodding in double-time, Arras jouncing, unprepared for the new rhythm. With Bess twined around him Arras felt as if he'd been tricked into a wrestling match, thankful his legs remained sedately clenched round Taubi's barrel.

"And to halt him?" Ask now, learn to control the bubalus or they'd obediently trample anything in their path.

"Twixt his horns, right on poll." Bess's legs now lolloped against Taubi's sides, striking Arras at irregular intervals. He considered asking P'roul how she was enjoying the ride, but didn't want to disturb her. Both she and Rawn were exhausted from their mindmelding efforts and the emotional turmoil of hearing such news. By all common sense, Bess should be mounted on Nauki with Jenret and Rawn behind her, Holly and P'roul riding behind Arras. But if directing Nauki took Jenret's mind off his fears for Doyce and Khar, it was fine with Arras.

"If this road is so good, why didn't we take it when we

were bound in the other direction?" He knew full well why
they hadn't—Jenret had been adamantly against it, declar-
ing the swamp route quicker. This was merely a passing
comment to provoke discussion, and provoke it did!

"Wha'? Yed t'ink Bullybess take yed inna swamp ta lose
you? 'Spect swamp fever ta kill yed, yer supplies, yer coin
be mine—easy?" Without looking, he sensed her hand hovering over his belt knife, ragged self-control just staying her
from avenging his implied insult.

"No, Bess." Best select his words with care, not further
rile her. "But I *do* want to understand. We hired you to
guide us, to protect us from our own arrogant stupidities."

Amazingly enough, she laughed, a hoarse, hooting wail
that made Taubi's ears perk and flap. "Ho, boy! You Canderisians big on 'unnerstanin,' huh? Doan unnerstan much,
but willing ta learn. Awrful dumb country yed come fra!"

That piqued him as much as he'd piqued her. "Madame,
I am *not* Canderisian! I'm Marchmontian, born and bred,
and proud of it!"

She thumped his back. Damn, he wished he could see
her face, read her expression. "Ah, touchy, touchy! Holly
wanna 'unnerstan,' yed wanna 'unnerstan.' Sorry! Listen—
I bin feelin' guilty as zin! Jenret right, when coast flooded,
swamp route faster. Course I know, how you t'ink he know
odderwise?" Now she was pummeling his back between his
shoulder blades, Arras increasingly sore but still intrigued.
"I give in, *neber* t'inkin' Canderisians—and Marchmontians—take fever so hard! Misjudge ter'ble! Hu-miliating to
lose clients, no matter how stupid-stubborn dey be. Bad
luck!"

"Well, we all toss the dice and lose at times. It was a
kindness to let Jenret believe his decisions would lead us
to Jenneth sooner, even though we fell ill." Clearing his
throat, he dared another question. "Who's this Momsvaert
you told Holly about?" That, too, seemed strange, that a
man could command a group of hooligans and no one
seemed to protest overmuch.

"Eb'ryone know him." Bess hawked and spat, then fell
silent. "How I know your Doyce friend meet him? Only
cause I know twitchy-Wycherley now, hear he having
marchant problems, that I find pieces fit. Dagga boys to

rob and steal, sneak if can, bash if can't—easy nuff way ta liberate trade goods."

"But hasn't anyone else suspected this, attempted to do something about it, report it?"

For once no sarcasm tinged Bess's voice. "Not if dey like life. Which yed choose: Shortage'n goods or shortage'n life?"

What had Doyce gotten herself into? More troubled by Bess's wary admission of fear than he cared to admit, Arras cast around for something neutral to discuss, chose an old standby, safe in any land. "Is it going to storm, or will it blow by us?" The air still felt like storm, embracing him closer than Bess's wiry arms, but the clouds seemed to be thinning.

"Doan know. Tink it hold off bit longer. Jes be storm, not big gale like afore."

"Well, at least Taubi and Nauki like mud." At the sound of his name, Taubi rolled a big, brown eye back at Arras.

"What that Doyce woman like? Flashy pretty-fine like Jenret? What? Desperate hard ta choose twixt child and wife."

"Don't worry." Risking disaster, Arras gave Taubi's neck another tap and held on tight as the bubalus jounced faster. "He made the right choice."

Finding a rock to his liking, Diccon settled cross-legged on top to wait for the ghatten to catch up. Gave him more time to think—not that that had helped before. If Pw'eek couldn't reach Jenneth, could he? And more important— should he even try? Both Bard and Davvy counseled caution, to not rush in like a lackwit bursting with fulsome cries of joy at being reunited with Jenneth. It might be too shocking, too great an adjustment for her mind to bear, suddenly being plunged into a new reality, even though it was her old one.

For a moment he had to laugh at himself—good old Diccon, forever rushing ahead without a second thought. How often had he tumbled head-over-heels into some new enthusiasm? All his life, most likely! Now here he sat—like a stodgy toad on a rock—plagued not only by second thoughts, but by third and fourth thoughts as well! What to do? How to proceed? His insides were paralyzed with indecision, his mind wavering, bungling each plan. Mama'd never believe it! At that his smile faded. How was Mama, Khar? Had Papa and Uncle Arras and Holly reached them yet? Lady help them all—disaster on all fronts! But for now his only concern *had* to be Jenneth, not only because of his own wants, but because he'd been entrusted with rescuing her, making their family whole again.

M'wa and Kwee had convinced Pw'eek to stay with them, not go skulking back to watch over Jenneth, brooding at her inability to reach her Bond. Poor Pw'eek! Half of her frayed with worry about Jen, the other half in paroxysms of delight at having Kwee restored to her, and Kwee in equal raptures at her sister's return. With more will-power than he'd thought he possessed, Diccon'd avoided the hut as well, his brain ajangle at her nearness. Had continued doing so today to avoid the temptation, still baffled as to how to approach her.

What if . . . what if Jenneth didn't feel the same about seeing him? What if his own twin, his other half, rejected him? Didn't need or want him any longer? Mayhap Bard or Davvy *should* contact her first! Cancel, revise, erase, emend! He'd have worried a hole in his paper if he'd made notes, and he was sure he'd worn a hole in his brain as well!

He stared up at the sun, stretched, listening to the wind riffling the branches, talking among themselves. If only they'd tell him what to do! That old apple tree at home could probably offer some sage advice, had been their silent confident for years. Go back to the beach, rejoin Bard and M'wa, Davvy and Luykas? But all they'd do would be argue some more about what to do. The lack of a clear-cut answer, an action to be taken had already driven him here; he and the ghatten had escaped, itchy, unable to sit still, coiled tense to *do* something! No, explore some more—walk, run, even—see the lay of the land. It couldn't hurt. Then mayhap he'd be fit to endure another endless discussion.

"Come on, ladies. Let's go." They were still so young— so curious and captivated by anything new, eager to pounce and bounce, abandon their woes, live fully in the moment.

Hard to believe they'd grow up, undertake the solemn duties of Seeking truth. Even harder to acknowledge that he must, too.

Mouths upcurved in secretive, satisfied ghatti smiles, they came padding side by side, and Diccon was touched by their similarity: usually he viewed them as totally dissimilar in appearance and attitude, just as he and Jenneth differed in so many ways despite their twin-bond. Tails high, both crooked leftward in a question, the two tilted their heads at the same angle. Yes, Pw'eek was larger, blockier, but their body conformation was the same. In the dappled light the difference in their markings grew less pronounced, though the calico's white mustache and chest did stand out. Kwee's coloration was a more gentle, diluted version of her sib's.

"Snack?" he cajoled to hurry them, hardly surprised as Pw'eek broke into a rapid trot that left her sister two lengths behind.

"Oh, yummies? Oh, so good!" she trilled, caressing his shin, sleeking up the back of his leg so fast she nearly buckled his knee when her shoulder slammed it from behind. "Me-OW-a-WOW!" Dipping some trail mix from his pouch, he divided it between the two, guiltily adding a few more nuggets to Pw'eek's portion.

"Well, she's had slim rations lately," he apologized to Kwee, tickling her ears. *"She's had to hunt alone, unlike some other lucky ghatten I know. She didn't have M'wa to help."*

Licking her chops to cleanse the crumbs from her lips, Kwee eyed the empty space in front of her sib, the way she casually side-glanced Kwee's dwindling mound of food. **"Slim pickings, mayhap. But hardly slimming—as you may have noticed!"**

"Well, not everyone can be as lithely lean as you, sweedling," and laughed as she preened, casting flirtatious glances at him. *"Now, shall we ramble some more? Or go back to the beach?"*

The ghatten shared an incomprehensible look, Kwee leaning to lick her sib's face, and the two began mutually grooming, necks serpentining, heads dipping and rolling, eyes slitted in ecstasy. Pw'eek pulled free first, her pale, spring green eyes locked on his, imploring, but for what he

couldn't judge. **"This way, yes?"** But before he could answer yea or nay, Kwee had already bounded down the trail,
stopping every few strides to launch even more coaxing,
come-hither glances his way. As if he could resist!

"All right, all right, I'm coming." Well, lacking a clear
choice—just as he did regarding Jenneth—any road might
prove as rewarding as another. Though given the looks of
this untrimmed, tangled trail, he'd be too busy ducking eye-
poking branches and unwinding creepers from his neck to
his ankles to dwell on Jenneth. Just as well, because sometimes if he stopped worrying things like a puppy with a
slipper, just let everything collect in the back of his mind,
the pieces floated together and fit. Jenneth usually did that
when faced with problems—while he'd already have waded
hip-deep in them. Well, give it a try. Belt knife in hand, he
slashed through the worst of the offending vines, slithering
between or under others as he went.

"Can't catch me!" Kwee sang out, a saucy tail-flick teasing him further along the track.

"And when I catch you?" he shouted, joyously caught up
in the mock chase. *"That's what you should worry about,
you scamp!"*

'Twasn't fair, it absolutely wasn't fair! She hadn't meant to
pry, poke where she shouldn't—besides, it wasn't much of
anything at all! Circular glass plates, some gears, a crank,
metal spheres mounted on bracket-thingies. With the belt
broken like that, it didn't even work! Not that she had any
idea what it *did* when it did work. Hadn't she put it back
together careful as could be—rewrapping the canvas, patching the tears, even found some twine to tie the ropes together where they'd frayed? Had shoved it back in place
under the table, near good as new, vaguely disappointed
that it hadn't proved more entertaining.

For Pommy to yell like that, face scarlet to his hairline,
his neck cords bulging, accusing her of meddling, spying,
poking and prying! On and on and on, venom spewing out
of him, working himself into a rage—and the way he'd
looked at her! Aqua shivered, hugging herself. As if she
were some ghastly creature, foul, sly, slinking, sneaky—

"worse than a perverted ghatti!" he'd screamed, whatever
that was. When she'd tried to stutter some word of apology,
explain, he'd lost all control, slapping her hard across the
face! "Stay clear of that, or I'll toss you back, let the sea
have you!" he'd screamed before stalking off to join Hirby,
hovering outside, wringing his hands, face screwed in anguish. Throw her back? His precious Aqua? What had she
unwittingly done?

It hadn't felt right to remain any more, too painful and
humiliating to docilely stay at the scene of her shame, so
she'd wandered further from the hut than she ever had
before, past the stream, even. Anywhere and nowhere was
fine with her, and she fingered the three lucifers snug in
her pocket. If Pommy found she'd taken them from his tin
box, he'd accuse her of stealing as well! It just *wasn't* fair,
nothing was fair! Eyes constantly staring at her, making her
skin crawl, and those whispers trying to hiss and sizzle in
her brain. Things wanting *out,* things wanting *in*—not a soul
ever asking her how she felt about it, just doing it to her!
Well, she wasn't going to slink back, lick Pommy's hand!
Everything so hot and burning, flaming in her mind!

The track had closed in, overgrown, though she could
spot the cut marks where someone had slashed it back not
so long ago. Everything grew too fast, too exuberantly here,
lush yet lurking to grab at her hair, drape clinging spider
web-ick across her face. Made her edgy, itchy, they did, but
at least the storm had blown by them. Still windy, but a
blue-patched sky, stringers of clouds running fast and free,
probably chasing after the storm.

If only she were flying free, no longer imprisoned by not
knowing who Aqua was, no longer fettered by guilt for
invading Pommy's privacy, no longer so thwarted, frustrated by everything that swarmed 'round and 'round in
her brain but would not coalesce! Close enough to touch
sometimes, as if a friendly hand stretched out to her, yet
she didn't dare extend her hand to bridge that empty gap.

Could almost *see* the hand sometimes, a boy's hand, callused, clean-nailed—she giggled, someone had made him
use the scrub brush! A kind face came with the hand, not
handsome, just ordinary-nice except for gorgeous blue eyes
so dark with concern. Unlike Pommy, he liked kitties, she
could tell . . . Oh, wasn't everything bad enough as it was,

without her populating the very emptiness that beckoned her! She feared and yearned for what existed on the other side, most of all to see if *she* existed there.

She was going to *explode*, she knew it, her head would simply burst! And Pommy had struck her, the man who'd rescued her, saved her life. Damn Pommy! Damn Aqua, whoever she was! Damn the tendrils and vines and greedy, grabbing fingers and hands within and without! All wanting a piece of her, a piece of what? Of who? Desolate, eyes teary, head tucked low, she swept her arms in front of her, breast-stroking through the greenery. Batter and bash at me, and I'll bash back! A satisfying snap and rip as she tore the branch free, let it drop and trod on it. She was as strong, as clever, as *good* as the blue-eyed boy in that empty place—not like Pommy swore she was!

But the branches and vines apparently realized they'd had enough, been bested—at least temporarily—and she stumbled ahead, tripping over a final snatching root. Burn it all down, that's what she should do, burn it and burn it and burn it. . . . ! On hands and knees, sobbing, she finally lifted her head, discovering she'd stumbled into a clearing, the sky arching eggshell blue and tranquil overhead, the sun smiling down, not pounding at her. Toward the rear of the grassy expanse, a tree, somehow what a tree was supposed to be—a big trunk, tall, its boughs lofting upward, its leaves polite and proper, not dangling to clutch and caress her. Slowly she pushed herself onto her feet and walked to it, tentatively placing both hands on its crevassed bark, so utterly, wonderfully familiar, and began to cry in earnest. It felt so good, sturdy as an old, intimate friend. Finally, tears spent, she stroked the bark and sank to sit with her back against the tree, supported by its companionship, her thoughts drifting . . .

"Phew!" Breathless, face and arms and chest sticky with sap and dusted with flower pollen, he burst into a clear space, almost like a small meadow back home. Wiping his knife on his hip, he sheathed the blade and resettled his belt. *"You imps, where are you?"* Hard to see in such dazzling light after the living green canopy that had shielded him. Any time he'd hesitated, spent too long hacking or studying an easier way round, under or through, one ghatten or the other had popped up to tag him with a paw and dash off, rippling with soundless ghatten giggles.

Shoving his hair back with green-stained hands, he idly wondered where they'd hied off to this time. Returning should be no problem—he'd hacked a path wide enough for a two-horse team. Well, wide enough for a pony. *"Kwee? Pw'eek? Come on, I need a rest. No more tag, you've run me ragged."* Squinting, he made out Pw'eek to his left, frozen with one paw still lifted in midair. Mayhap the brilliance was playing tricks with his eyes, but her outline blurred, as if she quivered with emotion. Odd that ghatten didn't play "Statues" very well. Whatever had transfixed her evidently boded no danger because he couldn't sense any radiating fear. Rubbing his eyes, he gazed rightward to spot Kwee in a near-identical pose, utterly fascinated by something he couldn't see.

As he waited, curious how long she'd hold her pose, he finally detected something from the corner of his eye, out-of-place, foreign to the shaded base and heaving roots of the giant beech midway between the two ghatten. Whatever it was had halted the scamps in their tracks, and anything able to do that deserved a more thorough examination. Except that he couldn't pierce the dense shadiness surrounding the beech, the shape elusive now that his eyes had finally adapted to the sun. If it was alive, it might startle easily, but he took one step and paused, took another and gasped, slapping his hand over his mouth to mute the sound. Jenneth! It was Jenneth—it *had* to be—curled up like a baby rolapin, asleep beside the tree, her dark hair pillowed on a root!

Blessed Lady, what now? Retreat, abandon her in fear of panicking her? Mayhap lose her again? What? If he went rushing at it all wrong, he might never right it, never have a second chance to try again. *"Kwee, Pw'eek? What should I do?"*

"Follow your heart, your instinct," Kwee advised, never shifting her gaze from Jenneth, while Pw'eek stealthed two steps ahead, again halting with her forefoot in the air. With a pang he noticed it was her poor little foot with its missing toe. **"Oh, my Jenneth! Please hear! Please listen!"** Pw'eek's

mindvoice crooned, strained and high, overlaid with a tremulous purr that threatened to veer out of control. Tearing
her eyes from her beloved, she counseled, **"You never forget your ghattenhood together."**

A deep breath did nothing to steady him, but somehow
he *knew*—mayhap his muddled mind *had* molded a plan
when he wasn't aware of it. Mayhap the tree had planted
the seed of an idea in his mind. He forced himself into a
carefree amble, letting it make whatever sounds it would.
Let some part of Jenneth hear him in advance, not awake
her in startlement, convinced danger lurked nearby. Horrible to awake with a jolt, heart pounding, breath quick. How
he hated it when it happened to him!

Heart pounding as recklessly as if he'd been the one
rudely awakened, he squatted near her sleeping form, close,
yet distant enough not to intimidate. Her pale skin showed
sunburn and peeling, still pinkly raw in spots, though healing. Dark crescents beneath her closed eyes, a gauntness to
her face, a sad dismay even sleep could not erase. "Good
afternoon, sleepyhead. Rise and shine," and prodded her
ankle with a knuckle, not daring any further touch.

Her eyes popped open, those hazel eyes with their spangles of blue-gold and green, their mother's eyes. A wariness
flickering in them, but she didn't scream or try to bolt, just
kept staring at him with a painful intensity, measuring him
within and without. "Hullo," he said matter-of-factly and
stood, stretching down a hand, inviting her to clasp it. Call
her Aqua? Pw'eek said the man called her that, that she
responded to it. Or Jenneth? Mayhap neither right now.
Folding her legs under her like a fawn, she held out a hand,
hesitant but compliant, and he brought her to her feet in
one easy move, forcing himself not to swing her into his
arms, hug her tight.

"Hullo?" she said back, stifling a yawn, but he could feel
the tension in her hand, the way it shot down her arm.
"I'm dreaming, aren't I?"

Not knowing if she might bolt, he released her hand and
lightly grasped her shoulders to shift her right side against
the beech, her back toward him. Quickly he positioned himself back to back with her, his right hand atop the crown
of her head, his palm sliding across until it struck his own
head, experienced a wave of relief that he might, just *might*

actually have grown! "I'm taller than you, Jen, finally!" his voice all high and trembling. "And *high* time, I'd say!"

"Are not! You're standing on a root again—cheating!" A gasp and she whirled to face him, hands over her mouth. "Diccon? Oh, Diccon!" Tears in her eyes, tears in his as he roughly grabbed her, hugging her hard, rocking back and forth with joy.

She hugged him back, laughing, crying, pounding his shoulder blades, nestling her forehead against his collarbone. "Oh, Blessed Lady! I know who you are, I know who I—" and broke away, dropping to her knees as she cried, "Pw'eek! Oh, dear one! How could I—" A blurred bundle of calico fur slammed into her lap, practically toppling her as she butted her head under Jenneth's chin, trilling joyously. "It was *you* knocking at the doors in my mind, and I couldn't remember how to let you in! Why I should, or who you were!" Squeezing Pw'eek tight, she wrapped her other arm around Diccon's leg, intent on bringing him down beside her on the grass. "And you are *not* taller than I am! I've *always* been taller!"

"But mayhap I've grown up looking for you," he whispered in his mind, wondering if it could possibly be true.

Done sniffing at Jenneth's scabbed knee, Kwee tilted her head and regarded him. **"Oh, it is—truly—my silly human."**

Hand in hand, Diccon and Jenneth lagged along, the ghatten bouncing round their feet and chasing each other, whizzing up tree trunks to launch themselves at their Bonds, supremely confident they'd be caught in loving arms. Unable to contain himself, Diccon pranked as happily as the ghatten, tickling his sister's neck with a creeper laden with deep orange trumpet blossoms, garlanded her with them. Grabbing a giant leaf with a cuplike depression at its base, Jenneth reciprocated by tilting it, soaking Diccon with dew that trickled inside his shirt.

"I *have* to go back," she explained again to Diccon, "I can't just leave, disappear without saying good-bye." A tremendous surge of giddiness swept through her, everything around her vivid with the most vibrant hues she'd ever witnessed, absolutely shimmering with life. Things boringly

familiar from her short life as Aqua now appeared achingly
new and unaccustomed to Jenneth's eyes, and this would
be the final time she viewed them thusly, must absorb every
unique particle, impress them on her new—or rather—her
old mind. Some things from her sojourn here would be
irrevocably lost, but other, far better things had been
regained.

What she'd refrained from mentioning was the racing
shame and anger still coursing through her at Pommy's unjust treatment. But regardless of that, she owed him a farewell and a heartfelt thank you, more than that. Knowing
Diccon, she doubted if he had two coppers in his pocket
to recompense Pommy, but somehow she believed Pommy
would scorn a monetary reward, desire something intangi-
ble, more difficult to grant. What to say to Pommy, how to
say it? Assuming he'd returned, of course.

Diccon, still beaming—she'd never seen him quite so
sappy-looking, or so glowingly beautiful to her eyes (her
brother?)—swung their hands between them. "Kwee's contacted M'wa. Bard and Davvy and M'wa'll be along quick
as a wink. Guess Luykas's staying with the launch, doesn't
want to intrude on a family reunion." Pulling Jenneth to
him, he brushed a piece of petal from her hair. "How'd
you get here, anyway?"

"I don't know, I can't really remember that—not yet.
Mayhap not ever." She sighed, brow crinkling as she sought
to recall it. "I can summon up the night I went overboard,
how cold and wet and scared I was—how brave Pw'eek
was," a fond smile at the ghatten. "Bits and pieces of the
time I was adrift are coming back to me, but I can't tell
you exactly in what order. And . . . and the horror of
waking up one morning and finding Pw'eek had floated
away! Off on her own adventures, no less." Stopping, she
knelt to gather up Pw'eek, staggering upright and masking
the lower half of her face behind the ghatten. "Armful,
isn't she?"

Somehow Pw'eek wriggled and flexed until she reclined
like a baby in Jenneth's arms, white belly exposed, all four
feet kneading the air, a front paw occasionally grazing Jenneth's cheek, batting her nose. "Oh, poor little missing toe!
What happened?" Jenneth kissed the scalloped foot, bent
to kiss the exposed white belly. "My lily belly!" More som-

berly she glanced up at Diccon, blowing a clump of loose fur from her lips. "Anyway, I was *so* thirsty and hungry, and the sun was *so* hot, it all just went on and on and on . . . as if there'd never been a beginning, and no end in sight. The next thing I distinctly recall is waking up in Pommy's hut."

"Who is he, this Pommy? Young, old? Well-spoken? Native or not?" The all-too-casual tone, especially on the last question made Jenneth pause. What Diccon was wordlessly asking within her head caused her hesitation. It had never occurred to her, couldn't have, given her limited frame of reference as Aqua.

"I'm not . . . sure. You mean, is he an exile . . . a convict?" She exchanged a glance with Pw'eek, but the ghatten seemed unsure as well. "He's not from here, I don't think— he sounds Canderisian to me, not that I'm sure what a Sunderlies accent might sound like."

"Sort of a lilt to it, and a slur sometimes. A bit like Uncle Arras when he's excited, but that's not exactly it. Sort of a tropical sway to it." His body attempted to demonstrate.

"Tropical sway to it? That explains everything! How could I have missed it?" She snorted disgustedly, began to giggle as Diccon reddened. "Do that thing with your hips again!"

"Brat!" His affectionate punch stung more than his words. "Know-it-all, persnickety brat!"

But she ignored him, wanting to hurry, play out the conclusion and have it over, done. Get it over with, make her peace with Pommy, see once more and then no more—the beautiful tanned skin with freckled shoulders, the china blue eyes, the blond hair bleached almost white despite that foolish straw hat he wore. The man who'd handled her as competently and thoroughly and tenderly as he would have a baby, and yet the involuntary reactions of her body hadn't been those of an infant but of a woman awakening to her own sensuality. Don't think of that—no!

"Pommy's friend Hirby sounds different, not as well-spoken." Shaking her head, aware of how little she had in the way of clues, she sought for a better explanation. "No, that's not right, not fair. I don't think he's always 'all there' inside his head. He *could* be a convict, exiled for something terrible, something so ghastly it ate away at his brain. Hints he's dropped, well, they make sense now that I know—that I know I'm me, I mean. But that's only one possibility, one that fits your penchant for melodrama. Mayhap he was hurt, or shipwrecked just as I—"

"Jen—" the rest was lost in a retching cough, nerves warping his vocal cords, "Jen, did either of them, did they ever . . . do anything . . . ungentlemanly." His words tumbled and tripped over each other in his urgency. "Did they, er, so to speak, ever vio— I mean, because if they rav— er, uh, because if . . . taking advan—"

"Did they rape me, you mean?" Faster to finish it for him before his tongue tangled. Bending, she poured Pw'eek from her arms in a slow spill of butterscotch and gray calico. Didn't want him to see her face, he could read her too well, might even be reading her now, and some things were private! "No, they did *not*. Nor even attempt it!"

Mayhap that explained a part of her shame, her anger at Pommy—the only emotion he'd shown in touching her had been compressed into that one slap. That in a way she'd *longed* for something from him—deeper, more complex, more intimate—beyond the touches that had inflamed her body. Those strokings and cleansings, his painstakingly thorough rubbing with the aloe cream, had been a revelation, so sensual that her body craved his touch, desiring things she hadn't known she wanted—or at least hadn't wanted with such passion. If they had come together in that hut—in this circumscribed world that Aqua inhabited—it would have felt right, proper. A way to repay him for salvaging her, if nothing else.

"Fine, good!" Too brusque, almost, his lower lip truculent as he scrutinized her too, too thoughtfully. "Then we needn't draw straws to see who whips him first, beats him to a bloody pulp."

Almost in sight now, the hut's faded thatch peak just visible over the treeline. Claiming Diccon's elbow, she swung him round, made him meet her eyes, though he still needed time and distance, some way to separate himself from his discovery of what she'd felt toward Pommy. Daughters, sisters, mothers should never harbor lustful thoughts, be women first. "Don't let Uncle Bard even think anything like that—nothing! Do you hear me? You know

what happens if he's provoked!" Their eyes locked, each
cognizant of what one of Bard's berserker rages could accomplish in the way of mayhem.

"I promise. I'm no fool. Davvy had to whale him a good
one alongside the head when we were captured." Her eyebrows sailed up, but she decided that confidence had better
wait until later. "Only way to keep him from making things
even worse. We'd already found trouble enough, thanks to
me." Her surreptitious movement caught his eye, her free
hand slipping into her pocket. "Jen? What've you got
there? Hand them over!"

Reluctantly she withdrew her hand, opening it palm-up
to display three lucifers. "I'm *not* going to use them! I'm
too old for that!" Hating herself for wanting to possess
them, needing them to calm her, protect her, she cajoled,
"You trust me, don't you? Don't you, Diccon?" It just felt
better, safer, gave her more control to know she had them.
Aqua had needed them even more than she, but Jenneth
could be trusted with them, she told herself.

How Diccon hated indecision—that was all too clear
from his expression. He wanted nothing more than to
snatch the lucifers from her, yet he yearned to trust her.
From over Diccon's shoulder she glimpsed Pommy striding
down the trail toward them, then halting, almost like a stag
at bay, his head thrown back, intense, noble, but destined
to forfeit her in this final struggle. He couldn't keep her,
force her stay. Would he break free—flee, run from the
inevitability of her leaving? Why should he? Not when he
had every right to be here—they were the interlopers, intruding in his life. Pommy hated intrusions.

"Pommy! Wait, don't go! It's so wonderful!" Forgetting
how upset she'd been with him, Jenneth dodged by Diccon,
running toward Pommy, the lucifers tucked in her pocket,
safe and secure.

*"Pw'eek, don't let her fixate on them, you hear me? We'll
all be sorry."*

Pw'eek stopped, folding to cleanse a spot on her spine
just above her tail. **"*My* Jenneth, *mine* in certain things,
not yours! She and I, *we* decide what we do with them!"**

❧

She wished it would rain, the anticipation worse than the pounding, wet droplets. Hells, she was already soaked through, the air moist enough to wring, weighing down on her as if it were a burden to be carried. Bess had been able to lift Arras off his feet, but Holly was convinced the weather weighed far more. A smudged sky, sullen and swollen with rain, scowled, equally dissatisfied with the delay, the interminable pause that made it feel as if time stood still. Not to mention she'd become glued to Nauki, the bubalus's plodding gait tossing like a ship at sea. Better or worse than the swamps? Damned if she knew! *"Rain, dammit!"* Holly shook her fist at the sky. *"Just get it over with, let'er rip!"*

"Won't work." P'roul licked at damp fur, made a face as it clumped and stuck. **"Acts of Nature, whatever. Same with tides."** Without warning she arched on Nauki's back and rowled at the skies. Jenret wheeled from his spot beside Nauki's left horn, his bare chest sweat-slicked, eyes haunted.

Behind Holly, Rawn grumbled, **"Unnecessary and indulgent. Haven't we worries enough?"**

Balancing front paws on Holly's shoulder, P'roul stretched her pink nose toward Rawn, who'd draped himself across Nauki's loins, black blending with black. **"Sorry, sire. But it** *feels* **good, even if it solves nothing. I'm frantic about Merowmepurr, too."**

Stripped to the waist like Jenret, but with a red band tied round his forehead and his sash limply draped round his throat to absorb the perspiration, Arras caught up with Nauki, scratching him behind a loppy ear. The bubalus leaned his head into the searching fingers, moistly huffing. "I saw a flash of lightning westward—storm's rolling in faster." He studied the sky, nodding. "I give it to the count of fifty and the rain'll start. Any takers?"

Still unresponsive, Jenret jerked Nauki's halter rope as if that would speed the beast along. Irritated, Nauki gave a blubbering snort and shook his head, setting the line swinging like a children's jump rope. She knew—as did Arras—how Jenret mentally monitored Doyce's every breath, every thought. Arras had confided that Jenret was spanning a greater distance than most Resonants ever attained, a dauntingly exhausting effort to remain in continuous contact—especially without a reciprocal mindvoice meeting one halfway. Right now, nothing else mattered to Jenret, everything around him subsidiary to the intense mental link he'd so painstakingly strung to support Doyce. If Khar were to—Holly forced herself to say it—die, Doyce would need that support and more, physical as well as mental consolation. Just watching him wearied her, yet he'd found sufficient strength to support that thread of communion as well as almost bodily drag Nauki behind him.

Interrupting Arras's chanting count, Holly dug into a pocket and held out two silvers. "Two that it takes double," and joined him at "ten, eleven, twelve," their voices goading each other to speed the count, change the rhythm. If only Jenret would grant himself some respite. As marvelous as her bond with P'roul was, they both relished a certain amount of mental privacy, and Holly couldn't help musing that Doyce might yearn for some seclusion, privacy for her pain, her disquiet over Khar. Jenret's "presence" might soothe, but not his unrelenting oversolicitude.

"Marker!" Bess sang out, pointing to the side of the road where a squared stone stood, its carved number partially obscured by riotous creepers. "Ha! Bubalus makin' better time'n yed thought. We be ta Neu Dorp soon." Drawing up her knees, she placed her bare feet squarely on Taubi's back and rose, rooster-crowing and flapping her arms.

Startled, Arras lost count, but Holly never faltered, grinning as she passed fifty, then sixty, smooth and even, doing her best not to rush. It never occurred to Jenret she might be equally frightened for Theo. If anything happened to Theo . . . no, don't even think it, don't borrow trouble in advance. Imagination easily outstripped reality, and thinking something disastrous *couldn't* make it happen! "Seventy-three, seventy-four," she flicked Arras in the ribs with her toe, tauntingly jangling the two silvers just beyond his reach. But at "seventy-five," the skies bled so freely they might have punctured by a multitude of archers.

"Damn! Which of us wins?" she grumbled.

"*Nobody* wins—don't you see, that's the point!" Jenret's haggard blue eyes battered at her forced complacency, boring into her with something closely akin to hatred. "Nobody wins! No matter what you do, how you do it, how hard you try, *nobody* wins. *Ever!*" With a dismissive wave of his hand he indicated the highway ahead, the pounding rain turning it into a ribbon of streaming mud. No one spoke, the only sound cutting through the drumming rain was the sharp clack-snap of shutters being slammed, apparently at a house invisible from the highway.

She couldn't read him as intimately as Arras, though she'd come to understand him better on this journey. For all his outward bravado his inner sensitivities buffeted him more severely than anyone else could. Let him talk it out, release some of his pent-up frustration and fear, not carry the burden alone? Or would he lash at anyone trying to help? For some, sharing was equally shameful, an admission of weakness. Well, mayhap she could offer Doyce some solitude. "What do you mean, 'nobody wins'?" Right now she'd settle for breaking even, no one suffering any losses.

"Any idea where Doyce and Theo and the rest are right now? Arras, do you know where Harry is? Well? Do you?"

Arras, Resonant himself, stood stock-still, rain splatting against his bare chest, his mustache hanging limp like some little drowned creature. Strange, he still looked dressed, the paleness of his torso, his upper arms contrasting like a clinging white shirt against his tanned neck and face, his forearms. "Damn! At sea . . . wasn't very specific, was it?" Holly had an overpowering urge to cuff P'roul for not explaining any more, but she'd been so distraught she probably wouldn't have absorbed any of the details. "Can't get much, not at this remove, not with his mindspeech blundering worse than a drunkard. But I can tell *where* he is—where they *all* are!"

"Precisely!" Exuding a sort of grim satisfaction at having proved his point, Jenret strode on, tugging Nauki after him.

Rapping Taubi on the neck, Bess brought the bubalus up beside its partner. "Where they bein'? More trouble now?" Equally clueless, Holly gave a shrug, hands gripping P'roul's shoulders tighter than the ghatta liked.

"P'roul, has Khim told you anything more? Where are they?"

"Hadn't wanted to say—since there's nothing we can do." Fur plastered flat, P'roul looked half her normal size and twice as miserable as her Bond. **"Arras can explain— or Jenret. Bess might as well hear, too."**

"Arras?" Holly swiped her face with the inside of her elbow, unwilling to let the water blur her vision. Wondered why she'd bothered, Arras's forbidding expression a twin to Jenret's. "Arras, Jenret? Somebody, please—tell me!"

Wringing first one side of his mustache and then the other, Arras stared downward, unwilling or unable to meet her eye. "They're 'at sea,' right enough—in a boat, a rickety little craft riddled with leaks. A boat, mind you, crammed with nine adults, sixteen children, and two ghatti. An overloaded, leaky boat in the midst of a storm."

Eyes closed, willing herself to blot out the image, Holly whispered a prayer. Theo loved messing in boats, always had, but never in his life had he sailed the open seas. Rowboats and canoes, fine. And tacking in a borrowed, one-man sailboat with a sail not much bigger than a pocket hanky, that was the sum total of Theo's sailing expertise. What had Theo gotten himself into now!

A piercing whistle cut through Holly's thoughts, alarming Nauki. Bess sat astride Taubi, fingers to her lips. "Where dey tryin' ta land? Where dey sailin' fer?"

"The weather's so bad, they don't know if they dare land or even where they can—if they're being pursued. They think they've cleared the mouth of the Mbujiki River," Jenret replied.

"Huh, huh, huh!" Chewing at a knuckle, Bess stared upward, her free hand sketching the air, oblivious to the rain stinging her upturned face, sluicing her hair straight back from her forehead. A vigorous blink, a headshake, and she grinned. "Mebbe chance! What sail hoisted?"

Jenret's answer meant little to Holly, but apparently meant something to Bess. "Neu Dorp be likely safe, but never make it if boat so bad—'nother day sail, at least! Storm'll drive'm in inta rocks off Rookery Point, 'zuming zey doan sink first."

Jenret spat. "How comforting!"

"Damn right it comforting! Hustle by Neu Dorp 'n hustle plippety-plippety-plop ta Rookery Point. Beg, borrow, steal boats, coils'n coils of rope! Tell townfolk head fur beach, spread nort and south, lightin' fires at the good landing sites. Gif yer friends somet'ing ta aim fer! Haul'em in if dey sail close nuff!"

"Madame, I'll take any chance—slim to none—rather

than do nothing." Jenret walked straighter, taller, giving
Nauki an affectionate but emphatic tap on his neck to hurry
his pace. Holly, though, let her tears mingle with the rain.
Bess had mentioned Rookery Point once, the number of
ships that had foundered on its hazardous, rocky coast.
True familiarity with the waters was needed to navigate
such dangers. If Bess had eased Jenret's burden, she'd
shifted much of it, all unwitting, to Holly. *She* should have
been out there, not Theo! At least she could swim! Her
mind's eye conjured up a vision of Theo sinking, little children clinging to his neck, his waist, as he struggled to float,
save as many as he could. Theo, who sank like an anvil!

**"You told yourself before not to let your imagination
run wild. You can't forecast the truth any better than you
can the weather! Nor can I!"** P'roul's ears dripped, water
beading her whiskers. **"Show some spunk, some spirit!"**

Here she was, bemoaning fate when P'roul bore a
double-woe—both her sib and their mother aboard Theo's
floating colander. *"Sorry, dearheart. Give Khim my love
and—"*

**"Have her tell Theo you love him. I know, I did
already."**

Half-mesmerized by a towering wave that looked more like
an impregnable wall, Theo screamed "Hang on!" at the top
of his lungs, praying his passengers would hear, heed his
cry. No evading this one, not a prayer, despite his fervent
pleas. The objective was to ride *over* the waves, not punch
through them! All he could do was ease the rudder, hope
the boat didn't meet the wave broadside.

The wave enfolded them and he flung his arms round
the tiller, hanging on for dear life, because this escape had
taught him how truly dear it was. The boat emerged like a
lumbering, primitive beast, water sluicing off its rotted half-
decking, some pouring into the sea, the rest filling the hull.
Coughs, retches, and curses mingled with the frantic splash
of bailing as he turned the boat shoreward, he hoped. The
storm had harried them, sent them fleeing ahead of it until
he'd lost any real sense of where they were or where they
should be, making landing nearly impossible. Now it was

merely improbable. "Everyone accounted for?" he shouted
over the wind. "Then bail, dammit, bail!"

He tried to calculate how long they'd been at sea, but
couldn't even tell what time of day or night it was. Roughly
midnight when they'd gathered at the warehouse, the argument, the fight, Honoria finding the boat, picking up Dannae and her crew . . . and then the storm. Had to be
morning, even past noon, not that any sun would confirm
the fact. Time had a way of compressing or stretching itself
taffy-slow during crises, he just wasn't very good at telling
which.

At some point they'd clumsily lashed themselves to the
boat's rib cleats and side braces, the necessity terrifying
Theo as badly as the thought of even one child being swept
overboard. If the boat went down, so would they all,
trussed in place like haliday fowl. Which presented the
lesser evil: drowning together or drowning alone, swept
from a loved one's embrace?

The rain beat faster, then seemed to pause for breath, a
squall of some sort; either it'd taper off, or they'd out-
distance it. Or they'd . . . no, don't think on it. Lady save
him for a fool, was Khim still patiently crouched at the
bow? He'd not exchanged a word with her for so long, and
the nightmare fantasy of her being tossed free, desperately
paddling as the gap between them grew, left him physically
ill. Insides heaving in panic, he vomited, not caring where;
he'd lost whatever his stomach had held early on. *"Khim?
Darling, are you there? 'Speak me!"*

With little rope to spare, the children taking first priority,
Lindy'd rough-braided a harness for Khim from fabric
strips and some leather lacing from Corly's vest. At least
Khim could sink in her claws, cling like sin when need
arose, but the hammering waves could have proved too
potent to withstand. *"Khim!"*

"Wargh!" Meaningless, hardly standard ghatti vocabu-
lary, but he was reborn at hearing it. **"I've swallowed water
every which way! Bloated!"** Reassured, he strained and saw
her sodden form, black against the wood's wet darkness.
Lovely, lovely vivid white chest and muzzle, feet!
"Mew'ph's fading," she warned, **"we've sheered out of
range."** On occasion the storm had lofted Khim's mindvoice high enough to reach Gander and the Seeker-Bond

pair stationed there. Like foolish innocents, he and Khim had hoped this enhanced contact would allow them to actually navigate north along the coast, Mew'ph's mindvoice serving as a "beacon" of sorts. *"Well, I'd assumed it wasn't doing much good."* Still, just knowing another soul had some inkling as to their whereabouts had been reassuring. *"I've headed us shoreward, I hope."*

"If I can raise Mew'ph again, shall I have Dymphna send out a rescue boat? Mew'ph swears her Guardians are trustworthy." Straining upward, Khim prepared to try again. **"Don't much care if they are or aren't. Nicer to be rescued and thrown in the dungeons than to keep sailing, hoping we'll stay afloat!"**

How tempting to passively wait for rescue! Except it wasn't that simple—they still had to remain afloat, as Khim had pointed out. How could a rescue team ever spot them, a lonely, low-riding speck on the storm-tossed seas? *"Don't. No point risking more lives."*

Oddly matched comrades in arms, literally, Honoria and Dannae made their way back, clinging to each other. Despite the storm Honoria still exuded a certain confident beauty, her drenched clothes accentuating her figure, her sleeked hair emphasizing the exquisite structure of her face. In contrast, Dannae's topknot had unraveled, making it look as if a baby squid perched atop her head. How she'd swum in that waterlogged, outsized robe still amazed Theo. The Lady might not have been guiding them, but She'd surely been guarding her and the children as they'd confidently kicked their way out to sea, convinced they'd soon ram into the next wharf piling! Too easy to become disoriented in fog and rain, misjudge harbor sounds, the strength of the current. However, if the Lady were truly watching over Dannae, Theo thought sourly, She'd have bequeathed Dannae a rescuer with a more seaworthy craft!

"Shake out some sail?" Honoria shouted, straining against Dannae's hand to lean toward him. "Gusts are dying down and the wind seems steadier."

"Good, we'll run before the wind . . . or limp, whatever." He swept his arm toward what he hoped was east. "I'm easing toward shore, trying to reach port, any port. My best guess is that we've passed the mouth of another river— even with the storm, the water seemed silty."

Mouth thinned in thought, she nodded. "Must be the Mbujki," and unexpectedly laid a hand on his cheek. Cold flesh collided with cold flesh, and then her warmth burned, reminding him how miserably wet and cold he truly was, hunched in the stern, the wind whipping him till he bent like a willow. At least the tiller gave him something to occupy his mind.

"How're Doyce, Khar?" A fresh gust tossed his words back in his teeth, but they'd guess what he'd asked. Theo didn't want to lose a soul, but to be reviled as the reckless Seeker held responsible for Doyce's or Khar's death would forever haunt him.

Hunkering against the gunwales, Dannae tugged her tether to gain some slack and bent forward so he could hear. "Doyce fares better than Khar, physically. Wounds not as deep." Spume flecked her, but she paid no heed, simply swept her hair back as if it were so much seaweed. "But Khar's condition's making Doyce sick with fear. Don't know if the ghatta's wounds are infected, or if it's exposure, but she's fading. She's not a young beast."

"Keep her as warm as you can." He rolled his eyes in mute apology. What a stupid comment! How were they to accomplish that?

But Dannae gave an amiable head-bob and raised her interlaced fingers where he could see them. "Got Siri, Smir, and Harry packed round so tight Doyce can barely see Khar. Smir swore it was a Sunderlies shell game—find the ghatta neath one scamp or another."

"Ozer and his brood?"

One hand on Theo's arm and the other beside his hand on the tiller, Honoria looked forward, lips moving as she tallied them. "All accounted for, but cranky, hungry, tired . . ." she drifted off, "as are we all. We're all at risk of exposure."

"In other words, everything's fine. We're still part of the Lady's greater scheme, have our roles to play." It dawned on Theo he'd not stammered once. Hell of a way to cure it: immersion therapy and stark, raving terror! Pass that tip to the eumedicos when they returned, if they returned. "If the tackles and braces still work, see if you can unfurl some sail. Mayhap I make this cannikin respond. Have it dancing

over the waves like a water sprite, obedient to my least
whim!" Holly'd be proud of him!

Every muscle, every sinew had gone brittle, ready to shatter
at the first blow. But oh, the first blow had already been
struck when Aqua'd unearthed *that* machine, his past swirling round his present in a viscous fog of memory, shrouding
his mind. "That was then, this is now," he chided himself,
"Aqua played no part in my past, has redeemed me from
it, given me a future."

But to see her now as she broke away—that young
stranger hanging so intimately close and familiar—to rush
toward him with such consummate joy animating her
face . . . Unbearable that someone else could induce, *had,*
induce a look previously reserved solely for him! That, and
the two ghatti frolicking around the young man's feet! Not
cats, but ghatti, those evil, wretched beasts who'd ruined
his past could casually demolish his future with equal ease,
blast his hopes! How had they come here, how had they
caught him and Aqua?

Hadn't he fled across the sea to escape them, left the
past behind except for those impulsively stolen drawings of
the machine, the one that could expose Resonants? No way
for them to hide, work their subtle wiles on Normal minds,
coerce them into seeing black as white! Once the glass disks
spun and the sparks flew, all Resonants within its reach
stood revealed, temporarily paralyzed! With dogged effort
he'd constructed his own machine from those plans, forearmed if ever it should prove necessary to unmask these
creatures here, protect life and limb.

Whether his meticulous reproduction actually worked, he
couldn't judge, had never discerned a Resonant upon which
to test it. Those who watched him spin the crank, set sparks
flying, simply stood, impatiently waiting for it to do something more dramatic than making their arm and neck hairs
prickle. On moving here he'd bundled it away with a sigh
of relief; he *had* outrun them all, Seekers and ghatti, Resonants. No, they'd not destroy him as they had Hylan Crailford, Bazelon Foy. Even turned *him,* Tadj Pomerol, into
their cat's paw, their unwitting instrument to strike down

Baz, the silver sickle slicing, slicing . . . through the creamy, olive-tinted column of his throat. . . . Had they returned now to see if they could make him strike out at his beloved Aqua?

Spinning round, he ran for the hut, momentarily unable to face her, not now, not like this, not raging and crying within. So dear, so precious, his gift from the seas, and now hovering on the brink, corrupted by this Canderisian stranger, a Seeker boasting two ghatti! Could he save her? Could he even save himself? What was there to salvage, other than the usual broken bits of flotsam and jetsam, nothing ever perfect, unflawed, nothing new with which to reinvent himself one more time? Except Aqua, and even she'd been far from perfect when he'd found her, so near to death, but he'd healed her, made her whole once more.

Hearing Tigger howling in the distance, he pounded up the path, praying that Hirby had arrived. Better than nothing—Hirby was his friend, as much as possible given his racketing thought-processes. Breaking into the tended space ringing his hut, he stood, panting, surveying his domain, yearning for it to remain like this, forever untouched by taint. But a shape moved, unfolding itself as it rose to stretch, step from his doorway into the sun. The man appeared made of sunlight, honey-gold skin, close-cropped, tight-curled hair perhaps once the same shade, though now gray-threaded. Funny, he looked as if he belonged here in the Sunderlies. A stranger—from Samranth, no doubt—but not an entire stranger like that Seeker-scum cavorting with his Aqua.

Rolling his shoulders to allay his stiffness, his face tired but contented, the golden man ambled toward him, hand outstretched. "Hullo, I'm Bard Ambwasali. Sorry to intrude, but we're meeting friends here—including a long-lost one, Jenneth Wycherley, who fell overboard from the *Vruchtensla*."

Reluctantly extending his hand, Pommy spasmodically jerked it away as a black-and-white form materialized from in back of the hut and halted, watchful. "Get it *out* of here!" Pommy screamed, voice shrilling. "Make it *go* away! Get that perverted beast *out* of here! You—get out, too!" Hands shielding his eyes, he trembled and twitched, fighting down another shriek as the interloper hesitantly touched his arm.

That touch—too much! The machete—where was it? Still lodged in the stump where he'd left it? On the bench? In the hut? Had Aqua tidied up after him this morning?

"Lady bless! What's distressing you so?" A new voice now assaulted him, footsteps, another outsider intruding. "Bard, send M'wa out of sight, if you would. Not everyone appreciates ghatti, I'm afraid."

Relieved at his compassionate tone, Pommy warily let his hands slide from his eyes, still hiding his mouth behind them. Mayhap it was safe to look, if that damned ghatt had gone. Please, please, Blessed Lady, let it have vanished! He stared at the new face, sympathetic brown eyes, brown hair unrulily falling over his forehead . . . stared and stared at a face etched in acid in his mind, no matter the years that had matured it from boy to man. No!

"Resonant spawn! Little wretch, demon scum! Grown now and come to defy me again!" He spat at the man's feet and raced for the hut's safety. "You can't make me kill what I love this time!"

No, all that painstaking labor, the expense, it hadn't been a waste! The machine, unbundle the machine, make it function! Oh, it wouldn't kill Resonants, wouldn't kill the Resonant boy—now man—who'd caused Bazelon Foy to stumble into the sweeping sickle's embrace, the killing kiss that Pommy'd directed at another. But it *would* temporarily weaken them, cause Resonants to collapse. Use it, and he could even the odds, right the past! Might work on the golden Seeker as well, mayhap on that scum seducing Aqua.

Damn, where was Aqua? Hadn't she been right behind him on the path? Diving through the door, he feverishly ripped at ropes and canvas. "Aqua, get in here! *Now,* darling! You'll be safe in here!" And Hirby, where was Hirby? He needed his brute strength, his unquestioning obedience, three against two—unless more spawn lurked without! Resonants and Seekers, invading his domain, menacing, imperiling everything he held dear! Ghatti crouching on every surrounding branch, ready to pounce! No, no, no, it wasn't meant to happen like this—not ever again! "Aqua!"

Barred from his usual cheerful banter, Dlamini brooded over Uma-Uncle, the old man's fretting almost palpable, shadowing each step like a cloud. Ask a question, receive no response beyond a grunt or a dismissive lift of a dusty, brown shoulder. Even when they'd mistaken their way in the swamps, Uma-Uncle had been a pleasant, wise companion, relating stories, funny or serious, or talking of the past and of the future—living in Mkjinka. Oh, how Dlamini ached to go there—for the learning, for the converse it offered! But now, nothing. Uma-Uncle gave him no more regard than a walking tree stump. Mvelase's eyes were red-rimmed, red-veined with wakeful worry. His silent disregard made Dlamini doubly lonely for Arras, Jenret, Bess and, of course, the beauteous Holly.

Those memories, while highly pleasant, caused him to stub his toe more than once. He, Dlamini, so modestly boastful with the maidens of his surefootedness! Here they were, in sight of the sea—his first glimpse of it!—and he was barely allowed to snatch a peek here and there along the path from which Uma-Uncle never deviated, day or night. Its swirling blues and greens, so many shades so subtly moving, flecks and patches of white rising and foaming, dissipating, only to reform and perform again. No matter how far he gazed, nothing marred its vast expanse, eagerly swelling to snuff the setting sun, quench it with a hiss. And then no morn would ever dawn again. He shivered. Ah, better to think on Holly!

Slipping his waterskin from his shoulder, he shook it to hear its liquid play, then offered it to his uncle. To make him take notice, Dlamini finally politely slapped his chest with it. Like someone awakening, Uma-Uncle took it and pondered it before pulling the peg with his teeth and shooting a stream of water into his mouth. And all the time his feet never missed a step, even though he never glanced at the path, ceaselessly padding along. By the gods, Uma-Uncle'd outlast a bubalus at this rate! Dlamini swore he'd worn more than one layer of callus off his feet, the glittering, harsh sand as abrasive as Uulbora's pumice!

"Will we arrive in time?" Probably pointless to ask, but

he needed to hear a voice, if only his own. "And we will finally meet your nephew, my cousin, Bard?"

Taking a last mouthful of water, Uma-Uncle tilted his head and made a gargling sound, neatly spat. Returning the waterskin with a head-bob of thanks, Mvelase finally looked square at Dlamini. "We will be in time for what we've been called to do."

The old man's legs scissored back and forth, but the tiredness crept through Dlamini's limbs, not his uncle's. Gods help him if Uma-Uncle took it into his mind to walk across the wide water they called the sea! Somehow he'd accomplish it, triumph as usual, though Dlamini might be hard-pressed to keep pace! Despite the fact his legs were longer, he skip-stepped to catch up with his uncle. "That's what I don't understand—what is it we've been called to do?" He wanted to protest that Uma-Uncle took a greater interest in this unknown nephew than in the grand-nephew so loyally by his side, refusing to acknowledge how tired they both must be.

Absently Uma-Uncle plucked an ivory flower from a stem bent in their path, never slowing his stride as he sniffed it, the delicate petals molding against his nostrils. "Ah, ah, ah!" his uncle cried as if he were in agony, slipping the flower inside the fold of his shoulder cloth. "We have come to take him home, at last."

Still puzzled, Dlamini stole another look at the sea, wishing for a robe as dazzlingly blue for gifting Holly. All of this journey had been a wondrous adventure, an unparalleled opportunity to view new sights, meet strange new people but, all in all, he was no longer sure if he cared whether he ever met this mysterious cousin. Enough was enough, and he yearned for home.

A horrific clamor struck his ears, a baying so harshly loud that it couldn't issue from any dog, at least not the quick-footed, middling-sized ones that herded their cattle. They generally controlled the herd with silent efficiency, preferring nips over barks to move the cattle. This sounded like a beast from blood-drenched nightmares, and the sight of it, half-dog, half-dwelecka fiend, bounding up the dunes at them, made him freeze in his tracks. But Uma-Uncle simply continued walking, swinging his staff. The beast halted, standing its ground directly in front of Uma-Uncle,

growling warning, its teeth viciously long and white in its
shaggy, matted fright of a face. Mvelase's staff flicked up
and over, slamming the beast across its snout, and it turned
tail, sprinting away ki-yelping.

Yes, brave grandnephew, was he not? To let an old man
face a beast like that unassisted. Shamed beyond belief, he
hurried after Uma-Uncle, his face burning. Oh, how he
wanted to go home!

Her hand lay light on Khar's flank, even that minimal pressure generating pain, though the ghatta refused to let her
remove it, reveling in her touch. Disorienting during such
intense intimacy, delving within the ghatta's mind,
sharing—nay, assuming, if she but could—her excruciating
pain, to realize Khar lay cushioned on a bed of childish
laps. In the middle, Harry hugged Smir and Siri, while they,
in turn, sheltered Khar as best they might from the drizzle
and spray, the cutting wind. Somehow she'd wedged herself
between Harry's and Smir's legs, her own knees angled
over Harry's, feet snugged under Siri's ankles.

It hurt to sit up, it hurt to recline, but it pained worse
to witness Khar in such extremity, to hover so near, all to
no avail. Either her fingers had gradually numbed, or
Khar's breathing had grown shallow, the rise and fall of
her striped sides retreating from her touch. Even her mouth
had pouched, its firm line lax, drooping in a way no self-
respecting ghatta would countenance, except in deepest
slumber. Within Khar's mind, fragments of the past whirled
and spun by like fallen leaves, fading, turning brittle even
as Doyce clung to them, reminding Khar of their life together, the past they'd shared. If the past faded, was there
a future? Even the present felt tenuous, so gossamer-thin
the slightest touch could tear the veil of life.

So, it had come to this . . . finally. Their beginnings
hazed, the end in view, the pyre's flames soaring high,
higher. And could she, *should* she fight against the end, the
emptiness, if it granted surcease from pain? Somehow she'd
never envisioned it ending like this, half-drifting, half-
sailing in a boat so leaky it could nearly drain the sea,
crowded by children and adults, no privacy for tears or

lamentations—or for tender farewells. Her own mind screamed, burned with an aching loss, bemoaning the injustice of it all—not like this, not right now!

"Oh, beloved . . . !" and found she could 'speak no further, brain afire, consuming the inadequate words of thanksgiving for their life together before they were uttered. Head tossed back, exposed to the elements, she loosed a silent wail of anguish, heartsick at her failure. Always too little, forever too late!

But in the midst of her self-flagellation, a childish cry of pain gradually registered, a small mouth icy against her ear, tiny fists furiously pounding her shoulders. "Auntie Doyce, please!" wailed Byrlie. "Please, oh, please—it's Mama!"

Loath to desert Khar, her own body stiff, resisting each command, she lumbered up, balancing against Byrlie as she assembled her scattered thoughts, determined what had frightened the child so. But the answer stared her in the face: Lindy, obviously in the throes of one her farseeing spells. A long, high shriek tore from Lindy's throat to wail with the wind, her blonde hair streaming and writhing, whipping across her rose-colored blouson, now a dull, rose-gray like a recent scar. Even competing against the wind and rain, her screams battered at all ears, children beginning to cry, terrified at such a bizarre outburst from someone they'd trusted to provide sanity and comfort all this long day.

Oh, Blessed Lady, don't force me to portion myself between two whom I love!

With dawning hope she noticed Gelya's stealthy approach toward Lindy from the opposite side, working her way around and over sprawled bodies, unobtrusive as a snail. But then, given Lindy's cries, her strained expression that sought to pierce nothingness, Doyce doubted Lindy focused on the here and now. Laboriously she shoved Byrlie into Corly's arms and continued on, hunching against the wind and rain that felt less real than the blaze within her mind. But Lindy spun a quarter turn, raising her arms to supplicate the skies as she cried, "Bard! No, darling! Davvy, no—don't! Please, Lady, not like this! Behind you! Don't die, darling, not now! You can *change* it, break the pattern!"

Closer, closer now, not that Lindy'd notice a tree toppling on her, and Doyce nodded to Gelya to move in tandem, pincer Lindy and drag her amidships. Readying herself to plunge forward, Doyce gaped as Lindy erupted in a mass of writhing flames, her body a pillar of candescent fire.

Fire! Yes, yes, so lovely, fire! Yes, just strike the lucifer! Let the flickering tongues of flame cry out! Distract them with their dancing death, their kindling life. Fire to cauterize the pain, light so bright it sears and blinds!

Flinching backward, faltering as she shielded her eyes with a forearm, Doyce watched Lindy's flame-wreathed figure raise an admonitory hand to the skies, shaking her finger as she called, "Jenneth, no! Put it down this instant! That's right, darling!"

"What in the world?" Davvy's eyebrows arched in puzzlement. "I've heard of people who can't stand cats, let alone ghatti. The psychological and physiological ramifications are well-documented in eumedico literature." Looking helplessly at Bard, he asked, "But what was that sputtering about demons and spawn?"

Hand on his sword hilt, where it had remained ever since the man had overreacted on seeing M'wa, Bard warily looked to his Bond for confirmation, dreading his answer. *"M'wa? That* is *who I think it is, isn't it?"*

Eyes never wavering, M'wa continued assessing each wisp of sound, each fleeting movement within the hut. **"Somehow, yes. Don't ask me why he's here, how he found Jenneth. But yes, he worked hand-in-glove with Bazelon Foy, almost his acolyte, Tadj Pomerol. He escaped in the confusion."**

"Uncle Bard? Davvy?" Bubbling with laughter, Jenneth bounded up and threw herself into Bard's arms. A deep ache retreated from his heart as he squeezed her tight and madly swung her around until she screamed with delight and locked her legs around his waist, just as she had as a child, just as Byrlie did now. Ah, Byrlie! To see Byrlie, to see Lindy—soon now! The pattern *didn't* hold, he'd broken the pattern, his heart had healed almost whole! It wasn't too late to start anew, rebuild himself, the people he loved in their own images—no one else's! A new world beckoned—except for this one monstrous artifact from the previous one.

Craving his share of affection, Davvy embraced them both, Bard mock-growling as he whipped Jenneth clear, then delivered her back. "I'm so . . . I don't understand how . . ." Jenneth gabbled, cheerfully shoehorning one sentence into another, ". . . so lucky! Pw'eek found me, *you* found me! I love you so—"

Yet in contrast with her words, Jenneth had already begun to break free of his embrace. Had he crushed the breath out of her? Or had something frightened, threatened her—that brute's nearness, mayhap? Attend to business, he told himself, the past isn't paid till Jenneth's in her mother's and father's arms.

"What's the matter with Pommy? Did you hurt him? What did you do?" Flinging tangled hair free of her face, she bent a look of fond reproach on him before anxiously surveying the hut. "I've never heard him like that. So scared and angry." With a coltish skip she started toward the hut, but Bard hurriedly snatched her wrist, smilingly refusing to release her. No—not until he was confident the man posed no danger to anyone, including himself. Though strictly speaking he hadn't been mad, Tadj Pomerol *had* been easily swayed, a follower, idealizing and idolizing the man he viewed as Canderis's savior from the Resonants. What these long years in this desolate spot had made of him, Bard couldn't yet determine, and preferred to handle that beyond Jenneth's earshot.

Joining them, Diccon breezily announced, "I didn't think we were racing, Jen. Where's your friend gone? I want to thank—"

"Well, *I* want to leave—now!" Keeping track over his shoulder, Bard began to draw them farther from the vicinity of the hut. "Let's head back to the boat, and I'll explain." *"M'wa, keep watch. Call me as soon as he sets foot outside."*

More perplexed than petulant, Jenneth stamped her foot. "But Uncle Bard, why can't I see Pommy? What's he done to anger you? After all, he saved my life!" Appealing to Davvy, she emphasized, "This *isn't* fair! Why's Uncle Bard

so set against him? Can't *someone* explain? Davvy?
Diccon?"

"Don't argue, Jenneth. Just go! I'll explain later." What
point in responding when he still hadn't answered Davvy?
Nor was he confident he wanted the twins exposed to what
he had to say. Before his eyes a nightmare from the past
had been resurrected, come rushing back to flood him with
vile memories, whether or not Davvy'd deduced Pommy's
identity. Could Davvy have forgotten what he remembered
with such sick certitude? Were children so naturally resilient that they walled out hurtful memories, went on with
their lives, unscathed? "Davvy, Diccon, take Jen back, the
ghatten, too. M'wa and I'll be along shortly, some unfinished business to attend to."

"But Jen deserves an answer, we all do," Diccon protested, his jaw set at a stubborn angle so reminiscent of
Doyce. "You really can't treat us as children any more, not
after what we've endured on this trip! After all, we're *sixteen*!" Twins, forever sticking together, just as Byrta had
stood up for him, and he for her, a double-dose of argument wearing down all but the most resolute. But Diccon's
eyes now revealed doubt, his bluster gradually deflating, as
though Davvy had quick-warned Diccon off.

"Come on, Jen. Uncle Bard'll explain later." Winding his
fingers through Jenneth's—and Bard recognized that little
maneuver so well, apply subtle pressure to bend back the
fingers and the person would follow meek as a lamb—Diccon drew her along. "Come, my furry ladies, Kwee,
Pw'eek!" His other arm snug at his sister's waist now, he
coaxingly chattered away. "You know Uncle Bard's as bad
as Mama when it comes to tidying loose ends. Let him
clear up things, and then we can come back and apologize.
Not to mention properly thank your friend. Wait till you
meet Luykas—you'll like him. And our launch, you'll never
believe how Bard—"

Bewildered, lagging as best she might, Jenneth stole
glances over her shoulder whenever she could. "Hurry,
catch up," Bard prodded, "I want someone dependable
with them."

Seemingly deaf to his plea, Davvy nervously circled his
head as if loosening a stiff neck . . . or spiraling back to
another day, another night, sixteen years past. Through the

open door, the small window, Bard watched fragmented movement, busy, purposeful. What was Tadj Pomerol up to? Packing—if the gods favored Bard. Or did Harharta's pact with him stand fulfilled?

"I don't want to remember!" Davvy wet his lips, his whisper ragged. "That abandoned cellar-pit, Lindy and I . . . prisoners . . . their sacrifices! You and Doyce and Eadwin saving us. I . . . I kicked at the dark-haired man . . . Baz . . . Bazelon Foy . . . juggled earlier that night . . . how Lindy loved it! He hit me, captured us. By the Lady, how he . . . hated, despised all Resonants! Wanted to kill us all without quarter! Killed Darl, killed Faertom and Garvey!" his tears fell freely now. "The blond man was with that dotty old woman—I didn't recognize him at first . . . He was so young, handsome, almost beautiful . . . not a hair out of place. Now his hair's bleached to straw, his face so tanned and lined. Oh, the loathsome things he screamed at me!"

"Now do you understand why I want the twins gone, you, as well?" Increasingly uneasy, Bard worked his sword in its scabbard. No excuse, no pressing need to draw it, but oh, how he longed for it in his hand, prepared for what might come.

Melting from his post without a lost motion, M'wa flowed beside him. **"People on the back path. And he's ready to come out. Carrying something—can't tell what. Doesn't look like a weapon, anything dangerous, though."**

Happy dog yelps split the air as a hairy, scruffy beast big as a calf pranced and leaped, gamboling around a large, unkept man with gaping teeth and mouse-brown eyes that veered between shrewd assessment and blank emptiness. Following close behind came two tall, lean men—one old, one young—with umber skin and honed features. The horns atop each staff riveted Bard's attention, made him frown with effort. What—why?

"Hirby!" Startled, Bard pivoted in time to see Jenneth break free from Diccon, her brother belatedly chasing after her. Damn, he'd been sure they were clear by now, should have been halfway to the launch! "It's a terrible mix-up! Go tell Pommy I'm fine, that everything's fine!" Fending off Diccon, she put Hirby's bulk between herself and her

twin, dodging and dancing round, the dog joining in the
romp.

By the gods, this wasn't a game! Without thought, Bard
loosed a venomous curse that meant nothing to his Canderisian friends, but caused the two strangers to regard him
with renewed interest. A sense of awe, a feeling of homecoming crept over Bard, and he took a hesitant step toward
them, unknown yet so very familiar, a sight it seemed he'd
waited forever to see.

" 'Ware! First things first!" M'wa's 'voice shattered his
trance, made him reluctantly tear his eyes away as Pommy
staggered outside, tenaciously hugging some sort of unwieldy machine to his chest as passionately as a loved one.
Placing it on a rude bench just beyond the door he divided
his glares between Bard and Davvy, defying either to venture closer.

A glass plate—Bard saw it reflecting the light, dust-hazed
as it was. No, two plates, tight together, set vertically like
a wheel, and a pair of metal arms or brackets that curved
out and up like graceful horns, not unlike the horns on the
strangers' staffs. A part of him noticed that Pommy's belt
cinched the gears, mayhap replacing a missing or damaged
part?

Apprehension became certainty: once before he'd viewed
a machine of this sort, similar, anyway. On the twins' naming day sixteen years past, Mahafny and Jenret had taken
a similar device outside and somberly smashed it. Rrmm!
RrrRrmm! Round and round, faster and faster, the man
furiously cranking, Bard grasping the full import of the
spinning disks too late as M'wa yowled, **"Get them clear!
Won't kill or hurt them, but it'll leave them vulnerable!"**
M'wa's whiskers rippled, almost sparked. **"Leaves them
with a sense of repletion!"** Bard had no idea what the ghatt
meant, but even he could feel the building static in the air.

"Pommy, what is it? What does it do?" Jenneth's voice,
full of curiosity. "Can I see—" RrmmRrmm!

"Davvy! Run—take the twins!" Raptly watching the
sparks now beginning to fly between the two balls, Davvy
ignored him, and Bard planted both hands on his chest,
giving him a rude shove. How long did he have? The
leather belt protested, slipping, screeching—mayhap the
machine wouldn't function properly. Again he bodily

forced Davvy back, more urgently this time. Davvy stood
nearer to the machine than the twins, hands at his temples,
eyes closing in ecstasy—unwise, given the intent hatred in
Pommy's eyes. "Get back, you fool! I'll handle this."

"No!" Struggling out of his stupor, Davvy grappled back
until Bard lost all patience, began to battle him in earnest.
"*You* protect the twins! This is *my* battle, Bard, *mine* this
time! Don't risk your life again for me!" Davvy's wildly
swinging forearm caught Bard a solid buffet on the temple,
almost toppling him backward over a strategically hooked
foot.

Damn, he'd thought Davvy too dazed for that trick!
Wrestling, thrashing each other like two disgruntled school-
boys while that machine slowly picked up speed!
RrrRrmmm! Mayhap the insanity was contagious. Whimpering, recoiling, the bulky, unkempt man skirmished with
Diccon, whose blows went wilder and wider as a muddled
giddiness swept over him. Still, it effectively kept Diccon
from running after Jenneth as she hurried toward Pommy's
side. And oblivious to it all, the huge dog was bouncing
and feinting, jumping stiff-legged at M'wa, unwillingly retreating but drawing the beast clear of the ghatten, as innocently transfixed as if they watched a circus performance,
enthralled by the odd goings-on of their Bonds and their
own sparking fur.

"Pommy, is it working right? I hope I didn't hurt it when
I unwrapped—"

The infernal machine grated and screeched louder and
louder, like a demon, snapping off sparks, a faint scent of
burning in the air, the friction between the plates burning
bits of debris lodged between them. Diccon slowly
swooned, the large man standing over him, bewildered, and
Bard belatedly grabbed for Davvy's collapsing form as Jen
cried, "Oh, Pommy! It's so, so . . . Oh, Blessed Lady!"

Quivering in ecstasy, she canted her hips, thrusting and
pumping at something invisible. To Bard's everlasting
shame, the sight of her arching hips, the realization she was
a woman, not a child, brought a surge of desire over him,
no longer an adoptive uncle but simply a man wanting a
woman—this woman. His unexpected, all-too-human car-
nality mortified him.

Leaping away from the machine as if galvanized, Pom-

my's face contorted with enraged betrayal as Jenneth
mimed the motions of sexual congress. "Damn you for a
two-faced slut, Aqua!" he shrieked as his open palm caught
her a stinging blow across the cheek. "Don't tell me you're
one of them, too, you Resonant bitch!"

Now Pw'eek scrambled up Pommy's leg, snarling and clawing, while Kwee leaped for the device, scrabbling against the
spin of the glass plates, her claws screeching. It wobbled, and
she clung grimly, rocking back and forth, until at last it toppled off the bench. The belt snapped, plates crashing and tinkling, armatures bending, and Pommy threw himself after it,
screaming incoherently, desperately scooping the scattered
pieces to him with one hand while distractedly fending off the
ghatten with the other.

Hateful! Horrible, hateful man! Weeping, wanting nothing
more than to run and hide, Jenneth stumbled along the
path behind the hut until she was forced to stop, too enervated, too confused to run further. When no hole big
enough to crawl into and die presented itself, she detoured
behind the hut, crouching against its reed and driftwood
wall, hugging herself tight.

Humiliating, hateful! In front of everyone like that! She'd
sensed the rising sexuality emanating from Diccon and
Davvy as Pommy's machine had roared faster, a firestorm
of lust sweeping over her as well. He'd caused it, teased
her along—and rejected her! Left her stimulated to a fever
pitch, unsatisfied, acting the wanton fool in front everyone!

Screaming, rage flaring . . . Bard roaring at Pommy . . .
now shouting for her, urgent, anxious. Couldn't face him,
no! Her hand sought her shirt pocket, fondling the lucifers
inside. Oh, yes, oh, yes, bad Pommy—not bad Aqua, not
bad Jenneth, but bad Pommy! More horrid shouts, the
crunch and crack of breaking metal and glass as Bard
kicked and stamped at the machine. . . .

Pommy'd hurt Diccon, he'd hurt Davvy, upset Bard, even
poor Hirby, and now he should pay! Disgusting! Peek
round the corner—see him groveling, clinging to Bard's leg,
whimpering over his stupid machine! A machine that revealed Resonants . . . And now her hatred truly ignited as

she realized what she'd experienced, what Pommy's device had originally been intended to do.

Take the first match, scrape it against the coral foundation, cup the delicate flame in her hands, coax it, make it catch. . . .

. . . Doyce was in flux, both herself and simultaneously Lindy, locked within Lindy's foreseeing, participating in her vision, lofted into a far-off now, pleading with Jenneth not to strike the lucifer, alter the immutable. The very core of her soul went molten—Jenneth prepared to play with fire, let her emotions explode in a roaring inferno that might ultimately consume her mind! Never before had Doyce sensed her daughter so rife with untapped power, prepared to wrestle with something beyond her ability to control, throwing her challenge before the empyreal gates of unadulterated, fiery light! Still entangled within Lindy's envisioning, trapped by Lindy's anguish, Doyce fought to let her mind soar free, beating frantically upward and circling to pinpoint Jenneth, find and stop her. A child's body saved from the sea, a child's mind lost to madness! Which way? How far . . . ?

. . . She smiled as Diccon and Hirby blundered down the path, shouting "Jenneth!" and "Aqua!" at every bush and shrub. "Aqua!" "Jenneth!" No, no one by either name here, just someone called Blaze. An errant breeze extinguished her lucifer and she thought she'd be consumed by rage. . . .

. . . The second lucifer, then. Strike it, strike it now! No, no! Not so hard, don't snap its wooden stem . . . !

. . . Hide it, protect it! Safe in her clenched fist! Smile at the handsome young man cautiously craning round the corner at her, such lovely ocher wrappings highlighting his rich umber skin. No, no need to speak. Hold up a finger, mouth "shh!", make him withdraw. Ready herself, savor the wait, soon, soon. . . .

. . . Nattering! Always nattering, annoying, intruding where he wasn't wanted, needed! So he'd delivered a few open-handed slaps across Pommy's face, a mild rebuke considering what the man had attempted. Not to mention what he'd set off in Jenneth, making her play the harlot, inciting equally lustful thoughts in his own brain, unbidden! *This* was the man who'd tried to kill Davvy once before, and now Davvy defended him, protected him!

Enough! It swept over Bard, waves of surging, seething fury, incensing him that someone, something always thwarted him, kept him from saving precious lives. He didn't know where Jenneth had fled to, couldn't make Pommy reveal her whereabouts. Davvy'd thwarted him on the beach at Goose Island, hadn't let him protect Diccon, protect him, find Jenneth sooner! Always Davvy frustrated him, simply by being who he was—Lindy's dearest friend. If he didn't take his hands off Bard's arms, he wouldn't be held accountable for what might transpire. Rage suffusing him, everything hazed with a red glow . . .

One tiny part of him still protested, *"And your dear friend as well, wanting to protect you from Pommy, return you to Lindy and Byrlie."* Some small, sane part of him acknowledged that, made him pull his punch, not shatter Davvy's jaw, merely knock him cold—just deserts for his interfering ways. . . .

Better yet, here was a suitable outlet for his rage, that fool scrambling for the machete under the bench! Ha—try that, would he? He dodged Pommy's machete blow, heard it whistling by his ear, a weird, cold beauty in its passing, the blade spangled by sunlight, gleaming blue-white along its edge. Whirl, slam an elbow into Pommy's gut, yes, an equally satisfying sound. Sword—unsheathe the damn sword, make space to parry and thrust, slice and stab, hack, even. Why bother with finesse? Center, center his vision to focus on this threat, nothing else remained, mattered as much as exterminating this man. Now he'd finish what had been left unfinished. . . .

. . . *"No! Don't! Mine!"* A white paw with an indentation swatted the smoldering spot, swatted again, claws raking burning fragments free. Push the ghatten away, gently blow on the flame, whisper its name, your name, make the serpentine red line eat faster at the shredded reed, burn deeper, burst into Blaze! Pick up a burning splinter, press it to another reed, another frond. Create a flaming hoard to protect Bard from Pommy's wrath! Let it be her consummation, consume Pommy for spurning her! Yes, yes, a little flame here, another there, passing itself on, replicating itself, crackling, snapping, devouring . . . !

. . . The world spun black beneath Doyce's gliding thoughts, refusing to yield its blazing secret. Beating at it with invisible hands that burned and blistered, kicking at it with boots that charred and smoldered, she felt the conflagration within Jenneth closing 'round her. Obdurately, Jenneth's mind fought back, resolved to have its own way.

"Beloved, embrace my strength . . . use it!" Khar urged her, **"Take of my eyes, my heart, my wisdom! Save Jenneth, save yourself . . ."** and the beloved mindvoice faltered, too weak to follow as Doyce surged higher, searching.

"Jenneth, darling! Don't do it! Fight it, don't let it claim you! Fire won't change the outcome—some must live and some must die." Her throat closed tight, eyes burning with unshed tears, her heart hollow. Oh, Khar . . . for some must live, and some must die! *"Drop it, drop the lucifer, darling!"*

"Mama?" A cry of relief. *"Oh, Mama!"* . . . .

The world revolved around two men, both in the throes of their own private madness, circling and feinting, testing and taunting. Bard had the advantage, knew it with keen pleasure, the sword's reach longer than the machete's stubby length. But ah, this Pommy *was* good, twirling the machete till it formed a whirling shield, changing hands, balking him, constantly balking him. In the distance—not so distant, really, it just seemed so—the growls of an enraged ghatt and dog locked in mortal combat, two ghatten now screeching their fury as they joined the fray.

Go for the wrist. The machete pivots around the wrist. The scent of smoke invading his nostrils, distracting . . . What? Fire? Flames of rage outside his own domain of fury, not fueled by his own private fires . . . ? Jenneth, playing with fire again, when she'd been told so many . . .

"DON'T DO IT!" A voice, yet not, booming out of no-

where, echoing from everywhere. He heard it despite his
lack of Resonant skills, and it unnerved him to the core.
"FIGHT IT, DON'T LET IT CLAIM YOU!" Gods help
him—the Lady goddess, Harharta and all the other gods of
his ancestors—that was Doyce! She couldn't be here, that
command couldn't be directed at him, yet he half-froze,
wondering where she was, almost anticipating Lindy's and
Byrlie's arrival. To hug them, tell them how much he loved
them, start anew . . . And at that moment of hesitation
Pommy's machete lashed out and snapped his sword in two.

So, so, the world was revolving, was repeating itself. No
new patterns, just old ones despite his hopes. Always it
came down to doing it again, doing it better, doing it
right . . . So like that desperate day in Marchmont when
Byrta had died in his place, saving his life. His sword
snapped in two then, Gregor wielding that giant broadsword with supreme grace and casual confidence. Byrta!
Her severed head flying off and away as she blocked the
blow meant for him. *"Byrta, I'm coming!"* He gave an exultant cry as he dove toward Tadj Pomerol's stomach, burying the remaining length of his sword just below Pommy's
rib cage, concentrating on driving it upward, blind to the
machete blow slicing through the base of his neck. *"Byrlie!
Papa loves you, always!"*

Time stood still as Bard died—at rest, at peace, and at
home at last in his beloved Sunderlies. Doubled over,
clutching her knees, Jenneth sobbed, but her tears weren't
necessary to quench the fire she'd already guiltily doused
and kicked apart. The others stood unmoving, Davvy woo-
zily propped on one elbow, rubbing his jaw, Diccon and
the unkempt Hirby in a sobbing embrace, still breathless
from charging back on hearing Bard's screams of blood-
lust. At last, the two dark strangers with their ocher waist-
wraps, the ends scarved across left shoulders, walked with
solemn grace to Bard's body, prostrating themselves in
front of it.

"What now?" asked the younger one, tears streaming
freely.

"We anoint the body, robe it, take him home," replied
the older man. "It is what his soul called for us to do."

"But, but . . ." the younger man pointed a shaking finger

at M'wa, limping toward them, black and white coat blood-ied. "What of him, his heart-beast?"

The older man held out his hand, stroking the broad head, caressing the once supple curve of spine. "He may journey with us or not—as he wishes. A piece of the Sunderlies is embedded in his soul. He, too, has been forsaken, separated from his heart and home."

Unable to "see," able only to sense her daughter, Doyce now stood beside Lindy, their arms linked around each other's waist, swaying, staring out to sea, sharing—in extremity—the vision as it had unscrolled to its bitter conclusion. Yet despite her immeasurable relief at hearing Jenneth's voice, Doyce realized by degrees that another familiar, beloved bond had fallen silent.

"Khar? Beloved! 'Speak me, I beg you!" Sagging against Lindy as the enormity of this severing sank in, her knees went weak, her mind flooding with emptiness. Follow her beloved into the void? Retreat, rejoice in what still remained to her? The world around her had been effaced in one sweep, devoid of color, shape, or sound, all laughter stilled, the talc scent vanished, the warm purrs now an icy avalanche of nothingness, the perfect petal pink of a nose . . . fading, fading, blankly white. . . .

Haggard with shock, Doyce fainted, slipping through Lindy's arms into the water slowly sloshing in the hull.

Sweet Lady, bless them both! Reeling from what he and everyone else aboard had witnessed, a mass of surreal flames and momentary unbridled power, Theo's hands trembled, swinging the tiller as Doyce slumped, Lindy half-cradling her as she too collapsed. The spell Lindy'd suffered in the kitchens had been minor compared to this full-blown manifestation, the future she'd viewed had been mere moments from occurring, was now completed. Somehow the future had enmeshed Doyce as well, drawing her into a reality he didn't dare begin to envision. The Lady had had no choice but to let it unfold.

But who had died—Bard? Or Davvy? A wave crashed over the crumpled figures, children's and adults' heads re-emerging as water sluiced out, still stunned, awestruck, still unsure where or how or what they truly were after what they'd witnessed. Guiltily Theo firmed up the wobbling tiller.

"Oh, poor M'wa!" Profound sorrow weighed Khim's speech, but did she grieve because M'wa's life hung in the balance from the same danger stalking Bard, or because Bard *had* died? With a yowl that literally forced each hair on his head to rise and sent a shiver down his spine, Khim's keening sorrow grew more frenzied, filling his ears, his brain. **"Merowmepurr! Merowme?"** Not Khar, as well? Nightmare upon nightmare! It made him yearn to join her, throw his head back and wail at the havens for their loss.

Still staggered by the drama just concluded at the bow, Oordbeck made for Theo on hands and knees, wincing and cursing when the boat's roll forced his weight on his bad arm. Grabbing a bucket as it floated by, he began to bail one-handed, face gray with shock, fumbling for words. "Trouble . . . nothing but trouble! Years, you hear me? Years I've worked long and hard . . . and honest . . . and not a stitch of it—trouble, I mean. Then, no warning, mind you," he slammed the bucket against his knee, flinching as it dented, as if another illusion had died. "This! Trouble pouring down! *Why*?" Bereftly he searched Theo's face for an answer.

Silently commiserating, lacking any adequate answer for Ozer or himself, Theo simply shook his head in lieu of a response. Unjust as it was, he hated Ozer for his whining, his complaints, his wrinkled, waterlogged skin that probably looked exactly like his own. How could Oordbeck be so insensitive, so unaware of what had transpired, while Theo had to silently suffer, unable to even console Khim! Couldn't the man sense how the world had shifted, momentarily shying in disbelief at this disaster?

No, Ozer had no reason to know about Khar, what it had meant for both Doyce and Khar when the ghatta had given so unselfishly of her waning strength. Don't waste energy over things he couldn't control, it was his job to keep their boat afloat, aiming toward land, no matter what happened to Lindy or Bard, to Doyce or Khar. "It was-n't,

I m-mean, i-it's not our f-fault. Th-things just h-happen
some-t-times." He shrugged an apology.

Bucket over his bent knee, Oordbeck slammed it with his
fist. "Bad enough you export your criminals here without
exporting your personal troubles as well! Then you stick
me in the middle of it—fine! But couldn't you have left the
little ones out of it?" Tears streamed down his face.

Fumbling though his pockets, Theo pulled out a handkerchief, wringing it out and handing it to Ozer. "I'll g-get us
out of this, s-somehow—I promise." How, he didn't know,
but if he didn't, who would? He hoped he had more control
over the boat than he had over fate.

Glowing behind them and to their right as they toiled along
the highway, fires sprang to life—one, two, three—each
slowly burning brighter, more confidently, as the oil-soaked
wood finally caught. Fire in such fog and rain, an act of
faith, a reason to hope. Jenret's faith, his hope, flickered
like the fires, nearly guttering, then blazing high again.
Each bonfire dotted a suitable landing spot along Rookery
Point's inner curve; another bouquet of flames blossomed
in the dark, tentative, cringing at the elements at first, but
gradually blooming a full-blown orange-red. If Bess had
succeeded, runners from Crookerton had carried word
around the point: launch any craft suitable for rescue purposes in the storm. Look for a small, single-masted vessel
making limited headway under scant sail, loaded and low
in the water, and clueless where to put ashore.

Arras lofted a question ahead to Bess, leading the bubalus. "Are you positive these are safe landing sites—no
shoals or reefs to rip them wide open?"

To Jenret's febrile mind this was hardly a tactful question
to indiscriminately bellow into the dark, given the carnival-
like crowd at their heels, all heading for the beach to help
however they might. Indeed, it stunned him that Arras had
risked it

**"Because that's usually the sort of discourteous thing you
blurt?"** Ruddy glints from the distant fires glittered in
Rawn's eyes as he sprawled across Nauki's broad neck,

claws shallowly hooked into the beast's dense shoulder hair.

"Why we light'em, else?" Bess spun, hands on hips, jaw pugnacious. "No bonfire on tip of Rookery, big man. That easier ta reach den shore here—if yed doan mind rocks."

One foot miring in the mud, Arras cursed, grabbing Taubi's horn to remain vertical. "My apologies, Bullybess. On the Marchmont coast it's not unknown for some to lure ships onto reefs, plunder the remains, comb the beaches for anything cast ashore."

"Ho! That happen here, sometimes. 'Course Bess not know much bout such, strickly speakin'." She fiddled with the coils of rope draped over Taubi's flanks until she'd readjusted them to her liking. "But I tell each village most precious cargo be sixteen liddle'uns. 'Poor'n pocket, soft'n heart,' we say here." Unable to resist, she added, "Not 'soft'n head' like you."

They labored up the verge from the highway now; once crested they'd begin their descent to the dunes and the beach. Jenret tried to attend to his footing, scrubby beach plums and ramblers snagging and stinging, cracking wetly underfoot as the bubalus plodded through, creating their own path. Carrying a double-yoke slung over one shoulder as if it were a sapling, Holly trailed after him, the slope too irregular for the bubalus to be teamed.

His body automatically labored, leg muscles tired, back aching, brain detached, near-numb. *"Too late, too late,"* his mind chanted with monotonous regularity. *"People will die, people I love. Caught in the middle, near enough to watch Doyce drown in the distance, not near enough to save her. And Jenneth, Diccon? What if . . . if things go wrong there? Has my fickleness doomed everyone I love? Never able to choose between my trivial pride and the people who give my life meaning."* Bowing his head against Nauki's shoulder, he struggled for control, drinking in the laboring beast's steamy warmth, it too uncritically giving its all for him. Just as the people around him, friends and strangers, were all uncomplainingly doing.

"Rawn, what can I do? I've got to do *something!"* Even the ghatt had exhausted his store of wisdom, mutely raising his massive head to rub it beside Jenret's ear.

Cresting the rise, they paused, Jenret staring out to sea,

as if he alone could pinpoint the tiny boat with its precious cargo lost somewhere in the endless waves and wind, the enfolding gloom with its rain that still drizzled without cease. A few of the bravest (or most foolhardy, like himself) of Rookery Point's populace had manned their dories, and a fishing smack, cautiously cruising the waters as they banged on pots, rang cowbells, and blew whistles, but the sound floated back to Jenret, not out to sea. A two-masted ketch remained in Neu Dorp for repairs, damaged from the last storm. The lure of rushing out in one of the boats had sorely tempted him, but for once he'd acknowledged his limitations, left it to those better able. Nor could he exercise his worries, pace back and forth on a dory. A wry grin at such honesty, it would tickle Doyce no end.

Though he'd seen the sense in Holly's plea for him to grant Doyce some peace, not fetter her with his own fears, he guiltily let his mind roam, urgently seeking hers, wanting to let her know how hard everyone was trying to rescue them. No matter what befell them, good or bad, she and the others should derive some hope, comfort from knowing that they weren't alone, that others thought and prayed for their welfare. Nor would he stint on meting out the love and loyalty due her from his heart to hers. He'd bankrupt a thousand mercantiles to have her in his arms again, bankrupt all of Canderis to ensure the twins were there as well!

But what his mind encountered was a fiery image whose scorched wings made it crumple, grief welling from it, not at the fall but at the loss of the anchoring support—Khar feebly clawing at the fringes of life. Sagging to his knees, Jenret flung a desperate arm round Nauki's neck just as Bess gave the beast an encouraging goad to send it down the steep, slick incline, Taubi tight behind.

Jouncing, skidding on his knees over rocks and through beach plum, he fought to scramble to his feet, Nauki uncomplainingly dragging him, practically hurtling them both down the slope. Fingers sliding through coarse, wet neck hair, he skidded beneath Nauki's belly, wallowing through the thick, churned mud, praying a giant hoof wouldn't smash his head. If Nauki missed, Taubi was still to be reckoned with, half-walking, half-slithering, almost nose-to-tail with his partner.

"**Hold!**" Rawn commanded, curt and to the point.

"**Tuck!**" Jenret complied as best as he could, Nauki shuddering to a halt above him, braking by leaning back on his powerful haunches. "**Now!**" Hands, Holly's and Arras's, yanked him clear, jerked him upright. Rawn's midnight shape loomed over Nauki's head, paws prodding at one ear or the other, guiding the beast.

"Are you . . . ?" Not bothering to complete her question, Holly ran deft hands over his arms, his chest, Arras doing much the same down both legs, checking, Jenret supposed, for bruises or broken bones. Ah, that would be the least of it! Mind jarred more than his body, he brusquely broke away and stiffly sidestepped the rest of the way down as fast as he could, panting with fear.

"Rawn? Did you hear? Can you 'speak Khar at all? Jenneth—how does she fare?" Doyce's final cry still rang in his brain.

His 'speech tinged with such hopeless loss that Jenret's heart nearly stopped, Rawn cried out bewilderedly, "**Never did I think she'd journey on before me! They're both so far beyond us!**" And Jenret knew that Rawn referred to something far more dauntingly final than mere physical distance.

To encounter Rawn's dark despair, all hope abandoned, chilled his very heart. His dear Bond's anguish and his own stubborn refusal to let Doyce's love languish, die without protest, made him square his shoulders, savagely shove an errant lock from his forehead. *"Would you seek them to the ends of the world—or beyond—old chap?"*

His tail snapped once, then hung, limp. "**But where would we seek . . .**"

"Rawn! We are Seekers Veritas, we seek the truth, no matter how it disguises itself, no matter where it leads us!" Fingers digging into Rawn's neck and shoulders, Jenret massaged the ghatt, intent on driving away his despair. *"Go to the Elders, old friend—find Kharm! Find Matty Vandersma. Do that, and I'll do my part—even if it's the last thing I ever do in this world or the next!"*

"Come on!" he shouted, swinging his arm wide, enticing, inviting Rawn to follow. "Let's get down there, set things up. With any luck, we've work to do!" Fear, even the worst fear in the world, could be mastered by making a supreme effort, by giving his all to do something.

Halting sideways, he waited for Arras to catch up, hands locking on his brother-in-law's forearms to slow his descent. "We can *do* it, Arras! We *will*! Things may go from bad to worse, but we're not doomed yet, I can feel it, potentialities beckoning me. And no, Nauki didn't kick me in the head!" Arras clung forearm to forearm with him, silently questioning, his eyes dark and worn. "Promise me one thing, though!"

Leaning back, half-closing his eyes to focus, Arras said one word, wary. "What?"

"If Rawn and I don't make it . . ." Needing the contact, Jenret roughly hugged Arras. "Oh, never mind! We *will* make it, Doyce and I, Khar and Rawn, together somehow, somewhere!"

Knees locked, fingers loosely woven below her waist, she looked from one body to the other, back again, silently musing. So . . . this was death, not nice and neat like Grammie Inez's had been, not the "blessing in disguise" that Mama and Aunt Francie had murmurously labeled it between tearful bouts. Real, harsh, death, still hot and blood red, the color of anger and enflamed hatred. Flies already whizzed and whined round the bodies, hovered before diving down to sample them, pronounce them satisfactory. No, it wasn't satisfactory—it was death.

"Like what animals do to each other." Pw'eek swatted at a fly, jumped and snapped at another, intent not on play but on driving them away. **"To survive, to live, mostly. Sometimes to protect what they love, yes? I killed birds and rodents to eat. Would have ripped out Pommy's eyes— or worse—for hurting you."**

"Yes, Pw'eek is very brave, valiant." And so she had been, Jenneth thought. A rust-colored crust slowly formed in Bard's hair, damming the blood as the sun dried it. *"Were they animals, then, or men?"*

Grappling with everything that had happened to her and because of her this day, Jenneth wondered if her very soul might overspill with sorrow for both Bard and Pommy. She had been rescued—twice—and two had died. She'd not cried, holding her tears in abeyance by an act of will. Death

was akin to exploring an uncharted emotional landscape,
and she was still seeking a compass. So many aspects
needed to be surveyed in a new light—Bard on the roof
deck at Windle Port, sharing his heart with her; Pommy so
gently spreading the lotion over her skin. Ways and ways
of being adult, parts of being adult, and so much more,
including death and life, things that couldn't be changed.
She was no longer Aqua, no longer Blaze, she was Jenneth,
but a part of her wasn't the same, newly matured, still
questing after her life.

Davvy, pale as ashes, finally looked up at her from where
he knelt by Bard's body. Easy to see that her unnatural
composure unnerved him, stripped away some of the self-
control he fought to project, though she didn't mean to
make it harder on him. Would screaming and wailing,
throwing herself on the ground and beating it with her fists
change a thing? If so, she'd gladly do it time and time again
for Byrlie, M'wa, Lindy.

"Jen, you shouldn't . . . please don't stand there staring
like that. It's . . . unseemly." Abruptly rising, he reached
for her wrist to move her away and stopped short, following
her gaze to his bloody hands. "You've soot all down your
cheek and neck." He thrust his hands behind his back like
a guilty child. "Go wash it and see to Diccon."

Ah, it was allowable for him to snap at her, because he
didn't dare snap at the elderly dark-skinned man who also
stood staring down at Bard. He seemed as attentive to
death's aspects as she, so perhaps it wasn't an unnatural
reaction, Davvy the one unable to look squarely at its
countenance.

"Will you excuse me while I see to Diccon?" she asked
formally and turned on her heel. She knew how Diccon
was reacting, could hear his strangled retching. Best get a
basin and some water, a rag or two. If she couldn't yet
comfort herself, she could comfort others, wished for a silver platter to pass it around on beside the cold baked
meats.

Poor Hirby! She stooped to drop a kiss atop his head as
he sat holding Pommy's hand, Tigger piled on his lap while
Hirby wept into his fur, the poor beast's tail nervously wag-
ging. "You loved him, Hirby. So did I." Had she? Or had
she felt for him the way Tigger felt for Hirby? It was all

so complex, these shadings and subtleties of emotions to discover, sort out.

Returning, she sponged Diccon's face, only to have him roll over and vomit again so hard that tears were forced from his eyes. "Wha . . . what about Lindy, Byr-lie?" Diccon sobbed, holding Kwee much as Hirby held Tigger. "A . . . and M'wa?"

Oh, Lady sustain her, M'wa's pain! There was a being who deserved a whole serving tray of solace! Had everyone disregarded him, each so enmeshed in insular grief they'd forgotten he was the chief mourner? "I'll be back," hurriedly she swiped at Diccon's face again, loving him for being so genuine with his emotions, able to let them pour out. "I think we're making it more difficult for Davvy by being here. Let's see about going back to the launch and your friend Luykas when I get back." He nodded, blowing his nose on the rag, his wondrously long eyelashes beaded with tears.

M'wa? Where was he? Not at Bard's side as he'd been those first few moments of disbelieving shock. Panicking, she darted from one spot to another, hunting for him, afraid that grief had driven him into a physical and mental wilderness where he'd retreat so far they'd never locate him. *"Pw'eek, darling, have you seen M'wa? Where is he? How is he?"*

"We're by the palm tree!" Her precious ghatten knew what it felt like to be lost, alone, had obviously sensed what M'wa was suffering, even if she'd been too distracted to do so.

Silently, solemnly, she walked toward the palm, hearing its whisking rustles. M'wa huddled beside the young, umber-skinned stranger's leg, close but entirely separate unto himself, a finger-span apart but oh, so distant. Forehead against forehead, white star against butterscotch-gray, M'wa rocked against Pw'eek, their eyes slanted tight. The young man she'd shushed held a world of pain in his voice, whispering, "His heart has broken. Each piece chimes its pain as it falls away. Can you hear it?"

Nodding, she rested a hand lightly on each furry neck. "I . . . I think Pw'eek and I, my brother and his Bond, should go. But I don't want to leave M'wa alone."

"Don't worry, I will watch over this marvelous beast. We

are cousins of a sort." His eyes looked older than her first fleeting glimpse of him had indicated. And he, too, had wept over Bard. "Go ahead. I must help Uma-Uncle with his plans, but I will console my cousin's heart-beast."

Suspicious, Theo squinted at the tiny gleam of reddish-orange in the distance. Nice, pretty, it was—and distracting. The way it danced and flittered like some luminescent insect . . . except insects generally moved huge distances, considering their size. This pretty "insect" was a positive homebody, staying in place. Lady protect us, I'm so damn tired I'm seeing spots before my eyes, so bloody exhausted . . . He yawned, looked again. Still there. Wasn't lightning, not a fly-speck like that. Not a low-lying star or rufous planet peeping through the storm clouds. Hallucinations—why not? As long as he realized what they were, he could fight them . . . or be entertained.

All through this night, or this day, or whatever it was, he'd clung to the tiller until his hands resembled bird-claws. Without food, without rest, he'd outwitted the seas, made this tub of an overloaded boat almost obey. His whole universe had narrowed to a square-butted craft mayhap two meters wide (let him stretch out at the widest point and he'd give a more accurate measurement) and five small Oordies long. Total population: twenty-five humans, two ghatti. No corpses as yet, and stubbornly screwed his eyes to block his tears.

Only a matter of time, only a matter of time until Khar completely faded away, mayhap Doyce following after her. Why had she—why had they—soared so far beyond earthly reach? Except that they'd give, always had, unselfish in their love, their devotion to duty. Why should this be any different? With effort he let his facial muscles slacken.

They'd dropped off to sleep, one by one, strewn around the boat as best they might, heads resting on slack shoulders and laps, propped against the gunwales. He'd not had the heart to awaken anyone. He'd have to, soon, because someone had best start bailing again . . . No, no rest for the weary. No rest . . . but if rest meant drowning, he'd remain awake forever and a day and the next as well. . . .

Ah, so he wasn't the only one awake. Ghost-pale, eyes dark-circled, Honoria made her way back. "That fuzzy reddish speck—did you notice? I think it's a signal fire, a bonfire." She pointed at his private hallucination. So, it wasn't exclusively *his* any longer? "Right over there. Might be another, too," she swung her arm, holding it still with effort as he sighted along it. "Unless I'm seeing things. See it?"

You sea, you sea, you see the sea, he hummed to himself. "Really?" he added politely, if tardily. Taking him by the shoulders, she shook him till he wobbled, then readied herself to slap his face. He recoiled, one hand erasing his slack grin and pocketing it. Fine, if she wanted serious, he'd play serious. "Is it really a beacon?" He thought about it some more. "For us, belikes? Beckoning to us?" Oh, he'd done it now! *Beckoning beacons, beaconings becking, I sea the beaconings becking in the see what I can see* . . .

"I think it's a shore beacon to signal any poor souls lost in the storm." Honoria paused, pinching the bridge of her nose, sliding a finger and thumb on each eyelid. "But some beacons are hoaxes. It could indicate a safe harbor, or it might be meant to lure us, wreck us on a reef." That, too, had a nice ring to it: *wreck on a reef . . . beckoning wreckoning.* . . . Would Honoria like such lovely, interlocking words?

But Khim interjected, **"It's a good beacon! P'roul just told me so! Aim for it, Theo!"**

Although Honoria might baffle him, his Bond's word was truth, and Theo leaned on the tiller, determined to make the boat's prow point at the red dot. Suddenly invigorated, he hauled one-handed at the braces to help the boat swing round, home in on the light. *"Tell P'roul we want cha! Nice hot cha, nice dry clothes, nice dry beds . . ."* Without warning a rudder pin sheered off with a crack, the tiller bucking, and Theo found himself bodily flung atop Honoria. He, Theo, never crudely rude, indecently pawing . . .

Her strength surprised him as she heaved him off, struggling clear to haul on the brace, let the sail do part of the useless rudder's work. "Bloody rat-assed rudder!" she snarled. "Come on, Theo, help me reset the sail! Give us a chance—just a little chance, that's all I ask—to sail, to drift, whatever . . . in the right direction! Or anywhere near it."

He was awake now, achingly awake, aware of every sore spot, every minor wound and strain, his empty belly, his near-empty brain. So fill it up, think! "Wake everyone, have them start bailing. See what we can use for a rudder, a plank from the half-deck, anything that's not part of the hull! Then help me judge how to alter course." Possible, remotely possible that as long as the boat floated, they could make way with just the sail, shifting their weight to ease it right or left, point their prow on that lovely ruddy beacon. If the storm didn't blow harder again, if they didn't spring any more leaks . . .

"Khim, my sweet. Don't you dare lose P'roul! Tell them we're limping in, don't let that beautiful fire die down!" By the blessed Lady's butt, he'd get out and push if he had to!

Khim sounded put out at such high-handed orders; as if she'd lose contact with her sib if she could possibly help it! **"Frankly, you'd make a better anchor than a rudder. You never did float well, too bony, not enough fat."**

Waves pounding him, his footing precarious on shifting shells and pebbles churning underfoot, Jenret took a deep breath as he stood, stripped naked, in waist deep water. How did the Lady balance faith and fate? One dory had broken an oar, another had a loose thole pin hampering them. No hope there, unless they could maneuver together, create one serviceable dory out of two. So far they'd not been able to signal the third dory or the smack to alter their courses. Somehow he'd known it would come to this impasse, and he was determined to wait no longer, each moment an eternity as Doyce's need grew.

The rope chaffing his waist was a lifeline—in both directions. If he could swim to the disabled boat with this line, they might be able to haul it into Rookery Point's safer waters. The bubalus stood yoked, their patient backs to him and the hock-deep water. And if he failed, couldn't swim the distance, the others could always reel him in. Except why be reeled to safety if he couldn't reach Doyce, the boat?

"Rawn, go well, fare well. Find what you're Seeking, my friend. I'll do my part."

But Rawn was already engrossed in mapping the ghatti spirals in his mind, the Spirals of Knowledge he must ascend to reach the Elders with his plea. Without his intercession, Jenret's success or failure wouldn't signify. **"My Bond! My joy!"** floated back to him, and he imagined the black ghatt gnawing his knuckles, whiskers bristling, side teeth nipping just enough to remind him how much of a fool he ofttimes was.

Crouching, he waited until the wave reared, dove through it and came up gasping, stroking with a fierce overhand. How long that'd last, he'd see, and kicked harder. Soon he'd have to conserve himself, ration his energy, or burn out before he reached his goal. Breast stroke when he couldn't lift his arms anymore. The rope tugged, wanting to tangle with his scissoring legs, so he took greater care, submerging as the next wave rolled at him. At least Arras and Bess played it out efficiently, not too much slack, not too much pull. *"P'roul? Am I on-target?"* Though he'd known her since ghattenhood, P'roul's mindvoice seemed out of place in his mind, barely filling the void of Rawn's necessary desertion. But Rawn had his own task, P'roul hers as well, though she'd pulled double-duty: tracking Khim and the floundering boat, and ensuring Jenret didn't swim wide in the dark and the rain.

"Fine, wiggle-worm straight." P'roul was Rawn's daughter, but she had Khar's humor. Stretch the arm, cup the hand, face dipping as he rolled from one stroke into the next, driving his arm down and past his side with all his mustered force. Kick, kick, kick, work from the hips, be efficient—the kick originated at the hips, powered the driving feet. Flailing didn't help. Breathe, now hold as the head rolls through the water, breaking the surface just long enough to steal another breath, then shoot into the wave. Yes, it *was* calmer, more regular the farther out he swam, the waves' destructive force intensifying as they pounded the shore.

Already his arm muscles burned, pain shooting down his sides, warping vulnerable gut muscles. A stitch in time out here would let him drown nine times sooner. Legs going leaden, too, so he'd ease up slightly, conserve himself. Funny, feet pushed, arms pulled. *"Doyce, darling! I'm coming! Hold Khar tight, don't let her slip away. Don't you slip*

away. Rawn and I love you too much to let you go!" Was
it selfish to love someone so deeply, did it bind, obligate
them in ways he'd never considered? No sense to admit
how selfish he was, she already knew—still cherished him.
And he'd always judged her so levelheaded! Snorting watery laughter, he stroked on.

So tentative, so distant, even as each stroke shaved away
the margin of separation, he heard it. *"Jenner? So hard . . .
to hold Khar. Even in my mind . . . everything slipping . . ."*

The wave slapped his face, stung, his throat burning as
water shot up his nose. Careless fool! He spat, swallowed,
the salt sting scouring his throat. An ear plugged with
water, no time to wriggle a finger in it. Count it off, find a
rhythm. Lady bless, no extra breath to let him sing, but he
could think the words, coax Doyce to remember as well,
connect her to his heartline so she wouldn't drown in death.
*"Oh, Matthias did ride, with his ghatta beside, as they sought
out the truth of it all . . ."*

*"With Kharm as his guide . . . all falsehood defied . . .
they rode out so straight and so tall . . ."* Weakly Doyce
had joined in, muddling the words, mixing verses, but making an effort. At some point as they'd exchanged verses,
he realized he'd switched to a breast stroke, legs convulsing
like a feeble frog's. Every so often P'roul's soft voice urged
him leftward or rightward and he'd obey, glimpsing an occasional gray vision of the boat from his temporary vantage
point atop a rising wave. Each time the boat disappeared,
it grew more painful. Find something else to sing, it did
help, distracted his mind from the fact that his breastbone
wanted to split down the middle like a wishbone.

> *If you must love a rambling man,*
> *Don't cage his fancy-free.*
> *Just let him wander for a span,*
> *And he'll rush home to thee!*

So he always had and always would, he realized as P'roul's
frantic words jarred his brain. **"Running out of rope! Can
you reach yet?"** Shaking his hair out of his eyes, he drove
himself upwards with a flurry of kicks, rising as high as he
could, searching, searching. . . . Damn it to the hells and
beyond! He could see the boat skittering along broadside

to him, make out a rise of rocky outcropping looming not far ahead, the water boiling around them in an erratic pattern.

"About twenty meters, I guess," he told P'roul. *"Enough?"*

"No! Expect to feel like a hooked fish right about—" Even given the scant warning, the backward plunge was more intense than he'd anticipated, dragging him under and down, fighting, finally rising, anxiously treading water within the confines of his leash. Let an eddy catch him, a wave flip him just right, and he'd be jerked under again. He didn't think he could take that, not without notice. Lady help him, even if he could work free wet knots, untie the rope and swim to the boat, it would do no good! Mayhap the rope would float, but he'd never find its loose end again. A nautical version of finding a needle in a haystack.

"Have Khim tell someone to swim out, meet me with a rope!" Kicking just enough to keep his head above water, letting its buoyancy cradle his rubbery arms, he watched them bob limp as a drowned man's. It dawned on him then. *"Just not Theo, he sinks—"*

"Like a stone," P'roul finished for him. Normally it was a joke, but not this time. **"Get ready, someone's anticipated you, already on the way!"**

Again, kicking as hard as he could, he jetted himself upward in time to see a slim, pale figure, obviously female, take an arching, shallow dive. Honoria? A flash of naked arms and legs, the steady, regular splash of her strokes, her breathing rapid as she churned closer. "Here!" he shouted, popping up again, waving his arms, "Here, over here!"

Strange, once he'd daydreamed of seeing her naked, and now that he could, he didn't care, because it wasn't the mind and body he loved. She'd offered him adventure and teasing enticement, flattered his ego, and he'd so nearly succumbed. Grabbing his shoulders in nervous relief, she nearly dunked him, finally stopped bearing down on him and let herself float, leaving a steadying hand on his shoulder. "Don't lose your end, whatever you do," he implored, wondering now how they could tie the ropes together, not risk dropping one end or the other.

"Slipknot, not wise but expedient." She gulped air greedily as she fumbled with one hand, bringing the drooping length up out of the water. "Left a long tail on it." For a moment it looked obscene, her hand closed round it like that, and comical as well, because for once she was resolutely innocent of the vulgarity. Unable to help himself, he laughed at himself, at life.

Rawn toiled slowly, deliberately, up the bank, casting about for a spot where he wouldn't be interrupted by tramping feet, shouts. Vain hope, but he needed as much peace and quiet he could find for this endeavor. What Jenret had asked, indeed, begged him to do was foreign to his reserved nature, leaving Rawn full of misgivings, too-aware of failing before he'd even begun. Yet even without Jenret's special pleading, he'd have essayed it on his own—for Khar, for Doyce. Sometimes all a middle-aged—nay, elderly—ghatt could do was hope, and try.

Sniffing fastidiously, shaking a paw at the hateful damp, he located a patch of pleasant-scented grass, noticing a talc-like scent to the soil, almost claylike here. A poignant reminder of Khar's lovely, elusive scent, and if he wavered, that scent would dissipate until it became a mere memory of longing and regret. Circling, pressing the sweet blades into a bowl-shaped nest, he settled, twitching at the drizzle. Why, why couldn't it be Khar attempting this? She was so adept at climbing the Spirals, 'speaking the Elders. On the beach below Jenret waded into the water, his body so absurdly pale and puny against the sea's dark rush. Would he lose one or the other, mayhap both? Not to mention Doyce, his next most-beloved among humans?

He'd never disdained the Elders and their advice, cryptic though it was; it was simply that he rarely felt a need to consult them. Egotism? He washed a forepaw thoughtfully. Living so closely with Jenret, mayhap he'd steeped unwittingly in some of that pride. Jenret dove, and he winced at the white body slicing the water, the sea's chill as shocking as if someone had doused him full in the face with a bucket of water. **"Ah, my Bond, we are too old for this!"** but he refused to let his anguish reach Jenret's mind, cripple him with more doubts.

It was just . . . the Elders were all very well and good,

had their place, just as he'd accepted his own lesser one, content with it. Worry about growing in wisdom, circling through the Spirals, and a ghatt might hamper himself when it came to coping with an urgent matter in the here and now. Of course he'd learned the Major Tales of ghatti history, loved hearing them, reciting them when no one was near, his quiet reverence undetected. But to barge uninvited straight up and around the Spirals, begging, pleading, demanding?—no, that wasn't his way.

But tonight it was, must be his way. If only a moon or two would light his path, some stars at least, some bright track arrowing toward the Elders. What anchored him here and now was a fair, furless body thrashing the waves, and an extravagantly striped furry form, so hurt and still, adrift in a distant boat. Had he any right to beg this boon, this favor? All beings, ghatti and human, reached an end-stop at some point in life, except for the Elders, immortal and near-immortal, privileged souls not quite flesh, not yet spirit, who dabbed a paw in both worlds. A trade, mayhap? That appealed as fairer, more just, but how would that affect his Bond, Jenret?

"Stop borrowing trouble!" He crouched, ears back-bent as he hissed at himself, at his fears. Atremble, he let his mind reach, soar awkwardly into the ether, claws snatching at the First Spiral. Ha, oops! **"Concentrate, you dust-brained, good-for-nothing ghatt!"** Yes, up and easy through the First Spiral, round the curve and press into the second. He'd not forgotten how, after all! Licking his chops, he eased along the Third Spiral, testing his mettle. **"Oh, Elders, hear me! It's Rawn. Been a while—too long, I admit—but I'm here now. A word in your collective ear, if you please."**

The hum and thrum of ghatti voices, a soundless rush of words, impossible to comprehend. Not exactly soothing, even a bit irritating, like a fly buzz-bumbling in one's ear. Needed more height, obviously. How high had he climbed the last time? Damned if he could remember. Come to think of it, when *was* the last time? Damn exhausting labor, pussy-footing round and round, uphill all the way! Easy now and push, dig in those hind claws, don't slip!

"Ghatt up a tree?" a voice murmured as another asked, **"How will he get down?"** **"Funny old ghatt . . ."** **". . . midnight black."** The teasing had a good-natured ring, but he didn't relish it, all the same. And then, a voice he recognized, Swan Maclough's other half, Koom. **"Rawn, old mate! Is that you? Missed you up here. Khar checks in with some regularity, but you—never!"**

Lips drawn back to reveal worn teeth, he fought to catch his breath, spring into the next Spiral before it twisted past. **"Koom, my ruddy friend! Greetings! Think you could scare up the great Kharm, Mother of us all, and her bond, Matty Vandersma?"**

"Oh-ho . . . full of himself, isn't he?" **"Prodigal comes curving-swerving up, thinks we've been waiting with bated . . ."** **". . . bated . . ."** **". . . breath."** Nips and tweaks at his ears and whiskers, his tail, and he lashed it to chase them clear. **"Flex a paw, beckon . . ."** **". . . truth comes . . ."** **". . . or so . . ."** **". . . thinks."**

"I'll hunt you down, Spiral by Spiral, if I must!" he howled, glaring at the wisps swirling by him, untouchable, unreachable. **"This isn't for me, I swear! It's for Doyce Marbon and Khar'pern!"**

With effort Rawn dragged himself into the Fifth Spiral, unmolested, the wisps backing clear, writhing and twisting amongst themselves, communicating, questioning. The air tasted thinner up here, sweeter but thinner, didn't fill his lungs, provide the strength he needed. Every muscle quavered, threatening to tumble him tail-over-ears, shorn of hope, as nakedly exposed as his Bond.

Damnation! Something butted his rear, hard! Knock him off, would they? Swinging about with a simmering hiss, claws slashing the air, he struck wide just in time. Somehow, despite their youth and innocence, their lack of training, Pw'eek and Kwee had joined him—ghatten probably incapable of reciting a Minor Tale, let alone the first Major Tale!

Twinkling, sparkling with newness, their fur dusted with the future, their ghatten forms slowly dissolved into a luminous nebula of purrs, reflecting and absorbing a million as yet unformed tomorrows he'd never witness. So much past, even wider vistas of the future, and he but an insignificant speck of here and now, not even worthy of being cosmic dust!

As the hallucination glowed and thinned, Rawn shook his head, clawing toward the Sixth Spiral, praying his shaking haunches could push him higher. Oh, for a friendly boost from behind! Even an impulsive tail-nip would do the trick, but naturally not one Elder would obligingly annoy him! Now where had Koom gone?

The air at the Seventh Spiral was absolutely ethereal, so insubstantial he wasn't sure how it supported his groaning, inert body, filled his straining lungs. It floated above, beyond all being, his eyes seeing everything and nothing within its radiance. And still the ultimate Spiral imperiously beckoned. . . .

It loomed impossibly steep and slick, immateriality polished by the myriad paws of ghatti past. One misstep and he'd slither down on his ear, speeding faster through each corkscrew curve, only to crash, his body bursting, his life leaking out. Wheezing, whimpering, he steeled himself for the swift, savage descent, the end-stop of his life. And Khar's as well, you weak-limbed, weak-willed failure! Laboriously bending a paw pad to his mouth, he sank in his teeth until the blood flowed, the pain sharpening his mind, overriding his failing body. Tight on his belly, he dragged himself along, refusing to glance ahead or back, a trail of bloodstained paw-prints in his wake. Suddenly the shifting shape of human hands reached out, seizing him behind the shoulders and lofting him high, the world whirling. Panicky, his eyes bedazzled, he couldn't see.

"Dear old Rawn!" A male voice, affectionate, a bit reproving. *"So like dear Jak's Tah'm, just as Khar so resembles Kharm."*

"Matty?" Rawn dared not hope, yet believed despite himself. **"Khar'pern's sorely hurt, her life ebbing, draining away!"** He swallowed hard, bowing his broad head in humility. **"Doyce clings so tight, their Bond so strong, that she may follow. It's just that it's not time yet—it can't be!"** Now he reared back, boxing at the wisps, driving them back, defying them to taunt or mock him again. **"Take me in Khar's place, if you must! But spare them!"**

"Ye-Ouch!" a voice protested as the wisps formed and reformed into a lavishly striped ghatta who lacked the white markings that distinguished Khar. The stranger's circular pattern dizzied and dazzled him, spun his thoughts 'round and 'round and 'round. . . . His stomach heaved. **"Always so blunt and bluff, aren't you?"**

Oh, no! That voice resounded in the very essence of his soul, a voice that remained with all ghatti, from ghatten-hood to death and beyond, the voice of the Mother of them all, Kharm. He'd swiped Kharm on the nose! **"Forgive me!"** He quailed, submissive.

"So, you seek to question the Truth of death?" "... death." "Death ..." came the reverberating whispers all around her, neither joyous nor sad, just speculatively rising and falling.

Now he must try, risk reproach, denunciation, even failure. Blunt, eh? Drawing himself up, he 'spoke. **"I seek not the Truth of death—of that there can be no question—but the *time* of death. Some things remain undone, can be accomplished only by Khar and Doyce. Are you ready to select another Bond-pair to carry the burden in their stead?"**

"Truth ..." "Time ..." "... time and truth." "Always time ..." "... for truth." The whispers crashed and banged and bruised, his ears ringing. **"Time ..."** "... and tide ..." "... and truth!"

"What does that *mean*?" he rowled.

A finger firmly tickled the joy spot behind his left ear, and despite himself a ragged purr leaked out as the finger gently traced a line on his forehead against the fur's grain. *"Poor old Rawn. Not the sort for abstract puzzles, what with your life so focused on the here and now."* Matty's fingers worked their way down, massaging Rawn's spine, lingering just above his tail.

"Jenret's been puzzle enough for me!"

"Oh, no truer words were ever spoken!" Matty's laughter boomed, and Rawn bounced. *"Kharm, darling? Is it truly time? You're the one who'd know best, not I."*

A considered, judicious pause. **"It depends. Think of tides, Rawn, glad tidings, tides turning. You've traveled out of time and in time. . . . Now, farewell."**

So this was what Khar had meant about dealing with the Elders, riddles, conundrums, never, *not ever,* an outright answer! It was up to him to winkle it out, discover the truth as he glided down and down and around. . . .

❧

She'd struck off smartly for the boat while Jenret fussed with the ropes, but had slowed by imperceptible degrees, colder, more enervated than she'd expected. Hardly part of her grand scheme of things! Lifting her into the boat without capsizing it would be a rare treat, she'd be bruised from head to heels, no doubt, everyone clumsy from exhaustion.

Why had she ventured this, volunteered without being asked? Wasn't there someone else aboard who could swim, at least paddle—that flabby dagga boy, Ozer's dead-plain sister-in-law? Or was selflessness catching from that Shepherd? Well, she had no immediate plans on becoming the Lady's martyr! Altruism wasn't a skill likely to advance agents, let alone prolong their lives.

If she didn't know better she'd swear the boat looked smaller, more distant than before. Tired? Of course, but just bobbing up and down wouldn't get her there. Think of something else, contingency plans, anticipate the unexpected.

What was galling was the effort she'd expended on this whole mission, and Vaert now probably thumbed his nose at her from somewhere. Mettha'd find a solution for that. Hindsight being what it was, clearly Vaert'd carried more weight with Geerat than she had; she'd mistakenly congratulated herself on convincing him not to kidnap the children. From the beginning she'd underestimated Vaert's reach and power, allowed personal hatreds to crowd in, color her judgment, the assignment plagued from the start in some indefinable way.

And what was that blasted root-toot-bangety-clang that crept up out of nowhere, made her miss a stroke, forget to duck a wave? Stroke evenly, stroke. Tiredness didn't matter, just mind the repetition. Slower, yes, but consistent.

She'd misjudged Wycherley. Momentarily she slipped under the surface to massage a cramp from her calf, fingers so stiff she could barely make them work. A gasp of air, and she continued doggedly paddling, determined not to succumb to the pain. Ah, Jenret, a handsome, malleable man, definitely not immune to a pretty face and figure, easy to lead round by the nose or lower. Or so she'd initially thought. While he might be a business dilettante, he'd had a fair knowledge of his mercantile workings at his fingertips, wouldn't let her make assumptions without support.

The pain bit deep into her side now, twisting, knotting, making her gasp at an inopportune moment, gag and choke as the water poured down her throat. Ah, ah! Not easy to swim with your knees pulled tight to your chest! She needed to rest so badly, just float, relax, let the water slip over her like cool, fresh sheets sliding over clean, bare skin! Closing her eyes, she imagined it, sighing with pleasure.

No rest for the weary . . . or was that wicked? Straighten slowly, breathe calmly, work the muscles free and easy. Where the hells was that damn boat? Sailed away for sunlit seas and left her? But what had caught her up short was overhearing Jenret and Doyce singing tonight, had had—to be frank—no compunctions about eavesdropping by ear or by mind. Amazing to uncover a sappily sentimental vein within herself that she'd have indignantly denied harboring—would have ruthlessly excised long ago if she'd known of its existence!

Mayhap their love had seemed more poignantly real because she'd juxtaposed it against her own memories of "love" in that boat with young Janacz and his cohorts. Ironic to sail on that very same boat when she should have commandeered it to a new life long ago! Best to avoid that sort of love, its depth and demands and devotion—do without it. Had done so even within her own brief days of marital bliss, once she'd found Wolfaert considered it his just due . . .

Oh, why think on that . . . ? Intractable pain wound through her again, contorting her, wrenching each muscle to its will. . . . The spasms froze her muscles, seized them so tight she couldn't move. Damn it, not even breath enough to cry for help! Fight, damn it! Bring your head up, breathe!

Forcing her brain to function, stop mulling over the past, Honoria Wijnnobel strove to map out the fight of her life with her usual clinical precision, suspecting she would lose. . . .

Fingers unrelentingly locked on the gunwale, Dannae knelt in the sloshing water, praying for forgiveness. Whatever her previous misguided opinion of Honoria, the woman had exhibited true bravery, a physical courage exceeding Dannae's own. The sight of two wet, naked bodies feverishly striving to unite the ropes while the waves pounded them about left Dannae muttering snatches of prayers, each plea lapsing in favor of a more potent one for the Lady's ears.

Corly crouched against her, his breath heavy in her ear as his fingers formed the eight-pointed star, though not very proficiently, she noted. Again, did it matter? What counted was that he cared, attempted to pray. Not a bad lad, really, just one of many who'd detoured, begun walking a disobedient, sinful path till he'd fallen on a new one. It happened often in the Sunderlies, especially in Samranth. A wave crashed over the blonde head, and Dannae held her breath until she saw it again, flinging streamers of hair.

Surely the Lady couldn't truly have believed "If not in this life, then in another." That *had* to have originated with some follower at least minimally content with his lot in life—enough to eat, a place to live, people to love and be loved by, a moderately decent job that didn't flay the soul. Without such things, dignity turned to ashes, the spirit's fire faltered and was snuffed. The body might prevail, but the soul, the spirit, fled. Fine to hope for a better tomorrow, a better future existence, but today counted as well, had to be lived as honorably, as honestly as one could.

"Dannae, Shepherd Dannae!" Corly had been shaking her by the shoulder, for how long, she couldn't judge. Unlike the others, he now had no eyes for the unfolding drama in the water, the recalcitrant ropes refusing to join together. "Over there!" Pointing, he half-dragged her round to face the bow. "What's zat over there?" Water seethed white, churning, exploding as it burst over the obscene blackened fangs of rocks ominously looming just above the surface. Horrible crashing, smashing sounds assaulted her ears, made her want to cower, seek cover.

"Rocks!" Worse, she could feel the boat gravitating toward them as if mesmerized by the ravening teeth, unable to maneuver clear or make headway toward shore until— and if—the ropes were spliced, the towing begun. Lady help and aid us! To be so close, so near to rescue only to be dashed on the rocks, their boat shattering, bodies flung about and crushed against the rocks before lifelessly sinking into the depths. Abruptly, the boat slewed, then lurched, though she could still sense the current hungrily sucking the bow toward the outcropping. The towline! They'd connected it at last! Distant figures highlighted by the bonfire on the beach began to move with new energy, faint cheers floating, resounding across the water. Her own enthusiasm boiling over, Dannae pummeled Corly's back while he gave her a rib-cracking hug and let loose a string of high-pitched whoops that sounded sweetly in her ears.

Slowly, slowly, the boat eased on its new course, the tow rope straining taut and straight from the bow, then dipping beneath the water, invisible. Just where it disappeared into the sea, one pale face bobbed, glowed almost luminescent. But there'd been two moments before—where was the other? Where was Honoria? Had she pulled herself back along their lifeline, willing hands drawing her into the boat, clutching her chilled body close to warm it? No. None huddled round a chilled figured plucked from the sea's bosom; instead, all eyes strained toward shore.

Concerned, Dannae scanned the waters, especially toward the spinous rocks appearing and disappearing behind the frothy spume of lashing waves. If the boat had been carried that way, wouldn't a body be drawn in the same direction? Whitecap, whitecap. Lathery white suds. All the pallid, foaming bits broke into irregular patterns, couldn't be Honoria. Then, as if summoned by her gaze, a marble-pale head broke the surface, a few feeble kicks flurrying the water before the body sluggishly resubmerged.

Unfair! Dannae seethed at the injustice of it all, refusing to accept that the Lady had called Honoria to Her bosom now, of all times. "Blessed Lady, it's me, Dannae. Take Honoria home to You if that's truly Your desire, but think it over again. Not that You'd make a mistake, but a misjudgment, like. It gets powerful confusing keeping track of us squiggly humans, like trying to watch an anthill from above. But some of us truly need to atone for things here, now, not simply do better in the next life." Or was she a meddlesome fool? For all she knew, this was Honoria's progress beyond previous lives!

Again Honoria rose through the waves, still fighting to stay afloat. There! That was sign enough! Wait for another and it might be too late. Shocking Corly to the very marrow

of his being, Dannae slipped out of her sodden robe and—
holding her nose—jumped overboard, gasping as the water
engulfed her, bubbling by as she sank, then popped up. As
the boat rocked from the abrupt shift in weight, heads
turned to see Corly with one hand modestly covering his
eyes, the other vigorously pointing after her.

Ignoring them, Dannae put her mind to her task. Well,
the Blessed Lady certainly knew Her Shepherd couldn't
swim and would resolve the problem one way or another
in Her infinite wisdom. Dannae snorted saltwater at the
option she'd not considered. Well, she'd survived an earlier
swimming lesson, and that had gone—her arms and legs
flailed, churned—er, swimmingly. Yes, cup the hands, paddle, paddle; kick, kick. The Lady worked miracles when
She chose, and if She'd concentrate on actual, rather than
divine guidance this time, Dannae'd be well pleased at discovering she'd not swum to Canderis!

It helped that the currents 'round and within the rocky
fangs drew her to it, let her angle toward the deceptive,
shifting spot where she'd last seen Honoria. A weak shaft
of moonlight cut through the mist and drizzle. Another true
sign, or Dannae'd eat her hemp belt and sandals in penance. Honoria's head fleetingly reappeared, only to loll, roll
facedown the way a weary soul burrows against a comforting pillow to block out noise or light. "Honoria! Hey, Livotti, you gutless coward! Worse than gutless—spineless,
too! Kick those legs, kick, kick! Come on, stick your nose
in the air—tis what Livottis do best!"

With difficulty the face turned toward the taunting voice,
her expression peaceful but bewildered, as if rudely interrupted at some momentous task. And so dying was, thought
Dannae. The superiority, the standoffishness that marked a
Livotti had been washed away by the waves.

As if it were important to clarify why she wasn't kicking,
struggling, Honoria whispered, "Can't. Too . . . crabby."

Exasperated, Dannae spouted a stream of water as she
plowed ahead, bashing the waves. Well, wasn't that just like
a Livotti—crabby as all get out! Then it dawned on her: the
phrase used by those who played frenzied pick-up games of
kick ball, or raced each other. How sometimes they'd flinch
in pain, a muscle spasming in a calf or thigh, a stitch in
their side doubling them over. "Caught a crab" they called

it—a cramp or spasm. It struck swimmers in the harbor, some, even the best, would unexpectedly drown. "Don't worry, I'm coming for you!"

Just as Honoria's outstretched arm began its trailing descent, her head already submerged, blonde hair a mantling aureole around her, Dannae caught the slender fingers and pulled for all she was worth. Gathering the slack body to her bosom, she screamed as something wrenched at her topknot. Sea monsters—plucking a plump, tender morsel to devour!

"It's me, Theo!" gasped a very un-sea monsterish voice from behind her neck. "Hang on to her, and I'll hang on to you! I've a keg for a floater."

· A relief, that, considering what she'd heard about Theo's lack of buoyancy. Ever curious, she twisted, straining to see his thin face. "How'd you get enough rope? We used all the rigging for our share of the line."

His long, strong legs frog-marched beneath her, tickling the back of her thighs, his arm now across her left shoulder, his hand tucked snug under her right arm. Pleasant, cuddlesome, somehow. Honoria's head pillowed against her breasts, she let her body stream out white against the sea. "Tore up your robe, I'm afraid. Blame Harry, 'twas his notion. Added our shirts, trews, whatever we had. Some of us will land bare-naked as the day we were born."

"As long as we land, Theo, the Lady will avert Her eyes, I'm sure. 'Spect She's seen it all, anyway."

Theo laughed, a whoop that warmed her heart and more. "In all of its infinite variety, do you think?"

"And plentitude." Ah, thank the Lady for giving her such an ample form because Dannae'd discovered she floated like a cork!

"Ho! Come to me, come, come!" Eyes straining to separate sea from sky, Arras backed up the beach, coaxing the bubalus along, signaling his needs to Holly and Bess as they directed Nauki and Taubi. Hooves squeaked against wet sand, setting his teeth on edge, as did the startlement of elongated shadows racing across the sand at him, Bess's and Holly's tense expressions momentarily engulfed by even deeper darkness. Some shadows writhed and twisted, cast by the bonfire's soaring flames; others ran beside their owners as people rushed to help where needed.

He licked his lips, tasting the salt of sweat and sea, refusing to glance at the welter of activity behind the bubalus. First too little, and now too much rope. The dangers of the excess rope preyed at him; as they gained ground, laboriously brought the boat deeper into the bay, more rope was reclaimed, must be dealt with. The bubalus couldn't continue plodding up the dunes and pulling with all their might; the steep grade might drag them over.

"Hold, hold!" Hand outstretched to halt them, Arras waited as Rookery Point folk strained at the rope to hold it in place, ensure none of the slack was paid out. Why the hells didn't they have some sort of reel capable of winding up the excess? What they had resembled an oversized bobbin, though that wasn't right, either. A weaver's shuttle, mayhap? Somehow it seemed important to be able to accurately describe it: a timber mayhap a shy two meters long, its middle narrow-waisted as a timer-glass, and with each end concave. Two deep, L-shaped notches had been carved into it, one near each end. Francie'd know what to call it; she used miniature versions to store her broidery floss.

While the villagers fought to hold steady, floundering, losing their footing in chest-deep water, others hurried to wind the slack round the "shuttle," flipping it end-over-end with a monotonous chant. Somehow, when done correctly, the tension at either end kept it from unspooling. A muffled curse as someone's fingers snagged beneath the rope. Under this much tension it could crush or slice off fingers if a body wasn't careful.

At a villager's nod that they'd spooled as much slack as possible, Arras dropped his hand, shouting, "Come, come forward!" Holly and Bess, each with an arm draped over a thick bovine neck, whispered endearments in droopy ears, urging on the bubalus. They could just as easily do without him, but this supervisory role allowed him to face seaward, reassure himself that Harry was safe, Doyce and Khar, and all the other wretched souls. He wished, for Holly's sake, that he could spy Theo.

"Jenret!" He pitched his 'voice to sound hearty, but not so much as to startle him. *"Work yourself back hand-over-*

hand, someone will meet you halfway if you're too tired.''
Himself, most likely. That he'd do, and gladly, in recompense for Jenret's bold rescue effort. He fought a nagging
disquiet that Jenret might vanish, slip under the waves, too
exhausted to continue—just as Honoria had disappeared
only moments ago. At first he'd disbelieved his eyes, seen
it too late, and said nothing to anyone, since there was
naught he dared say. He'd learned early and hard as a
military commander that one never threw one life after
another, unconsidered. Whatever strength Jenret still harbored must be used to save himself, not squandered in a
hopeless task. He assumed she floated lifeless in a pale
wash of hair somewhere beyond the boat, relieved his view
was now obscured.

"Want to make sure . . . the knot holds," and Arras could
almost hear Jenret's teeth chattering with cold and exhaustion. *"Nori's back safe?"*

"Mmph, believe so." Thank the Lady P'roul was too busy
to call him on so a blatant lie, and that Rawn was nowhere
to be found, though that in itself left him uneasy. Enduring
this could unnerve the heartiest of souls, and considering
Jenret's and Rawn's bond . . . *"To me, easy, yes, yes!"*
he encouraged. *"How're Doyce and Khar faring?"* They
mattered to him—deeply—but if only he could ask how
Harry fared! He'd contrived a bit of mindspeech with the
lad, but the emptiness in his arms wouldn't be assuaged
until he could hold Harry close. And then, he decided,
throwing forbearance to the winds, soundly whip him for
prematurely aging him!

"About the—" Jenret surged into the air as if shot from
a bow, both arms outstretched, exultantly slapping the
water as he descended, dipping under the surface for a
moment before bobbing back up. *"Yes! Rawn, old boy! He
did it, Arras! Without Rawn, what I've done would have
meant nothing!"*

Baffled, wondering if his old friend were hallucinating,
Arras stumbled backward, tripping again as his heel
slammed something solid yet yielding, heard a mournful
hiss. "Rawn?" Had he trod on the beast's paw, his tail?
The beast was too dark-hued to readily discern. *"Rawn, old
friend? Do you need me? Please, mindwalk if ye will!"*

"Tide's turning." Never had he heard Rawn sound so

feeble, worn thin. **"Boost me on Nauki so I can see Jenret!"**

Fearing he was fulfilling a final request, Arras gently scooped the ghatt into his arms, amazed at how light Rawn felt, scarcely any burden despite his bulk, as if he'd abruptly diminished, shrunk in size. Laying Rawn along Nauki's wide back, Arras caught a hint of whiteness like a trace down his forehead, started to brush off what he assumed was sand, only to halt, chilled to realize it was a white blaze. Unsteadily clambering upright, wobbling with each plodding stride, Rawn slashed at Nauki's rump and flung himself at Taubi with an ungainly twist of his once-supple body. Still, his claws scored the beast's flank as the ghatt plunged into the gap between them.

With a lowing, disgruntled moan the yoked team dug in their powerful haunches and sprang ahead, the boat shooting shoreward, men and women roaring and cheering as they hauled in the line, others wading out, securing the boat. **"A little more speed was necessary."** Stiffly, Rawn regained his feet and limped clear, collapsing on the sand. **"Awfully large hooves, but they're kind-hearted beasts. Didn't tread on me, though I richly deserved it."**

Arras knelt, softly stroking the white streak on Rawn's head with a finger. *"Impetuous as your bond, aren't you?"*

A wheezing purr answered him. **"Only when time and tide turns so fast."** Arras wasn't sure what it meant, but suspected Rawn and Jenret knew the cost only too well.

Elbows on knees, forehead buried against the back of his wrists, Davvy wondered if his head would ever stop aching—or his heart. Twilight now, the air still, the sea murmuring soft in his ears, a ceaseless dirge, a wistful lament to Bard's death. Dead? Oh, dear, Blessed Lady, how could he be dead? And with his death . . . the freedom to dare think that Lindy could be his. Wasn't that the most despicable, detestable thought in the world? He was beneath contempt. . . .

A cool wetness pressed against his forearm, and he belatedly realized that Hirby stood beside him, exuding kindness from every pore, patiently holding a tin mug of fresh water.

With a nod of thanks he took it, pressing its coolness
against his temple. Raising his eyebrows at Hirby, he indicated the bench beside him, and the man settled, giving a
simple sigh of relief. Devoid of words, they watched Dlamini work with scrupulous care to obliterate the blood-
soaked ground where Pommy and Bard had fought and
died . . . where *he* should have fallen in Bard's stead. Senses
wound to fever-pitch, he swore he could hear each grain of
sand jounce and collide as Dlamini scattered them, his raking palm frond whispering of woe as he smoothed the
earth.

Without looking he knew how Mvelase hovered over
Bard's body on the other side of the hut, putting his finishing touches on the corpse. Unfamiliar herbs and oils, un-
guents, their scent almost soothing; lengths of strangely-
printed cloth to lovingly wrap the body. What then, he
didn't know, refused to contemplate. From the sand and
dirt fresh-ground into the knees of Hirby's trews, the raw
blisters on his hands, the slump of the massive shoulders,
he judged that Hirby had observed his own private rituals,
laid Pommy to rest. Oh, how he craved rest as well, simple
sleep without dreams, not to have to think how he'd . . .

Vision blurred, head pounding from Bard's blow, he'd
literally pushed his private misery aside, assuming the dispassionate mind and mien his eumedico training required
as he'd squatted to examine the bodies. It had proved both
more and less difficult than he'd imagined, a familiar task,
only the setting strangely surreal, though why it should be,
he wasn't sure; death could and did occur anywhere.

No breath, no life lingered in either Bard or Pommy, and
Davvy'd continued to clamp down on his own grief and
emptiness as he'd considered what must be done to give
death its due. It had been far easier to let the man who
called himself Bard's grand-uncle take charge while he'd
dealt with the twins. Diccon's reactions he understood, the
boy purging sorrow from his system, but Jenneth would
take longer to heal, exploring the loss in some deeper re-
cess of her soul.

Sipping the water, prodding his jaw where Bard had hit
him—his final contact with Bard a blow—Davvy pondered
what to say to Hirby. The man appeared content to sit
silently, staring into nothingness, humming under his

breath. Finally he forced himself to speak the formulaic words. "I . . . I'm sorry about your friend." Hirby deserved more, had suffered a loss as well. "Sorry this happened. We didn't know the past would haunt us here. Pommy couldn't have known he was resurrecting the past, either, when he saved Jenneth."

Dolorous, mouse-brown eyes regarded him, Hirby's lower lip trembling in his bird's-nest beard. "Will Aqua come back to say good-bye to Pommy? To Hirby and Tigger?" He shifted, hitching himself along the bench, working his big hands together. "Pommy lied to Hirby 'bout fetching crawdiddies that day. Didn't want to share his gift from the sea." His face screwed up, a wail of pain and loss to crack the skies. "Always shared with him, I did! Nobody left for Hirby to share with no more!" A faintly hopeful look, "Less Aqua stays?"

"No, Hirby." Davvy patted the man's knee, gave him a one-armed hug. As Mvelase walked toward them, he forced himself to think, consider what must be done with the body, how to tell Lindy and Byrlie about Bard's death, if they should view the corpse. Lindy, yes. Byrlie, he wasn't sure. What right had he to even presume those decisions were his to make!

Without warning, everything within him spasmed. Oh, blessed Lady, what of M'wa? Like a puling coward he'd run away from any thought about M'wa, outracing the stink of his own fear. M'wa's world had ended today.

With quiet dignity Mvelase stood before them, immeasurably foreign and yet so formal. "You would see your friend now? To remember him as he was, not as he ended?"

"I . . . yes, thank you." How many dead bodies had he looked upon during his years as a eumedico? Peaceful deaths akin to sleep? Passings of gnawing, wrenching pain? Violent, unpredictable deaths from lethal accidents? But rarely did he view the body later, once it had been prettified, neatened to match the memories of family and friends. Somehow it mocked death, smoothing away its rough edges to make it more palatable to the grieving kin. But he needed this, needed this time above all for a final look at Bard, something to partially obliterate his brutal end. Mayhap call forth the finer images of Bard he carried in his heart, near-canceled in a wash of blood and berserk intent. As he stood, Hirby rose as well, slipping his hand into Davvy's as Tigger gave a piteous whine from beneath the bench.

The scent of smoke and damp ashes still strong in their nostrils, they moved around the hut to the site Mvelase had painstakingly prepared before moving the body. Should he have let Mvelase gain control like that? Take charge of the body? Hirby's sweaty hand engulfing his, he stared at his feet, observing each step on this final road to farewell, forcing himself to lift his eyes and contemplate his dearest friend, his dearest rival.

Bard had been laid on a rough bier of planking and fragrant boughs, his honey-tinted skin smooth and unlined, his face at peace. Strange how he looked, so exotic, yet so peaceful, a necklace of nuts and seeds with a carved stone amulet around his neck, his wrapping cloths of saffron and ocher and black block-printed with birds and animals Davvy couldn't name. Familiar and yet so unfamiliar except . . . for the black-and-white ghatt huddled in a still mound at his feet. Unable to sustain M'wa's gaze when the ghatt raised his eyes, a profoundly deeper grief battered him and, like a coward, he concentrated instead on Dlamini, his cleaning done, and now stationed at semi-attention at Bard's head, his staff with its horns erect like a marker. Why hadn't he noticed before how much he resembled Bard except for the shadings of their skin?

"At dark we will start home with him," Mvelase stated matter-of-factly. "A journey of many days, but when we reach our lands, his soul will rejoin his body, be eased at having found his home."

For one crazed instant Davvy panicked, convinced Mvelase meant that Bard would live again, his spirit and soul reunited, his life rekindled. But it at last dawned that Mvelase spoke truth of a sort: Bard had forever been an uneasy wayfarer in a land he could never claim as his own, despite his birth. Had tried desperately to fit in, had proved an honorable Seeker, a tender husband and father, no matter how foreign these lives felt to him. In truth, he'd at last come home.

Except Mvelase refused to take one thing into account, and Davvy greatly feared he might be forced to destroy

Bard's peace in death so that the living might feel at peace. "You can't leave, not yet. I don't know when, I don't know how, but we must find his wife and daughter, let them say their farewells. I'm sorry, but it's not your place to determine where Bard's body will lie."

Now what had he gotten himself into? Not to mention Diccon and Jenneth and Luykas? For how long in this heat could they serve as honor guards to a decaying corpse? And all in the vain hope that Lindy and Byrlie would magically appear?

"They will come—soon." M'wa 'spoke him with an inexorably sad certainty. **"Tell Uma-Uncle we shall wait, then accompany him."**

Dropping to his knees, Davvy rested one hand on the ghatt's back, his other hand on Bard's cool, bare foot. *"M'wa, we can't wait forever, we don't know where—"*

"The Vruchtensla will bring them, will meet us." Puzzled, he relayed M'wa's terse statement to Mvelase and watched Hirby's lips begin to move, muttering and mumbling. Mvelase did not look well-pleased at the news, and Davvy feared he might use force to complete his self-appointed task. How Mvelase and Dlamini had come to be here was beyond him—why should this prove any different?

"Mayhap meet halfway?" Hirby asked diffidently, eyes squinting with shyness. "Start journey for your friend, carry your friend closer to his loved ones?"

Hirby looked as if he'd hatched an idea, chest swelling with pride as he continued. "Take your launch, we can sail body across bay to Calcanis River. Say good-byes there, then take launch upriver." A dirty-nailed hand patted at Mvelase. "Closer to your plains, your home, make your journey faster."

"Done," Mvelase announced. "Simple men's ideas are wider, wiser than our petty disagreements."

As the beach erupted with jubilation, Holly gave Taubi a hug and let herself be swept along with an exuberant tide of people wading into the surf. From both land and sea, bells and whistles, pots and pans raucously celebrated their success. If one more eager hand clutched it, the poor little boat would undoubtedly crack into pieces, drop straight to the bottom. Unmindful of her boots she plunged ahead, staggered by the sea's coldness, the chill rippling up her legs, her whole body flinching as others splashed her in passing.

Arras was already manhandling a protesting Jenret toward the bonfire, a woman hurriedly draping a blanket over his shuddering wax-white form. His almost-maternal gesture as he tucked the blanket close and high round Jenret's neck touched Holly's soul, unbidden tears welling in her eyes. Next came unbidden laughter at the way some things never changed: objecting, casting off the blanket, Jenret argued with chattering teeth to return to the boat, to Doyce. Nor did she blame him, because what drove him, drove her. Sparing a moment to pray for Doyce and Khar, her anxious eyes continued scanning the sea. What she wanted above all was to feast her eyes on Theo, find how he fared. Then she'd decide whether to kiss him or kick him for fretting her so!

With a whoop and a gladsome cry of "Papa!", Harry strained on tiptoe on the bow, waving both arms until he caught his father's attention. A shallow dive knocked two rescuers under as Harry swam like a fish for shore, encouraged by good-natured cheers. Relieved another distraction was past, Holly eagerly searched the bobbing, moving heads for Theo until someone suddenly thrust a small, blonde child—practically as naked as the day she'd been born—into her arms, and she automatically swung to pass it along to the woman behind her. Each time she made some progress toward the boat, yet another barely-clothed child landed in her arms, until at last she recognized Byrlie being conveyed along the human chain.

"Sweetheart, are you all right?" Holding her tight, clinging a moment longer than necessary, given the waiting arms anxious to pass another child to warmth and safety, Holly pressed a kiss on her forehead. "Byrlie, have you seen Theo?"

Tilting her head, Byrlie regarded her, and Holly shivered at her prolonged silence, at the wide, blank gaze focused so far beyond her. "Papa's dead, you know," and the child sagged in her arms as if she'd needed the release of saying that, of having someone acknowledge it.

"Blessed Lady . . . hold him close!" Choking as if a wave had overswept them, Holly fought for breath, the horror crushing her lungs. How, how could the child know, be so sure? Had Lindy had one of her farseeing spells? Clamping her lips on the tumult of questions straining to spill out, Holly had no option but to hug her again and hand her along, another child already coming her way. Were the others hurt, dead as well? Jenneth, Diccon, Davvy? Not after all this, not after suffering through so much! And damnall, *where* was Theo? By the Lady, was that a dagga boy wading ashore, swaggering mien undercut by rolls of baby fat over his drooping skivvies, wet blue-and-yellow feathers flopping against his cheek? Had he just winked at her? Was the whole world in microcosm here tonight to witness this?

As she saw Doyce and Khar being lifted out of the boat, Holly broke her link of the impromptu human chain and waded deeper, stumbling and going under as someone accidently collided with her. Breaking the surface, she bellowed, "Theo! Theo, dammit, where are you?" No doubt about it now—she'd whale the daylights out of him when she got her hands on him! Oh, to get her hands on that bony, scrawny, so dearly loved form! *"P'roul! Khim! Where's Theo?"*

"Back here!" Her white markings like patchy, floating fog fragments, Khim 'spoke her from the stern. **"Tow him in, hook three for the price of one! But hurry, please! He's tired."**

Tow him in? She swam now, faster and far easier than walking through water this deep, forcing it to yield and let her pass. *"Is he swimming, Khim?"* The idea of Theo swimming or, more accurately, thrashing like a maniac to keep his nose above water, was not to be contemplated. *"I swear, Khim, explain fast—or I'll dunk you!"*

Resting a hand on the stern, she let her weight tilt the boat enough to put her nose to nose with Khim. Although Khim looked mildly annoyed, falanese glee had gained the upper hand, or paw—as if the ghatta found this highly diverting. At last she took pity. *"Theo's out there stark naked with two women—two! Quite a sight! One woman's naked, too, and the other's practically so!"*

Slack-jawed, Holly pondered the idea of Theo at sea with . . . with naked women. Oh, dear, how rich! She could hold over it his head forever! Once she'd determined he was all right, that is. Bashful, modest Theo—cavorting with naked women? Theo himself—naked? Well, he'd apparently learned how to stay afloat. Notions of inflation seizing her, she dunked herself to quash them, came up shouting, "Theo!"

"Holly?" echoed back a dear but muffled voice. "Get us in! I'm n-not s-s-sure Honoria's g-go-ing to m-make it—s-s-she nearly d-drowned!" While it mimicked Theo's familiar stammer, she could hear his teeth clattering with cold. Lacking even the normal amount of body fat most people had, he must be half-frozen!

As Khim darted starboard to paw at where the line was secured, Holly let out a bellow for aid and fumbled for the line. He didn't sound that distant, mayhap only fifteen meters or so, but the wave action was choppy, the remains of an eddy. At first her seeking fingers grabbed what felt like a string of wet laundry, strips of shirts, pantaloons, trews, skirts, knotted one after another. With a curse she disgustedly cast it aside, only to curse with greater fervency as she fumbled after it—this explained why everyone was half-clothed! Wrapping it round her elbow and wrist, straining backwards, she planted her feet on the seabed and heaved. Other hands grabbed the laundry line, Bess, nose barely above water, hooking her belt and bodily hauling her backward until her footing came firmer. *"Khim, he said Honoria's with him. Who's the other woman?"*

"A mostly naked Shepherd—female, by the way. Gloriously buoyant! Though if they let Honoria sink, no great loss!" To Holly's puzzlement, Khim sounded absolutely peevish, but she had no time for that as the odd trio floated into view. Theo, one long arm wrapped around a wooden keg, clasped a round-faced, hearty-looking woman to his breast. What struck Holly most of all was her cropped hair—so short on the sides and back and a long, untidy plume rising from the center like a radish stem. The woman, in turn, cradled Honoria to her, the pale face, the equally pale hair streaming like spilled milk as it mingled with the dark waters.

It all came together in a rush, left Holly shamed at not

thinking, not caring. Mayhap she and Theo had mistrusted Honoria from the start, but Honoria had been the one who'd volunteered to swim out to meet Jenret with the towline. The one whose well-being not a one of them had considered, as long as Jenret was safe. Had she deemed Honoria expendable? Did her act of heroism nullify what else she'd done—spooking Doyce's horse, turning the custables into lethal grenades? If, *if* she'd done those things. Gritting her teeth, unsure precisely what to believe, Holly strained with a will, then stretched until her hand locked on Theo's bare shoulder. "Drop your feet, you can touch bottom here."

Still keeping a hand under the Shepherd's arm—and she, Holly judged, couldn't touch bottom except on tiptoe— Theo sputtered, "G-get h-her in—quick! We n-nearly l-l-lost her t-to the un-dert-tow round the r-rocks. D-d-dannae r-rescued her when the r-rest of us were t-too b-b-busy worrying a-bout s-saving ourselves!"

Amazed at the woman's lightness—did spirit weigh more than flesh?—as Theo transferred Honoria to her, Holly plowed through the water, ignoring its tug, ignoring any aid. Theo'd passed on his responsibility to her, and she'd not shirk it. Somehow she'd make this right, figure out the truth of the matter. Shaking wet hair out of her eyes, she realized the beach now swarmed with new figures, at least a dozen horsemen.

"Has anyone seen Honoria Wijnnobel?" came a woman's voice from astride the lead horse. "Is she here, safe?"

"Here!" Holly shouted back. "I've got her right here!"

Springing from her horse, a woman dressed in worn shades of black and navy and brown came splashing through the surf to force a flask between Honoria's pallid lips. "Treat her with care," the woman warned as she tilted the flask. "She's the best operative I have. And from the looks of things, I'd say she's done a credible job, given the ambiguities we accidentally threw in her path."

Hands grasping under her shoulders, behind her knees, more hands working to unwind her arms from Khar's quies-

cent form. "No!" she screamed and flailed an elbow, ready
to bite and kick if she must.

"Pass the chazza o'er," a voice soothed. "Make it sore
sight easier on us all." Another voice, "Gotta git yed a-
shure, ma'am. Lest yed wan ride boat alla way."

When had his singing gone silent? She missed it, its ability to push back the dark of Khar's absence, and now he
was absent, too, leaving her with an uninhabited heart.
Alone except for the hands so insistent on trying to rip
Khar free from her. Poor Jenner, struggling to save her on
his own, so many things to do at once that his singing had
faded away. But she *had* found momentary mirth in his
mental image of that rope end, her dear so suddenly prudish, almost skittish!

"I can't let go of her," she muttered, hazy as to whom
these voices belonged to, or the hands, but concluding they
meant to be helpful, even if they didn't understand that
lacking her touch Khar would surely stumble down that
final step. "*Must* hold on, under . . . stand?" Could she
make it any clearer to these witless souls?

"Jenret!" Her cry came piteously weak, so she switched
to mindspeech, "*Jenret! Where are you? Help me, don't let
them take Khar from me!*"

"*Darling, don't fret! I'll make it right . . .*" but within
that, Arras's voice broke in, "*I'll handle it, Jenret. Just a
subtle suggestion, an intimation barely brushing their minds,
and they'll believe it their own idea. Not strictly proper, but
called for.*"

"Huh," a new thought dawned on the first voice, "if'n
chazza means sa much ta her, lez not part'm. Mebbe a silly
beast ta us, but not ta her. S'awkward, but we kin make a
four-chair."

The prodding hands returned, lofting her clear of the
boat, hands hoisting at knees and thighs, hands braced
under her armpits and fanny, leaving her bent in the middle
to cradle Khar. Water swished against her bottom, across
her lap, and she tucked Khar under her chin, trying to
shrink upward, afraid the ghatta's head might slip
underwater.

"Be out shortly, ma'am. Hard holdin yed up sa high,
beggin' yer pardon. Can't keep yed completely clear of
the water."

"No matter. Believe I was already wet." Her human con-
veyance gave an appreciative laugh, and she wondered
what she'd said to provoke their mirth.

"Doyce, I'm coming!" A certain suppressed anger coursing through Jenret's 'voice—over her? What? *"If Arras will
be kind enough to unhand me!"*

*"Only if we're agreed, you pigheaded man! You can
barely carry Rawn, you're so exhausted. I'll bring Doyce
and Khar the rest of the way to shore."*

"You'll carry Rawn, my second most cherished . . ."

"Just hurry! Khar's so far gone . . ." she cried in anguish.

Splashing, reckless cursing, and she felt herself passed
like a parcel into a single set of arms, arms that felt so
utterly familiar and safe that she could almost believe . . .
that Khar might live, that she could have Jenret and Khar,
Jenneth and Diccon to love, not have to choose. Whiskers
brushing her arm, mustache brushing her cheek—what?
Ah, Arras maneuvering to hold Rawn tight against Khar—
the ghatt's whiskers had tickled her.

As Jenret staggered under their combined weights, she
sensed dry land beneath his feet as he ran higher up the
beach, could feel his pounding heart, the rise and fall of
his ragged breathing. And beside them, matching them
stride for stride, Arras with Rawn.

"It's not too late," Rawn reassured her, gruff as always,
and though her eyes burned and blurred, she discerned a
streak on his head. Quite dashing, in fact. Would Khar
think so if she ever returned from her dormant state to
see it?

Privacy, blessed privacy at last as Jenret laid her on a
blanket, stretching his stark-naked length beside her. Blan-
kets piled over them both, Khar snug between them, Rawn
as well, cocooned against the world, hidden from death.
With intense care Rawn began thoroughly grooming Khar
from her nose down, giving each individual hair his undi-
vided attention, licking life into her. If she held her breath,
would it be transferred to Khar?

But that was impossible to attempt, Jenret making her
gasp as he repeated words she hadn't heard for years. *"I
surrender, heart, mind, and soul to you if you will share
yours with me."* He cradled her head between his hands,
his lips moving from her forehead, to her own lips and,

finally, over her heart. *"Do you remember those words,
Doyce? Do you?"* he asked more urgently. *"I said them
and I meant them when I agreed to marry you. But somehow
we both forgot how to share, became selfish of giving of
ourselves without even realizing it. But the damage can be
undone."*

A thousand fears, large and small, real and imagined,
swept over her, and hesitantly, she mentally reached to
stroke his mind, willing him to invite her to enter without
impediment. What she read there convinced her, told her
that he would be her safe harbor if she would be his, no
matter what storms of fear or mistrust swept through and
tried to wreck them.

"You're allowed to borrow, not steal outright," he chuckled. *"Yes, a safe harbor for our bodies, a safe harbor for
our minds and souls—and damn the storms! I hate being
seasick!"*

Beside her Rawn shifted, working lower, concentrating
on the spot over Khar's heart.

" . . . **Beloved** . . . ?" Puzzled, weak, Khar sounded in
her mind and the completion made Doyce's heart overflow.
**"Rawn said . . . to mention that Kharm and Matty say . . .
'hello.' Silly old ghatt . . . did the spirals for me . . . for us."**

A safe, snug haven of laughter and gaiety, mellow with
food and drink, even music—one of the sailors squeezed a
concertina—and golden lantern light that gallantly held the
dark, the sea at bay. This party aboard the *Vruchtensla*
marked their last night in the Sunderlies, their final opportunity to bid farewell to friends, old and new, before they
returned to Canderis.

Praying to the Lady for strength—or sudden deafness—
Doyce listened with mounting admiration as Harry piped a
credible ditty on the fipple flute loaned by Tuck. As the
flute and concertina swung into a rollicking tune, children
and adults began to dance, tentatively and then with growing confidence, an intricate chain of clasped hands, changing bodies weaving a pattern of excruciating, ever-changing
beauty before her eyes. True happiness consisted of such
transitory moments as these.

Lantern light reflected on the earrings, the ball and hoop that Diccon and Kwee, Jenneth and Pw'eek displayed with such self-conscious pride at their novelty. Technically they hadn't yet earned them, hadn't finished—let alone commenced—the Novice course of Seeker Veritas training. With gentlemanly ceremony Diccon waltzed by with Talie, one of Oordbeck's brood, his face still pale beneath his tan, expression solemn, a foretelling of the man he'd soon become. Jenneth hectically juggled partners, out-dancing them all, face flushed and elated.

It had been Lindy who'd suggested the premature gifting, much to Doyce's consternation, calmly unclasping the earrings Bard had gifted her with as a child. His and Byrta's, and against all fashion, Lindy had worn the double set, two in each ear. "I'd like . . ." her eyes were swollen but her voice composed, even a hint gay, "I know Bard'd be deeply honored if the twins and ghatten wore them. And so would I." From tight beside her mother, Byrlie had proffered a small, blue-velvet pouch as well. "Bard meant for Byrlie to wear M'wa's and P'wa's sets when she grew older, but she agrees with me."

Hiding her mouth behind her braid-tip, the child nodded her confirmation. "They belonged to Seekers—the very *best* Seekers," she emphasized. "Oughta stay with Seekers." Momentarily overcome, Doyce could only nod her thanks while Lindy continued outlining her plans for their leave-taking. And what a leave-taking it had become, she thought, as her foot tapped time to the music.

Grandly sweeping by, Dlamini graciously passed along one dancer after another left-handed, refusing to surrender Holly, beet red at such unabashed admiration but gamely holding her own, never missing a beat. Sailors whirled small and medium-sized Oordbecks right and left, lofting some into the air—including the two newest members of the Oordbeck brood—Smir and Siri. Hampered by his broken collarbone, Ozer had shrugged and grinned, saying that he'd never notice two more. Gelya and a middle-aged sailor danced slowly, occasionally defying the pattern to ensure they returned to each other's arms, while Captain Thorsen appeared reluctant to release Dannae. Given the proprietary looks that both Corly and Theo shot their way, Doyce feared three-way fisticuffs but decided Dannae would take a broom to them all.

Of course, the high point of the evening had been the secret plan to gift the new Bond-pairs with their earrings, though no one could have predicted Diccon's reaction. Too much anticipation, mayhap, his eyes wide as Jenneth and Pw'eek stood bravely still, not a murmur, not a flinch; even Kwee had evinced a decidedly unbouncy stoicism as her turn came and went. But before the needle could even pink Diccon's lobe, he'd swooned, keeling over in a dead faint. Hardly a stellar performance for a future Seeker! As Davvy had noted, smelling salts in hand, it was a good thing Diccon'd not had his heart set on a eumedico career!

"Doyce, darling—time's running short. The Captain wants the launch back before the tide turns." Sidling behind her, Jenret cradled Khar in his arms, Rawn by his side. How peculiar to see that faint white blaze on Rawn's coal-black head! And miraculous beyond belief to have Khar alive—and grumpy as only an invalid could be—in Jenret's sheltering arms.

His lips brushed the back of her neck in sympathy and solidarity. *"Rawn and I've already said good-bye. We thought you two would want to make your farewells in private."* Touched by his empathy, she nodded, mouth tight to avoid weeping, and took Khar in her arms, sniffing the scent of talc that always rose so sweetly from her. So light, but so resoundingly alive, and reveling in her embrace—thanks to Rawn and the blessed Elders!

Walking toward the bow, she passed Honoria and Mettha Prinssen—Security Chief, not flower-arranger—awaiting Dlamini and their final passenger in the launch. Mvelase and Bess, Hirby and Tigger had remained ashore, readying their precious burden for its journey up the Calcanis and east to the Naukkilari Plains, home. Bess had apparently decided to journey with them, visit Mkjinka.

"Go well, Honoria," she said with reluctant respect. "Thank you for your efforts on behalf of Wycherley-Saffron and the other mercantilers. My best to you and Mettha and the rest."

Planting a cool kiss on Doyce's brow, Honoria had the grace to look faintly embarrassed. "Never for an instant did I realize how much woe I caused you and Jenret—it seemed a perfect cover!" And then, more earnestly in halting mindspeech, *"Truly, there was never anything between us. But if I'm not on duty the next time I visit—beware! I may try again—I'm not a gracious loser!"*

"Then I'll be forewarned—and forearmed—so remember that!" To Doyce's delight, Khar demanded the last word, stretching out a white paw, claws extended, that deliberately raked Honoria's arm without breaking the skin.

Never could she genuinely like Honoria Wijnnobel, but value her abilities—yes. But Honoria hadn't been the one they'd come to bid farewell.

Nearly invisible in the shadowed base of the foremast, even his white forehead star dull, M'wa sat, tail precisely wound around his feet, eyes rarely shifting from the lonely lantern on shore that marked where his beloved Bond waited.

With awkward care Doyce folded herself onto the deck, nestling Khar in the bowl of her crossed legs. Motionless until they'd settled, M'wa rose to greet-sniff Khar and rub his chin across Doyce's knee. *"Are you sure, old friend?"* She felt guilty, supremely selfish, but she'd willingly play low and dirty if it promised success. *"Are you sure it's right to desert Lindy and Byrlie—when they need you so?"* Again, the ghatt stared toward shore, his neck straining, his silence eloquent as an answer.

Finally he 'spoke. **"They love me, but they truly don't need me."** M'wa shifted, flexing his claws. **"They need each other now to heal—and they have need of Davvy as well."** His next words came in a passionate rush. **"How can you be so deliberately blind?—you two above all, who sense with each fiber of your being how the Bond calls from heart to heart!"**

"Peace, M'wa." Bandages white around her midsection, Khar unfolded from Doyce's lap, stiffly planting one paw in front of the other until she shoulder-bumped M'wa, wreathing herself round him and sitting close. **"She knows too well. Surely you remember how stubborn she is when she decides someone's worth loving. Don't blame her for trying, even though in her heart she admits she's wrong. Relinquishing someone she loves runs against her grain."**

Mayhap it was moonlight, but a glimmering amusement sparked gold-green in M'wa's eyes, bringing them to life.

"Oh, Khar, has she gone all broody since surrendering the twins to adulthood?"

Miffed, Doyce contented himself with a mock-swat to the top of his head, and unresisting—always so reserved, so controlled—he permitted her to pull him closer, licking her cheek as she bent her face to his. *"Oh, M'wa! What times we've had together! All of us! I can't let you slip away like this, not to . . . to wherever. . . ."*

"Ah, but for me, it's not a separation, but a reunion. To be truly home, truly whole again—Byrta with P'wa, Bard with me. The oneness calls to me and I can't chance losing it again. Good-bye, dear friends. You live in our hearts, just as we always shall live in yours."

Gently breaking free from her embrace, the black-and-white ghatt padded away, the high white stocking on his left hind leg momentarily bright, his long, black tail swaying its farewell in the night. The concertina, alone this time, squeezed out the poignant verse of a favorite Sunderlies tune.

> *Where are you going?*
> *'To Samranth, to Samranth.*
> *Why do you sail*
> *To the Sunderlies shore?*
> *The law says that I've sinned so*
> *That I am exiled,*
> *Ne'er to see home again,*
> *Just these damn isles!*
> *Ah, my past crime's been paid for,*
> *my new life begun,*
> *Under the sun, under the sun,*
> *On the Sunderlies shore!*
> *Seeking the sun in the Sunderlies!*

Mickey Zucker Reichert

To Order Call: 1-800-788-6262

Kristen Britain

GREEN RIDER

As Karigan G'ladheon, on the run from school, makes her way through the deep forest, a galloping horse plunges out of the brush, its rider impaled by two black arrows. With his dying breath, he tells her he is a Green Rider, one of the king's special messengers. Giving her his green coat with its symbolic brooch of office, he makes Karigan swear to deliver the message he was carrying. Pursued by unknown assassins, following a path only the horse seems to know, Karigan finds herself thrust into in a world of danger and complex magic....   0-88677-858-1

FIRST RIDER'S CALL

With evil forces once again at large in the kingdom and with the messenger service depleted and weakened, can Karigan reach through the walls of time to get help from the First Rider, a woman dead for a millennium?   0-7564-0209-3

To Order Call: 1-800-788-6262

DAW 7

John Marco

The Eyes of God

Akeela, the king of Liiria, determined to bring peace to his kingdom, and Lukien, the Bronze Knight of Liiria, peerless with a sword, and who had earned his reputation the hard way, loved each other as brothers, but no two souls could be more different. And both were in love with the beautiful Queen Cassandra. But unknown to anyone, Cassandra hid a terrible secret: a disease that threatened her life and caused unimaginable strife for all who loved her. For Akeela and Lukien, the quest for Cassandra's salvation would overwhelm every bond of loyalty, every point of honor, because only the magical amulets known as the Eyes of God could halt the progress of Cassandra's illness. But the Eyes could also open the way to a magical stronghold that will tear their world apart and redefine the very nature of their reality.

0-7564-0096-1

To Order Call: 1-800-788-6262

MERCEDES LACKEY

The Novels of Valdemar

Exile's Honor

He was once a captain in the army of Karse, a kingdom that had been at war with Valdemar for decades. But when Alberich took a stand for what he believed in—and was betrayed—he was Chosen by a Companion to be a Herald, and serve the throne of Valdemar. But can Alberich keep his honor in a war against his own people?

"A treat for Valdemar fans"
—Booklist

0-7564-0085-6

To Order Call: 1-800-788-6262

DAW 24